By BRIAN GARFIELD ⸺

Fiction
WILD TIMES
RECOIL
DEATH SENTENCE
HOPSCOTCH
THE ROMANOV SUCCESSION
KOLCHAK'S GOLD
THE THREEPERSONS HUNT
TRIPWIRE
GANGWAY! (*with Donald E. Westlake*)
DEATH WISH
LINE OF SUCCESSION
DEEP COVER
RELENTLESS
THE LAST HARD MEN
WHAT OF TERRY CONNISTON?
THE VILLIERS TOUCH
VALLEY OF THE SHADOW
THE HIT
WAR WHOOP AND BATTLE CRY (ED.)
THE LAST BRIDGE
THE VANQUISHED

Nonfiction
COMPLETE GUIDE TO WESTERN FILMS
I, WITNESS: True Personal Encounters With Crime (Ed.)
THE THOUSAND-MILE WAR: World War II in Alaska and the Aleutians

BRIAN GARFIELD

Wild Times

————————— SIMON AND SCHUSTER · NEW YORK

Designed by Eve Metz
Manufactured in the United States of America

1   2   3   4   5   6   7   8   9   10
Library of Congress Cataloging in Publication Data

Garfield, Brian Wynne, date.
    Wild times.
    I. Title.
PZ4.G2315Wi   [PS3557.A715]   813'.5'4   78–15610
ISBN 0–671–24374–8

FOR IAN AND JEAN

Contents

8

BOOK ONE

Denver Shooting Match

THEY HAVE ASKED ME to set it all down for a book and I am pleased they still want to know about the old things. I mean to set down an account of it as straight as I can but you have to keep in mind that I used to have something of a reputation as a liar.

When they asked me to write this book they wanted mainly to know about the Wild West Shows before we are all dead who dreamed them and created them. My life has been more than Wild West Shows— I am sure most people who still recognize my name in 1922 already know that—and as long as I have the opportunity to set the record straight in these pages I would like to refute some of the nonsense about me that has appeared in lurid fictions.

I am not so different from anyone else, but when the truth is mixed with lies to become legend it becomes difficult for anyone later to go back and sort out the realities. I am glad to have this chance to put to rest both the dime-novel fictions and the catcalls of detractors. I have an opportunity and an obligation to try and restore balance to a story that has been tipped way out over the precipice of plausibility, and that is what I shall do.

Not too long ago when I made my last public appearance in Denver I overheard a young sporting man say to his lady friend, "The trouble with Colonel Cardiff there, he actually *believes* he's Colonel Cardiff."

Yes and no. I know who I am. I am Hugh Michael Cardiff. But I am not necessarily the fellow from those dime novels.

9

My life in public began when I was grown to nineteen years old and went up against Doc Bogardus in Denver. Everything that has happened to me since then started from there, so I believe that is the place for me to start this story.

. . .

I was over in Ouray that spring. There was still a bit of snow and we spent most of our time indoors taking our meals and drink in Dick Maurice's place which has become a landmark nowadays in all the memoirs. Actually it was a primitive place with a pinewood bar and a few mirrors and handmade furniture. The ornate construction came later after the place burned down in '71 and Maurice rebuilt it like an Italian palace.

An artist drunk to his hair roots was on his knees painting a woman's face on the floor in imitation of the one we'd all seen up in Central City. The roped-off floor was surrounded by a crowd of us watching the painting take shape and egging the poor fellow on.

"You got the eye too close to the nose there, bucko."

"What's the matter with her mouth?"

"Let's see a little more of them teats there. You ain't got no call to be bashful about it."

"That's the strangest-looking nose I ever seen."

"How come she got red eyes there?"

"Because she's advertising, you fool, this place sells red-eye, don't it?"

Then a boy about twelve came in with a roll of posters under his arm and I saw him bend Maurice's ear at the bar. Dick Maurice shrugged and nodded, after which I saw the boy go over and nail one of the posters up on the wall. The boy left and we all walked over to read it. The poster drew my interest because it was topped by an illustration of a Springfield rifle. Over behind me some of the miners didn't have any interest in it at all; I remember hearing a loud disputation about the impeachment proceedings against President Johnson.

I still have a copy of that poster. Somebody gave it to me years later and I kept it.

A CHALLENGE TO MARKSMEN
From the World-Famous Rifle Champion
DR. Geo. P. BOGARDUS

Through courtesy of the Denver *Gazette,* and at Great Expense, Dr. Bogardus will appear for one day only at W. F. Skinner's farm, Denver, Colo., ready to accept challenge from ANY SHOOTER IN THE TERR. Targets to be glass balls, to be thrown into the air at 25 yards rise. Challengers' choice of muzzle-load rifle, metal cartridge rifle, pistol, revolver or musket; shotguns not permitted. Sporting bettors invited. Purse, provided by the *Gazette,* to be

Winner to be decided as best-of-100 shots. All Challengers Eligible.
Competition to take place 2:00 P.M., Saturday 25th April 1868,
W. F. Skinner's farm, Denver, Colo. Terr.

I'd been working a timber shift with a Ute Indian boy called Bear
and he had his nose pushed to the window trying to see the poster; they
didn't allow Indians in saloons. Still don't today.

He asked me what the poster said.

"They've brought this Dr. Bogardus down to Denver. Shooting contest. A thousand dollars to the winner."

"And you got a gleam in your eye." Bear went around to the door
and I met him there. He said, "Who's this Dr. Bogardus?"

"Claims to be a world-famous rifle champion."

"You ever heard of him?"

"No. Some kind of Easterner, I guess."

He looked at me. Bear was all right, a big lump, always happy about
something or other. He said, "Well I guess I'll have to find me another
wood-chopping partner," and he went away down the street. He let his
call sing out back toward me over his shoulder: "Good luck in that
shootin' contest, Hugh."

I was going by the name of Hugh Smith in those days because I
wasn't sure if they still had a warrant out on me in Kentucky.

In the morning I caught a lift over the mountains on a bullion wagon,
twenty-six-mule team; they were happy enough to have me because
they knew my reputation with a long gun and the hills had some road
agents in them. We didn't encounter any trouble though.

Denver in that spring of 1868 was raw and crowded and maybe a
bit pretentious. It's grown up a good deal now but even then it was big.
There were buildings the likes of which I hadn't seen since I was a boy
and my father took me over to Vicksburg. Tall buildings, three stories;
horse trolleys in the streets; weather lamps on poles at the street
corners; two-pump fire engines drawn by eight white horses; a big insulated icehouse; more people than I guess I'd seen at any one time
in my life up to then. I remember particularly that there was an
amplitude of women, all shapes and sizes. That was Friday and the
schoolbells rang, after which the streets flooded with children.

It was a long-ago time and there were things it takes an old man to
remember. I recall there must have been two dozen mountain men
in their strange wild getups wandering around the city gawking. They
still existed then. Beaver pelts were still currency and those old mountain men hung on to their lives, stubborn but they had a right to be.
Once a year after the spring thaw they'd come down out of those

Wyoming mountains to Denver which was the nearest city and they'd see the elephant and tie one on. Then they'd head back to the Tetons to set their traplines again. They were gamy and most of them didn't speak much English; mostly they were French. Some of them had been in the Rockies pretty near fifty years. I'd known old Grandfather Tyree down in Arizona so I felt at home with the mountain men but some of the citizens of Denver tended to cross the street when they saw one coming. Most likely it was to avoid the smell.

I found a room in a boardinghouse and spent the evening exploring the wickedness of the fandango district but I had a degree of prudence even in those youthful days and I knew better than to get myself drunk the night before a shooting match. I didn't touch a drop that night and I would like to emphasize that fact because there have been some accounts of the shooting match written by people with faulty memories who have tried to make out either that Bogardus was hung-over or that I was. A true shooter knows better. I know I had nothing to drink and I know that Bogardus' eyes were clear.

The noise in the fandango district was considerable. They didn't have the gas lamps yet but there was a profusion of whale lamps and a lot of light came blazing from the saloons and gambling parlors and bawdy houses. Piano and fiddle music, a lot of it, mingling in the street into a calliope cacophony, and barkers in red cutaways and beaver hats outside the establishments hawking the delights to be found within. The walls sported posters advertising the talents of singers and dancers. Every window had a copy of the Bogardus shooting-contest poster.

I went inside one saloon to see what it was like and when I passed through the doorway I was struck in the face by the noise and smell. There was a small platform stage with a three-piece band stomping earnestly and a big-chested girl kicking her leg forward in the San Francisco cancan style. She had a good loud singing voice, off-key but piercing. Smoke hung under the low ceiling, a fog of it, redolent of stale whisky and strong sweat. Men didn't bathe much then.

There were some keno and faro tables and I guess maybe a poker game or two. The faro barkers were yelling out bets over the crowd. I felt hemmed in; I withdrew after a moment and went out. I went on down to the Platte Club and tried my luck against a chuck wheel but I lost four bits on the first roll and discovered I had no interest in it; I was too keyed up by the prospect of the shooting match.

I made my way into quieter streets and walked a long time until I began to get cold. I was thoroughly lost by then and had to ask directions. A tough watched me cross one intersection; he was thinking about rolling me for my poke, I suppose, but he had a look at my worn clothes and the size of me and he thought better of it. I hadn't filled out all the way at nineteen but I was big enough to make that sort think twice.

I had a mind to read a chapter or two of the new Charles Dickens that I had found in the sundry shop but the morrow's match lay heavy on me and I slid the old Hawken rifle out of my scabbard and examined it fretfully.

There has been a lot of tomfoolery and inaccuracy in some accounts of that match as to what kind of rifle I actually used. That Hawken rifle had been my companion for nearly as long as I could remember. Long use had put a silver shine on it. The wooden buttstock was disreputably scarred and pitted. I always kept it clean and thoroughly oiled and I'd replaced the cap lock several times over the years but the fine Kentucky steel barrel had a long way to go yet before it wore out. It was a workman's rifle, that's the point I want to emphasize. They have made a legend out of those days now, of course. They arm us all with silver-plated gem-studded rifles that might look fine in a jeweler's window but would get a man laughed off the plains. If my rifle was shiny it was only the shine you get on the seat of pants you've worn too long. I had to black the sights with charcoal to get rid of the glare. It was simply a St. Louis-sold .46 that my father had bought from the Hawken Brothers direct by mail in the year 1856 and it was their standard manufacture but I will say that was of a very high standard. They were made one at a time on hand forges and lathes and the brothers did not sell any second-rate work. The best rifle of its time was the Kentucky long rifle; and the best Kentucky long rifle was the Hawken. Mine was twelve years old and it had seen a lot of lead through the bore and it had been rained on and mud-crusted and scratched and polished bare by riding in saddle scabbards but I'd never bent it or used it for a pry bar. And that's probably enough about that.

I took it apart that night as Kevin Tyree would have done, down to the last minuscule piece, and cleaned everything with exact care. I set up the scales and weighed out my powder charges in precise grains and sealed them up in paper. I sorted through the conical lead bullets —I was still using the mold Kevin had designed for me—and pouched them in my chamois pouch. Put out a tin of percussion caps, tore off enough cloth wadding for patches, gathered my oil tin and chamois and charcoal-pitch and set everything neatly on the commode by the bedroom door.

The Hawken had supported me most of the past three years. It got me a job as a contract game-meat hunter for the army post down by Mesilla and that was where I'd developed the game of shooting for pennies: a penny a shot against anybody who cared to shoot against me. Any old target. I amassed a lot of socks full of pennies before my reputation betrayed me and it got to the point where nobody was willing to shoot against me. When the army's meat contract ran out in 1866 I'd moved on north to Santa Fe and worked all summer for a cattle outfit there, a Spanish outfit, until the wanderlust infected me again. With Libby on my mind I'd ridden south again; the only way I felt I could shake her image was to keep tracking new ground. I wintered in and around Fort Griffin, Texas, living off my rifle—hunting game and selling it in the town and shooting against local marksmen for anything up to four bits a shot. I still had John Tyree's horse and saddle; that first year I'd accumulated a traveling kit and learned how to carry everything I needed without weighing down the horse.

In the summer of 1867 I'd gone to work for a long-bean cowman who was rounding up loose stock in the chaparral breaks of the Big Bend country—another summer pushing cattle; and I guess learning all the time. I kept my books about me, of course, always reading when I had the chance and getting ribbed for it.

I moved north at the end of that season, working my way slow, on the drift—at that time it wasn't a dishonorable calling, you were welcome if you worked off your keep where you stayed. There was always a little outfit at the end of the day's ride, man and wife and little kids, where they were glad to swap you a meal and a roof for your muscle and a few hours' work. I was eighteen years old and a boy that age hasn't much use for a great deal of money. I made my way. Sometimes it was a near thing but I always had my ingenuity and my rifle. Hunger isn't a threat to a man who can handle his rifle. I expect I have eaten more fresh-killed venison meat than most white men in the world.

I spent a good part of that winter honing my shooting skills. I'd set myself the task of teaching myself to shoot from the back of a running horse because I'd seen some Comanches do it down in the Panhandle and it struck me as a useful ability to develop. It took me half that winter to train the horse not to be gun-shy—you let somebody shoot off a rifle next to your ear and see how *you* like it—and the other half to train myself. This one was a new mount; I'd played out the Tyree sorrel in the Big Bend. I'd spent more money than I could afford on the new animal because I had to have a knee-trained mount; I bought it after a great deal of dickering with the vaquero who'd trained it. It was a two-year-old blue roan when I got it, trained as a cutting horse, sharp as a Bowie blade. That horse could swap ends like a bird.

In February I'd started north out of the Rio Chama country—following the buffalo, hunting from the back of the horse. It was a hazard because wherever the herds went the Indians went as well and even if there hadn't been any Comanche warfare the past season or two I didn't want to chance a run-in. I sold some buffalo meat to the towns on the trail but when the Comanche moved in too close I left the herd and rode on over into Colorado. Following my nose into the Rocky Mountains because I'd never seen them before. I didn't remember well enough all the things Grandfather Tyree had taught me about the mountains and I paid for that when the blue roan poked a foot into some wild man's bear trap. Snapped the leg clean and I had to do away with the horse and then I was afoot. Arrived broke in Cripple Creek a week ago with nothing on my mind but Libby.

. . .

They have drawn some pretty absurd pictures of us in the sensational fictions. I will tell you as best I can what I looked like as a young man. Later of course there were photographers and you have seen those tintypes and rotogravures but they always dressed us up for those.

In my late teens I was so big it sometimes was an embarrassment because I felt the description of the bull in the china shop had been invented with me in mind. I have never been fat but I had my father's wide Welsh shoulders and chest. I never thought much of the color of my hair; I suppose you'd call it sandy—it was too dark to be blond and too light to be brown. That was before it turned white on me.

By the time I got to Denver I'd grown a long mustache to make myself look older. It drooped down over the corners of my mouth and I used to wax the points after the fashion of the day. The wax tended to darken it and that is why the newspapers and dime novels later referred to my hair and mustache as "tawny."

I had little scars here and there from inevitabilities: a fall, a fight, the flail of a doctored cow's hoof. I'd been stung by a scorpion in the Big Bend and fanged by a diamondback rattler in Mesilla; I'd been sick with the poisons but I lived—those creatures aren't deadly except to infants and the infirm, dime-novel legends to the contrary. I've known a lot of men who got bitten by rattlesnakes. I never knew one of them to die from it. It's things like that—the irresponsible melo-dramatics of the sensation writers—that made up my mind to write this account when they asked me to. It is time somebody put the ridiculous in its place and told the truth as it was.

I used to sleep on the floor all the time and that gave rise to another legend about me, something to do with my wildness. The fact was they didn't make beds long enough to fit me. That's why I slept on the floor. I have shrunk a bit, the way all old people do, but in those days I stood six foot five and a half inches in my bare feet. I enjoy sleeping in beds just as much as the next man does. But I never found a comfortable one out West in my youth. That's the reason—the only reason—I used to sleep on floors.

. . .

15

An old man tends to ramble; you must forgive me. I started out to tell you about the Denver shooting match.

The Skinner farm was decked out like a fair. Flags flapping in the wind; big blue refreshment tents; a great crowd spilling across the buffalo grass from the trees down by the river to the barnyard. Above the sycamores you could see a lot of snow still heavy on the high Rockies. Riding in with the flowing crowd of arrivals I thought it was a splendid place, full of beauty. I wished Libby were there to see it. She was as strong on my mind as ever.

They'd constructed a platform with a roof and open sides above the pasture rail fence. The platform was bedecked with Union flags and gay buntings. Several chairs sat upon it in the shade. The crowd milled with a thrumming murmur of pent-up excitement and I shared in it. I saw men in expensive suits and hats rubbing shoulders with workingmen, all of them drifting from one knot of people to another. The women's dresses made splashes of color.

I tethered the hired horse among the ranks along the corral fences, pulled the cinches loose and made my way up across the barnyard toward the big red tent that sported a banner sign, REGISTRATIONS. I saw money change hands all around me—sporting men making their bets. There was a lot of loud laughing.

I had the Hawken slung over my shoulder in its scabbard and the heavy kit bag in my hand. I stood in the long queue until it was my turn, then bent over the roster to sign myself in. I had a bit of hesitation there. I'd been going by the name of Smith but that was on account of something six years ago and a thousand miles away and I was sick of hiding furtively behind a false name so I dipped the pen in the inkwell and wrote in a bold hand across the page *Hugh Cardiff—Mill Springs, Ky*. It gave me a good feeling.

Most of the signatures were X marks followed by names printed in pencil by the registrar, who was a bald man with a little badge on the lapel of his cutaway coat identifying him as C. S. Roe of the Denver *Gazette*. I returned the quill pen to Mr. Roe and smiled at the next man in line as I turned away toward the rail fence.

It is strange, I suppose, the sort of thing you remember about times long ago. In some ways I can remember those days better than I remember anything that happened last week; they tell me that's one of the attributes of growing old. But the thing I remember most about that moment at Skinner's farm is the hats.

The headgear worn by the men and women in that crowd was marvelous in its variety and finery. Silks, beavers, bowlers, sombreros, flowered chapeaux, sunbonnets, slouch hats, flat-crown farm hats, high Texas ten-gallons, plaid soft caps, California vaquero hats with their mile-wide brims, narrow little porkpies, army shakos with their stiff inclined flat tops and short bills, pale cavalry campaign hats with one side pinned up, blue artillery hats with curled brims, mountain leather hats with the brims turned down, parasols. Hardly a man or woman was hatless. I was one of the few. I owned a hat—buckskin, flat of crown and brim—but I had judged it too disreputable for the gallant occasion of the day and I'd left it in the boardinghouse. In any case I do not shoot while wearing a hat. It tends to trap the smoke around my eyes.

My shirt was fringed buckskin that I'd bought from a Comanche trader in Fort Griffin and my trousers were cast-off army britches and they were a bit greasy but the best I owned; only my belt and boots were expensive—Texas leather expertly tanned. I felt out-of-place amid the dark suits and flamboyant outfits and peacock hats around me but the scabbarded rifle on my shoulder granted me status: most of the men in the crowd were spectators—I was a contestant.

I made my way close to the rail fence. It was half an hour short of the commencement of the match but a throng had lined up along the railing and I had to stand on my toes to see over the row of hats. A beaver top hat makes any man as tall as I am. Over to my right was the bunting-bedecked platform; I had no doubt the judges and organizers would take their places there. Beyond the fence the gunning ground was a wide pasture, its far end bounded not by a fence but by a high cliff of pale red stone. Backstop for the bullets; I commended the good judgment of whoever had selected the pasture for the match.

I discerned great mounds of glass balls at intervals along the fence and I tried to make my way closer for a better look at them; I pried gently into the crowd and someone nearby was saying, "What do you make them, inch, inch-and-a-half diameter?"

"They're two-inch, I heard the man say."

"Still, twenty-five yards, flying through the air . . ."

"Separate the men from the boys, that's for certain."

Clustered around the heaps of glass balls were numerous young boys in shirtsleeves, maybe eleven years old or thereabouts. They were joshing one another the way kids do—feigned assaults, punch-ups to the shoulders: displaying their uneasy nervousness. I felt it myself but I was trying to hold it in, out of sight.

I backed out of the compressed knot of spectators and walked out into the open behind the judges' platform. I unslung the long rifle and drew it from the scabbard, rested the butt plate on the ground and folded my arms over the upended muzzle; closed my eyes and talked silently to myself: *Gentle down now, just relax, it's just another shoot for pennies, what the hell, you do it every day.*

"Hugh Smith, ain't it?"

I opened my eyes. He'd startled me.

I didn't recognize him. A young man, maybe my own age; more than a head shorter than I. A round sorrowful hound-dog face, brown hair and startling silver eyes; slim but not gaunt—a small man and young but not fragile. Pinstripe suit, bowler hat. Two long-barrel Colt's Navy-model revolvers thrust through his black belt.

He said, "I saw you shoot in Santa Fe. My name's Caleb Rice."

He gave me a firm handshake but not a knuckle-crusher. He was glancing toward the crowd at the fence. "You seen the glass balls?"

"Yes."

"I hope those kids got straight throwing arms." Caleb Rice pointed toward the red cliff. "We'll be shooting toward the northwest. But if a kid throws off to the left any, we'll be shooting right into the sun later in the day."

It was something I'd already considered. If I had any choice I'd pick a spot as far over to the left as I could get. There was a dogleg in the fence down toward the left and the shooters at that end would be aiming more like due north.

I said, "You got a rifle?"

"I use these." He touched both hands to his Navy revolvers. "It's what I know how to do." He had a sad kind of smile: it didn't tip his eyes up. "Like I said, I saw you shoot in Santa Fe. You might as well have been a road agent the way you took money from those folks. They none of them had much chance. But I can hold my own, you or anybody else." He was still smiling, to take the edge off it; he squinted up toward the high platform. "There's Doc Bogardus now."

I turned to have a look.

The man climbing onto the platform was tall and heavy. He wore a black suit and a narrow-brimmed black hat and a heavy neat black beard that put me in mind of General Grant's pictures. He carried his bulk with a posture of importance. From the cut of the expensive broadcloth suit it was hard to tell whether he was muscled or simply fat. I said, "Looks like a businessman."

"He is. His business is shooting. He won the British national championship last year at Bisley."

"Never heard of it."

"I read it in the *Gazette*." His smile at that time disturbed me; it was so doleful. Later on I would get used to it. "There's a lot of money in shootin' matches." He tapped the barrel of my rifle with his fingertip. "If you know how to earn it."

"A thousand-dollar purse is a lot of money."

"He didn't travel all the way out here to Denver just for that. It's the side bets. You got any money down on yourself?"

"Bets? No."

"How much you fixing to bet?"

"I hadn't thought about it."

"How much you got on you?"

"About thirty dollars I expect." From shooting for pennies and bits in Cripple Creek.

Caleb Rice said, "I've been to one of these things before, over in Galveston. The only way you make it pay off is bet your money where the odds are best. If you think you're going to lose then bet on somebody else. Bet on Bogardus or bet on me."

"I'm not going to lose," I told him. "Anyway I don't know anybody else. I've never seen you shoot, nor Bogardus."

"You'd be safe betting on me."

"How do I know that?"

He said, "Because I'm the second best pistolman around and the first best is Wild Bill Hickok and I don't see him here today."

"You think you can beat Bogardus?"

"I believe I can. It's short-range shooting. The advantage goes to the pistolman."

"I don't see that."

"A lot easier to lift a handgun a hundred times than a rifle. Look at Bogardus there—carries all that fat, his arms bound to get tired out."

On the platform Bogardus leaned out from the edge to judge the angle of the sun. He looked shrewd.

Caleb Rice said, "You want to bet your thirty dollars on me, there's a barker over there giving twenty-to-one odds on me. You could win yourself six hundred dollars."

"They put odds on every shooter here?"

"If they never heard of you they put fifty-to-one against you. I believe folks have heard of me, some."

It put an idea in my head. "I believe I will put down a bet."

I walked away toward the barker, passing two men who were speculating whether Governor Seymour would win the Democratic nomination for President. I had no idea who Governor Seymour was. I have never paid much attention to politics. Except for Teddy Roosevelt I have never voted. It only encourages the rascals.

I waited for the barker to complete a transaction. He had a thick tally book and a pocket lined with sharp pencils. He was a square man with red burnside whiskers and a friendly freckled look.

"Yes sir, how can I help you out today?"

"Do you have the name Hugh Cardiff on your list there?"

He ran his finger down the page. "How long ago did you sign?"

"Maybe twenty minutes."

He flipped the page over. "Here you are then. Cardiff, H., Esquire."

I snorted at him and the barker chuckled in a shy way. "Well I guess wrong once in a while. Taken a look at your shirt and britches and decided you couldn't read. No harm done." There wasn't any "esquire" on the list after my name or anybody else's.

I said, "You can call me esquire anytime you like. Have you put odds on me?"

"For how many balls?"

"Tell me how it works, then."

He said, "You'll get a hundred balls. The odds I give you depend on how many you think you can hit."

"How many does Bogardus think he can hit?"

"He claims he'll hit them all. His previous competitions he's averaged ninety-six."

"That's pretty good."

"Surely is. Are you betting on Bogardus?"

"I'd rather bet on me," I said.

"You ever shoot in a match contest before?"

"Not like this one. I've shot for pennies and such. I've never been beat."

"You shouldn't ought to tell me that. Might shorten the odds if I decided to believe you. But then I'd have to know who you shot against."

"I mostly didn't get their names."

I wasn't exactly lying to him. I have been accused of fraud in that match but I told no lies. My real name is Hugh Cardiff. I didn't mention the fact that shooters like Billy Dixon and Antoine Leroux had been bested by me under the Hugh Smith name. But there's no law that I know of prohibiting a man from keeping his mouth shut. Maybe it's true I strung them along that day but in the end it's the shooter's skill that counts, not his name.

The barker said, "Look here, my name's Cletus Hatch. Come over here a minute with me."

We walked toward the fence and Cletus Hatch pointed through a gap in the crowd. One of the mounds of glass balls glittered just beyond the fence. "You ever shot glass balls on the rise?"

"No. I've shot just about anything else you can throw up in the air, right down to a one-bit piece."

"Let me tell you how this is going to be, then. There's twelve piles of glass balls, and twelve crews of boys to toss them. There's twelve on-the-line judges, one on the fence behind each position. Up on the gazebo there you've got the match judges, three of them. Now there's seventy-odd men signed up so far, we'll likely end up with pret' near a hundred contestants. One of the judges draws the names out of his hat and the shooters go up on the line, twelve of them in the first batch. The glass balls are used because it's easy to see when one's been hit. Any ball that doesn't shatter before it hits the ground is chalked up as a miss. You understand?"

"Sure."

"Now when you get up in the line there'll be eleven other shooters on either side of you. The smoke and noise are going to be something fierce. You'll get ten balls to shoot. You've got to hit at least one of them or you're ruled out and you withdraw to the spectators' line behind the fence. The next shooter then takes your place. Now as long as you hit one or more of the first ten throws, then you get ten more throws. Again you've got to hit at least one of the ten. And so on, right up to a hundred throws. The point is, there ain't time to give every amateur a hundred tries to see if he can hit one glass ball. The one-in-ten rule squeezes out the amateurs and saves time."

"Fair enough."

Cletus Hatch said, "The line judges keep score on each contestant. After every man's had his one hundred throws, the top scores are tallied. That decides the winner."

"What if there's a tie?"

"Then the shooters involved in the tie have to square off against an additional ten balls each, and if it's still a tie they shoot another ten balls after that, and so on until somebody wins."

"How do they divide up the handgun shooters from the long guns?"

"They don't. It's free choice of weapons to every man."

"Revolvers and repeaters—they get to shoot as many times as they like at the same ball while it's in the air?"

"Rules say you only get one shot."

"What's Bogardus' weapon?"

"Repeating cartridge rifle. Henry rimfire. Fifteen-shot magazine. Forty-four-caliber."

"That's a heavy weapon."

"Not his. He gets his rifles hand-worked personally by Mr. Oliver Winchester. They're said to be lightweight and of perfect accuracy. Now you wanted to know about the betting and I'll lay that out for you. There are no odds on anything up to nine balls, since you've got to hit at least ten out of a hundred to stay in the competition. From ten balls to one hundred the odds increase with the number of hits. Odds against you are on this table here."

He showed me the front page of his tally book.

BALLS HIT	ODDS AGAINST
10–19	1 to 1 (even money)
20–29	2 to 1
30–39	7 to 1
40–49	12 to 1
50–79	25 to 1
80–90	40 to 1
91–100	50 to 1

"Those are the odds against unknown shooters."

"You mean if I hit better than ninety out of a hundred you'll pay me fifty dollars for every dollar I bet?"

"That's the stake."

"What odds do you put on a fellow beating Doc Bogardus?"

"One hundred to one," Cletus Hatch said promptly.

In the poke I separated the coins by feel. When I drew my hand out it held two gold coins: a twenty-dollar double eagle and a five-dollar half eagle. "Put me down for two separate bets. Twenty dollars at a hundred to one that I beat Doc Bogardus."

Cletus Hatch's red eyebrows shot up.

I said, "The other five dollars at fifty to one that I hit more than ninety glass balls."

"Remember now, you hit only eighty-nine or ninety and you lose all your money, son. The fifty odds start at ninety-one. That's a risky bet."

I said, "I'd bet it all on beating Bogardus, you see, except I've never seen him shoot."

"That's sensible." He took the money out of my palm. "Wait up now, I'll write you my receipt."

.   .   .

Walking over toward the line with Cletus Hatch's receipt in my pocket I was thinking: If I beat Bogardus I'd win the thousand-dollar purse plus $2,000 on my twenty-dollar bet and $250 on my fifty-dollar bet. That came to $3,250. If I didn't beat Bogardus but still hit more than ninety balls I'd win $250. If I fell down and broke my shooting arm I'd still have the five dollars that was left in my pocket to pay my boardinghouse landlady and the stable where I'd hired the horse. I'd learned never to bet my last money on anything, no matter how sweet it looked, and that was a resolve I didn't break for a very long time.

I knew I could hit more than ninety glass balls and I was pretty sure

I had a chance to beat Bogardus as well but then there must have been a lot of shooters there who felt the same way. Hardly a grown man in Colorado didn't have a gun and none of them would have signed up against Bogardus if they didn't think themselves experts. Tell a man you could outshoot him and it was like telling him you could beat his time with his woman. Those were gun-proud times. Most of the older ones had pioneered. They shot straight the first time; those who didn't were just as likely buried somewhere back on the prairie.

I saw young Caleb Rice through the crowd and remarked again the hangdog sorrow pleated into his comical face. He was fiddling with one of his wood-handled Navy Colts. I made my way toward him and heard a man say to his lady companion, "Bogardus beat the army competition team last summer at Springfield Armory Range. We're in for some first-class shootin' today."

Caleb Rice looked up at me in an edgy sort of way. "You get your bet down?"

"I did."

"On me, I hope."

"Not exactly."

"Here I thought you'd be smart. I'll tell you something—Bogardus ain't never shot a match west of the Missouri before and I believe he's made a mistake coming out here. What do they know about real shooting back East? I believe Bogardus will go home from here with his tail between his legs. It ain't him worries me. But some of these other gents—I know some of these boys. Shoot the feather off a Cheyenne's head at half a mile. You see that old-timer there? That's old Fitz Bragg, he rode with Kit Carson against the Navajo, he hunted all over these hills with Bridger and them-all. That old boy can shoot the whiskers off a cat."

I said, "You're shooting against glass balls, Caleb, not against Fitz Bragg or Doc Bogardus. Just keep that in mind, you'll be all right."

He took a deep breath and threw his head back; for a moment he closed his eyes and then he clapped me on the arm. "Thanks. I had the jitters there."

We turned and joined the throng pressing toward the gate. The shoot was about to begin.

The thing I would like to make clear is that it wasn't blind luck that brought me to Denver that day. If it hadn't been that match it would have been another one. I was not just another drifter out to try his luck. I'd fixed my goal in mind at the age of sixteen down in the Tubac country of Arizona Territory. Down through the years I've seen countless young men who caromed from pillar to post, always expecting that someday they would decide what they wanted to do with their lives, what they wanted to make of themselves. I never had that indecision. I knew from the beginning that I intended to be the champion rifle shot of the world.

Of course there's many a slip, and the road to hell is paved, and a young man's fancy turns—in sum, I shouldn't have had a sand fly's chance of achieving so lofty a goal. But I will say this much for it, even then: at least it *was* a goal. It separated me from the rootless and the windblown. It provided me with sins I came to regard as virtues—ambition, pride. And for a little while there it looked as if it might even keep me out of trouble.

. . .

C. S. Roe of the Denver *Gazette* climbed up on the gazebo and hollered for attention. When he got the requisite silence he addressed us in a thin high ringing voice.

"Now the judges here be Mr. Pease, Mr. Mackenzie and Mr. Harrison, known to every man in Denver, and their decision will be final as to the competition scores.

"Shooters will stand twelve men in a line and they will shoot at will, there being twenty-five feet between each man and the next man in line.

"A line judge will stand behind each shooter, and the line judge's decisions will be final as to whether a throw was fair and whether a ball was hit. If any ball is thrown too wide or too low, and judged unfair by the line judge, then that ball will not be counted against the shooter unless he fires at it, in which case it will be entered in his score as a fair throw.

"Each shooter will shout '*Throw*' when he's ready each time. The boy will then throw a glass ball to a rise of twenty-five yards above and ahead of the shooter.

"You may shoot at any time before the ball hits the ground, but under no circumstances is any weapon to be discharged in such a way as to put risk to spectators or men in the line. There are constables here prepared to make immediate arrests. This is a gentlemen's sporting meet and we mean to see it remains genteel. Constables have been instructed to arrest anyone who acts disputatious about anything whatsoever.

"We have ninety-six registered shooters. I believe you all know the rules of exclusion. Each shooter must hit at least one of every ten balls thrown, else he is disqualified. Shooters may choose their own rate of speed, but as soon as each man finishes his string he must retire behind the line so that the next man may take his place.

"Names of the first twelve contestants have been drawn from Mr. Pease's hat and I will now read them off. As your name is called, please take your place ahead of one of the mounds of glass balls you see along the fence. And good luck to each and every man.

"Mr. Samuel Thompson. Mr. Fitzroy Bragg. Mr. Ephraim Jenkins. Mr. Caleb Rice. Mr. Calvin Ludlow . . ."

Mine wasn't called. I pried my way along the fence, had to skirt the heaps of glass balls and the groups of kids. I found a place to stand down near the end of the fence where the crowd was thin. Caleb Rice had made a run for the left-end position the instant his name was called and he'd beaten Fitzroy Bragg there because Bragg was too old to run fast. I knew the yarns they spun about Fitz Bragg. He was one of the famous ones.

I saw the old man grin impishly at Caleb Rice because obviously they'd both had the same thought about the angle of the sun. Bragg wore a store-bought suit and a bowler hat but it didn't disguise him; you could see by the way he moved that he was an outdoorsman. He reminded me quite a bit of old Grandfather Clement Tyree with his weather-whacked leather in place of skin and his crinkled eyes that had squinted into a lot of sun-beaten distances. And he had that same slow-moving gaunt grace.

The three of us were strangers to one another that day in Denver. But when you're drawn to someone it's not surprising your paths cross again. I would meet up with each of them later on—in wild and different circumstances—but when it happened it didn't surprise me. You read histories and memoirs of those times and sometimes you can't help but wonder how those old-timers kept crossing trails so constantly. There were little cliques, of course, and to some extent they were separate from one another, but for example you can pick up any book about the late '60s and the early '70s and you'll see how Wild Bill Hickok and Buffalo Bill Cody and Texas Jack and a whole crowd of them kept intertwining, while farther south and west there was a constant flow-together of younger fellows like the Earp brothers and the Masterson brothers, and there were some—like Billy Dixon and Fitz Bragg and Caleb Rice and me—who time and again kept meeting up with fellows from both these groups. From the long view forty or fifty years later it starts to look like a lot of suspicious dime-novel coincidence but it wasn't. We didn't have much of a population west of the Mississippi in those days. There was a circuit of boom towns. Everybody rode it. Farmers didn't, of course, but then nobody wrote dime novels about farmers.

I keep digressing.

I was watching Caleb Rice and Fitz Bragg at the left end of the shooters' line. They were next to each other, separated by about nine yards of grass. Caleb looked over his shoulder and gave me that sorrowful smile when he recognized me; touched his hatbrim with a finger-tip and winked at me and hauled one of the long-barreled .36's out of his black belt.

I made a couple of cut-cotton patches and stuffed them in my ears. "Fire at will."

"Throw!"

"Throw!"

The cotton distanced the shots in my ears; they snapped like Mexican fireworks. I watched Caleb shoot. He set his feet and his shoulders lifted high, then settled—deep breath. "Throw." A glass ball soared up over his head and I saw the Navy revolver rise smoothly. The glass ball glistened in the sun. It hung poised for a brief instant at the top of its climb and that was when he fired. I saw the Colt kick up in his hand as it discharged. Before the sound reached me I saw the glass ball shatter. It made a pretty cascade of rainbow pieces that arched toward the meadow.

"Throw!"

The line judge on Caleb's position was a friendly-looking gent with puffy red cheeks and a whisky-blue nose. He was right beside me. He tipped his silk hat back and hooked his elbows over the rail fence behind us. He didn't take his eyes off Caleb when he talked to me out the side of his mouth. "This boy's worth watching."

Caleb hit his third ball and called for another throw. I looked over at the old man, Fitz Bragg. He was using a French rifle, a needle gun. Short barrel, lightweight, repeater. *Throw.* A shower of glass shards.

The racket kept popping and I was glad for the cotton in my ears.

It surprised me how quickly it went. The experts wasted no time between shots and the rest were soon ruled out by inaccuracy. New shooters began to move into the line almost at once and I listened for my name to be called.

Up the line I saw Bogardus move into a vacated position. It was all very democratic: Bogardus had his name drawn from the hat just like everybody else. I moved along the fence to get a better look.

Bogardus took up his stance like a violinist with the lever-action Henry repeater braced into his shoulder so he wouldn't have to lower the rifle to jack each new round into it. Two boys behind him at the base of the pile of glass balls began to make alternate throws and Bogardus' rifle began to speak.

The crowd behind the fence at my back clustered forward until it became a tight steaming mass. Bogardus' rifle cracked with businesslike rhythm and glass broke *pop-pop-pop* where he was shooting. Pieces of two or even three balls would still be falling into the grass when he hit the next one; the two boys were throwing as fast as they could.

Bogardus ran through the fifteen cartridges in his magazine without missing a single ball.

I'd always thought myself a sharpshooter. But I'd never seen anything like the display Bogardus was putting on. Sometime in later years in my reading I ran across a definition: *Genius is the art of making something look easy.* By that definition Doc Bogardus was a genius. He made it look absolutely effortless.

I began to realize I was going to have a hard time winning my bet.

A man stepped forward then and handed Bogardus a fresh rifle, took away the empty one and retired to clean it and reload it. Bogardus resumed with hardly a break in the metered rhythm of his shooting. He stood fat and steady, his head hardly stirring, the rifle moving gently to seek each toss. No wasted movements. The mechanisms of those rifles must have been honed to perfection: I saw Bogardus lever new loads into the Henry merely by flicking his right hand open and shut. Empty copper rimfire shells cascaded from the breach and formed a pile around his boots. The man was a shooting machine.

· · ·

Fitz Bragg's short needle gun cracked steadily and sometimes it blended with the snapping of Caleb Rice's revolver. The two of them completed their rounds almost simultaneously and I saw them grin at each other. Then Caleb came back to the fence waving his revolver overhead to the judges on the gazebo to indicate he was surrendering his position. I went along the rail to meet him. "How'd you do?"

"I missed three."

The line judge said, "Four. Your score's ninety-six."

"I make it three." Caleb said it with that kind of amiable soft voice that makes you look again. It was the first time I realized that about him: he wasn't a man to mess with.

"You fired at one of them twice, and it was your second shot that took it. That don't count, son, by the rules of the contest. It'd be unfair to the shooters with single-shot weapons, you see."

"Well I didn't know that."

"You can check out the rules if you like. They're posted on the fence over there." The line judge sniffed. "Your job to shoot 'em, bucko, mine to count 'em. I've got no ax to grind here."

"I won't dispute your word then. Four it is. I'll take ninety-six— I don't think anybody will beat it today. Wind's coming up. I missed two on that account."

The judge smiled a bit. "What about the other ones, then?"

"Plain carelessness on both of those. I misjudged the rise." Caleb took my arm and walked me off to one side. "Your turn coming up soon, I reckon. Tell you a trick I learned a while ago. Lick your finger, moisten your windward ear. Gives you a handle on the wind. A gust makes your ear cold. Those glass balls are hollow, the wind pushes them around more than you think."

"Why thanks."

"You did me a good turn back there when I got rattled. Calmed me down and I'm beholden." His face was grey with smoke. "Anyway you won't beat my score."

"*Next shooter up, please. Mr. Hugh Cardiff.*"

    · · ·

I went into the line fourth position from the left and that was satisfactory. My line judge was a little tiny fellow in a bulky beaver-pelt coat. I shook hands with him and introduced myself. "How'd Bogardus do?"

"Ninety-six out of a hundred."

"Then he can still be beat."

"Yes sir," the little fellow drawled, not giving anything away, but I could see he was amused. "That a Kentucky Hawken?"

"It is."

"Pretty old one, ain't it?"

"Pretty near as old as I am." I stepped forward to take up my position and looked over my shoulder at the boy. "How's your arm holding out?"

"Fine, sir. We've been taking turns."

"All right. I shoot about five a minute with this old muzzle-loader. Give you a chance to breathe between throws."

"Yes sir. Thank you, sir." Boys in those days were polite.

"You ready?"

"Yes sir."

"Let's go, then."

I put my back to him and lifted the Hawken, snugged it into my shoulder and tested my footing.

"Throw."

    · · ·

I saw the ball soar overhead, sun winking along it, and I had time to remind myself the sun glare would be on the left side of the ball now because it was nearly three o'clock in the afternoon. I aimed a fraction to the right of the point of light. When the ball reached its apex against the sky I squeezed the shot and lowered the rifle to reload without bothering to watch the target. I knew I'd hit it.

Paper cartridge, ramrod, percussion cap. Lift the rifle. "Throw."

    · · ·

I shot the first twenty without a miss. Behind me a crowd began to gather.

I turned to the throw-boy. "Let's let the rifle cool down a minute. No penalty for that, is there?"

"No sir. You take all the time you want." That was the line judge; he was watching me with friendly admiration now.

The rifle was hot in my hands. I saw Caleb Rice in the crowd alongside the barker Cletus Hatch. I walked over to the fence and crooked my finger at Hatch.

"Anybody besides me bet money on me today?"

"Nope. Nobody ever heard of you."

"I may have given you a fast shuffle," I said. "You might have heard of me under the name Hugh Smith."

"I've heard that name, yes."

"What odds would you put on Hugh Smith?"

"About half what I gave you. Except on beating Bogardus. Those odds are the same for everybody."

"Then change the odds on my five-dollar bet, will you? I'll feel better."

"I'm obliged for your honesty."

I saw Caleb watching me with a speculative and dubious eye.

Then the crowd parted obediently as Doc Bogardus marched forward. He planted his bulk before me, the fence separating us, and looked at me from under his dark hatbrim. He was tugging his thick U. S. Grant beard. I couldn't be sure if there was a smile behind the beard but in any case I smiled at him. Not cocky or anything. I was just being friendly. All sorts of stories have come down across the years about that first time we met face to face. Now I'm going to write down how it really went.

Bogardus just looked at me for a moment, maybe smiling, maybe not, and I heard someone say, "We got four ninety-sixes so far and we got better than two dozen shooters still to go. Powerful marksmen here today."

"You watch this big youngster here. Way he's going he's like to beat ninety-six. He ain't missed a ball yet."

"With an old Kentucky muzzle-load, no less."

I swabbed out the bore with a cool oiled patch. Loaded her up and glanced at Bogardus. I guess I was waiting for him to say or do something but he didn't; he just watched me. I didn't feel any threat coming off him. He didn't rattle me, nor, I think, did he intend to.

I went back to the line and spoke over my shoulder to the boy. "You ready?"

"Yes sir."

"Throw."

. . .

There was a corner of my mind, separate from the rest, that kept track of the numbers. Twenty-three was my first miss and I heard a gush of sound from the crowd. I was annoyed because I shouldn't have missed that one; I'd thought it was a hit, I wasn't looking at it—I was reloading by the time it hit the ground but I heard it burst on impact and I heard the crowd.

Then I remembered what Caleb had told me. I wet my finger on my tongue and moistened my left ear.

The breeze fluttered cold. Batting the glass balls around, giving them lift. The wind must be freshening.

Now I took more time with each shot, testing the air before I called for the throw.

Down the line the steady racket of gunfire continued. Another expert over to the right somewhere drew some of the crowd off but when I looked back after my thirty-first shot Bogardus was still there, standing like a great black rock, watching with his big dark eyes, and I still couldn't discern the expression behind the beard.

I shot without missing again until the fifty-third ball. I don't know what happened with that one. It seemed to jink to the side just as I squeezed the shot. Maybe the wind, but I didn't feel it on my ear.

By then the crowd had massed again and there was no more talk around me. They watched me in silence. After the sixtieth shot I waved the throw-boy back; the rifle was so hot I could hardly hold it.

Doc Bogardus spoke for the first time in my hearing. His voice was as deep as a cave echo. "Someone bring the lad a bucket of water."

.   .   .

My eyes burned from the smoke. My arms were beginning to ache. I propped the rifle upright against the fence and revolved my arms in their sockets to loosen them up.

Bogardus said, "Take your time now."

"Yes sir. Thanks."

"Mighty heavy work with a long rifle like that. Started my own career with the same weapon. Hawken Brothers. That was back before the war."

A youth came up lugging a wooden water bucket; Bogardus waved him forward. "Make way, gentlemen, please. Set it down here, boy, that's good." Bogardus leaned against the fence and extended a hand toward me. "Mind handing me that rifle?"

I was uncertain but even then I knew the only way you could find out whether you could trust a man was to trust him and see what happened. I lifted the rifle through the fence. I felt a twinge in my left arm: a warning.

30

Bogardus took it from me, upended it and unceremoniously plunged the muzzle into the water as deep as it would go.

I was shocked.

Steam sizzled loudly and made a cloud above the bucket before the wind took it away.

Anger lanced through me. I put both hands on the rail ready to vault it.

Bogardus held the rifle upright, muzzle-down in the water. He spoke calmly. "No harm to the rifle, son. My word on it."

I hesitated.

Bogardus said, "Hawken steel can take it. The damage occurs if you heat it up too much, not the other way round. Understand me?"

I suppose I was gawking; I don't remember replying. Bogardus tested the breech plate with his finger. "Cool enough now." He lifted it back through the fence. "Run a dry patch through her, then a light coating of oil. Good as new. She starts to heat up again, put her back in the water."

There was a buzzing murmur back through the crowd. "Never seen the like." And: "Man must be crazy, hot steel in cold water—bend that rifle like a lariat." And: "Canny enough from a dude that sees he's gettin' beat."

Bogardus swung around quickly. "I'm betting one hundred dollars the boy makes his first shot. Come on, have I got any bettors?"

The crowd swayed back away from him. Bogardus wheeled again and I saw the contempt in it; now he faced me. "Go ahead, son. Pleasure to watch you work."

I dried the bore and oiled it, loaded and lifted, and tried to ignore the twinge in my left arm. "Throw."

A hit.

I looked back and saw the hard smile in Bogardus' eyes; now I knew what his smile looked like. I rammed a load home and capped the rifle. "Thank you."

"My pleasure."

"Throw!"

. . .

Number seventy-four was my third miss. I had to attribute it to a faulty bullet: possibly a bubble in the metal that threw it off plumb. Three down. I had to make twenty-six straight hits to beat the leaders.

Eighty, eighty-one, eighty-two. Shooting slow, shooting steady. Wait for the wind to settle. Eighty-three. The rifle heating up again; I plunged it without hesitation into the bucket.

Bogardus was still at the fence. The last competitors were moving

31

into the line. Rattle of gunfire; acrid stink of powder smoke; no talk at all in the crowd now. My eyes were gritty and raw. My left shoulder was causing real pain by now and I knew it was the old break where Vern Tyree had shot me with the exploding gun. Nothing I could do about it except ignore it.

I pulled the rifle out of the bucket, dried it, oiled it, rammed a fresh load down, capped the lock, settled the butt plate into my shoulder socket.

"Throw."

Eighty-seven.

Ninety-one.

Ninety-three.

Take it easy now, just take it slow, there's no time limit, forget the numbers, take each shot as you find it, one at a time and no thought to anything else, forget the damned pain.

"Throw."

Ninety-four. Ninety-five.

The crowd behind me seemed to vibrate with silence. A steady shrill whistle piped in my ears despite the cotton wadding; it always gets like that after the first half hour or so. I let the rifle hang down at arm's length and tried to gather strength; moistened my ear and dragged the Hawken to my shoulder. "Throw."

Ninety-six.

"Come on over here, Elizabeth, watch this boy. Four to go. He's hit all but three."

"Throw."

Ninety-seven.

"Throw."

The glass sphere floated up. Sunlight, getting a bit lower now, rippling off the smooth surface. Red raw grit in my eyes. Throb and twang in the shoulder; it was bad now. Watch the ball. Sudden cold lash of air against my moistened ear. Watch for the jink to the right—feel that gust? Wait for the pause at the top.

Squeeze.

Ninety-eight.

Paper cartridge. Ramrod. Cap. Tongue, ear. Lift the rifle. *Forget the pain.* Easy now.

I didn't call for the throw. I lowered the rifle and dragged my sleeve across my eyes to wipe away the wash of tears—part of it was pain, part of it was the eyes trying to clean out sulfur irritation. Was that metal getting too hot again? No; not yet. Just take it easy now. Two to go, that's all. You can do it easy. Eyes dry now, all right. Lift the rifle. Settle down. Good.

"Throw."

I watched that one break. Ninety-nine.

A muted explosion of vocalized emotion from the crowd; and then a hush—in fairness I have to call it a hush. I could hear it distinctly, even through the ringing in my ears, when someone back in the crowd sucked air through his teeth.

Gentle now. The last shot.

I lifted the rifle.

"Throw."

The sphere floated into the sky. The sights lifted to meet it. No wind this time; an easy shot. Curving a bit off to the left there, lead it steady. Turn.

The twinge in the shoulder made me gasp. It passed; but now the ball was falling and I felt the gust against my ear as I squeezed the shot off.

The groan ran through the crowd.

I'd missed.

. . .

We had six finalists tied at ninety-six. We drew lots for the sun-side advantage and Fitz Bragg won the shortest straw. Far-left position. Then a Texican, Caleb Rice, me, a Denver sporting man and at the right-hand end Doc Bogardus.

It didn't seem to alarm him. He came down the line to speak briefly with each shooter. When he came to me he smiled through the beard. "What's wrong with the arm?"

"Broke it once. Shoulder acts up now and then."

"Have that seen to when you get a chance. And buy yourself a light-weight repeater rifle for these competitions if you mean to stay in the shooting game. Even as big as you are, you'll do better if your arms don't get tired."

"Thank you."

"Good luck to us all, then." Bogardus went on down the line. Over the years the "feud" between us filled a lot of newspaper space but the fact is that off the shooting line I always liked and admired Doc. He was a gentleman.

I looked to my left. Caleb stood with his eyes on the ground at his feet, a Navy revolver in his hand, waiting for the signal to start. Uneasy, unnerved; it was evident in his stance. I spoke softly: "Hey, Caleb."

It brought his face around. His eyes came up. I winked broadly at him.

The slow mournful smile pushed the shadows back from his face; he straightened up, breathing deep.

Down at the end of the line Fitz Bragg spat a brown stream of tobacco juice into the ruined grass.

C. S. Roe climbed up on the gazebo. "Your attention please, gentlemen. This is the elimination round. Shooters will fire ten throws each. You know the rules. All right, it appears all contestants are ready? Fire at will."

"Throw."

. . .

My shoulder gave me trouble and I was late on two of the ten but I managed to hit them before they reached the ground. One of them was so low when I hit it that the bullet ricocheted off the pasture.

That round knocked off the Denver sporting man and the Texican and Fitz Bragg; they each came in with nine out of ten but it wasn't good enough because they were up against Bogardus and Caleb Rice and me, and each of us made every ball.

It was a surprise to the crowd when Fitz Bragg missed his tenth shot; apparently something went wrong with his needle gun but the old man took it in good spirit and I saw him nodding happily when he headed off to collect his bet winnings from Cletus Hatch. Well-wishers clustered, clapping him on the back; he was a popular man everywhere in the West.

"Second round, three shooters, ready on the line please, gentlemen. From the left: Mr. Caleb Rice of Beaumont, Texas, shooting the Colt's Patent Navy model revolver, caliber point-thirty-six. Mr. Hugh Cardiff of Mill Springs, Kentucky, sometimes known as Hugh Smith, shooting the Hawken long rifle, muzzle-load, caliber point-forty-six. Dr. George Bogardus of Danville, Virginia, shooting the Henry rimfire repeating cartridge rifle, caliber point-forty-four. At your will, gentlemen, commence firing."

. . .

On his third shot Bogardus missed.

A shout went up from the crowd but then Caleb missed his fifth shot and it left the prize open to me.

But pain kept jabbing my shoulder and I fluffed my next-to-last shot and it tied the three of us up again; yet another round to go and I doubted my shoulder could take it.

Caleb said, "You had us for a minute there."

I cooled the Hawken in the water bucket and walked around in small circles swinging my arms in great circles, trying to squeeze the smoke out of my eyes, fighting the dizziness of fatigue and the painful whistling in my ears. It was no help realizing the other two had most of the same difficulties.

34

Bogardus walked over and stood between Caleb and me. "Gents, I salute both of you. Whoever wins this round, I believe in my heart there are three champions of this meet."

Someone in the crowd said, "You boys can beat the fat dude. Don't let him soften you up."

I glared at them but couldn't single him out. Bogardus, for his part, made a point of ignoring it. He turned away toward his position and I said, "It's an honor shooting with you, sir."

"And for me the same, Mr. Cardiff." I saw the twitch of the smile behind the beard before he went by.

I dragged the Hawken out of the bucket and swabbed it out.

It was past four o'clock and the sun was well down in the sky, the breezes more fitful than ever. The light was changing; tricky conditions for shooting. Skill really wasn't the issue any longer; it was a matter of endurance.

The Hawken seemed to weigh a ton. "Throw."

A hit.

I was still in this thing; I wasn't beaten yet.

Load, lift. "Throw." A hit again and I settled back into the rhythm of it. Load, lift. "Throw."

I heard an outburst of emotion from the crowd but I didn't break my rhythm to investigate it; possibly one of the others had missed a shot. I broke my third ball, then the fourth, the fifth. "Throw." The sixth.

A murmur rumbling through the crowd. Never mind; not my concern. "Throw." The seventh—a hit. Tears of pain from the arm; I could hardly move it. Moisten the ear. Lift—*lift*. Aim. "Throw."

The eighth: off-center but still a hit; I watched that one, watched the fragments of glass twinkle earthward and paused with two shots left to wipe my eyes and swing my arm back and forth before I loaded for the ninth shot.

I was lifting the rifle when a shout burst from the crowd, a great explosive groan—one of my opponents had missed a shot, that was for sure, but I continued the steady rise of the rifle to my shoulder. "Throw."

Arc of glittering glass, wind on my ear, the shoulder now grinding with steady throbs of pain that weren't nearly as distracting as the earlier stabs. Squeeze. Take the recoil tight and easy.

A hit.

Load, lift.

"Throw."

Aim, follow its rise, wait for the peak. Sunlight on glass—I could actually see the silhouettes of the Rockies reflected in the glass before it burst into tiny bits and rained across the grass and I heard the ear-splitting great roar of the crowd as I turned and plunged the hot rifle into the water bucket and realized, when I looked up at the faces beyond the fence, that I'd won.

BOOK TWO

Westering

LOOKING BACK over those events that took place more than fifty years ago I can see that I have not explained very much about myself or how I came to be what I was. I like to think I might have ended up a champion rifle shooter no matter how things had started out, but the fact is it was the war that put me on the road that carried me to Denver and I feel obliged to tell you a bit about that because there have been some wild representations about it in the fictions that pass for fact about me.

For instance I was never a Pony Express rider, as some would have it. The Pony Express was a short-lived institution of 1860 and 1861. I was born in 1849. So much for that idiocy.

Or: for instance—it has been asserted that I got the idea that led to my invention of the Wild West Show from watching the dancing and acting-out and manly contests of a Plains Indian powwow when I was captured as a boy by Cheyenne warriors who burned my parents' log cabin and made off with me and my baby sister. I have a copy of the magazine that contained that account. Now that yarn is wrong in so many different ways I hardly know where to start. I have no sister. (I had an elder sister but she died in infancy.) My parents did not live in a log cabin. We lived in Kentucky, on a farm, and the Cheyenne do not range nearly that far east. Indians never burned our home, nor attacked our farm, nor troubled us in any way for that matter. My father died in the war and I will tell you about that in a moment. I have seen the activities of Plains Indian powwows but that did not take place until I was a grown man. And I did not get the idea for the

37

Wild West Show from Indian powwows. I got it from a Negro cowboy's prank.

. . .

I did not know my mother. She died giving me birth.

My father's name was Michael Hugh Cardiff. It is the name with which he was christened but actually it wasn't the original family name. His father, my grandfather, had come across from Swansea, Wales, about the time Jackson and Lafitte were defending New Orleans; my grandfather's surname was Llewellyn-Lowyd and the men who admitted Immigrants to Baltimore asked where he was from, and thinking no one would have heard of the town of Swansea my grandfather named the nearest large city, which was Cardiff; he was written down in the book as Cardiff and so it remained.

My father was born in Pennsylvania; his father was a coal miner. The old man died in a mining accident in 1837 when my father was eighteen years of age; after a suitable period of mourning and clearing-up, my father married his sweetheart, Bettina Rogers, who was distantly related to the Rogers who sought the Northwest Passage. My father had a bitter dislike of the coal mines for reasons that must be obvious. He took up farming, failed in his first attempt and went west with his pregnant wife to Kentucky, where my sister was born and died on the same day. For some years thereafter my mother feared attempting to have another child but then in 1848 she became pregnant again and her fears—and those of the doctors—were proved sensible because they had to cut me out of her womb and she did not survive the loss of blood.

My grandmother was still alive then; she and my father raised me on the farm near Mill Springs. She died of the typhus in 1859 and I still remember the funeral.

My father was a fine marksman and put a .25 flintlock rifle in my hands upon my seventh birthday and trained me in its uses.

My father and my grandmother, like so many who pioneered the green hill country, were unlettered. It was my father's ambition for me that I not grow up illiterate and ignorant. We had no schools for farm children in those days of course; the town had its school but we were fifteen miles out. A trip into Mill Springs on the backs of our plow horses was an adventure and infrequent, and possible only in the dry seasons.

It was for those reasons that my father undertook an arrangement with the son of a neighboring farm family to tutor me three days each week. I was my father's only son and it was not until long afterward that I realized that circumstances had soured him and he had invested

38

all his hopes in me; he had no ambitions for himself. I was to be his vindication.

The neighbor family were pariahs because they were Jews. In those days if you were a Welshman you were expected to mine coal; and if you were Jewish you were expected to be a tradesman. The Singmans were farmers and this threw our families together in a strange way because we Cardiffs were Welshmen yet we didn't dig for coal. No one quite knew what to make of the Cardiffs or the Singmans.

The Singmans had a son seven years my senior. His name was Isaac. He was very small, slight, myopic, unsuited for farm work. I knew him at first as a cool youth, aloof, distant—he was my tutor and he administered my lessons strictly. When I was nine he was only sixteen but I regarded him as a middle-aged man; actually he had a keen wry humor but he displayed no playfulness to me. I suppose I feared him. He had been raised by several generations of bookish people: they had grandparents and great-grandparents living on the farm with them. Proud people. Devout and demonstrative. Isaac was a kind of black sheep because of his restlessness and curiosity. He would make painful trips afoot to Mill Springs to raid the town's school library for books; he would read anything he could get his hands on—if there was nothing else he would read the labels on flour sacks; I imagine he memorized the St. Louis catalogs. At least twice a week we'd see him trudging by our gate with a heavy sack over his back, filled with books. It was a thirty-mile walk and it took him all day. With the sack slung over his shoulder he'd walk along at a steady pace with a book open just under his chin. Often he'd devour an entire book during the hike. It was a wonder he didn't break his neck. He tripped and fell quite often but he must have had a muse looking after him.

Isaac taught me to read and taught me the hunger for it. I have four passions in my life now: arms, books, my woman and the rapture of an audience in the arena.

At first my father and grandmother were suspicious of Isaac. I suppose he was different from them and from the people they knew.

My grandmother died; then it was just the two of us, my father and I. And Isaac who came three days of the week to tutor me, for which my father paid him five cents or the equivalent in produce. Isaac turned the money over to his family for his keep, as he rarely did any work on their farm.

My father was neither a born farmer nor a successful one. About the best he had to say for the life was that it was better than mining coal. He took no interest in it. The farm was a burden and he kept it only because it supported us. Whenever there was an excuse he would put up the tools and take down the rifles—our food came as much from hunting as it did from the furrowed ground. We sold meat and pelts to supplement the farm's meager providence. By the time I was nine years old I was the equal of any man in the valley on the hunt; by the time I was eleven I was far the best hunter in that district of Kentucky. My father boasted of it: he took pride in my prowess, as it reflected on his tutelage.

My twelfth birthday came on the twenty-sixth of January, 1861, and that was when my father made me the gift of the Hawken .46 long rifle. At that time the rifle was several years old.

Often we would come in from a hunt with raccoon and possum in our kits, sometimes a deer slung on a shoulder pole between us, and we'd find Isaac waiting on the porch reading his inevitable book; we'd skin out the game and then I'd go to my lessons with Isaac.

Penny dreadfuls have made our early lives out to have been ceaseless dire adventures. In fact the only adventures of my childhood, before the war came, were those in the novels I gaped over. I must have committed the Waverley novels to memory.

At first the war passed us by and we heard of it only as distant news. The border skirmishes had not touched our valley and politics were matters of indifference to the people there; there were no slaveholders in the county, nor any inflamed spirit of abolitionism. I recall the valley as a pretty little place, soft and green, locked away from the rest of the world. There was only one road out and it forded half a dozen streams to reach Mill Springs. There were fourteen farms in the valley; most of it was still uncleared wilderness where my father and I hunted. Fourteen families and none of them interested in war.

At first we could only hear the guns like distant storms; then at night we could see the flashes. Then on the far hills on a sunny afternoon we saw the slow-moving dots as the advance scouts for opposing armies felt their way toward one another.

. . .

Like deer in a hailstorm we just had to hunker down and wait it out. We heard the peppering of distant musketry for days and we kept hoping the armies would pass on by and have their battle somewhere else. Some of the boys my age went off to spy on the warfare; like anybody else I had my curiosity but my father kept me close at hand. "I imagine there's principles and things a man might risk getting shot for. If a thing be worth living for then it ought to be worth dying for. But this war's none of our concern, Hugh. I can't say I hold with owning slaves but I can't say I hold with going to war over it. Your grandfather told me they did away with slavery in the old country and they did it without going to war. And anyway it may be this war of theirs is over the slave question and it may be it's over something else. I don't pretend to comprehend these things. You can fight to defend your land when it's invaded but we appear to be invaded by both sides just now and I can't see as either of them be determined to protect us. We've no allegiance."

My father was born in Pennsylvania but he had a Welshman's song in his voice; he'd been raised among the immigrants.

He said, "If you feel like you must fight for something, that's something else, but I don't see the sense of mixing in strangers' troubles. We'll just be keepin' our heads down until they pass by. You hear me? I want no tomfooling around. You could get yourself killed."

"Yes sir."

. . .

The Battle of Mill Springs was fought on the far side of that range of hills but some of it splashed over into our valley and the hungry soldiers of both armies made free and easy with the crops and stores of several farms over toward the west gap. When we got word of that my father loaded the rifles and set them ready by the door. "They can kill each other if it's what they want. But they'll not steal our food." He was getting angry now. My father always had a slack rein on his temper.

This was January of '62 and I was about to turn thirteen. I was on the skinny side and hadn't yet started to sprout tall and my voice hadn't begun to change. My father would talk to me as if I were an adult but he looked upon me as a child.

When the musketry rattled closer down the valley he began to pack the kit bags we used when we went on overnight hunts. "I think we must fade into the hills and wait them out."

"What about the farm?" I asked.

"It's your life I'm thinking of now." We shouldered the kits and our rifles and made for the hills three miles behind the south pasture.

We never got that far.

. . .

Where we always crossed the creek my father had made a path of stepping-stones. There had been quite a bit of early snow that season and the creek was higher than usual. Water birled off the chain of stones and a few of them were an inch or so beneath the flow. My father considered the crossing and the trees on the far side. It was a cool afternoon but not downright cold; much of the snow had melted but there were wet white mounds of it on the shaded banks—everything was dripping. "They like to lie up in ambush in places like this," he said. "We'll cross one at a time. You wait till I'm safe on the far side. Hear me?"

"Yes sir."

He pressed his fist gently against my cheek and I waited in the thicket while he set out across the stones, holding the rifle across his chest for balance. There were oaks along the banks, some of them old and stately; the shadows were deep. It was late in the day. Sunlight fell through the trees aslant and dappled the surface of the creek. There was mist low along the ground, greying the greens. I knew of a beaver dam upstream a few hundred feet but I couldn't see it. We'd known of it for several weeks. Now I heard the banging of the beavers' tails—they'd got a late start and they were busy forting up for the winter. We planned to set traps in the summer when the young beavers were grown; pelts still brought fair prices at that time.

My father had crossed nearly to the far bank when I saw a streak of reflected light high in a tall oak at the bend downstream. My father also seemed to pick it up in the corner of his vision; I saw his head lift and turn. By the time I shifted my gaze to search for it the wink was gone; but then after an instant I saw a puff of smoke there.

My father cried out and the sound was overwhelmed by the delayed snap-*bang* of the rifle in the tree. My father tumbled into the water and even as he was falling I saw him yank the rifle to his shoulder and let fly. Slower to react, I began to raise the Hawken but by then the hidden rifleman was crashing down through the branches, breaking off twigs, making a long howling racket.

I rushed into the stream and slipped on the stones; I lurched and stumbled through the icy chill water toward my father who was struggling up from the water onto the far bank. Before I could reach him I saw the strength run out of him. The rifle fell from his grasp and he collapsed half on the bank with his leggings still in the creek. The fast flow began to push his boots around.

I dropped to my knees at the water's edge and reached out to touch his face. He saw me, tried to speak but he hadn't the strength. He died within those few seconds.

A ray of sun lanced through a hole in the trees and fitfully illuminated his profile, leaves blowing across the light. That remained vivid in my memory ever afterward—the cranky puzzlement still registered on his face.

I saw where the ball had taken him—glancing down through the hollow of his collarbone: he had been leaning forward reaching for the bank and it must have penetrated straight down into the heart to kill him that quickly. What massive strength it must have taken for him to shoot his killer and then drag himself to shore.

But then we Cardiffs have never given up easily.

Fragments of panic flitted through me; I had no idea what to do; what flooded me was an unthinking desperation, a child's wild outcry—I needed my father; I became petulant, angry with him for failing me;

then grief poured through me and I remember the chill of fear striking for the first time, belated but terrible. I was alone.

The little trench spade was strapped to my father's pack and I thought to bury him but I seemed unable to move. I must have remained there without stirring for quite a long time.

Then I heard the approach of hoofbeats. Coming from upstream.

Several horses. The way they ran forward I knew it must be soldiers —they'd heard the shots and were coming to investigate.

The danger galvanized me. I clutched my rifle and slipped into the trees, retreating downstream along the bank, running.

I almost tumbled over the soldier. He lay where he'd fallen crashing from the treetop. His head was twisted unnaturally—broken neck. With a harsh uncaring need to know, I hooked the toe of a boot under his shoulder and rolled him over.

He wore a dusty blue uniform and a corporal's stripes. His face was young, dark, unexceptionally round but I stared into it as though I could find something important there: I suppose I was looking for a sign that he acknowledged my father's retribution.

My father's bullet had punctured the corporal's tunic at the shoulder. Not a mortal shot; it was the fall that had killed him.

I was filled with a peculiar irrational disappointment. Staring at the dead man I felt hollow-throated and nauseous, listening to the advancing ring of hoofbeats.

The horsemen pounded into the thickets and began crashing around, not far above where my father lay on the bank. I wheeled into the oaks and ran for my life.

   . . .

I heard them bulling about for hours. They'd seen my tracks in the wet snow; probably they took me for a Confederate sniper. All they knew was that one of their own lay dead and that a stranger, a farmer, lay with a bullet in his heart. Possibly they assumed the fancied fugitive rebel had killed both men.

They searched in high anger. I heard their voices now and then. I was high in an oak, tears and sweat streaming. I heard someone call for dogs; fortunately there were none nearby.

After dark they kept up the search and I saw torches moving through the forest. But I'd covered my tracks well and I knew if they hadn't found me in daylight they had little chance at night; nevertheless I shivered with terror—suppose they camped and waited for morning light?

But they had a war to fight. After a time they went away. The torches were extinguished. I heard their horses dwindle into the night.

But they might have left a sentry. I stayed in my tree.

43

I'd had glimpses of them, heard men speak of their friendship for the dead corporal. Evidently he'd been a popular fellow, a keen marksman as well; something of a legend among them. He'd been sent out by his unit—they were Union dragoons—to work as a sniper against the rumored rebel spies who were thought to infest the hills. I worked it out that he must have posted himself in the high oak overlooking the bend of the creek so as to ambush spies who came to drink or water their horses. Personally I had never seen a spy and wondered how you would know one by sight. A spy, by definition in those days, was any combatant who didn't wear a uniform to identify his allegiance. The corporal—I suppose he had mistaken my father for a spy. Or perhaps he was one of those men who shoot anything that moves for the sport of it.

In any case he was dead and I couldn't mitigate my grief by raging and swearing revenge. I wept the night through.

Toward morning I ventured back to where my father had fallen but the body was gone. It put a new fear in me, one I couldn't define—I had visions of my father's ghost prowling the oak thickets. Then I saw two mounded graves where the troopers must have buried the men side by side. There was a strange and fitting justice in that.

It was possible the dragoons had left a man behind on guard. I moved with silent caution, shivering in the cold. Made my way half a mile downstream in the river-edge trees, then at dawn struck out through the wild thickets that bordered the back pasture of the Singman farm. The cocks crowed and everything seemed at peace; during the night I'd heard the far rumor of warfare beyond the range but now everything had gone silent.

I saw a fox slink into the brush—perhaps it had spent the night eyeing the Singmans' fenced flock of chickens. I slipped across the barnyard and knocked softly at the back door.

Isaac's mother let me in. She was up and dressed, feeding the iron stove to prepare breakfast for the large family.

My memory of that morning has gone hazy with time; I do not recall with any exactitude the conversations or events. Probably it is of no great importance. I was overwhelmed by terror, a sense of being lost.

I must have blurted out a half-coherent account of what had happened.

"And the sniper?"

"He's dead."

"Did you kill him then, Hugh?"

I only shook my head but they took it for something else and later I heard them telling one another in awe that I had avenged my father by killing a Union corporal.

44

I remember being cuddled and soothed. It put me to discomfort—I was not used to being pawed by women and I was at the age when such attentions embarrass a boy.

There was a great rushing about to feed me and bathe me and treat the scabs and sores of the trivial scratches I'd suffered scrambling in trees and thorn thickets.

Isaac was not at the farm that morning. He had already departed on his hike to Mill Springs. His parents had tried to dissuade him from going because of the danger but Isaac had insisted that the armies were off in the opposite direction. He was twenty years old and capable of making his own decisions; the Singmans were not a stern family and it was not in them to forbid him to go. Isaac was engaged to marry a girl called Rebecca who lived in the town. It was one reason he never postponed his semiweekly walks to the library at the school in Mill Springs.

Isaac's uncle, an itinerant peddler, was at the farm that day. He had his name painted in a faded crescent across the side of his wagon but you could hardly see the legend for the wares cluttered across it: J. V. SINGMAN. I never found out what the initials stood for. J. V. Singman was on his way west; he intended to get out of the war and do his peddling where he didn't risk being plundered and killed, whether by accident or by Jew-haters using the war to conceal their murders. He intended to take his business with him. The vehicle seemed to contain or suspend every device and gadget known to man. He was mostly bald, a gentle slender man perhaps sixty years old, good-humored, easy. When one of Isaac's sisters annoyed him I recall he said with a twinkle, "You should have a cold winter and a short blanket and long legs." The Singmans were a big close warm family and sometimes love filled their house like the heavy scent of fresh rising bread in an oven.

A sweet wine, meant to relax me and soothe my terrors, put me straight to sleep and I must have remained unconscious most of the day. I was exhausted, having crouched wide-awake and shivering all night in the high fork of an oak.

What brought me awake in the evening was the disputations of loud voices coming through the thin door from the front room. I had no trouble hearing what was being said; the Singmans were not bashful about exposing their feelings. Anger shook the walls of the house.

Isaac's father was on at Isaac, who had returned sometime while I slept: "For your own good you must leave."

"I'm not running away," Isaac shouted. "It's what they want."

"Do you care what they want, then?"

"Do I owe them the satisfaction of giving it to them?"

Uncle J. V. Singman put his calm voice between them: "Your father is thinking of the best thing for you. Why not come with me to California? When feelings cool down you can return."

"This is my home. I shan't be driven from it by plowboys."

"It may be your hospital if you stay," the uncle said in his wry way. "From what you say, they would break you in pieces like fish bones. Pride goeth before fish bones, I believe."

Isaac's father said, "Go. Go with your uncle. You'll be in the best hands."

"There are no books on the prairie."

"Suffer. It won't hurt you."

J. V. Singman said, "I leave in the morning in any case. I must be cross the rivers before the ice melts. It is up to you, Isaac, but you know you're welcome with me."

It went on; I fell back into sleep as if drugged and did not reawaken until nearly dawn, when I padded into the kitchen and fueled the coal stove. By the time Mrs. Singman arrived I had the coffee bubbling and she thanked me; she asked me how I felt. She would have kept talking endlessly but Isaac arrived, gaunt and skittish, his eyes hollow as if he hadn't slept at all. "Good morning, student."

I only nodded a greeting; when he was in one of his moods he scared me. He reached for the coffeepot and I saw the tremor in his hand—anger, perhaps fear. He poured himself a cup and sat down and stared at the steam rising off the black surface of the coffee. "Although I'm sure my sorrow is of little help to you at this moment, I'm sorry about your father."

I said, "Why are they after you? And who is 'they'?" I blurted it; a child's curiosity is overwhelming.

To my surprise he answered with a smile. A twisted smile, full of irony. He said, "Well I am very much in love, you see, and I suppose Rebecca is not so much in love with me."

"What's that got to do with anything?"

"Let us just say that I tried in certain uncouth ways to persuade the young lady to do certain things she was reluctant to do. Let us say my passions were inflamed beyond the capacity of conscience to dampen them. And let us say the young lady escaped my grasp and ran shouting to her brothers. Fortunately while they were searching for me in the stable I was being transported out of town under cover of a tarpaulin that lay draped across the bed of a convenient and unsuspecting farm buckboard. It carried me in the wrong direction and I had to jump off the wagon after we had got clear of town and make my way back around the town by a long and circuitous route, which explains the tardiness of my return home last night. I am sure the four brothers are awaiting my return to Mill Springs with blood in their eyes, and equally certain that if I don't return within a suitable time to offer myself up to their manly punishments the four will descend upon this farmstead like a plague of six-foot locusts in search of retribution for a crime which, in the end, did not take place. My offense was not consummated, you see, but I imagine the intent is what matters."

Mrs. Singman said, "Wild oats, merely wild oats. A young man is expected to sow a few here and there before he—"

"Mother, it's no use making excuses, is it? I'm guilty enough."

"Pooh."

"My principal concern is with the fact that I am what you see, a runt. Rebecca's four brothers appear to have been sired and damed by Percherons."

"It's just as well to break it off. In five years she'll be as fat as the rest of them."

"I admit to a degree of cowardice," Isaac continued as if she hadn't interrupted. "I've thought through the night. Father and uncle are quite right. I must absent myself for a while."

"You'd best take Hugh with you, then."

Isaac reacted to that with openmouthed surprise. When his glance came around to me it didn't appear too friendly. "What do I want with him?"

"He's killed a Yankee soldier. They'll be after him for a spy. He must flee."

"I didn't kill anyone," I said. "Where'd you get that idea?"

"Yesterday you said—"

God knows what I'd said yesterday; but I knew I couldn't have claimed to have killed the corporal. "My father killed the soldier. I'd have done it myself if I'd been quicker, I guess."

It occurred to me then, for the first time, that my father quite possibly had saved my life by shooting the corporal out of the tree. I'd have been his next target.

Mrs. Singman said to Isaac, "It doesn't matter who killed the soldier. If they make inquiries they'll learn Michael Cardiff had a son. Everyone in the district knows that much. They'll assume Hugh committed the murder."

"It was no murder."

Her troubled eyes evaded me. "Hugh, we've done you a terrible wrong."

Isaac pushed his chair back with impatience. "What are you on about?"

"Yesterday we told the others about Michael Cardiff's death." Her voice was small; she winced when her eyes touched mine. "The word is all across the valley by now. We had understood that young Hugh shot the soldier. That's what everyone was told."

"Mother, you've condemned him. The word will reach the soldiers sooner or later—the valley flaps with loose tongues."

She clasped my hand. "Hugh, I beg your forgiveness."

"I guess you'd better ride with us," Isaac said with no evident pleasure.

I withdrew my hand. "I think the battle must have moved on by now. I doubt they'll come back. They've got more important things to concern them."

Isaac said, "I wish it were true. But they take a dim view of spies and people they take for spies. They execute them. As an object lesson, they say." He stood up. "Anyway what were you planning to do? You can't work the farm by yourself."

"I hadn't thought about it."

"Well you can't stay here, that's certain. Not now."

"I don't know . . ."

Mrs. Singman said, "Will you forgive me?"

I did, of course, but my predicament simmered slowly into my awareness. I'm not sure I had any real fear of the soldiers coming for me. I thought it unlikely. But I could not return to the farm. I had to put my father's death behind me; the wound was still open.

And I confess the child in me wanted the adventure. In those days westering was every boy's fondest dream.

The Singmans took it as settled that I would depart with Isaac and J. V. Singman, and I gave them no argument. Isaac's uncle seemed pleased to have me along. The three of us on the hard seat said our farewells to the family—there were tears all around—and we set out that very morning, pausing at our farm only long enough for me to pack my few belongings. There was no sign soldiers had been there. But I cried when I took my last look around. I made Isaac and his uncle wait while I ran down through the thickets to my father's grave. It was undisturbed. I remember speaking to him in that solitude; I can't recall what I said—a farewell of some kind. I remember mainly a grinding anger in me, caused by the fact that of the two graves I didn't know which was my father's and which his killer's.

We turned the stock out; the other Singmans would collect the animals and look after them. In my kit I took the title deed to the farm but I knew it was worthless; when the war passed on and affairs became straightened out, the bank and the tax people would confiscate the farm. Or perhaps it would become another spoil of war. To this day I don't know what became of the farm or who lives there. I have never

48

wanted to go back. I had happy times there but it was not a happy place. I remember it mainly as the place where my father was murdered.

.   .   .

We traveled several weeks to make Paducah, then Cairo, because the armies were engaged across our path and we had to detour far to the north. The roads were treacherous with winter. Occasionally we came across the spoor of skirmishes and battles—artillery craters, forests chopped to pieces by minié fire, fresh graves and bloodstains, the lingering afterstink of smoke and blood and battlegrounds, swarms of flies on the rotting carcasses of army mules and horses. I learned to loathe the smells of war.

We crossed the frozen Ohio River on the nineteenth of February; the ferryboats were frozen into their piers and wagoners were lashing their vehicles across the ice. We made the crossing without incident and traveled upstream along the Mississippi. I had passed my thirteenth birthday, unnoticed, back along a Kentucky road.

At Cape Girardeau we were ferried across the Mississippi by a flat-boat that charged a stiff fare; J. V. Singman parted with it grudgingly.

We had a large tent aboard the wagon in which we made camp each night; the tent had a fire hole and I do not remember any extreme discomfort during those winter nights. But one of the horses went lame near Jefferson, Missouri, and the three of us didn't have enough money among us to buy another. For that reason our progress was delayed while J. V. Singman traveled from farm to farm to peddle wares. Finally we made a trade for an eight-year-old plow horse; it took more than a week thereafter to coordinate the new horse with the old in the traces.

It was J. V. Singman's plan to make for Santa Fe and thence to California by the southern route; this required that we cross the Southwestern desert by spring—otherwise we would have to wait out the summer months somewhere en route, perhaps in Santa Fe itself. The delay at Jefferson therefore rankled Isaac's uncle and he was in a poor humor for several days.

It was just before we left Jefferson that I learned of the extent of my jeopardy. It came by purest chance and Isaac's obsession with reading.

Isaac showed me the newspaper. It was a Yankee broadside; he'd picked it up in the mercantile while we were stocking the wagon with foodstuffs for the journey. I no longer have the paper, nor recall precisely what it said, but the announcement held in substance that one Hugh Michael Cardiff, age 19 (indeed!), of Mill Springs, Ky., was being sought for the ambush murder of Union Army Corporal Paul Ordway, age 20, of the First Michigan Light Rifles. I was described as a Confederate spy, height 5′ 3″, weight 120 pounds, hair brown, eyes

49

grey. A warrant for my arrest had been issued by the military government and anyone knowing my whereabouts should make contact with, so forth.

Evidently some member of the Singman family or a neighbor had repeated and garbled the false story of my having killed the soldier; my subsequent flight only confirmed the Yankees' belief in my guilt.

That was when Isaac suggested I change my name. For the next six years I became Hugh Smith.

. . .

I had my first look at the prairies that winter.

Neither law nor morality crossed the Mississippi in those days, or so it was said.

We followed the Santa Fe Trail into the Southwest across a prairie where the creeping trains had left deep ruts and rusty junk heaps of equipment tossed aside to lighten wagons and the ashes of burned Conestogas. We came occasionally upon bull trains, timidly eager young faces peering out from the flapping canvas, and we passed Kickapoo Indians, trappers, hunters and scouts from some of whom we gained valuable advice and information. Twice we were caught in heavy snowstorms; one delayed us two weeks.

Today the journey can be made in Pullman comfort; smooth graded roads link most of the towns for motorcars. Many of those towns did not exist then. Towns that had been settled before the war had been deserted when the troops were recalled to the East. Sometimes we went twenty days or more without sighting a human habitation; we had only our maps and the stars to guide us; and if we made twenty-five miles in a day it was exceptional—fifteen was the average.

Memoirs of westering have been published in sufficient number to fill libraries and it is not my purpose to replicate those. Our trip was difficult but without extraordinary incident until after we crossed the Rio Grande and made our dusty way into Gadsden country. In that desert J. V. Singman fell ill with a debilitating fever. We debated whether to turn back to the nearest town, Mesilla, some eight days behind us; J. V. Singman refused, urging us to press on—"I shall live or I shall die, and if it's the latter then it won't matter to God or myself where it happens." His wish to see the Pacific Ocean had become an obsession by then.

. . .

When the wagon threw a wheel it didn't surprise us because the road was badly chewed up where it shelved along the side of the mountain. J. V. Singman was exhausted in his illness and we made a bed of sacks for him in the shade of the cliff before we set out to retrieve the castoff.

Unhappily it had been the near-side back wheel and it had gone right down the steep pitch into the dry canyon bed far below. We had a long scrabbling climb to the bottom. The wheel was far too heavy to lift along the path of rock handholds by which Isaac and I had come down; we had to thrust a stout stick through the hub and roll the wheel half a mile down the canyon bed to the point where the road met it. Then we struggled up the road, rolling the big wheel between us. It went slowly because Isaac was unusually slight for a full-grown man and I, of course, did not yet have my full growth.

We paused at intervals to dig the most offensive rocks out of the surface and pitch them over the side; we didn't want it happening again on the downslope because the wagon's momentum might topple us all over the side next time. The road was in disrepair because the Overland Stage people had abandoned it more than a year ago when the war began. It didn't take any longer than that for the desert to ruin a road: hailstorms, wind-driven sand clouds, flash floods, avalanches of clay and stone.

The sun made a furnace of the canyon. Sweat kept stinging my eyes and we had to stop frequently. It took us a good part of the day. If the road had been any steeper we wouldn't have managed at all; but the route had been graded for Butterfield coaches and that was why we'd chosen it.

Ever since El Paso it had been one breakdown after another. All three of us were sapped near the end of our endurance, especially uncle J. V. Singman.

I watched Isaac inspect the castoff wheel with his spectacles pressed up against the bridge of his nose. "There's a split in this spoke. Get the binding wire, Hugh." Also there was a bad dent in the iron rim but nothing could be done about that until we found a smith.

We ate dry tack and drank cold coffee and went to work. Nosebags hanging on the horses. From the wagon's endless bounty of tools and hardware Isaac extracted an iron jack to raise the sagging corner of the wagon. We fitted the wheel onto the axle and drove wedges into it and thrust a new cotter bolt through the securing hole. I smeared it with grease. Then we went to gather up J. V. Singman and put him in the wagon because we still had two hours' daylight left for traveling but when we touched him he was dead.

• • •

Through the next hour Isaac wept at intervals and cried out in his anguish—great emotional displays. I never knew what to do at such times. I sat to one side in silence; I didn't want to intrude on Isaac's grief. I later learned to appreciate the value of such demonstrations of passion—they were cleansing to the system. Far better than bottling things in. But at the time I lacked those understandings; I'd wept for my father and I was certain I had no tears left for anyone else.

I watered the horses and waited uneasily while Isaac chanted prayers. A lizard darted from one spot of shade to another; large birds circled high beyond the cliffs; the heat was heavy and without sound. Pale boulders loomed precariously above the roadway where it twisted sinuously toward the dry-bed crossing at the bottom.

Finally I realized Isaac was speaking to me: "It is time for the burial."

. . .

I slept fitfully and was aware once or twice that Isaac was not asleep. He sat like an Indian, blanket-wrapped beside the grave. We hadn't been able to dig far into that hard soil; we'd covered the body with mounds of rocks.

In the morning I built up the fire and heated coffee but I hesitated to speak to Isaac. I wasn't sure whether some sort of ritual was involved in the silent vigil and I didn't want to disturb him but I felt a restlessness to get away from that place.

Finally I proffered a cup of coffee and Isaac stirred. He turned away from the grave before he tasted the coffee. Then he shrugged the blanket off his narrow shoulders. "We should press on."

We hitched the team and packed the wagon. I took the reins. Isaac climbed onto the seat and looked at the empty space between us. Then he looked off toward the grave.

"Can we go now, Isaac?"

"All right. Yes."

. . .

The wagon jolted along endlessly with lunatic rattlings. I no longer noticed the racket. The sides of the vehicle were pendant with pans, traps, tools, gewgaws and gimcracks. When a peddler wagon approached a farm it announced itself from a mile away.

For three days we followed the Butterfield route across desert flats. Our map was accurate and we found fresh springs by the ruins of an adobe Overland Stage relay station. The depot had not fallen apart by itself; its log rafters were charred and things had been smashed up. Based on what we'd heard in Mesilla, we judged it to be the work of Jicarilla Apache.

Our map was a cheap print of the Butterfield route and carried a legend at its lower corner, "Based upon the survey of Cooke's Mormon Battalion, 1849." Frequently during each day Isaac would unroll the map and compare its indicated landmarks with features of the landscape; he would align things with his pocket magnetic compass. I thought it was unnecessary because we were simply following a marked road, but Isaac was nervous about everything. "It pays to be certain of our bearings. Mapmakers have been known to make mistakes."

We talked very little of anything except the moment-to-moment details of each day's journey. The two of us were very young to be on our own in that wilderness. It was several days before either of us could bring himself to discuss the future, even in the most tentative terms.

Somewhere on that vast creosote plain we crossed what was generally acknowledged to be the artificial boundary between the areas known as New Mexico and Arizona. The Gadsden Purchase district had only been U.S. territory for nine years or so; prior to that it had been part of New Spain and Mexico and therefore most of the inscriptions carved in the rocks above the springs were in Spanish but we could make out some of the numerals. The inscriptions dated back as far as 1703. You can still read them. We left our own signatures in the stone as well: *Smith - Singman - April 1862.*

We camped west of the spring so as not to frighten off animals. In the dusk we crept back to a hill overlooking the water. It was up to me to shoot meat for the pot because Isaac was shortsighted. While the light was still good I measured the range with my eye and estimated it at two hundred yards and knew I was correct within ten yards one way or the other. The Hawken was charged and loaded—in this country you always kept it that way—but for certainty I replaced the percussion cap before I laid the rifle out beside me and we settled down to wait.

Flimsy clouds scudded overhead, reflected in the pool by the spring. We'd had to come around to the east of the water because we had a west wind; it put the sunset sky in my eyes but that couldn't be helped. I pulled the hatbrim as low as I could.

It went nearly full dark and I was giving up hope when I saw movement in the rocks above the ruined coach station. They came down to the water strung out in a nervous line, snorting and snuffling, snouts weaving back and forth: peccaries, the small wild boars of the desert. The Mexicans called them javelina.

By now the light was poor for shooting but we needed fresh meat and I waited until I had a pig motionless at the water's edge and squeezed my shot with care. The racket banged my ears and the big rifle jarred my shoulder and the flash of muzzle flame lanced red in my eyes—it blinded me for a moment but I didn't need to see the pig to know it was down. You can always tell what I aimed at by what I hit.

The meat was tough but we ate it gratefully. Isaac said, "I'm not certain what we'd do for food without your shooting eye. It was unwise of me to resent your accompanying us at first. I apologize." He cleared his throat. I looked at him, waiting for him to continue. Isaac had not shaved in some weeks; his black beard was becoming full and thick. Finally he voiced his thoughts:

"I suppose in a practical sense I am my uncle's heir now. The wagon and its inventory are mine. I imagine it would have been his wish that I continue on to California and attempt to establish the business he would have established."

"Is that what you want to do?"

"I never quite saw myself as a merchant, I confess." I believe he was talking mainly to himself. "A teacher perhaps. But there are opportunities for advancement in commerce—even wealth. I don't mind seeing myself as a rich man someday." Then he laughed. "What does it matter? We probably won't get to California at all. They told us we were fools, didn't they? In Missouri, in Texas, they told us—the deserts, the mountains. Red Indians."

"We've come this far. We haven't been attacked."

"They may await us around the next bend."

In Mesilla the word was the Apache had gone south into Mexico for the winter mostly because there was no one left to raid north of the border. Comanche rarely came this far west, it was said, and once you crossed the line into the Arizona district you were likely to encounter more gila monsters than hostile Indians. And the gila monster was the rarest creature of all.

There were tribes along the rivers—Papago, Mohave, Paiute—but they were farmers. That was what they told us in Mesilla. But then in the next breath they said, "Of course you can't count on nothing much. Last year Cochise raided across the border, took out every Overland depot between Lordsburg and Tubac, killed fourteen white men, run off three hundred head of stock. And there's still a few ranchos along that stretch around Tubac. Pete Kitchen's place, the Tyree Grant, the Baca float, three, four others like that—stubborn damn fools wouldn't see fit to pull out and wait the war, they done forted up and they going right on running cattle down there. Prime target for Apache raids if you ask me."

.   .   .

In the next two weeks the country changed, desert giving way to grassland. The map led us to the Santa Cruz River and we followed it along the Butterfield road up into a range of hills thick with scrub oak. To the south was the Baca float—one of the Spanish land-grant ranchos—and to the north was Pete Kitchen's fort but we saw neither of those establishments, passing westward through one range of green hills after another until we rolled into the village of Tubac in early May. We learned here of the battle at Shiloh and the Union occupation of New Orleans; these were reported dutifully in the local newspaper, the only one in the territory, but the war was a distant thing to the people there.

A blacksmith repaired the damaged wheel for us and we went into the shops where Isaac measured out his coins and made purchases with care. We remained three days in the village, at the end of which we examined the horses and judged them sound and rested. We wanted to press on quickly so as to get across the Yuma desert before summer. At dawn we left the river and the adobe village behind us. The country ranged up ahead of us, a stretch of easy hills: we would top one and see the next. There were pockets of water and groves of sycamore. There would be terrible desert farther west but we didn't brood on that; we'd worry about it when we reached it.

On the map that region was marked *Hidalgo-Ruiz Grant;* that legend was taken from the 1849 survey. Nowadays the property was known as the Tyree Grant after the name of the family that had bought the land after the Mexican War of 1848. The map showed that we would be several days on Tyree land before we reached the rim of the Sonora desert leading to Yuma.

I saw the occasional steer out in the high grass and hoped California would look as good as this Arizona country. Great red cliffs broke through the green hills, looming tall, pocked with caves. Now and then we would pass a log corral and an adobe house; we would exchange greetings with the line vaqueros. I picked up a word of border Spanish here and there.

My destiny was changed on the third morning out of Tubac. We were climbing the eastern slope of a long hill, indistinguishable from a hundred others we'd climbed. I planned to stop and rest the horses at the top. As we neared the crest I heard the bellow of a big animal in distress and I stood up on the wagon's seat to search it out.

Ahead of us the rutted wagon track curled down to brush bottoms and skirted a boggy mud pond. The commotion was down there in the bog.

A saddled horse tried to heave itself onto dry land but it wasn't the horse making the racket. I saw a longhorn bull in the mud, plunging and heaving in panic—it bellowed again and a small figure clawed toward the bank, desperately trying to avoid the flailing hooves.

A rope was noosed around the bull's neck; that told the story. The little boy had thrown his rope over the horns and dallied it to the saddle and tried to pull the bull out of the sucking bog but the horse had lost purchase on the slick bank and fallen in, tossing the boy into the bull's path. The bull was plunging for the bank and in the next instant the boy would be crushed.

My hand closed over the breech plate of the Hawken. It was cocked by the time the butt struck my shoulder and without pause I laid my cheek along the stock and took aim. I had time to think: *Four hundred yards and remember it's downhill.* Then the bull heaved up, forelegs coming free of the mud, poised over the boy's spine, and I leaned forward to meet the rifle's heavy recoil. The shot rang flat; through the smoke I saw the longhorn shudder from the impact.

A reflex lunge but the bull was unbalanced and plunged to one side into the mud beside the scrambling boy.

On the seat Isaac was peering nearsightedly toward the bog. "What is going on?"

I watched the boy swim for the bank; lowered the rifle and drew the ramrod. On the bog the longhorn subsided—a twitching of musculature, then death.

My hands began to shake and I sat down abruptly.

      •   •   •

The boy was lathered in brown mud and we scraped the worst of it off him before we tied his horse to our tailboard and lifted him onto the seat.

The boy clawed at the caked stuff on his face for a while, shy, not looking at either of us. Isaac said, "What's your name?" and the boy only gulped like a fish. Isaac was gentle, amused: "We'll take you home if you'll tell us where it is."

I felt a bit weak just then. I was looking at the size of that bull and thinking how I might have made things worse if I'd shot wide by only an inch or two, if I'd stung that bull instead of killing.

A man on horseback came down the road at full gallop, drawn from some distance away by the sound of my gunshot. The man had a Mexican hat and a Mexican saddle with the big flat saddlehorn but he wasn't Mexican. He had a red beard and blue eyes and freckled hands. A man built square and sturdy like a keg.

The horse came from full gallop to a precise halt beside our wagon and I marveled at the grace with which the rider held his seat. The man's blue eyes took things in very quickly: I saw him look only once at the bull floating dead in the bog, the tracks and slicks along the bank, the boy's horse tied up behind us.

He had a big deep voice. He directed it toward Isaac. "You shoot that bull?"

There was a hint of accusation in his voice and it made me speak up. "No sir. That was me."

The man eased forward, his palms stiff-arm against the saddlehorn. Peering at the small boy. "You all right, Kevin?"

"Yes sir, I guess."

It was the first time the boy had spoken. His voice shook; the fear remained in him.

I endeavored to smile. I tapped the boy's arm with a gentle playful punch. "You're all right now."

Isaac said, "Is he your son?"

"No, he's young Kevin Tyree. His daddy's John Singleton Tyree. I expect you know the name—you're on Tyree land."

"I've heard it. My name is Isaac Singman. My young companion here is Hugh Car—Smith, late of Kentucky."

The red-bearded man swung his horse closer alongside and reached out a brawny arm to shake hands with Isaac. "Harry Dreier. Manager on the Tyree Grant." An embarrassed grin crossed his face and I realized he was younger than I'd thought; probably twenty-five or so, no more. Then I looked down and noticed another thing. By turning his horse around to shake Isaac's hand Harry Dreier exposed his right leg to our view and it was a wooden peg from the knee down, socketed into a holster at the stirrup.

Harry Dreier glanced at the dead bull again. "Kevin, I thought you was going to get around that old bull and drive him back to the herd. Not run him straight into a bog."

"I'm sorry, Harry, he ran faster than I thought." The boy managed a little smile. He caught me grinning at him and that animated him: suddenly he jumped to his feet on the wagon. "Harry, my friend saved my life. He shot that bull and it was just going to jump right down on me."

"Where'd you shoot him from, son?"

"Top of the hill. Back yonder."

It made the man look around; I saw his eyes measure the distance and grow a little wider. "What's the rifle—Kentucky?"

"Yes sir."

"That's remarkable shooting, son. Remarkable."

Isaac said, "There are sporting gentlemen in Kentucky who'll put their dollars on him as the best rifleman in four counties."

"Remarkable," Harry Dreier said again. "Well you-all come on up to the house now. We'd better get that mud washed off you, Kevin, before your mother mistakes you for an Innun pickaninny." Turning his horse to guide us away, he added, "That was an expensive old bull. We'll have to break this just the right way to Mr. Tyree."

And that is how I came to the Tyree ranch in the spring of 1862.

BOOK THREE

The Tyree Grant

NOT TOO MANY YEARS AGO I journeyed to Prescott to take part in the celebrations that marked Arizona's statehood. There were parades and horse races and all manner of fooforaw to mark the acceptance of the forty-eighth state into the Union. I gave a little shooting exhibition.

Several of the speechmakers, in the courses of their interminable stentorian tedium, saw fit to pay lip service to those pioneers who founded the Anglo region, tamed it and brought civilization to it. Among the names called on the roll of honor were such as William S. Oury, Pete Kitchen, John Slaughter, General Crook and of course John Singleton Tyree.

That's about the only time you hear of John Tyree anymore—a name among several; a footnote in the state's history books. "Pioneer cattleman." Sometimes on the wistful heavy-drinking night of July Fourth the old-timers still prop up saloon bars while they spin yarns to one another about how John Tyree tracked his daddy's killers to Mexico with a hang rope or how he outwitted the Apache warrior Ibran or how the Tyrees damn near shot Hugh Cardiff to pieces. The yarns can get pretty wild.

It is true that I was shot by one Tyree and nearly shot by another. There is no truth at all, however, in the canard that I was shot for stealing a horse. I can understand how that rumor started but it has no basis in truth. The two incidents were years apart.

. . .

59

John Singleton Tyree was not a tall man but he was broad-chested and strong. His face was half-covered by the droop of his black mustache and his long hair was unruly—he never took to slicking it down the way some men did. He had an extremely square jaw that jutted from beneath the mustache and there was great power in his stance and in his deep-set eyes. When I first met him I sensed a tough strictness.

I was awed by the size of the house. Harry Dreier took us into the parlor and introduced us to the rancher.

The boy Kevin said, "This is Hugh Smith and he's going to be my best friend."

"All right, Kevin. Get along and get the mud washed off you."

The boy went out, led along by a fat waddling Mexican woman. Later I learned her name was María; she was cook, maid, mistress of the house staff, general factotum and *dueña*. Good-natured in her way; but I never saw her smile.

As soon as Kevin was beyond earshot John Singleton Tyree turned on Harry Dreier with volcanic force:

"By God I am amazed at you. You let him out of your sight—the boy's ten years old. Left to you he'd never have seen eleven. By the dear Lord God, Harry, I'm inclined to make your left leg the equal of your right and then ride you off this ground."

Harry Dreier stared at John Tyree's boots and never lifted his eyes. I noticed the peg leg was wobbling just a little under his weight. He was hiding it pretty well but he was twang-taut.

I heard the nervous sawings of Isaac's breath. He stood beside me with his hand gently on my shoulder; we both had our hats across our chests as if it were a funeral or we were suitors. In the big thick-walled room John Tyree's laughter rang with sudden shocking force: it made me take an involuntary step backward. Isaac's hand fell away.

"All right, Harry, I expect you're as shaken up as I am—and God knows you won't let it happen again."

"That's for a fact."

"Then get out until I cool down."

Harry Dreier stumped away without another word. The heavy door whacked gently shut behind him.

"Now then," John Tyree said, "tell me about yourselves."

.   .   .

It was the first time in some months I had sat down to a meal at a dining table in anyone's home and I felt shy under the inspections of our hosts. My hands seemed to have lost the feel for knife and fork, we'd been eating out of camp pans for so long. All their eyes seemed to be on me.

60

There were six in the Tyree family—eight at table that night, with me and Isaac. There was John Tyree at the head of the table and Mrs. Tyree at the foot—she was a stout woman with brown hair tied in a bun behind her head; stern most of the time, but she had a good smile.

There was Grandfather—John Tyree's father—his name was Clement Tyree and he didn't speak much but I liked the twinkle of the eyes above the cracked parchment of his cheeks. His large hands, gnarled and dotted with age spots, never stopped moving.

Then there were the children, three of them, ranged along the table at John Tyree's left hand. Kevin was the youngest. Bathed and fitted into clean clothes he proved to be even smaller than he'd appeared in the bog—so slight he was almost frail: a thin-faced child with wild hair as glistening black as his father's, as dark as the older two children were fair.

The eldest was Vernon Tyree—known today, to readers of this account, as Major Vernon Tyree, the famous showman. Vern at that time was fifteen—he was two years older than I—and even then he was nearly as big as his father but he hadn't filled out yet and it made him look slat-skinny and awkward because of the great width of his shoulders. He had strong handsome features and I suppose I was a little in awe of him. He was my senior and that is an age when one or two years make a significant difference among boys; and Vern Tyree had the look of a boy who would be the leader in anything: leadership would fall naturally on him, he'd be one of those people to whom everything would come effortlessly.

Beyond the two boys sat the girl whose eyes never stopped twinkling with mischief. She was twelve years old and she had the head-tossing arrogance that girls have. Her name, I learned, was Elizabeth but everyone except her mother called her Libby. During the meal Libby addressed many frivolous questions to me—there was a challenging mockery in her face—and I fended them off without grace and resented the ways she found to embarrass me. She seemed to enjoy it, my discomfort fueling her fervor until her father said mildly, "That's enough, girl." He was very fond of her. She uttered protests of innocence; pout; sullen silence—but then I caught her twinkling at me.

Isaac was talking in his slow deliberate voice—the answer to a question Mrs. Tyree had put to him. "My uncle and I were setting out for California, you see."

Mrs. Tyree looked at me when she spoke. "Then the boy isn't indentured to you?"

"Only by friendship, madam."

"An itinerant orphan—such a shame. How old are you, Hugh? Fourteen?"

"Thirteen, ma'am."

"The boy ought to have a home," she told her husband.

. . .

The legs of the wooden bed were set in open tins of whale oil to keep scorpions and centipedes from climbing into the bedclothes. The *dueña* left a basin and pitcher of hot water on the commode, reminded me to shake out my boots before putting them on in the morning, and departed cheerfully enough. In the night I heard a guitar and the soft run of Mexican songs, several men singing.

I slept well in the unfamiliar bed but I was awake at dawn. Dogs were yapping at something down among the outbuildings. I scrubbed myself with tallow soap; there was a chill in the morning air and I toweled dry in a hurry. When the cook's triangle rang I was sitting on the edge of the bed waiting to be summoned.

The meal was served by the *dueña*, María Maldonado; she went in and out of the room with a dry swishing of thighs. The parents and children were all at the breakfast table, although Grandfather Clement Tyree was absent; Kevin said, "He's five miles up in the hills by now. He likes to ride the line."

John Tyree spoke a lengthy grace and I saw Isaac bow his head politely. Isaac looked drawn; I wondered if he had a touch of fever.

Through a window I saw ranch hands on their way into an adobe cook shack below. I was surprised by their number: dozens of men.

Isaac ate silently with his eyes on his plate; either he didn't feel well or something was heavy on his mind. I watched him with some anxiety while I fended off eager questions from Kevin and prying banter from Libby. At the head of the table the elder son, Vern, was in conversation with his father about horses.

John Tyree's glance traveled down the table toward Isaac. "Mr. Singman, have you had a chance to think over our conversation of last night?"

"I'm still thinking on it."

"The desert to the west is arduous."

"I understand."

They called it the *jornada del muerte*—journey of death. It was said human bones served as milestones.

John Tyree said, "I won't press for an answer," but he was looking straight at me and I became uneasy.

Isaac said, "Thank you. We'll stay a few days at least. How does that suit you, Hugh?"

"Fine—fine."

After breakfast young Kevin was eager to show me around the ranch and I went from place to place with awed fascination. The house was a low sprawl of adobe, old walls with deep-set doorways and windows. According to the Spanish fashion it was built in a square around an open quadrangle. A galleried veranda ran around all four sides of the patio and all the rooms had doors leading off the veranda.

Along the outside of the house another veranda, the *portal,* ran the length of the front wall, deep in shade. Kevin showed me iron shutters across the windows, slitted with gun ports. "Apache," Kevin said matter-of-factly. Log rafters protruded at intervals from the walls like railway ties, high up. "They call those *vigas.*"

A clay jug hung in a net of rope suspended under the veranda ceiling; this was the *olla,* filled with drinking water that stayed cool in the heat of the day through evaporation.

I said, "What happened to Mr. Dreier's leg?"

"Harry? A colt stomped his foot. He got the gangrene. Come on, I want to show you the rest."

We went into the patio. There was a well in the center of the courtyard. "That's so the Indians can't cut us off from our water."

In all I counted nearly thirty doorways opening onto the courtyard. "I never saw a house with so many rooms."

"They built it a long time ago, you know. The Spanish hidalgos. It was a real big family, I think seventeen children and all. Now we go outside this way."

"How'd your folks come by this place?"

"That was Grandfather Clement. He was out here a long time. It was before I was born, I guess. He used to hunt and trap and stuff like that."

We went back through the hallway to the outside. A hairy brown dog the size of a pony came to its feet bristling but Kevin spoke quickly: "All right, Lobo, all right." He rubbed the dog's muzzle. "Let him sniff you. He's a good dog but you need to let him get to know you."

"What kind is he?" After a moment I scratched Lobo's ear and the dog's tail twitched with tentative friendliness.

"I don't know. Just a dog. He's a good tracker. Last month he killed a coyote that came after the chickens."

The house dominated the ranch; it was on the hilltop. You could see miles of grass country—hills around the valley and sawtooth mountains on the horizons, blue in the morning sky. Beyond the cook shack stood a village of vaqueros' huts and barns, corrals, tack sheds, various outbuildings. Kevin dutifully identified them all for me. There was a cantina and a smithy and a dry-goods and general store that Kevin called "the sutler's" where the vaqueros could buy their needs, and there was an adobe chapel with a bell tower. "The padre's a circuit rider. He comes once a month to say Mass and hear confessions."

63

"Are you Roman Catholic?"

"Presbyterians. But the hands are mostly Catholic. What are you?"

"Methodist, I guess."

"What's that?"

"I think it's something like Presbyterian."

"The fellow you're with, he's a Jew. I heard my father say."

"Yes."

"I never met a Jew before."

"He won't bite you."

"He's awful small for a full-grown man."

"Big enough to get along," I said.

I realized then that he was sizing me up. He was shy but once in a while he had a brash quick grin. "You going to fight my brother Vern?"

"What for?"

"You're as big as he is."

"I got nothing to fight him about."

"That don't matter," Kevin said. "You and Vern, you'll have a fight, I bet you."

"Why don't I fight you instead? That'd be easier."

"Wouldn't be fair. You've got to pick on somebody your own size." He pointed toward one of the corrals. "That's where we keep the studs. We got an Arab stallion, all the way from Cairo or someplace. You want to see him?"

. . .

The afternoon rain came with a sudden viciousness typical of desert storms. After the brief downpour I saw rivulets cut their way down the hillsides. On the trail I'd learned enough to head for high ground—the sheltered gullies were death traps in flash floods. Beyond Lordsburg we'd seen the remains of a Conestoga wagon that must have been carried several miles at high speed: the debris was scattered along hundreds of yards of arroyo bottom. We'd found bleached bones of oxen nearby; the flood must have taken them too. If there were human bones we hadn't found them.

Those things happened, westering, and the published memoirs are full of them to the point where you get the impression that pioneering was nothing but hardship and catastrophe. At that age I took every day as a new adventure, it's true, but in many ways life in those times was as commonplace as it is now. Pioneer settlers mostly were ordinary people; some, like John Tyree, owned a special brand of power and courage—but even John Tyree was not a wild man. We weren't savages. Civilization followed wherever the settlers went. The Tyrees, for example, lived thirty miles from their nearest neighbors, and in country that Easterners thought of as a brutal wilderness; but they lived much as people live today.

That evening Isaac took me into the front room and we found John Tyree and his wife and the foreman, Harry Dreier, assembled there; Isaac glanced at me and I saw his eyes moisten as he turned away. John Tyree said, "I'll speak for you if you like."

"Perhaps . . ." But Isaac's voice caught and he didn't finish. He nodded his head fitfully.

I went very still and felt a knot in my chest. I watched John Tyree's stern face.

It was Mrs. Tyree who broke the silence. "Hugh, a boy your age needs a sound upbringing. You need schooling, you need a home."

"Yes ma'am. I expect we'll settle down to that when we get to California."

John Tyree said, "Mr. Singman's likely to have his hands full in California. He'll be in an itinerant trade—he'll be plying from town to town."

Isaac's face was averted from me. Mrs. Tyree said, "It would be a hard life for a boy."

Isaac gave a little jerk with his shoulders. He stood with his head lifted as if in defiance; I saw his fists clench at his sides; but he did not speak.

John Tyree said, "We're in your debt, Hugh. We owe you the life of our son Kevin."

"Sir, you don't owe me anything. I didn't do it for pay."

Mrs. Tyree said, "Your friend agrees with us that you'll be best off in a home where you have the steady care of a family."

I saw it then. "You want me to stay?"

"We'd like it very much, Hugh."

I said, "What I did for Kevin cost me a few grains of powder and one bullet. It cost you a blooded bull. I think maybe I'm the one who owes you, not the other way around." It was nonsense; the lame words embarrassed me immediately. I felt the beat of my own heart, suddenly strong in my ears. I found myself looking at Harry Dreier. The peg-legged foreman smiled a little as if to reassure and welcome me.

John Tyree said, "What do you say, then?"

I blurted my answer: "I'd just as soon go on to California with Isaac if it's all the same to you, sir."

Isaac closed his eyes. "I'd rather you stayed here, Hugh. It's for the best. It would be a favor to me if you could stay on with these fine people. We'll meet again, when you're grown—we'll promise each other to do that." He opened his eyes; he was looking toward John Tyree

65

then and I saw something unbending in John Tyree's face and it made me realize the unspoken statement between them: *He is a Christian boy and it would not do to have him raised by a Jew.* No one had said as much in my presence but I knew without doubt that it had been stated between them in my absence.

I said, "I mean no insult but I've got my own debts and I mean to help Isaac make his way to California. He needs my good eyes and my rifle, you see—he's got the myopia, he can't shoot or anything."

"Remarkable," said Harry Dreier. It seemed his favorite word.

Mrs. Tyree said, "Your loyalty is admirable, and it's the measure of your quality, Hugh, but Mr. Singman won't need to shoot. He'll carry all the food he needs—we shall see to that. And there are no hostile Indians west of here."

Isaac said, "I'm grown now, Hugh, you don't need to worry on my account. I'm asking you to stay."

"You don't want me, then."

"It isn't like that. Don't act like a child—you're beyond that and we both know it."

I left the house to think it out. Behind me I heard them talking among themselves. I walked along the hillside away from the ranch, picking pebbles out of the yellow grass and tossing them at scrub oaks. The sun was well down and the puddles were drying. I watched vaqueros lope across distant hills. Moving dark spots there on the slopes were grazing cattle. Clouds scudded across the east and I saw a bird very high—probably an eagle. My eye measured it and I thought for sure it was too far for a shot even if I had the Hawken. And anyhow my father had taught me never to shoot an animal I didn't need to eat.

They were strangers, that's what it came down to. I thought about living here with them, under the roof of the strict stern Tyrees, and then I thought about Isaac and California—Isaac with his love of books and poems. I started throwing stones again, throwing hard, whacking them into the trunks of scrub trees. I had a good arm and it took up a rhythm, *whack-whack-whack.* I picked up another handful of stones and kept at it, never missing.

The hands began to ride in and I grew hungry but I stayed out in the grass until I heard the ring of the triangle; then I went along to the house. Mrs. Tyree on her way into the dining room told me to hurry and wash my hands. By the time I came to supper they'd started without me.

Libby's arch questions annoyed me this time and I kept growling at her until her father told her to leave me alone. Kevin started up an excited monologue about a horned toad he'd caught. Talk ran past me, elusive and unimportant. After supper I went out on the *portal* with Isaac and listened to him read verses from a leather volume of Byron he'd found in the house. Finally he said, "You'd better turn in."

I awoke once during the night and thought I heard the clatter of the wagon but it might have been a dream.

Another time I came awake sweating and lay an hour with my eyes open trying to make up my mind on the matter of staying or going; but I fell to sleep again and didn't awaken until an early dark hour of the morning—far past midnight.

Isaac had a compass, he knew the desert enough to have got this far, he had the Mormon Battalion map, he would be fully outfitted by the Tyrees. I knew all that. I also knew the stretch of desert along the Gadsden line from here to Yuma and beyond was known as the *jornada del muerte* with good reason. We'd heard plenty about it in Mesilla. *Break an axle out there you're a dead man.*

Sweat broke out on my palms. I knew the sound I'd heard earlier in the night had not been a dream.

Abruptly I was up and moving. I stuffed my few belongings into my pack and gathered up the Hawken rifle and went out through the courtyard and the hallway into the ranch yard.

Our wagon was gone.

The dog Lobo came out of the night with a suspicious growl; I spoke softly and rubbed its head. The dog fell into step and accompanied me past the cook hall and the tack barns to the corral.

I dropped a hackamore over the first horse I could reach; led it inside the barn and found a blanket and the most disreputable saddle in sight. I had to adjust the stirrups for my height.

The horse gave me a hard time when I tried to fit the bridle-bit between its teeth but finally I had it in place; then in the dim starlight outside the barn I scribbled a brief note on a leaf torn from my old copy of *Ivanhoe: I will have the horse and saddle returned as soon as I can. Thank you. Hugh Smith.* I propped it on the peg from which I'd taken the saddle.

I climbed up, fighting the horse; I was not an accomplished horseman by any means. On occasion I'd ridden our plow horse back in Kentucky but that was a far cry from this spirited vaquero's mount.

The dog barked once and backed away. Finally I brought the horse under control, lifted the reins and rode out of the silent yard.

    · · ·

I had seen the map often enough to know the route Isaac would follow and I had no trouble picking up the wagon's tracks at dawn when the horse carried me out of the last range of hills onto hardpan flats.

My seat was sore by then and the insides of my knees had been rubbed to blisters by the chafe of the stirrup leathers. I kept shifting the Hawken because there was no place to scabbard it. Finally I stopped and dismounted and tied it crosswise along the back of the saddle, using the concho thongs. Then it got in the way when I got back on the horse; I lost my balance and fell.

The horse danced away and I felt sudden fright. I ran after the animal but that made it all the more skittish; it trotted fifty yards away up the trail and looked back at me, rolling its eyes.

For a minute I closed my eyes; then I walked slowly toward the horse, talking in a soft way: "Whoa now, gentle down now."

The horse kept prancing away. I began to panic and of course that made it worse. Finally I had run myself out and sat exhausted on a rock glaring at the horse.

In the end I was able to grab a trailing rein; then I stood facing the horse and talked to it a long while to calm it; and finally I climbed up awkwardly to get past the rifle. My seat settled toward the saddle and the horse let go with a mischievous burst of cartwheeling and plunging; I all but lost purchase again. I grabbed everything I could reach, locked my ankles around his belly and hung on.

Finally the horse settled down in disgust and I sat exhausted, gathering breath before I gigged it forward and guided it west, waiting for the hammering of my pulse to quiet down.

. . .

Isaac had several hours' head start on me but I'd worked it out that he'd have to stop early, on account of the heat and his early start, and I expected to close the gap sometime that day. The wagon was slow and anyhow Isaac would be conserving the animals for the desert ahead; by now he probably wasn't more than fifteen miles from the ranch and by tonight he probably wouldn't be more than five or ten miles farther. Back in Kentucky he'd have walked that far in a day.

By midmorning I was regretting I hadn't thought to bring along a canteen of water.

. . .

Someone had impaled a cow skull on a post. It grinned at me as I approached. I kept lifting my hat and dragging the sleeve across my face but nothing helped. In later years I learned from the Apache how to make do in the desert but I had none of that knowledge then.

Tan-grey corrugations of earth lay before me endlessly. The road was well beaten and I knew Isaac was ahead somewhere but I could see several miles and nothing moved on that expanse.

I rested the horse ten or fifteen minutes, squatting in the animal's shade holding the reins, studying the landscape the way a hunter seeks game: checkerboarding the desert in my mind and searching each square before shifting scrutiny to the next. A bird flitted about; something disturbed a clump of green-grey weeds nearby; but in the distance nothing stirred.

Isaac might be resting in the shelter of an outcrop, or he might be broken down or trapped in some mishap, or sick with dehydration, or . . . It was no good crossing this desolation alone. I felt the lonely brass taste of fear; I tried to imagine how Isaac must feel.

There was little vegetation on the rim of the desert. Here and there grew cactus, brush, the occasional hat-size clump of sage, the spindle tracery of ocotillo—each bit separated from the next by yards of sand-clay and grey stones. To the west it grew even more sparse; the farther hills appeared completely bare of everything but rocks.

As I penetrated into the desert the footing became harsher. In my mind, listening to the talk of deserts, I'd pictured sand dunes like those portrayed in the illustrative plates of Arabian adventure stories but it wasn't like that—the *jornada* was a jagged country, little ranges of mountains built of sharp boulders, valleys of clay and hard-edged flotsam of dark rock that looked like the volcanic tailings we'd seen back beyond Mesilla. Fried and shriveled by the sun.

I began to feel dizzy during the white-hot afternoon and started to wonder if I'd make it through to nightfall. It had been foolish not to bring water.

. . .

The afternoon became a dream of hell. I could see little; everything was hazed in rising heat waves.

My legs were abraded so badly I tried to ride with my feet up against the pommel but it knocked my tailbone painfully and I couldn't hold my balance; I got off and stumbled ahead, leading the horse. My legs hardly carried me.

. . .

Sometime in the late afternoon I sat down and tied one of the trailing reins around the ankle of my boot to make sure the horse wouldn't run away, put my hat over my face and lay back in the hot sand of the road thinking to rest a little while before I went on. My lips were bleeding where I'd picked at the chapped skin. Pain radiated up from chafed knees and thighs. My tongue felt enormous, like a rock in my mouth.

When I awoke it had gone full dark.

I had a great deal of trouble getting to my feet and then discovered I had to sit down again to untie the leather rein around my boot. The

69

horse whickered, probably expressing its thirst. When I crawled into the saddle the horse seemed to wobble.

I winced with the agony of it when my knees slid down against the stirrup leathers but I kept thinking of Isaac out there alone and finally I got the horse moving down the road at a steady trudging gait.

Not far along the road I discovered the remains of a campfire. The coals were cold but the wind had not yet scattered the ashes so I knew it was fresh. It had to be Isaac's fire; there was no evidence any traveler had come after him. A cold fire—how could he be that far ahead? I felt a weight drop through me; it made a hollow emptiness of fear.

I looked up toward the sky. The quarter moon was well over west. Bright stars; a lot of them; the Milky Way was distinct. I'd learned the stars as we'd traveled west—it was one of the many things in which Isaac took an interest and he'd shown me the constellations in the pages of an astronomy book. Isaac had to use the book because he couldn't see the stars.

Now I realized something was wrong. The moon down west—I'd slept far longer than I'd thought. It was after midnight, perhaps close to dawn.

And Isaac would be traveling by night.

While I'd slept he had gone rattling on into the desert, putting miles between us.

I set out doggedly after him. My throat was constricted with a terrible pain.

It was no good turning back now even if I'd wanted to: it was too far. My only chance was to catch up with Isaac.

   . . .

The miles became vague; my head swam; thirst and saddle pain made the world swirl about me, unreal, distanced. My eyes began to swell and I had increasing difficulty holding them open. The horse plodded at its slowest pace, worn out and dried out.

The plum-colored light of false dawn began to spread across the rock plains. I tried to keep my grip but felt myself slip off the saddle; I hadn't strength left to hold on. I fell hard, hip and shoulder, but even the pain didn't snap me awake. I heard the horse stumble a few paces away and stop.

I thought I heard a distant familiar clatter: the rattle of the peddler wagon.

I tried to rise. In my mind I formed the words I would shout. But everything was absorbed into the red wash that flooded my eyes. Light swirled away.

   . . .

I came awake choking: drowning.

A rough callused grip at the back of my neck. It lifted my head off the ground. Someone was forcing water into my mouth. It ran down my chin, soaked my shirt.

"Isaac?"

I gulped and swallowed and fought to breathe.

The canteen was removed from my lips. "That's better."

I recognized Harry Dreier's voice. "Drink a little more now. Take it slow."

I sipped and coughed. Then Harry Dreier laid my head back on the earth. I felt the wetness of something moving against my face—a bandanna, soaked, rinsing my skin.

After a while I was able to see. I had no voice; I spoke in a whispered rasp. "Isaac . . ."

"He's fine, son. He got this far, he'll get the rest of the way. He's on down the road quite a way by now, I expect."

"I heard the wagon."

"Maybe you just thought you did." He was looking over his shoulder. "You surely wore out that horse, boy. You'll have to ride double with me. Let's see if you can stand up."

Helping me to my feet he said, "Next time you try something like this, Hugh, try and remember to take a canteen?" Then he shook his red head. "Remarkable. Purely remarkable." I limped toward the horse; I'd have fallen without his grip. He said, "I'm glad you're still alive. John Singleton Tyree would've skinned me otherwise. You want to do me a favor, boy, don't try any more tricks like this while I'm around."

I went faint with pain when he put me up on the horse.

. . .

I was abed with fever for a time. Mrs. Tyree was concerned that I might have suffered a heat stroke. The *dueña* swathed me in cool herb compresses to leech out the evils. Finally after some days I was up and around, albeit wobbly on my pins, and when Vern Tyree first saw me abroad he said in his dry drawling way, "Well look here now —it's Old Saddlesores up on his hind legs again."

The name stuck to me like a burr.

. . .

None of them rode me for stealing that horse; they understood. Once John Tyree took me aside. "Do you intend going after your friend again?"

"No sir. By this time he's in California or he's dead."

"He's not dead, count on that."

I said I would; but in truth I wasn't confident. The season was late for desert passage, the heat rising daily . . . But I have never been one for brooding.

I came to know the three Tyree children well. In a way I believe I brought them closer together, as I served as a bridge between Vern and the two younger ones. It was Vern's inclination not to spend much of his time with them; he was older; he made it a point to get off with the vaqueros when he wasn't in Mrs. Tyree's schoolroom. When thrown together with his brother and sister he tended to ignore Libby and to pick on Kevin with lofty contempt. Kevin tried to hide his fear of Vern —he was spunky enough but small; and he took little interest in the things that most impressed Vern. Kevin had a curiosity about small animals and book facts and mechanical things. To some extent I believe the episode in the bog had made him skittish: he never talked of it but he stayed close to home and I never saw him out with the hands. Harry Dreier frequently lurked near Kevin, wherever he might be on the ranch—I would emerge from my studies and find Harry Dreier carrying Kevin piggyback or playing horseshoes with him. One afternoon Vern came up from the corral and watched Kevin riding around on Harry's shoulders, the peg leg stumping up little puffs of clay, and Vern said, "You'll turn him into a sissy. He's halfway there already. Come on, Harry, we got work to do."

"You can try talking to me that way after you've grown up a little more," Harry Dreier replied; but a few minutes later he walked away down to the barn with Vern and after that Harry spent less of his time with Kevin.

Libby was a pest. I suppose all little girls are pests to growing boys. She had a rocking horse that squeaked abominably; she was forever blowing soap bubbles from a corncob pipe. Mischief was her greatest pleasure.

Mrs. Tyree administered to our education in a small L-shaped adobe chamber they'd set aside as a schoolroom. Her desk was a rough pine table in the center of the L; the three girl students sat in the short room to her right and the half-dozen of us boys sat in the long section. If a boy misbehaved and Mrs. Tyree judged the offense insufficient for application of her switch, she would make the boy sit with the girls; this humiliation was more than a young boy could bear and usually the mere threat of it was enough.

The wooden benches were hard and made us squirm but Mrs. Tyree kept us hunched over our pencils and tolerated no misbehavior. The children ranged from an eight-year-old-girl named Rosalia to Vern Tyree who was, at fifteen, the oldest student. Aside from the three Tyree children and myself the students were all Mexican, children of ranch hands; these were the ones who were willing to do their lessons in English. The others had to look after themselves. Mrs. Tyree was proud of her students: "They'll need that kind of gumption if they want to get anywhere in this country today. This is the United States now."

Of course there was some dispute about that. The United States was at war over its very existence. But it was clear enough we were in Anglo territory at least; no matter who won the war, the Gadsden country wasn't likely to be ceded back to Mexico.

I must repeat that frontier families of those times were not primitive savages as they are so often made out to be by the Manifest Destiny orators who point back to the crudities of the pioneers, apparently in order to show how far we have progressed in gentility since those days. In many ways I am not sure we have progressed at all. The Tyree family, for example, had a well-filled and well-utilized bookcase of substantial size, over which was painted a motto, GOOD BOOKS ARE OUR BEST FRIENDS. Most of the volumes had been shipped at considerable expense over tremendous distances. For myself, before I left the Tyree Grant I must have read every book in the shelves at least twice through.

．　．　．

In the afternoons when schoolwork was ended for the day we were dispersed to our chores. The elder boys worked on horseback and this was the emblem of pride by which we were distinguished from the younger children who performed their chores afoot. Now and then, saddling up or riding past the barns, I would catch a small child's envious eye on me—the child with a pitchfork or tar bucket in hand peering up at me as I loomed overhead on horseback.

At first I remained an indifferent horseman and because the nickname fit me too well I resented it mightily: Old Saddlesores. I knew I rode like a bag of flour. Sunday afternoons the children would fly across the pastures playing ferocious games of steal-the-bacon with prize flags tied to trees at either end of the field; in the early weeks I found myself outmaneuvered and outridden by little Libby and it infuriated me. She would laugh in my face as she eeled past on a wildly pivoting horse, dangling the prize flag just out of my reach until I could stand it no longer and leaned too far out of the saddle and fell painfully to earth while she galloped away screaming with delight.

Vern, who rode with an Indian's effortless grace, was too old to stoop to childish games but now and then he'd ride by and watch our galloping tournaments. On a hot Sunday in June I found him waiting for me when I came riding off the meadow nursing a bad bruise on my hip where I'd taken the force of a tumble. Vern put his horse alongside mine and accompanied me toward the barns. "I've seen you shoot that big rifle. You're pretty good for a kid."

"For a kid?"

"All right, Saddlesores, take it easy. You're pretty good. All right?"

"I'm better than that."

"If you say so. But on that horse you're pretty bad."

"You trying to pick a fight with me?"

Vern laughed at me. "No. Trying to make a trade."

"What kind of trade?"

"I'll tell you what, Saddlesores, I'll teach you how to ride like a vaquero, you teach me how to shoot. How's that sound?"

. . .

I have to guard against an old man's tendency to attribute things in retrospect. It would make for tidier truth if I could maintain that Vern Tyree and I were rivals from the beginning. That was not the case, however. I liked him. I believe he liked me.

Along with my liking for him was an admiration that was tinted by envy; I have to admit that. I had to work for things that came easy to Vern. I made myself into a fine horseman under Vern's tutelage but it was long hard work that needed concentration and sent me to bed many a night with bruises and sore bones. (So much for the correspondents' claims that I was a "born equestrian champion.")

Vern was rangy, growing toward his full height then, an exceedingly handsome boy—he had his father's square jaw, a bold blade of a nose, high wide cheekbones, the good grey eyes of an outdoorsman; all of it crowned with his mane of yellow hair. He did everything well, everything he set his hand to. He had a good quick mind. If my greatest fault was stubbornness then Vern's was impatience: both with himself and with others. If something didn't come to him quickly he grew petulant and tired of it. For example Harry Dreier tried to teach us the game of chess. I slowly mastered the game. Vern found it elusive; he soon abandoned it. I still believe he would have proved a far better chess player than I, if he had only stuck by it. But he did not find it worthy of his concentration.

That was a difficulty he did not have with marksmanship. Vern took to it as a salmon takes to swimming.

All it needed were a few quick pointers to correct the natural mistakes he had been making. He'd been yanking the trigger of his rifle, pulling his aim off; I taught him to squeeze steadily. He'd been flinching —the natural result of jerking the trigger; that was easily cured. He'd been closing one eye to shoot—always a mistake; why halve your vision? He hadn't taken sufficient interest in the proper mold of his bullets or the measure of his powder; I taught him the principles of consistency and care. This last was the most difficult for him to achieve, as it required a stubborn kind of dull repetitiousness that was foreign to his quicksilver nature. But the rewards of that bit of drudgery were so immediately apparent to him that he subordinated himself to that particular monotony.

Within a week it was clear Vern had the makings of a first-class shooter; within a month he was well toward mastery.

I began to realize that Vern's natural accomplishments were not as truly effortless as they appeared. He learned quickly, it's true. You only needed to teach him something once; he never forgot it. But that was a skill that required sharp focus. Vern had the ability to bring astonishing concentration to things if they interested him. He was like a good hound—put him on the scent of something and nothing could distract him.

In the evenings after supper we'd retreat to the lean-to that housed the forge and I would teach Vern how to heat lead to the proper temperature before pouring it into the molds and how to crack the fresh bullets out gently so as not to mar them. I taught him how important it was to keep his rifle clean and oiled: any speck of imperfection could throw the spinning ball off its path. I showed him how to measure powder precisely into paper wads and seal them for fast loading. "Otherwise you end up pouring powder down the bore by guess and by God."

Actually all I did was teach him the things my father had taught me.

* * *

Grandfather Clement Tyree spent most of his time away from the ranch buildings. At first I saw very little of the old man. Kevin told me, "He likes to be alone a lot."

There were times when I liked to be alone as well. I would take my rifle off into the hills and set myself the challenge of picking off targets at longer and longer ranges. On those wanderings I often found myself wondering about Isaac, hoping he'd made California safely. I tried to picture California. I'd never seen an ocean.

* * *

I took aim on the tassel of an *agave* that must have been at least five hundred yards away across the mottled hills. Squeezed off my shot and stepped aside to peer past the smoke.

A miss.

Well, I thought, it was an awfully small target.

"You got to figure the ground between, Saddlesores." The voice made me bolt: I wheeled and saw Grandfather Clement astride a fallen cactus a few feet behind me.

"I never heard you come up."

75

"I don't make a whole lot of noise when I move." The old man watched critically while I broke a paper wad with my teeth and poured the powder into the Hawken. When I thrust the ball home and capped the lock he said, "Mind if I give her a try?"

The old man fired from a position on one knee; he scarcely seemed to take aim but I saw the *agave* tassel burst in the distance. Grandfather Clement handed the rifle back to me and braced a palm on his knee to stand up. He moved slowly but he still had great strength in his towering frame.

"Keep in mind you're shooting across uneven ground, son. Shadows down on the slope there, bright sun on the rocks over yonder. Sun makes the air move. You get air blowing up from those hot stones, air settling down toward the shadows. I expect you missed your shot because you didn't count on the wind rising off the rocks there. You shot over top of it. You want to keep such things in mind."

The old man winked at me and turned abruptly. He was soon out of sight and I couldn't hear him at all.

. . .

One July or August day—it was so hot that very little work was being done; the vaqueros could be seen motionless under their hats wherever there was shade—the Spanish doctor from Tubac, whose name I do not recall, paid a call in his canopied dogcart. He visited at regular intervals to see how Mrs. Tyree was getting along with her rheumatism. On this occasion he carried several letters that had arrived by Wells Fargo dispatch from California. Mrs. Tyree had a cousin in Sacramento and there were two or three items of business as well but also there was a letter addressed to "Master Hugh Smith, I/C/O Tyree Grant, Village of Tubac, Arizona District, Territory of New Mexico."

I recognized the handwriting and it put a fullness into my throat.

When he handed me the letter John Tyree said, "Safe and sound in California, as you can see." He even smiled a bit.

I went off by myself to read Isaac's happy letter.

My dear Master Hugh,

It is my profound hope you have fared well under the wing and tutelage of Mr. John Tyree and his good family, and that you have not thought too harshly of me for having left you in their care. They are, I believe, of excellent repute and character, and you will do well to abide by their inculcations.

I have found California to be something less than the Promised Land; nonetheless its climate is for the most part serene, its populace desirous of trade goods, and its byways sometimes pleasant in the traveling. I arrived at the port of San Pedro in need of wagon repair, as neither the desert nor the

76

ensuing mountains had been kind to our weary long-journeyed vehicle, and found that smiths here—like innkeepers, haberdashers, shop chandlers and even ladies of easy persuasion—have an astonishingly low opinion of the value of a dollar. Nevertheless I look upon the future with rapt anticipation, and am upon my way to the Sacramento Valley to ply my wares. If you should discover the time to drop a brief note to your harried friend, merely enough to reassure him of your continued good health and well-being, be assured it will reach me if it be addressed in care of the Wells Fargo shipping office in Sacramento, California.

There is a dismaying paucity of books of good quality in these parts.

I beg you look to your lessons, dear Hugh, for a man is but what learning makes of him. The mind is a precious jewel, and needs constant buffing and polishing. Especially on these primitive frontiers of the wilderness one must be extraordinarily careful lest one allow the mind to wither.

In warm friendship and the heartfelt hope that the Fates treat you with every kindness, I remain,

Your friend and obedient servant,
Isaac

. . .

I saw very little of John Tyree. He owned what was for those times a considerable enterprise; he had little time to devote to children. In any case he was an aloof man. He presided at the evening meal, a formal distant figure; most days that was the extent of my contact with him.

But I grew up with the children. We were close: I might have been one of them.

. . .

Vern and I rode out on our first hunt together. Kevin trailed us on his pony. Vern tolerated his presence with the understanding that he would keep out of our way.

We rode down the Santa Cruz through grass hills under the shadows of timbered summits, a cool wind riding off the mountains. Lobo, the big brown dog, trotted inquisitively in our wake.

Just short of the ranch boundary I saw buzzards rising from the tall grass and we went that way down a long hillside to find the remains of a Tyree longhorn with an arrow through it. The birds had picked it to pieces but there were evidences of knife blades at work and Vern studied the horizons angrily. "Yaquis, I guess." The dog was sniffing at the carcass.

Kevin said, "That's not a Yaqui arrow."

"How do you know, snot?"

"I just know. I think it's Chiricahua Apache."

Vern grinned at me. "Mighty Indian fighter here. The snot hasn't got two brain cells to rub together. Everybody knows Chiricahua don't range this far west."

"I still think it's Apache." Kevin broke off the feathered half of the arrow and thrust it through his belt. "We'll find out when we get home. What you want to bet it's Apache?"

I was studying the tracks. "Two men. Moccasins, on foot—no horses."

Kevin said, "You see that, Vern? I was right. Apaches hunt on foot."

"So do Yaquis. I never heard of Apaches around here."

We rode into the valley, following the river because our quarry was wild Canadian duck for the holiday table. It was nearly Christmas by then. The ducks sometimes would lie up for days in the slack eddies of the Santa Cruz and if you were lucky you could bag a brace or two before they flapped out of range.

Vern had cajoled his father into giving up his prized repeating rifle for the day—a five-shot revolving Colt's Patent rifle, caliber .44 inches. Harry Dreier had offered me the use of his Greener shotgun but I declined the offer with thanks. I didn't like shotguns and preferred to stay with the Hawken even though it was no one's idea of a bird gun. My father had told me, "A shotgun chews up half the meat. Shotguns are for people who can't hit what they aim at. Which is not after being my weakness and damn sure isn't yours."

Vern had loaded the Colt rifle and carried an extra loaded cylinder in his belt pouch. It gave him ten fast shots without reloading and I tried to tease him about it: "You need ten shots to bag a brace of ducks?"

"I don't see the point bagging one or two and letting half a dozen get away clean."

"What do you want to do, wipe out all the ducks in the valley? How many can you eat?"

"Let's just see who brings the prize home, Saddlesores."

Back in Kentucky if you went for duck you went in predawn shadows and waited in a blind but out here there wasn't much surface water and the ducks were either there or not there; it didn't matter what time of day you went. It was past noon when we emerged onto a prow of land that overlooked a bend in the river and I spotted the floating dots on an eddy a thousand feet from us. We tethered the horses in the piñons and made our way down on foot.

Kevin tripped but I caught him in time to prevent a racket; Vern whispered angrily, "Wait here, snot."

"Let him come along. He'll keep quiet."

Vern glared at me. "He's your lookout, then."

Kevin gave me a grateful apologetic smile and we resumed the stalk.

For a target as small as a duck you wanted to get right in close and we crept forward nearly to the riverbank, screened by cottonwoods, chilly in the deep shade. I kept a look all around, as I always do, because you don't want to take aim on a seven-pound duck only to be surprised from behind by a thousand-pound bear.

Nothing disturbed the copse except a few bantering wrens. Vern made hand signals and we separated by twenty yards to keep out of each other's field of fire; Kevin trailed silently at my heels, wide-eyed with excitement, mouth open to silence his breathing.

I got down on one knee and laid out my patched bullets and paper powder-wads close to hand. I opened the tin of percussion caps and placed three of them by the ammunition, closed the tin again and put it away in my pouch because it's no good scattering caps across the earth and I wasn't going to have time or desire for more than two or three shots.

I saw Vern beside a white-boled cottonwood setting out the loaded spare cylinder by his left foot. Then I had no more time to watch Vern; I was readying to shoot, withdrawing the long ramrod from its place beneath the Hawken barrel and laying the rod out with my powder and ball.

I braced an elbow on my knee and laid the rifle snug against my cheek and held the trigger while I eared the hammer back so that the cocking action made no telltale sound. Behind me I heard Kevin's breath catch in his throat. Lobo, a good and patient beast, sat panting behind us, sniffing the day.

On the flat water the ducks swam slowly, varicolored in the sunlight. Dancing ripples of light stabbed at us from the surface of the river. Down toward the bend was a trivial whitewater where the flow birled off rocks. I had a look behind me and winked at Kevin and was about to look to Vern for the signal to begin when Vern's rifle fired without warning.

Briefly angry with him, I settled my aim as the ducks began to take flight, flapping and running across the eddy.

Vern's first shot had killed a duck. I quickly found a target. The racket blended with the sound of Vern's second shot; two ducks plunged flat—three dead now and that should be ample for the Christmas pot. I reloaded the Hawken without hurry, not intending to shoot again.

But Vern's Colt repeater roared again and again until I stared at him in astonishment.

With absolute concentration he was leaning over his sights, firing and cocking and firing again, puffs exploding from the breech and muzzle one after another. Above the pond ducks were getting into the air and falling back, slaughtered by Vern's salvos.

Finally the woods were silent. I collected my gear and stowed it and carried my rifle across to Vern.

He was getting to his feet, deeply flushed, his eyes wide and glistening; breathing through his teeth. Slowly the gloss went off his eyes. He grinned at us. "Count 'em. Count 'em, by God."

Nine broken ducks floated on the pond, one of them mine. Two more carcasses on the riverbank beyond.

Vern had killed with every one of his ten bullets.

I said, "You must be awful hungry."

. . .

Lobo was no bird dog. Vern ordered Kevin into the water to retrieve the ducks. The Santa Cruz is barely a stream by Kentucky standards; the water came up to his knees, no higher. The boy made several trips and finally emerged with the last carcasses. He stood dripping, stared down at the heap of charnel and abruptly dived into the undergrowth. I heard him retch.

"Squeamish snot." Vern made a sound in his nose and squatted by the river, putting his hat aside; he splashed water over his face and slicked his hair back with his palms. He wiped his face in the crook of his sleeve. "You ever see shooting like that, Saddlesores?"

"Why'd you want to go and kill all those birds?"

He stood up, clapped his hat on, grinned at me. "Because I liked it, you stupid turd."

. . .

When we brought the string of ducks home Vern made a ceremony of turning the Colt rifle over to his father. "Ten shots, ten ducks." It was all Vern said.

But John Tyree's reaction didn't appear to be the one Vern had expected. He thrust the rifle back into Vern's hands. "Take it and clean it before you give it back to me." And he turned away.

Mrs. Tyree said in a distant quiet voice, "We can give them to some of the hands, I suppose."

John Tyree stopped and looked over his shoulder at me. "You shot one bird, Hugh?"

"Yes sir."

"How many could you have hit?"

"Three. Maybe four."

"With your single-shot Hawken."

"Yes sir. I know I'd have had three. I couldn't warrant the fourth— it'd depend which way they flew, whether the trees would've got in the way."

"But you shot one bird and stopped."

"Vern seemed to be bagging enough ducks, sir."

Brooding, John Tyree left us without further talk.

80

With feelings I sensed but did not fully understand, I avoided Vern for several days after that.

. . .

Kevin and I crossed paths with Grandfather Clement Tyree when we were putting the horses up. Kevin showed him the shaft of the arrow we'd taken from the butchered steer. "Vern thinks it's Yaqui but I think it's Apache."

Grandfather Clement only had to glance at it. "Chiricahua Apache. I taught you better than I thought, Kevin."

Harry Dreier stumped forward from the barn's shadows. "That'll be the third steer we know to've been killed by Indians this season. Many more of them, we may have to take steps."

Soon after the New Year, we did just that.

. . .

I put the horse toward the ridgetop at a quick trot, lifting the Hawken from the scabbard. To either side of me the line of horsemen advanced toward the crest: Tyree riders, rifles up.

Grandfather Tyree lay at the top on his belly with his hat off watching the valley beyond, waving us forward.

I crested the ridge and saw the Indians and put my horse to a gallop.

Four of them hunkered around a dead steer. A single horse stood beyond them—most likely a pack animal to carry the meat.

It was only a quarter-mile run and no man, not even Apache, can outsprint a galloping horse on open ground with that short a lead. Three of the Apache stood up slowly and showed their empty palms. But the fourth wasn't giving up. He made for the ground-hitched packhorse, snatched up the halter rope, made a leap onto its back and kicked the horse into a run, clinging to its far side for cover.

I heard voices.

Harry Dreier: "Shoot the horse."

Vern: "Kill the damned Indian."

John Tyree: "Let Hugh have the shot."

I drew rein; the trained horse swirled to a halt and I took aim.

I'd seen the skittish way the horse had shied when the Indian had run toward it. It told me something about that horse. There were saddle-size rocks scattered along the valley: I chose one ahead of the fugitive and settled my aim and waited for the Indian to ride close. The range was perhaps four hundred yards.

When I judged it the right moment I fired. Then with the explosion whistling in my ears I gigged the horse to one side to see through the smoke.

The bullet tore off a sudden white patch of stone. I heard Vern jeer: "You missed." But it was enough to spook the Indian's horse. It broke stride, shying, stumbling. The Indian pitched off.

I put my horse forward at a dead run, recharging the rifle at the gallop: paper cartridge, ramrod, percussion cap. I circled past the three Indians at the carcass and kept going full out.

The fugitive Apache was on his feet trying for the horse but the animal was well and duly spooked. It wouldn't let the Indian come near. It shied, backed away, reared. The Apache gave it up and began to run—long strides toward the crest; beyond it lay badlands where a man could lose himself in seconds.

I heard Vern's angry voice behind me: "Kill him for God's sake." But I plunged on, spurring.

The Indian was nearly at the crest when he looked back and saw me bearing down. He quit his run then, stood and turned and waited for me. A knife came up in his fist, defiant.

I stopped the horse ten feet short of him. Trained the Hawken on him. I tried English: "Walk back down the hill." It had no effect. Then I tried Spanish.

His eyes responded to the Spanish. He began to walk. I circled back, keeping out of reach of his knife. I gestured with the rifle and finally, with reluctant practicality, the Apache dropped the knife.

He was wide-chested and his legs were sturdy but from up close I realized he was only a boy, hardly more than my own age.

I said in Spanish, "How are you called?"

"Do you care?"

"*Su nombre.*"

"Mexicans call me Ibran."

After another half-dozen paces he looked back and said, "Why ask questions of one you intend to kill?"

On the way I caught up the skittish horse and led it along.

Ibran wore only a breechclout; not even moccasins. He was brown, not red; his black hair was tied back out of his face by a leather band. His bare feet trod the stony ground with indifference. But he was lean—thinner than he should have been.

His three companions stood together under the guns. Tyree riders sat horseback in a circle around them and there was a conference going on among John Tyree, Harry Dreier and Vern. Up on the hill behind us Grandfather Clement was mounting his horse to come down from his ambush blind.

I drew up beside Vern. The Apache called Ibran walked over to join his companions. None of the Indians spoke.

Vern said, "Leave them hanging. The word will get back to the rest of them."

Harry Dreier said, "It's the fifth steer they've taken this season. We got to do something, for certain."

I said, "They're just kids. Look at them." None of them looked more than fifteen. "They're hungry."

Vern said, "Then they should've hunted whitetail or javelina instead of Tyree beef."

John Tyree's head came around. His scrutiny touched me and went on toward Harry Dreier. "What's your opinion, Harry?"

"I don't think they want killing. Butchering a steer when you're hungry—is that worth being hanged for?"

"They were prepared to take that chance when they did it."

I caught Ibran watching me. I couldn't tell whether he knew what was being said.

Vern's lip curled back. "What would you do, Harry, just turn them loose and let them do it again?"

"I don't know, boy. It ain't up to me." Harry turned toward John Tyree. "Waiting your signal, sir. You give the word."

"I wonder what that word ought to be." John Tyree brooded at the Indians. "Hugh's right. They're not even grown men."

"They're grown enough to've killed us if the positions had been reversed," Harry pointed out. "You think they'd hesitate?"

"No. But I like to think there's a distinction between us and them. I like to think a civilizing influence means something."

"Might be something different if we had courts of law down here, sir, but there's no jail we could put them in."

"It's a fine dilemma, Harry."

Vern said, "We've got to kill them. What's it matter whether we shoot them or hang them?"

"Vern, listen to me and remember this while you grow up. Remember it clear. Killing doesn't answer questions. It doesn't solve problems. It usually causes more difficulties than it ends. If we kill these four boys we'll have trouble from the entire tribe. Can you comprehend that?"

"You mean we'll let ourselves get scared off by four redskin brats."

"Four redskin brats and four thousand adults who care about them. Don't you understand what I'm talking about?"

"I guess I do. But I believe we've got to kill them. As an example."

Abruptly John Tyree looked at me. "You haven't expressed your opinion. I've heard Vern's. What's yours?"

I examined my rifle. The sun glanced off the oiled breech plate. I had Ibran in the corner of my vision, Vern to my left. Old Grandfather Clement joined us and sat on his horse watching me.

I said, "I'd brand them, I think. Brand them and send them home."

Harry Dreier's eyes popped open. *"Brand* them?"

Grandfather Clement was chuckling.

I said, "It'd hurt like hell, and they'd carry it the rest of their lives to remember us by. Most likely their friends will laugh at them every time they see them."

"Fourteen years old," John Tyree said in wonder.

Harry Dreier said, "Remarkable."

. . .

All through that spring of 1863 I carried the stench of burnt flesh in my nostrils and I remembered the expression in Ibran's face when we turned the four branded Apache loose and rode away, leaving them with the beef they'd killed. I hadn't fathomed that expression at all. Was it gratitude, or hate; or only contempt?

. . .

Antietam. Fredericksburg. Lincoln proclaimed the Emancipation. Draft riots in New York City. The threat of intervention by Napoleon III. Chancellorsville: Lee whipped Hooker but lost Stonewall Jackson. And Grant took Vicksburg.

Vern spilled the names off his tongue as if they were personal friends. He devoured the reports that came in erratically from travelers and the Wells Fargo dispatches. Vern took a keen interest in the war. He second-guessed the generals until he earned the teasing of the bunk-house crew: El Señor Generalissimo Vern.

The battle at Gettysburg was fought early in July; we received the news in September. Vern went about the place trumpeting the Yankee victory.

The Tyrees had traveled too far from their roots in Scotland to keep much allegiance to any particular place except the land that John Tyree now bestrode. It was like my own home in that respect; John Tyree's attitude toward the war might have been my own father's. "I can't see going off to fight and die in the service of slavers or financiers. They're each as dastardly as the other."

I spent a good deal of that summer and autumn tracking stray cattle through chaparral; I learned to enjoy loneliness. Gradually I became the provider of game for the Tyree table because the fewer cattle you butchered the more you sent to market. At least twice each week I'd ride in at suppertime with fresh meat on the crossbar saddle of my packhorse.

Most often I rode the far reaches of the Grant alone; now and then I went in company with Kevin or Vern. Very occasionally Grandfather Clement would join me on some far hillside, never explaining why he chose my company.

84

Grandfather Clement was an old man filled with youth. He was near seventy and owned a fund of fascinating tales from the fur-trapping days. He had guided Brigham Young.

I led him on, loving his outrageous tales; many of them were obvious lies.

"My wife's father came out with Daniel Boone, or anyhow that's the story that got around. I never knew the man. He went off when she was a little girl, out into the French country—that's what it was then, French, the Mississippi valley. We heard tell he was with Lewis and Clark later on, and I guess he got himself killed in the War of Eighteen and Twelve. We never knew for sure.

"My own family farmed over near Vicksburg until the floods washed us out. Folks went back to Virginia. I married my good woman, rest her soul, and she raised up young John while I was off gallivanting. Never was much responsibility in this family until John came along. Spent more than half my life going from one Indian woman's bed to another, I did. Shot a good many moose and buffalo in my day.

"I used to take jobs now and then when I needed money for powder and shot or drinking whisky. Brought in plenty pelts for Mr. John Jacob Astor's company, I can tell you.

"Made three rendezvouses up in the Green River country, old Bridger and them, I knew all those fellows. Old John Nelson—I ran with him two years, we guided the Mormons to Utah together. I trapped all over the country in the thirties there and I guided four trains out to Oregon in the forties.

"I knew the tribes, you see, I'd slept with women in half them camps—Cheyenne, Arapaho, Ute, all of them. Good people, some of them. Some brute savages too. People generalize about savage Indians or noble Indians they don't know what they're talking about. They run to different stripe, tribe to tribe and man to man. You keep that in mind now. Like anybody—you got to take an Indian like you find him.

"My last Indian wife, I remember her fondly now. I took her to me when she was fifteen years of age. Southern Cheyenne woman a little on the plump side. Found her down there in the Llano Estacado. She never quit smiling, never did until the day the fever took her. We even settled down awhile. That was the last job I ever had working for anybody else. Not far from here, over to the Chiricahua country, I ran a relay station there for the Butterfield Overland people. Close on twelve years ago now. Then I come across this land grant here, this ranch, found out it was up for grabs on account of the Gadsden Purchase and the voiding of some of those Mexican-Spanish titles. I claimed it for the Tyree family and to my surprise John and Marjorie came right along when I told them to. First time they ever listened to me. I been drifting in and out of here ever since. Guess I'm about done drifting now.

"Three summers I spent with the Comanche, you know. Followed the buffalo up the plains. Pawnees was at war with the Sioux up there—they always are. Pawnees are all right, you can get along with most of them. There's worse lives, I expect. You ever been in a big city, Hugh? No? Well I mind that's the worst life any human creature can endure. Indians got the right idea there. Don't ever sell Indians short, Hugh, they may have strange ways but they know what's important and what ain't. Summer of eighteen and forty-four I was riding with the Navajo up in the Acoma country . . ."

Once he opened up the old man would talk himself hoarse, his tongue following the peculiar and usually disjointed track of his thoughts, curving and doubling back and crossing its own backtrail like a bear in search of tasty grubs. His swollen arthritic hands would ride up and down with powerful violence to punctuate his talk.

Grandfather Clement was an astonishing marksman and taught me things I'd never suspected, particularly concerning things like the behavior of wind across uneven ground and the convection effects of colors. Those were lessons he'd learned on the Great Plains where you had to make long shots count because the game could see you coming from far off.

It was not impossible, he showed me, to bring down a whitetail buck at a range of half a mile if your rifle was big enough, your powder charge heavy enough and your hand steady enough. But it required an abundance of varied knowledge because if you misjudged any of a hundred factors then your bullet might go six inches or six yards wide.

"It's rare in my experience to find two young shooters as promising as you and my grandson Vern. In fact I expect it's unique. I mind Carson could shoot near as good as me but I never met another man that took to the rifle the way you and Vern does. You want to watch out for young Vern, there—things come natural to him, he don't need to work for them the way you do, but just the same he's a learner, that boy. He ain't lazy. You want to watch out he don't best you." Then the old man chuckled a bit. "That kind of competition's good for the both of you. The way I size you both up, it should put the keen edge on both of you."

Then he said a strange thing; he said, "I don't like to say this about my own grandchild, but the day may come when you oughtn't turn your back on Vern. You understand my meaning, Hugh?"

But then immediately he turned impish. "Let me show you a little trick now." I marked the glint in his eye. Grandfather Clement picked up a stone no bigger than his thumbnail and placed it in my hand. "Toss it up in the air for me."

"How high?"

"Just toss it easy there."

I flipped the stone ten feet in the air and the old man lifted his rifle to waist height. Shooting from the hip he blew the stone out of the air.

I must have gaped at him, for he laughed at me. "Think you can do that?"

"I doubt it a whole lot."

The old man reloaded. "I'll let you in on a secret now. That there's the easiest kind of shot to make. I used to impress hell out of Navajo and Ute with that kind of tomfoolery. You know the trick, ain't nothing hard about it."

"From the hip? A target that small, on the move?"

"Well now that's the trick. In the first place you can forget how small it is. It's only eight, ten feet from your rifle muzzle. Hell, that's point-blank. That little stone close up, that's the same as a barn door a hundred yards away. You take my meaning?"

"But it's moving . . ."

"Not a whole lot. You hold your fire until it tops out. You shoot it right at the top of the arc. It's stopped rising and it ain't started falling. It's just hanging there, see? That's when you shoot." He winked at me. "You try it, you'll see. Like falling right off a log."

It amazed me. The old man was right.

I was able to do it from the first shot—as long as I fired from the shoulder. Aiming.

Hip-shooting was another thing entirely. That was like learning to shoot all over again.

Grandfather Clement taught me well.

· · ·

The rifle was the link between the old man and his smallest grandchild as well. Kevin had a keen fascination for the mechanics of things. He took up the study of ballistics at the age of eleven.

Kevin had fragile shoulders and he didn't like the kick of a big rifle and he never could stand much noise; he never learned to like shooting. But he loved the precision of the mechanism. With Grandfather Clement's help he made himself into a first-class gunsmith. Then he turned his attentions to the chemistry of gunpowder and soon he was mixing his own, refining, experimenting.

Sometimes late into the night you'd hear the ring of Kevin's tools at the forge. Some nights Mrs. Tyree had to march down there in her nightdress and drag him away by the ear.

· · ·

In the autumn of sixty-three I had another letter from Isaac and was pleased to read that his trade was prospering in the Sacramento country. "Another year's peddling and I feel I shall be able to open an emporium and stock it with the best and sturdiest goods. I have come to like the trading life. But I keep my books about me and hope you do the same."

Books were scarce on the Arizona desert but I did my best to come by them.

· · ·

Longstreet was defeated at Knoxville; President Lincoln spoke at Gettysburg; and Henry Ward Beecher preached in the East. So the newspapers told us. They were weeks out of date by the time we saw them.

It was early 1864 then; and Vern had announced his intention of going off to war. His parents attempted to reason him out of it. Vern curbed his tongue and did not argue back but one morning we found a note from him on the breakfast table. We learned he'd taken his best horse and saddle and his father's prized Colt repeating rifle.

Mrs. Tyree went around long-faced and John Tyree saddled his horse. He announced he would be away for a week or more. He took Lobo and a hunting rifle; I believed he intended to track Vern down and bring him home. Leading a packhorse he rode away and we all were anxious for him.

He was gone ten days and returned unshaven and alone. It turned out he had not made any attempt to catch Vern. He'd gone off to be by himself and work out his demons in solitary hunting. He brought with him a brace of mountain cottontails that made good eating and a tale of having seen Apache camps in the high peaks.

Sometimes the Indians went into the mountains in winter to hunt out sleeping bears in their hide-ups. John Tyree said he and the dog had spied on one of the Apache camps. "They were cooking the bear and had some unholy ceremony going on. It went on for days. I traveled about my business but I could hear them and see the fires several nights running."

Grandfather Clement said, "Apache respect the spirit of the old bear. They dance and make their prayers to make sure the spirit rests easy. Avoids trouble later on."

· · ·

We had a brief note in March from Vern. He had got as far as Missouri where he'd joined up with a militia unit. He said they were breaking up their bivouac and striking out east to join up with Grant's armies. Vern was in high spirits; the letter boasted of victories to come. "I am already made sergeant and hope a lieutenancy soon."

"He'll get his fool tail shot off," John Tyree grumbled but it was the casual pride of a loving parent.

. . .

The job of branding the Tyree herd in that spring of 1864 was a hard chore because the cattle had multiplied in unusual numbers during the previous mild year. It took several weeks to comb the Grant and bring the herds together on the various branding grounds; then it was the age-old battle with mother cows to get their calves away long enough to mark them with the iron and castrate all save the lucky few males.

John Tyree sold some of his cattle in Mexico and some to California buyers who brought their crews overland at infrequent intervals to collect the herds. I recall four or five such occasions during my growing-up spell at the Tyree Grant; they all blend together in my recollection—there was always drinking and whooping and the music of the *baile* late into the night.

Winters are never severe in that part of the world; I believe we had snow only once in three years, a faint early-morning dusting that melted and evaporated before noon. But the winter of '63–'64 had been unusually mild and the hills that spring seemed unusually overcrowded with wolves, deer, coyote, mountain lion, bobcat, jackrabbit, quail and the kind of predatory beast that walks on two legs and steals his neighbor's provender.

It was a band of such thieves that brought misery to the ranch that summer. Buzzards led one of the hands to the south line on the seventeenth of July. Grandfather Clement Tyree lay in a gully, shot dead by a musket ball.

. . .

I had to put my handkerchief across my nose and mouth to shut out the rotting stink of it. Insects clustered, drinking themselves drowsy in the old man's blood. Each man studied the signs in the earth and in subdued voices we deciphered the incident.

Grandfather Clement had tried to surprise a group of three horseback cattle thieves—almost certainly there had been three of them. But his arthritic hands had slowed him down and he'd been killed before he'd had a chance to get his second shot off. The first shot had drawn blood from one of the thieves.

Tracks in the hardpan were indeterminate. We lost the spoor near the border and turned back for the night; even I with my keen eyes couldn't tell which way the murderers had gone. The soil there is flinty and does not take sign.

Near midnight we gathered below the house. A slight rain had begun. John Tyree and Harry Dreier stood in oilskins under a lantern in the open barn doors. "We'll want four men with us. We know my father shot one of them. Shouldn't be too hard tracing a wounded man— he'll be seen—but—"

Harry Dreier interrupted him: "It's my experience those kind of people are just as likely to leave their wounded behind to fend for themselves. We'll find the wounded man quick enough but that don't speak for the others."

"We find the wounded man, Harry, he'll point us to the others. I can promise you that. Bald Ernie, I'll take you and Rojo, you're the best ground trackers on the Grant. And we'll have the dog. Raul, all right, you and Manuel. That's it then. More than six of us and we'd be unwieldy. We don't want to look like an invading army. Saddle your mounts."

I stepped forward. "I'd like to go."

"I guess not, Hugh."

"I'm the best shooter you've got, sir."

"I don't expect it'll come to that," John Tyree said. "I'm fixing to hang these men."

. . .

We buried Grandfather Clement in the rain. Libby clung close to Mrs. Tyree's skirt under the parasol. John Tyree read the service from the family Bible, Harry Dreier holding a lantern under a sombrero for John Tyree to read by. Feelings welled through me, drawn by the grieving drone of John Tyree's voice. I'd grown fond of the old man with his tall yarns and his erratic humors.

It was still raining when I went up onto the *portal* with Kevin and the women. Behind me I heard John Tyree speak in a voice from which all expression was withheld:

"Let it be a hard reminder of the hazards of line riding. I want the hands to travel in pairs at all times from now on."

The six riders slid past in the night on steaming dark horses, by twos and almost silently. I watched them pass through the yard lights. Then they were gone on, Lobo trotting after in deadly soundlessness. The night absorbed them all.

I felt a soft hand on my shoulder; I heard Mrs. Tyree begin to weep.

. . .

Kevin hammered at the anvil; I was casting lead into my bullet molds. Libby appeared, squinting against the firelight in the forge. "Mama says it's time you went to bed."

"In a minute." Kevin's hammer rang.

"She says now. You want to be dragged to bed by your ear again?"

Kevin put the hammer down. "I got to put the fire out first, don't I?"

I said I'd look after it. I had more lead to melt.

Kevin went grudgingly from the shed. But when I looked up Libby was still there.

If in this narrative I have not dwelt upon the subject of Libby Tyree it is for the excellent reason that young boys make a point of paying as little attention to small girls as they can. Like the other youths on the ranch I had avoided Libby's company whenever possible. Small girls were regarded as pests. They lived in their own world. What Libby and her fellow female children did for amusement I had no idea. Girls were mysteries.

Up at the house a door closed, the sound faint in the night—Kevin going inside. Abruptly Libby said, "We had another letter from Vern."

"How is he?"

"They made him a lieutenant. They fought a big battle near some river, I can't remember the name."

When I didn't reply she said, "Well I think it's pretty good. Not everybody has a brother who's a hero."

"Sure enough." I spilled six gleaming bullets from the mold onto a patch of felt cloth. Then I picked them up one by one in my gloved hand and examined each for flaws.

She said, "Why don't you ever look me in the eye?"

I looked Libby in the eye. "Is that better?"

"I just wondered if you were scared of me." I saw her restrain a giggle.

"What am I supposed to be scared of?"

"I don't know. Boys are supposed to be scared of girls."

I said I was not. It wasn't altogether true.

She said, "Do you want me to go away?"

"You can stay or you can go."

"That's fine hospitality." She flounced out and slammed the door.

That night when I was trying to get to sleep I had a picture in my mind of Libby in her homespun. She was growing into a little woman— she was fourteen then, about to turn fifteen. I tried to put the picture out of my mind.

. . .

John Tyree returned with Harry Dreier and the four vaqueros and the dog seventeen days after they had left. They returned as they had departed: in the rain, in the dark.

I heard the horses; rose from my bed and leaped into clothing and hurried out to meet them.

I found them unsaddling in the barn. A rank steam came off the horses. Rainwater runneled down from the trough of John Tyree's hat.

"Hello, Hugh. How's the news? Everyone all right?"

"Everything's fine, sir. Did you—?"

"We did what we set out to do." John Tyree walked past me out of the barn. He never again spoke to me of the subject.

Later Harry Dreier told it to me.

"They stood by their partner and that was their undoing. We had the scent by then and old Lobo tracked them right down. They holed in, back in a canyon down there in the Yaqui country outside Caborca. The dog got in there and took off a few pieces of hide. They had their hands full with Lobo and we managed to disarm them. We found a cottonwood and we stretched them right there. White men, Texicans, if it matters. Scalphunters I expect. They canceled the bounty on Apache scalps down to Sonora a while back and a lot of these raw-hiders taken to murdering and stealing since then. Anyway these particular three won't trouble anyone again."

Nothing more was said. After that, whenever I rode out on my solitary hunts I missed the old man sorely.

. . .

Christmas again and the New Year. It came in without word from Vern.

An increasing tide of pilgrims flowed across the ranch heading for the Yuma Crossing. They carried tales of devastation back East: Sherman in Georgia, Grant in the border states.

The new Homestead Law had beckoned the pilgrims and the war had driven them; between these forces they continued to multiply and stories came back from the *jornada* of growing cairns of bones along the desert. Even in wintertime the ill-prepared innocents sometimes were not strong enough to survive the passage.

There were rumors of war deep in Mexico as well: risings against the government of Maximilian and the French army.

But then they are always fighting in Mexico. Even as I write these pages there are rumors Pancho Villa is somewhere in the Sierra raising a new army.

. . .

I turned sixteen and the shirt cuffs stopped halfway to my wrists. I had to learn to stoop to get through doorways—a difficulty I still experience.

It all came at once that spring. Every few weeks I had to unlace my stirrup leathers and let them down a notch. I recall spending the season in agonized embarrassment as my voice cracked and dropped into its present booming baritone register. My gawky limbs always seemed longer than I was used to. I kept walking into things, knocking things over. Libby laughed at me a great deal and a hot flush would spread across my face every time.

From my new height I found myself looking down on Harry Dreier and John Tyree and all the vaqueros. Mrs. Tyree measured us all by backing us up to the doorjamb but I no longer fitted inside it without cracking my head; she had to take my height by standing me against one of the veranda pillars. I remember the day I'd gone six foot four inches: Mrs. Tyree said, "My goodness, I don't see any sign of it stopping, either."

It was after supper. From the kitchen window emerged the clatter of dishes—María, growing even fatter, with her hands in the suds. The song of a concertina wavered up from the cantina. Starlight on the yard turned the earth silver. Mrs. Tyree settled in the rocker and a fan of lamplight fell across her through the open door and I remember taking note of the creases in her face, the way her hair was more grey than it had been. She watched me with a grave concentration that made me uncomfortable.

"We don't have much chance to talk, just the two of us."

"No ma'am."

"I'd been hoping by this time some of your reticence might have worn off."

"I'm not sure what you mean by that, ma'am."

"You keep to yourself too much, Hugh. You don't let anyone get close to you. Do you think that's fair?"

"I never meant to give offense, ma'am. I'm sorry."

"Sit on the step if you're a mind to—you don't need to stand there like a common hand with his hat in his hand." The rocker began to creak as Mrs. Tyree swayed gently back and fro. "I wish I knew what you were so afraid of."

"I don't guess I'm afraid of anything, Mrs. Tyree."

"Then why do you keep your distance so?"

"I am obliged for the things you've done for me, ma'am, but there's no way I can ever pay you back for them. I expect I don't feel too good about that."

"Poor Hugh. Is that it—are you trying not to increase your debt to us any more than you must?"

"Maybe something like that."

"Put it right out of your mind, then. Whatever we've done for you we've done because we wanted to, not because we felt we had to. No one's kept ledgers on you."

"You've fed me and bought me clothes, given me saddle and horse, schooled me . . ."

"And you've worked like a beaver to earn them. It's not as if we'd been supporting a shiftless lazybones, is it? Be fair to yourself. Who's put the meat on our table for the past three years?"

"Just the same, ma'am—"

93

"All we ask is your love, Hugh, but it's the one thing you've reserved from us. I find this very awkward but it must be said. We would appreciate some sign of your affection. You're always courteous, and always cool. I find it painful sometimes. You're such a good close friend to Kevin—can't you be a friend to his parents as well?"

Her words seemed to break something down inside me. I found myself crossing the veranda and picking up her hand. I had a frog in my throat and had to stop to clear it. "I'm sorry, ma'am, I never meant to do hurt. You've made a wonderful home for me here. I'll try to do better, I promise."

I saw the moisture in her eyes before she averted her face. "It's all we ask."

After a while in her shrewd way she added, "You know, Hugh, it's not disloyal to your father's memory to take another family into your heart."

    .   .   .

The first shot knocked the tin spinning and I kept it rolling without missing a shot and felt great pleasure for Kevin. He had worked up a new gunpowder formula and had designed the conical bullet molds to a new configuration of his own creation. They had a remarkable accuracy.

The horse whickered and I turned quickly to see what had alarmed it. I saw a rider coming up the slope, threading clumps of manzanita.

It was Libby. "I heard the noise and knew it must be you. Does Kevin's new invention work?"

"Works fine."

"He'll be delighted." She dismounted from the high sidesaddle. I stepped forward awkwardly, not knowing whether I should offer a hand, but by the time I reached her in my indecision she was standing by the horse and her smile changed, infected by a sly humor. "You'll have to learn to be faster than that, Hugh."

She handed me the reins with a mock imperiousness and I led the horse away and tethered it beside my own. Libby talked at my back: "Actually they were going to send one of the hands out to find you but I said I'd come."

"Find me for what?"

"To bring you the news." I turned and found she was watching me with her face tipped to one side. "The war's over. The South surrendered. Vern's coming home."

"That's real fine." I fingered the rifle and smiled at her and noticed how her breasts thrust the homespun.

She gave me an up-from-under look, mischievous, typical of her. "I'm not sure you want him to come home."

"Why shouldn't I? Vern and I are friends."

94

"You've sort of been the big brother around here since he went away."

"Well I don't know about that."

She said, "Do you know why Vern joined the Yankees?"

"He had an itch for action."

"I don't mean the war. I mean why he picked the Yankees' side. We're more or less from Virginia, you know, we never were Yankees."

"He always seemed partial to the Union side."

"Yes. But why?"

"I guess I don't know," I said.

"Because he could see they were winning, that's why. That's Vern all over. He didn't join up till he knew which side was going to win, did he?"

"He wasn't old enough. You're not being fair to him."

She said, "You wouldn't be like that. If you picked a side it would be on account of what you believed in."

"How do I know? Maybe." I made myself busy reloading the Hawken.

She tapped her foot occasionally until I looked up. She pouted at me. "What do you believe in, Hugh?"

"I don't know. What do you mean?"

"What would you fight for?" She leaned forward. "Would you fight for me?"

"Why would I have to?"

"Sometimes you're stupid. Exasperatingly stupid, do you know that?"

"I expect I must be. I don't know what you're talking about."

She delivered a dramatic sigh.

I finished loading the rifle and wasn't sure what to do. Finally I took to hefting the Hawken to my shoulder and snapping my aim at imaginary targets on the horizons. I went around full circle.

She was still watching me. "What do you want to be, Hugh?"

"Be?"

"I don't think you want to be just a cowhand or a wanderer like my grandfather. My father says he suspects you'll make your mark on the world. I believe him."

"He said that?"

"I heard him."

Her eyes were large and serious and, I thought, soulfully illuminated. She was a girl of soaring beauty and it took no great feat of imagination to find in her the qualities that were embodied in the heroines of the romantic novels that were all the rage then: their skins of purest alabaster, their throats swanlike, their hair silken, their forms divine, their cheeks pale, their eyes lustrous deep liquid pools. In actual fact

95

Libby probably was none of those—she was a ranch girl, though not a tomboy, and was hardly pale or fragile; nevertheless no one could have denied she was beautiful. Heartbreakingly beautiful. That afternoon I believe I comprehended it fully for the first time.

She said, "You know there's one thing you do better than anyone else. Even my grandfather said so."

"I'm a good shot."

"You could be the best shot in the world."

I said, "I intend to be."

"You're joshing me now."

"No."

She managed to be both grave and mocking: "I believe you may just do it, too. You've got that kind of stick-to-itiveness. Everybody says so."

"What do *you* say?"

"Well I *cer*tainly hope you make *some*thing of yourself. I shouldn't want to waste my time with anyone ordinary."

"I see—now I'm wasting your time?"

"You try my patience, Hugh Smith. Ask yourself why I came here instead of letting one of the hands ride out with the news of Vern. I wanted to see you alone, you silly goose." Her eyes grew a bit wider as she stared at me. "If my mother knew we were alone out here she'd skin me."

"Then maybe you ought to get back."

"She doesn't know I'm here."

I felt a warm flush spread under my cheeks. It made her laugh spiritedly. "There—I've made you blush, at least. That's a start."

She flustered me. I wheeled in anger: lifted the rifle, pulled the trigger; a hasty shot and it missed the sage clump by a foot. The sudden discharge alarmed the horses and I made a grab for reins.

Libby said, "Did that make you feel better? You missed, for heaven's sake."

"You don't even know what I was aiming at."

"All right, then, you were aiming at the dirt off to one side of that sagebrush."

I put my shoulder to her to cover my embarrassment when I reloaded the rifle. Nerves made me spill half the powder. Finally I looked at her to find out why she wasn't giggling.

Her lips were parted. She still had her merry look but her nostrils were flared and her eyes had gone opaque. "Did you mean what you said about intending to be the best shooter in the world?"

"I don't josh about that kind of thing." I was trying to be casual and matter-of-fact as boys will; actually it was the first time I had voiced my ambition to a living soul—perhaps, indeed, it was the first time I had ever voiced it to myself. That was an important afternoon in my life.

Libby said, "Did you ever kiss a girl?"

"Did you ever kiss a boy?"

She threw her head back and closed her eyes. My heart raced. After a moment I set the rifle down and took a tentative step forward.

Impatiently she opened one eye. Then she smiled and closed it.

I felt Libby's spine beneath my fingers, cool through the cloth of her dress. Her eyes opened fully then and seemed to shine. "We both ought to learn how, oughtn't we?" Then she stretched up on tiptoe and kissed me on the mouth.

.   .   .

In the night I stood out away from the house on the hilltop. I shoved my hands in my back pockets as Harry Dreier often did. Threw my head back to look at the stars—the constellations were vivid and put me in mind of Isaac's astronomy book. I thought of Vern's homecoming, thought at length of Libby, thought of my wondrous discovery that day: I was going to be the champion shooter of the world.

At the time it didn't seem at all an unrealistic goal.

.   .   .

Wanting to get an early start I gulped bread and coffee in the kitchen and carried my hunting gear down to the barn while it was still dark. I picked out a mount from the *caveja* and had it saddled when Harry Dreier stumped into the barn with his tally book and pencil. "You got enough provisions?"

"Enough for four days."

"That ought to do it." He moved closer to the lantern and consulted the tally book. "So far we've got back creased cards from eighty-two people. We'll slaughter a steer and Rivero's packing in a wagon with Mexican fixin's but quite a few folks are partial to quail and nobody'd mind much if we had a couple of sides of venison. You taking both those pack mules?"

"Yes."

John Tyree intended it to be a wing-ding celebration that would set the territory right back on its ears.

They'd be coming from a hundred miles around. The vaqueros were stitching tents to accommodate the overflow of guests; two men had made a run with the buckboard to Caborca for a load of lumber for cot frames; a wagonload of tequila, mezcal and pulque was on its way up from the Sierra Madre; there was a keg of fireworks from Guaymas. Cases of crystal goblets had been ordered up from Mexico City but the *juaristas* had ambushed that particular pack train and we would have to make do with clay *ollas* from Tubac.

I said, "What if Vern doesn't show up in time?"

"Expect he will. He said he would. Vern generally does what he says he's going to do."

I looped several lariats onto the packsaddles and led the three animals out of the barn. Lobo wandered down from the house and sat down by Harry Dreier's peg leg to scratch his ear with his hind foot. I ruffled the dog's neck and was rewarded with an elaborate yawn that bared great teeth. Harry Dreier said, "You want to take him along?"

"No. He's not a hunter."

"More of a killer. But he earns his keep, don't you, old dog?" Lobo wagged the tip of his tail and cocked his head alertly as he did whenever anyone spoke to him.

Violet strips of dawn lay across the mountains. I sorted out the lead ropes and gathered the reins to mount. Harry Dreier stepped back. "Have yourself a good hunt."

"Thanks. I expect to." I clucked at the mules and led them out of the yard, heading toward the dawn.

• • •

It was my intention to ride east into the Patagonia ranges where the game was bountiful: the green hills had plenty of water. I had the secret hope of bringing home a special delicacy for the feast—a mountain sheep or a pronghorn antelope. They were scarce this far south; if any were to be found they'd be in the Patagonia highlands. I'd had more than three years to learn this country and now I aimed the horse straight at the mountains, knowing exactly where I meant to penetrate them.

An hour after sunrise I crossed the Tubac-Nogales road; another half hour and I was splashing the animals through the lazy shallows of the Santa Cruz River. Then it was a steady climb away from the cottonwood bottoms. I kept the animals down to an easy pace to conserve them.

When I topped the first high ridge I breathed the animals and hipped around in the saddle to look down my backtrail. The river valley was grand in the morning sunshine—a wide splash of colors fading pale toward the desert hills to the west. From up here you could see fifty miles.

Looking back that way I discovered two riders coming up from the river. Following me.

I made a face. Then I dismounted to wait.

They rode up with bright expectant faces and I scowled at them both. "Have you got permission for this?"

Kevin said, "Sort of."

Libby flashed her dazzling smile at me. "We left a note."

"I don't suppose there's a way I can persuade you to change your minds?"

"No." She wore a Mexican hat against the sun and her favorite short Spanish jacket; she looked slender in a divided riding skirt. Her eyes flashed at me, merry green, and I thought how long I'd known her before I'd realized she had green eyes.

Kevin said, "We can help a lot, Hugh. We can be your beaters. Drive the game right to you."

"I haven't got enough food to keep three of us."

"We brought our own."

"Thought of everything, did you?" Cross with them, I squinted toward the mountains and then gigged my horse forward and led the mules over the ridge without waiting for them.

They caught up and accompanied me cheerfully. Mrs. Tyree would want to send someone to retrieve the children but John Tyree would veto it: he'd trust me to look after them.

The children, I thought. Kevin was thirteen now; he'd never be tall but he was no longer a child. And Libby was near sixteen. Maybe they wouldn't clutter it up as much as I feared.

I gave Kevin the lead ropes of the mules and led the way into the trees. Every now and then I got down off the horse and inspected the earth for sign. In the lodgepole shadows the earth was bare; tracks were easy to pick up among the dry needles. There'd been deer along here a while ago, heading for the succulents higher up.

The midmorning sun flickered through the treetops like a moving signal lamp, keeping pace with our progress. It was cool in the pines but I didn't unstrap my coat; I wanted my arms free for the rifle. My nostrils absorbed the rich pine-forest smells and my ears kept track of a woodpecker's rattle and a variety of birds talking to one another. The horses carried us along gently, hoof-falls muffled by the conifer needles underfoot; there was the squeak of saddle leather, the occasional snort and swish of tail. I looked back and found Libby's eyes on me—green and laughing.

We came out of the rim of the forest and I pointed toward a peak across the canyon. "Mule deer, five or six. A few hours ahead of us but they're just browsing, not moving fast. They'll be on the near slope there."

Kevin searched the mountain. "How do you know that?"

"I know their habits. Look, you two want to help, ride up the head of the canyon and make your way up toward the timberline. Come across through the scrub oak up high there. You'll be upwind that way, they'll pick up your scent and move back down toward me. That way we won't have to carry the carcasses so far. All right? But keep it quiet until you get around them. If they spot you too soon they'll be over the mountain and gone."

"We'll be quiet." Kevin looked over his shoulder at Libby. "You coming?"

"I'm feeling lazy. You go ahead—you don't need me."

I gave her a quick glance but she was looking at Kevin and I couldn't see her expression. She said, "I'll look after the mules if you like."

Kevin's face changed a bit. His glance shifted from Libby to me and back again. I felt charged, uncertain; a pulse throbbed in my throat. I didn't look at Kevin, but busied myself taking out the Hawken and examining it. I listened to the slow thud of hoofbeats starting up. When I lifted my head I saw Kevin riding away, hat tipped back, making a point of not looking back at us.

. . .

We dismounted. I felt myself drawn into her green eyes. "I don't know, Libby . . ."

"We wanted to be alone together, didn't we?"

"What if he looks back?" Kevin was in plain sight climbing toward the head of the canyon.

Her hands slipped around behind my neck. Her lips were shockingly soft.

She said, "I want to fill up with you."

"Libby . . ."

"What?"

"Nothing. I just love the sound of your name."

She traced my lips with a fingertip. I stole a glance up the mountain. Kevin was crossing the hogback at the head of the canyon, dwindling into the pines. I was consumed with a boyish lust to learn the marvels of the wonderful soft secrets of Libby's body.

I cannot be sure what might have happened had not Kevin's progress along the steep mountainside disturbed a shale slide.

. . .

The avalanche made a racket that exploded the mule deer out of the pines. They bolted down the far slope at a steep angle and I only had time to disentangle myself from Libby's arms and reach to the scabbard. There was time for only one shot, for my ammunition was on the far side of the saddle. The range was something short of three hundred yards and I made the shot count.

. . .

We packed the buck down to the valley and pitched our skinning camp on a mound of open ground above a loop in the Santa Cruz. I cleaned and bled the carcass and hung the meat on stout cottonwood branches; afterward I rummaged my pack for the towel and the cake of lard-and-ash soap. Kevin had my Hawken in pieces on his blanket; cleaning it with patient care, his face still red from the embarrassment of having spooked the game prematurely.

I went down to the river beyond a screen of trees, stripped down and went into the cold shallow water with the brick of soap. It was very near here, just a few hundred yards downstream, that Vern had shot the ten ducks.

It has always been my habit to bathe after skinning an animal out—another teaching of my father's and indeed of his father's before him; though he was a coal miner my grandfather had a reputation as a wild-game provider, both in Pennsylvania and before that in Wales, where he had been punished more than once for poaching.

Nowadays we are told it is important to bathe on such occasions to wash away the blood and other substances in which microbes may fester. I doubt my family had any knowledge of microbes; it was a matter of good manners and comfort. The point I wish to make is that not all frontiersmen were filthy. Unlike some, there were those of us who bathed whenever we had the opportunity.

I was lathering healthily when Libby came along swinging our three canteens, impish mischief in her face. I backed up, sitting down primly in the river and regarding her with an intimidating scowl that only raised the pitch of her laughter.

"Go on," I said, "find your own spot."

"Why I think I like it here so much I may just sit here all day long. And what do you think of that, my love?"

"You're a wicked woman."

"Yes I am." Another giggle bubbled to the surface. But there was a flame of carnal curiosity in her eyes and abruptly she put the canteens down and shrugged out of her jacket and sat down to tug off her boots.

I said, "What do you think you're doing?"

"I'm getting in the water with you."

She was no longer laughing. I said, "Now wait."

"What for?"

"It's not a proper thing, Libby."

"Pooh." She set the boots aside and stood up working at the buttons of her blouse.

Then I heard the roar of an angry voice behind me: I wheeled and saw the horseman across the river—fifty yards away, no more, advancing at a grim trot, his body swaying to the motion of the horse, blue uniform, officer's epaulets, face shadowed by a pale campaign hat with a cocked red feather.

The horse reached the bank and didn't pause: it came right into the shallows and came across as steadily as a machine. The rider's very silence became menacing as he advanced.

"Oh my God," Libby murmured behind me, "it's Vern!"

. . .

I spoke over my shoulder: "Get on back up the hill now." But she didn't go. I felt her weight behind me, felt her hand upon my shoulder; she was barefoot in the water, her blouse half open, facing Vern in defiance.

I was in a shamefully ludicrous position, sitting naked in the water, my chest and bare shoulders exposed. Had I been Vern I must have burst into laughter. But Vern did not laugh, did not smile; his mouth did not twitch at all—he was unamused, angry, indeed enraged.

I said, "Welcome back. Welcome home, Vern."

The horse came out of the water just a few yards from us and Vern stepped down onto the bank, moving with sinewy grace. His eyes never left us. I had time to notice distractedly that he had become a man and that his face seemed to have been shadowed by war: crow's feet around his hollow eyes, creased brackets around his mouth. He was very thick through chest and shoulders now, heavily muscled.

Libby said, "You look foolish with that look in your eye, Vern. Welcome home to you and stop looking like that. Hugh and I were only joshing."

Still he did not speak a single word. With unhurried deliberation he removed his hat, pegged it on the saddlehorn and withdrew his rifle from the scabbard.

Before I could break out of my embarrassment and disbelief Libby was plunging toward him. "Vern, no, for God's sake stop this."

Vern swung his arm up backhand across Libby's face and she stumbled back with an outcry. I was galvanized by that. The rifle was coming around and I launched myself from the water in cold sudden knowing terror: he meant to kill me without a word.

In that brief hurrying instant I saw white-hot wrath and a glistening hunger in Vern's strange face. It drove cold deep into me. The rifle was rising and in panic I swatted at the muzzle, caught it with the flat of my palm, deflected it; I flailed the heel of my fist against his forearm and the rifle fell to earth.

I tried to get a grip on his arm. "Vern, listen to me . . ."

But he wasn't going to be talked to. I saw his boot coming but not in time; the boot caught me on a bare shin and knocked me down spinning in a shock of astonishing pain.

. . .

Fighting is a children's enthusiasm. I had had my share of dust-ups. I was not a bully, however, and rather than enjoy fights I feared them because I knew nothing of the science of combat and I tended to lose control.

A real fight between two angry men is quite different from the staged wrestles and dust-ups we contrived in the arenas to entertain audiences. I have seen expert pugilists at work in the ring and admire their precision but they are professionals and capable of calculation. I had had my fights, as I say, and probably had won more than I'd lost simply because of my size and reach; but when the red throb of hot fighting anger is in my blood I have no skill, no cleverness—I am dominated entirely by anger and fear, as I'm sure most men are, and I lash out by instinct rather than design, the whole affair becoming a matter of energy and desperation and panic.

Certainly I did not want a fight with Vern Tyree. He was a soldier trained in the arts of death. I had enough presence of mind to realize that if he got the upper hand he would kill me.

      .   .   .

Libby was yelling, a wild sound, and I saw Vern's shadow loom, the boot swinging at my face. I fended it off with a lunge of my arm; the boot slithered in my grip but I twisted with desperate strength and Vern fell with a windblown grunt. I recall smelling the saddle sweat on him; I do not recall the fine points of what followed. We went at each other in unchecked violence, raging abandon. I am sure he fought with more precision than I did; but I had the desperation of survival, the certain knowledge that he meant to take my life.

We inflicted hurts on each other; a wild and clumsy scuffling, hampered by the mud we churned up. I remember at one point stumbling to my knees, mud under my hands. I curled my fists and when Vern ran at me I flung a handful of muck in his face.

It stung him, blinded him, and in a corner of my vision I was dimly aware of movement on the bank—Kevin, appearing from the camp, drawn by the noise. Vern clawed at his eyes and spat mud from his teeth. He was down on his side—he must have slipped and fallen; I do not recall striking him. Then I realized he was lifting a rock in his fist. It was heavy enough to have laid my skull open.

I rushed him but the bad leg gave way and I fell—Vern's arm rising overhead with the rock. I recall the cringing stab of terror. Then a vicious whipping sound and the blur of something that swung against Vern's belly with the hard slapping sound of the flat of a cleaver striking raw beef.

The rock fell harmlessly and I saw Vern stagger back bending double and hugging his belly in pain. Sweat sprang from his face and sucked-in breath hissed through his teeth.

It was Libby, she'd hit him with the rifle, swinging it like a club.

Vern wasn't stopped. A wild outflinging of his arm slammed across Libby's breast. She fell with a cry. Kevin was there; I think he must have been trying to pull her away from us. Libby's cry was anguish. It exploded inside me and drove me to my feet. Vern was walking around aimlessly, still bent far over in pain, and in my rage I drove my knee up into his face. I heard it and felt it: the brittle snap of cartilage. His nose.

In the back corners of my attention I was aware that Libby was moaning somewhere and that Kevin had scooped up the rifle.

Blood streamed from Vern's nose and I swung clumsily with my fists like a small child, doing no real harm I'm sure, never really hitting him, blundering up against his protecting arms, but it must have raised his guard for I remember launching myself suddenly—a leap of panic: both feet hard into his unprotected belly.

He went down with my legs buckling against him; I fell across him. I heard the air drive out of Vern with a grunt of exhaled pain.

My weight and wildness had done him in. I scrambled to my feet. Kevin wordlessly handed me the towel I'd left on the bank. I wrapped myself in it, shivering, and touched Libby's cheek: "Are you all right?"

She nodded, mute in her terror. Kevin gulped like a fish, his Adam's apple plunging.

On the ground Vern rolled over and began to crawl around blindly like a crushed beetle.

My shin throbbed terribly where the edge of Vern's boot had struck; I tottered and sat down. Faintly I heard Kevin speak—I turned and scowled at him. "What?"

"I said don't shoot that rifle."

I only realized then that I had Vern's rifle in my hand. I must have taken it away from Kevin. I stared at the rifle—it coursed through my numb mind, one of those stray random thoughts from nowhere, that it was the old revolving Colt's rifle that had belonged to Vern's father. The one with which he'd shot the ducks.

I must have gaped at Kevin because he said, "When she hit Vern she bent it. She bent the rifle. Don't shoot it. It could blow up."

My mind was not capable of sorting his words. I absorbed what he said only slowly; then I threw the rifle from me. I bound the towel tighter about myself and struggled to my feet and searched Libby's face. "You sure you're all right?"

She could only swallow. Her eyes went past me down to Vern who was doubled into a ball sucking air, jaw lurching up and down, face pasted with a crust of blood. She shuddered against me, buried her face against my chest; her voice came up to me muffled: "He must have gone mad in the war."

Possibly, I thought, but the madness I'd seen in Vern was one I'd seen before. It was the same look he'd had in his face that day he'd killed ten ducks with ten shots: the hungry naked glisten.

I had a furtive look at him. He lay on his side with his knees doubled up, whimpers of agony escaping him. Kevin had stripped off his own shirt and soaked it in the river; he was daubing gently at Vern's face and Vern made no protestations. Perhaps he had too much pain to be aware of Kevin.

His eyes came open, swollen and dark; they rolled toward me, assumed focus, clarified with recognition and drilled into me, driving me back. Libby turned quickly in alarm but then for a moment nothing stirred. I stood for an unreckoned length of time pinned by his eyes while the cunning and rage trickled back into him. I spoke as calmly as I could: "Vern, forget it. Gentle down. There was nothing going on between your sister and me except in your imagination."

He averted his face then and I thought it was over.

I looked away from his ravaged agony and glanced behind me, saw the slow wheeling descent of a buzzard and realized it was curious about the meat I'd hung in the sun. I had better get up there and scare it off or we'd lose half our venison.

I took a step and heard the sudden scramble of quick movement behind me and turned, alarm spearing through, in time to see Vern fall on the abandoned rifle.

He was very fast: rolled over lifting it as he sat up on his knees. He hunched over the rifle, still unable to straighten up against the pain, but I saw him ear back the hammer of the rifle, a deliberation on his face like that of a small child concentrating on a meticulous task.

Kevin was shouting: "No, Vern—*no, no,* that rifle's not—"

His voice must have been drowned by the earsplitting explosion. It was an astonishing and untidy sound, a compound of blasts, things rattling, heat, shock, a great force that knocked me flat to the ground.

It was as though I had been struck by a falling tree.

.   .   .

Sharp pain stabbed me. At first I couldn't find it. Then it localized: my left arm. From elbow to shoulder. *He's shot me!*

I saw no blood, only a strangely slanted groove indented darkly into the flesh. But when I tried to move I knew the bone was broken.

A red haze washed over my vision. Trying to see through it I squinted in terror toward Vern, waiting for the next shot.

He was collapsing. His arms went out to break the fall. And there didn't seem to be anything but blood where his face had been.

. . .

I must have passed out for a time. Then I lay alert but powerless, as if the will had been leeched from me; very calmly I watched Kevin work, binding splints to my arm with calm efficiency—it was something he could do, a mechanical task for his hands. He was talking in a dull voice and the words penetrated my consciousness as if they came from a considerable distance.

"   must have slammed all the caps back against the recoil plate because all the chambers went off, everything blew at once. This wasn't a bullet, Hugh, it was the barrel that hit you. Can you hear me yet?"

I must have made some sound because he continued: "It could have torn your arm right off. Two, three pounds of steel. It was all bent out of kilter, you see. It just blew up."

My mouth was dry. I started to speak and choked. Coughed, swallowed and resumed: "Is Vern . . . ?"

"His left hand. And his eye . . ."

Libby wavered in my uncertain vision, leaning toward me. "Hugh?"

Kevin said, "I think he's all right."

She said, "We must try to get them home."

. . .

I stood in a blank misery on the *portal* and heard people moving through the house—singled out the thud-stump, thud-stump of Harry Dreier's gait. The doctor's dogcart was drawn up by the end of the house and across the yard a group of vaqueros stood in a knot outside the sutler's keeping vigil: every now and then their hatbrims would turn as they looked up toward the lamps of the house.

It was cool, dim, silent. The dog Lobo climbed onto the porch and sniffed my boot and went back into the shadows to curl up. I heard his claws scrape the floor as he scratched something.

I could see straight through the high dining-room windows through the farther window into the courtyard where I had a glimpse of fat María carrying a great steaming caldron toward Vern's bedroom. I tried to adjust my arm in the doctor's sling but nothing seemed to reduce the ache and throb. The ride back from the river had been a nightmare of agony. At times I'd wished for the ease of unconsciousness that blessed Vern. Every few minutes we'd stopped to make sure he was still breathing. He was alive but he'd known nothing of the pain of the journey.

Most of the force of the explosion had blown forward away from him because of the position of the recoil plate. Vern had held the forestock in his left hand and when the rifle blew it had ripped the flesh off his palm and buried a sliver of steel in his wrist. Pieces of the rifle had flown forward like minié shrapnel; the single largest piece, the barrel, had caromed off my arm, shattering bone. The simultaneous blasts inside five cylinder chambers had peeled the metal back from the chambers like unfolding jointed limbs: I'd seen the wreckage and it looked like a spider. The rifle's hammer had been torn off its screw and driven violently up into Vern's face, taking a little skin off his cheek and glancing off the bone of the brow over his right eye. It had not penetrated the skull but it had cut his eye.

They came out of the house, the doctor talking in slow reassuring tones. I hung back in the shadows and Harry Dreier stopped on the *portal* while John Tyree walked the doctor out to his buggy; Harry turned and found me in the shadows and came toward me from the lamplight, thudding on his wooden leg.

I said, "Will he be all right?"

"Nothing's ever certain, I guess. The surgeon thinks his hand will heal. He may have lost his eye. It'll need poultices and probably he'll be wearing a patch over it for a while. The surgeon says there's only one prescription that can produce answers—tincture of time. Vern will have some scars at the very least."

I watched the doctor climb into the buggy, refusing John Tyree's invitation to stay the night. The buggy clattered away.

Harry spat to one side. "He's alive at any rate. If he finds any good sense he'll be grateful for that."

John Tyree approached us and Harry glanced that way, then stumped away. The proprieties were such that his presence would have been rude. He knew that John Tyree meant to speak privately to me.

I had to steel myself for it. Stepped forward so that he could see my face.

He gave me a long scrutiny. "How's the arm?"

"How is Vern?"

"Alive," he said bleakly.

I nodded, mute.

John Tyree stood with his hands in his pockets rocking from heels to toes, still examining my face. There was a hard angry challenge in him. "Vern talked awhile. He said some things I hope he'll regret— said you'd done sabotage to the rifle, for instance."

"No sir, I didn't do that."

"I know. I've heard Libby and Kevin on the subject." His stare discomfited me. He said, "It's a hell of a homecoming for my son."

"Yes sir. I am sorry."

"Have you anything to say? Anything to add to what's been said? Anything to confess to me?"

"Only that I'm very sorry any of it happened."

I saw Harry in the farther shadows—listening but not intruding. John Tyree knew he was there.

John Tyree said, "It was a tragic coincidence that he happened to come down that valley just as you were hunting there."

"Natural route home from Santa Fe, sir. Isaac Singman and I traveled down the same valley."

"What I'm trying to get you to talk to me about, Hugh, I do not believe my son attacked you entirely without cause. He is not a madman."

"Maybe he thought he had cause." I wanted to be away from him then; I felt a squirming resentment; but I stayed and faced him.

He said, "I'm giving you ample opportunity to speak to me, man to man."

"There's nothing I can say that will change things. We were joshin' in the river, sir, Libby and me. Vern took it for something else."

"Is that all you want to tell me?"

"Sir, I think it is."

He drew a deep breath and seemed to hold it a long time; finally he exhaled and his hand went under his coat. A cold emptiness settled in my chest—I saw the revolver emerge in his fist.

He said, "You were naked before my daughter."

"Not the way you think."

My heart began to pound. Disregarding my words John Tyree cocked his revolver. "That's how you repay our kindnesses."

I heard Harry Dreier step forward. I held John Tyree's eyes. He prodded my chest with the weapon.

I had to stand my ground. "You're mistaken."

"Pack your tack," he breathed, "and be off my land. If you set foot on this Grant again in my lifetime I'll set Lobo on you."

"No sir. You may as well shoot me now. I won't leave this place if my leaving means I admit to something I did not do."

"Your nakedness before Libby is all the truth I need to know." The revolver lifted toward my face. I saw Harry Dreier behind him. There was nothing Harry could do but I saw his agony.

John Tyree said, "You saved Kevin's life once. If it weren't for that I'd nail you to the barn. To my mind this cancels the debt between us." He lowered the revolver. "I give you your life. Take it and go." His voice shook, barely under control.

The revolver lay back in his fist, unaimed but still cocked; still between us. I stared at him over the gun. "I did nothing. I love Libby— I wouldn't hurt her."

"Don't speak of love in my hearing. Not after you've exposed an innocent girl to your nakedness." He lifted the revolver again—not as a weapon but in a strange gesture like that of a brimstone preacher calling down the wrath of God. "Go! If you intrude on me and mine ever again I'll do you in! Do you understand me?"

I don't know where my courage came from but I met his fevered eyes and spoke in a dead-calm voice. "If you besmirch Libby's name— if I ever hear it said I was driven off this land because I befouled her— I'll come back to settle it. I won't have lies told about her. Not by any man—not even by you."

He was looking up into my face and I saw he did not truly comprehend what I said; there was too much anger in him, checked only by his righteousness, his stern sense of justice: he would not murder me but beyond that he could make no concessions.

It became between us a silent contest of wills. I could not look away then because it would have been a confession of a guilt I did not feel.

After a time I saw his rage building and I spoke. "I'll go because I'm asked to go. It's your home and you have the right. But I've done you no offense. Put that gun away—then I'll go."

His thumb rested on the drawn-back hammer of the revolver. "I ought to kill you." Then without another word he turned his back to me and strode into the house. The door closed forcefully behind him— the *portal* seemed to shake—and I stared after him, suddenly trembling.

Harry Dreier said, "All right."

"What?"

"I'll help you pack your things."

"I'll do it myself."

"I'll just tag along then."

"What for?"

"You're not to see Libby on your way."

"You too, then, Harry?"

"I don't think unkindly of you, Hugh. A young man's got his oats to sow—I sowed my own, your age. If she'd been somebody else's daughter Mr. Tyree would feel the same. But she's his own and a father can't help how he feels about his flesh and blood. Don't write to her either—your letters would only be intercepted and burned. I'll talk to her after you've gone. Don't fret yourself. She's young, so are you. Don't think about her, don't ever come back looking for her—put her clean out of your mind. You'll find plenty willing women up the trail, I promise you that. And they'll find you."

"Harry, I've kissed her twice in my life and that's all I've ever done to her."

"And can you promise if you stayed it wouldn't come to something more?" He reached for the latch and opened the door for me. "Let's

109

go, son. And if it's any comfort I've been proud to know you. You ever need a friend . . ."

But it was not Harry's friendship that obsessed me. It was Libby's love.

I walked straight toward her door but Harry restrained me calmly. With my arm in such pain I was not capable of overcoming him.

I took only the few things I had brought with me from Kentucky; those and the clothes on my back and the saddle and horse that Harry picked out for me. "You'll keep the horse and saddle. They're yours. A man doesn't take a gift back, once given." But I took nothing else. The rest were things that belonged to the Tyrees—books, mainly. I left it all behind.

Harry extinguished the lamp and walked me outside the barn leading the horse; he shook my hand and helped me mount—one-armed I was awkward. I pulled the hat down tight against the wind. I kept looking up toward the house but Libby's window was around the far side and I could not see it.

Harry stepped back. On the *portal* I saw a stern figure watching me: John Singleton Tyree. Lamplight threw frosty glints off his eyes. He had a rifle in his hand, held loosely at arm's length.

I said, "If he tries to punish her . . ."

"I'll see he doesn't, Hugh. Go with God." Harry touched his hatbrim.

I felt torn by conflicting impulses but finally I lifted the reins, had one last look at the house and rode out of the yard with tears wet against my cheeks.

I was not to return to Arizona for five long years.

BOOK FOUR

From the Plains to California

WHEN I LEFT ARIZONA I was on the drift for a while, absorbed by the flow of war veterans and adventurers who sought their fortunes in the West. I have told how I spent those few years; they brought me eventually to Denver where I met Caleb Rice and Fitz Bragg and where I squeezed out a rifle victory over Doc Bogardus.

Two weeks later there was a shooting match at Bent's Fort, again featuring Bogardus, and Caleb Rice went along with me to that one. Bogardus was pleased to see me and we shared a meal during which he told me some of his experiences. The match itself went well for him—too well as far as I was concerned: Bogardus defeated me soundly, 97 balls to 93, and in fact I came in fifth that day. Caleb shot 95 and Fitz Bragg 96 and Wild Bill Hickok 96 also. It was my first look at Hickok. Even then he had a flamboyant reputation. He was an outsize character in every way.

For a brief span of fourteen days I had been the champion rifle shot of Colorado Territory but Bogardus took the title from me at Bent's Fort. Caleb and I, liking each other well enough to travel together, followed Bogardus to Leadville for yet another match—that was in the early part of June 1868—and on a cool cloudy afternoon I matched shot for shot with Bogardus right up to the tie-breaking aftershoot. It was just the two of us, Caleb and some others having dropped out in the first run of one hundred balls, and I kept up with Bogardus for two strings of ten but then my arm gave out and he whipped me handily in the third elimination round—he shot ten to my seven. I nevertheless managed to win quite a few thousand dollars betting on myself.

We shot a fourth match that June at Central City but by that time the word was out across Colorado and very few contestants chose to shoot against us; there were only fourteen in the match. My arm was increasingly troublesome. Bogardus admonished me yet again to get myself a lightweight repeater and have my shoulder examined by a surgeon; then he proceeded to wallop both Caleb and me by shooting 99 out of 100 balls, a score neither of us approached by half a dozen. Afterward Bogardus judged he had taken the cream off Colorado's sporting money. He bade us an amiable farewell and departed for the East. I did not meet him again for some years.

●　●　●

I awoke with a blinding headache and the feeling that three Arapaho were trying to scrape the moss off the north side of my tongue. I eased my eyes open but the light burned me and I closed them.

Caleb said, "Here, have some coffee. I laced it with a few hairs of the dog."

"Lordy."

It tasted terrible. I drank it down and almost gagged. "I hope we had a good time last night."

"You weren't drunk. That's a hangover from a Mickey Finn."

"What?"

"I lost track of you. Found you about midnight where they dumped you out behind the icehouse. Your pockets were cleaned out. You must have hit a low dive or two. It's a good thing you didn't have your poke on you. It's still in your saddlebag there—I saw to that."

I rolled painfully out of my blankets and considered our camp. The trees dripped with a residue of drizzling rain. I ducked back into the tent. Then I realized I had seen something in the camp that didn't belong there. I squinted at Caleb Rice. "Whose wagon is that?"

"Yours. Studebaker wagon and four matched bay horses. I got no notion what you plan to do with 'em, but you own 'em. I found the bill of sale and put it in your saddlebag. If I was you I'd put my money in a bank somewheres. You feeling well enough to listen to a proposition?"

"What proposition?"

"You've won a lot of money. I ain't. I was too damn cocky, as usual. A-hundred-to-one odds sounded too good to me. But you see where it's left me."

I said, "You could've helped yourself to my poke and ridden out for Texas, couldn't you? If I was Mickey-Finned."

"Well I never pictured myself as a thief, much."

"I'm beholden," I said.

"You being rich and a man of leisure and all, you may not take an interest, but I wonder if you've done any calculating on what you're fixing to do next?"

"None."

"Just expecting to lie around and live off your wealth?"

"I don't aim to fritter it away. Maybe you're right, I'll put it in a bank."

Caleb's face hovered over the little fire. "Listen here, suppose we team up, move around from town to town, stir up some shootin' matches with the local gentry? We could make our fortunes. I'll take on the pistolmen, you take on the rifle shooters. There's plenty of rich mining strikes up in these mountains. What do you say to it?"

"I'll think on it. You know what gravels me?"

"No. What?"

"Why ever did I buy a Studebaker wagon and four matched bays?"

"Beats hell out of me."

"I remember buying them right enough. Had something in my mind. But it's vanished."

Later I woke up and remembered. I'd been a little drunk and a little maudlin, remembering the past, and I'd been thinking about Isaac Singman, how nice it would be if I arrived in California and made a present to Isaac of a handsome brand-new peddler wagon and matched teams of horses.

Sometime, I told myself, *I'll do just that.*

But right then I was content to set off with Caleb Rice to skin the sporting gents of Colorado.

.　.　.

I vectored out away from the running buffalo, climbing toward the crest while the herd ran on toward the river. Caleb sat his pinto until the stragglers thundered past him and then rode across the track to join me. Down by the water I saw a great bull lift its head and blink toward the sky. It was an arresting picture, softened by the haze of tan-yellow dust. *Thinking about winter,* I judged. *Thinking it's time to walk south.*

Caleb dismounted and propped his Sharps .50 against his knee when he sat down. He hadn't used it today, preferring his revolvers, but you always carried a rifle anyway.

He said, "I'm fixing to go blind from the dust. I'd admire to call it a day and turn it over to the wagon boys if it's all the same to you."

"Suits me. The horses are tired anyway." I slid the Spencer into its scabbard.

He looked back down the line of mounted corpses. "I feel like I might be sick directly." Then he climbed back aboard his pinto.

It wasn't noon yet but it would take the railroad's packers the rest of the day to hoist the carcasses aboard their wagon train and drive them back to the railhead for butchering. I sloshed the canteen around. "I want something stronger than this."

"Reckon I'm of the same mind."

We rode over the top of the ridge and saw below us the meat wagons stretching out in a half-mile line, the drivers clustered around a fire up front. The meat cutters had their own fire farther back because nobody could stand the smell of them; but they earned fifty cents a day which was twice the wage of a driver and so the meat cutters put up with their own stink.

We rode to the head of the wagon line. Oxen stood in their yokes chewing grass, shooing flies with their tails. The boss driver looked up but didn't get to his feet; he only watched us over the rim of his tin coffeecup, sipping from it, dislike plain in his eyes. We were boys as far as the drivers were concerned—neither of us was yet twenty years of age—and to them it wasn't fitting we should get contract hunters' pay while the boss driver and his men had to settle for two bits a day. Of course if they could've shot as well as they hated they'd have been making hunters' pay too.

What I said was, "They're all yours."

The boss driver inclined his head half an inch to indicate he'd heard. It was the sum of the exchange.

I spurred away east with Caleb at my stirrup.

Neither of us spoke for several miles. I tried to ignore the lurching of my belly. We crossed one gentle rise after another—the magnificent Great Plains. Finally the railhead came in sight over south in the distance—I spied the chuff of smoke from a work train's locomotive. The line of laborers and wagons was strung out two or three miles along the roadbed. You couldn't see them for the cloud of dust but you could hear the ring of their hammers even from this far away.

We gave the construction a wide berth and rode on. Eastward the rails vanished into the distance. Along one stretch just beyond the bone-pile the bare earth was stained almost black. That was where the cutters had butchered last week's buffalo kill to feed the multitude of railroad workers. The smell and the flies hung in the air even now. It sickened us; we lifted the tired horses to a canter until we were beyond the odor and swarm.

Caleb said, "You happen to count your kill this morning?"

"No." It got to the point where you turned into a mechanism. You didn't think about much of anything at all.

"I did," he said. "You know you killed forty-nine buffalo today?

Seven magazine loads. Forty-nine shots. You didn't miss a one."

"Didn't I?" I said it without interest.

"I fancy that's a new record, Hugh. Old Billy Comstock's been going around calling himself Buffalo Bill ever since he killed forty-eight last spring."

"No," I said, "Bill Cody shot sixty-nine a few weeks ago for the Kansas Pacific, didn't you hear?"

As far as I know Cody's record stands to this day and certainly I'd not have had the stomach to best it.

In those days we wasted nothing. Hides, tallow, bones, meat, feces—everything was put to use. We'd learned that from the Indians. There were markets for bone meal and buffalo robes; the droppings—buffalo chips—made good fuel for campfires in the treeless plains. Meat fed the workers and tallow went for soap: everything was used or sold and the railroads profited handsomely.

As far as we were concerned it was honorable to hunt buffalo on the run. From the back of a running horse.

Later the politicians decided to annihilate the herds to subjugate the Indians by starving them. Human vermin who called themselves "hunters" went out with wagonloads of rifles and set themselves up in stands. They would shoot from fixed positions on the ground from long range. Buffalo had poor hearing. Those gunshots would sound distant and directionless; as long as the "hunter" kept his distance he could shoot at the herd all day and they wouldn't stir. I believe the record kill for that kind of shooting came to something over one thousand buffalo in a single day. In most cases those animals were left to rot.

Because of those people I have hesitated to call myself a buffalo hunter. But I confess I was one in the days when there was no end to the buffalo in sight—they numbered in the millions—and when we shot only enough animals to feed the railhead camp.

Nevertheless I found no pleasure in it.

. . .

The horses carried us unhurriedly over the undulating Nebraska plain and a little past two o'clock by my snap-lid pocket timepiece we came in sight of Fort McPherson. Caleb sat up straighter on his saddle. "Maybe some new sportin' ladies arrived by now."

"If they have they'll be on their way out to the railhead." The town was drying up. They'd be pushing on now, pitching the tents and the red lanterns forty miles west for the next camp.

"Well hell, what are we coming back here for, then?"

"I can't speak for you," I said, "but I'm fixing to draw my pay and look for another line of work." I was starting to talk the way Caleb talked—his Texas twang was infectious.

When he made no reply it made me feel defensive. "Look, there won't be any buffalo here by next week. They're heading south. I haven't much ambition to tangle with the Oglala around here but they're a lot easier to get along with than the Arapaho and Cheyenne south of here. You want to follow the herd south, then I expect we'll need to part company."

Caleb gave me a sorrowful look. "Trouble is, right now I don't know but one way to draw down forty dollars a week."

"We could go back to shootin' contests."

"We milked that dry, Hugh. Everybody's heard of us. They know you and me can shoot rings around the rest of the world. Ain't much left right now except meat hunting for the railroad. Listen, next week these railroaders will still need food."

"Not from me. I can't stand any more killing. Money just gets to costing too much when you have to earn it this way."

"Well that's easier to say when you got a few thousand dollars in banks."

"Whose fault is that?"

"All right. Anyhow I don't much feel like disputing with you. I don't sleep too good myself. But I wisht I knew another way to make good wages."

I said, "Are you telling me you haven't saved up anything at all? Not even enough to sit out the winter?"

"Well I took a bad turn or two in a few card games. Paid Wild Bill pretty high for poker lessons."

I laughed at him. "You're a foolish man, Caleb Rice."

"Yes sir, I reckon that is so. But I can tell you this, I don't feel much like wintering in a Texas line shack. You know I don't intend to spend the rest of my life on the drift. I have got me a powerful urge to settle down and make something of myself."

"You do? Since when?"

"You look at old boys like Billy Dixon and Old John Nelson and Fitz Bragg. Wasted their whole lives wandering these prairies and what have they got to show for it?"

"I don't believe they carry a whole lot of regrets around with them in their saddle rolls."

"Hugh, sometimes you're a caution. Ain't you the one always telling me how you intend to be the champion rifle shot of the world?"

"That's me. We're talking about you. I never saw much ambition in you before."

"I don't want to end up stumbling into a saloon at the age of sixty years and have to spin brags about the good old days so's folks will buy drinks for me that I'm too poor to buy for myself. There's better things than that for a man to aim for."

"I am pleased to hear these grown-up responsible sentiments."

He ignored my joshing.

"I'd kind of like to have me a family and a decent place to lay my head and some honest respect from the folks around me."

"You want to run for public office, then."

"Now quit pulling my leg, Hugh."

The drab town in the distance drew us in slowly like a fisherman's taut line. The army's stockade was the only real structure; the rest of it was impermanent: a portable metropolis they called "Hell on Wheels." It had blossomed with the railroad's arrival. A few of the tents sported wooden false fronts but they were the kind that could be dismantled and moved on to the next site. Some of the establishments were merely wagons—chocked down, pegged out, enlarged by canvas canopies and rickety lean-tos. Several men were folding their businesses as we rode in; they were loading everything into their wagons to move on.

Young Wyatt Earp, who was always a diehard, even then, still had his tripe and keister set up in front of one of the saloon tents.

"Step right up here, gentlemen, and test the keenness of your eyesight. You can make yourself some money right here if you think your eyes are quicker than my hand. The only thing you need to make me sleep out on the plains tonight is good eyesight and a modicum of sporting blood. Here you see three walnut shells, which you can buy in any general mercantile, and I have here just one small green pea, slightly hard with age. Now all you need to do, gentlemen, is determine which shell the pea sits under. Now who's going to be first to take a chance?"

He had a good strong voice and a little crowd had gathered around him—seven or eight, no more than that. We rode on past. I only met him a few times in my travels and always found him to be a charming and handsome but slightly shifty fellow. I ran into him in Denver once and found him selling phony gold bricks to cowboys at one hundred dollars a shot. I cannot claim to have been his intimate but I know this much about him: he has never been the marshal of anyplace. Thirty-five years ago he was a charlatan by calling—gambler, pimp, confidence man, what-have-you. A likable fellow for all that, very handsome and hungry for fame. He is still like that. He is a bit older than I am, I think.

We left him to his monte pitch and rode on up the little slope and into the fort, where we drew our wages in the paymaster's office and signed out, took a tongue-lashing from a smarmy lieutenant for quitting without notice, rode out of the fort and sat our horses watching the town shrink. We saw Wyatt Earp ride away. By next week there wouldn't be much more than scars on the earth to mark the town's passing; four days ago there'd been three thousand men in the camp.

We cleaned our guns and stowed them with the other gear in my handsome Studebaker wagon. I saw to the matched teams of bays in the rope corral. Then we walked into what was left of the town and ate a meal of pinto beans and bulldog gravy, buffalo meat, cornbread, canned peaches and coffee. Afterward we bought a jug of whisky.

. . .

Caleb Rice has become famous of course, although perhaps not nearly as famous as he ought to be—some others with their flair for publicity have stolen much of his thunder; you would be amazed how many of the exploits attributed in the legends to other heroes were in fact performed by Caleb Rice.

It was Caleb, not Hickok, who faced down John Wesley Hardin in Abilene; and it was Caleb, not Wyatt Earp, who brought an end to the outlawry of John Ringo in Arizona. But all that came years later.

I have never quite comprehended the perversity of legend. There were men on the frontier—particularly in the later days—men like Bill Tilghman, Tom Horn, Tom Smith. Giants astride the earth. Burton C. Mossman, Bucky O'Neill. These were heroic men by anyone's measure.

Mossman I remember particularly well—a small man in stature but he organized the Arizona Rangers and with just twelve good men cleaned up the entire outlaw-infested territory which extends to a size big enough to cover the whole of New England.

Yet no one has heard of these men; instead the legends have accrued to gentlemen the likes of the Earp brothers and Billy the Kid—people of no account. Maybe it is easier to construct a myth around a man when you don't have to be limited by facts.

I set out to speak of Caleb Rice and perhaps it is time someone spoke for him; Caleb was not an apple polisher and had little truck with writers, unlike Cody and Earp who often traveled around with dime novelists and correspondents in tow.

We had trailed together half a year by the time we quit the railroad buffalo job. At first I had taken him for a wanderer. He was a cheerful youth good with his pistols and in the camaraderie of camps and saloons he put on the amiable show of a footloose fellow: "There's a lot of elephants I ain't seen yet." Gradually I came to learn there was a good deal more to him than that.

In his thoughtful moments—they were not infrequent—he proved himself an uncomplicated philosopher to whom matters of principle and virtue were more than words. Honesty was not merely a habit with Caleb; it was a law of existence without which human affairs were not possible. I once saw him almost cripple a bounder in Bent's Fort who had fraudulently sold a hamstrung horse to an unsuspecting dude. If a merchant mistakenly gave him too much change Caleb was scrupulous enough to travel miles out of his way to return it.

Yet he was not above putting the twist to sporting gamblers. He was capable of using the truth to effect a lie. Early in the summer he had whipped up considerable custom for our shooting contests in the mountain towns and camps by boasting unashamedly about my prowess and his own. He bragged so loudly and so arrogantly that every man who could hold a gun in his hand was infuriated to the point of accepting our challenge. In its way it was a kind of fraud but Caleb found nothing dishonest in it; it amused him mightily.

For my own part I tended to disparage my marksmanship among strangers—in its way a far more dishonest pursuit, I admit; but then I have earned my reputation as a liar.

Caleb had his blind spots. He could not tolerate the kind of weakness that masquerades as gentility: he could not abide a coward. In his later years, as a peace officer, he respected the brave outlaws against whom his trade pitched him but he despised the sneak, the sort of criminal who hired others to do his dirty jobs. It was an attitude that reflected his own dignity but sometimes it served him ill; it caused him to loathe and underestimate certain kinds of people, particularly businessmen, and Caleb never learned how to be politic with men he considered soft. It caused him no end of difficulty and grief over the years, inasmuch as the very people he despised were usually those empowered to rule him—the merchants of the towns that employed him.

Just the same, Caleb Rice was a humorous man and no one who did not know him seems to have got that straight. When we first went to work for the railroad it was through the good offices of Fitz Bragg, who was hunting for the Union Pacific himself and recommended us; and on one of those midsummer sorties Caleb planned out a hooraw that remains in my mind as one of the great moments of my life on the plains.

A few of us had camped a few miles from the railhead camp in order to be away from the noise and stench. We had three or four wagons there including my Studebaker. A young fellow had hooked up with us three days ago. His name was Owen Fairleigh but nobody called him anything but the Pilgrim. The Pilgrim provided a great deal of entertainment for us even though most of it was unintentional and the Pilgrim for the most part seemed oblivious to the amusement with which we all regarded him.

He was a young accountant from Ohio and he knew the West of yellow newspapers and penny dreadfuls and he could be counted on to announce frequently that he was a dead shot and intended to lay out any hostile redskin who came within a mile of him, after which he intended to count coup by slicing off the savages' heathen scalps. On one occasion I had tried to explain to him that counting coup and taking scalps were not at all the same thing but the Pilgrim knew everything and told me I was ignorant. The Pilgrim was an expert and was not to be argued with.

He came replete with a whacking great Dragoon .44 revolver, a big black sombrero, cartwheel spurs and boots with heels so high he tottered. He was plump and his eyes tended to be more watery than steely but he was very big—as tall as I and thirty or forty pounds heavier—and he had a big round voice that he employed freely in the quashing of disputes.

That particular evening the Pilgrim was busy cleaning his oversized revolver and Caleb Rice watched him from our side of the campfire, sipped his coffee and murmured to me, "We all set now?"

"I expect we are."

"Son of a bitch has sure got it coming to him." Caleb couldn't stand the sight of the Pilgrim. He believed the Pilgrim to be a coward at bottom.

Over beyond my wagon was a lump of blankets that purported to be Fitz Bragg asleep. That was for the Pilgrim's benefit. The other hunters were playing cards around their fire.

The Pilgrim finished playing with his horse pistol and holstered it and came swaggering toward our fire with his thumbs hooked in his ammunition belt. When he reached down for the coffeepot Caleb said, "Don't look around, Pilgrim, but we seem to have some visitors out there."

The Pilgrim went bolt still.

I stretched elaborately like a man ready to turn in; under my breath I said, "I count at least four hostiles by ear, Caleb. How do you tote it?"

"Five. Definitely five. Maybe more of them farther out where we can't hear them."

With exquisite timing an owl chose that moment to hoot across the buffalo grass and it nearly exploded the Pilgrim out of his boots.

I smothered a giggle and said, "I reckon we better have ourselves a little turkey hunt, boys."

The Pilgrim swallowed. "Right now?"

Caleb nodded toward the west. "I just seen a feathered war bonnet move behind them bushes." A creek was down there and there was a good deal of brush. The Pilgrim searched it, round-eyed.

With his face all screwed up the Pilgrim hefted his enormous revolver and pulled back the hammer with both thumbs. The old Dragoon model hadn't been made in nearly twenty years; probably this one had belonged to his grandpa; it weighed nearly six pounds fully loaded. It had been designed as a horse pistol—meant to be carried in a holster fixed to the saddle—and it took an exceptional man, or a fool, to hang one of those things on his thigh where it would thump and bruise and weigh him down.

Of course, the Pilgrim was exceptional, he surely was that.

Now he squared his shoulders and began to stalk toward the river. His spurs made a great racket. Caleb and I had to cover our mouths with both hands to stifle our snickers.

We went along just behind the Pilgrim, crouched over. I drew my Remington revolver and Caleb brandished his shotgun.

"Keep it quiet now," I warned.

"Stick together," Caleb said. "We don't want 'em taking us one at a time."

I caught Caleb's wry glance: *And we don't want the Pilgrim shooting one of us by mistake.*

We crept through the night until something stirred in the bushes.

There was a little squeak in the Pilgrim's throat. He sought to cover it by clearing his throat manfully. Any Indian within half a mile could have heard that.

I had to wait before I regained a sufficiently straight face to whisper, "Hold your fire till we're sure of our targets."

The Pilgrim trembled from hat crown to spurs. He tripped over a rock and almost fell down. I winced—he could have blown his foot off but fortunately the Dragoon had a heavy trigger-pull and hadn't gone off.

A shadow figure flitted from one bush to another, silent and sinister.

The Pilgrim didn't see it. I saw Caleb's eyes roll toward the sky— *God give me patience.*

I touched the Pilgrim's shoulder; he jumped. "Hold it up a minute," I said. "Look over yonder."

After a moment the shadow figure obliged by dodging between bushes again. In the starlight the Pilgrim's round face whitened. He whipped his gun up fitfully. The shadowy villain leaped from the bushes and ran across into deep darkness behind a tree. The feathered head-dress bobbed like a signal flag.

The Pilgrim's gun roared.

Muzzle flame lit up the night and the blast was earsplitting. The kick all but knocked the great revolver from the Pilgrim's hand. I heard the slug whine off wood somewhere.

The tree opened up with gunfire then. Flames lanced toward the stars—a quick tattoo of shooting—and the Pilgrim yelped: the huge revolver twirled gracefully out of his hand and skittered when it hit the ground but by then the Pilgrim was hotfooting it back toward the camp.

Caleb nearly had a seizure. Fitz Bragg came up from the tree trying to reload his rifle but he was laughing so magnificently that he kept dropping cartridges. I tried to contain the laughter that whooped through me; we weren't finished yet.

Fitz removed the feathered war bonnet and tossed it aside.

I picked up the Pilgrim's Dragoon and almost lost my balance. "Lordy. You know how much this blunderbuss weighs?"

"Come on," Caleb said.

Fitz led the way into camp and we found the Pilgrim under the wagon.

He looked up beseechingly. "Innuns, Fitz! Swarming with them! Hostiles! Get ready for an attack! They got Cardiff and Rice!"

Then he saw Caleb and me crouching behind Fitz, casting anxious looks over our shoulders out past the firelight. I pressed the Dragoon into the Pilgrim's hand. "Get ready to hold 'em off."

"You ain't dead?"

"Not yet," I said grimly.

"Maybe," the Pilgrim croaked, "maybe we shouldn't do anything reckless . . ."

Caleb said, "You said you wanted to scalp some Indians. Here's your chance. You or them."

"Here," Fitz said, "I think the Pilgrim got himself wounded, by damn." He dragged the Pilgrim out from under the wagon. The Pilgrim pawed and whimpered.

I fired two or three shots off into the darkness. "We're surrounded by hostiles!" Over at the other campfire I saw the rest of the boys wince and groan.

Fitz was ripping off the Pilgrim's shirt. He exposed some pink soft flesh and splashed the dregs of our coffee on the Pilgrim's bare back— "Sure enough, Lord Jesus he's bleedin' something awful there."

The Pilgrim tried to reach around and feel his back. When his hand came away wet and warm he made a strangled noise and flopped out on his face.

We all collapsed in a wild helplessness of mirth. One of the boys called from the other fire, "You ought to be ashamed of yourselves."

"Hey there, boy." Fitz was shaking the Pilgrim's shoulder. "Hey, you just got hoorawed, boy, you got your leg pulled."

But the Pilgrim was oblivious.

I plucked the Dragoon revolver from his limp hand and fired it into the earth until it clicked empty. Just in case the Pilgrim should wake up and decide it hadn't been as funny as we thought it was.

"Smart," Fitz Bragg remarked.

Caleb was still chortling. "I wouldn't fret it. Pilgrim couldn't hit the broad side of a barn from inside the barn."

"Nevertheless," I said, "I'd hate to get shot by accident with that thing."

Fitz put the coffeepot back on its rock by the fire and pulled a branch out of the fire. Its tip was burning. He examined the brand with a gleeful kind of insanity and turned toward the Pilgrim.

I said, "What are you fixing to do with that?"

"We ought to give him a scar across his back to show for it."

"Now come on, Fitz, fun's fun."

"The hell. He's got to have the scar to show his grandchildren, ain't he?"

Caleb said, "Damn fool won't live near long enough to have any."

I said, "Put that back in the fire, Fitz. He'll have scars enough before his life's over."

Reluctantly the old mountain man returned the brand to the campfire. "You young bucks gone soft nowadays."

After a while the Pilgrim began to squirm. I watched him come around.

"What happened?"

Fitz said, "We drove 'em off." But then his face began to twitch.

.   .   .

Before I interrupted myself I was speaking of Fort McPherson and the day Caleb and I resigned from the buffalo-hunting trade.

Early November it was, in the year 1868, I cannot remember the exact date or day of the week although perhaps I ought to be able to, since in a number of ways it was a singular day in my life.

Half the establishments that remained were being packed up; fourteen left before nightfall. The sun tumbled out of sight. A work train chuffed through toward the west; a mud wagon came straight through town without stopping—a gambler, a pimp and six fancy ladies aboard and a horseman outrider whom Caleb and I recognized. The horseman rode up to us with a brief nod, no smile, and regarded us for a moment before he spoke. It was Hickok, his pearl-handle revolvers glimmering softly in the twilight against his tawny clothes, the long hair hanging down over his shoulders. In the photographs of him that I have seen his hair appears pale but actually it was brown, considerably darker than my own. He was traveling with the whore wagon and obviously he was heading on to the new camp to play cards and entertain the sporting ladies and generally impose himself on folks: everybody knew Wild Bill and everybody considered him a peacock but he did make those pearl-handles sing; there wasn't a better pistolman in Nebraska, not even Caleb. Hickok could drive corks through bottles with his Navy Colts. He drank too much to be dependable but he had flair and color. Most folks liked him although most folks also kept a certain distance. He had few close friends, if any.

He was tall—nearly my height—and bulky, tending toward fat. But no one mistook him for a soft man.

He nodded to both of us. We were passing the jug between us; we sat with our backs propped against the spokes of the back wheel of my Studebaker. Caleb lifted the jug in a gesture, inviting Wild Bill to step down and take a drink, but Wild Bill declined. It wasn't discourtesy, just laziness—he didn't want to climb off his horse and Caleb didn't want to get to his feet.

Wild Bill said, "There's word on the trail a fellow's looking for you." He was looking at me when he said it.

"What fellow?"

"Name of Tyree. From down Arizona way."

"Which Tyree? You happen to catch a Christian name?"

"If I did I don't recollect it. If it's important then I'm sorry."

I said, "I expect if he looks hard enough he'll find me all right. Thanks for the word."

Watching Wild Bill ride away to catch up with the mud wagon Caleb gave a reproachful belch. "I'll have another crack at him one of these days."

"He beat you fair and square last time. He'd just do the same thing again."

"The hell. I was drunk."

"So was Wild Bill."

"You think you could beat him, Hugh?"

"Not with handguns. Not yet anyway. I need more practice."

"You stick to your rifles, old son, I'll stick to these here. God created men, Colonel Colt made them equal. And he made me just a little bit more equal than anybody else."

"Excepting Wild Bill."

"Well maybe."

"You ever kill a man, Caleb?"

"Expect I did, if you count a backshoot Mexican thief as a man. How about you?"

"No."

"Why'd you bring that up, then? Something to do with this Tyree fellow that's looking for you? Who is that?"

"There's three Tyree men. Father and two sons. I wish I knew which one it was." Maybe it was Kevin. Next to Libby he was the Tyree I most wished to see.

But I had a feeling it was Vern. Along the trail when they told you somebody was "looking for you" it didn't generally mean a friendly visit.

In the growing dusk we watched the town die before our eyes. One saloon tent remained open to the last. A dozen men milled under the open lean-to at the bar, which was simply a plank thrown across two kegs. A few lamps threw desultory light around. Doubtless these stragglers had remained because they felt a need to draw breath before plunging on to the crowded madness of the railhead.

On the open tailboard of a covered wagon a fat man in dusty black clothing stood caterwauling to the customers. He had a good loud voice and it carried to our camp:

"I stand before you tonight a man who has met that villainous blackguard, Demon Rum, and emerged triumphant from the contest to come before you good folks and spread the true humble gospel of Temperance. My friends, think you upon the seductive influence of King Alcohol upon our vigorous unsuspecting youth—recall, if you will, how the Demon leads us to pain and regret, to riotous debauchery and the agony of besottedness, from the hoary bloated gout of habitual imbibing to the final inexorable Hades of Delirium Tremens. And so I say to you, my dear friends—cast off the chains of bondage! Discard your wayward ways! Join the Good People of this Earth in solemnly pledging to Abstain, now and forevermore—Abstain from Any and All intoxicating Drink! *Abstain!*"

Somebody at the bar shouted out at him, "Oh, shut up, Bob, come on inside and have a drink."

Caleb passed me the jug. "Go on, take a pull. We ain't hardly dented it yet."

"No. The whisky's giving me no pleasure tonight."

Huge grey moths rustled around the single lantern on the side of our wagon. Up at the fort somebody was bellowing orders to a detail. A few small campfires burned among the tepees where the tame Pawnees had their camp. A horse whickered. I looked up at the stars and the whisky transported my mind back to things of earlier recall: another wagon under the same stars—Isaac Singman and his uncle J. V. I remembered the astronomy book.

Caleb interrupted my reverie: "It's a crying shame. You see all that gold coin in the paymaster's office this afternoon?"

"Lot of money there."

"A fellow could walk in and take it. All it needs is a cocked gun. Live the rest of his life like a king. Too bad neither one of us is gaited that way. I never tried stealing. You?"

"Thought of it once or twice but my hands always sweat."

We heard the quiet approach of soft-leather footsteps. I twisted around to look past the wheel rim. Caleb said, "Who's coming?"

"That fat gent. The one that was lecturing on temperance."

Caleb snickered. "Offer him a drink."

The fat man came in sight puffing from the climb. "Gentlemen."

"How do."

"Name's Robert W. Halburton. Most people call me Bob, be that as it may. Mind if I seat myself?"

"Pull up a chair there," Caleb said, "and have a drink."

"My pleasure, sir." Halburton twinkled at our surprise; he produced a flat metal flask. "First-class elixir here. Cures warts, hangnail and the social disease. Join me?"

"I'll try anything," Caleb said with reckless courage. He put the flask to his mouth. His eyes went wide; I saw his Adam's apple go up and down.

Caleb lowered the flask with a beatific smile. "Now that's sippin' whisky."

"Kentucky aged," the fat man assured him.

I said, "I thought you were a teetotal man."

"I'll tell you there, son, we all enjoy our little jests. Now you'd be astonished how many free drinks I get pressed on me by jokesters thinking to corrupt me. Many's the man I've drunk under the table with his own bought-and-paid-for liquor."

Caleb burst out laughing. I said, "You could've fooled me for certain. I took you for a genuine saloon buster."

"I suppose I've made my share of converts to sobriety, which pleases my sense of irony." Halburton settled his rump gingerly upon the sod; I passed the flask back to him after appreciating its contents and he drank with the reverence of an experienced imbiber. "Now I'm told you two gentlemen go by the names of Rice and Cardiff. Which is which?"

"I'm Caleb Rice. This here's Hugh Cardiff."

"You perhaps can tell that I'm from the East?"

"Yes sir, I reckon we calculated that."

"New York, in point of fact, is my home and headquarters. New

126

York City. I am a writer, in the sometime employ of the *New York Illustrated Weekly,* a great publication for which I bear the title frontier correspondent. It's my task to bring to thousands of avid readers the exploits of our foremost pioneer heroes out here in this rugged wilderness of savage beasts and redskins. Why, only last week I filed a lengthy dispatch recounting an exclusive interview with none other than Wild Bill Hickok himself."

"Shouldn't be too hard," Caleb remarked. "Feed Wild Bill a few drinks on the cuff, he'll talk you to death."

Halburton cleared his throat. "Be that as it may, you and I may know the drab facts of reality but my readers want titillation. The excitement of high adventure. Bold heroes astride the vast open landscape. All that buffalo shit."

Caleb laughed. "All right, now I believe you. But you surely do pile it deep."

"Horseshit, buffalo shit and bullshit, my good friend, are my stock in trade. There's not a man alive today who's half so adept at wielding the shovel as your obedient servant. Gentlemen, you are looking at the champion bullshitter of the world."

I said, "I'm always proud to meet a fellow champion. Pass me that flask again."

. . .

"You might be amazed," Halburton told us a bit later, "how many successful dispatches I've filed the morning after hanging around whorehouse parlors listening to the brags of the patrons."

"No sir," Caleb drawled, "I don't think I'd be amazed at all."

"Be that as it may. I'm always on the lookout for new heroic adventures to relate to the gaping readers back home. And I was about to say, in point of fact, it was just such a whorehouse encounter that has led me here to Fort McPherson tonight, to seek out, in particular, two legendary heroes of the plains named Cardiff and Rice."

It elicited Caleb's snort of laughter. He opened one eye and rolled it toward Bob Halburton.

I said, "You have got our undivided attention here."

"I thought I might. Wouldn't you like to partake of the contents of this flask again?"

"I might have just a sip."

"Please and be my guest."

The whisky went down warm and gentle. I handed it over to Caleb.

Halburton said, "You're the champion rifle shot of these parts, I'm told, and your friend the champion pistoleer?"

I said, "I am indeed, but my friend here might not be able to make such a statement without getting powerful arguments from a few other old boys around here. Hickok for starters." I sniggered at Caleb. I admit I may have been a trifle splooshed but I felt a warm happy attack of lying coming on me.

I said, "Why, sir, if you're seeking out genuine heroes of the plains you don't need to look any further than this wagon wheel right here. Cardiff and Rice, why they're the stuff that true-life legends are made of. Why from the time I fought off a hundred Indians when I was a Pony Express rider to the time Caleb here rescued the Colonel's daughter from old, uh, Red Hand's camp while I killed that great Cheyenne war chief with a single rifle shot from a range of two and a half miles across a fierce wind—"

"Sure enough," Caleb murmured, "there ain't never been a real genuine hero out here half as tall as my partner Hugh." He rolled his eyes toward me.

We had Halburton enthralled. I waxed expansive. "I mind the time Caleb and I were carrying dispatches for General Phil Sheridan through hostile Indian country. We got ourselves jumped by, oh, must have been at least forty Cheyenne. Old Caleb took care of thirteen of them with his two Colt revolvers, the ones you see right there in his sash. He fired twelve bullets, you understand, but one of them killed two Indians. Of course I had my own hands full at the time there, took care of ten, twelve Indians with my fifty-two-caliber Spencer rifle, the one you see over yonder in that scabbard, and then when Chief Feather Hat jumped me with a knife, why I just twisted right around and scalped him with his own war knife. Now you know Chief Feather Hat stood eight feet tall. Minimum. Biggest Indian ever born. But he was no match at all for me, no sir."

Bob Halburton beamed at me. "Mr. Cardiff, I do believe you have a future as a news reporter. You have the proper ability to report the straight facts without embellishment, I can see that plain and clear."

Caleb muttered, "Lord help us," and closed his eyes.

Halburton was scribbling furiously in his notebook. He glanced at Caleb and said, "Be that as it may."

. . .

The sun in my face brought me awake and I stirred. Halburton was gone. Caleb snored under the wagon, flat on his back with his hand draped protectively over the jug from the saloon. I went around, as arthritic as an old man, feeding and watering the stock and building the fire for breakfast coffee, for which I felt a powerful need. I'd slept against the wagon wheel and my spine felt pleated by the spokes.

Caleb came to the fire squinting in pain, clutching his cup tremulously. "How long did you stay up lying to him?"

"Until I ran out of yarns. He was starting up on a third notebook. He's fixing to write a dime novel about us."

"Think of that," he said without enthusiasm.

"Said we should watch out for the book. It'll have the name Ichabod Zachary on it."

"Who?"

"He doesn't use his own name to write those things."

"I wouldn't either. Whoo boy. I got a head on me like a buffalo. Pour me some of that black stuff."

After a time I said, "We ought to set our minds to planning. What are we aiming to do?"

Caleb stretched his arms. "I can't say for you, partner, but I'm aiming to head back to Colorado and get myself a law job. It came to me in my sleep that was what I was cut out for. Police deputy."

"You're locoed up for sure. That's dangerous work."

"Not if you can handle your pistols it ain't. They know me back in Colorado, you know. My name'll scare the fight out of the hellions. It's the kind of job that gets a man respect from folks." He looked at my face and scowled. "Now don't you go funnin' me."

"You don't know the first thing about law work."

"Reckon I can learn. Reckon it can't be that hard. I expect you're forgetting all those Indians I fought off with you—Red Hand and Chief Feather Hat and all. When you and me was the heroes of the plains."

"What kind of flowers you want me to send to your funeral?"

"I'm going to set out for Denver this very day." Caleb stood up. "You coming?"

I considered the drab army fort and the ghost town on the slope. For sure I wasn't staying here. "I'll ride along with you a piece, at least."

⋅ ⋅ ⋅

I wintered in Fitz Bragg's camp in the Tetons. That was a curmudgeonly gathering of rapscallions, five of them in number. They said they were weary of society and anxious for solitude—I've never seen such constant jabbering and drinking and laughing and arguing as I did that winter.

As the youngest member of the party (by nearly forty years) I was treated somewhat as chore boy but I also learned from those old-time frontiersmen about winter survival and dealing with Indians. The old men had lessons to impart and I spent that season absorbing what wisdom I could. Like Grandfather Clement Tyree, each of those old men had devised his own tricks and techniques of shooting and living.

Later someone suggested I could have done better by apprenticing myself to a polished competition shooter like Doc Bogardus but I dispute that. These were old men whose very survival had depended solely on their wits and their rifles since they were young. I could not have had better teachers.

I expended a fortune in ammunition that winter. I would go out alone to shoot. I would talk to Libby, confiding my schemes and ambitions, pointing out to her the beauties of that overwhelming land, talking about our future—how many children would we have? I pledged her my love forever.

Our tents were pitched along the Snake River in the lee of the Tetons When the weather was poor for hunting we would fish through the ice. On other occasions we ranged quite far into the passes, traveling on snowshoes by twos and threes; we hunted caribou and bighorn sheep, snowshoe rabbit and bears and skinned them for trade. Once we tracked a grizzly three days through the snow, shot it and had to pack it all the way back to camp on travois. Fortunately it was mostly downhill; the bear weighed the better part of a ton. We ate all the meat we killed and cured the pelts before we stacked them to freeze.

I never traveled without my saddlebag of books but that was a long winter and I must have read each of them half a dozen times. I grew heartily sick of Sir Walter Scott.

Occasionally we ran in with Shoshone and Sioux. On the plains to the east the army was involved in a winter campaign against some of the tribes—Custer had a regiment in that—and as a result the western ranges were a bit more populous with Indians than usual. Our dealings with them were standoffish encounters, not hostile but neither were they friendly. Both sides remained distantly correct and polite. We had no trouble. One of Fitz's companions tutored me in the sign language of the plains. We had a little difficulty with pilferage and on one occasion a pair of Arapaho kids tried to make off with our horses but we put a stop to that and sent them packing with quirt welts across their backsides and a warning that we'd use our rifles next time. Before we dispatched them from our camp we gave them a little exhibition of our shooting skills. Evidently they were impressed; they did not return.

In the March thaw before the floods we broke camp and dragged our laden travois to Fort Laramie where we got a fair price for our pelts and drank a great deal to celebrate our farewells. It was an amiable parting but I am sure we were happy to see the last of one another. At least I for one had had my fill of their raucous company.

. . .

In Denver I hoped to strike up a shooting match or two; also to look up Caleb Rice and see how he had fared. I was disappointed on both counts. No one had forgotten my victory over Bogardus the previous spring and I found no sporting blood among the Denver gents. As for Caleb, when last seen he had been on his way to Bent's Fort.

At that time in Denver there was an establishment that belonged to Mattie Silks. I had been introduced to the parlor and its occupants by Doc Bogardus on my previous visit to Denver and now I repaired there to reacquaint myself with one or two young ladies who had struck my fancy in 1868.

I had been in the mountains half a year with five old men and therefore had no urgent wish to depart Mattie's hurriedly. I was there three days, never once setting foot out-of-doors.

. . .

Later in the week I waddled down to the Farmers & Merchants Bank to deposit a bit of the money I had earned from the past year's buffalo shooting and hide hunting. Added to my previous stake, which I had won in the shooting contests a year ago, this came to a tidy sum. Financially I was quite a successful young man, possessing nearly ten thousand dollars to my name. A canny instinct led me to break up this holding into a number of deposits, none greater than two thousand dollars, which I placed in accounts with various banks in the town on the assumption that one or two of them might fail but not all of them at once. I am known to have been extravagant at times but never altogether stupid about money.

With enough gold coin in my poke to see me through the coming weeks I returned to Mattie's to collect my warbag and blanket roll. When I entered the parlor I found Wild Bill Hickok there with two buxom ladies. He summoned me with a lift of his jaw.

"I hear you wintered out with Fitz and them. Wonder you haven't gone deaf from all the old-hen cackling."

"They're good old boys."

"I should have done the same," he allowed. "Lost my roll to Buck Courtwright in an honest game."

"This Courtwright must be a hell of a card player then."

"I had a bad run of cards but just the same you're right, he's not a slouch. Listen here, Hugh, I need gainful employ. They've offered me a job over in Abilene, city chief of police. Peace marshal. They want a man to keep a lid on the cattle crews from Texas. Now I've accepted the job but I'm going to want a deputy I can trust behind my back."

Then he just looked at me while he fondled the two ladies. His eyes were guileless. It was early in the day and he was still sober.

I said, "You asking me to be your deputy?"

"Yes I am. You're big enough to throw a scare into those rebel trail boys."

"I am honored by your trust," I told him, "but law work isn't my line. But I'll tell you what, you ought to talk to Caleb Rice about this. He'd make you a first-class deputy."

"He would, yes, but he's gone to California."

"Is that a fact?"

"That's what they told me at Bent's Fort. Got himself a job in Sacramento, deputy constable or the like."

"Good for him."

Hickok said, "Look here, it's not as if you've got anything better to do. I need a deputy. The pay's good. You get to keep half the fines you collect."

"Well it so happens I do have something to do and no offense intended but I don't see the point risking my neck every night on the street of a Kansas cattle city that I don't care two beans about. But I do wish you good fortune there."

"Thank you kindly," he said, and called for a drink. I noticed he didn't offer to buy me one. I'd have refused anyway.

Wild Bill then withdrew the two pearl-handle Navy Colts from his sash—he never wore holsters to my knowledge, always carried his pistols thrust through his sash—and placed them behind him on the parlor bar. It was partly for comfort and partly a kind of talisman; it was something he did when he felt he was among friends; by disarming himself he showed his trust. Actually he carried a .41-caliber Deringer up his sleeve. He did not confuse politeness with foolhardiness. I suppose most people who knew him had seen it. Wild Bill found frequent cause to have a gun in his hand.

He took a sip of sour mash—Mattie served only the best—and closed his eyes to enjoy it. His first of the day, I suspected. When he opened his eyes they were directed at me. "I ran into that fellow again who was asking after you."

"Tyree?"

"This time I took his Christian name as well. Vernon Tyree?"

"I know him."

"Said he was looking to meet up with Hugh Smith. Of course by now he knows you're traveling under the name Cardiff."

"It's my name."

"I always calculate a man's name is whatever he chooses to call himself." Wild Bill smiled; it made me wonder whether on occasion he himself had used an alias.

He said, "This was in Santa Fe in December. Your friend was heading back for his home in Arizona but he said he had a powerful urge to meet up with you. Seemed kind of disappointed when one of the boys informed him you were wintering in the Tetons. I expect that was out of his reach, him having to go back to his cattle farm in Arizona. Handsome-looking young gentleman, he is."

"Patch over one eye?"

"Why no. A scar or two on his face but I saw no eye patch. Why?"

"Well I'm glad to hear he didn't lose it."

"You shoot him in the face or something, Hugh?"

"No. He shot himself. You might call it an accident."

"Well I'm not inclined to pry."

"Did he say anything else?"

"Said he'd heard a lot of bragging about you winning rifle competitions. Said he'd admire to best you in a rifle target match. I didn't shoot against him so I can't say whether it was a windy."

"He's a good shooter."

"As good as you?"

"I'm not sure. Maybe even better."

"In that case I'm sorry I didn't have a match with him. I'll bear what you say in mind for the next time I cross his path. Always enjoy a hard competition—it brings out the best in me." He grinned at me; Wild Bill had a truly engaging grin, you couldn't help responding in kind I think it was a shame he was killed so young. I did like him.

But it is a good thing I was not tempted by his offer of a deputy job. Later I heard how he had been in a gunfight in Abilene and got rattled, perhaps the result of too much corn whisky, and shot his own deputy to death by mistake.

．　．　．

Fitz Bragg was like a bad penny in my life at that time.

Wild Bill's news about Caleb's move to California had rekindled my interest in traveling to that strange country. I had it in mind to strike up some shooting contests there; it was my ambition to be the champion rifle shot of California. And it seemed an excellent opportunity to look up Isaac Singman.

I tossed my few belongings in the back of the Studebaker and set out on the trail.

I arrived at Bent's Fort in April 1869. I was twenty years of age.

Bent's Fort was a major oasis for wagon pilgrims; trains broke up and reassembled there, depending on their destinations. Major trails crossed at Bent's Fort—from the plains, from Texas on to the Rocky Mountain mining discoveries and the Southwestern desert territories and California beyond.

I found Fitz on the edge of town dickering with a wagon-train captain. He was trying to pick up work as a guide or contract hunter. In part his aim was sentimental: it was to be the last season for that kind of westering. By the end of the summer the transcontinental railroad would be completed. We who knew those early days are dwindling in number; when you can cross the United States in Pullman comfort in a few days' time it is hard to imagine those days when the same journey consumed many months and imposed great discomforts and sacrifices and great triumphs as well. There is little triumph or accomplishment in making a three-day train ride. I like to think of those early days as a grindstone. They separated the gemstones from the pebbles. Either they ground a man down or they polished him up. I made my first wagon trip west at the age of thirteen and I shall always take pride in that.

      .   .   .

Fitz's train was bound for California by the southern route, through Cook's Canyon in the Peloncillos and along the San Pedro and Gila rivers. To a point it was the same trail Isaac and I had pursued. I had the ulterior ambition to pay a call on the Tyree ranch once the train approached within forty miles of it. With that in mind I dispatched a letter from Mesilla to Harry Dreier. I watched the Overland coach carry it away.

Our train had sixteen wagons: a small party by pioneer standards but there were few emigrants nowadays—most Easterners intended to wait out the completion of the railroad. Our party was ambitious. They were a close-together group of Indiana farmer families who'd got crowded off their land by a coal-mining combine. They were hardworking people who aimed to settle rather than prospect and they meant to get to California ahead of the railroad while the best land was still available for homestead.

Because of our small number we were vulnerable. The increase in traffic since the war had inflamed resentment among the Indian tribes and skirmishes were on the increase. Where Isaac and his uncle and I had passed safely through a thousand miles of Indian country in our solitary wagon, now no one felt safe traveling with fewer than a hundred companions. By those standards we were dangerously small in number.

But we had one defense the others had lacked. We had Fitz Bragg.

A day out of Santa Fe with Comanche to the east and Apache to the west Fitz and I left the train and proceeded with a few trade goods along the Rio Grande until we had found a small hunting party of Mimbreno Apache. "Ain't easy to outwit an Apache," Fitz observed, "but you can trick any man if you know his blind spots."

I found the Mimbrenos a very humorous group of young men. They kept turning pranks on one another. It was difficult to get them into serious conversation and when finally Fitz managed to get them smoking and listening he went through a long rigamarole by way of preamble: Apache dialogue was elaborate with ritual and circumlocution.

Fitz explained how we had a small bunch of wagons bound for California with thirty-seven people *loco en la cabeza,* mostly women. These women were crazy in the head, Fitz declared, and that was why none of the big wagon trains wanted them along. Fitz didn't mind traveling with them because everybody knew he was a little crazy himself.

This made a few of the Apache look searchingly at me but they were too polite to ask the obvious question.

They listened with increasing gravity to what Fitz had to say and they went away rather quickly at the end of the parley.

After that we had no trouble with Indians. The word got passed down as a matter of course from one band to the next, from Comanche to Jicarilla to Chiricahua to Papago to Pima to Mohave to Paiute. Indians wanted nothing to do with crazy people, especially crazy women. It was the most dangerous kind of medicine to tangle with crazy people because you never could be sure they wouldn't witch you. You gave them great respect and wide berth. All sorts of demons of the Indians' pantheistic world inhabited the souls of crazy people.

We saw a few Indian hunters along the way thereafter but they kept their distance and we had a pleasant trip until we got to Fort Huachuca where I planned to leave the train for a few days in order to ride across the Patagonia country to the Tyree Grant. But there was a letter waiting for me at the fort and it changed my intentions.

It was from Harry Dreier.

16th May 1869

Dear Master Smith-Cardiff,

I have your letter from Mesilla and hasten to reply. It would be unwise for you to do what you said.

We hear about your shooting matches and I know Mr. Clement would have been rightly proud of you.

I have had your previous letters at frequent intervals and am grateful to you for keeping me posted on your progress in the world. However if you had hidden hopes that I would show your letters to Miss Libby, you were mistaken. I have never shown her them nor even mentioned them and I do not intend to. She needed no far-distant skylarking from you. She is nineteen years old, a true young lady. She has had numerous gentlemen suitors and no time for truck with dead memories. It has been four years and you must stop carrying a torch about.

Miss Libby has been sent back East where her mother and father wish her to take a finishing-school education.

Your present letter mentions Miss Libby five times. You exasperate a body, and I am led to wonder if you ever intend to grow up. She is far away out of your reach. She felt, at that time, that you had run off and left her without so much as a good-bye, and while I explained that you had no choice in the matter, she felt betrayed all the same, and if she thinks of you at all now I am sure it is not with any fond regard. You always were a stubborn youth but you must learn to accept that things change. You must grow up and forget her.

You may recall our old dog Lobo. He died last winter.

Young Kevin has set up his own smithy shed and serves as gunsmith and tool fixer to all the hands. He sells rifles and pistols of his own design to our hands and to passersby. I carry one of his rifles myself. It is of excellent balance and accuracy.

Master Vern has taken over some part of the running of the Grant now that John Singleton Tyree has become entangled in a foolishness of legal claims over the property. A Spaniard came over here from Barcelona claiming the Hidalgo Ruíz people had no authority to sell the Grant. The Spaniard has presented himself as the real owner of the property. The case is expected to go before the federal claims court. The matter has my employer in a state of weariness and irritation.

The Spaniard has called upon us a few times. He goes by the name of César Núñez and has got real drawing-room manners but I sense meanness underneath. I imagine that we shall win in the end, possession being what it is and Núñez being a foreigner, but this matter has taken some of the salt out of my employer. His hair has gone grey, can you believe that? He is only twelve years my senior and I am barely thirty-one years old this month.

I should advise you that when Master Vern discovered that we had known you under a false name and that your real name is Cardiff, he made inquiries through the post, under the assumption that if a boy travels under a false name he must have good reason to hide the true one. Master Vern ascertained that a warrant for the arrest of Hugh Michael Cardiff is outstanding in the state of Kentucky. Vern has grown up some in these years and it is not in his character to do a man in the back, and I do not believe he has any intention to alert the peace authorities anywhere along the routes of your travels, but I imagine that, should you set foot on the Grant, he would incline toward placing you under arrest and having you delivered back to Kentucky in chains. I render this advice to you in the hope of discouraging any idea you may harbor of visiting us. I believe you would dislike to tangle with Vern now. He is a robust strapping young man and knows his own mind. He is every bit a first-class shooter.

I wish you all the very best in the future.

Your very good friend,
Harry Dreier

It was like Harry to make no direct accusations: I had fooled him as well as Vern, traveling under a false name, but he made no complaint of that. Harry was a forgiving man.

At first his letter made me tense and anxious with fear and when the Santa Cruz deputy sheriff paid a friendly call on our train I was ready for a dispute with him. If the warrant was still out on me there might be shinplasters in circulation.

The deputy had a look around our camp to see if there were any known felons among us. It was mainly a matter of form. I knew that; we'd undergone the same thing in other towns. And Fitz told me not to fret myself. The name Hugh Cardiff had been bandied all over Colorado and Nebraska, he pointed out, and nobody had arrested me yet. He had a twinkle: "Maybe nobody's had the nerve to."

The deputy looked me in the eye and shook my hand. He smiled and there were no secrets behind the smile. I watched him ride away; I was wondering what I'd have done if he'd tried to arrest me.

Fitz said, "If it's six years ago and a wartime charge besides, ain't much chance anybody'd bother sending you back to Kentucky."

Vern Tyree might, I thought. He'd do it out of grudgement if I strayed into his reach.

I had no cause to confront Vern then. I cannot say whether I had any feeling it was bound to come. It might have been wiser to face him then and have it done; but that is the wisdom of hindsight.

   • • •

A few days later we camped on the Rillito in the shade of cottonwoods between the army's adobe layout at Fort Lowell and the village of Tucson. As it was the biggest town we would visit this side of our destination, most of the pilgrims elected to lay over an extra day to shop in the Tucson emporiums and replenish their supplies. Fitz and I went along to "see the elephant" and I made the acquaintance of a young lady who went by the name of Crystal. She was a forlorn little creature. Fitz commented later that she looked underfed. By comparison with most of the sporting ladies of that time she was surely slender; but then I am strange that way, I have always preferred my women lean. Libby was slim too, of course.

In the morning we began to organize the stock and there was the usual racket of hitching-up. Fitz was saddling his favorite pony and making ready to ride out ahead to scout the trail—a formality, really, since it was a well-beaten road. But Fitz was never a man to shirk. He had a job and was being paid to do it and he intended to do it properly—hangover or no hangover.

That was when a disreputable-looking fellow on a mule rode up among the wagons and dismounted by my Studebaker. He was a mass of scars; he wore a round black hat down his back suspended from his throat by a thong and his hair looked as if someone had tugged it out in tufts. He was a trifle under ordinary size and moved with a distinct limp, the kind that told you instantly that it caused him pain to walk. By his garb I took him for a hard-luck prospector. Assuming he meant to try his hand at begging a grubstake I moved to head him off but Fitz caught sight of him and beamed. "Albert, you son of a bitch."

"So, Fitz. You're keepin' well?" The man pounded Fitz about the shoulders and Fitz's face crinkled into a smile so intense he seemed on the verge of tears.

"Ain't been less than a coon's age, Albert. You got a few new scars there, too."

"You know how it is, Fitz, they use Albert for a pincushion always." The prospector spoke with a heavy accent—German or Dutch, I thought.

Fitz said, "You still the chief?"

"Still and always. They cannot make do without Albert."

"Good for you, son. This here's my trail partner, Hugh Cardiff."

The prospector sized me up and shook my hand. He said to Fitz, "You always have had the good sense to pick a man big enough to hide behind, I will say that for you." He smiled at me with surprisingly straight white teeth. "Pleased to make your acquaintance, friend Cardiff. Are you the man who shoots bumblebees at one mile away?"

I laughed at that one. I hadn't heard it before.

"Not only that," Fitz said, "but I seen him hit two bumblebees with the same bullet." He said it with a straight face too.

There was a clatter of tack and gear, a multifarious creak of rigging and leather—the wagon train readying to span out. Fitz reached for his reins. "Here, why don't you ride along with me a spell, Albert?"

"I can't, I must meet the crook over at the fort." At least that was what I thought he'd said; later I realized I'd mistaken a word. Albert touched Fitz's sleeve: "I heard you was here, I want to talk with you." He took Fitz off toward the wagon. I couldn't hear what they said to each other. I watched our elected captain walk forward leading his horse; he interrupted the two men, asked Fitz a question, got Fitz's nod of agreement and mounted his horse to lead the wagons out.

Fitz and Albert strolled off to get out of the trail, both of them leading their mounts, still deep in conversation. I could see enough gestures to realize Albert was trying to talk Fitz into something and Fitz went from reluctance to interest to uncertainty. Finally Albert whapped him about the shoulders again and got on his mule and rode off toward Fort Lowell.

Fitz and I rode out ahead of the train and it was a long time before he spoke.

We curled out west around the spur of the Santa Catalinas. It was desert country but we were surrounded by mountain ranges of various sizes and colors. Fitz kept squinting off toward the boulder-strewn peaks west of us. Abruptly he slapped his fist down against his saddle-horn. "Damnation. I may be old but I ain't dead yet." He turned a suspicious eye upon me. "You know how old I am?"

"Not exactly. You never said."

"I am sixty-one years old, that's all. A man can expect threescore and ten if he lives right, ain't that so? Means I got a good nine years left in me."

"Sure you do. You'll make a hundred, Fitz."

"Damn right I will." He squinted belligerently toward the mountains again. "Albert's right. I'm gonna do it."

"Do what?"

But he didn't answer right away. He was working something out in his mind; I watched the emotions chase one another across his mobile face. Then he said, "They're rising."

"What?"

"All over. They wiped out Fetterman up north and now Albert tells me they wiped out an army column over to Apache Pass."

"Indians?"

"They're getting crowded, don't you see?"

"Fitz, what are you on about?"

"Manifest Destiny, boy. Like the orators say. Manifest Destiny. The white man's bound to progress all across the land. The Indian's in the way."

We went along for a while in silence. The sun climbed and heated up. Fitz said, "General Crook's taken command at Lowell. Albert's got himself a commission to raise a troop of professional scouts."

"Albert?"

"Sure. That lame little gent's the best Indian tracker on the desert."

Suddenly it dawned on me. "Albert. You mean that stove-up tramp is *Al Sieber?*"

"Bet your ass he is."

And that was how I met the famous Al Sieber for the first time.

.   .   .

We made our way along the cutbank rim of the Rillito, following the road through creosote thickets. Behind us I saw the dust of the wagon train coming along. The Rillito was dry—water only ran in those arroyos in flash-flood season—but if you dug down just a few inches you'd hit water under the bed. We always followed dry rivers whenever we could. In that part of Arizona the surface waterholes are few and far between.

Fitz said, "Albert said he could use me. Think of that. An old man like me."

"You'd do him proud, Fitz."

"White folks need protecting, don't they? These Apaches are rising. Bound to be a good deal of trouble the next few years." He was talking himself into it and I let him go on. He said, "Three, four days more we'll be west of Apache country. Won't be any trouble after that, so long as you know how to keep them alive in the desert. You still got that map in your warbag? I can mark out the water for you. Your only hard spot would be the dunes west of Yuma. You get through those you'll be fine."

My heart gave a jump. "You intend to quit the train here?"

"I'll put it to the captain. I've seen you through the rough patch. You can handle it from here, Hugh."

"I've never been in California in my life. But I'm obliged for the respect you put in me."

"Our job's to keep them healthy to their destination. You can do that as good as me. You're a trail master, Hugh, I never rode with a man that learned faster and I've never known you to forget anything that needed remembering."

"I've had a good teacher, haven't I?"

"Thank you kindly." He flashed his smile at me. "I'll ask the captain if they'll cut off my contract. If not I'll stay on to California. I won't go back on anything without everybody agrees to it." Then he added, "They'll release me from my word, I count on it. Because they know what fine hands they'll be in."

I felt a swell of youthful pride. Fitz threw his head back and bayed out his whoop. "*Hoo-raw*. I'm going to chase me some Indians again."

Fitz stayed on with us until we made the flowing river at Gila Bend. Then with the wagon party's blessings he rode away back toward Fort Lowell. I watched him dwindle. On the last visible rise he waved his hat in a circle overhead and I echoed the gesture and then the train was mine. It was a heady responsibility for a twenty-year-old.

I pointed them west and headed for California, where I would find new adventures and my life would take a new course.

BOOK FIVE

The Sacramento Fire

AT YUMA the Johnson-Jaeger Steam Navigation Company ferried our wagons across the Colorado River to the shore of California. Paddle-wheel steamboats churned the shallow river but soon thereafter we were shagging across the loose sand of the California dunes. It was slow hard work corduroying the wagons across log-roller supports, pulling each log out from behind the wagon and laying it down in front to make a continuous track. Sometimes we made less than a mile in a day. But Fitz had prepared me for it and we did not run dry.

In time we hit the hardpan flats and picked up the pace crossing the Mohave country. It was as hot as Beelzebub's drawers but we traveled that stretch mainly by night and I had Fitz's instructions as to where to camp, where to find water and where to seek forage for the animals.

We had one encounter with a batch of Mohave Indians and it got sticky for a bit there because my Plains Indian sign language didn't get through to them but one of them spoke a bit of Mexican and we managed to sort things out by bribing them with a few doodads, a worn-out horse and two skinny beef cattle.

There weren't really enough of the Mohaves to pose us much challenge but I could see the resentment that smoldered in their faces and I knew Fitz was right. The pilgrims just kept coming into the land, more and more of them every season, and the Indians everywhere felt crowded. Pretty soon they were going to push back. I felt sorry about it and some confused.

It wasn't right against wrong. It was two different rights against each other. I have always felt that was the way of it. Nobody was to be blamed. I never held with the notion that the Indians ought to be killed off the way you timbered off a homestead in order to farm it. Indians aren't trees. But neither was it right for a few hundred Indians to be dog-in-the-manger about tens of thousands of square miles that they weren't making much use of anyway.

There just never was an easy answer to it, to my way of thinking. I did not much like the way things worked out but I am not sure I could have proposed any wiser solution. I did my best in my own small way, always gave out plenty of honest jobs to the Indians who worked in our traveling shows, gave them the opportunity to keep their dignity and hold their heads up.

It was June when we made our destination in the rich valley of the Sacramento River. A raw new farm town called Courtland sprawled by the river and I could see the shine of anticipation on our pilgrims' faces as we approached. It was fine land, lush and wide, summer-warm although the peaks off to the east were white with snow.

We made our last camp in a copse by the river just a few hundred yards up the road from the town. The train's elected captain made a tiresomely eloquent speech in praise of my work in guiding them through the wilderness. After this mustering-out nonsense, which touched me, I accepted my pay and went into town, the thought of saloons and sporting ladies uppermost in my mind. I felt a bit on the lonesome side. I no longer had much in common with farm people.

The next morning a delegation of our pilgrims went along to the land office to see the homestead maps. The women strung long rope lines of laundry through the trees and the scent of lye soap drifted strong along the riverbank. I put my Studebaker onto the Sacramento road and went along slowly on account of my hangover.

The wide road followed the river and I had some excitement when a paddle-wheeler appeared, all glittering brightwork and vivid paint: the *New World,* skimming downstream at high speed. Passengers waved from the decks as the ship slid past me at a good thirty miles to the hour. I lifted my hat in the air and whooped them on.

Toward evening I got into a traffic of buggies and wagons and horsemen all converging on Sacramento city.

"Hello there, friend, what's all the excitement?"

"Nothing especial. It's Saturday evening."

"Why I'd forgotten. Would you happen to know where I might look to find a peddler by the name of Isaac Singman?"

"If he's in town you'll most likely find him down in the commercial district there, trading for goods. Just keep to the river when you come in town. Ask around when you get there—most folks know Singman."

"Thank you kindly."

There were huge railroad yards at the terminus, several locomotives throwing smoke, jackbooted men pouring off the passenger carriages from the Tuolumne and the Sierra Nevada. Sacramento had a throbbing fandango excitement like nothing I had seen outside Denver. Hoots of laughter; in the distance an occasional high-spirited gunshot; cacophonies of jangling music from honky-tonks. There were dry-goods and ship chandlers, low dives, Chinese cafés, establishments of all sizes and kinds. It was dark by then but most of them were wide open and crowded. The streets were thronged. Here and there I'd see a pigtailed Oriental in billowing sleeves, a Negro freedman, a Mexican in his sombrero, a Paiute in a big round black hat, a Modoc in skins.

Ahead of me a rubbish van's horse had collapsed in the traces and I patiently eased the Studebaker through the crush. Two yapping dogs squirted across the street and a kid on a high-spirited steed tried to keep his horse from rearing in alarm. A man with revolvers in two holsters stood under a corner lamp pole with his lips peeled back from the cigar he was smoking. A polished hansom deposited three sporting gentlemen in front of a gambling parlor and a water wagon came along, scattering pedestrians, wetting down the dust of the street.

I asked directions twice and finally came into a wide thoroughfare behind the piers, lined on both sides with freight barns and corrals. There was little traffic here. Some distance away a heavy freighter was drawing in, pulled by sixteen oxen with a driver on the high seat and a whip-handler on horseback.

"I believe you might find him over yonder to Halstead's."

"Thank you kindly."

A long wooden sign hung on chains, its legend painted in a faded crescent that must have been luridly ornate before the weather had got to it: F. W. HALSTEAD—FAST FREIGHT—GEN'L MERCANTILE DELIVERY. Painted wings adorned the word FAST.

I stepped from the wagon onto the loading platform and walked through a high wide doorway into a cavernous space most of which was filled with stacked goods—harness and plowshares, fenceposts, rock salt, bolts of cloth, carpetbags, lanterns, hats, boots, spools of wire, flagons of whale oil, beds and chairs, tent poles—but I didn't stop to inspect anything. I was looking for sign of human occupation. No one stirred.

In dimness at the far end of the warehouse a door stood ajar and lamplight spilled through it. I picked a path that way.

143

It was an office, as cluttered as the rest. A space had been cleared around the roll-top desk and two men were there—a heavy yellow-bearded man and a small figure on a stool hunched birdlike over the desk pecking at ruled pages with the nib of a pen, darting out fitfully to the inkwell, scratching busily on the dry paper. He wore a bottle-green coat and eyeglasses.

I tipped my shoulder against the doorway and smiled. I watched Isaac remove his wire-rim spectacles, blow the dust off them and put them back on, hooking them over one ear at a time. He looked up at the yellow-bearded man. "Three thousand for the lot, then."

"I make it forty-four hundred and fifty."

"Impossible, Franklin. I've got my expenses to consider. Wagons and oxen and crews. The distances involved . . . Three thousand five hundred. My final offer."

"I'd lose on it. You're a valued associate, Isaac, and for you I'll accommodate to forty-two hundred, but only on condition you never breathe a word of it to my other customers."

"Thirty-seven-fifty. Absolutely as high as I can go."

"We're talking about ten wagonloads of goods, Isaac."

"Twelve loads, Franklin. I can't overload my wagons. Think of the terrain they must climb."

"That's for you to judge. Most of the traders would settle for ten."

"Most of the traders have no view to the long term. To crowd these goods on ten wagons would cost me several oxen dead of exhaustion. I prefer to reach my destination with livestock intact. In the long run it's a saving, not to mention the matter of respect for God-given life."

"You're a queer bird, Isaac."

"Mrs. Deauville doesn't wait supper for tardy tenants. I must be on my way. Let's settle this matter."

"At forty-two hundred."

"At four thousand. The figure we both knew we'd agree on from the beginning."

The yellow-bearded man laughed. "It's yours."

Isaac drew out a pouch and emptied it on the desk. "Four thousand, if you care to count it." He winked at the yellow-bearded man.

"You've yet to short-count me. Now you'll have the loads out of here by Monday closing, yes? Otherwise I must charge storage against you."

"Agreed."

I rapped my knuckles against the jamb. "Isaac."

The narrow shoulders jerked. Isaac squinted at me through the dusty lenses. "Yes? May I be of service?"

Then his face changed. "Hugh!"

He rushed beaming to embrace me. "I've been expecting you. How wonderful."

. . .

Ten—10¢—Cents
BOLD HEROES OF THE PLAINS
Authentic Exploits of CARDIFF and RICE
—Legendary Frontiersmen—
A Narrative of True Wilderness Adventure
WILD REDSKINS! SAVAGE BEASTS! OUTLAWS!
From the Pen of
ICHABOD ZACHARY
Famed Frontier Correspondent

Thus had legend preceded me. I stared upon the dime novel with its bright-hued illustration of two improbably muscular heroes in buckskin astride prancing white horses. Blazing guns in every hand. Glamorous rescued damsels adoring the two men with worshipful eyes. Hordes of snarling Indians in hot pursuit.

I laughed until I was blind with tears.

Then I handed it back to Isaac but he waved it off. "Keep it. You should have it."

We emerged from the warehouse and I asked Isaac what he thought of my Studebaker wagon and the teams.

"I allow I find them formidably handsome. I doubt I've seen such outstanding bays since we departed Kentucky."

"They're yours."

"What did you say?"

"Are you deaf, then?"

"I've never had such a gift in my life."

Then he sparkled and soon his talk ran on at high speed. He'd begun with a single wagon—Uncle J. V. Singman's wagon—and he had eighteen to his name now. For some years he had supplied goods to the remote mountain camps but most of them were turning into company towns: prospectors had finished off the easy pickings and the big companies had taken to demolishing entire mountains with waterspout monitors, washing the ore down by the ton. "Not much future there for a man like me. I've turned much of my effort to the new farm communities. But soon there'll be a dwindling market for my shops on wheels—I can see the handwriting. It's almost time for me to build my emporium and settle in."

"You sound as if you might be thinking about getting married."

It made him laugh. "Not many respectable ladies take much romantic interest in an undersized shortsighted Jew. Now and then I've encountered a woman with a gleam in her eye and a calculated smile. The kind who'd marry you on the chance you'd make her wealthy. But no thank you. I prefer the company of my books and my landlady. Mrs. Deauville is seventy-three years old and tart as a lemon but she plays a fair game of chess. Do you attempt the game?"

"Not often."

He turned anxious. "Do you still read, then?"

"Every chance I get."

"That's all right then. Now tell me all your news."

. . .

We found a spot for the wagon and stabled the bays. Isaac's boardinghouse was in a quiet street. Mrs. Deauville was tight-lipped and lean; she set a spare table. I didn't wonder Isaac was still thin as a boy.

I remembered something. "You said you'd been expecting me. How came that?"

"Yes, I completely forgot in the excitement. A stout gentleman gave his name as Halburton—"

"That's the fellow who wrote this dime novel."

"No, that gentleman's name is Zachary."

"It's a name he uses when he writes. Did you meet him?"

"Someone told him I was your friend. He sought me out and told me you'd be arriving here. He implored me to ask you to go to him at your earliest convenience. He's residing at the Occidental House."

"But how did he know I'd be turning up?"

"I'm afraid he didn't say. There's one way to find out, of course. Go ask him."

"In a while," I said. "I've another friend, Caleb Rice. Is he around here?"

"Young fellow not much more than my size, proud of his pistols?"

"That's Caleb."

"He's a county deputy, I believe. For the sheriff. His office would be up in Ransome."

"How far away is that?"

"Four hours' ride. Three on a fast horse. But if you're thinking of going there I might advise you it's a sudden town."

"Bandits?"

"No, it's a farm town, they've been having trouble with the mining companies."

"I didn't think there'd be much cause for mixing those two groups."

"It seems the gold monitors have been washing deposits of tailings down into the farm valley. I don't know much about it, really. Your friend was dispatched there to keep the peace. Humorous young fellow."

We were in Mrs. Deauville's sitting room pushing chess pieces around by the yellow light of a whale lamp. I had gone rusty but not so much that I couldn't see I was losing the game. I made it as hard as I could for him but Isaac checkmated me in the end.

"Well fought," he commented. "Your mistakes were at the beginning rather than the end. Now that you've warmed up we'll have a real game." He began to set up the pieces.

"Let's save it for next time. Where's Halburton's hotel from here?"

. . .

The Occidental House sprawled the length of a city block and sported a dozen elegant shops under the overhang of its veranda. Balconies overlooked the intersection, staid with banks and a block of law offices and such. I threaded the heavy Saturday-night pedestrian traffic and made my way into the lobby and found it a vast room of dark wood and deep leather and draperies. Each chandelier must have had sixty candles. I thought of the fat man in the dusty coat delivering his hoarse temperance lecture outside a crude tent-saloon at Fort McPherson and the comparison struck me with amusement.

Heavy armchairs contained worthy citizens brooding over news-papers; there was a gathering around a big table, men with pungent cigars and loud talk about Leland Stanford's railroad empire and the burning issue of hard gold versus greenbacks. Through the open doors of a saloon room issued the warbling European voice of a *chanteuse* and the strings of a small orchestra. I made my way to the registrar's desk and inquired as to Mr. Halburton's whereabouts and the clerk began an investigation of the registry but a uniformed bell captain leaned forward: "Mr. Halburton's in the game room, sir. Up there."

I followed his pointing arm: went up to the mezzanine on the wide carpeted treads of an immense stair, then followed the railing with the open lobby beneath me until I reached a leather-padded door where a black-suited man who must have weighed fully three hundred pounds stood with his arms folded forbiddingly.

"Looking for Mr. Halburton."

"I don't know as the gentlemen wish to be disturbed. I'll ask inside. Your name?" He looked me up and down and disapproved visibly of my outfit.

"Hugh Cardiff."

His eyebrows lifted at once. Perhaps he was a reader of dime novels. He disappeared through the leather-covered door and I stood by the rail overlooking the swirl of people in the lobby until the huge man emerged and spoke: "You may go in."

I squeezed past him and found myself in a short corridor. A door at the far end stood ajar and I heard the rattle of cards ashuffle. When I pushed through the door I found myself in a large room filled by six

147

circular tables: faro, poker and whist were in progress and the room was silent with tension—I heard only the crisp slap of dealt cards and the quiet ring of gold on velvet.

At the near poker table Bob Halburton looked pleased with his cards. It was draw poker—a game I knew well enough to avoid.

I stood behind him waiting for the players to finish the hand. Halburton had a substantial pile of coin before him and it grew again when he gathered in his winnings. I tapped him on the shoulder and he looked up with recognition and then pleasure. Then he stood up and scraped the burden of gold coins into his overturned bowler hat. "My business appointment has arrived, gentlemen. Been a pleasure taking your money."

One of the players said, "Don't take it too far away, Bob. We'll want a chance to take it back from you."

"At your service tomorrow evening, gentlemen. Hugh, shall we find a quiet spot?"

I followed him out to the mezzanine. He seemed if anything a bit stouter than he'd been in Nebraska; perhaps it was the bulk of his dark suit. He was chuckling. "It's almost a crime taking their money. I've got a flask of good sour mash in my room if that'll suit you? I've got a proposition to put to you and we'll want privacy."

"Sour mash always suits me, Mr. Halburton."

"Call me Bob. I expect we'll be seeing a lot of each other. I'm glad you got here—I was beginning to doubt my information." We were walking up a flight of stairs. He puffed between bursts of words. "Traced you as far as Bent's Fort—a month ago. They said you'd taken a wagon train—out here."

"You came all this way to see me?"

"I did indeed." We went along a carpeted hall; he inserted a key in a door.

The bed had been turned down and the drapes shut. A pair of boots stood by the door freshly shined. My companion went around the room turning up lamps, then shouldered out of his suit coat and produced from a wardrobe shelf the same flat metal flask he'd shared with us at Fort McPherson. He passed it to me and sat down with a grunt on the room's only substantial chair; he waved me to the bed and I sat on its edge.

I lowered the flask. "It's still sippin' whisky. Only the best for you." I watched him, reserving trust. "I saw your dime novel."

"Which one?"

"How many are there?"

"Six at last count. Two more in the presses for publication this season."

"You write fast."

"Snails don't get rich in my trade. How'd you like it?"

"Haven't had a chance to read it yet. I only saw it an hour ago."

"When you get a chance read it. You do read, don't you?"

"Yes."

"Thank God."

"Why?"

"Because it's easier to memorize your lines if you can read."

He had a pull from the flask while I digested the implications of his words. He belched and wiped his mouth. "Do you play poker?"

"Not often."

"You're not a gambler then?"

"I'd as soon gamble on my shooting. Never had much interest in playing-cards. It always looks kind of childish."

That provoked his smile. "A bit of play never hurt a man, you know. You're too damned serious for your age but it's not to be denied you're the most startling commodity to strike the world since Mr. Judson's book on Hickok and Cody. You're a celebrated certified hero. The Cardiff-Rice books have been outselling the other dime series by five to one."

Abruptly he tossed the flask. I caught it in midair without spilling a drop and kept a straight face against his grin. He was inspired to say, "Remarkable reflexes. As I'd expected."

I smiled crookedly to show I wasn't altogether bewitched by his line. I had not forgotten his boast that he was the world's champion bull-shitter. He was not merely a liar but a persuasive one.

"At first the thought came into my mind we might serve the public by putting you on the lecture circuit. Chautauqua, the library societies, podium and stump. Audiences would pay handsomely to hear from his own lips the tribulations and triumphs of an authentic frontier hero."

I said, as if unmoved, "Of course I'd have to grow a beard to cover up the fact that I'm not old enough to vote."

"I shouldn't fret myself about that, Hugh. You're tall enough to command any audience. But I said to myself, Halburton, any dolt can stand on a platform and deliver speeches. No, that's not for Cardiff and Rice. Far too static. These are men of action, I told myself, and they must be presented to audiences in a vehicle that justifies both their stature and their reputations as men of heroic principle and superhuman prowess."

"I like it better when you stick to plain language, Mr. Halburton."

"Bob."

"Bob, then."

He nodded as if he counted it a victory. "The opera houses of every city are crying out for the fresh, the novel, the exciting. They're put to sleep by the familiar mortgaged-farm stolen-will tedium of ordinary melodramas. Think what we can bring them, Hugh—the fresh hot taste of great true adventure!" He leaned forward as if to take me into his confidence. "Be that as it may, have I pricked your interest?"

"Maybe."

I was stringing him of course. His excitement was infectious even if it were sham. But it seemed important not to let him see my interest. An idea had already begun to churn in my head.

He said, "I've written a theatrical play. *Heroes of the West*. It's your story, Hugh, the true authentic adventures of Cardiff and Rice, reenacted on the great theatrical stages of the world by the original heroic participants in the flesh."

He thrust himself to his feet and began to stride back and forth, belly pushing ahead of him, animated by enthusiasm. "It will be the sensation of the decade. Nothing like it has ever been seen under the proscenium arches of the world. I've planned a schedule for a grand tour. Starting in New York City at none other than the Astor Palladium—perhaps a six-week engagement, enough to whet their appetites. Then triumphant appearances in Philadelphia, Boston, Providence, Baltimore. So on, so forth."

He stopped in his tracks and beamed at me. "What do you say, then?"

"Do I get to read this play before I give an answer?"

"By all means. By all means. I have a copy for you, right here somewhere—where is the damned thing now?" He was rummaging through a portmanteau, flinging things feverishly about. Then with a cry of discovery he produced a thick sheaf of papers bound together with wire and tossed it across the room to me.

I caught it and glanced inside. "What's Caleb got to say about all this?"

"Prepared to join us on a moment's notice. He's eager to begin. You need merely say the word, Hugh."

His uneasy bark of a laugh seemed to come in the wrong places. He appeared to be far more on edge than I was. I had yet to make up my mind whether he was genuine gold or whether he was likely to turn green after a while.

I let the silence grow. He began to fidget. "You can't turn me down. You can't *let* me down."

"I could. You could pick up any vaquero off the prairie and put him onstage as Hugh Cardiff. Nobody'd know the difference."

"They'd know. Mark me now—you're the spit and image of the heroic model. Hickok has a paunch, Cody is half-drunk most of the time, Texas Jack has scars under his beard, even Caleb Rice has the visage of a senile monkey. Alone Caleb would not sell half a dozen tickets. You're incorrect in assuming I'd have an easy time finding a substitute for you. I have learned in an adventurous and checkered life that one must never defraud when truth will suit as well. Why present an imitation Hugh Cardiff when the real Hugh Cardiff is available?"

He began to talk with wild gestures. "Hugh, you must know this. You possess what is called in the theater a presence. Very few have it. It's not an attribute that can be learned. It exists in a few men, God-given, and you are one of those few. You need merely enter a room to become its focus of attention. I can't define it. Lee has it, Grant does not have it. I knew this about you when I first laid eyes on you under a wagon in Nebraska. That you were a star of immense magnitude merely waiting to shine in full glory."

"I've seen playactors strutting onstage in Denver," I said. "I haven't got much use for them. A grown man making a fool out of himself spouting words somebody else wrote for him."

"You'll grow to love the applause."

"Will I?"

"At least make the attempt. It could mean your fortune."

"I've already got a fortune. A small one, anyhow."

Halburton took a hurried pull from the flask and brooded a while at the floor. Clearly in search of the right words he spoke slowly and without his former bombast. Very soft. "I offer to place the world in the palm of your hand, my young friend."

. . .

With his play under my arm I let myself out of the room and went along the busy Saturday-night streets atremble with excited anticipation. We had left it that I would consult with Caleb before informing Halburton of my decision. Halburton had agreed to that: Caleb would confirm everything he'd told me, he said.

A tour of the cities of the East—it was heaven-sent. How better could I seek out Libby Tyree?

No; there was no chance of my turning Halburton down. But I hadn't wanted it to show. Even then I had a canny sense of bargaining position.

In high elation I went along to Isaac's boardinghouse and broke the news to him.

. . .

Church bells rang through the warm morning. I sat on the porch plowing through the turgid prose of Bob Halburton's dime novel. Now and then I must have snorted; on occasion I was forced to laugh aloud, startling the families that hurried past on their way to church.

151

I could not reconcile the Halburton-Zachary yarns with any reality I had ever known. I had never fired in anger at an Indian; Bob had me slaying entire tribes. There was no relationship between the swooning damsels of *Bold Heroes of the Plains,* their crinolines and heaving bosoms, and the tart earthy sporting ladies who had been my only feminine companionship. Bob's characters talked in language I'd never heard; I imagined that the meanings of many of his words must have eluded most readers who were not as well-read as I. The book described feats that were physically impossible for man, horse or gun. It showed its hero—a seven-foot Hugh Cardiff whose fists could smash six villains at a blow—scaling great cliffs by his fingernails and wrestling grizzly bears to death; it had Cardiff and Rice, in a single chapter ("In Which the Villains of Hell's Hinges Are Taught a Lesson"), dispatching thirty-four felons—I counted them—while rescuing the Colonel's fair-skinned daughter from "a doom that she contemplated with far more trepidation than that with which she gladly would have greeted her finite end."

The door squeaked open and I looked up to see Isaac with the wire-bound script of Halburton's play in his hand. Isaac's lips twitched in an effort to hold back amusement. "I have a bit of trouble picturing you getting your mouth around some of these speeches."

"So do I."

"But with your sense of horseplay I think you'll have a grand time of it."

"I don't want to make a fool of myself."

"Keep it in the spirit of good fun and you'll have nothing to be ashamed of. I know it's preposterous but no more so than the romances and novels you once loved to read so much." He pressed the play into my hands. "And now I must go to Franklin's and summon the men to load my shipment. You're off to Ransome for the day, are you?"

"To see Caleb."

"Enjoy the ride then. I'll expect you tonight or tomorrow." He went off down the street, his clothes a bit baggy but his stride chipper: he still walked at an incredible pace.

I smiled fondly at his back.

. . .

Guns went off sporadically, the sound slightly muffled like fireworks, and I found Ransome's main street deserted except for an angry delegation of citizens who prudently stood in their Sunday best behind the shelter of the courthouse which was the only stone building in the town. Caleb was in the crowd and I saw a crisp white bandage about his right hand. He looked as if steam were ready to burst from his ears.

The sound of gunfire continued and my hearing placed it in the direction of the general store, which from the street appeared to be deserted.

In the crowd several men and women were delivering simultaneous harangues. Their loud voices ran together, trampling one another, and I could make out no distinct phrases.

I dismounted as Caleb emerged from the enraged gathering. He greeted me with the bassett-sad smile to which I had become accustomed on the buffalo plains. "You picked a fine time." His Texas twang made it emerge as *fan tam*. He held a revolver in his left hand, dangling toward the ground. The haranguing went on. Caleb walked me around behind the courthouse. We could still hear the peppering of shots from down-street.

"What's going on?"

"A few of the singlejack bruisers are taking the general store apart. A lot of stray ammunition flying."

"What's a singlejack bruiser?"

"Toughs. The mine companies hired them to throw the fear of God into these farmers down here. Must say they're doing a fine job of it." He brandished his white-wrapped hand. "I went to arrest them and one of the bastards shot me. Can you imagine that, Hugh?"

"Bad?"

"No. Ripped some skin off the back of my hand and frayed the tendons some. I can't use it right now, though."

"Are you any good left-handed?"

"Just fair." He wore a respectable grey three-piece suit and a bowler hat and I could see under the coat he was carrying his revolvers in under-the-shoulder holsters, the John Wesley Hardin design from Texas. There was a small tin badge on his lapel.

"I said, "How many in there?"

"Four. They fancy themselves pretty good with pistols. They took a notion they could demolish the store and everything in it. That's what they're at now."

I listened to the fitful shooting. "They'll run out of ammunition."

"Not likely. They got the storekeeper's entire supply of powder and ball. The storekeeper's the one with the loudest voice over there. He's been stirring the farmers up against the mines. So the mines sent their singlejack bruisers down to teach the storekeeper his manners."

"The mines don't seem to harbor much respect for the law, do they?"

"Singlejack bruisers *are* the law, to their way of thinking. They're lawfully deputized by the mountain counties. Of course their jurisdiction don't extend down here, and mine don't extend up to the mines. It's one of the finer points you learn about this business after a while. Law and outlaw can depend on whose bailiwick you happen to be in."

"Down here they're outlaws and you're empowered to run them in, though. Is that right?"

"Sure. All I got to do is walk in through that hailstorm of bullets and arrest the four of them. I'm sure they'll be polite about it and all." He didn't bother to summon the energy to smile. "I am fixing to wait until they leave the store, or chop it down into matchsticks too small to cover them, and then I am fixing to pick them off from ambush. Unless you got another suggestion."

"It might be kinder to get them out of there before they finish destroying the storekeeper's livelihood."

"Well I don't think too much of that old boy anyway. He's a loud-mouth son of a bitch, I never did like him. Makes my job hell around here. If he'd quiet his mouth down we'd all have a gentler time."

"Aren't you supposed to protect the property of the citizens hereabouts?"

"To the best of my ability. That's what I'm sworn to do." Now he did smile; a lazy sort of grin. "And that's what I'm doing. I expect to enforce the peace to the best of my ability. Just as soon as those old boys get done wrecking Fancher's store. Come on over here and set awhile, tell me what ructions you've been up to."

"Hold on a minute."

He turned back to scowl inquisitively. I said, "You scared of those bruisers, Caleb?"

"You bet."

"You really intend to pick them off?"

"No, I was joshing. I ain't gaited that way. I'll let fly at them when they ride away. I'll miss, of course. I can blame that on my left hand."

"Then it's your intention to let them go scot-free."

"Sometimes that's the best way. Sooner or later they'll meet their justice. Those kind always do. But they ain't killed anybody and I don't see the point spilling blood over this."

"The storekeeper might take a different view."

"I can see you disapprove of my attitude here."

"You seem to have changed some."

"Old son, I am making a fine living here. I get fifty dollars every month and half the fines I collect. I don't take bribe money from anybody, I treat everybody fair and I uphold the law to the best of my ability. I will face a froth-mouth killer if I have to but I don't see the sense getting killed over a little hooraw here. Nobody wants to get killed over that."

I understood then. I had to smile. "The truth is, you can't shoot worth a damn with your left hand, can you?"

"Never tried." He was sheepish. "God's sake don't let on to anybody."

"You want me to get those four out of there for you?"

"Think you can?"

"Sure I can. Didn't you read that dime novel?"

"Son, you're forgetting, I was there when you told him all those lies. Don't go and get yourself hurt now."

"Don't fret yourself about that," I told him. "If it's not worth your getting killed, it's surely not worth mine. I haven't even got a badge."

"You're welcome to mine."

"I think I'd rather go without it."

. . .

Later it was in several of Bob Halburton's dime novels how I shot it out with the four singlejack bruisers and wiped them out to a man. That is not what happened. I will tell the truth of it now.

I left my weapons on my saddle and walked up to the street leading my horse toward the store. Not being an absolute fool I kept to the same side of the street as the store so that they couldn't see me coming until I was right at the corner of the store. They were whooping themselves hoarse in there, having a fine old time. Guns going off, bullets chipping away at the walls, ammunition ricocheting all around the street. There wasn't a single intact windowpane in the vicinity. I heard bullets smash things up inside the store—shatter of glass, gurgle of flowing liquids, a crash now and then whenever something fell down.

I had to bellow to make myself heard.

"Hey you in there."

I did it several times and there was a lull in the volleying. I heard boot heels stump toward the front of the store. No one appeared but a voice came at me: "Who's that?"

"A sporting man."

"You don't sound like Sheriff Rice."

"I'm not. He's over there behind the courthouse, shot in the hand."

"What you want, then?"

When I spoke I kept moving back and forth a bit, crouching sometimes, so that they wouldn't be able to fix my position by the sound. I didn't want a barrage coming through the thin wall of the store at me. I said, "I'm a sporting man."

"Friend, you already said that."

"They tell me you gents are the best shooters around."

"You just come on inside and we'll prove it to you."

"I'm unarmed. I want to talk."

"What about?"

"A sporting proposition."

There was a murmured conference inside. Over at the courthouse several heads appeared at the corner, attracted by the sudden quiet. I waved them back out of view.

The mutter subsided within the store and the same voice summoned my attention. "What sporting proposition?"

"A wager." My horse fidgeted; I took a shorter grip on the reins. "I've got a fine horse and saddle here. Them against your twenty dollars I can shoot straighter than any of you gentlemen."

There was a brief silence followed by a bark of laughter after which all four of them commenced to roar, spurring one another on to greater hilarity.

When the laughter dwindled I lifted my voice. "I ought to warn you, wherever I go I seek out the finest shooters and challenge them to a match. I don't get beat very often."

"What's your name?"

"They call me Hugh Smith." It wasn't exactly a lie.

"Never heard of no Hugh Smith."

"I'm new to these parts."

"Let's have a look at this horse and saddle."

They were intrigued, then. I smiled to myself. No man, least of all a tough, likes to believe he can be bested as a shooter. I had challenged their pride; they were bounden to accept the challenge.

I said, "I want your warrant you won't shoot me down. I'm not armed. My guns are on my saddle."

"Come around front here and we'll take a look at you."

"Just so you don't shoot me for a lark."

"What do you take us for, murderers?"

"Do I have your word you won't shoot me?"

"You do."

I put the reins in my teeth and led the horse around the corner, holding my hands out and open where they could see them.

Through the shattered windows I had a dim image of shattered gloom. I took a position directly before the veranda platform. I could not see the four men inside; they were not exposing themselves to view.

"Right handsome gelding. What's that, a Texas rig?"

"Galveston, yes sir."

"We ain't coming out there in the street. Not with Rice lurking around there."

"Then I'll come inside. If you've got any targets left in there."

"I guess we do. You come right on inside."

   •   •   •

I could hardly credit the shambles.

"Friend sporting man, are you stupid or crazy or just drunk on Sunday morning?"

I sought out the owner of the voice and found the four men ranged across the rear of the store. Dust hung thick in the air, powdered motes drifting. It was like the ruination of Gomorrah. I sneezed.

Looking about me I said, "Sizable termites in these parts." It elicited a few chuckles and the four men picked their way carefully through the debris, approaching to take a closer look at me. I did the same to them. They were for the most part unremarkable, all of them dressed in plaid and butternuts and jackboots. The leader was not the biggest of them but he was big enough to loom over most men and you could strike a sulfur match on that jaw, I thought.

I was distracted by the damage they'd done. I had never seen such purposeful wreckage in my life. Nothing was intact.

"My name's Jack Malloy and nobody has ever beat my skill with shooting iron. You certain you want to part with that horse and saddle?"

"I don't intend to part with them. I intend to match them against your twenty dollars. You gentlemen have twenty dollars among you, I assume."

"That horse and saddle must be worth at least a hundred." Malloy was suspicious, and rightly so.

I said, "I'd say I was offering fair odds. I was the champion shooter of Colorado Territory."

"Colorado Territory's a long way off." Malloy squinted through the haze. One of his companions had a coughing spell. Malloy said, "A sensible man wouldn't risk his life for twenty dollars. What's your real game?"

"I'll tell you how it is, Mr. Malloy. I was set upon by road agents on my way here from the Tuolumne and they made off with my poke. I stand flat broke in my britches. I'm on my way to Sacramento for a big shooting match and I need twenty dollars for fresh clothing and tonsorial grooming because I always like to look my best when I shoot a match."

"If you're the best shooter around, how is it you allowed yourself to be bested by road agents?"

"I never fight the drop, Mr. Malloy." I looked pointedly at the revolvers in his big fists.

He said, "We could just take the horse and saddle."

"I expect you could. But then we'd never know which of us was the better shooter."

He smiled in response to that and I knew I had him.

．　．　．

They cleared a sort of path through the distressing wreckage. At the far end of it the store's cash counter remained standing, after a fashion; its face of boards was holed and splintered. On the countertop I placed twelve candles—stood them upright in melted wax and ignited their wicks. Then I returned to the opposite end of the room where the four men watched me with scowling skepticism.

I counted up their weapons surreptitiously. Each of Malloy's companions carried a repeating rifle and a six-shot revolver. Malloy had a rifle and two revolvers. I had no arms; mine were outside in the street on my horse.

Malloy said, "Let me get this straight now. You are offering to take six shots, no more. You're offering each of us to take six shots apiece. That gives us twenty-four shots to your six. It don't make sense."

"I'm betting I can extinguish more candles with six shots than you gentlemen can with twenty-four. Don't you like the wager?"

"Friend Smith, I have taken candy from babies, so to speak, but I never in my life took anything easier than I'm going to take that horse and Galveston saddle."

"We'll see then." Calculating quickly, I added in an offhand way, "Your choice of weapons, of course, but personally I'd recommend we use rifles."

"In other words that's your specialty, is it, the rifle?" He laughed at me. "We'll use pistols."

"Suit yourselves."

"That means you got to use a pistol yourself. It's only fair." He leered at me.

"Fair enough," I agreed. "Shall I use my own or will you make me the loan of one of yours?"

"Use mine," he said, handing over his left-hand revolver butt-first with a magnanimous flourish. I inspected the chambers and found it fully loaded. The weapon was a .44 Remington Army model. Six shots, percussion-capped, top-strapped with a groove sight. I had taken that into my calculations. My own revolvers were Remingtons, the same model; I was familiar with its balance and it was not for nothing that I had spent the winter in Fitz Bragg's Teton camp honing my revolver skills along with the others.

Malloy and his companions set their rifles aside, propping them against walls, and we stood five abreast facing the twelve burning candles.

I said, "I'll fire the first six. Agreed?"

"Go right ahead, Mr. Smith." The four revolvers lifted lazily. None of them was exactly aimed at me. But neither were they averted.

When I raised the borrowed Remington I was careful to keep it pointed at the candles at all times. The boys were a little drunk and a little nervous. I meant to give them no cause for alarm.

"I'm going to commence shooting now."

When no one raised objection I cocked the revolver and put my concentration on the flickering candles. The distance was some thirty feet. I squeezed the trigger.

A flame writhed violently with the passage of the bullet. But it did not go out. I had missed.

"I forgot to mention," Malloy drawled with amusement, "that one tends to pull off just a wee trifle to the left."

"Thank you kindly," I said in a dry way, and made my adjustment. Assuming that as a natural course he had lied to me I set my aim a fraction to the left, rather than the right.

In the confined space the racket was deafening and I understood now why Malloy had conducted the entire conversation in bellowing shouts. His ears must be ringing frightfully.

I nipped the right-hand wick off; the flame went out. I had the Remington's aim now and I fired the remaining four bullets quickly. I did not miss. I'd extinguished five candles. Seven remained.

I turned graciously and returned the revolver to Malloy, who dropped it into his holster and scowled at me. "You wasn't just joshing us, was you?"

"No sir. Do you want to give me the twenty dollars now or do you want to try for those candles?"

Malloy exchanged glances with his companions. Each of them kept flicking startled looks at me. It was one thing to shoot a target the size of a man. It was another to shoot at the tiny flame of a candle that was hardly bigger than the bullet itself.

I said, "You've got twenty-four chances. All you need to do is hit six of them. You don't need to hit seven."

Malloy growled and lifted his revolver, planted his feet, closed one eye, squinted along the barrel and took a great long time steadying his aim. Then he began to shoot, and after a moment his companions raised their revolvers as well and began shooting angrily. Two or three candles went out. I suspected they were blown out by the concussion, rather than hit by bullets, but it was a matter of indifference to me. I folded my arms and smiled upon them.

It took very little time for them to empty their revolvers. Four candles still flickered on the countertop.

When the barrage ceased Caleb Rice's loud voice called forward from behind us:

"All right, folks, fun's over. Hands up and turn around."

     .   .   .

He manacled the four of them together with handcuffs. Malloy and his men glowered. Caleb said cheerfully, "You did look just a little foolish the four of you standing there with empty guns in your fists."

I said, "They owe me twenty dollars."

"If they've got any money left after they've paid their fines and served their sentences."

"I won't hold my breath," I told him.

Caleb turned his hound-dog grin on Malloy. "You got nothing to be ashamed of. You just got outshot by Hugh Cardiff himself. It'll give you something to talk about in the saloons. When you're an old man and they let you out of jail."

Malloy said, "Cardiff. I should've known."

It seemed my reputation was growing.

That is the truth of how we bested the four singlejack bruisers. As can be seen, no one was killed. Caleb and I had set the plan in advance and he had entered the rear of the store during the shooting, holding a shotgun left-handed ready to make the arrest as soon as the four men had emptied their guns.

I taught myself a valuable lesson that day. Whenever possible it is better to outwit a man than to outfight him.

• • •

I returned that evening to Sacramento intending to await Caleb; he looked forward keenly to being a theatrical celebrity and it only remained to give in his notice to the Sheriff's Department and await the arrival of his replacement. I thought I would spend the few days enjoying the fleshpots of Sacramento and the company of my old friend Isaac. Also I had it in mind to attempt the provocation of a few shooting matches in that prosperous city.

I stabled the horse and was returning on foot to Isaac's boardinghouse—was just coming around the last corner toward it—when I scented smoke in the twilight and saw the glow of a fire over the rooftops.

It appeared to be some distance away, down toward the river. A big fire; now I heard the clang of the engines. A church bell took up an insistent rataplan. It occurred to me it was Sunday evening and probably no one had been abroad along the riverfront's commercial streets; that was how the fire must have eluded earlier discovery.

Isaac came boiling out of the house pressing the stems of his eyeglasses to his temples. "Infernal racket. . . . My God, that's down toward Halstead's . . ."

I went with him. By the time we reached the corner we were running.

• • •

We found the riverfront choked with running men and heavy smoke. Two pump-engines stood askew along the quay. The horses were rearing and volunteers were unhitching them. Several men leaned up and down against the pump handles and long streams of citizens paid out the hoses from which river water spouted against the fire. Someone had smashed through the doors of an implements warehouse and men stood in the splintered opening tossing mint-new metal buckets and wooden casks to anyone who would catch one. They were passing the buckets to and from the pier where several youths lay belly-flat dipping them into the river. The noise was a bedlam of hoarse yelling and smoke-coughing and the scuff of running boots and clank of metal and hiss of steam but mainly it was the roaring thunder of a great fire that had consumed a hundred feet of buildings and was reaching for more.

Hawking smoke I dodged into the line and became a piece of the chain, bucketing water up the queue. I saw Isaac dart through toward the cross street and remembered the cluttered warehouse up there where Isaac's shipment was.

Smoke rolled across the hardpan and it was difficult to see much. Nearby a strong man stood astraddle, braced against the pressure that bucked out of his hose nozzle. The man stood like a urinating giant but a sudden spurt knocked the brass nozzle from his grip and threw him asprawl. The hose curled like a whiplashing snake; the force of water dashed men flat and I dived out of the queue, pounced on the nozzle with both hands and dragged the hose toward the fire, playing the high-arching stream across the murk above me. Someone cried: "Is anyone inside? Does anybody know?"

"How the hell did this thing start?"

"Christ a'mighty, didn't anybody see it? How'd it ever get this big?"

"These old warehouses nothing but dry timber. . . ."

There was a terrible grinding racket—a roof collapsing somewhere in the rolling smoke. I fought the pitching nozzle to keep the gout of water directed against the fire. Men ran up behind me and grappled with the leaping hose. Someone behind me uttered a half-strangled question: "How the hell did you hold that thing by yourself?"

By the quay I saw half a dozen men still trying to unhitch the fire horses and get them away from the smoke before they might panic into destruction. A fierce clanging announced the arrival of a third engine somewhere but the smoke was so thick I could not see it.

Our massive spout was driving a hole through it, thrusting the fire back and scattering the smoke. I followed the stream forward into cleaner air. It was mainly because I had to find a place where I could breathe. The nozzle fought me and I humped it forward with all my strength and ahead of me the wall fell back, tipping slowly at first and then going down with a rending outcry of noise.

Through the sudden opening I saw that the fire had leaped the street beyond and was attacking everything within the block.

And in the flickering blaze I saw a diminutive figure stumbling back, arms flung up across his face, driven back by a wash of heat but surrounded by flames, nowhere to shelter. Isaac.

"*Hold this damn thing.*" I roared the words at the man behind me, released the nozzle to him and ran full-tilt back to the river stripping my coat off—dragged the coat through the water to soak it, wrapped it about my head and chest, ran for the side street and shook off the protesting arms of a fire warden who tried to restrain me.

I took a great gulp of smoky air and held it in my lungs while I ran under the arching waterspout. I batted into the furnace blast and tried to remember where from this point Isaac had been.

A ball of flame vaulted overhead—just beyond me. I recoiled from its livid heat.

The wet coat began to sizzle. I found my footing and plunged ahead. There was no flame here in the open street but the fire had sucked the air away; it was a wall of heat against which I threw myself—nothing to breathe, it was like trying to swim in boiling molasses. My legs began to fail.

I tried to suck wind but only seared my throat and coughed it out. I would have to turn back. . . .

Then a brief opening in the red caldron, a glimpse of a dark shape huddled small—I dodged a falling beam, hurdled a heap of embers and found Isaac motionless there.

I scooped him up in my arms and peered about me through slits of pain and realized I'd lost my bearings but it didn't matter because the fire was everywhere around us and there was no way out of it.

I was coughing hard then, great spasms that felt like ripping out the flesh of my lungs, and Isaac was too heavy to hold any longer but I put one foot in front of the other and I moved.

A hard blow knocked me down. It pummeled Isaac right out of my arms.

Then I felt the fresh wetness of it and realized they had found us: they were hosing us down—it turned the street instantly to mud and I slid and fell when I tried to pick Isaac up but finally I got balanced on one knee and heaved him up across my shoulder.

I charged into the spray. It dashed back and forth across us. Head down I waded into it. The main thrust of it went overhead, otherwise I would not have been able to move against it. Over the roar of the fire I could hear faintly the men's shouts of encouragement.

Then nothing would hold out any longer and I felt myself drop and that was the end of it.

.   .   .

It was a barn of some kind, lamplit, filled with retching and the hacking of burnt-out throats. I tried to open my eyes farther but they stung me beyond relief. To breathe was agony. I coughed weakly and saw a hazy face swim near: "Laudanum here, Mrs. Klaus—this man's in pain."

Out, in, out again. Once more I awoke and there was less noise in the place—murmur of voices, someone cursing in a steady monotone. A hand gently shook my shoulder. "Hugh?"

I tried to speak. It only brought on a spasm of coughing.

"It's Bob Halburton, Hugh. How're you making it? Can you see?"

I cracked my eyes open and had a vague impression of his bulk. I formed a whisper: "Is Isaac . . . ?"

"He's alive. You brought him out safe." He pounded my shoulder. "Listen, my friend, you're too valuable for any more of these real-life heroics. I've heard of your exploit in Ransome this morning—two adventures in one day—it's meat for a dozen more dime novels. But be that as it may, you're a fool for danger, my friend, and you've got to learn to look after your hide. You want a pull at my flask? Here, I'll leave it with you. Don't let the sawbones find it."

Then he was gone and the cold metal pressed into my hand.

. . .

A different bed, a silent room, the distant sound of conversation somewhere in the house. And rain, soft against roof and windows.

I wheezed and tried to sit up. There were plasters on my hands. My feet hung over the end of the bed.

Mrs. Deauville came in. Her ancient face brightened instantly. She asked how I was; I whispered I was fine; she indicated disbelief but she smiled. I asked after Isaac. She said he was weak but would be all right. I allowed I was hungry and after a few moments Mrs. Deauville returned with a bowl of soup; she sat by the bed and helped me because my bandaged hands made awkward work of the spoon.

She propped my pillows behind me and I leaned back. "How bad are my hands? Tell me the truth."

"You had frightful blisters. The doctor had to lance them. He said they may give you pain for a fortnight. But they'll recover. Mainly he was concerned for your lungs—you'd inhaled a great deal of smoke. But you seem to have been breathing easily today."

"What day is it, then?"

"Tuesday evening."

"Isaac?"

"You've saved his life, you know. But he's been badly burned. His face and hands . . ."

"His eyes?"

"No, he's not blinded. He'll be quite all right, most likely. He'll bear scars and he may be short of breath. I'm afraid he's very low—he lost everything in the fire, you know."

My head drifted back against the pillows. My eyes fluttered shut. "Everything what?"

"I don't know that much about it, Hugh. He says he's bankrupt."

. . .

In the morning I was unsteady but on my feet; I made my way across the landing to Isaac's room. The cubicle was cluttered with the best of Mrs. Deauville's furnishings. Isaac's figure seemed too small for the brass bed. He was sitting up with a comforter across his lap. His face and hands were wrapped in white; his eyes peered through openings in the plasters. I said, "You've the look of one of those Egyptian corpses they keep digging up."

"I'm glad you are fit, my young friend, but it was an intolerable foolishness to risk yourself after an idiot such as myself."

"Why the hell did you go in there?"

"My goods were on those wagons. It's gone now, every stick. Wagons and goods both." He lifted his bandaged hands in a gesture of resignation. "I suppose I meant to rescue what I could. I didn't stop to think. I went because I had to go, that's all."

"You'll start over."

"Or get a job."

"You must have something left."

"A few wagons, elsewhere. Not enough to cover my debts." He made a hollow sound I took for laughter. "Franklin has my gold. I have a little heap of ashes."

His eyeglasses were on the counterpane. He did not put them to his eyes. "I've worked diligently nearly seven years to build up a business. All gone in a flash. Such is fate. Possibly no one ever will know what caused the fire. I suppose it hardly makes a difference in any case. Perhaps if my creditors are kinder than I expect them to be they may allow me to keep the use of one wagon. I'll be an itinerant peddler again. I suppose it wasn't such a bad life."

"What are your debts?"

"Enormous. Seven thousand, perhaps eight thousand. It will take years to repay them."

I said, "We came out from Kentucky as partners, remember? Let's renew the partnership. All I need to do is sign half a dozen bank drafts."

He blinked at me through the bandages. "Charity, Hugh? No thank you."

164

"It's not a gift and it's not a loan. I'm investing in a partnership. What do you say?"

"I say you ought to keep your money until you need it."

"You'll make it grow for me. An investment."

His bulky white hands lifted and spread apart. "Hugh . . . what can I say to you?"

"Say you'll take on a partner. And stay away from fires."

. . .

And that is how, in the summer of 1869, I boarded the Central Pacific train from Sacramento in the company of Robert Halburton and Caleb Rice, bound for fame and fortune on the theatrical stages of the world.

BOOK SIX

Heroes of the West

BY THE TIME we set out for the East the country was spanned. Central Pacific had met Union Pacific at Promontory Summit, Utah. The railroad—which Caleb and I, in our way, had helped build—was completed. With a certain excitement we took passage across the nation only five weeks after the rejoiceful celebrations.

I recall it was only a few months later that the Suez Canal was opened. In that one year the world became much smaller.

. . .

The first photograph ever taken of me was made during that trip. Bob Halburton needed photographs of us for the lithographer's use as a basis for engraving advertisements for his play.

We stopped off in St. Louis where we were outfitted with elaborate wardrobes and hangovers, and enriched by several hundred greenback dollars the result of a shooting match we organized extemporaneously.

The photograph shows us standing, leaning on the upended muzzles of our rifles. Actually we were posed inside the photographer's shop against a painted backdrop of trees and with potted shrubs set before Caleb's legs to conceal the fact that he was standing on a crate to minimize the difference in our heights. I hasten to add that Caleb Rice was not such a dwarf as his detractors make him out to be. He stood five foot five plus his boot heels and I expect that was within the average range of height for men in those times. It was I, not Caleb, who was something of a freak. Until Bob costumed me I had always tended to wear boots with very low heels to minimize my height. In the boots he provided in St. Louis I found myself looming almost seven feet tall.

From numerous old illustrations the world is familiar with the fringed buckskin costumes of the frontiersmen, although most people may not realize that those pretty Indian-style fringes served a useful purpose—they provided the practical man at all times with a ready supply of thongs and twine. Basing our costumes on those traditional working clothes, Bob Halburton conspired with a St. Louis tailor to create skin-hugging pure-white chamois tunics and leggings. The effect was startling.

Later I saw Buffalo Bill Cody's costumes, and even recently I have seen Tom Mix in moving pictures wearing outfits not dissimilar to those Bob Halburton designed for us, and in fairness to Bob I must point out that Cody first trod the boards in 1872 and first went out with his arena show in 1883, while Caleb and I opened in New York City in Bob's play in November of 1869. So much for the trumpeted claims of origin and invention. The creation of the Wild West performance was Bob Halburton's and Bob's alone.

He outdid himself in St. Louis. We wore tooled holsters and soft polished white calfskin boots. And Bob found us the biggest hats in the city, under which our locks—especially trimmed and combed for the photographer—flowed to our shoulders. Neither Caleb nor I had enjoyed a haircut since we had hunted buffalo on the plains; long hair was the style of the times and in common with many others of that day we both had cultivated the length and sweep of our mustaches.

I have been asked why we wore our hair in that long fashion and I have heard numerous idiotic explanations for it. Originally the mountain men let their hair and beards grow for two practical and simple reasons: there were no barbers handy in the Rockies, and heavy hair was protection against the weather. But on the prairies after the Civil War it became a point of honor with the hunters and plainsmen to let their hair hang long as a taunt to Indians and rawhiders seeking white scalp-locks. A good long handful of hair was easily grasped and therefore a sporting challenge; and any man who cut his hair short was thought a coward. Custer, Cody, Dixon, Hickok, Lillie, Selman, Bragg and many others set the style; few dared risk the ridicule of going against the manly fashion. Later, when long hair became an anachronism and a curiosity, it became a matter of showmanship among Wild West troupers to retain the plains style of hairdress. We might not have been so easily recognized in crowds had we looked like every hen-pecked citizen of the mob.

. . .

"It's all right for you," Caleb growled at me. "Folks won't likely hoot at you. They take one look at a sawed-off runt like me in these duds and my friends would never stop laughing till they died." He wheeled upon Bob Halburton. "I ain't going to do it. I ain't going to wear these things."

It took us several days to calm him down.

. . .

Entraining for the East we followed the Ohio River through country as soft and green as the Kentucky of my remembered childhood. Caleb and I occupied the hours studying our copies of the play, attempting to commit our parts.

I have always had a keen memory. I can recall the pitch of a man's voice speaking to me forty years ago. When I was a boy Isaac would quiz me endlessly about the details of my reading. I learned to remember everything. Soon the habit became ingrained.

In any case it is true that I was able to recite my entire part, in all three acts, before our train reached its terminus in Hoboken; much to Bob's satisfaction.

Caleb, however, was not a man to whom written words had much meaning. He had been schooled in an orphan asylum in Texas but he did not read for pleasure. His lips sometimes moved as he perused newspapers. And his memory was easily distracted; he had only one mnemonic excellence: he remembered faces. Show him a "Wanted" shinplaster once; five years later he would spy a man across a room and remember the reward poster. But he could never keep his grip on words.

It was Bob who thought to train him vocally. After we settled into our lodgings in New York we employed an elderly stage actor to recite Caleb's speeches to him line by line. Caleb would repeat each line by rote. In that manner after some weeks he was able to get through his part without too much prompting.

From the beginning, however, Caleb had misgivings about his new-found thespian career.

. . .

Signorina Maria Sabattini was a leading lady of operettas and melodramas in Europe. Bob Halburton explained that he had brought her to our shores, at great expense, to favor our audiences with the glorious fresh face of an internationally renowned actress.

I was a bit dubious about this. Maria was haughty and tended to ridicule her two male co-performers; that much I could accept; but her thick Italian accent did not vouchsafe her portrayal of a beautiful red Indian maiden and I began to suspect that our play might inspire more laughter than thrills.

We rehearsed throughout that hot steamy summer, first in available lofts, later on the very stage where the play would open. The Astor

Palladium was a great dim dusty cavernous place; backstage it reeked of soot and sweat, as did the entire thronging city for that matter.

As I was the first to have committed my part I was more free with my time than the others in the cast. I employed my liberty in the search for Libby Tyree.

. . .

"How old did you say?"

"Nineteen. Nearly twenty now."

"A little old for finishing schools, wouldn't you say?"

"I wouldn't know. Never been to one myself."

It elicited the correspondent's polite chuckle. We were backstage. I was attempting to answer his questions for the benefit of readers of the New York *World*. The correspondent was a man of middle age with skin very pale except for his nose. He was scented faintly of whisky although it was hardly noon yet. It was July, my fifteenth newspaper interview since our arrival, and I realized by then that alcohol was the occupational habit of most newspapermen.

The correspondents seemed to have some trouble deciding how to deal with me: an uncertainty whether to laugh at me or quake in their shoes; and being imbued with youthful high spirits I played my own games with them, stringing them along, pulling their legs, terrifying them and charming them by turns. I told outrageous lies. In this I was encouraged by Bob Halburton. "It makes for the best copy. Keep it up. Hooraw the boys—they'll not soon forget you."

As Bob had been one of their own number prior to his success as a dime novelist and theatrical entrepreneur, the habitués of the fourth estate knew him well enough to approach Caleb and me with skeptical suspicion. At first their columns about us were arch and derisive.

It remains to be seen whether the two scouts, who advertise themselves as prodigious warriors, may yet be able to perform so heroically upon the stage. Caleb Rice in particular strikes, upon first acquaintance, as rather a trifle woebegone and undersized; while Hugh Cardiff seems suspiciously well-spoken for so rough-and-ready a presumed Westerner; and unless they may have found their way near to the Spaniards' fabled Fountain of Youth, both scouts appear uncommonly young to have committed so many as one-tenth the number of exploits attributed to them.

. . .

After a short time, however, we seemed to melt some of the ice of our initially frigid reception; and soon the *Herald* was welcoming us after all:

Cardiff is an uncommonly large and handsome fellow, straight as an arrow, and appears to move with a lithe and charming natural grace, utterly without the bombast usually associated with stage art. One may be moved seriously to doubt that the Messrs. Cardiff and Rice are destined to pose threat of serious dramatic competition to Booth or Beerbohm Tree, but nonetheless the two young scouts have proved attractive and amiably refreshing additions to New York's theatrical society this season. Thus far, at least, the two heroes' fabled revolvers have remained in holster, and no undue fireworks have exploded in the vicinity of the Astor Palladium, where Mr. Halburton's widely heralded production of *Heroes of the West* is expected to open its doors to the public on 3rd November.

. . .

I sought information from the correspondent of the New York *World* and he endeavored to help. "I don't know much about such schools myself. There must be a list of them somewhere. Are you sure the school is in this area?"

"I'm not sure of anything. It's the first time I've been east of the Mississippi since I was thirteen years old."

He made a note in his pad. "Interesting point there."

"There must be someplace I can find this kind of information."

"Have you tried an inquiries agent? There's a detective in South Street—reliable man."

. . .

Abner Wingate had muttonchop whiskers and pallid blue eyes that watered. His black hair was a trifle greasy and twisted tightly against his skull in ringlets. But the correspondent had said he was reliable.

Wingate's office was a shabby hideaway amid the saloons and ship chandlers of the East River waterfront.

"What service may I perform for you, then? You may rely completely upon my discretion—please don't fear to be candid within these walls."

Through the open windows the rancid stink washed in: dead fish, livestock droppings, salt, alcohol, tobacco, the open gutters. An autumn wind sluiced across the estuary, picking up these flavors and conveying them through the second-story office, roughing up Wingate's papers. Down through the open window I could see tars and loafers, cigar boys, topcoated businessmen, orangewomen, ships' officers, merchants, washerwomen, newsboys and harlots mingled in steady idling streams. Freight wagons and hacks plied the narrow turnings and smoke drifted from the stacks of steamships; and above the roofs I could see forests of masts and rigging—the dwindling remainder of the clipper fleet. There was a racket of shouting and singing—fishermen and peddlers hawking their wares.

"What a refreshingly sentimental assignment," Wingate observed when I had explained my mission. "I'll take it on with pleasure. My work's so often sordid. I'm a veteran of Mr. Allan Pinkerton's organization, Mr. Cardiff, and you may be assured that if anyone can find your young lady it is I. You've come to the right man. Now then—you say the girl was sent East by her parents from Arizona. The question arises, how did they pick out her school? They must have seen advertising. Do you happen to know which Eastern periodicals they may subscribe to?"

. . .

The school was out a bit to the west of Philadelphia, a six-mile ride in a hansom from the nearest railroad depot. There were lovely elms and maples about the place, their leaves rainbow-hued: it was October. Girls in prim and pretty dresses flowed across the lawns, giggling at the sight of me. The headmistress said, "I'm sorry you've had such a long journey in vain."

"You've no idea at all where she might have gone?"

"She matriculated this past June. After an elapse of nearly four months, who can tell where she might be? She left in the company of a delightful girl with whom she'd formed a fast friendship. The Merriams are on the Main Line, not more than twenty-five miles from here. But I'm sure Libby would not have extended her visit with them this long. Isn't it most likely she's returned to her home in the West and her parents?"

It was possible. Anything was possible.

I went calling on the Merriams.

. . .

"Yes sir, I see. And who shall I say is calling?" He was a Negro but he spoke with an English accent. It disconcerted me. I gave my name and the man in livery left me in the foyer while he disappeared within.

There were several copper-plate daguerreotypes propped in a cluster on a small table and I occupied myself with their inspection. It was a house unlike any I had ever been inside; coming into the grounds along the gravel coach path through tailored woods and wide lawns I'd had my first look and been taken aback. It looked as if it must have been designed for a president or a king. Four white pillars of massive girth towered forty or fifty feet high to support the veranda. I saw a love seat suspended on chains from a tree limb, for a swing.

In the foyer Wellington boots stood in a military row awaiting their need if it should rain: they were lined up according to size and I judged there must be two dozen occupants of the house, all with distinct foot sizes; then it occurred to me the boots might have been placed there for guests. I marveled.

I heard delicate footsteps and turned away from the daguerreotypes; the portraits depicted several stern men in tight collars and dark coats

—each copper plate a likeness of a different man but all of them obviously related. Five brothers, I guessed. Their faces shared strong tidy features. They seemed to range in age from twenties to forties.

The woman who came to meet me was recognizable at once as one of them. She had the same heart-shaped features. She was small to the point of fragility; her hair was white and fine; she must have been in her sixties but she carried herself briskly.

"Mr. Cardiff? Come in, won't you? I'm Louise Merriam. Libby's told me so much about you."

My heart leaped. It was the first confirmation I'd had that Libby still thought of me.

. . .

She led me into a sitting room the size of which amazed me. The ceiling was lofty. Luxurious furnishings were clustered in groups. Displayed about the room on tables were sturdy metal models of railroad locomotives. They appeared to be working models. Each had a little brass plate to identify it. The brass plates all included an engraved line, *Merriam Steam Locomotive Works, Pa.*

"How nice of you to call. Would you like tea? Whisky perhaps?"

"No thank you, ma'am. I don't want to keep you."

"Nonsense. How nice it is of you to call."

"I should have written. But I was on my way back from the school and took a chance someone would be in. I've got to get back to New York this evening."

"I'm so glad you came. I enjoy company—I rattle around so in this big house now." Behind her polite smile was a gentle concern; I could not make it out. "Libby is not here, Mr. Cardiff."

"Did she go back to Arizona?"

"No."

"Perhaps your daughter could advise me where to find her, then. I'm anxious to see her."

The lady looked away, clearly discomfited. "I don't think that would be a good idea."

She traced a model locomotive distractedly with her finger; she spoke without looking at me. "I know Libby's fond of you, and I know her regard for you was something she was forced to conceal from her family. But that's in the past. Her life has changed now."

Then she looked directly into my eyes, her head thrown back. "Are you as strong as you look?"

"I'm not sure I take your meaning."

"You must steel yourself."

"Ma'am?"

173

"Libby is in Virginia at the moment. With my youngest son. They were married ten days ago."

. . .

I rode the express back to New York in a dazed state of mind, little noticing my surroundings or the passage of time. I nearly missed the last ferryboat.

Mrs. Merriam had been considerate but there was no cushioning that blow. I was rocked beyond understanding, beyond believing.

The wedding had taken place in a church at Cheyney on the twelfth of October. The groom was Stephen Chandler Phipps Merriam—twenty-three years old. Mrs. Merriam referred to him as "Phipps" and insisted he was the best and smartest of her children. She showed me his portrait —the youngest of the five men daguerreotyped in the foyer—and gave me a press clipping. Later on the train I read it several times until the words penetrated my befogged consciousness.

Phipps Merriam and his four brothers had inherited a hugely success-ful enterprise from their father, who had succumbed to an illness in 1867; he had been a designer and builder of railroad locomotives. Phipps, who had undertaken a classical education at those institutions that attracted the sons of the very wealthy, had entered directly into the family business concern at twenty-one. The newspaper cutting referred to him as "a young mogul of Philadelphia commerce." Within the past year or two Phipps had extended Merriam interests into the production of coal, the development of petroleum fields in western Pennsylvania, shipbuilding on the Delaware—steam packets to replace the retiring Atlantic clippers—and Western railroads. Assuredly an energetic and ambitious young man. But none of it told me anything about Phipps Merriam that would explain why Libby Tyree had married him.

My lodgings were in a theatrical boardinghouse not far from Madison Square. I arrived exhausted; it was quite late; but I found I could not face the empty rooms and I repaired to a rough saloon.

Sometime in the day I awoke with miserably pounding head and an abdominal malaise that should have done me in. It took a long time for me to collect myself. When I faced myself in the shaving mirror I discovered great welts and bruises about my face and torso. I had no recollection of the fight. One of my eyes was swollen almost shut.

Bob Halburton took one look at me and grunted in disgust. I at-tempted to explain things to him. I sat backstage holding my head in my hands. I spoke until I was dry; I poured myself out to him.

He left me alone for a while after that. Our opening was fast ap-proaching; the play remained unwieldy—Bob kept rewriting sections of it and rehearsing the troupe till they were ready to drop. I went through the motions with them but my heart was not in it. I hardly attended anything. Caleb had to remind me to eat. Bob would have to speak three or four times to get my attention.

Finally Bob took me aside. "You've got to stop this."

"That's easy to say. I'm sorry—what can I do?"

"You can stop this mooning around. With all the madness just now I've hardly time to drop everything in the rush to mollycoddle you. You've lost your *objet d'amour*—very well, the world hasn't come to an end. The woman's married another man—she's done with you. Get it off your mind. You've been stumbling over lines you had letter-perfect a month ago. You've been muttering through your part like a drunken sleepwalker. Your distractions are disturbing the entire ensemble. You've an obligation to them, you know. Who can poor Caleb lean on if not on you?"

"I can't help it, Bob."

"God save us from moonstruck calves. Listen to me—you've an obligation to the company and to Caleb and to me. Who's paid your bills, Hugh? Who made you a celebrity of the nation? Who brought you East in the first place? You've a debt to me—and I mean to enforce its payment."

He waved his flask in my face, his exasperation barely contained. "We're two weeks from our opening! I can't have any more of this."

"I'll try. I'm sorry, I'll do my best."

I was a romantic; I was very young and in many ways simple about things. I allowed my youth to provide an excuse for actions that were selfish and churlish and self-indulgent. It did not occur to me that four years had passed and that she might have changed completely: she might be fat by now or as skinny as one of Phipps Merriam's steel rails; she might have turned petty and strident or gone wild with the reckless frivolity that had once been such an endearing part of her character; she might have turned ugly, she might have turned dull. But I credited none of it. She was the woman whose image I carried in my heart and I allowed of no imperfection because I loved her and I found it impossible to believe she did not love me; and I was heartbroken.

· · ·

I gave all I had to the show but it wasn't enough: I could not put Libby from my mind. Eleven days before our opening I left notes for Bob and Caleb and entrained for Virginia with an address in my pocket on Abner Wingate's notepaper: "Mr. & Mrs. Stephen C. P. Merriam, I/C/O Blaisedell Downs, nr. Arvonia, Cumberland County, Virginia." He had not volunteered his source of the address and I had been too preoccupied to inquire.

One train took me to Washington, D.C.; and another to Richmond. I sat straight on the wooden coach seats watching the countryside click by, neither reading nor conversing, hardly even thinking—just willing the time to pass. I wore my most conservative clothes, a dark tweed three-piece suit I had acquired in a shop in New York to discourage the stares that came my way when I dressed in Bob Halburton's fringed plains regalia. A bootblack had polished my walking boots to a military gloss and I wore a narrow bowler hat and, upon a chain across my waistcoat, a silver snap-lid watch. I felt I was prepared to face the Virginia gentry. My only concession to my background was the small .31-caliber five-shot Wells Fargo revolver in my belt. I never traveled anywhere without a firearm, especially in the teeming East which was then (as it is now) far more dangerous to the traveler than the West.

In Richmond I hired a buggy from a black liveryman and asked directions to Arvonia. It proved to be a considerable drive and I was compelled to lay over at an inn in Powhatan as I didn't wish to call on the Blaisedell estate at an unseemly hour of the night.

I tossed the night unable to sleep, rehearsing the speeches I had contrived to get me into Libby's presence.

In the morning I bathed and shaved with care and set out upon my way. I arrived shortly before noon in Arvonia, asked the way to Blaisedell Downs and found it two hours later amid the groves and meadows of a beautifully rolling section of hunt country. I saw no indications in this gentle lovely land of the ravages of war or Reconstruction; but behind me the towns had cowered.

A neat whitewashed fence ran for some miles along the edge of the Blaisedell property. It carried me to a gateway arch and a long elegant driveway entunneled beneath the archways of tidily groomed elms. As I trotted forward in the buggy I heard the faint and distant rumor of dogs baying on the hunt.

. . .

It was as one might dream a gentleman's country estate to be—the way I had pictured such homes from my readings in English novels. There were paddocks and lawns, numerous outbuildings, a large Georgian house shaded by immense maples and oaks; all the buildings were white, so clean they might have been painted afresh only yesterday.

The gravel drive made a horseshoe loop before the veranda. I tethered my buggy horse to a post in the shade and began to walk toward the wide steps. My approach did not seem to have caught anyone's ear. The place seemed deserted; I guessed they were out on the hunt. I prepared myself to wait; but I went up onto the veranda in any case and lifted my fist to knock.

I was arrested by a sound so faint I wasn't sure I hadn't mistaken it. I turned my head to catch the sound more fully against the flats of my eardrums and it came again—a lurching sob of a woman's breath.

It did not come from inside the house. I went along to the end of the veranda and peered back alongside the house. I saw a high thick hedge tidily trimmed. Behind it a woman wept softly.

I looked around me in a kind of alarm, feeling an interloper. No one was about. If there were servants they were occupied elsewhere.

The sobs of distress continued and I vaulted the veranda rail and found my way along a path to a gap in the hedge. Through it I saw a tailored little garden—a fountain arching merry bubbles, globes of azalea and rose bushes, slender tall cypresses, flagstones and a lawn; and on a sheltered lounge-swing I saw my Libby in tears.

A slender young man sat with his arm about her shoulders.

. . .

The young man stiffened as I appeared. His movement must have alerted Libby, for she drew herself up and tried to compose herself. The young man came to his feet, obviously ready to repel the intruder —he cut a faintly pathetic figure with his dainty fists clenched, his narrow pale jaw thrust forward belligerently. As I approached, Libby dabbed her eyes with a bit of lace and looked up at me. Her eyes cleared; her face changed.

"Hugh." She whispered my name and her eyes went wide.

The young man indicated his surprise—evidently he knew my name —but his fists opened and he became uncertain. I could not decipher his reaction. I knew one thing: he was not Phipps Merriam. He was nothing like the daguerreotypes. He was frail, olive-skinned, black-haired.

Libby tried to laugh gaily but it caught in her throat. She turned her face away to hide. "Oh Hugh—what a moment you've picked to come calling."

"Libby . . ." All the carefully rehearsed speeches fled my mind. I stood tongue-tied. I reached for her hand; it was ice-cold.

But she did not withdraw it. Her face came up—wan, swollen and damp with tears, but even more beautiful than I remembered it.

And then she plunged into my arms with a great bursting sob. "Oh Hugh! I'm so glad you've come—you've answered my prayers."

. . .

The young man cleared his throat. Awkward with embarrassment and pointedly not looking at us he said, "Elizabeth, I—eh—I shall post myself on guard on the—eh—ramparts." He spoke with a French accent; he uttered a self-conscious laugh and hurried away toward the gap in the hedge.

Libby cried herself out against my chest. I held her tight against me. Her body shook; through the delicate fabric of her beige dress I felt the warmth of her. A great tenderness welled up inside me and I held her until I felt my heart would burst. She burrowed the top of her blond head into my throat and raked my back with her fingers and pressed herself to me with a violence and desperation that alarmed me —it was as if by crushing herself to me she could draw strength and courage from my body into her own. "Libby, my darling, my love— what's wrong? What is it?" I kept murmuring to her, trying to soothe her.

Finally she was empty of tears. She subsided to stillness, her face hidden against my lapel. Then with a tiny laugh she threw her head back. "Even in that ridiculous tweed you still smell of gunpowder. I've always remembered that—it's your scent, no one else's. The perfume of cordite and sulfur. Gracious, I must look a sight. How can you bear to look at me?"

"You're so lovely. . . ." It was all I managed to say before my throat constricted. I had to swallow; I tried to smile. "What ever's wrong, Libby? What's happened to you?"

She slumped against me again; this time it was exhaustion—she wanted my support. I lowered her gently until we sat side by side on the swinging lounge. She took my hand in both of hers and examined my fingers as if they were totally unfamiliar objects. After a moment in a small voice she said, "I've made a ghastly mistake with my life, Hugh."

"I could have told you that, Libby, but you didn't wait for me."

Before the words were out I regretted them but there was no recalling them.

But she was not offended. "I was impatient. Greedy. I was desperate, Hugh, and I thought you were lost forever. *I just didn't want to be poor.*"

"You're not making much sense."

If she heard my words she gave no sign of it. She said in a preoccupied voice, "If he were cruel to me I think I could understand that. I could even live with it. My God, it's his indifference I can't stand. . . . It's as if I weren't there at all. How can I live like that? A piece of furniture . . ."

"Libby, please try to make sense. I want to help you." I looked up toward the hedge. The young man was no longer in sight. "Who's the French fellow?"

"Jean-Paul? Oh, he's a dear. He's been my only comfort." She released my hand and gathered herself, clasping her hands primly in her lap. "I'm sorry. I didn't mean to put on such a ridiculous display. I wasn't myself—an unguarded moment—you must forgive me, dear Hugh."

"Tell me then."

She said, "I don't know how you found me—I daren't ask. But you've come like a knight in armor, Hugh. I've never needed you as I need you now."

"I'm here, Libby. Whatever you want of me. Anything."

"My mother is dead, you know."

"I'm sorry. I hadn't known."

"Pneumonia. Last spring."

I thought, that must have been the very time I'd gone by the Grant with the wagon train. Harry Dreier hadn't said a word of her illness to me. Probably he'd withheld it to spare me grief. Or to keep me from bolting onto the ranch.

"I couldn't go to the funeral. I'd have got there much too late in any case. But there was no money."

"No money? How's that possible?"

"They've taken the Grant away from us."

.   .   .

There was bitterness in her voice. "A man from Spain claimed he was the real owner. . . ."

"I know about that. Harry Dreier told me about the dispute."

"Harry? How could—?"

"We kept in touch. He didn't dare go against your father but I wrote to him regularly and he kept me posted about things."

"Dear Harry," she murmured. "He's such a fine man. Now he's on the drift, I suppose. Looking for work somewhere. Well he'll find a good position, I'm sure of it. Even with one leg he's a better man than most with two."

I waited for her to go on. Her hands fidgeted and began to caress mine; I'm not sure she was aware she was doing it. Her eyes had an abstracted gaze. "First my father was driven to the wall by the enormous legal costs of carrying the fight from one court to another. All our money went on that. All of it. And then the worst cut of all—we lost the Grant."

"The courts gave it to the Spaniard? How could they?"

"My father thought it was politics. Washington trying to placate the Spanish government for some reason or other. No one really knows, Hugh. The point is we lost everything. And then two months ago my father went back to the ranch for the last time to gather up our things. The family's things. The Spaniard was there, of course, with his new crew. No one seems quite sure what happened. They had words. My father was so proud. They came to blows, or perhaps it came to shooting. I'm not sure. My father is dead, Hugh—killed by the Spaniards. They said it was self-defense. There was a posse waiting to drive my brothers off when they went there. Vern and Kevin had no choice, I believe. They were forced to turn away. They were escorted out of Arizona by peace officers and put on warning not to return to the territory."

"Dear Lord," I breathed. It was a lot to absorb at once.

"Kevin's in Denver now. He's working for a gunsmith. One day perhaps he'll open his own shop." Her voice was very small. "Vern came East. He's somewhere in Virginia—he visited us here last week. I think he may be in Richmond or Charlottesville. Gambling, mostly."

She drew a deep breath to steady herself. "As for me, I found myself suddenly poverty-stricken. I hadn't a penny to my name. I found myself on the mercy of my school friends. I knew that wouldn't last very long. They'd soon tire of extending charity to me. I had to do something, you see. Phipps had been sparking me since we met last winter. He's a very determined man. Once he sets out to acquire something, he must have it. He's very spoiled. Nothing has been denied him. And of course he's very rich, very successful—everyone said he was the greatest catch of the season. How the girls envied me." She almost broke into tears again; she contained herself only with great effort. I pressed her hands anxiously.

Her face dropped; the fall of her fine hair concealed her features from me. "What a nightmare it's been, Hugh."

"If he's mistreated you I'll—"

"Mistreated? He's never lifted a finger against me. He's as polite and distant with me as he'd be with any servant." She looked away into the fountain, or perhaps beyond it. "That's what I am now, Hugh. A scullery maid—someone to tidy up after him, turn down his bed, lay out his suit for the morning trip to the office, make sure his coffee's warm when he wants it, be invisible except on public occasions when I'm to be his ornament. Like a jewel to be worn on his waistcoat. The honeymoon lasted just forty-eight hours. Since then he's visited my bedroom exactly twice."

She said the last in a whisper.

"Libby . . ."

"No. I suppose I deserve every bit of it. I married him because I was terrified, Hugh. I was frightened of poverty. I'd never been poor. I couldn't face the fear of it. I married him for position, money. I can't deny it."

"You never loved him at all?"

"I never even liked him."

"Poor Libby." I lifted her hand, kissed her fingers, pressed them to my cheek. "If it's a mistake it's not the kind you ought to have to spend the rest of your life paying for. I can see you've paid enough already."

"But what ever can I do? He'll never let me go. In the Merriam family it's unthinkable."

Gripping her hand I rose to my feet. "Where are they? Out on the hunt?"

"Yes. They'll return soon."

"Come on then."

"Where?"

"I'm taking you away with me."

. . .

There were servants in the house but they left me undisturbed; evidently Libby's acceptance of me was enough to reassure them.

I allowed her to pack only one valise. "There isn't time. I don't want to have to shoot it out with the whole hunt party."

I tossed the valise in the back of the buggy. The young Frenchman hovered nearby with a shy smile. Libby went to him quickly. "Jean-Paul —you'll keep my secret."

"But of course. I shall purloin your things and take them with me to Chad's in Oyster Bay. You have the address? Good. You can let me know where to send them."

"You're a darling, Jean-Paul. I shall miss you."

I must have glowered darkly for Jean-Paul recoiled from her embrace. He gave me a sickly apologetic smile, not without charm, and I took Libby's arm to lift her into the buggy. Jean-Paul said, "It is for the best. I wish you both a great love and happiness. *Au revoir. . . .*"

We went down the drive at a good clip. I said, "He's a strange fellow."

"He's a . . . friend . . . of the youngest Blaisedell son. We only met three weeks ago, when Phipps and I arrived here, but Jean-Paul has become my closest friend in the East." She gripped my arm. "You don't need to worry about him, Hugh. We're friends, that's all. Like sister and brother."

We reached the gate and turned into the road. Again I heard the baying of the hounds. "They've cornered the fox. It won't be long now."

She said, "Where shall we go?"

"Anywhere. Does it matter? We're together. It's been so many years, Libby. . . ."

I had my arm around her. She pressed herself to me. "My darling," she murmured.

In the distance I heard the volley of shots, the fox meeting his end.

. . .

Phipps Merriam might not know who had abducted his wife and he might not even notice her absence at first but soon he'd know she was

181

gone. He'd question the servants; he'd learn she'd driven off in a buggy with a tall young man. Jean-Paul would throw up a smokescreen of some kind but in the end they'd come looking for us. I didn't think it prudent to return to Richmond; that was the first place they'd look.

Charlottesville lay across the mountains to the northwest. There was a railroad there. We went along in that direction, staying to the main well-traveled roads because our passage would draw less interest there. I felt we had a fair lead on any pursuit but nonetheless I was comforted by the revolver under my coat.

It was a dreamlike experience. I had not yet accepted the reality of it; too much had overcome me too quickly and I hadn't the capacity to deal with it. I simply rode with the moments. Libby, the dream of my life, was at my side and we held each other close as we rode across the Virginia countryside through a cool dry clear autumn afternoon.

As we approached the hills it began to grow dark and I sought an inn. We found one in a village astride the main road. As I tied up the buggy and helped Libby down I looked into her eyes. I had my hands about her waist. She came down to earth with her hands on my shoulders and pulled me down; I tasted her kiss—as startling and soft as it had been the first time on an Arizona hillside.

Neither of us spoke. I lifted our two small bags out of the buggy and went with Libby into the inn.

We were given one room, as man and wife, and neither of us corrected the innkeeper. When the bedroom door shut behind him we fell into each other's arms.

The clothing of those days was not designed for lovemaking and by the time we had shed each other of stiff celluloid collar, whalebones, shirt studs and endless paraphernalia we were laughing like children. In that high humor we fell upon the soft bed together and Libby's laughter pealed high at the sight of my long legs hanging out over the foot of it.

That night I took my love—the adulterous taking of another man's wife—and we did not sleep at all until dawn.

   . . .

We could not bear not to be touching each other. We went circuitously into the mountains; we dawdled in country villages—we stayed a full night and day in a primitive lodging in the pines where we could smell the raw new whisky of a nearby still. We loved each other to exhaustion and the excitement of it was only enhanced by our danger. I shall not dwell on those happy hours, for they were all too brief and they were ours in privacy.

On the third day we drove into Charlottesville. In those days it was a pretty town; perhaps it still is. I have never returned there although my memories of that day have been gentled by time and succeeding events; nevertheless they are not memories that I shall ever cherish.

The three days that led us to Charlottesville, however, are days that shall always remain warm deep in my heart. We spent them learning each other, rediscovering each other, exploring the changes that had taken place in ourselves. We had grown up; we were no longer children playing at love. Whatever Libby found in me I presume she must have found it pleasing. I know that I found in her a remarkable woman. Her body was perfection, her smile blinding, her love heart-filling. She told me of Philadelphia, the people she'd met, the things she'd done. She wasn't the frivolous lass of our youth; she'd become a woman in every way. When not in school she'd spent a good part of her holiday time working as a volunteer in hospitals and soup kitchens during the previous year's Panic. She had seen the ravages of poverty there; she had done her best to assist the stricken; but the experience had driven home when her own family had encountered tragedy. That was why the prospect of her own poverty had filled her with such dread. "I saw them grovel. I knew I could never do that. I'd kill myself first. It's not money, wealth, privilege, any of those things. It's the loss of dignity I couldn't bear. My sin is the sin of pride. Oh Hugh, we never need to be rich as long as I have you. You're all the dignity I shall ever want. Your love for me is something I can take all the pride in the world in."

Then we reached Charlottesville.

.   .   .

I reconnoitered ahead, going on foot from the back street where we'd parked the buggy; I meant to explore the railway station myself on foot, for I doubted anyone would recognize me. If they were on the search they would undoubtedly recognize Libby first. That was why I left her behind me.

My fears were realized. I saw three young men lounging about the depot. They were not waiting for a train; they were watching the faces of everyone who approached the station. They had a determined air and one of them sported a badge that winked on his coat. He carried a shotgun in the crook of his arm.

I returned to the buggy. Libby watched me with tight expectant eyes. She saw my face and knew, without being told.

"It's no good, is it?"

"We'll just have to keep driving. We'll drive this buggy clear to Manhattan if we have to."

"They'll only be waiting for us there. They'll figure out who you are, Hugh. Vern will figure it out if the others don't. I've never told Phipps about you but he knows about you. Something he said once. I'm sure Vern told him. Vern still hates you."

"Then we'll head west."

"No. You'd never forgive yourself for letting down your friends in the show. After a while you'd begin to blame me. You wouldn't be able to help it."

"Then we'll face them."

"It's no good, Hugh. I've chased it around inside my mind in every possible way. We've had a few days of happiness—more than some people have in a lifetime."

Her tone alarmed me. "Libby—"

"You haven't much time. You must be in New York in time for the opening."

"It doesn't matter. Nothing matters but you. We'll go to Colorado. No one will ever find us."

"And hide the rest of our lives? We'd finish by hating each other and hating ourselves. We can't go on with it, Hugh. I'm going back to Phipps."

"You can't. I won't let you."

"I'm going back to him," she said with firm strength, "and I'm going to press for an annulment or a divorce. I shall not let up until he grants it. Then I'll be able to come to you with my head held high. And we shall never need to step aside from anyone. It's the only way for us, can't you see?"

I knew she was right but my heart could not bear to part from her. "Then I'll go back with you."

"No. You must open your play. And if you went back with me you'd get into a fight with Phipps or Vern or both of them—and whatever the outcome, how could we live with that?"

"You've turned into a wise woman. Wiser than I like. I can't refute the sense of it—but by God I can't let you go." I pressed her to me.

"You've got to, Hugh."

. . .

I watched the buggy until it was absorbed in the turnings of the road. Then I picked up my valise and trudged through the town to the depot.

The young constable gave me a close look as I went to the ticket window but no one attempted to stop me as I boarded the northbound train.

I felt a shambles. Clinging desperately to the hope that our separation would be brief I rode the train into the night with tears damp upon my cheeks.

. . .

In New York my co-actors and our writer-director were hysterical in their relief. I tried to pull myself together, to put anxiety and self-pity aside, to fill the hours until I would again have my woman in my arms.

I forswore strong drink and of course sporting ladies. I plunged fever-ishly into my work.

What helped turn the trick was Caleb's desperation. He so vividly needed a staunch friend to lean on that I was unable to think about my own concerns. As our premiere night loomed, Caleb succumbed to panic.

． ． ．

Bob Halburton began to have trouble with the finances of *Heroes of the West* before we even opened the show. Late in September on Black Friday the manipulations of Jim Fisk and Jay Gould had sent the price of gold plunging. Some of the financial support promised for our play failed to materialize. Bob turned red in the face and occupied himself with heavy drinking and bitter complaining about spineless cads who turned back on their commitments.

In the end he was able to float a loan from the printers who were his partners in publishing the Cardiff-Rice novels but he was not pleased by the reprieve. "They have strapped me over a barrel. It's nothing less than usury. I despise the cretins for kicking a man when he's down."

Bob had not only written the play; he was our producer, our director and our mentor. He hired the hall, raised the capital and shepherded us through our endless rehearsals while simultaneously working with the backstage crew to design scenery and properties. In addition he had assigned himself an acting role in the play: it suited his humor to play a villain.

On the night of our opening in November the city had been surfeited for a week with gala posters and newspaper broadsides advertising our grand spectacle. Before the curtain went up I was hard put to say whether Caleb or I was the more unnerved.

Heroes of the West had been elaborated and refined for months. Bob meant to provide New York's jaded appetites with something that was more circus than drama. To that end he had employed no fewer than sixty tame Potawatomi Indians from Illinois to dress up in feathers and warpaint upon our stage; our cast also numbered several greasy and dastardly villainous henchmen, most of them recruited from the water-front docks of Hoboken and Brooklyn. The stage scenery included a large number of real trees, their dead leaves painted green, and an actual waterfall, activated by some sort of steam-powered recirculating pump that was a mystery to me. Scores of rifles and pistols were em-ployed in the program and it was one of the stage manager's duties to ensure before every rehearsal and performance that the weapons were indeed loaded with blank cartridges, lest our pantomime massacre become a real one.

． ． ．

In rehearsal Caleb and I had found our speeches to be silly mouthfuls but we had taken Bob's word that the conventions of the stage were different from those of ordinary discourse. In any case we enjoyed the acrobatic pursuits of our action scenes, which occupied substantial portions of the play, and we had great hooting fun as we worked out carefully designed routines that involved leaping, pirouetting, somersaulting and shooting.

For several reasons the powder charges in our blank cartridges had to be reduced to nearly nil. Otherwise the stage would have been obscured in a haze of gunsmoke, the noise would have deafened audiences in the confinement of the theater, and the cast would have risked serious powder burns. The unfortunate result of this necessity was that our guns popped with insipid little cracks hardly louder than the slap of a palm upon a mosquito. Then a week before our opening Bob came upon the idea of employing the orchestra's drum section to punctuate the battle scenes with sharp-pounding drum rolls. This device added great reality to the proceedings.

After all, the play purported to depict true events.

. . .

We could hear them crowding down the aisle beyond the heavy curtain. Bob came along from his dressing room looking splendid in his villainous regalia—he wore a cutaway coat, a stovepipe hat, a brilliant green brocade waistcoat, pearl-handle revolvers like Wild Bill's, and a fake mustache the tips of which extended far out beyond his cheeks. He was beaming. "We've taken in more than three thousand. Every seat in the house is filled."

Behind the lowered curtain Caleb and I took our places by the campfire. The half-dozen Indians who were to attack us after our opening dialogue concealed themselves among the trees. Caleb, standing opposite me by the fire with his arms crossed on top of the upended muzzle of his rifle, was trembling so violently that the rifle set up a rataplan against the boards of the stage. The stage manager, a quick-thinking fellow, rushed from the wings with a folded pad of cloth which he slipped under the buttstock. He smiled up at Caleb. "Stage fright happens to everybody. You'll be fine as soon as things commence."

Caleb clenched his jaws and stared in panic at the thongs across the chest of my costume. He did not say a word.

I was feeling a pleasant rush of confidence by then. I could still hear the quiet hum of conversation from the audience; it sounded warm and friendly. Then the murmur subsided. It meant the house lights had gone down.

The flare of a match drew my nervous eye to the wings. It was

Halburton lighting one of his noxious cigars. He grinned at us, touching his hatbrim with his index finger. Then he leveled the same finger at the stage manager, who signaled a stagehand to turn the big wheel; and the curtain began to rise.

. . .

The footlights struck me painfully in the eyes; I could see nothing but blackness beyond them. And suddenly I envisioned great slavering monsters in that darkness—I could hear them breathing.

Mine was the opening line of the play. I knew the line well. I must have uttered it a thousand times in rehearsal.

I was utterly blank. I gawked at Caleb. He gawked at me.

The curtain continued to rise and a sudden deafening burst of applause from the audience nearly bolted me out of my boots. I saw tendons twang at Caleb's throat; his eyes went even wider. The rifle in his hands shook with a frenzy that must have been visible from the farthest row of the top balcony.

For my part I felt calm, relaxed, utterly comfortable. Detached.

So detached that my mind was a complete blank.

. . .

The applause died away. Silence loomed about us. I was unable to stir a muscle. My eyes were fixed upon the top of Caleb's hat. In the audience someone coughed impatiently.

I saw Caleb's Adam's apple plunge in a swallowing spasm. Then amazingly he spoke. A word—a croak—then he cleared his throat and spoke out in a loud crisp voice:

"Well you done pretty good on the buffalo hunt today, Hugh. And I got forty-two buffalo myself."

Thus prompted, I seemed to regain consciousness. I must have grinned ludicrously with my relief. "Why yes indeed, Caleb, I believe I shot forty-nine buffalo this morning. I did quite well on the buffalo hunt today. And you got forty-two buffalo yourself."

Caleb smiled then. He hung his rifle in the crook of his arm and slouched around the campfire, picked up a long straw and settled it in the corner of his mouth so that it bobbed up and down as he talked. It was exactly the way he would have behaved around a real campfire on the solitary plains.

For just an instant there I hated him. After the trouble he had caused during rehearsals here he was taking to it like a duck to water while I stood facing him with my mouth flapping silently and the next speech completely lost to my memory.

But at least a partial sort of consciousness had returned to me and I said boldly, "Wait till we tell Wild Bill Hickok about that. He's never shot forty-nine in a single run, nor even forty-two. I imagine he'll be plenty impressed. He might even buy us a free drink, the old tightwad."

None of it was in the script. But it elicited an amiable laugh from the audience. My confidence began to grow.

Caleb brought us back to the rehearsed lines. "Well say, Hugh, I hope the Indians aren't lurking about."

"We'd best keep our eyes peeled," I agreed. "You want to see to our trusty steeds there, Caleb?"

Soon the Indians attacked us and things warmed up and my stage fright was lost in the heat of battle—it was a job to avoid some of the tomahawks that our Indians wielded with unusual enthusiasm; even though the ax heads and knives were papier-mâché the hafts were real enough. Then we were blazing away with our six-shooters and the drums were pocking away. And we were having a high old time.

. . .

As the final curtain came down the house rocked with a tumult of applause and Bob Halburton's beaming grin stretched until I thought his jaw would split. The ovation truly thundered. As we stepped forward for our curtain call Bob shot between us and draped his arms about our shoulders; we took our bows together and Bob was shouting above the roar of the crowd:

"Boys, we have arrived!"

. . .

It is quite possible the world will never look upon its like again. From the beginning of the action—"The Indians are upon us!"—to the final tumultuous blood and thunder, *Heroes of the West* brings an exuberant vitality to the New York stage such as it has not seen in many a year. Nor has the jaded city ever witnessed such an incongruous and anachronistic complexity of imbecilic drama, renowned players performing boisterously but execrably, voluminous gunfire, wild acrobatics, exuberant bombast, interminable lectures, spectacular settings, infantile melodramatics, hand-wringing sentimentality and, on the whole, wonderful mindless artless diversion. Everything about it is constructed and performed as woefully as it is possible to construct and perform; yet as an exhibition of two remarkable men it is filled with a curious charm and grace, winning for the two rough frontiersmen the goodwill of its happy audience.

Indubitably it appears that our eccentric long-haired Western scouts are assured of being the lions of the season; and the name of playwright-novelist Robert "Ichabod Zachary" Halburton is assured of enduring fame.

. . .

The reviews in general were jocular and forgiving, less derisive than simply amazed. We were the talk of the city. Great queues formed at

188

the ticket office; within two days we were sold out nine weeks in advance.

Invitations arrived: a ball, parties, tea with literary lions and the leading families, politicians' banquets, charity bazaars. Every door was open: the city was ours.

We met many of the Four Hundred; we met Boss Tweed and Edwin Booth and members of the family of John Jacob Astor. We met pugilists and painters, mediums and poets, and we shared knowing smiles with them—all of us were freaks on parade for the entertainment of the rich; but we didn't mind. We were well-fed and fawned over.

And of course celebrity draws women—of all ages and forms—as honey draws bears. Caleb and I were all but smothered in billowing waves of women. It has been said Caleb went through the women of New York like a scythe through Ohio wheat; as for myself I withheld temptation by dedicating myself to the day when Libby and I would be together. I had several letters from her—they were poor substitutes for her presence but I kept them close to my heart and awaited the day of our reunion.

. . .

The run of our show was extended into February 1870, then March; we were filling the theater every night of the week. Caleb and I estimated what our shares of the profits would be and we counted ourselves rich men. But the assumption proved premature as we soon learned.

In the meantime Caleb became quickly jaded with fame; he found it a strain after the first heady weeks; in time he stopped accepting invitations and remained in his rooms most of the hours he was not onstage. By March he had turned into a recluse and I had to drag him away from his lodgings merely to ensure that he ate his meals. He became steadily more morose and irritable; he drank. I could not figure out what was ailing him and he refused for a long time to confide. I suppose he dropped hints: he would mutter darkly about "playacting" —but I was too dense to interpret them.

Early in April we were to open *Heroes of the West* in Baltimore. With the enormous success of the show we had booked a number of additional cities and extended the lengths of the engagements; it was planned we would return the spectacle to New York in the autumn of 1871 to close the circle and end the tour. But as we approached our closing night at the Astor Palladium Bob summoned Caleb and Maria and me to his dressing room. I had never seen Bob so ashen and anguished. He was not drunk. He did not look at any of us directly; he waved us to chairs and darted surreptitious sidewise glances at us.

"Be that as it may," he muttered; he tried unsuccessfully to smile.

Maria Sabattini regarded him without warmth. She had a pair of black-olive eyes that had seen everything and were surprised by nothing. During the entire run of the show she had kept to her own friends and acquaintances; we rarely saw her except on the stage; for my part I had been content to have it that way—her charms were confined to those she was able to project across the footlights.

She was wise in the ways of entrepreneurs; she was onto Bob Halburton before he even spoke. Taking one look at the set of his face she said, "You are not-a paying us."

"Your salaries of course," he murmured. "You've been getting those right along." Our salaries amounted to seven dollars a week, each, for Caleb and me; and five a week for Maria.

"Our shares," she said impatiently. "Nobody works-a for five dollars a week."

"Your shares, my share." He threw up his hands and blinked rapidly. "My friends, fortune has turned against me."

I glanced at Caleb. He was scrutinizing Bob narrowly.

I said, "You can't have lost that much in card games. You can't. It's not possible."

"I suppose it might be possible, given the high rollers in these parts, but no. I have not played cards with the company's money. Even I am not that foolish." He was beginning to regain his bluster.

Maria said in her odd voice—it managed at once to be flat and shrill —"But there is-a no money, yes?"

He spread his palms wide. "There is no money, yes. Are you familiar with the term 'selling short'?"

. . .

I said, "How bad is it?"

"My young friend, it could be worse. Indeed it could. Just think. We might not have our health."

Caleb in his quiet dangerous voice said, "How much of my money did you lose?"

It made Bob draw himself up to his full medium portly height. "Now just a minute. None of it was *your* money. None of the money would have been yours until, if, as and when it was paid over to you by the company."

"Words," Caleb drawled. "How much?"

"A goodly sum, I fear." Bob glanced anxiously from one of us to the next, never quite meeting eyes. "Look upon it this way, I beg you. None of you is faced with debts. None of you faces bankruptcy. You may be broke but you are paid up with your landlord and, be that as it may, your prospects are assuredly bright."

Maria sighed theatrically. Then she slipped her hand out—a sinuous gesture—until it came to rest palm-up. "My ticket back-a to Milano please."

"I shall manage that shortly, I promise you."

She folded her arms and looked on stonily. After that moment she did not speak again.

Bob sat down. He braced his palms on his knees and stared at the floor as if overcome with nausea.

I said, "I just don't see how you could possibly lose all that money. We've been taking in fortunes."

Caleb said, "I knew he'd find a way. This thing's been sour from the start. We never should have—"

"Please, Caleb." Bob lifted his head reluctantly. "I must try to explain it. I had your own interests at heart. I'm guilty of misjudgment and miscalculation, but not malice."

I said, "You'd better tell us what happened. In simple language we can understand."

"We were over a barrel, weren't we? I had to borrow capital from my printer in order to open the show. Do you recall that? Yes. We had to agree to pay a very high rate of interest on that money. The printer said it was a high-risk investment. He demanded usurious interest. I had no choice but to agree. It was that or fold the show."

"All right. Then what?"

"We had four months' grace. The printer's note comes due this Monday, April fourth. At that time we must repay his investment— the principal—and also we must pay the interest in full."

"How much?"

"Does it matter? We haven't got it." He endeavored a weak smile. "Don't you see? I was trying to safeguard your shares of the profits. I invested our receipts because I was trying to earn enough extra money to pay the printer's interest without sacrificing our profits."

"But your investments didn't gain. They lost."

"In a nutshell, yes. I put some of it in shares. Mainly those have appreciated. We have a small profit there. I shall sell those tomorrow. That will pay for Signorina Sabattini's boat fare and it will put a bit of traveling money in your pockets. But the printer will remain unpaid, and of course he will slap a libel shinplaster on this show. We'll be unable to open it anywhere in the nation without being closed down immediately by marshals. And I, of course, will be forced into bank-ruptcy, since I haven't the money to repay the printer."

When none of us replied he went on, speaking as if the silence un-nerved him and needed filling. "I examined the market with care, don't you see. I observed that the stock of Consolidated Railways was soaring far too high. I observed that the company had spread itself too thin, too fast. I felt it inevitable that the fragile structure must tumble down. It was only a matter of time before it all collapsed. Anyone could see that. And I'm still convinced I was correct—I simply miscalculated the length of time it would take. Consolidated is still riding high. Much higher, in fact, than it was when I sold the shares short."

Caleb said, "What the hell does that mean?"

"It means simply that I sold stocks that I didn't own, expecting the price to go down. Instead, the price has gone up. I am committed to deliver a certain number of Consolidated shares to a Beaver Street broker on Monday morning. I shall have to buy those shares, at the current inflated market price, in order to deliver them to the broker at a much lower price which we agreed on four months ago."

Bob cleared his throat. "If the price had indeed gone down, as I expected, we'd have realized an enormous profit. More than enough to cancel the cost of the printer's loan."

I said, "You've not only lost all our profits from the show. You've gone into debt beyond that?"

"I'm afraid I have, yes. I shall owe some thirty thousand dollars."

I said, "You're just possibly that most foolish man I ever met. Do you know that?"

"I can hardly dispute it at this moment."

Caleb said, "You gambled with our money. Not your money. Our money."

"That's true. I was doing it in your interest."

"You should have asked us first."

"I know that now."

"What it amounts to, you stole it from us."

"You could put it that way. I'm at your mercy. No bravado, no bluff. I throw myself at your feet." Bob lifted his bloodshot eyes with effort and met Caleb's angry hound-dog stare.

Caleb looked at me. "We ought to hang the son of a bitch."

"Caleb, it's only money."

It made him snort with disgust.

Bob said, "In a nutshell, then, I am something over sixty thousand dollars in the hole. Ten thousand to pay the printer's interest. Twenty thousand that should have been our profits. And thirty thousand out of my pocket. I needn't add it's a thirty thousand I haven't got in my pocket." He stood up and thrust out his chest. "I'll earn it back someday. I'll pay each of you in full."

Caleb said, "I don't guess we ought to hold our breath waiting on that day." He went toward the door.

I said, "Where are you going?"

"I'm going to pack my gear and go back where I came from."

"Hold on, Caleb. Let's work this out."

"Nothing to work out. We're finished here, ain't we? The show's closed, ain't it? I can't stand this city anyhow. I'm going. You coming?"

"In the first place people have paid good money for tickets for the rest of this week. We owe them a show."

"They can go plumb to hell. Them and their money." Caleb never had anything like my regard for an audience.

He saw my disapproval and he tried to explain himself. " 'Fear not, O salts of the earth, for Cardiff and Rice are here to save you from the depredations of yonder vile red villains.' " It was one of his lines from the play; onstage he always managed to forget half of it or skip past it—it was the first time I had ever heard him recite it correctly. He did so with a contemptuous curl of his lip. "I was ready to quit anyway. Ain't no way I could've stuck out another year of this rubbish, nor even another month. I just ain't cut out for playacting. No two ways about it. All right, then, he's made up our minds for us. Maybe losing our money he done us a favor. At least that's the way I'll try to look at it." He pointed his thumb over his shoulder in the direction of Bob Halburton. "But just don't ask me to trust him ever again."

With that Caleb reached for the latch but I blocked his exit. "Hold on a minute. If you want to quit the show that's up to you. But we've got four more performances to finish. We gave our word on that."

"*He* gave *his* word on sharing out the profits."

"What are you telling me, Caleb? That your word's no better than Bob's?"

"Aagh," he said in bitter disgust. "Hell, I'll finish out the four nights, I reckon it can't sink me no lower than I've already sunk. But after that you can just watch my dust."

I said, "I don't believe he meant to steal from us."

"Believe what you want."

"All right, he was greedy. He wanted to make extra money. But he meant for us to share in it. Don't you believe that?"

"What difference does it make? He lost the damn money."

"I think we owe him a little help here, Caleb. He's got himself between a rock and a hard place. You find a friend in a whipsaw like that, you try to help him out of it."

"Hugh, you are too soft. You're too forgiving a man. You ain't going to survive long that way."

I said, "We owe him, Caleb. You know we do. Without Bob there's a whole lot we'd never have seen and done. Why we're famous around the world, you and me. Bob did that. Doesn't that count for anything at all?"

"Just what do you want me to do there? Reach down and dig in my pocket and come up with thirty thousand dollars?"

"We could do that, you and me."

"What in tarnation are you talking about now?"

"We could make that money back. On Sunday."

. . .

That Sunday, the third of April 1870, proved to be one of the signal days of my experience. In some ways it ruined my life for years to come; in others it set me onto new courses that may have been all for the best. I cannot say how things might have gone if it hadn't been for that chilly grey Sunday afternoon; I only know my life would have been markedly different.

Bogardus came of course, and Frederick Butler and Oliver Winchester and Jonathan Gregg and numerous other first-class shooters of the day. The crowd was not great; we'd had less than a week to issue our challenge and set up the meet. We shot in the Brooklyn Driving Park. It was a select group; the contestants were few but there was an enormous crowd of spectators—through our contacts among the correspondents we'd made sure several newspapers announced the forthcoming match. The news piqued New Yorkers who were curious whether we were windbags; the competition attracted a great crowd of skeptics and sporting bloods.

There was no possibility of our attracting the kind of betting odds we'd had in Denver. Our Colorado scores had been published; our reputations were known, although in some quarters there was a sense that exaggerations had been perpetrated in our behalf by the newspapers, journalism in those days being known more for its flair than for its accuracy.

I had something short of three thousand dollars remaining from my savings—the rest of my capital was invested in Isaac Singman's California business—but I was not free to wager all of it; we had to hire the Driving Park and pay the cost of glass balls, ammunition, judges, throw-boys, marshals and ticket takers. We charged spectators ten cents a head for admission but this did not appear likely to offset expenses. As things turned out four thousand spectators came and the marshals had a devil of a time finding space for all of them without risking them in the line of fire.

I wagered two thousand dollars—half on Caleb, half on myself. In order to raise odds I had to bet on our hitting ninety-five balls or better out of one hundred. In that manner I was able to raise odds of twenty to one. It meant if either of us hit ninety-five we would win $20,000; and if we both succeeded we would win $40,000.

It was known that even champion shooters like Bogardus often turned in scores of ninety-one or ninety-three in such matches. To bet on scores as high as ninety-five required gambler's courage on Caleb's part and my own; but it was the only way we were able to raise sufficient odds. To my mind the reward was more than worth the risk. I did not wish to see Bob Halburton bankrupted and possibly jailed for fraud and embezzlement. I owed him a great deal.

. . .

We attended the meet in our best theatrical regalia—that was at Bob's suggestion. "Put on a show for the folks." Once into the firing line I knew I would shuck my hat and tunic but in the meantime I strode about, decked out in my white buckskins and glad of their warmth against the grey chill. The afternoon threatened a drizzle.

Because of the crowd and the confusion we had a late start; it was nearly half-past two and the light was poor. The glass balls would be hard to see on the rise because there would be no sun glint on them. In my many years' travels I have found remarkable distinction between the light of the West and that of most other parts of the world; the Far West has a much brighter sun and my eyes are attuned to it and I find the rest of the world perpetually half-dark. Inevitably this has an effect upon the keenness of my vision in soft-lighted regions.

There was also the matter of our being out of practice. Once he agreed to the scheme Caleb participated wholeheartedly; he was never a man for half measures. But we had shot only a few times since our arrival in the East nearly a year previously.

All in all we both knew we would need to concentrate more closely than ever before. Otherwise neither of us could possibly meet the goal of ninety-five balls.

Certainly the last thing I needed was distraction in the person of Vern Tyree.

. . .

Bob Halburton rushed about coddling judges, organizing the marshals, thundering and cajoling. The mob swelled and swirled, voices becoming angry with the delays. Doc Bogardus joined Caleb and me by the rope rail that had been set up to keep the spectators back. There were grey strands now in Bogardus' black beard but his eyes were alert and I recognized the twitch of his smile. "I'm glad to see you've equipped yourself with a lighter weapon and a repeater at that."

I was using my Spencer rimfires for the match; they fired a heavy buffalo charge but I was most accustomed to them after the Hawken.

Bogardus said, "How's the shoulder?"

"It's given me no trouble."

"Did you ever have it seen to?"

"No. Never seemed to find the time."

"If it troubles you come and see me. I'm a genuine doctor, you know. It's not merely an honorary title."

"I didn't know that."

"I keep up a part-time practice. Surgery." He turned to Caleb. "You've still got your Navy Colts I see."

"If they're good enough for Hickok I expect they're good enough for me."

"Yes, they're remarkably accurate weapons when kept in proper tune." Bogardus tipped his head back to inspect the low sky. "Let's hope it holds off." Then he ambled away toward the valet who held his rifle cases.

A reporter who saw our exchange from a distance evidently assumed that Caleb and I had traded insults with Bogardus; in any case the next day's newspapers reported that we had had a row before the shoot. There was no truth in it at all but the story fueled the rumor of the rivalry between us.

Bob Halburton called the meet to order. Standing on a dais he announced the rules of the competition. Judges withdrew names from a hat and the shooters moved into the line, Bogardus among them. My name was not called; I waited behind Bogardus' heap of glass balls and watched him shoot. The heavy damp air seemed to mute the sound of shooting; and as always I had my ears stuffed with cotton. There were thirty-odd competitors and several of them were gadfly sporting bloods of no ballistic distinction; they were quickly ruled out by the one-in-ten regulation. Caleb went into the line and the spectators crowded forward to watch him shoot. There was great excitement in the crowd. Breath misted before people's faces. Caleb cut a fine slender figure with his snapping revolvers, shooting quickly and surely, never hesitating; like Bogardus he used two ball-throwing boys, working alternately, and fired his first six shots with such regularity one could have set a tune to the rhythm. He paused only to switch the second revolver into his right hand—six more shots, and not a miss. When he stopped to replace the cylinders in his revolvers he turned and grinned at me. None of the Denver uncertainty this time; Caleb had grown up, he was a professional now. And it relieved me to see he had not gone rusty for lack of practice.

Bogardus, the shooting machine, went through four rifle magazines before he missed his first shot. All the shooters were doing well, I thought; apparently I had misjudged the ill effects of the light. In truth there was no glare against the eyes and I assumed this was compensation for the lack of highlights. As I watched the throws I saw the glass balls were clearly visible; there was no difficulty about that; and the still-damp afternoon promised no risk of wind.

My name was called and I moved along the line to take my place. One of our Potawatomi Indians from the show had volunteered to second me; he brought my rifles along and prepared to reload the spent magazines. I talked briefly with the throw-boy and turned to accept the first rifle from my second. I happened to glance down the line where a boisterous group of young bloods was just arriving. They pushed through the crowd toward the dais; they made a good deal of noise—loud talk, hard laughter. From where I stood they looked like a pack of rich young ne'er-do-wells—their clothes foppish and expensive, their behavior ill-mannered and arrogant. They talked with the arch nasal silliness that I suppose has always been typical of youths with too much money, too much idleness and too little dignity. There were six or eight of them. They held my attention for only a moment and I would have put them out of my mind except for the sudden glimpse of a familiar face. He came through the group toward the podium. "So sorry we are late. May we still sign up?"

It was Jean-Paul, the frail young Frenchman from Virginia.

He looked down the line and caught my eye. A broad smile crossed his face and he nodded a greeting.

Then I saw Vern Tyree step into sight through the knot of young fops. He had a cased rifle under his arm.

I went bolt-still.

Vern's appearance had altered little. His shoulders were still wide, his chest heavy, his limbs muscular, his carriage proud—the same yellow hair; he was still extraordinarily handsome. There was a ridge on his nose where I'd broken it and I could see the traces of scars on the cheek below his eye—like duelist's cicatrices. As he shifted his grip on the cased rifle his left hand seemed awkward. It worked deftly— he was not disabled—but his hand was slightly deformed. All that must have been the result of the rifle explosion five years ago.

Then he looked up. I detected venom in his recognition. It was gone in a flash. A thin hint of a smile crossed his features and he came toward me.

The ball-throwing boy was waiting my command; the line judge scowled; but I stood behind the line awaiting Vern's approach and watching him withdraw the rifle from the fleece-lined chamois case.

It was, I saw, a Colt's revolving rifle. Of course it wasn't the same one that had blown up in his face. But it was the same design, the same .44-caliber model. It looked brand-new.

He draped the empty case over his shoulder and came on toward me bouncing the rifle casually in the circle of his loose fist.

Bob Halburton's attention came around toward me—perhaps someone had pointed out to him that I was delaying the proceedings. Bob's face gleamed unhealthily; he had been at the flask for hours. I saw his eyebrows lift in inquiry and I understood he was asking me if he should admit the latecomers to the company of shooters. I delayed reply. Vern advanced toward me and Jean-Paul hurried forward to interpose himself between us. Vern shot him one glance and then ignored him, stopping a few feet from me with his feet slightly apart and his features composed into a peculiar unfathomable smile. The gnarled left hand had gone into his trouser pocket—that was before he took to wearing gloves at all times—and he jingled coins and regarded me baitingly. "It's your shoot. You going to let us enter?"

"You're late, as you can see."

Jean-Paul said, "An unfortunate delay of the train." He was nervous and I realized he wanted to make sure no trouble took place. Perhaps Libby had appointed him peacemaker but I thought him a sorry choice for the job.

I feigned indifference. "Sign up if you want." I gave Bob Halburton a glance and an affirmative nod of my head and an inclination toward Vern and Jean-Paul.

"Now I thank you," Vern said dryly. "You didn't happen to be in Virginia a few weeks ago, did you?"

"Me?"

"I'm right sorry I missed you. I looked for you in Colorado a few years ago—thought we might find out who was the better shooter. I guess we'll have a chance to find out today, won't we, Saddlesores?"

"That's what we're here for, Vern."

He made as if to turn away; then he looked back at me through hooded eyes. He spoke very low: "You'll die before I do, Hugh, and that's a promise." Then he walked away from me.

   . . .

It set me off to a poor start: the ripples of his parting threat disturbed me. I was unable to discern Vern's purpose or intentions. He appeared to know it was I who had run away with Libby in Virginia; yet his accusations had been oblique, his challenge indirect.

I began shooting and missed two of the first twenty; I realized I had to ignore everything but the contest; finally I settled into the rhythm of the match.

   . . .

It was a good day for Caleb—he hit ninety-six—and a bad day for Bogardus, who ran a string of four misses before he realized his rifle had fouled; he took it with equanimity and retired from the field with a score of ninety-one. I was surprised by the performance of Jean-Paul, who was firing a French needle-gun revolver as delicate as his person

198

but turned in the respectable score of eighty-seven. He had the eye of a first-class shooter.

A few others shot in the low nineties but Caleb was the man to beat. Being out of practice I shot at a slow pace, taking my time with each ball, feeling no urgency. When Caleb finished his run I was on my thirtieth ball; when the last shooters came into the line I was on my sixtieth or thereabouts and I'd missed only those early two shots. The old confidence had returned and I knew I would be all right so long as I did not force the pace: speed is the first excellence to deteriorate in the absence of constant practice. It takes a while longer before the eyes lose their accuracy or the hands their habits of aim.

I became aware that Vern Tyree was attracting a splinter of the crowd and I inquired of the line judge how Vern was doing. Shortly thereafter the word came back to me that Vern had shot forty-one glass balls before missing his first.

I had no evidence to support it but I believed he must have trained himself strenuously for this match. He had belittled its importance by addressing himself casually to the topic but Vern had never been casual about anything; I remembered the passions of his childhood dedications to horsemanship and marksmanship. It was not in Vern ever to admit he was second-best to anyone at any pursuit he thought important.

He meant to best me on the shooting range. And abruptly, because it was so important to him, it became important to me as well. I have always been a competitor; no more than Vern did I have any desire to come in second-best.

I settled down and shot with painstaking care.

   . . .

I missed my sixty-seventh. Vern was shooting fast with the Colt; he too was into the sixties with only one miss behind him to my three.

He was too far down the line for me to observe; I had periodic reports of his progress from the line judge as I changed rifles or paused to rest my arms. The shoulder began to twinge. I had hoped the imperfection would have healed in the past year. It was not yet very painful—I was using a much lighter rifle than I had employed at Denver—but it was enough to warn me.

The line judge said, "He's missed his second one. He's up to seventy-two."

"Thank you. . . . All right. Throw."

   . . .

Bang of discharge, shatter of glass, murmur of crowd through the cotton stuffing. Gunsmoke acrid in the still-damp air. A few light drizzle drops sizzling on the hot gunmetal. "Ready? Throw." Eighty-three, eighty-four.

"He's missed his third one. He's up to ninety-four."

"Thank you. . . ."

A click and a sharp pain in the shoulder now each time I lifted the rifle; it was quick and did not linger and I simply waited for the pain to subside before I called for the throw.

Eighty-nine, ninety.

"He's finished. His score's ninety-seven. You can still tie him, Mr. Cardiff."

Ten to go and I could not afford to miss any.

Somehow I did it.

. . .

The elimination round was announced by one of the judges from the dais. By that time Bob Halburton's speech was too slurred for oration.

From our opposite ends of the line Vern Tyree and I approached the center where we would stand side by side to fire the elimination match.

I saw a vein risen and throbbing above his eyebrow, the scar embossed by anger.

Caleb stood nearby, his chin tucked in with suspicion and disapproval: I had told him everything about my past—clearly he was no more easy in Vern's presence than I was. There had always been a madness in Vern; you never knew when it might surface.

The crowd surged forward. This was drama beyond the price of their admission: a dead-heat runoff between two Wild Westerners. I don't suppose anyone knew Vern Tyree's name at that time—the match brought fame to him, even as it imposed obscurity upon me—but his handsomeness and his skill and his arrogant carriage ensured avid public interest. Besides, as the unknown he was the underdog. I could hear the bets being wagered amid the sportsmen in the crowd.

Vern wore a sawed-off sheepskin-lined saddle jacket against the chill. He had removed his sombrero for the shoot and his long hair fell plains-fashion about the sheepskin collar. He wore a revolver and a knife in his holster belt; he stood in Texas boots; he was every inch a Westerner, to the delight of the crowd.

When I offered my hand he refused to take it; I was not surprised. I could smell whisky faint on his breath but certainly he hadn't consumed enough to affect his shooting. He said in a quiet voice, "I'd as soon use your head as a glass ball but I guess there's a law against it." Then he smiled, up to the eyes. "You set the pace, Saddlesores, it's your duck hunt. I still recall the time I shot ten to your one. You remember that?"

"I remember a lot of things, Vern."

"So do I, you know." With the deformed left hand he touched the scar on his cheek. "They tell me you put a Pinkerton man on my sister. They tell me you went down to Virginia."

"You believe everything you're told?"

His cold smile played on me. I said, "If you want a fight, Vern, don't hide behind your sister for an excuse. I'm ready to accommodate you." I felt child-foolish but I also felt obliged by the circumstances to speak that way. "Or would you rather have me back away? What kind of satisfaction are you looking for?"

"Right now I'm looking for the satisfaction of winning this shooting match."

"Would that be enough for you?"

"Maybe—maybe."

I said, "That's too bad then. It's a satisfaction I won't give you."

He was still smiling oddly. "Well I am sorry then," he said without contrition. "Let's commence." With a whipping jerk of his wide shoulders he turned away from me and stalked to his position.

I saw Jean-Paul watching. He still held the graceful needle-revolver in his hand as if he'd forgotten it was there. He was looking at Vern. Then his glance came around to my face. I could not interpret his smile.

.   .   .

We shot ten to ten in the round. There was no money in it; I'd won Bob Halburton's stake for him; this was a matter of pride and private challenge.

The second round went nine to nine; the third ten to ten.

My rifles stood in the water bucket. Vern swabbed out the bore of his Colt, replaced the cylinder, dabbed a piece of burnt cork against the front sight. He swung toward me with the rifle at the ready position—for a moment, seeing the blaze of his eyes, I thought he was going to shoot me.

"That's cool enough," he said. "Let's go."

The fourth round we shot ten to ten. I had fired one hundred and forty times. The shoulder was deteriorating; now I had steady pain—an agony almost unbearable when I lifted the rifle.

It might have been easy to miss one or two and end the pain but as Caleb would have said I wasn't gaited that way.

We fired a fifth round—nine hits each. I missed the tenth shot because my arm refused to lift the rifle high enough.

.   .   .

His face was venomous. It was if there were no one in the park save the two of us. The scars were raised on his face, white against the red flush. "Understand this—I'll beat you out on this shoot and on any

201

other shoot you choose to enter and in every other way there is. And I expect one of these days I will end up by killing you, but not right away."

I gave him a long steady gaze. "Tell me why."

"You know why."

It was the sum of his answer. He wheeled toward the throw-boy. "You ready? Let's resume this."

I tested my arm. The pain was almost blinding but I elevated the Spencer to my shoulder and I knew I could hold it there for seven shots, levering the mechanism without removing the stock from my shoulder.

"Throw."

. . .

The muscles began to bind because I was not accustomed to holding the rifle in a raised position for such a length of time. It was Bogardus' method, not mine. But I made it work.

The sixth shot, the seventh; not a miss. Then I had to hand the empty rifle to the Indian. I lifted the fresh one to my shoulder with my good hand and slowly moved the aching arm until my hand touched the forestock. It was as if a dull blade had impaled my shoulder and begun to twist there. I fastened my grip about the forestock and waited for my eyes to clear. I heard a gasp from the crowd—Vern missed his ninth shot. He made the tenth. Then I felt him watching me. I had to make three in a row to beat him, two of three to tie him; I was not sure I could hit any at all.

I squeezed my eyes shut and breathed deep. Then I took my stance. "Throw."

The recoil grenaded through my shoulder. I all but dropped the rifle. I was weeping with pain then; I had to wait for my eyes to dry.

"Throw."

I saw it burst, knew I had at least tied him, knew I could not possibly endure another round of ten shots; I had to end this now.

I summoned my will like steel hoops about me—peered dry-eyed down the carbine barrel—felt a pain unlike any I had ever experienced before—and called for the throw.

The glass ball soared. The front sight of the rifle moved too slowly to meet it. The ball began its drop. Pitching forward to hold it in my sights I squeezed the trigger and saw the ball shatter less than a foot above the earth.

Stunned by pain I fell to one knee. I jammed the butt of the rifle against the earth and clung to it for support with my good hand; otherwise I'd have tumbled on my shoulder. I looked up through tear-blurred vision at Vern, hearing the applause come off the crowd in waves.

Even anguished as I was, it flooded me with an extraordinary savor—it is something no one can explain who has not felt it. I had learned the taste of it upon the theatrical stage but this carried to a far greater intensity. The crowd thundered its acknowledgment of my victory and I relished it, took it to my soul, enveloped it.

In that moment Vern was forgotten, I do not know how briefly.

But as my eyes cleared I was arrested by Vern's face because I had seen that expression before. I had seen the madness in him twice before; I saw it again now.

    . . .

He did not stir. He made no threatening act. His right hand rested across the revolver at his waist; he only stared at me—livid, his eyes large with malice, nostrils flared, lips compressed. I could hear his breathing and see the short bursts of it in the form of mist upon the air.

I hated him then; I was thinking of Libby, thinking it was Vern who had driven us apart.

I did a cruel thing then. Climbing weakly to my feet I began to turn away from him and in doing so I said, "You're still second-best."

Lightheaded with pain I wove an unsteady path toward the dais to collect my prize. It was of no account, a simple store-bought brass trophy cup we had purchased to award to the winner as a token of his victory. But now the two-handled cup assumed an importance to me—it was the symbol of my victory over my enemy—and I was determined to claim it.

I smiled and nodded to acknowledge the congratulations of spectators and fellow shooters and judges. People swirled past; my vision was unclear; I must have stumbled and staggered like a drunk. I carried the rifle in my right hand all but forgotten. Caleb came along. He clapped my hat onto my head and draped the tunic across my shoulders. I winced even from that gentle touch. He was speaking, a high-spirited whooping and laughing. I did not attend his words. Bob Halburton summoned me onto the dais and made some sort of a speech and presented me with the trophy. I tucked it under my right arm and once again acknowledged the tributes of the slowly departing crowd. It began to drizzle in earnest; the white leather of my outfit became dotted with dark spots of moisture. It had greyed, fouled by powder smoke.

I propped myself hip-shot in the corner of the dais rail and awaited the subsiding of my pain. Bob Halburton seemed glassy with drink; Caleb was pounding him about the shoulders and trying to convince him his fortunes were restored but Bob's only response was a loose foolish grin.

Well-wishers flowed past the dais, some of them reaching up to shake my hand; I had to set my rifle and trophy down. I saw some of the rowdy bloods in whose company Vern had arrived but I did not see him; I thought perhaps he had crept away to nurse his spiritual wounds in privacy.

I began to regret my cruelty to him. The margin of my victory had pushed past Bob Halburton the dime novelist almost capsized. Bogardus approaching the dais I remembered his gallantry in Denver—*Gents, I salute both of you. Whoever wins this round, I believe in my heart there are three champions of this meet.* That to Caleb and me: a pair of callow young bucks, but Bogardus was not a man to whom manners were important only in polite company.

I felt ashamed. It would have cost me nothing to be gracious to Vern.

Bogardus tramped heavily up the steps onto the dais. When he pushed past Bob Hamilton the dime novelist almost capsized. Bogardus implanted himself before me and I took his expression for physician's concern. "That shoulder's causing you terrible pain, isn't it? I fear for that arm. Will you let me see to it?"

"I don't think I could get through another shoot like this. Thank you and yes. It's a great kindness."

"Nonsense. It's my profession. Good, we'll have a look at it then. Perhaps it's not a serious thing." Then he smiled behind the beard. "You shot a hell of a match today. I assume you've not even kept in practice. With that in mind it's a remarkable performance indeed."

"You'd have done as well but for luck."

"No. I was a bit jaded—otherwise I'd have caught the problem sooner. Perhaps it will teach us both a lesson about overconfidence."

"Doctor, win or lose it's always been an honor to shoot in your company."

He accepted that with grace; then he looked past me. Caleb was propping Bob Halburton on his feet and still trying to convince Bob of his good fortune.

"Shooting is your great dedication," Bogardus said to me, "but it is not your friend's. He has the aptitudes but he lacks the drive. He'd be just as happy if he never shot another competition."

Then his smile went a bit crooked. "That makes him fortunate, you know. He'll never be the prisoner of the demons who possess you and me. I shall go on shooting until I drop—and you're cut from the same cloth."

"I reckon I am. Yes sir."

"It's something we both might benefit from, you know."

"What do you mean?"

"It keeps getting harder to stir up challengers for shooting competitions. One's fame precedes one. Haven't you found that to be the case? And it's a difficulty that can only continue to worsen."

Then he tugged his beard with a sun-darkened paw; he twinkled. "Now just suppose two champion shooters, evenly matched, equally celebrated, were to appear before the public in a sequence of shooting matches, the totality of which would decide the ultimate national championship. Suppose we made public issue of the powerful rivalry between us for the championship. Suppose we invited all upstarts to see if they can't upset us—and offer them attractive betting odds."

I saw his point and smiled. Bogardus continued to stroke his beard. "I do believe we'd draw the crowds and the heavy bettors. What do you say?"

"I'd like to think on it. Right now I'm contracted to Bob Halburton's show."

"You're a shooting man, not an actor. Just as I'm mostly not a doctor any longer. We belong on the shooting line, you and me. Look at the truth, Hugh—there's a hundred thespians, a thousand, ten thousand of them who can act rings around you. I've seen your show. It's a curiosity, it's an enjoyment, but your name won't go down in history beside those of Langtry and Booth. You cut a striking figure on the stage but if you don't mind my candor you're a third-rate actor. On the other hand put a rifle in your hand and I believe you're one of the two finest shooters on the planet today. I count myself immodestly your equal but I accept no one else into this company. To be sure a man can have an off day but over the long haul you are the only shooter I've ever met who gives me pause. And you've got better than twenty years on me. When I grow too old the crown will be yours alone. Can you possibly throw that over for a dreary sawdust career in second-class melodramas no one will remember a week after they've closed?"

I said, "You talk as good a line as Bob Halburton when you've a mind to." But I warmed to the notion. It struck immediate sparks in me, kindled my fires: I was on the point of responding when a disruption drew my attention.

Three big men bulled their way toward the dais, thrusting people roughly aside as they approached. Two of them wore bowler hats and carried truncheons. The third, leading them toward us, was Vern Tyree. His face was set into lines of savage satisfaction.

The three men mounted the dais like wardens at a hanging: deliberate and enginelike, susceptible to no diversion. They brushed past Caleb and Bob Halburton. They thrust Dr. Bogardus aside. Vern stood face to face with me and suddenly jabbed the index finger of his gnarled left hand into my chest.

"This is the man."

One of the bowler-hatted men revealed a badge. "Federal marshals. You are Hugh Michael Cardiff?"

"I am."

"You are under arrest."

"What for?"

"We have a fugitive execution warrant from the state of Kentucky on a charge of willful murder in the first degree."

. . .

In a flash the two Navy revolvers were in Caleb's fists. I heard distinctly the clicks of the mechanisms as he drew the hammers back to full cock.

In a calm voice he said, "Let's see the warrant first."

The chief marshal regarded Caleb's revolvers with more surprise than fear. With slow care he withdrew a folded document from his coat. He opened it and held it up before Caleb's gaze. I saw Caleb's eyes whip back and forth from the warrant to the marshals.

Had it not been for Caleb I might have submitted to arrest. Caleb knew the story of that warrant from my own lips. He knew the fraudulence of the charge; and as a Texan he had contempt for Yankee warrants.

Caleb said, "Hugh, this is a fugitive execution warrant. You understand what that means?"

"No."

"They issue them against fugitives who've been convicted and sentenced for hanging offenses."

"Wait a minute." I turned to stare at the chief marshal. "I was never tried. They never convicted me."

"Read the warrant, son. Under martial law during the war a fair number of spies were tried and convicted *in absentia*. You've been sentenced to hang." He fluttered the paper at me. "Tell your friend to put up his weapons, it won't do him no good."

Caleb said in his patient voice, "I think you ought to skedaddle, Hugh."

"Well I don't—"

"You don't get this yet, do you?" A revolver waggled toward the flapping paper. "That's dead-or-alive, Hugh. They can shoot you on sight."

The junior marshal chose that moment to swing his truncheon toward Caleb. There was the roar of a Navy Colt. The marshal stumbled. He teetered for balance and I realized Caleb had neatly shot the heel off his boot.

The marshal reached for the rail and stood chagrined; one foot on tiptoe.

Caleb said mildly, "That was foolish."

206

The marshal's face turned baleful but he did not speak; there was no need to.

Caleb said to me, "Go on. Get. You got no chance here."

There were still hundreds of people churning about the dais. The amazing thing is that none of them seemed aware of the drama being played out on the platform. Not even Caleb's shot alarmed them. The afternoon had been filled with shooting and most of them must have been half-deaf from it; one more shot was hardly calculated to startle them.

I was in a state of heightened perception in which everything seemed to take place very slowly. I was aware of many things at once—above all my own confusion and fear.

Vern Tyree stood half-hidden behind the chief marshal; I was never unaware of his presence. Bob Halburton slumped uselessly to the side. The judges had edged away from us. The Indian with my spare weaponry looked on, uncomprehending. I thought I saw Jean-Paul moving along just below the dais but I wasn't certain. There was a lot of talk around us; the crowds eddied. Caleb's revolvers dangled casually from his hands and did not point at anyone in particular but their threat dominated us all. The chief marshal breathed in and out deeply and visibly—his thoughts were transparent: he was trying to calculate a resolution to the scene that would not involve the risk of injury to the crowd. The junior marshal lifted his heelless leg and massaged the bottom of his boot with his palm. No doubt it stung.

The chief marshal slowly folded the warrant and pulled back both lapels of his coat to expose the suit underneath. "We are not armed with guns."

"That simplifies," Caleb said. "Go on, Hugh, go on now."

"Where?"

"Anywhere."

"That's the same as nowhere," I said. "I can't spend the rest of my life with that hanging over me. I'd better go back to Kentucky with them. I can straighten it out with the truth."

"Don't you get this, Hugh? They ain't going to try you. They ain't interested in your testimony. You're already sentenced to hang. You go back to Kentucky they'll just put a rope on your neck and that's the end to it. You listen to me—I know the law." His hound-sad face tipped toward me. "Get!"

I am not sure to this day what I would have done if the choice had been left to me.

I saw sudden movement in the corner of my vision. I responded from instinct—threw up my arm to ward off Vern Tyree's approaching blow. It struck my wrist. He swung at me with another hand and that was all it took: suddenly and crazily we were fighting and it was the bank of the Santa Cruz River over again but this time it was as brief as the wink of an eye—I saw the revolver swoop. He used it as a club. It struck my chest and knocked me back.

I heard Caleb's shout. I flailed for balance; I was bent to one side and that was when Vern slammed the revolver down upon me.

It struck on the point of my bad shoulder against an inflamed fire of pain. It shattered through me like a hundred knives thrust into every sensitive nerve of my body and I could not fight that overwhelming pain; I heard my own scream, my eyes rolled into darkness, I believed I was dying and I plunged eagerly to meet the relief of death.

And in truth I very nearly passed in my checks that time.

BOOK SEVEN

Trailing Apache

I WAS ALERT in flickering bursts separated by periods of unknowing. I was bound up tightly as if in ropes, jouncing in discomfort inside something that moved. I felt it pitch to a stop.

A voice—Bogardus'? "Don't let him move yet." Then the vehicle, for it was such, swayed with weight as someone dismounted. I heard his footsteps diminish. There was a muted racket and a mechanical chuffing nearby and I was aware of faint rancidity in the air—waterfront aura. I felt helpless in my weakness, exposed and vulnerable and ashamed—it was the first time in my life my big body had betrayed me.

I heard footsteps return—more than one man. Fear pricked me.

Bogardus spoke in a soft voice. "Here's our friend." Then for a bit I passed out completely. I came awake in the open—on a pier, I guessed; a man loomed beefy and vague in the night. The nearest lamps were aboard a ship at the far end of the dock.

I had an imprecise impression of three men moving around me of whom Bogardus was one and I thought I recognized the second; the third appeared only as a man in nautical garb, officer's cap. Bogardus said, "This is Bill Dwayne. First officer. He'll be looking after you both." Dim light shone against the officer's white teeth.

Bogardus' companion lifted pieces of luggage off the back of a hansom and the ship's officer took the cases from him. "I'll take these aboard. Give me five minutes to set the deck crew to errands on the starboard side. Then bring him aboard and take him directly below. You know the cabin."

Then the officer addressed himself to Bogardus' companion, a slight man whose nervous movements were familiar to me. Jean-Paul. "Stay below until we've set the pilot off the ship. That'll be around dawn. After that you'll have the freedom of the ship. All right?"

"Yes, and I thank you."

"Paying well enough for it, ain't you?" The officer walked away with the luggage.

Bogardus bulked in the steamy cool darkness. "A hell of a thing, is it not? I wish there were another way."

"He will be all right, Doctor."

"I expect he will. I'm confident he and I haven't seen the last of each other. One day perhaps a presidential pardon—but not for a long time to come. With Grant in the White House there's little chance of setting aside the verdict of a Yankee military court."

"He will be safe with us. There will be time to heal."

"It's a fine thing you're doing for him."

"A promise I made to . . . a mutual friend," Jean-Paul said.

Bogardus said, "Bill Dwayne's a good man. His wife's a second cousin of mine. You won't be hurt by trusting him. Well—I judge it must be time to go."

When they picked me up the pain drilled through me and my consciousness dwindled but it seemed important to hang on to reality. I clung to the pinpoint of awareness and felt myself carried, smelt the cologne that must have wafted off the young Frenchman, heard the creak of rigging and lap of harbor water. The ship's deck throbbed with the chug of its engines. Occasionally those carrying me would lurch and I stifled the outcries of pain. I could see and hear; I lacked the ability to speak—it would have required a concentration of effort that lay beyond me.

The compartment contained narrow cots bolted to the bulkheads; there was one small porthole. The luggage from the hansom was under the cots.

"Cramped quarters," Bogardus said, "but they'll do. It won't be forever, will it?" He kept his voice right down.

"You had better get ashore."

"Jean-Paul—"

"No need for talk, Doctor. He is in your debt far more than mine. One day he will thank you himself."

"God be with you then." And Bogardus went.

Weak and morose I lay wondering what was to become of me.

    . . .

I was bound up in cotton plasters about my shoulder and chest, the arm strapped to my side. It looked a professional job. I came out of sleep feeling drunk and lightheaded. The pain still accompanied me but it was inexplicably distanced.

Jean-Paul lay on his bunk against the opposite bulkhead reading a book—something in French; I could see the title on the cover. He became aware of my stirrings and looked across. "Awake?"

He smiled and sat up. "You feel as if a fog, yes? Don't be alarmed. The ship's surgeon has given you morphium for the pain."

"What happened?"

"We're at sea."

"Yes. Going where?"

"France. Brest first, then my home."

My head swam. "My God."

"You've a great deal to get caught up on, *mon ami,* but there is plenty of time for it. We shall be twelve days more at sea."

"What happened to Caleb?"

"He's quite all right. We'll talk when you feel up to it."

"I'm up to it."

Jean-Paul had a quick smile that was almost a grimace. "Very well." And he proceeded to tell me of the occurrences since the moment when Vern Tyree struck me down.

.   .   .

Caleb, believing for a moment that Vern had killed me, went into a frenzy and had to be restrained to prevent his shooting Vern; this was done by Bogardus' interposing himself between them—Bogardus would have been a difficult obstacle for Caleb to shoot around. Vern took refuge between the marshals while Bogardus tried to calm Caleb.

Jean-Paul mounted the dais at that point, having fought his way through the crowd to get there. Bogardus examined me briefly and informed Caleb that I was alive but in need of immediate medical attention. The two marshals insisted that I must be taken to jail but Jean-Paul, fearing I would not receive proper surgical care there, held everyone at gunpoint while Caleb and Bogardus carried me off the field.

Jean-Paul then leaped away into the crowd and, from the way he told it, enjoyed the sport of leading the marshals a merry chase. He was able to give them the slip, after which he made his way to Bogardus' lodgings, waiting across the street until policemen had come and gone; he was relieved when they did not arrest Bogardus.

Jean-Paul joined Bogardus that evening and they repaired to the house of a friend of Bogardus' in Brooklyn Heights—the house where I had been taken. Caleb was there looking after me, along with the young doctor who owned the house. The surgeon was a colleague of Bogardus'. Bogardus had chosen the place because it was nearer the shooting park than any hospital and it would not be suspected by the police.

In the morning Caleb surrendered to the custody of the marshals and spent twenty-four hours in captivity but finally he was turned loose upon payment of a stiff fine and on condition that he depart the state of New York immediately. When Jean-Paul last saw Caleb he was on his way to the ferry, planning to entrain for the West.

Bob Halburton, appeasing his creditors with the winnings from the shooting match, had provided Bogardus with every penny he could spare for my assistance. When last seen Bob had been off to his quill pen and his pot of wild imagination, planning to write further novels of the adventures of Rice and Cardiff in order to restore his fortunes. Bob was often down but never for long.

Jean-Paul showed me an article in the *Sun* about the Brooklyn shooting match, my victory, the arresting marshals, my sudden and mysterious disappearance; the emergence of a previously unknown Westerner, Major Vernon Tyree, as the surprise challenger for the title of best shooter of the match. A considerable space was devoted to a fanciful recounting of Vern's Civil War record as scout and cavalry officer. I doubted much of it was true; it had the ring of a liar's yarn. And I knew Vern had never been promoted to major.

The closing of the play *Heroes of the West* was dismissed in a passing paragraph.

As for Bogardus, he had told the police that I had regained consciousness in the buggy on the way to the hospital and had leaped from the buggy and made my escape on foot into the alleys of Brooklyn. His story was impossible to disprove and Bogardus had not been arrested.

In Jean-Paul's case an order had been issued for his deportation from the United States but he had anticipated it by going aboard the steamer with me.

As for me, I had arrived in a sorry state at the house of Bogardus' young surgeon friend. The surgeon, with the assistance of his wife and Bogardus, and with Caleb and Jean-Paul looking on, had operated upon me with his knives and sewing needles. After the surgery I had been sewed up and bandaged. I had slept forty-eight hours under the influence of morphium before Bogardus was able to complete the arrangements for my escape by way of a ship berthed at Perth Amboy. I had been spirited from Brooklyn by lighter, transported from one Perth Amboy dock to another by hansom and carried aboard ship—as I knew—by Bogardus and Jean-Paul.

Jean-Paul said, "I know nothing of medicine but Dr. Bogardus had a long discussion with the ship's surgeon and he can explain to you the condition."

.   .   .

The surgeon was a stringy man with wisps of grey hair and a face that was not likely to be surprised by anything at all. Not an unkindly

212

face; merely a jaded one. I came to suspect he was a steady user of his own stores of morphium. But the drug did not seem to dull his mind or his capabilities.

He sat on the edge of Jean-Paul's cot and lifted his hands so that I could see clearly. He made a fist and inserted it into his cupped hand. "The shoulder joint. Ball in socket—like this." He twisted the fist within the cupped hand. "Normally the ball rides properly inside the socket. It can't fall out because the lips of the socket hold it in place. Now I'm told you must have had an old break to the upper arm, and that old injury had driven the arm bone very hard up into the socket. At that time you suffered trauma to both the ball and the socket. Under certain conditions it must have given you great pain. I'm trying to keep this to layman's language. Do you understand me so far?"

"Yes. Very clear."

"All right." He went on, unsmilingly matter-of-fact: "Some of the cartilage had been crushed by the old injury and this left the joint in a weakened condition. I'm told this recent injury was caused by a heavy blow to the top of your shoulder. Normally such a blow might cause only a bad bruise; but your shoulder had already suffered an injury and when you were struck this time the socket bone shattered."

He splayed the fingers of the cupped hand. Now the fist flopped loosely amid the open fingers.

"That was the condition of your joint when you were operated upon by Dr. Bogardus and his colleague. The arm was hanging from nothing but muscle and flesh. The surgeons did their best to knit the shattered socket back together. They reset all the pieces of bone and sewed you up. You'll always have a mass of scars on the skin of your shoulder and upper arm but I imagine that will be the least of your troubles. You're very tightly taped up at the moment. You must not move *at all* without assistance. Understand that? If you move it may pull those bone fragments apart. I doubt any surgeon would be willing to open you up and reset them again. The risk of sepsis would be too great."

I watched him without comment. He sighed quietly. "In the end—perhaps eight or ten weeks from now—you will be able to start working the joint and see whether it functions. I have no idea whether it will or not. I wasn't present during the surgery. Dr. Bogardus thought the chance of full recovery would be remote and the chance of partial recovery rather slim, but he said he has great faith in your strength and recuperative powers. It's a question, you see, whether they patched together enough remaining bone to give you a workable socket for the joint. I can tell you this much from my own experience with similar wounds in the Crimea—I doubt you'll ever have anything like the freedom of movement you used to have in that arm. I'll be surprised if you ever lift it to shoulder level. In fact you may have to face the possibility you'll not lift it more than a few inches away from the perpendicular."

He shook his head. His eyes were bleak but his sympathy evident. "I'm sure the surgeons did their very best. But I fear they didn't have much left to work with."

. . .

It is the left arm with which a right-handed shooter lifts the weight of his rifle. Without the use of that arm I would never shoot again.

Weighed by that knowledge I also was burdened by my exile.

It was a time of gloom. I hardly attended Jean-Paul or the surgeon or the few others who occasionally visited me in my imprisoning compartment. I wondered what difference it would have made if I'd submitted meekly to the marshals and gone back to Kentucky. Was hanging any worse than what lay ahead of me? A cripple doomed to wander the world never setting foot in his homeland. I could not help thinking bleakly of the legend of the Man Without a Country.

I was in a dark fugue, a dirge. There was no word from Libby; there had been time for none—she would hardly have had the news of my disappearance by the time I took passage from Perth Amboy.

Half sick with throbbing pain, silly-headed with morphium, I endured somehow—often by distracting myself with rage. Clearly it was Vern Tyree's instigations that had set the marshals upon me. If it had not been for Vern that old warrant would never have been extracted from the dusty files in which it must have been buried. And it was Vern who had crippled me.

Vern, my enemy; Libby, my love; brother and sister. There was nothing to think about but the two of them; and nothing to do but think about them. The dilemma was insoluble. I felt myself plunging slowly toward madness.

. . .

Jean-Paul's surname was Cavaignac; he was distantly related to the French general who had been dictator in 1848, the year of Jean-Paul's birth; Jean-Paul was something of a black sheep and had journeyed far through Mexico under the rule of Maximilian, and California and Texas and Louisiana. He admitted cheerfully that he was a ne'er-do-well and had little intention of ever becoming a sober productive member of society. Determined to take his enjoyments wherever he might find them he had made his way from New Orleans to Atlanta and then north into Virginia, letting one introduction lead him to the next, carousing and gambling his way from place to place, bringing with him a hilarity and a suave charm which he bartered for companionship and lodging. When

214

they grew tired of him in one place he went on to another. "Everyone is always happy to see me arrive," he told me, "and happy to see me depart. I have learned not to overstay my welcome."

"How did you get to be such a friend of Libby's?"

"They are all so stuffy, her husband and his family. I think I was to her, what do you say, a fresh breath. I made her laugh."

He saw my suspicious squint and was amused by it. "I only made her laugh, you know. I am a rogue but not so much so as to steal another man's woman, and certainly not foolhardy enough to steal a woman who appears to belong to *two* men—or three, if you wish to count her jealous brother. And in any case I do not take her fancy, though I confess she takes mine. Her heart is reserved for you—you know that. I must tell you about Elizabeth—your Libby. Her devotion to you is something extraordinary. Never have I seen anything like the wretched unhappiness she felt when she came to her senses after marrying that pig. You know she did it out of terror, nothing else."

"When she returned to Blaisedell's—did they treat her badly?"

"No more badly than one might expect. When she returned from your adventure together she said nothing to anyone. Her brother attempted to force her to say that you had kidnapped her against her will. She was wise enough to neither deny nor confirm the charge. She remained silent. Nevertheless her husband and her brother were in terrible tempers. They were on the point of going to the constables and having a warrant issued for your arrest on a charge of kidnapping and assault, which is to say rape. I believe I managed to persuade them that such a warrant would not be enforceable if the chief witness refused to testify against you. And even they could see that Elizabeth intended to provide no testimony of any kind. I could only admire her strength. She was icy and distant with her brother, never discourteous, and the same with her husband. She confided only in me. From her confidences I was afraid she might break down at any moment but she carried through splendidly."

"She intends to have an annulment," I said. "Or a divorce."

"I know. She put it to her husband straightaway."

"And?"

"The poor man was stunned by it all, of course. He's an oaf but I had to feel sympathy."

"What did he do?"

"He plunged back into his business affairs as if they could purge him of his trouble. Elizabeth continued without mercy to press him for a decision. She has made it clear she's prepared to leave him in any case, should he refuse to grant her wishes."

"Then she'll be free of him either way."

215

"Probably. One never knows how things will turn out. I know that Phipps had not collected himself enough to answer her at the time when I left. In the meantime Elizabeth has taken a flat in Philadelphia. She refuses to live under the same roof with him."

"Why did you come to New York? Did she send you?"

"Yes. When the advertisement of your shooting competition appeared in the newspaper she knew her brother would go there. She was afraid for you—correctly, as it turned out. She asked me to look to your protection."

"I want to repay you, Jean-Paul. I don't know how I can but—"

"There's nothing to repay, *mon ami*. I've done you a service because I am hopelessly and unrequitedly in love with your woman."

. . .

Two shocks awaited me in Brest. One was a letter from Philadelphia, conveyed by a faster ship than our own. It had been sent to the shipping agents, to Jean-Paul's attention, and he brought the letter into my cabin and slit it open with his fingernail, dropped it in my lap, gave me the benediction of his *c'est-la-vie* smile and left me in privacy to read the letter.

Dearest Hugh,

In my heart of hearts is a hope that this letter will never find its way to you, that perhaps it would be better if you did not hear from me at all and assumed the worst of me; for to be hated for neglect may be preferable to being hated for betrayal. And yet I must write this letter to you, although it is the most difficult thing I have ever done. I could not live with myself otherwise.

I still do not know how to begin what I must tell you. I have started this letter a score of times and burned a score of half-written pages. There is so much to tell you so that you must try to understand, and there is so little that I understand myself.

I remember the chaste novels we read under my mother's tutelage when we were children together. I have never seen myself in their hand-wringing heroines but now I wring my hands and must grovel for your forgiveness.

You have never met Phipps Merriam, my husband. You do not know him. I did not know him myself until now; I did not count on his relentless cruelty, his single-mindedness, the evil of his arrogance. In sum, dear Hugh, I did not credit him with strength, and in that I was tragically wrong.

When first I met Phipps it was at his home, to which I had repaired for a visit to Phipps's sister, with whom I had become fast friends in Miss Tewksbury's school. Upon our first meeting, Phipps took me aside and told me that I had captivated him, that he intended to marry me, and that I must take his wild statements seriously because he was offering me an empire. That is how he put it. He said, rather gaily, that if I married him I would soon find myself the wife of a great leader—a senator and perhaps even a president.

At that time of course I dismissed his boasts as the empty bragging of a rich and frivolous young man. I did not know him. I came to realize very quickly that there was nothing frivolous about him; but by then I had forgotten his initial boast.

I should not have forgotten it, for Phipps certainly has not. He is preparing a campaign for a seat in the Congress this fall. He intends to carry on from that base into the Senate. He is driven with ambition and will permit nothing to stand in his path. Having already proved his supremacy in the world of finance and industry he now seeks to prove it in politics.

Oh, how can I say this? How can I convey it in the cold etching of ink upon paper? I ought to be touching you, clasping your hand, searching your marvelous calm outdoor eyes with my own. I see your face before me even as I write these words but I can touch nothing but this cold pen, this blank paper.

I must plunge ahead and simply say it.

I am with child. I tried to conceal my condition from Phipps, knowing how it must complicate matters between us. I moved out of his house into my own flat; I admitted none but a few carefully chosen friends as visitors. But through the treason of one of them, I know not which one, the truth of my pregnancy was reported to Phipps.

I am to bear the child in July. It is not Phipps's child. He knows this.

Three men—employees of the Merriam interests—arrived at my flat last night. When I refused them entry they forced the door and bore me off to an office in Market Street. I was thrust into a windowless room where, after a few moments, Phipps joined me. He shut both doors and bade me sit upon a chair. He remained upon his feet, hands clasped behind him in that pompous way of his.

He demanded to know the name of the father. I said nothing. He pressed his demands; he became argumentative and threatening. I revealed nothing. Finally I saw that he realized I was not prepared to reveal your name. He suspects you are the father, of course. Just as he suspected it was you who "abducted" me in Virginia. But I have been determined not to give him the satisfaction of confirmation of his suspicions. I told him he was free to believe whatever he cared to believe.

Facing me like an inquisitor in that bare little office—I found it a cell—he spoke quietly and firmly, with a self-possession I found new to him. It is, I gather, the air he puts on when involved in his business dealings. It is an air of supreme confidence, brooking no possibility of contradiction. He is young, of course, and has not been tried by failure; nevertheless in his possessed calm arrogance he is most persuasive.

He said—these are his words—"Understand this, Elizabeth. The child is my child. That is what the world will know. That is what the child will know. That is all anyone will ever know."

When I did not reply to this, he went on in the same unnaturally calm resolute way, pacing back and forth within the narrow confines of the cubicle. He said flatly that he had the presidency in mind and that the country would not elect a divorced man or a cuckold to the presidency.

Then he chilled me to the bone. He said, "It will, however, elect a widower."

Without putting it in words Phipps made it quite clear to me that he was prepared to see both me and the child killed rather than give us up. He made oblique reference to the possibility of accidents. He described the power that his wealth provides him. He told me the story of a clerk in one of the Merriam companies who had absconded with a sum in embezzled funds. He told me how the Merriam interests had patiently sifted clues until they ran the fugitive clerk to earth in the Argentine and brought him back to America, along with what remained of the money he had stolen. His meaning was clear: there is no escape.

I fear not for my own life. If I cannot be with you it matters little if he kills me. But I am to be a mother soon and I must vouchsafe the future of my child.

Our child, dearest Hugh. You are exiled and I imprisoned; it is clear the fates have never had in mind for us a happy destiny. Through my own foolhardiness we must keep apart. Sometimes, as in this pressing darkness of my chamber, I feel I cannot bear it. But I shall. For the sake of your child I shall bear anything. I pledge to you that your child will grow straight and tall as its father, and with as much honor and courage; that much I can warrant, for as its mother I shall shield it from the evil influence of my husband even as I provide it with every advantage Phipps's wealth can bring.

But the world may never know the child's real patrimony. I fear if it were revealed Phipps would not hesitate to murder. He is a ruthless man.

Forgive me, my darling, and remember me always as I shall remember you—with all my love.

Libby

. . .

As I read the letter there was a long suspended interval of unreality and disbelief—like the moment when the skinning knife slips and you see the blood pump from the cut but you don't feel the pain yet and you wait for it.

Then I put the letter down and it clubbed me.

I swam in opacity as if in a nightmare. I do not know what savage acts I may have committed. The fire of red anger burst inside me and thereafter for a very long time the small red glow of rage burned inside me—years passed before it was extinguished.

I do not know how otherwise to put it: my heart was broken.

. . .

When in my groggy dismal rage I looked up the sun was falling aslant through the porthole across Jean-Paul's features.

"I must return to America," I croaked.

"No. You would be hanged for it and Elizabeth would suffer. And the child as well, I fear."

"You read the letter?"

218

"You've been in such a state, *mon ami*—as if completely drunk. You were shouting. I felt I ought to read it. I've left it safe in your valise there, among your books."

"I'm going back," I said, "and I'm going to kill Phipps Merriam."

"If you wish to hang. After they've hanged you, do you suppose Elizabeth and the child will be happier?" He managed a wan smile. "She is right, you know. You've no choice. And in any case you cannot return to America—have you forgotten the warrant?"

"Warrant be damned." But I lay back, exhausted. "What am I to do, Jean-Paul?"

"Recuperate. Then think of the future."

"Future." I growled the word in bitterness. Nothing seemed to matter. "When do we go ashore, then?"

"I am to leave the ship in a little while. But I fear you cannot do the same."

"What?"

"It seems that the empire of Napoleon III intends to humiliate Prussia at any cost. We are on the verge of war here, *mon ami,* and there is a great xenophobia—strangers are not admitted without the proper papers and I'm afraid you have no papers at all."

"I've never needed papers."

"Just so. In any case this ship's next port of call is Tangier. After that the Cape of Good Hope, I believe, and the Indian Ocean. You'll have pleasant voyages I'm sure, while your body recovers its strength. Your passage is paid and you've good friends in the captain and the surgeon."

I reeled from the shock of that; and hardly noticed when Jean-Paul took his leave.

It was the last I ever saw him. He was killed, I was told, in a duel some months later during the Franco-Prussian War. *Mon ami.*

.   .   .

It was a hot dry cloudless day off Ceylon when the surgeon dismantled the straps and plasters that bound my arm to my body. "You'll have no muscle control at first. . . . The tissues have been stationary. . . . You must expect a considerable degree of atrophy. . . . With time and exercise you'll see how much use of it you're able to regain."

He helped me off the edge of the bunk to my feet. I stood swaying, rocky; I almost fainted, weak from the months of confinement.

I scowled at the arm hanging flaccid by my side—shriveled, white, peeling; I looked up at the surgeon and he nodded assent and I tensed the muscles to lift the arm.

It did not move at all.

.   .   .

We were battered by a typhoon and the ship laid up for repair in the Portuguese colony of Macao. I shall not dwell on those weeks and months; a distinct melancholia hung about me like a mist throughout that time. I recovered much of my strength except for that of the injured arm; I was able to use the left hand only for small chores that required little strength, and could not lift my arm from the shoulder but only from the elbow. My only excellence—the skill that separated me from other men—was marksmanship, and since I could not hold a rifle I felt abandoned by the Fates. I took work where I could get it—by the beginning of 1871 I was working as assistant to the Dutch overseer of a rubber plantation in Java, keeping books for him, plodding through each day without thought for the next. I began to accept the idea that I was a cripple; but as my body strengthened so did my will, and if I could not lift a rifle nonetheless I could prove myself with pistol and revolver, and I set out to train myself to do everything with the handgun that I had once done with the long rifle. . . .

In time, restless in exile and hating the tropics, I went to sea again.

. . .

The hammock swayed with a sickening rhythm. A big man in filthy grey tatters prodded me with his truncheon. "Get up, it's your shift."

"What?"

The fo'c'sle stank of rotted bilge; I came back blearily to awareness.

The ship slid hard over almost on her beam ends. I was half out of the hammock and clutched its rope while my feet skittered on the sharply tilted planks.

"You mean I slept through *this?*"

"A ripe gale sure enough," the bosun said. "Get aft—there's a lot of cleaning up for you."

"I'll just bet there is."

"And take it easy, lad." His concern was generous enough; it was caused by the fact that I had a useless arm. Men with two good arms had a hard time in seas like these.

The wooden hull creaked alarmingly—great snaps and groans of sound. The fo'c'sle was all but deserted; one or two men were still there, shouldering into sou'westers and sea boots. I followed the bosun up the ladder onto the open deck.

Foam lashed the bows and combers tried to break over the windward rail and I was tossed past the hatch cover; I gripped a line and struggled to get my feet under me. I saw crewmen bent over the lee rail, their faces all but buried in the sea; they looked ghostly in the weird light. It must have been midmorning, for I had gone off watch at dawn, but the storm had leached the sky of color and storm lanterns were lit and hung swaying violently, shifting the shadows and upsetting equilibrium. Men were shouting and I saw several tars roll past me on what must have been urgent errands but the patterns of their movements seemed rough and aimless.

The bosun flung a few words at me—"Hang tight, lad!"—and was off pell-mell toward the pilothouse ladder.

The smash of the sea was a frightening racket; behind it dimly I heard the steady growl of the packet's inadequate steam engine. She was built mainly for sail; the engine was auxiliary and had been installed as an afterthought. *Venus de Mer* was only twelve years old but she had seen better days and too many rough seas. I saw she had a few yards of canvas up, no more; an excess would have stripped her of her masts in this blow.

A Portuguese tar, very pale, spun past me and made a grab for a boom overhead. Hanging there he gave me a petulant glance. "By damn we are upside down!" Our plank bottom slapped into a trough of water —everything jarred loose, I lost my grip and went spinning hard against the bulkhead, clawed blindly and found a handhold—and saw the Portuguese run yelling down the canted deck. He fell and slid, pitching down the deck until a bulkhead stopped him hard.

A lantern broke loose and fell, scattering flames; but the sea soon extinguished them and I saw the lantern fly into the waves. We heeled ponderously over onto the opposite precarious keel and a swinging boom broke loose of its lashings with half a ton of sail bundled to it— I saw it whip around and knew it would not stop in time. There was a high grinding racket, a rending snap; the ship went over once more and the heavy boom smashed right through the starboard rail like a giant spear, lancing into the ocean to be swallowed in foam.

Dimly I heard the master's cry: "Keep her into the wind, damn you!" And I saw figures scaling the rigging. I made my way slowly aft along the slippery deck, judging each step, waiting for a pause in the shifting, my hand leaping from hold to hold. A freak turn of wind again brought the master's voice to my ears: "Larboard the helm, you bastard!" I saw the bosun reeling across the afterdeck. Men bawled and clung to anything. In the sick green dimness I waited the roll of the deck and when it passed its crest I let loose my hold and let gravity take me: I half-fell, half-slid to the galley hatch. A great sheet of water crashed over me. I could not find a handhold on the hatch; I felt myself carried up by the water, away from the deck—it was a terrible sensation. I was choking, the sea in my mouth and nose. I was turning somersaults and then the ocean slammed me down, flattened me against hardwood; the sea ran away, rippling foam, and I gasped for life. The ship dropped stern-first and I saw the galley hatch. With impetuous desperation I dived for it and made my grip fast. The sea broke over me again but I held. When it retreated I stood bending my back, hauling the hatch cover open; I got down through it somehow and brought it down slamming above my head, secured it and clung trembling to the ladder.

In the eerie lamplight the galley was a shambles stinking of vomit. One of the cooks was lashing himself to a stanchion; the other was trying to pick up fallen caldrons. I dropped to the deck and gave him a hand; we wedged things wherever we could. A sudden vicious lurch hurled me against the bulkhead without warning; my nose hit the planking. I felt the warmth of blood in my nostrils and heard the muffled run of my own oaths. The world rocked underfoot and I did not see how we could get through this blow alive.

. . .

Like all storms it blew itself out and we were still afloat, albeit damaged—we'd lost a foremast boom and several spars, a section of main-deck rail and a good amount of supplies and cargo that had been lashed to the open deck. The off-watch took an inventory after we had made jury repairs and afterward the first officer informed us that because of the loss of stores we would have to make an unscheduled port. We had been blown some distance off our course and the nearest port was Dar es Salaam and the captain expressed concern about that because there was some dispute among the sultans, the British, the Germans and the Portuguese as to which power held sway over that section of the East African coast.

It was November; I'd been aboard *Venus de Mer* nine months. We flew a British flag but the captain was French, the ownership Norwegian and most of the crew Scilly Islanders. She was a random coaster hauling cargoes of convenience on an irregular circuit; in my months on board we had hit such varied ports as Tangier, Cape Town, Macao and Djakarta. The ship was due for a refit and we were on our way back toward Europe with a cargo of sisal and coffee beans for Southampton when the blow hit us in the Indian Ocean.

For my service as galley assistant I earned a pittance and was free to leave the ship and its service in any port of my choosing but I had no keen desire to be stranded nearly penniless in any of the rancid African or Asian harbors where we had dropped our anchor.

During the first leg of the voyage I had been watched with care by the first officer and the bosun. One-armed I was a subject of dubious regard; if I had not pulled my weight I'd have been left ashore. But I was strong and willing enough; my left hand was not completely paralyzed and I had sufficient use of it to enable me to handle kitchen chores, although I'd have been useless in any attempt to climb rigging or haul sail. I was quickly accepted as an apprentice crewman; I liked my fellow voyagers well enough; the officers were no more brutal than any others of those times; and for a time I persuaded myself that I had a fine opportunity to see exotic parts of the world.

I learned a bit of seamanship as well and by the time we made port in Dar es Salaam I was regarded as one of their own by the Scilly Islanders; I numbered them among my friends. The bosun especially I found to be an upstanding and even-handed fo'c'sle chief; I taught him chess and spun him yarns from the classics I'd read, and he taught me the ways of the sea. It was not an altogether unpleasant year in my life but I was pursued by my old demons—the sense of exile, the loneliness for my loved one and the aggravating realization that my life had been taken out of my own hands: I was being buffeted from pillar to post with no evident purpose or goal. In the retelling of it I suppose it appears I had led a most adventurous life for a man of my tender years— I was but twenty-two then—but in truth I felt merely chagrined and resentful of the fact that I was not the master of my own fate.

We rested nearly three weeks in Dar es Salaam while the primitive shipyard rendered repairs. I found it a pleasant place. The harbor was a horseshoe of sand beaches shaded by great palms; the town was little more than a village dominated by a fort that had been constructed by Portuguese slavers. Nothing of particular note happened to me during my visit there but forever afterward I recollected those few weeks with warm nostalgic ease. Many years later I returned there briefly and found my memories had not misled me; Dar es Salaam is indeed a lovely place.

We plied our way through Suez—my first experience of the canal— and stopped long enough to view the pyramids and sphinx; I was awed as all visitors have been since the beginning of time; we called in at Piraeus, then Naples, and I acquainted myself a bit with the antiquities of Athens and Rome, fleshing out their stone reminders with memories of my readings in the classics. We passed under the guns of Gibraltar and made our way up the Atlantic to Southampton and there, in January of 1872, I bade my shipmates farewell, took my luggage and pistols aboard a steam packet bound for the Americas, and—this time as a paying passenger—once again turned my face to the ocean.

I had a sort of goal, vague and ill-defined. I knew I could not spend the rest of my life on the drift. I had a longing to settle, to put down at least a tentative root. I could not return to my native country—not yet in any case. But I could linger close by, in a land that at least was familiar to me.

Steaming toward Mexico I had only a faint notion of the future and certainly I had no idea that I was bound for loves and adventures such as I had never dreamed of.

. . .

I went ashore in Veracruz on the fourth day of March 1872. I found it a hot and filthy place the stink of which offended my foreign nostrils intolerably. There were swarms of insects—they hovered over the open gutters and went for blood. And the beggars clustered like flies.

Huge carts with two wheels of solid wood hauled each day's bounty of corpses through the city. It was an abscess, a running sore. I bought a horse and set out immediately to get away from it, heading north, riding slowly in the heat.

I followed what roads I could find, heading inland; I had purchased a map of dubious accuracy and used it as a general guide, stopping occasionally at peons' farms to ask directions. My border Spanish had gone rusty with disuse but I found it coming back to me.

Along the deserted trails I practiced with my revolvers. I had plans for those; also it was bandit country and I did not intend to be taken helpless.

I rode without hurry into the borderlands that lay just south of the Arizona line. I knew the country a bit, having traveled there a few times with Tyree riders, and I recalled it as a land that was harsh in its climate but respectful of a man's privacies. Yaqui country for the most part—thinly settled, dry, wild. The idea of such a land held a metaphysical appeal just then; I needed that sort of demanding solitude, to test myself against the wild while I sorted out my life and tried to lay plans.

I arrived in the border town of Nogales on a bright warm afternoon and sat my horse on the Mexican side of the fence looking through at the other half of the town which was in Arizona Territory. A thin traffic of wagons and pedestrians passed through the border gate. Troopers of both armies stood guard and there were government officers inspecting those who crossed through. I remembered the inside of the American customhouse from my childhood: the walls were papered with shinplaster posters of wanted men. I had no doubt my own face was among them. It was the handicap of fame that I was too celebrated to be neglected by the government.

I knew I could get across the border easily enough if I chose to. But then I would have to sleep with one eye open and cocked permanently over my shoulder. I would not live like that.

I brooded upon the border gate for the longest time, after which I took myself off to a cantina.

. . .

I prescribed for myself a toot; I doubt I enjoyed it very much but it seemed the thing to do. After a period of revelry and at least one brawl I awoke when a door opened and the sun came in against me like an explosion. I squinted painfully at my visitor and had a vague image of a long-stemmed woman wearing velvet gloves up to the shoulders and a brown-red Spanish shawl. I examined the lace and upholstery of my surroundings and saw an embroidered sign in a frame: *"No vulgarity allowed in this establishment."*

The woman tossed me a glance on her way to the dressing table. She walked unsteadily; she was drunk. She said, "Your poke's in your trousers over there, safe and sound."

"Thank you kindly."

"Wasn't enough in it to be worth rolling you. But I'd take better care of it I was you." She prospected for pins in her hair, letting it fall loose, reaching for a brush.

I said, "Did I get your name?"

"You never asked. All you wanted to know was did I talk English. You said you was lonesome for somebody to talk English with."

"I'm asking now—what do you call yourself?"

"Unless I want me, I usually don't call."

But she took the edge off it with a soft smile and glanced at me in the mirror. Her hair was heavy, a long dark red like polished wood. She hauled the brush through it with long rhythmic strokes. "Name's Maggie."

"Thank you, Maggie. What do I owe you?"

"You paid downstairs in advance."

"This your place?"

"I just work here. For a while anyhow."

"You expect to move on from here?"

"Customers get tired of the same old faces."

Hauling on my trousers I counted the few coins in my poke and placed one of them on the dressing table at her elbow. It was a gold quarter-eagle.

She smiled a bit. "You can't afford that. It's more than you paid for the night."

"What day is it?"

"Tuesday, I expect. I ain't rightly sure."

Then I'd been hoorawing three or four days. The pain in my head and the taste on my tongue confirmed it.

"Well," I said, "thanks, Maggie," and I left her brushing out her hair and reeking of cheap whisky; I went into the painful sunshine and made my way down the outside staircase.

225

I had breakfast and coffee somewhere and had trouble recalling where I might have stabled the horse. Inquiries led me to a dirty stucco livery stable that might have been white once. I found my horse and tack there safe and sound, parted with a bit more of my money and rode up the street to have a last look at the border gate.

It was an unhappy symbol of my exile and I did not brood on it for long. I put my back to it and rode south.

The shriveled arm was always with me and that increased the darkness of my mood but mainly the thing that discomfited me was the fact that my friends were denied me. Like Caleb and Isaac and Bob. And Libby and the child I'd never seen.

There was no one left with whom I wanted to share my life. I wanted to be alone and to be left alone. I knew I must go into the desert and make peace with my spirits and demons so that in some way I might make myself whole again.

I still could not lift my arm from the shoulder. The incapacity turned many chores into extraordinary efforts. Saddling a horse was difficult; tying knots could be tricky. Things took twice the time they should have taken.

I rode several days across the manzanita and organ-pipe deserts of northern Sonora, switchbacking and doubling my trail, seeking I wasn't sure what; I had only the mystical sense I would know it when I found it. What I needed more than anything else was time. I needed time to put things back together.

I'd earned money at sea but most of it had been converted into possessions now: the horse and saddle, the guns, the provisions and traveling equipment.

Therefore when I entered the town of Altar I set myself up at the front of the largest cantina on the plaza and in a loud voice issued my shooting-match challenge.

Altar was a desert town, mostly flat-roofed 'dobes. The young bloods of the town had their look at me and were unimpressed. A half-crippled gringo was no match for them, they decided, and I was able to attract substantial wagers.

I had ten or twelve challengers and the match went off Saturday afternoon much as I had expected it to. I fired revolvers—Remingtons, they were—and my opponents fired everything from hunting rifles to smoothbore muskets. I collected my winnings and prepared to leave town but a man was standing by my horse when I got there. He had a bottle of whisky half empty in his fist and looked mean-drunk.

I had seen him watching the shooting match. He hadn't participated in it but he had prowled behind us balefully. He was very small, hollow-chested, sickly of features but there was a cold danger in his eyes I didn't like. He wore dusty trail clothes and a black gambler's hat and I could see the handles of various weapons protruding from portions of his clothing. He was a white man and when he spoke his accent placed him as a Southerner—soon I realized he was from Georgia. He seemed quite young but illness had ravaged him and it was hard to discern his age. In any case he was older than I.

"You're Hugh Cardiff," he announced without friendliness.

"That gives you the advantage."

He ignored that. "From what I read in the newspapers you're worth a couple of thousand dollars alive or dead."

"Not here."

"Well it's not a long ride across the border, is it?" He had a nasty smile—bad teeth, cold eyes. "You shoot pretty well, I observe, but it takes more than skill to face another man's gun. Doesn't it?"

I thought, *I don't intend to die in this no-account street.*

I took him for an opportunist—one of those gringos who stole cattle in the territory and ran them across the border, sold them to Mexican ranchers and then rustled Mexican cattle to sell in Arizona. As I learned later—because I saw photographs of him and recognized him from them —I was quite right in my estimation but there was more to him than that. He was a killer of some renown. Probably it's fortunate I didn't know that at the time, although I doubt it would have intimidated me very much. He was so clearly a twisted man who relied on meanness to terrify everyone; he was the kind of man who takes pleasure only in others' fear or pain. It was easily read on his face.

Yet strangely he had a cultivated way of speaking. Once he'd been an educated man.

He said to me, "It wasn't too sporting the way you took the yokels' money there. They had no way of knowing who you are."

"It wouldn't matter. Nobody likes to be told he can be outshot. He's got to see for himself."

"You made it expensive for those Mexes to see for themselves."

Despite his melodramatic menace I found myself amused. "And you're appointing yourself their protector, is that it? Looking for an excuse to justify killing me for the bounty."

"Guess I don't need much excuse." He lifted the bottle toward his lips. He held it in his left hand and I knew instinctively that the movement was a ruse to distract me from the right hand which now went inside his *charro* coat.

I did not waste time with speculations. I still had the Remington in my hand; I'd just finished reloading it when I'd come upon him; now I took a leaf from Caleb Rice's book and fired almost without lifting the revolver. It knocked off the heel of his boot and he was both amazed and off-balance; I leveled the revolver at full cock and told him to go away.

I watched his back as he limped away. When he was beyond easy range I leaped on my horse and spurred away.

I never saw him again. I learned some years later that he was Doc Holliday. When I made that discovery I remember it made me chuckle but I confess it also made a chill run the length of my spine. Holliday reputedly killed more than fifty men in his short consumptive lifetime. I count myself lucky not to have been one of them.

The encounter had importance to me for another reason than that. It reminded me that I was on the dodge—that there was a price on my head. The wild border country was flecked with men who wouldn't hesitate to shoot me asleep or in the back if they knew the size of the bounty on me. And it was clear from my chance encounter with the diminutive border-jumper that if I remained around the crossroads towns I would be recognized in short order.

So I avoided towns.

The April heat drove me into higher country and I was on the track of a small herd of deer, riding through a pine forest with desert below me and peaks above, when I came upon a clear trickling stream. The deer had watered here and crossed over. Probably they were still in the vicinity. But I still had meat from a kill a few days earlier and I knew game would be plentiful in these mountains when I needed it; I abandoned the spoor in favor of exploring the stream. From the richness of the vegetation along its banks I judged it was not a mere snow runoff from the higher peaks; it obviously was a year-round creek and that meant a spring at the headwaters.

The growth was so thick I had to ride in the bed of the stream; there was no space along the banks. I followed it through narrowing canyon walls that loomed above me to towering jagged heights until only a slit of sky remained visible. The forest and shrubbery fell away, giving way to bare rock cliffs in which a tuft of growth sprouted here and there in the odd crack. Still I climbed—curious; and I knew if the passage became too narrow I could still back out and turn around.

The horse became uneasy but I pressed on, spurring gently. The canyon ahead turned out of sight. I rode into the turning and saw the walls fall away to either side ahead of me. Through the wide wingspread of this high rocky notch I saw white peaks beyond.

Springs bubbled among the jumbled rocks. There were several pools. All but one flowed away toward the stream I had followed. The final spring fed another stream that flowed trickling down the back of the mountain I had climbed. It went looping sinuously down a broadening green canyon that opened out into an extraordinarily pretty little meadow surrounded by pine forests that lapped up onto the steep mountainsides all around.

In the center of the meadow I saw a town.

. . .

Once it must have bustled and thrived. Now it was only the bones of a carcass, bleached and weathered and half-collapsed. There were two or three buildings of substantial size—they must have been shops and cantinas in their day. The rest were shacks built of logs or hand-hewn boards. Most of the roofs had fallen in. Weeds and bushes had over-grown what must once have been the central street. The creek ran down its center, spanned by three footbridges; and I saw where the builders had laid rocks across the bed of the creek to make a ford for wagons.

The air was cool and crystal dry and carried the gentle scent of the surrounding pine woods. I rode slowly among the dead buildings. Here and there I spied the droppings of game animals that had wandered by.

Behind the buildings I saw tailings along one slope half-hidden by a second growth of young trees; at one time it had been timbered off, cleared to make room for the diggings. I found the mine workings—bits of machinery gone to solid rust; and several open shafts leading into the hillside. From the debris and the color of the tailings I assumed it had been a silver camp. The mines probably had played out, the citizens gone on to some newer strike. I estimated the town must have been abandoned for at least six or seven years, perhaps ten. Not much more than that. There was still precious glass in two windows of one of the store buildings, although most of the shacks had had paper windows the shreds of which remained around the edges of the openings.

There was no mention of the town on my map and I found no sign-posts anywhere that might have given it a name.

They had discovered ore here, probably long ago; I found a stone foundation that must have been at least a hundred years old, for a great huge pine tree grew out of it. They had bored their tunnels into the hill-sides, extracting the ore—probably a small operation at first, a handful of miners working with hand tools; then the population had grown, per-haps in the 1850s from the look of the buildings, and machinery had been brought in. None of it had been of any great size—if they'd had to pack it in through that narrow gorge over the top then they'd have been able to carry nothing that couldn't have been packed on the back of a mule. A few wagons—I found the wreckage of two of them—probably had been brought into the valley in pieces and assembled here for use within the community. There was no sign of any wagon road leading out of the meadow.

I rode a lazy circle around the ruins and then returned to explore the town more closely. I dismounted, hitched my horse before the biggest building and climbed onto its porch with care, testing the footing—I did not care to plunge through a rotted floorboard.

I crossed the porch gingerly. A big door half-open on rusted hinges. I reached for the latch—and heard the snarl and growl of a beast.

. . .

I lifted a revolver in my fist. Cocked it and spoke. "All right, dog, gentle down."

I eased into the doorway to have a look at the beast that had menaced me with its warning voice.

The dog came toward me suspiciously, circling slowly, its toenails clicking on the wooden floor. I could not see very well into the interior dimness. My first impression of the dog suggested it was high and lean. As it circled toward me I saw the long snout and powerful jaws, the erect ears—a high chest and low haunches; a bushy long tail. I recognized the breed—German, the Alsatian shepherd.

Closer now and I saw how emaciated the dog was: the ribs made clear outlines, the fur hung from pointed bones. There was a decaying smell in the place and at first I took it to be the stink of small dead animals the dog had killed for food.

"What are you doing here all by yourself, then?"

My voice seemed to encourage the dog. It stopped and cocked its head a bit to one side, watching me alertly; its tail twitched fitfully back and forth.

"All right, I mean you no harm. You want to let me come in?"

With a degree of suspicion, reserving its decision, the dog backed away a few paces and stood wagging its tail tentatively.

I took two steps into the place. My eyes had begun to accustom to the gloom. I saw a keg-and-plank bar running along one side of the room; a few crude tables and chairs.

Nothing else remained of the saloon's furnishings; not even lamps. Everything portable and useful must have been carried off by the miners when they abandoned the town.

The dog whimpered and scuttled abruptly toward the bar. It circled behind the bar and came in sight again, head to one side, tail whapping back and forth; it barked lightly and only once—an impatient call rather than a threat. Then it spun around in a quick circle and looked at me again.

It was telling me to come and look.

I approached cautiously, my revolver ready. I detoured a bit wide so as to be able to look behind the bar without approaching too close to the dog.

A man's body lay there. The source of the smell.

"All right, take it easy. I'll have a look."

230

I advanced without sudden movements. The dog stood between me and the corpse but it allowed me to get close enough to see.

The dead man was in an advanced state of decomposition. Bones showed through the shreds of flesh. A heavy brown beard lay matted against the front of his frayed shirt; he was fully clothed from galluses to hardrock boots. He wore a holster belt but there was no revolver in it.

The shaft of an arrow jutted from his chest.

"Nothing I can do for him, dog. I'm sorry. You've looked after him, have you? Kept the scavenger beasts away. You're a good dog then. But hungry as hell, I expect. Come on then, I've got meat on my saddle."

I walked slowly toward the door, not knowing if the dog would let me leave the building.

But the dog seemed to have taken my measure and determined that I wasn't a thief or an enemy. I went backward through the doorway to keep my eye and gun on him. He followed me across the sagging porch and sniffed at the fetlock of my horse while I drew a strip of dried meat from a saddlebag and tossed it onto the porch. The dog examined it with a careful nose for a time before taking the first tentative bite at it. Then he devoured it ravenously—in the sunlight I learned that the dog was male, and even more emaciated than I'd thought.

I parted with most of my remaining venison to satisfy the dog's hunger. Later I learned he was an accomplished hunter but he must have stayed close to his dead master for the past ten days or more. Loyalty had overcome hunger.

I examined the dead man from a discreet distance. The arrow rode high in his chest, too high to have killed him very quickly. He'd been shot somewhere else, possibly some distance from here, and had dragged himself into the saloon, perhaps to fort up. He'd lost his revolver and, if he'd had one, his rifle; by now they would be the property of the Apache who'd killed him. For it was an Apache arrow—identical to the one Kevin had taken from a Tyree steer years ago; I recalled how Grand-father Clement Tyree had identified the shape and design.

I buried the dead man and found it hard work one-armed but decency required it.

That night I made my camp in a small shack with an intact roof. I heard the dog whining about the grave. But later as I rolled into my blankets the dog trotted into my shack, sniffed at me and settled down to sleep across the doorstep.

I had gained a new companion.

． ． ．

The implications of the arrow disturbed me and I spent the next day exploring the little valley. The dog trailed after me, apparently content with my company. I was searching for Indian sign—for any indication that the Apache might use this valley regularly for camping or hiding out. But I found no suggestions of any Indian presence. I was forced to conclude that the dog's master must have been killed by a hunter.

That day I learned that the valley was indeed locked away from the world: the passage through which I had entered by the springs was the only passable route in or out. The remainder of the meadow was surrounded by pine forests that flowed up mountainsides so nearly vertical they might have been cliffs were it not for the trees growing out of them. On foot it would be possible to climb in or out of the valley that way; but no shod animal could do so.

We went—the dog and I—back out through the gorge and without difficulty I picked up the tracks of the whitetails I'd pursued the previous day. They hadn't gone far. I bagged a small buck and packed it back into the valley behind my saddle. On the way the dog scared up a cottontail rabbit. I heard it crashing around in the trees for quite some time; finally the dog reappeared with the rabbit in its jaws. We had both secured our suppers.

That afternoon I set about fixing up the shack as my home.

. . .

I made myself as comfortable as the primitive conditions allowed. I gave the dog a name—Jim—and before long he was responding to the name whenever I called him.

I poked through the abandoned diggings, thinking to spot a vein of ore and occupy my time digging silver out of the old shafts. But if I came across any silver I did not recognize it. A few flecks of shiny metallic substance proved, on examination in the sunlight, to be nothing more interesting than pyrites and mica. I had to admit I was not cut out for a prospector.

In the stream that ran down the far side of the mountain beyond the gorge I found a few slow deep pools where I was able to catch small fish. I occupied myself with hunting and fishing and rereading the few books in my pack. Weeks went by, then months. I did not reckon time. I was engaged in a period of spiritual recuperation; I felt it would have to choose its own pace; I was content to drift through those days with no particular immediate concerns or thoughts of the future. Jim was all the companionship I wanted; I held rambling conversations to which he would respond with frequent tail wags and the occasional grunt or sigh. He was quite a vocal dog and enjoyed being scratched about the ears.

He did have an unhappy fascination for skunks. Twice that summer and fall I had to scrub him down in the creek with soap I made from wood ashes and animal fats; even so I had to exile him from my camp for a week or more on each occasion until the stink died away. I would toss him a strip of meat now and then and he would slink away with it, thoroughly ashamed of himself—but still it didn't prevent him from tangling with another skunk.

Jim proved a comical character and by amusing me kept my spirits up. He was the best possible kind of friend for me at that time, for I could utter absolute rubbish to him without fear of contradiction. I would maunder on for hours, telling him of my burning unrequited passion for Libby Tyree Merriam and my equally burning vengeful hatred toward her brother Vern. I would tell him wild yarns of my fictitious days of Indian fighting on the plains.

In that manner the days passed and I felt my soul begin to heal.

My arm did not progress so well. I had little more use of it then than I'd had the day I'd been carried aboard ship at Perth Amboy. The half-crippled state vexed me but my life from day to day was content; and for the moment that was enough. Still, with no one to witness my failures I began to experiment by exercising the arm in various ways. For months on end I would throw a lariat over a tree limb, hook my left wrist in its loop and haul the arm up and down with that sort of pulley arrangement. At first it was exceedingly painful.

·   ·   ·

I took note of it when the nights grew cooler. We increased our hunting forays so as to lay in a stock of meat which I then cured to see us through the winter. I thought of moving to lower country but the idea had no appeal; I had wintered in the Tetons—this was far milder country than that. In the end we stayed put. The snow became quite deep for a time and the horse had difficulty finding sufficient forage but we managed, all of us emerging somewhat thinner in the spring but healthy enough.

I was more than ready by then for a sight of the elephant and I saddled the horse when the passes cleared. With Jim trotting along on one flank I rode down toward the desert in search of a town.

·   ·   ·

In the next few months I made several forays into the village of La Cruz. I became friendly with its citizens and they with me. It was a small place and poor but it sported two saloons and a ladies' boardinghouse because it lay upon the conjunction of several roads that led back to mining camps in the Sierra. The Juárez government was laying track through the district and it was expected the village would boom in the fall when the railway reached it.

In La Cruz I bartered my pistol skill for supplies, striking up challenges and winning bets. By my second trip I was reduced to matching shots with traveling strangers because the villagers were wise to me but they were a good-natured lot and held their tongues when pilgrims answered my soft challenges with braggadocio.

The village lay on the rim of the desert where the mountains began and this placed it on the border between Apache and Yaqui country. Of the two tribes it was difficult to say which was the more intimidating to the citizenry: the Apache were a more sophisticated and clever people but they were nomads and crossed the area very infrequently; the Yaqui were primitive—often they actually resorted to the use of rocks as weapons—but they were always there, hovering about the fringes of settlements, sometimes begging for handouts and at other times burning and killing. The Yaqui of that area were not like the proud Yaqui of the high country; these were castoffs, scavengers who had been expelled from the tribes for one reason or another. The real Yaqui, the people of the high Sierra, are a remarkable people from all accounts— to this day they remain formally at war with the government of Mexico and I see no likelihood the government will ever subjugate them; for the most part it doesn't bother to try, merely leaving the tribes to their high-altitude strongholds and giving them generous berth. But that is hearsay and not part of my story, for I never ventured into that country and have no personal experience of the Sierra Yaqui. My encounters were with the lowland renegades and they were an inferior crowd although we had to respect their energy sometimes. They are an uncannily strong people. Today you see many of them working in the ports along the Gulf of California; it is nothing for a Yaqui dockworker, hardly more than five feet tall and weighing not more than 150 pounds, to carry twice his weight in grain sacks or bales.

Our trouble started in June because El Presidente Juárez had died and the government became chaotic and flaccid after his passing. Juárez, the passionate Indian, seemed to have held allegiance mainly by the force of his will—he was not a dictator; he was loved. No one was prepared to believe he was dead; no one had much respect for his successor, a man whose name I do not even remember although I believe he clung to the presidency for more than four years before being overthrown by the strongman Díaz. In the meantime there was considerable confusion among the people and opportunism among local tinpot tyrants who took advantage of the federal weakness and imposed fierce reigns on their provinces. The faraway government seemed to devote all its energies to passing bills safeguarding Juárez's liberal reforms but none of the new laws were enforced and in fact there was no law at all except that imposed by the local strongmen. Our particular tyrant—a Sonoran governor named Ignacio Pesquiera—was a verminous creature interested solely in the aggrandizement of his own private wealth and power; the only forays his troops ever made into our part of the Sierra were pillaging expeditions. The citizens were on their own.

The Apache took advantage of the disappearance of *federales* from the area. For some years, in previous decades, the Sonoran authorities had paid bounties for Apache scalps. Memories of those times rankled the Apache wanderers and a number of warrior bands swept periodically through northern Sonora committing raids that were more vengeful than practical. The instigator of these expeditions was a shaman who went by the name of Geronimo.

In July 1873, making my fifth trip of the season into La Cruz, I saw firsthand the evidence of Geronimo's brigandage. I found the village smoking in ruins and not a soul left alive.

   . . .

The lingering smoke spooked my horse and I had to tether it firmly some distance from the ruins. I went forward on foot, the dog following with care lest he burn his footpads on embers.

They had burned everything to the ground except for a few adobe structures the walls of which remained. The fire had destroyed several acres of brush and not a single tree remained in the village; only black skeletons marked the places where mesquites and manzanitas had stood.

The church had been built by Franciscans in the seventeenth century and its thick walls stood blackened by soot but intact. Before I reached it my nostrils told me what I would find within.

Most of the villagers had forted up inside. Likely the attackers had fired the thick wooden doors with flaming arrows and then gone in through the breach. It probably had not taken long—there were few guns in the village—and the slaughter must have been intense for a brief time. I was repelled by the air of that place and could not enter; I stood in the doorway with my hand over my nose and called out several times. I was not surprised when I heard no groans or other reply. Probably most of them had been dead or dying before the Apache had swarmed inside; the fire had consumed all the pews and the smoke inside the church must have been suffocating.

There had been fifty-seven people in La Cruz, fifteen or twenty of them children. It was possible some had escaped; I had no way of counting corpses and no way of knowing how many might have been burned to cinders. But there was no living thing anywhere in that square mile of charred earth. The village no longer existed.

There was no use in my remaining there any longer. I called Jim and hurried back to my horse and put my back to that place.

I had known those people. To this day I can remember many of them —the simple humor with which they fended off the dismal hardships of their lives.

I was saddened and grieved; for a time I did not think kindly of the Apache.

That was the frame of mind I was in when I met Flower.

. . .

It pleased me to call my horse Old Red-Eye, inasmuch as the name amused me and didn't make any difference to the horse one way or the other. The beast was a nondescript bay gelding some three or four years old; I had purchased it in Veracruz because it was the first tractable horse I'd found for sale there and not because it held any particular appeal for me. It was not until some years later that I was able to develop affection for any horse; I found the animals utilitarian but cranky and incredibly stupid—I know of no other animal on the face of the earth that will let a man ride it to death, for example, and I cannot count the number of times I have been kicked, stomped, bitten, crushed against trees or fenceposts, and bucked off by horses. The lion tamer in his cage with chair, whip and pistol faces no more peril than the human who innocently approaches a saddled horse.

Old Red-Eye had proved to be an irritable beast much given to shying violently from the least alarm. Through patient training I had taught him not to be overly gun-shy but I had been unable to cure him of his visual nervousness; loud noises did not alarm him but any sudden visible movement sent him wild. I marvel in retrospect at how long I survived in the company of that horse.

We were climbing toward the high passes, still ten miles short of the creek that would lead me up toward my valley. I was following a faint and overgrown trail through the pine woods. The sun over my left shoulder flickered intermittently, keeping pace with our progress, dappling the forest with patches of light here and there; pine smell was strong in the tinder-dry air.

Ahead of me and slightly to the north of the trail a flock of birds burst chattering from their positions. Jim was running a bit ahead of me and he stopped on the trail with his ears erect; I saw him close his mouth to sniff the air. I drew rein and examined the shadows with suspicion: something had spooked those birds.

In the hope it might be a deer I lifted a revolver and gigged the horse forward at a walk with the reins draped across my left hand. I tried to see into the deep woods but the country was dense.

Then hell broke loose.

I had just a glimpse of movement to my right. Then the horse lunged without warning—a wild kicking bolt that caught me unawares. The horse dodged out from under me and I was tossed right off and pitched toward the trail.

I alighted no more clumsily than necessary, rolling as I struck. Freed of my weight the horse plunged away, heedless of the pungent oaths I shouted against him and his ancestors.

Then I saw the snake.

I heard Jim's warning yelp. The rattler was in deep shade at the edge of the trail; my fall had disturbed it; I heard its scales hiss on the pine needles as it slithered into its attack configuration, coiling. Its head lifted, tongue darting.

The revolver was in my hand but I had fallen with my weight on that arm and I was propped against it, revolver in the dirt. The snake whipped at my crippled left arm and I tried to twist away but hadn't the speed. I felt the startling jab of fangs.

I rolled violently onto my back. Partway I was dragging the diamondback with me; then the fangs retracted and the snake whipped back. My right hand was freed of my weight by then. I fired without hurry and decapitated the snake.

Behind me Jim was barking in earnest and I took it for excitement.

My mistake was not in looking that way.

I sat up with my attention upon the two pinpricks welling droplets from my forearm. Under my breath I was cursing Red-Eye again because he had bolted fifty yards away into the forest and I'd have need of the water canteen on the saddle.

Fitz Bragg taught me the best way of dealing with snakebite and I cocked the revolver to get it done. The dog was still barking but even so, behind that racket, my ears caught some hint of sound that alerted me. At that moment it leaped into my mind that I'd seen a flash of movement across the trail just before the horse had bucked. Red-Eye had shied toward the snake, not away from it—something else had spooked the horse.

I turned to look behind me and saw an Apache standing in a crouch with his rifle trained on the dog.

It was easy to see his dilemma. He had a single-shot rifle. One bullet: shoot the dog or shoot the man?

I leveled my revolver on him and spoke:

"Jim. All right, Jim."

The dog stopped barking and stood ready to spring, well back on his haunches, ears laid back. The tip of his tail twitched hesitantly. He was far from a vicious animal; probably he would not attack a man under any circumstances; but the Apache didn't know that.

He stood bolt-still, a big brown man, his rifle pointed at the dog and his bleak eyes staring down the muzzle of my cocked revolver. A blank mask had descended across his face: I had the drop and he was ready to die.

Recognition poked at my mind and finally broke through: the scar

of John Tyree's brand on the Indian's cheek; the way he held himself—
I knew him.

He was a decade older, full grown now, his shoulders full, stomach
muscles gnarled, hands immense on the rolling-block rifle.

I said, "Ibran."

His eyes changed shape at my use of his name.

"Why don't you put the rifle away," I said in Spanish. "You won't
kill me—you still owe me your life. Don't you recognize me?"

Then his right hand came away from the breech of the rifle and
touched the branded T and there flashed through my mind an image of
Vern Tyree's making a similar gesture at a wintry shooting match.

Ibran said in Spanish, "You put the brand on me."

He let the rifle down, propped it against a pine and stepped away
holding his hands wide, palms out. There was a sheath knife at his side—
he wore only a belted breechclout—and he lifted the knife from its scabbard. For a moment I misjudged his intentions and went tense, lifting
the revolver toward him; then he reversed the knife in his grasp, holding it by the blade—offered it to me and spoke in a grave voice:

"For the snakebite."

"This is faster." I aligned the revolver carefully and shot a burn
across my arm.

The stinging shock sent me reeling; tears burst from me. But with
luck the shot had exploded the venom out of the wound and I only
hoped I'd done it quickly enough to prevent the spread of poison
through the bloodstream.

"I'll want the knife soon. But first I've got to build a fire to cauter-
ize it."

Ibran did not understand all my words but I saw him turn without
any break in his expression and begin gathering deadwood.

⋅ ⋅ ⋅

In the distance I heard the faint barking of several dogs and the pound
of log drums and chanted songs. I thought I could feel a vibration of
bare feet thudding the distant earth; perhaps it was imagination or the
beat of my own pulse.

I looked past the campfire and saw Ibran drinking from a jug; it was
pulque and I had the raw taste of it on my own tongue. He watched me
as if he were peering into strong light: with his head down and his eyes
narrowed. He set the jug down and his movements were precise and
very slow because he was drunk and didn't want it to show.

Ibran looked at the woman who sat near him—to one side and
slightly behind. She seemed deep in thought; she didn't notice his attention. Something preoccupied her.

I was trying to strike a balance between sobriety and courtesy: it

238

would have been rude not to drink with him and ruder still to be slaughtered for a faux pas.

He had broken out the pulque after I cauterized the bullet track with the flat of his heated knife—we soaked my bandanna in the pulque and wrapped it around my forearm. It didn't have the sickening pungency of carbolic but it was cooling. After that it seemed pointless to cork the jug.

The woman had come into our camp silently and with the darkness. I hadn't seen her come. I looked up once to reach for the jug and she was there, sitting as she sat now.

After a while she had spoken to Ibran in the Apache tongue, which I didn't understand, and he had responded with monosyllables. The easy affection in her voice made me assume she must be his wife. She was a slender young woman in a long black Mexican dress buttoned severely up to the neck. She had a small dark face and a mass of untidy black hair.

He and I had held fitful and desultory dialogues; they were brief and tentative—strangers feeling each other out. I assumed he had participated in the massacre at La Cruz and I was uneasy in his company to say the least. I was curious why we had not entered the camp where the crowd of Apache was celebrating in the forest—I could see the glow of their fires—but when I asked him he only drank again without replying. I tried a little joke but it did not amuse him; later I learned that nothing did. He had a dark nature and seldom laughed.

We had sat in silence for a long interval. Finally I ventured to stir and Ibran's attention came around alertly. He had a resolute self-assurance that made him seem older than he was. He watched me with tight expectant eyes, as he might have watched someone with whom he intended to lock in mortal combat. Danger twanged in him.

He stood up carefully, turning to leave the fire, and the woman reached out and hooked the jug away from him. His eyes argued with her but in the end he acquiesced.

When he walked away the woman brought the jug to me and I had a small swallow, grateful because my throat still burned with a touch of the snake fever.

She sat down, her movements quite dainty; by the grace with which she gathered her skirt under her she might have been in a Philadelphia drawing room. From the beginning I had discerned compassion in her. I said, "Is this all as strange for you as it is for me?" I spoke in Spanish; I knew she understood the tongue for she had smiled at an earlier remark of mine.

She said, "Until two days ago I was in a convent with no thought of any of this."

239

I was amazed. "But your husband—"

"I have no husband." Then she understood. "He is my brother."

I was surprised. "You don't look like him."

"We have different fathers. His father was killed when Ibran was a baby." She looked off toward the woods into which Ibran had disappeared. Again a trick of the wind brought to me the pounding Indian ceremony. "They have killed a bear," she said and I understood immediately for I remembered Grandfather Clement's description of the Apache habit of placating the spirit of the dead bear with ritual celebration.

"Ibran's wife is in the Chiricahua place," she said. I knew the area she meant. It was a rocky tangle of mountains in southeast Arizona; the whites called it Cochise Stronghold. "Most of the people are there."

In an easy voice muted by a great sadness she told me her story. She'd been abducted by Mexicans when she was nine years old—there'd been an ambush, several Apache had died: it was a camp of women and children and old people—the Mexicans had fallen on it with savagery but they had spared the children, bearing them off, feeling this would punish the Apache more than murder would. She had been raised in a convent orphanage and was now sixteen years old. I had thought her older than that; the severe black dress had fooled me.

Ibran had married into an influential clan and by his prowess had become the hunting leader of a Chiricahua band—a rare honor for a man so young. He had been with, but not of, the band that had raided La Cruz. The raiders were not of his tribal clan. He had accompanied the party only because a whisky trader had told him his sister was in the church at La Cruz.

Luckily Ibran had known where to look for her and had found her before the others invaded the rectory. He had stood guard over her while the bloodshed went on about them.

Of Geronimo's drunken raiders few were fully grown. There was no science to the raid and in Ibran's gloomy view little point to it. Geronimo, the witch doctor, had invoked a savage spirit among his foolish young followers and they were bent on frightening Mexican and Anglo settlers off the old Apache hunting lands. Ibran felt the attacks would only provoke the settlers to retaliate more brutally than before and of course he was right but I have observed that those who mete out terror never seem to realize they are only inviting revenge.

There has been a lot of nonsense about Geronimo. The newspapers made him out to be a great tribal chief. He was nothing of the kind—not in the sense that Cochise was a chief. Geronimo was a shaman, a medicine man. To some of the foolish Apache youths he was a messiah.

240

In the hierarchy of the tribes he had no official standing whatever—to most of the Apache people he was a notorious sort of outlaw; our own nearest equivalent would be Jesse James.

Geronimo was a clever brigand but as a soldier he took no real interest in war; his interest was in battle. Victory in a fight enhanced a man's prestige—he was of that old school. He never pursued any real strategy unless one counts Jesse James's campaign of retribution against the railroad as a strategy. It amazed us all that Geronimo succeeded as long as he did; after all, he and his bands ran wild longer than Jesse and Frank did. When I was drinking pulque at Ibran's fire Geronimo was one of the dancers paying homage to the spirit of the bear less than a mile from me; and it would be thirteen more years before he was to be run to earth in the Sierra.

Ibran wanted no truck with Geronimo's outlaw band. Ibran had an honorable calling: he was a master hunter among a people who valued that art above all others. War was not his pleasure. He was a moody realist not given to wild pointless provocations. Still, he was of the People: on the trail he had taken me for a tracker who might be guiding soldiers to attack Geronimo's camp and he'd been ready enough to kill me then.

She said, "He still is troubled about you. He has no trust in gringos."

"Right now I have little trust in Apache," I replied. "I saw what they left of La Cruz."

"You shouldn't blame that on all Apache."

"And Ibran shouldn't distrust all gringos. It cuts both ways. I guess we can't help what we are. Look, I'm called Hugh Cardiff."

She repeated my name, finding it curious on her tongue; with the Mexican inflection my name was pronounced "Jew" and when I had laughed at that in La Cruz they had taken to calling me El Alto to avoid what they thought was embarrassment to me.

She said, "I am called Arisa in the tongue of the People. The Mexicans call me Flor."

"Flor for flower."

"*Como?*"

"In English it's Flower."

She pronounced it carefully. "I think I like that."

"Then that's what I'll call you. I give you that name and we'll keep it a secret just between ourselves."

It made her smile. Her eyes danced with mirth and I was captivated at once by her pleasure.

I said, "What will you do now? Go back with your brother or return to the convent?"

"The convent holds too little for me. I was going to leave. I was to enter the novitiate this year but I didn't want that. Their gods are not mine."

"Then you'll go back to your people."

"No. I was tainted by the Mexicans—that's how the People think. It is why we're camped here and the others are over there."

She was a pariah from both the Indians and the Mexicans—from the one because of her upbringing and from the other because of her birth. Yet she seemed to take the dilemma with equanimity.

I said, "Then what'll you do?"

She tipped her face to one side; a quizzical and dreamy smile—she still had child in her. "Perhaps I'll stay with you." It was tentative, coquettish.

Sometimes you make a snap decision that colors the rest of your life. I said, "I would like that."

.　.　.

The sensation-mongers have written that I took a wild squaw to my bed in the Sierra Madre. In many respects that was gross inaccuracy. Flower was hardly wild; she'd spent nearly half her life in the tutelage of the Sisters of St. Joseph and she was considerably more civilized than a good many white women I'd met along the frontier. In any case I didn't abduct the girl and make a slave of her as the journalists so leeringly implied.

She was a practical creature; it was a cool courtship aimed toward a marriage of convenience. To Flower I must have been more refuge than paramour—she counted it good fortune to be offered the company and protection of a man who did not despise her for her color or upbringing. As for me, I cannot pretend I was smitten with love for her but the long solitary winter had wearied me of my own company and I knew I could not suffer another season of loneliness.

Her brother was her guardian in the Apache law—both her parents were dead—and under normal circumstances he'd have been empowered to sell his sister into matrimony in exchange for a price that could be measured in horses or other property. And I could see that the bargain would be agreeable to Ibran because I was offering to relieve him of an unwanted responsibility.

Still, it was a grave thing to sell one's sister to an outsider who was not of the People. It was a hurdle across which Ibran was reluctant to jump.

Finally I said to him, "What does it take to be an Apache, then?"

.　.　.

On a foothill crest we drew up our horses and Ibran leaned forward to take my reins. "Get down, Car-dee." It was the way he pronounced my name, the closest his tongue could come.

I dismounted and had a look out at the hardpan and slickrock plain. Yellow-red monuments a thousand feet high stood upon it like the discarded toys of giants.

Ibran got off his horse and handed the reins of both animals up to Flower. Without a word she turned and rode away—back toward our camp. But Ibran said, "Wait."

She sat with her back to us. Ibran came around before me and held out his hand, palm up. I saw what he wanted: I gave him my revolver. But he stood without moving and then I understood. I removed the cartridge belt and gave him that too.

Ibran slipped the knife from my belt sheath and put it in my hand— there was a knife in the waistband of his own breechclout—and then he handed the firearms up to Flower, after which he inclined his head, granting her permission to go. Flower glanced at me—it might have been concern but then again it might have been my imagination—and then I watched her ride away toward the shaded canyon. She did not look back.

We stood evenly matched, each of us armed only with a knife. Ibran gestured with his face toward the plain of monuments. "I give you till the sun is highest."

I said, "Any water out there that you know of?"

"I have never been here, Car-dee."

"That's fair enough, then."

He did not smile, although I felt he was tempted to. He said, "You see the far mountain there."

It was only a pale grey suggestion in the horizon haze; it had to be at least fifty miles from us, northwest across the uneven plain. Ibran said, "An Apache can go from here to there by the time tomorrow when the sun is highest. Can you do this?"

On foot, I thought, and I'm not an Apache. But what I said was, "I can try."

"And if I catch you first I will try to stop you."

"That's understood."

"I won't kill you—I won't have to. But the desert may do it without my help."

I said, "You just worry about getting there yourself. The foot of the mountain?"

"Yes, the foot."

"I'll be waiting for you there." And I set out down the slope into the plain.

.   .   .

From the foothill crest the distant mountain had been visible; from the edge of the plain it was not, having dropped below the horizon, but

243

I'd taken my bearings on a red-rock monument spire with the distinctive shape of an inverted metal funnel. I did not run; it would have been foolhardy. This was July on the high desert—not as crushing hot as the flats of Arizona west of the Tyree Grant but respectable all the same. The scientists who measure weather almanacs set their mercury thermometers in the shade some distance above the earth and they record temperatures up around 100 degrees Fahrenheit in those regions; this means the actual temperature in the sun along the surface of the desert ranges as high as 140 degrees—that dry sucking heat that scorches the skin as if you opened the cast-iron door of a hot oven and thrust your face inside. No, I did not run; I did not lope; I walked. I had fifty miles to cross and I was not a complete fool.

The fifty miles would be more like seventy by the time I made my way around the various obstacles that stood across my course. There were cutbank gullies, vertical ridge cliffs and gigantic sandstone chess pieces: from a distance they looked negligible but some of them stood a thousand feet high and half a mile wide and only a fly could scale them.

At intervals along the bases of these monuments the runoff water of flash floods had carved arroyos a hundred feet deep with precipitous sides and treacherous rims. Sometimes you didn't see these openings in the earth until you were upon them and then there was no way to cross—it was necessary to backtrack and go around the long way.

Two hours after my start Ibran would come after me and it would be his intention to prevent my completing the journey. If he succeeded it would be taken as proof that I was not good enough to be an Apache and therefore not man enough to marry Ibran's sister.

The test of skill and endurance is a ritual older than Ulysses and it is still held in high regard among the Indians; never mind that it had little to do with my worth as a husband—it would have been pointless to argue the matter with Ibran. He had his own conscience to salve: giving one's sister to a white man was difficult enough; giving her to an unworthy white man would have been unthinkable.

For myself, I played Ibran's game for a different reason. Call it pride.

. . .

My objective during that scorching afternoon was mainly to keep ahead of Ibran. I intended to cover most of the ground in the cool of the night and tried to save my strength for that.

I therefore took the gamble of wasting time and distance during the hot afternoon by attempting to lay false trails and keep out of my pursuer's line of sight. It entailed keeping to the bottoms of dry arroyos for long meandering stretches; when I came to patches of soft clay I went across them in oblique directions, walking backward and sinking my heels hard so that the tracks made me appear to have gone in the opposite direction. I wasn't sure it would fool him but it might confuse him, send him up the wrong tributary and force him to expend ten minutes here and a half hour there chasing false clues.

The desert Apache is born and raised on foot—he would rather steal and sell horses than ride them—and no matter that my legs were longer than Ibran's, the fact remained I had a severe handicap in experience and training. I also was limited by the weak arm—it made for difficulty in climbing.

I had engorged my system with water in the morning. So had Ibran. If I came across water before dark I would avail myself of it but I didn't intend to lose time searching for it until later in the day; I knew the desert well enough to realize that the people who die of thirst are mainly those who surrender to panic. There are a dozen ways to find water in the desert; if you know none of them you can die in twelve hours but it takes an extraordinarily determined ignorance. The easiest mistake to make is to overexert the body.

Conserving energy I went along at a studied pace, kept off the high ground and devoted equal attention to the backtrail and the ground ahead. I could not rule out the possibility of his getting around in front of me and jumping me from ambush; I kept alert for that and went along steadily.

The contours of the land carried me off course at times but it couldn't be helped; in any case I meant to make my speed at night.

I had a hat to shield my face from the sun; Ibran did not. I had boots; he had soft moccasins. My stride was longer than his, my body larger and therefore capable of storing more fluids. In theory I had the advantage.

But theory meant nothing. Ibran was Apache.

I had no advantage over him; the advantage I held was a superiority to most white men who come from civilized backgrounds and find themselves unawares in the great desert. I was no stranger to the desert, having spent my youth in Arizona and learned the lore of the plains from Tyree's vaqueros and Fitz Bragg's crowd of frontiersmen. At least I knew the uselessness of stopping to search for water. You could die that way, going around in circles.

You could die anyway; it was always a heavy risk; in the desert the only certainty was death.

I saw him once, early in the afternoon. I was cheered to see he was some miles behind me, coming along with a loose loping stride, moving with the effortless grace of a puma.

He was moving more directly west than I was; if he kept to that course he would pass well to the south of my line of travel. I knew I couldn't count on that—he'd pick up my sign soon—but I was encouraged by the distance that still lay between us.

I knew he couldn't see me; I stood in the shadow of a towering cliff. Having discovered him I then made my way around the end of the cliff and struck out northwest, keeping the cliff between us so that for a while I did not need to keep to low ground. It would be an hour before he came past the far side of that mesa; it was an hour I put to good use even though it was the time of the day's most intense heat.

My feet were beginning to rub raw inside the hot boots and I spared the time to sit down, tug them off and wrap my stocking feet in an extra thickness of cloth torn from my bandanna; then I went on, taking my bearings from the sun.

In midafternoon I came across a patch of scattered barrel cactus. They were good sources of moisture but I passed them by; if I hacked one of them open Ibran would see it and know I'd passed this way. I preferred to keep my feet on the trackless slickrock and endure thirst for a few hours more.

I kept a pebble rolling around inside my mouth to stimulate the flow of saliva. I walked alternately with one eye closed and then the other to prevent the dry-burning of eyeballs. I kept alert for rodent holes—twist an ankle and you were dead.

When I came to a hard-packed jackrabbit trail I put my feet along it and followed it as far as I could before it turned perpendicular to my course; there was no way on earth an Apache or anyone else would ever discern man tracks on that rock-hard trail. I used that and a dozen other game-hunting stratagems, forcing him to search, giving him no easy track to follow. We were playing the game by Ibran's rules but I meant to win it.

At first it seemed easy.

. . .

By late afternoon I knew I'd been betrayed by overconfidence and I was remembering the time I'd run away from the Tyree Grant in pursuit of Isaac Singman. This time there'd be no Harry Dreier to pick me up.

I was stumbling and short of breath, moving fitfully in a fog of the mind. My calves had stiffened up—the cramps of dehydration—and inside my swollen mouth there was no longer any saliva for the pebble to provoke.

All day I'd been approaching the upside-down funnel of rock that had been my first chosen landmark. It stood out ahead of me now, perhaps a mile away, perhaps three; my ability to reckon distances was fading. I was on the floor of a wash and I knew if I simply kept to it I'd arrive at the foot of the funnel but by that point the walls of the wash might be a hundred feet high.

246

Nevertheless I decided to chance it. If I climbed out now I'd be exposing myself to Ibran's view from any point within six or seven miles behind me.

I made a pact with myself: as soon as I reached the foot of the funnel I would rest, search for water and replenish my juices before proceeding any farther.

It never occurred to me that I would not get beyond the funnel in my journey.

. . .

Nearly sunset. I felt drunk and faint; I went ahead one uncertain step at a time. The walls loomed above me and the sun did not reach down into the narrow arroyo but the close air pressed its heat against me. The walls, forty feet high on either side, stood no more than twenty feet apart and the washbed was loose sand through which I moved painfully—it sucked at my boots with every pace. Ibran would have no trouble finding my tracks here but I was beyond caring about that.

I did not turn back; I was gambling on one thing. The arroyo flowed out from the base of the funnel-shaped monument; the monument itself was a steep pinnacle rising from the cone of its half-mile base. During some thousands of years enough rain had fallen on the monument to carve the deep gorge through which I stumbled. This suggested the possibility of a water trap at the foot of the funnel: if that much water flowed off the monument then it might have scooped itself a pool at the base. If that were the case then the pool would have become an oasis for desert animals.

And if animals used it there had to be a game trail leading out of the arroyo.

There were no animal tracks in the sand; therefore I assumed the game trail was still ahead of me: a route of access up through some cut-away fault in one of the cliffs.

. . .

Just on sunset I found the game trail. It clung, an irregular narrow shelf, to the side of a jagged tributary canyon that led steeply up out of the main arroyo. Looking up into the tributary I could not see the top of the trail; it was hidden somewhere beyond the bends of the vertical walls. But the hooves and paws of small animals had worn the path smooth and there was no question but that it gave access to the upper world.

There was still some question whether the other end of the trail—down the main arroyo into the deep shadows ahead of me—led to water. Possibly it led to a wet-season water hole that only provided a holding tank for runoffs; if that were the case it would be subject to evaporation and only intermittently contain a supply of fresh water.

We'd had no rain in months. And the ground was too dry to reveal whether the animal tracks were fresh or several months old; this deep in the gorge there wasn't enough wind to drift them over.

I looked for other evidences. Little tufts of scrub growth sprouted from the jumbled rock along either side of the washbed; there were stunted clumps of salt bush and sage, rock cactus, undersized mesquite and catclaw and manzanita—everything spiny and dry. But when I looked more closely, blinking to clear the film from my vision, I could see where the salt bush had been nibbled near the game trail. The half-eaten leaves had not yet yellowed around the edges; it meant something —jackrabbit perhaps—had taken a recent snack.

My spirits buoyed by this clue, I pressed on into the darkness.

The sky was still the deep blue of sunset but no daylight penetrated down the narrow sixty-foot chasm to the floor. Moving blind, I groped forward with my fingers trailing the abrasive surface of the cliff, testing each step.

I smelled it then: water. It drew me forward with triumphant satisfaction.

. . .

It was full night-dark above me by the time I found the pool. High stars threw the faintest of illumination into the chasm; my eyes, accustoming to the night, sensed rather than saw the rocks and brush into which I otherwise would have blundered. Solid objects were heavier masses in the darkness. Here I found a profusion of mesquites, gnarled brittle trees hidden away in the depths of the gorge but giving evidence that underneath at root level there was nourishing moisture.

The mesquites had dropped their peapod summer beans onto the porous rock and I crunched them underfoot and then I came around a great square boulder and found the pocket in front of me. The waterfall had scooped out a wide smooth bowl in the bedrock. Starlight glinted, reflecting from the still water.

I went down the slick tilt of rock, slithering on my rump, boot heels chittering to brake my slide.

At the edge of the tank I got to my knees and cupped a handful of water and held it under my nose to get the smell: if it had gone poisonous I wanted to know. There were other ways to get water—you could cut cactus open, you could dig beneath the mesquite roots, you could bundle cholla in your shirt and roll it up and squeeze moisture from it. But this was easiest—if the water was not contaminated.

It was covered with a scum, brackish; but it smelled good enough.

I fanned my hand back and forth to break up the surface scum. Then I sank my face into the pool, drenched my head, drank slowly, splashed water over myself, drank again and sat back thinking of the pleasure it would be to remove my boots and soak my blistered feet. But that pleasure had to be forgone. If I took the boots off I'd not get them on again; and water would only soften the skin of my feet. I would just have to suffer the blisters.

I washed and drank yet again, filling myself slowly, and remained at the pool nearly an hour to recover my strength and clear my head. The long night's march lay ahead of me yet—and I was certain I wouldn't have the luck to come across surface water again.

I urinated against a mesquite and returned to the pool to gorge myself with water and then I left the place, limping a bit on sore feet but much restored. My confidence was renewed and alertness returned. When I reached the foot of the game trail I paused to keen the night, turning my head slowly to expose the flats of my ears to all directions. I didn't want to encounter an angry coyote or javelina on that narrow ledge.

I heard nothing and began to climb, hugging the wall and moving slowly up the steep pitch in starlit darkness. My mind explored ahead of me: once at the top I would have to circle the funnel monument and strike out northwest across the plain, probably another thirty miles yet to the mountain that marked the far rim of this desert. With good fortune and not too many blind-canyon backtracks I might be able to cover twenty of those miles before day broke; the last ten miles, therefore, would be the toughest. I had to measure my strength out with that in mind.

Something stirred—ahead and above me.

I went bolt-still. It had been the faintest of sounds; it might have been anything—a gust of air against catclaw, the distant flutter of an owl's wings. But I waited, pressed flat against the wall, listening for it again.

Then I heard the earth crumble and saw clots spill away from the cliff. A little avalanche tumbled past, clattering its way down, and afterward I heard the bounce and slide and thump and grunt of a man falling.

. . .

I found him at the foot of the slide. There was enough starlight to see him by—barely. He began to sit up and I couldn't help it: I laughed at him.

"That's a clumsy way to ambush a fellow."

He snarled at me and tried to get up but when he put his weight on one foot it collapsed under him and I heard the hiss of pain indrawn through his teeth. He sat down again and clutched his ankle protectively.

The laughter drained out of me and I crouched to test his ankle. He winced when I touched it but we both had to know and he made no protest when I wrapped my hand around the ankle and moved it.

He never cried out but his head lolled to one side—he almost passed out. I took my hand away and straightened up, leaned my back against the steep canyon wall and brooded at him. "Ibran, you broke the damn thing. Now that's a pretty foolish thing to do way out here."

"The earth gave way," he said. "It was my error. I should have tested it."

I was sure he must have tested the rim before putting his weight on it. A fault in the cliff had given way under him but no one could have foreseen that in the darkness and in a way he was merely saving face by putting on a brave front and taking the responsibility for it; it would have been a weakness to put the blame elsewhere.

I didn't argue the point with him. We had a more urgent problem.

"Let's get you down to the water tank."

"I can crawl that far."

"You'll cut your knees to ribbons on these rocks. Come on—give me a hand, put your arms up here."

Pride made him reluctant but finally he gave in. He locked his wrists behind my neck and I put my good arm under his knees and picked him up that way and carried him slowly down the bed of the tributary. When we reached the floor of the chasm the going was easier and I hauled him to the edge of the rock pool and set him down gently.

Our approach scattered several small animals; I heard their feet skittering softly on the rocks. Ibran drank from a cupped hand. Then he threw his head back to glare at me.

He said, "You did well up to now. For a gringo."

"You want me to go over to that mountain to prove I can do it?"

"I see no point in that. I can hardly stop you now. In any case"—he showed his teeth—"I have caught you, haven't I?"

"I wouldn't put it quite that way."

He said, "How long, Car-dee?"

"How long what?"

"Before I can walk on this."

"I'm not a doctor. Six weeks, two months—it'll need to be splinted. I don't know for sure."

"We can't live here that long. There isn't enough water."

"Maybe it'll rain. Sometimes it rains in August."

"If it rains, Car-dee, we will be killed in the flash flood."

"True."

"Then I think you should leave me here and go back and bring the horses." He shrugged. "Or just leave me here and go on your way." He said it with equanimity; I sensed no bitterness. The Apache are practical about such things.

I didn't like the idea of leaving him to go for the horses. A water tank this size would attract predators—javelina in packs, coyotes, perhaps puma. Pinned down by his broken ankle and armed only with a knife Ibran wouldn't stand much of a chance if he found himself between a mountain cat and the water.

Besides, I was thinking of Ibran's sister. Two months would be a hard wait for her, not knowing what might have happened to us.

I stood up. Ibran didn't look at me. "You're going, then?"

"No. I'll set a few snares."

"This is foolish, Car-dee."

"Yeah, maybe." I went back along the trail.

. . .

We were three days and nights in that place.

I set traps Indian-style with advice from Ibran: noose snares sprung from overhanging branches and balanced-rock figure-four snares tripped by an animal passing beneath the rock. These had to be built with meticulous balance but I had the good fortune to be working along an established game trail where I knew animals would pass by.

By the second morning we'd taken an assorted bag: a small female coyote, several rabbits, a big chuckwalla lizard and a tiny kit fox. Ibran was in a bit of a delirium but he made himself as useful as possible skinning out the pelts, scraping off every morsel of meat and fat that otherwise might rot its way through the skin. We hung both the meat and the skins to cure in the sun; we built a fire well away from the water hole and cooked the meat up.

My main goal was the manufacture of a water sack and we used the coyote skin for that, stitching it up with sinews and making a carrying strap of rabbit hide.

I made a kind of rigid calf-high boot of mesquite roots and strapped it tight about Ibran's ankle; it was the best I could do by way of a splint.

During the third day I cut the sun-hardened meat into chunks and filled my pockets with them. An hour before sunset I filled the water sack from the dwindling rock pool and carried it up the slope to the shelf where Ibran lay in the shade.

We had spoken very little during the three days. Once or twice he had uttered curt speeches—"You must go. Why are you hanging around here?" But it had taken both of us, yelling and waving our knives, to drive off a thirsty puma the second night and I knew we couldn't stay.

I slung the water sack over my shoulder and stood above him. "Come on, let's go."

"Where? How?"

"I'm going to carry you."

. . .

We probably made six miles that first night. The foothills didn't seem any closer in the morning.

I picked a cutbank where we could lie up for the day in such shade as there was. I was staggering with fatigue; my muscles were cramped and so weak I trembled. It was as if a white-hot ramrod had been pressed against my spine.

Ibran said, "You're a very big hombre, Car-dee, but you can't finish this. My weight will kill you. You must not be such a fool."

"Get some rest."

. . .

I had assumed it would take three nights' traveling to carry Ibran back across the twenty miles we had covered in one day on the outward journey but I knew we hadn't crossed more than five or six miles that first night; and on successive nights my strength wouldn't be as great. I had to think in terms of a four-night trek now; it meant reducing our water ration and conserving food. From the tremor in my muscles as I lay down I wasn't confident we'd make it at all.

I slept fitfully. Insects whined in the heat; I kept awakening and batting fruitlessly at the air about my ears. The furnace-hot air was hard to breathe.

By evening I was neither rested nor refreshed but I hooked Ibran over my shoulders, stood swaying a moment and then began to walk.

. . .

We went forward by slow stages. My endurance flagged and I had to stop at ever shorter intervals to lay him down and rest. My legs had gone rubbery and loose; my back burned with agony from walking stooped under his weight.

For a while I rode him belly-down across my right shoulder—it was uncomfortable for him but he didn't complain and at least I could walk straight up. But when he began to retch I knew I couldn't carry him any longer in that position.

He kept trying to persuade me to leave him. It wasn't a gesture of noble self-sacrifice; it was his Apache practicality—better that one survive than that both perish. But I'd set myself the challenge and I've never been one to give up easily.

Still I doubt we covered more than five miles that night.

. . .

I slept that day, too exhausted not to, and came awake only when the sun went down; it annoyed me because we'd lost an hour or two—I'd planned to be on our way by half-past five when the heat began to wane but it was after seven, sundown, by the time we set out. I had trouble hoisting him on my back and tried to limit the number of halts that night because each time I set him down I wasn't sure I'd be able to pick him up again.

. . .

My legs gave out two hours before dawn. I lay flat on my back, my body jerking like that of a chicken just beheaded. Vaguely I heard Ibran's calm admonishments: "You see you can't do it, Car-dee. You have tried but it's too much. You must leave me tonight."

"Here, drink. Eat. Get some rest. We'll lay over here."

. . .

As always we were in a gully's ineffectual shade—a dangerous place in flood season but no likelihood of that now; there were no clouds. I slept after a fashion, feverish, jerking myself awake at times. A blood-red haze washed over my eyes when I tried to open them.

There were heat sores everywhere on my body; my lips were taut and cracked, bleeding now and then. My feet had swollen beyond pain and I knew I would have to cut the boots off to remove them.

Late in the day I awoke and heard the distant rumor of travelers—click of hooves on stone, thin song of voices. I roused myself to peer over the lip of the bank. Ants crawled across my skin under the rancid tunic and I scratched at them while I squinted through the pain and tried to focus through the shimmering waves of heat.

Six riders, two pack animals. Dusty uniforms, tired horses—a bit less than a mile away, quartering toward the northern end of the foothill chain. They were cutting across a corner of the desert to shorten the route from the southern hills to the northern ones. Provincial *rurales*—it was too far to recognize the uniforms with certainty but I knew of no other body of troops that would travel this region.

Ibran was beside me propped on one foot, his elbows braced against the rim. "Go on, call them over."

"I guess not."

"They have horses—water."

"*Rurales?* You know what they do to Apache."

"You're not Apache."

"I haven't come this far to be killed by those pigs," I said. "They live by rape and looting—saving lives isn't their way. If I had a gun it might be different."

"Six of them?"

"I shoot six times better than any of those."

"All right, I believe you, Car-dee."

He gave in too easily; it alerted me and I wasn't surprised when he tried to leap up on the bank. He was waving one arm and filling his

253

lungs to shout when I knocked him back off the rim and fell atangle with him into the washbed. He grunted with pain. I clapped my palm across his mouth and glared at him. "Keep quiet now, all right?"

After a moment his eyes cooled and he blinked acquiescence. I let him go. "Hurt your ankle?"

"A little."

I sat up and went to the bank and peered cautiously over it—they might have seen the activity. But the line of riders continued steadily toward the north, bearing away from us now. I let them go.

We had a strong moon. About midnight I laid him down on the rim of an arroyo, knowing it would be easy to shoulder him again— all I had to do was climb down into the arroyo and slide him across my shoulders without having to stoop down. We had to cross the arroyo anyway.

I stood on the rim looking southeast to get my bearings. The Sierra peaks were outlined clearly against the night sky. It was harder to make out the shapes of the foothills but after a while they shifted into perspective around the edges of my vision: the trick is to keep the eyes moving and absorb impressions from the side angles because the eyes are keener there—any hunter knows as much.

We still had seven or eight miles to cross. Flower was waiting in the canyon with our horses. We had only to get that far.

Seven or eight miles. Not far at all. Come on then.

I sat on the edge and slid down, got my footing and dragged him onto my back. Carried him with difficulty through the deep loose sand of the washbed and flopped him onto the far bank. I had a little trouble climbing it. Then it was a matter of lifting him again.

Without a word he curled his good leg under him and extended a hand. I gave him my arm and he hoisted himself upright and stood hopping for balance. I stooped to get the back of my neck under his belly and then heaved upright—it took three tries but finally he was slung across me, my right arm across the backs of his knees, and we went on.

It was merely a matter of putting one foot down, shifting the weight, swinging the other foot forward and transferring the weight again.

There was nothing to think about but the next step and then the next one.

False dawn caught us resting on a slickrock hillside with no shade in sight this side of the foothills and that was still a good four miles away. Four miles is nothing; a man can walk it in an hour, a horse can

254

cover it in twenty minutes. But as I looked at it I realized it might as well have been four hundred.

We had another day's heat ahead of us and if we waited for dark before starting out to cross it we'd never make it: we were down to the last ounces of water and the last few cubes of dried meat.

I said in a hoarse whisper, "I'm going to drink all the water. Take a sip now—I'll finish the rest. I need the strength more than you do right now."

"You're a fool, Car-dee. I speak to you no more."

He refused the water and I was too tired to argue. I drank it down, every last drop, and tossed the water sack aside. "Now we'll go," I said.

That was the last time I lifted him onto my back. I carried him some distance through the growing dawn light—maybe as much as a mile. Then I fell and he rolled away from me and I lay staring stupidly back across the plain we'd crossed. My cheek was hard against the flinty soil and my eyes blinked slowly, full of gritty sand.

I rolled onto my rump and put my hand stiff-armed against the earth to rise but my legs betrayed me and it was a long while before I got them under me and stood upright, feet braced apart, knees locked to keep from falling. When I picked up one foot to turn I almost fell over.

Waving my arm for balance I got turned around and saw Ibran up on one knee. He said, "You won't give up, will you?"

"No."

"You mean to kill us both."

"No."

"Then come here. If we have to do this your way . . ."

I was half-certain he meant to use the knife on me—for what reason I can't imagine but my mind wasn't tracking clearly. Nothing made sense anymore. I did as he bade: stumbled across to him and stood weaving.

He groped at my arm and used it as a handhold to pull himself upright. I all but capsized.

We leaned against each other; his arm went across my shoulders.

"Now," he said, "we walk together."

In that manner we set out blindly toward the hills, Ibran using me as a crutch while I used his weight to keep my balance. A three-legged beast, we swung ourselves awkwardly forward a foot at a time while the sun climbed into its remorseless orbit.

A time came when my vision darkened. I am not certain whether it was sunset or whether my eyes went black in high daylight.

I remember the last of it as a blind hands-and-knees crawling; inch by slow inch, nothing left but stubborn will.

The crawling grew ever more difficult; I thought it was my infirmity. But then I realized we were climbing.

I squeezed my eyes shut and popped them open in an effort to clear my vision—and had a blurred image of hillsides all around, rocks and brush, Sierra peaks beyond, starlit sky.

The foothills.

I looked at Ibran. His eyes were shut. He moved blindly, one hand moving forward, then a knee: the mindless repetitive action of a mechanism left untended.

Nothing left in him but habit. I reached for his arm but he kept moving and my grip slid away, too weak to restrain him.

My mouth worked: I croaked at him—"Ibran, the canyon. Over there."

He did not hear me, I suppose. He was climbing a slope like an inchworm and the camp lay somewhere over to the left. I pursued him and we both moved like creatures trying to swim in quicksand. I could not catch him.

Then I heard footfalls and Flower was there. Cool water drenched our faces, gurgling from the canteen; she went whimpering from one to the other, laughing and weeping, and later when I felt her soft touch I cried faintly, "Hold me tighter, Flower, then it won't ache so hard."

. . .

We had shared a skirting of death and it brought a peculiar closeness into the camp during the two or three days while Flower ministered to us with mud poultices and gentle kindness. We reset Ibran's shattered ankle with hard scrub-oak splints and waited there, in no particular hurry, recovering till we could ride.

In the evenings at sunset Ibran would sit with the last rays of light against his copper-brown skin and chant his quiet songs to the sky and earth. I listened with some interest, although I did not understand the words, for I found a comforting peace in his easy colloquy with the spirits. I didn't understand much about Indian ritual or the pantheistic spirits of the Apache world but I was impressed by the dignified matter-of-fact simplicity of Ibran's attitude toward his deities. Later I would learn more about the crotchety inconsistent demons of his world—they were humorous, spiteful, indifferent, petty, vain.

Ibran concluded his song and hitched himself toward the fire. I was sitting with my arms wrapped around my knees. After a while Ibran said, "You never mock at our ways, Car-dee, and I don't forget that."

I probably smiled because then he said, "White men are always talking. From all quarters I hear speeches from the whites and no two are alike. I'll tell you, Car-dee; I trust you because you don't make speeches."

It made me laugh a little and I rolled back on one elbow, pulling a straw to chew. Flower skewered meat on a half-dozen mesquite spits.

256

It was then that Ibran spoke to me, softly and from his heart, with words that never left me. In years since then his words have been repeated and printed and are known today, I suppose, to many a schoolboy; thanks in part to our Wild West Show.

He said, "I'll tell you about white men, Car-dee. They mainly do two things—they take, and they lie. You know when the old people first saw the white man they were happy when he came. They exchanged gifts with him, they fed him, they showed him where the water was, they helped him—helped him find the game, helped him find his way home out of Apache country. They befriended him. And so he filled graves with our bones. The spirits have given us a clean country here but the white man spoils it and destroys it, and all he gives us in return is laws. I'll tell you, laws never provided a man with a tree or a buck deer or a trout or a drink of water. These whites come more and more, and they take more and more, and what they leave behind they make filthy. They've put a curse on the country and a curse on us, the few of us who may see a few days more. Listen. If the whites had a country that always belonged to them, and some other tribe came and tried to take it away by force, what do you think the whites would do? You think they would go sit somewhere on a reservation and wait for the other tribe to move them again? Since the first time the white men promised we would never be removed, we've been moved four times. I think maybe you better put the Apache on wheels and then you can run them around wherever you want."

. . .

It was one of the few jokes I ever heard him make. Most of the Indians I have met are humorous people but Ibran always took a dark somber view of things.

I can tell you one thing about Ibran and people like him—the Apache and the Indians, mostly, whom I have met across the country. We cheated them, did our best to deprive them of their dignity, outlawed them, murdered them. But we never were able to enslave them.

. . .

We rode back to my ghost-town valley. Ibran said, "It is twice now my life is yours."

"I wasn't figuring to keep books on it."

"What?"

I said, "We're friends—let's let it go at that." In the Spanish tongue it has more force and more meaning—*amigos*.

"*Amigos? Sí, pero no. Hermanos,* Car-dee. *Hermanos.*" Brothers.

We sealed that with a locked-arm handshake and Ibran accepted my purchase of Flower: the contract was executed gravely by the payment of several pelts, two pistols and a pouch of ammunition with which

Ibran rode up out of the valley. He looked back once or twice as if still uncertain about leaving his sister with a closemouthed bullheaded gringo but at the top he waved and then he was gone. I did not see him again for a long time.

. . .

Flower taught me tricks of wilderness life I had not known. For instance I remember she would spread our blankets on red-ant hills. I had been alarmed the first time she did that. The mountains provided lice and other bugs that came to inhabit blankets after a while. The red ants ate these vermin and afterward it was a simple matter to flick the ants off the blankets. For similar reasons she had encouraged several spiders to build webs in the corners of our house.

It was near the end of summer by then. We had got along together for several months and things between us were matter-of-fact. She knew my heart had been claimed long ago by a white girl whom I expected never to see again. It did not matter to Flower; Indians are not prisoners of romantic love the way whites are. Or at least I thought not.

I recall that day because of the blankets and the ants; I recall we had not found any game that day and therefore I went out again the next day with the dog. In the high pass we found spoor and late in the afternoon I shot a whitetail buck.

I cut slits down the hind legs between the bones and the strong tendons and jammed the front legs through the slits; then broke the bones of the forelegs and turned them sideways across the slits like crosspins, making a sling of the animal so that I could put my arms through and carry it on my back like a soldier's haversack. That is how it is done; my father had taught me.

During the next few days Flower made pemmican of the venison meat by drying it in strips in the sun and then pounding it into powder and mixing the powder with melted fat. She packed this paste into cakes with the addition of wild berries and herbs. Preserved in this manner the meat would keep indefinitely and help see us through the winter.

At that time we treated each other with the awkward hesitations and uncertainties of near-strangers. We were learning each other but it took place with caution and at times with reservations.

There was a kind of courtesy between us and after a while it began to irritate me but I could not see a proper way to break through it. She might feel I was criticizing her. She might resent that; she was dutiful and did everything that was required of her with good cheer. I did not want to offend her because I did not want to drive her away.

Like her brother she had a capacity for withdrawing into impenetrable moods. These were rare with her but when they occurred they alarmed me. On more than one occasion she went several days without speaking to me. She was not angry with me, merely gloomy; she went about her work efficiently enough but her face was blank and at times I would catch her gazing off into the distance and apparently not seeing anything at all except the demons inside her.

The autumn came and we grew busier laying in meat for the winter ahead. The nights grew cool; there was snow on the high peaks now. Soon it would come down to us. One evening I came in with a carcass across my shoulder and found her on our porch staring at nothing.

I spoke and she failed to respond. She was in one of her moods again and this time I couldn't take it. I dropped the carcass to the earth below the porch and looked up at her. "I don't know where you are but I want you to come back."

"Do you?" She spoke in a dull voice and her eyes slowly focused upon me.

"When you get like this I might as well be alone here for all the company you are."

"I thought you preferred it that way. Sometimes when you look at me I think you would prefer I was somewhere else."

"Now that's not true."

"I'm a burden to you. You have to kill twice as much meat to feed me. With your bad arm it's not easy for you to carry it."

"That's nonsense."

Then she said, "I've tried to be a good servant to you."

"Servant? You're a silly fool, then."

The dog trotted off to drink at the stream. I hung my pistol belt over the horse rail. Flower stood up at the edge of the rickety porch and put her arm around the pillar and leaned her cheek against it, regarding me gravely.

I studied her and I thought how lovely she was, how delicate and sweet. I said, "You're still not sure whether to trust me."

She didn't reply to that and I said, "Where's the wisdom in marrying a man if you can't trust him? Flower, are you afraid of me?" I put my hand against her ribs; if I had been able to I would have used both hands and lifted her down off the porch.

She looked down at me with a thoughtful frown. "No," she said—as if she were surprised by the realization—"I'm not afraid of you, I'm only afraid I may displease you."

"And what would happen if you did?"

"You'd send me away."

"And you don't want that because you've no place to go."

"I don't want that," she replied, "because I want to stay with you."

259

Through the deerskin cloth I felt the warmth of her skin. She said, "Someday you'll go back to your white woman," and I saw tears in the corners of her eyes before she averted her face to hide them.

I gave a little tug and she stepped down off the porch. I put my arm around her and held her against me. She spoke into the turned hollow of my neck: "You stay so cool to me except when we're in bed. It's not the way I thought white men were supposed to be with their women. In the books I've read . . ."

I squeezed her. I had to laugh. "Flower, I'm sorry. Here I kept thinking it was what you expected of me. I've been afraid . . ."

"Of what?"

"Afraid you'd leave."

Then we laughed.

. . .

The winter came hard that year but we hardly paid attention to that. We invented our own language like children and made our own jokes and did absurd spontaneous things as if we were mad.

We weren't snowed in; the world was snowed out. I didn't want to be anywhere else.

One morning we stood in the doorway in our wolfskins after exhausting ourselves pelting each other with snowballs. We were covered with clinging white daubs. Along the valley the deep banks glared painfully in the sunlight. I said, "A lot of folks feel things break about even for all of us. For example I've observed that we all get about the same amount of ice. The rich get it in the summertime and the rest of us get it in the winter."

She laughed and nuzzled against me. "You're such a wise man."

I squeezed her against me. "You give me so much, Flower."

"I do?"

"Dreams I've never had before. . . ."

"What dreams?"

I did not tell her just then. But she had given me a rebirth of purpose. I hunted a great deal that winter but half my expeditions were only excuses to get out of sight of the house, which we had turned into such a replica of a real house in a real town that it boasted curtains and even smelled of wood oil and soap and fireplace smoke just as I remembered the aroma of my home in Kentucky.

I would strike out as if to go hunting but in another part of the valley I had rigged my exercise pulley and I spent painful hours every day hoisting my left arm up and down. I saw no sign of progress but was convinced, by a belief I could not have explained, that if I simply kept the thing moving it would sooner or later get the idea.

It has been explained to me in subsequent years by Dr. Bogardus

260

and other physicians that I was not justified in my expectations of cure. I do not understand anatomical mechanics but apparently the damage to my joint had been so severe that most of the key muscles had been torn away from their foundations and had atrophied; shriveled away from their original anchors those muscles would never again be of use to me. Only small secondary tendons and muscles were left attached to my arm and collarbone; these muscles were not designed to do heavy work like lifting the entire arm. I therefore had no medical hope of recovering use of the limb.

But I did not know that; and had I known it I would not have believed it.

Because of what the ship's doctor had told me I realized that the bone joint itself—the socket and ball—was likely to be misshapen and fragile. I was careful not to crack it; by very slow and agonizing degrees over the months I increased the length of travel of the arm and it was not until that following spring that I dared lift the arm above shoulder level with the aid of the rope pulley.

I endured pain and much disappointment in those daily exercises but I kept at it because I've always been stubborn and I was determined that my affliction would not be permanent. And in the course of that winter—it happened so gradually I was hardly aware of any change— I began to have a small use of the arm. One day I picked up the bearskin coat we'd made for Flower and I was helping her into it when she gave me a strange and delighted look.

"You used both hands to do that."

. . .

Events had sidetracked my course but I had set out in life with the ambition to become the champion rifle shot of the world and it was still my goal, even then.

She scolded me. "You didn't have to do this in secret."

"I didn't want to look a fool."

"Nonsense. I'll help you—I'll pull your ropes for you. You have one flaw, my husband."

"Only one, is it?"

"You are filled with stubborn pride."

I held her close. "You're my good luck, aren't you?"

She pressed her cheek to my chest. "Thank you for marrying me. My child will need a strong father."

"Your child?"

"*Our* child. He will come in the summer, I think."

. . .

In the spring I saddled Old Red-Eye and went down into the plains dragging our pelts on a travois. I sold them in Caborca in exchange for a milch cow and staples and certain supplies I thought the child would need. I tried to scare up a few shooting matches and managed to shoot two or three peso contests—enough for a pair of striped stockings because Flower coveted such vanities.

Caborca was crowded with young men and old and with women whose gay finery strove to hide the lines of dissipation upon their faces. The town by lamplight was more lively than moral. I found it unappealing and left quickly even though it was my first visit to anything approximating civilization in two years unless I were to count my previous forays to La Cruz.

I filled my saddlebags with books, most of which were in Spanish; Flower would help me learn to read them. And I found two *norteamericano* newspapers—great prizes for which I happily paid outrageous sums.

Phipps Merriam, I learned, was campaigning for the Senate from Pennsylvania—he held a seat in Congress. I was not surprised but felt pangs and it was good I was away from Flower for Libby occupied my thoughts for the eight days on the trail.

There was another panic in my homeland to the north. People were out of work everywhere.

I read that Caleb Rice had tried briefly to return to theatrical entertaining on his own; but as I might have predicted he didn't take to it. In St. Louis he had got angry at the spotlight following him about the stage and finally he pulled out his revolver, replaced a blank cartridge with a real one, and quenched the lamp with the bullet. There was some pandemonium in the audience as a consequence and the incident marked the end of Caleb's career on the stage. According to the newspaper he had taken employment as deputy sheriff of Ford County, Kansas, the seat of which was Dodge City.

I spent eight days on the return journey because the milch cow would not be hurried. As I rode I swung the weak arm incessantly; I had made a habit of it and would swing the arm whenever I walked or rode.

Flower was delighted with her striped stockings and put them immediately on her shapely legs and went to a slack eddying pool at the edge of the stream to admire herself in its reflection—a feat that proved comical because she leaned forward until she fell into the water, after which she stood at odd angles in ankle-deep water trying to see herself. Then she had to hang her things out to dry; unclothed in the sun she was a vision to me and I had been a fortnight away and I suppose it was not odd that we took our pleasure straightaway by the stream bank.

She slept awhile afterward; I watched her come awake in the late afternoon—she was smiling to herself, her eyes half-closed; she looked

262

warm and lazy. I tickled her and she sat up laughing. She cupped a handful of water and threw it at me.

We came to share an adoration that was freed of sentimentality by its flavor of affectionate ridicule. Whenever I was feeling low she would say, "Tomorrow you will laugh or I will leave for forever." And I would say, "Leave me alone or I'll send you away forever." What had begun as our fear became our joke.

In the summer our boy was born. He was a healthy brown-skinned infant with the voice of a steam horn. We loved him very much and named him Michael Ibran after my father and his uncle. Inevitably I called him Mike, as my father had been called, but Flower did not like the sound of it and never called him anything but Michael Ibran.

．　．　．

Michael Ibran grew at an alarming rate and I had to make one perilous trip down into the plains and purchase two pack-mule loads of grain to supplement the milch cow's meager forage through the winter.

In the spring when the boy was ten months old we discussed the future. Should we move to a town where the child could grow up among ordinary people? I had all manner of fantasies of the things I would do with my son as he grew up. I did not wish him to grow to be a half-wild creature of the woods. But in a town they would call him a half-breed; they would look askance on his Apache mother and one-armed father; and there was the strong risk I would be recognized and murdered for bounty.

In the end we decided to remain in our lovely valley. We had our lives together and we had love among us.

．　．　．

My life in those mountain years has been chronicled by numerous journalists and dime novelists according to whom I embarked upon one death-defying adventure after another. There were reputed battles with grizzly bears, rustlers, outlaws, mountain lions, Mexican soldiers and Yaqui.

No such encounters took place in fact except for my meeting with Doc Holliday which I have described earlier.

From season to season we led unexceptional lives in which the most startling changes were gradual ones. My hair slowly went white—I was still quite young then—and Mike changed from a squalling infant to a cheerful little boy. He was robust and like any child given to fits of temper and disobedience but seldom to complaint or illness. I remember only a few occasions when we had to rub his chest with eucalyptus oil to treat his trivial childhood phlegms.

In the summer of 1876 when Mike was two years old I ran across a few newspapers and realized what an eventful year it was up north in the United States. Custer's command was wiped out that summer and even the Mexican villages were filled with talk about that; there'd been talk of Custer's running for the presidency and everyone knew who he was. Then just a few weeks later Wild Bill Hickok was shot to death in Deadwood. I learned subsequently from friends who had known Hickok that he had died drunk and half-blind and morose, shot in the back out of carelessness; there was a general feeling among his friends that he had invited it—the next thing to suicide. I am glad I didn't see him in those last years; I prefer to remember him as I knew him, filled with vitality and gusto. He died old at thirty-eight.

That same summer Jesse James and his gang of robbers were shot up in the town of Northfield, Minnesota, where they tried to rob two banks at once but only succeeded in losing six of their number to the determined townspeople—three of the robbers were shot to death and three others, the Younger brothers, were captured and sent to prison. Jesse and Frank got away and continued to rob banks for some years; but their doom was sealed at Northfield in 1876.

It was an eventful summer all around. In our own quiet hermitage we suffered the greatest tragedy of Mike's first few years—the death from natural causes of the dog Jim.

Mike wept and wailed at great length that day. By nightfall he had exhausted himself and I carried him to his bed, pressing my cheek to his and rocking my head so that my whiskers must have scraped him; he complained.

"Get your sleep, Mike. I mean it now."

We sat by his bed until he dropped off; he lay asleep as if he'd tripped while running in sand.

Flower said, "Let's get him another dog."

. . .

I remember our pleasures mostly; there were few moments of drama and the seasons tend to merge in my memories. We brought a pony colt up from Caborca but I am not sure now whether it was the same year as Jim's death or another. The boy learned to ride in any event; by the time he was five he was a better horseman than I'd been at twice his age.

When he was six I began to teach him to shoot. And we read constantly—Flower and I read to ourselves, to each other, to the boy.

The new dog was more frisky than Jim had been; Mike and the dog played games happily. It was a nondescript spotted dog I'd obtained from a farm on the plain; it had no interest in hunting and I missed old Jim's company on my meat-gathering forays. But we were content. My

264

son grew taller; my wife did not grow fatter. We read, we indulged in jokes and games, and I believe we'd have been happy to grow old together in that place without ever leaving it.

I am inclined to skim lightly over those years in this account because they have little place in my history which after all is intended mainly to set straight the nonsense that has been perpetrated by sensational writers. And I must confess in candor that many of my memories of those years are too sweet to share. To be sure my recollections are tinged with bittersweet because of the way the idyll ended.

   . . .

I had a great faith that one day I would be able to return to my native land with my head high. I had rehearsed numerous schemes in my mind. When Mr. Hayes was elected president I sent by post a letter of appeal to him. It provoked no reply at all. Hayes of course was an Ohioan and a Yankee; I expected nothing better but would have been foolish not to make the attempt.

Presidential indifference did not discourage my ambitions. I had learned a great deal of patience. I was prepared by then to think in terms of years rather than moments.

I continued to exercise my left arm and although I never discerned any progress from day to day or even from month to month, nevertheless I realized—as Flower had—that my strength was improving. I had full use of both hands now; my grip was as strong as it ever had been. Along my chest and back a curious ridgework of musculature disturbed the surface of the skin, giving me a knotted look on that side of my body—I retain that ugliness to this day; there are lumps of muscle lying across the top of my left shoulder that give me a distinct imbalance, as though that shoulder is higher than the other, and in later years my tailors were forced to pad the right shoulders of my clothing in compensation.

What happened to me in those years was explained by Dr. Bogardus when he examined me some years afterward and observed incredulously that I was making small secondary muscles do the work of the great original tissues. I understand the specifics only vaguely; I know, however, that I never lost faith in my power to recuperate and regenerate. And by the time I began to teach my son to shoot, we were both able to lift our rifles.

   . . .

I see no point in dwelling upon it. In the summer of Mike's seventh birthday we made one of our infrequent trips to Caborca to stock up on staples and those few items of comfort that we could not provide for ourselves from the valley's bounty. There was some talk of fever in the area but we were not particularly alarmed; there were always illnesses rampant in that poor country.

We made our purchases and left to return to the mountains. By the time we reached our valley both woman and child were ill. Flower thought it would pass; and in any case I could not leave them alone for the days it would take me to find a doctor.

In a shockingly short time the smallpox killed them both.

. . .

I buried them on the hillside above our town. The view from there was lovely and it had been Flower's favorite spot in the valley.

My loss was complete. I can write nothing here that would convey the depth of that grief; I shall not try.

I lasted out the next weeks in the valley because I hadn't the will to go elsewhere but the pretty place was redolent with memories that brought me frequently to tears.

Driven by ghosts I began to assemble my few belongings, preparing to leave. I hope today the place remains as it was then, as I remember its beauty in the days when Flower and Mike explored it with me.

I was packed and ready to depart when I heard the dog's warning grunt and turned to see two horsemen descending from the springs, hooves throwing a bit of dust. They were coming openly but nevertheless I was glad of the revolvers in my belt: the long years in the hermitage had made a xenophobe of me and I suspected the worst at once—bounty hunters perhaps.

But as they drew nearer I recognized them, not without pleasure—Al Sieber, whom I had met only once, and my beaming old friend Fitz Bragg.

. . .

Fitz was riding a very old pony with a brush-scarred saddle and a dilapidated cracked-leather bridle both of which looked newer and easier used than Fitz's costume, which was greasy and ragged—his buckskin trousers reached only halfway to his ankles, evidently having been shrunk by too many rains, and the elbows of his pale red union suit showed through holes in the sleeves of his ancient army greatcoat. He carried a Hawken rifle that looked to be the granddaddy of the one with which I had won the Denver shooting match where I'd first met him.

Nevertheless he still moved with panther grace and his smile came quick and often.

Sieber was even more disagreeable and disreputable in appearance than I remembered him. His limp was accentuated, he seemed to have accumulated new scars on top of the old ones, and his hair mostly had fallen out altogether. Whether in English or in Spanish he still talked with an atrocious thick German accent. He was fully twenty years Fitz's junior but Sieber managed to look the older of the two.

We sat before the fireplace in my cabin, for the mountain evenings were always chill. I had imparted the news to them of my loss and Fitz had embraced me with silent compassion after which he produced from his pack a jug of pulque which we set out to exhaust. In a transparent attempt to cheer me up Fitz launched into a determined monologue that proved, if nothing else, that he had not tamed his ghastly sense of humor.

"Old Pete Rubio was a fine scout we had working for us out of Fort Lowell there, had only one weakness and that was an inclination toward bad whisky. He got to be damn near useless for the drinking and I knowed I had to cure him or lose him.

"So I went up into the Santa Catalinas there and like to kilt myself roping a big old black bear. Took me six days dragging that bear down to the fort—had seven, eight fellows helping me there—and we slipped a Mickey Finn to him. The bear, I mean. Knocked him right out and manhandled him into Pete Rubio's bed when Pete was sleeping one off.

"We was at old Pete's window watching there when he woke up and caught sight of his sleeping companion.

"Pete didn't bother to reach for his pants. He just run out in his trapdoor johns and crashed right into a trooper happened to be carrying a full tray of bottles for the officers' mess. They all bust but one and Pete emptied that one right down his throat before we could get to him.

"So we turned the old bear loose and then a Mexican traveler come through with one of them grind organs and a pet monkey. We borrowed the monkey off him and I chained the monkey onto the footboard of Pete's bed. Old Pete wakes up, he cocks one eye at that there monkey and the next thing we know he's taking aim with his six-gun and talking real grave-like, though there wasn't nobody in the room but him and the monkey. We was watching from outside the window. Old Pete says, 'If you ain't a monkey there, I reckon I'm in a bad fix. But if you *is* a monkey then *you* in a bad fix.' Then old Pete let off a rip-roaring barrage. One of them bullets killed that old monkey dead as yesterday and it cost me two months' pay to square it with the Mexican owned him. But Pete also succeeded in blowing off two of his own toes and for a while I thought we had him cured of drink.

"It wasn't so. He got himself drunk, real bad *borracho* drunk just the very next week, so I knowed we had to do something extra special for him. What we done, we waited till he drunk himself out cold and then we toted him along to the sutler's back room. Now we scared up some face powder from one of the officers' wives and let me tell you that was the hardest part of it right there—that stuff's harder to come by on an army barracks than gold dust. But we obtained it, had to pay Mrs. Archibald ten good dollars for it, and we went ahead and powdered old Pete Rubio good."

Fitz came down with a fit of laughing and we had to wait it out. When he got a grip on himself he resumed:

"We powdered his old face dead-white, you know, and then we dressed him up in his best Sunday black and we laid him out in an open coffin. Then we hung a mirror right over the coffin so's he could see himself and we all lined up to view old Pete lying in state.

"You should've seen his face when he woke up."

"Did it cure him?"

"Well sir I regret to say it didn't work out just the way we planned. It seems old Pete was so relieved to find himself alive he lit out for the sutler's bar and bought drinks for the house."

Al Sieber said mildly, "It was a waste of good energy anyhow because last month he went and got himself shot to death by Apache."

. . .

In the morning I tended the horses and returned to the house to find Fitz pouring coffee. Al Sieber was still fast asleep, working off the pulque. Fitz managed a subdued grin. "*Qué pasa,* Hugh boy?"

"I was fixing to ask you the same question."

Through the open door Fitz indicated his dilapidated horse. Then he pointed around to his saddle and rifle. Then he indicated his threadbare clothes. "You can see how I prosper, son. What you see is all there is—seventy years' gathering."

It made a profound impression on me and I recollected it often over the years.

Al Sieber sat up. "After breakfast we have a talk."

. . .

We went along the abandoned street scuffing soil with our boots. A pair of binoculars hung by a strap from Sieber's gnarled neck; he limped along, slow-moving with evident pains, and the best his scarred face could do for expression was to twitch now and then as if to drive away flies. But his eyes—pale blue and set in deep weathered folds—were among the brightest and cruelest I'd ever faced.

Finally he led the way over to one of the old buildings and sat down with a grunt of relief on the crumbling porch. "Beautiful morning," he asserted, giving the sky half a second's uninterested scrutiny.

Musing, Fitz Bragg said, "Up on the plains the railroads done drove the price of hides up to five dollars apiece. Some years ago, but I expect you been out of touch, son. Been a big shoot-up there where we used to hunt. In three seasons I hear they slaughtered near five million buffalo. See, the railroads make their money off settlers and they can't get settlers if there's mad-angry Indians so I guess they decided to starve the Indians off the plains by doing away with the buffalo. You remember how we used to talk about Manifest Destiny, Hugh? Well that's sure what we got. They kicked the Sioux up into Canada and the Cheyenne, the Arapaho, the rest of 'em down to the Nations. It seems like the up-standing citizens down our way, over to Arizona Territory, taken the same kind of idea in mind, and we got orders a while ago to move the Apache off the south reservation there and shift them up to Camp Verde north of Phoenix, over east of Prescott in that desert wash country."

I said, "Did you put them on wheels?"

"What?"

"Nothing. Something somebody said to me once."

"Hugh, we want to ask you for a little help. I know this ain't a fitting time for it, what with your grief and all, but—"

"What kind of help?"

Looking awkwardly at Sieber he hitched at his trousers with the flats of his wrists and then his hand described an arc encompassing the mountains above us. "You've hunted these hills awhile. Down in Caborca they told us you been up here nigh on a dog's age. You know this country."

"And?"

"Well it's kind of like this, Hugh old son. We, uh . . ."

Al Sieber stood up and pulled his Levi's down from his crotch. "I will say it straight, Mr. Cardiff. After the removal notice numerous Apache jumped the reservation."

"Which is understandable."

"I agree. But we have a job, your friend and me. We are paid to protect white people. Now we have got the Apache Kid running loose over in Chiricahua country with a crowd of killer Indians and we have got Geronimo loose over in New Mexico someplace with a hundred Mimbrenos and Jicarillas. Hell has busted out, Mr. Cardiff, and many people is getting killed."

"I'm sorry about that but what do you want from me?"

"We have also an Apache problem here got. Here is this range, in the Sierra. There is a rough band, mostly Chiricahua young men who have been peaceful hunters. They have made a war now. Somewhere in these mountains they have a *ranchería* that they use for a base. From here they are raiding across the border. They've burned places and stole horses and killed some people."

Fitz said, "What he means, Hugh, we've got plenty good scouts but none of them know this country here."

I was astonished. "You want me to scout for the American army?"

"Yes."

"Hell, you're in Mexico. You can't bring troops down here."

"No troops. We bring the scout company," Sieber said. "Indians mostly, a few Mex and breed scouts."

"How many Apache in this *rancheria?*"

"Maybe forty, maybe sixty."

"Scout troop, that's what—twenty men?"

"Twenty-four."

I said, "You're crazy, you know."

"We don't fight them this time," Sieber said, "we talk to them."

I was looking at Fitz's face; his evasiveness gave me a premonition and I said abruptly, "It's Ibran. You're asking me to hunt down my own brother-in-law."

Fitz nodded weary assent. "For his own good, boy."

I laughed bitterly in his face.

Fitz scowled at me. "Look, old son, sooner or later we going to run him down anyway. We got permission here from Mexico City and from this Pesquiera in Sonora. We can spend all summer tracking—in the end Ibran's going to get dragged home or killed, ain't no other choice to it. Now the quicker we catch him up, the easier on him."

Sieber pointed toward the pass where the springs were. "Our scout company is on the other side camped. We can ride today if you've a mind to."

In a kinder voice Fitz said, "We got orders from the army, Hugh. We got to go after him with or without your help."

Sieber was still looking toward the pass. He said, "Five, six years ago was a massacre at La Cruz not far from here."

"Ibran wasn't part of that."

"Ibran is Apache—that's mostly what the Mexes know about him. The Mexes catch Ibran before we do . . ."

He didn't have to finish that. His eyes rolled around owlishly toward me and just then I hated the old German. I said, "You want me to ride for the Yankee army when the Yankee government's still got a price on my head so I can't go home."

Fitz said, "That ain't fair, Hugh. Wasn't Al Sieber or me that put a bounty on you. And you don't see us down here collecting it either, do you?" Then he smiled, not without warmth. "I expect we got you between a rock and a hard place. I'm sorry a bit but you ain't got much choice but to help us out."

Sieber said, "For this job you get temporary commission, deputy chief of scouts. That carries the rank of lieutenant colonel and the pay is three dollars fifty a day and found."

"Lieutenant Colonel in the Yankee army." I laughed out loud.

Sieber gave me an odd look—sour, perhaps pitying. Then he said, "There has been a treaty signed. Between Washington and Mexico City. For the extradition of criminals it provides."

Fitz wheeled to face him. "You wasn't going to use that, Al."

Ignoring him Sieber went right on: "The army is prepared to pass the Hugh Cardiff warrant to the authorities of Mexico and request that you be arrested and extradited to the United States of America."

I said, "But if I go along with you there won't be any extradition."

"That is so."

"You bastard."

"You can shoot me down, perhaps, but it will not help. This was not my idea."

"Whose was it?"

"General Miles."

"He the one you answer to?" I asked.

"Yes. I am chief of scouts for his regiment here."

I knew of the general. Nelson A. Miles. He had a fine reputation and I knew he had the ear of Phil Sheridan who was in command of all the frontier armies and answered directly to Washington. I knew also, from the newspapers I'd gathered on that last fateful trip to town, that the political flavor of Washington had changed: a reform wing under Garfield had won the election; Garfield had been assassinated and the Vice-President, a man named Chester Arthur, had become President. Arthur had not served in the Union army.

My thinking just then was cold and deliberate. My family had been taken from me and now even the dubious freedom of my exile was being threatened. I wanted to be left alone but that was impossible; my only alternative was to fight and I did so.

I said, "I've been on the dodge a third of my life from a fugitive warrant that's nearly twenty years old and based on false evidence."

"I cannot help that."

I said, "I'll do the job for you, Sieber, on one condition."

"Yes?"

"I want a pardon from the President."

. . .

Sieber said evenly, "I ain't the President."

"You want me to do you a service. Then you do me one."

"I can't anything promise."

"You can promise to take it up with Miles and Sheridan and make a strong case for me. Look, Sieber, if I bring this off you can tell the generals they owe me one Indian war that didn't happen."

"You think a great deal of your importance."

"Well you see where shy modesty got me. I'm sitting here in a ghost town begging a favor of a cripple."

"You got a funny way of asking for it."

"I'm not asking you, Sieber. You owe me."

"Suppose I say no?"

"Then you'll have to chase me. You and the Mexican army both."

Sieber looked at me awhile and then went through the elaborate mechanisms of getting to his feet. When he was as upright as he was going to get he said, "I will talk to Miles and I will make him promise he talks to Sheridan. Beyond Sheridan I cannot anything promise. You know that."

Fitz said quietly, "I'll see he puts his shoulder to it, Hugh."

Sieber gave him a brief look and Fitz smiled coolly at him. Sieber said, "I have given my word to the man. I don't keep my word by half measures, you know that."

"Yeah, I know it but Hugh don't." Fitz said to me, "Al keeps his word, Hugh. He'll do it."

It was the best I was going to get. I said, "All right."

．　．　．

The village in the distance was like a crusted sore on the drab earth. The sun, only two diameters above the horizon, drew the sweat out of us. Dust rose into my eyes and teeth as we cantered forward. Two dozen men in a ragged double file.

The tracks turned southwest. From the quantity of windblown dust that had filled in the hoofprints I could tell how long ago they had passed here but I didn't need to speak; there wasn't a man in the company who couldn't read sand as well as I could.

Knowing where to look I had led the scout troop on the second day to a mountain valley I'd hunted twice. It was my third choice and proved the right one; we'd found their ample spoor—they'd made no effort to conceal the evidence they'd been there. But we were a few days too late and their tracks led us down out of the mountains and now we were tracking the band along a sand plain. I was puzzled because they had come down off the Sierra and rambled unhurriedly about the desert and now seemed to be circling back toward the mountains. The aimlessness did not make sense.

Off to our left the hot little desert village had a cemetery look. The Indian party had skirted well around it—almost as if they were deliberately avoiding confrontation.

Toward noon we scented the bitter aftersmell of fire and came over a hill to find a burned-out farm, a place of not much account; a dried old man sat off away from the ashes a bit, gaping at us empty-eyed as we approached. We stepped down and the old peasant told us a simple story—the Apache had come, they'd burned him out, they'd stolen his half-dozen horses and ridden away. They'd taken his rifle away from him and left him to watch; they hadn't molested him.

We climbed into the foothills. The track was much fresher now. We came upon green horse droppings, soft and warm. Vivid-hued butterflies hovered around the fresh dung.

In midafternoon with the Sierra looming above us we made a halt. I sat down under the trivial shade of a creosote bush and tugged off my boots to cool my feet, which smelled like strong vinegar by then; we'd been trailing five days. Fitz went off to water the desert with his urine and when he came back, buttoning his pants, he said, "Your old brother-in-law might's well have sent out engraved invitations."

I nodded gloomy agreement. A bird passed overhead with a steady wingbeat and I rubbed my face, which was covered with dust and insect bites; it felt hot and prickly.

A lizard sat in the shade under a rock, the pulse beating in its throat. In the silence I didn't hear Al Sieber's approach behind me and I was startled when he said, "The thing is, the Apache want a fight and we do not. We must remember this."

Up in that mountain meadow where we had cut their sign we had seen the ashes of big fires and the worn-earth indications that ceremonies had taken place. Summoning strength from witchcraft. Appeasing the spirits. Calling down wrath upon their enemies and invincibility upon themselves.

Then Ibran had led them down off the mountains, heading north. Intending to cross the border and raise hell but then they'd discovered we were behind them—probably they'd kept a watch on their backtrail and one of them had seen us riding down toward the desert. Now Ibran knew he was pursued. The knowledge had changed his plans. They must have decided to give us a trail to follow. They'd burned out the old peasant's farm to goad us; that was the only reason for it—they'd nothing against the farmer; otherwise they'd have killed him. They wanted us angry so they hung back, letting us catch up close, and they burned out the farmer and rode into the mountains and now they were waiting for us to chase them into their ambush.

Fitz was squinting up at the Sierra close ahead of us. "Perfect for it, I reckon. Timber country an hour ahead. What you think, Albert, maybe we lay over here till morning?"

Sieber came around in front of me and poked a finger toward me. "Is your country, is your brother-in-law. What you think?"

273

I knew Ibran well enough—knew his forbearance and his gloomy moods. It took a great deal to stimulate his rage but once kindled it would burn hot.

I had to agree with Sieber. "He wants a fight. He was heading for that town back there but then he saw us coming along behind him and decided we'd make a better fight for him."

"He ain't chicken, that's for sure," Fitz said, not without admiration. "That town would've been easier than us."

I searched the sunlit mountains above us. I shook my head at Sieber. "I never heard of anybody ever sneaking up on an Apache."

"Well I done it plenty times. Snuck up on you just now, didn't I?"

"I'm not Apache."

"Closest thing to it right now," Sieber said. "How long you been these mountains hunting? Nine year? Ten? You move like Indian, I see that all right." He pointed toward the peaks. "Now think like *him*."

I said, "You ever meet Ibran?"

"No. You're the only one among us knows him by sight."

"I don't belong here, I swear." I turned full circle on my heels to survey the horizons. Then I looked at Sieber's crew of army scouts. They slouched resentfully in patches of shade, sucking canteens or drowsing. Sieber treated them with contempt. They were Papago and Anglo and Mexican and Pima and Navajo and Yaqui and a few turn-coat Apache. There were no Negroes among them because the line troopers of the regular cavalry regiments were Negroes and it would have been a breach of treaty to bring regulars across the border and Sieber had left his Negro scouts behind because he didn't want mis-understandings.

They were dressed in oddments of clothing—not uniformed but they wore enough cast-off Yankee garb to identify them for what they were. Here and there a forage cap or high shako; a snug shell jacket, numer-ous pairs of dark blue trousers with cavalry piping. High laced Jefferson shoes worn in rough brogan style or black knee-high cavalry jackboots. Army-grey stockings. If nothing else had given them away their McClel-lan and shabrack saddles would have. Some of the Indian scouts wore their hair long and tied back with Apache-style headbands and most of them favored leaving their blouses skirted out rather than tucking them inside their waistbands but nevertheless they were clearly army Indians.

Twenty-seven of us in all. From the tracks we'd been forced to as-sume Ibran had added new recruits to his band; the sign indicated at least seventy.

"As you can see," Sieber said gently as though reading my thoughts, "the last thing we want is a fight. We would not stand a chance, would we?"

"I don't know how the hell you aim to get him to parley."

"In part that is up to you, isn't it?"

"You're asking blood from a stone, Sieber."

He sat down, moving a joint at a time and gingerly to favor his injuries. I said, "How long you been fighting Indians?"

"Maybe twenty-five year."

"What the hell for? You hate them that much?"

"Maybe."

"How many times have you been hacked up by Indians?"

"Bullets, knives, arrows, lances, clubs—hell, Colonel, I don't keep count. I'm like a real old army wagon. All replacement parts. Ain't hardly none of the original wagon is left."

"What do you keep fighting them for?"

"Well my job it is."

"That's all? A job?"

"Colonel, it is the thing I know how to do. It is the thing I do better than anybody else. I kill Indians real good. You make sense of this?"

"I just don't want Ibran killed when he's not looking for it."

"You want my word, Colonel?" For a moment his eyes blazed at me. I couldn't blame him for not liking a man who didn't seem to trust him.

But then I thought he must be used to it. A man who looked that disheveled and that disreputable—a man who boasted that he liked to kill Indians—wasn't likely to be taken on faith very often by anyone except a fellow Indian-hater.

I said, "He'll expect us to get a little scared of an ambush so he'll expect us to wait the night out here in the open before we go in there after him."

"So." Sieber's grizzled face twisted into something that passed for approbation. "First rule in war, if that is what you want to make it, is never let the enemy stampede you into doing what he wants you to do. You suggest?"

"I could talk to Ibran but it wouldn't do any good if he's already got his mind made up, which obviously he has, and if I didn't have any way to put pressure on him to change it."

"So?"

"Another thing to keep in mind. They'll be camped, they'll want to get their sleep and be all rested up for us because likely they'll want to run us around the mountains a few days before they set up the ambush after we're all dead-tired. So they'll camp tonight but naturally they'll post shifts to guard the horses and the backtrail." I waved my good hand around to indicate the scouts lounging about us. "These are good men you've got but I don't think they can get past half a dozen Apache sentries without alerting at least one of them."

Sieber rubbed his jaw. "The ordinary thing would be to stick knife in them—very quiet, you know. But would be better we don't kill any. They'll see we mean to talk peaceful."

I said, "If they camp on top of something they have us licked but I don't think they'll do that. Ibran's too good a hunter—he knows better than to get himself skylined. They'll be on a slope somewhere with a good view downhill."

"So?" The way he said it made it sound *Zo.*

"Hell, Sieber, you're the Indian fighter."

"You talk good so far. Finish it."

"If this were my hunting party I'd camp here right now, bivouac so they can see us bed down. Get a few hours' sleep. Then move out after dark, maybe around eleven before the moon comes up. Leave the horses here and a few men with them to show a little life in the camp. We go on foot and we go that way—northeast, cut around above them if we can. Settle ourselves up there before first light."

"And then?"

"We stay back a bit from their sentry line but close enough to shoot. These men handle rifles well?"

"If they didn't they'd be dead by now."

Fitz said, "You want to ambush their ambush?"

"No, I just want pressure."

"Pressure?"

I said, "There's only one way to do this and you knew that from the start. I have to walk into that camp. It has to be me because I'm Ibran's brother-in-law. Anybody else wouldn't get near him. So I have to walk in on my hind legs and talk him out of there. Wasn't that the reason you forced me into this?"

Fitz said, "We're trying to save some lives, Hugh, that's all."

"You just call me Colonel, all right?" I gave him a level look.

"Yes sir, Colonel sir." His grin was impudent.

"You call me Colonel right now because we'll do this my way. If I go with you then I'm in charge. Agreed?"

"No," Al Sieber said softly, "that is not agreed. I am the chief of scouts for the Arizona district and I am in charge here, partly because I have that authority but mainly because these scouts will take orders from me but not from you. You make sense of this?"

I brooded at him. I thought it out slowly and in the end said, "I have to trust you, then."

"You can."

"I'm not sure of that. If two or three youngsters in that camp decide to put up a fight can I trust you and these scouts not to shoot everyone down?"

Sieber said, "After this is over I will beat the shit out of you, Colonel, and tell you what a goddamn fool you are. But right now I will only say yes, you can trust me and my scouts to hold our tempers. We didn't come down here to kill Indians this time. I cannot more promises make. I am tried of this. You go in or you don't go in."

I watched him coldly. Sieber calmly took out a pipe and cut off a piece of Long Jack plug tobacco, inserted it in the pipe and pulled out a waterproof case of phosphorus lucifers. I watched him strike one of them on the sole of his boot and hold it to the bowl of the pipe.

"All right," I said angrily—anger to mask fear, it was. "I go in."

. . .

By Sieber's Horologe pocket watch it was half-past five. False dawn washed the rocks and I could see my breath before me; I felt the high-country chill in my nose and ears.

The silence was so intense I heard the crack of Sieber's knee joint and the creak of Fitz's holster. Keeping his voice right down Fitz said, "You got to reach Ibran before them others get aholt of you."

"*Seguro que sí,*" I muttered dryly.

Sieber tapped the face of his timepiece. "*Ahora mismo,* Colonel."

I sighed. There was no putting it off. I began to walk. Then Fitz behind me said, "Look a-yonder—up on the clift."

I could see four of them up there; I knew there must be nine or ten —Sieber had dispatched them an hour ago, his best climbers. They had a field of fire sufficient to enfilade the Apache camp.

I looked back at Sieber. He nodded his head as if to reassure me that the men on the cliff wouldn't get trigger-happy. But we both knew that if things came to a pass where those men had to start shooting, I was dead.

"You're covered the best we can," Fitz said. "All we can do."

I walked down toward the trees, keeping to cover as I went, moving from rock to rock. We were near the hilltop and beyond it across a narrow canyon loomed the cliff where the snipers had climbed. The mountains were crumpled folds, deep blue in the predawn light, patches of melting snow here and there.

This was timberline. A hundred feet below me the scrub trees began —piñons, scrub pines. The deep forest was well below; we'd walked up through it in the night, circumventing the Apache camp. Sieber was right—I knew the country here and it did make all the difference because neither he nor any of his scouts would have known where to look for Ibran's camp and left to themselves they'd have needed several days to find it but I knew the likely spots and had led the scouts directly here.

I moved with care, not wanting to draw fire. I carried no weapons, only a rolled white cloth under my coat. The cool wind bit my ears and my feet felt puffy from all the climbing. I got into the piñons and paused to take long drafts of the thin air and calm my breathing.

There was a bald mound about fifty yards beneath this place sheltered by a natural rock parapet in the shape of a V with its point at the lower end—ideal for a protected camp. It couldn't be infiltrated because there were open flats beyond the parapet and anyone approaching from below could be seen.

The bald mound itself provided a field of fire behind—coming down from above, as I was, I would come in sight of the camp and have to cross the open shale in plain sight of them. I'd hunted a bear across here last fall and taken note of the configuration of the land, realizing what an ideal campsite it made. There was a spring in the notch of the V; it fed a clear pool and the water then went underground to follow a hidden course down the watershed.

I looked behind me. The light was increasing but I couldn't see any sign of Sieber or Fitz or the scout troop; they'd posted themselves well, blending. They would give me a head start and then move in quietly behind me, close enough to burst into sight if it were required.

Moving onto the shale I took a deep breath and slipped the furled cloth out from under my bearskins. I had been moving very slowly and without sound. It was full dawn by now, nearly six o'clock, and I knew over on the east face of the range the sun was already up. I glanced up toward the cliff where Sieber had posted his long-range shooters. The sky above it was splashed with pink and yellow. In another five minutes the sun would appear above it and the Apache would have it in their eyes if they sought to shoot in that direction.

I unrolled the cloth—it was a six-foot flag with a stitched border; a seamstress at Fort Lowell must have made it up expressly to Sieber's order, inasmuch as I do not believe the army stocks white flags of truce as a regular issue. I lofted it slowly above my head and let the wind flutter it and rose slowly to my feet. I stepped forward, slipping a bit on the loose rock, sweating in the cold because I knew I was being watched now. I held my left hand crooked at the elbow with the open palm well out from my body so that they could see I was empty-handed and I made no effort to be silent as I crunched forward on the shattered footing. Several times I nearly turned an ankle; the shale was terrible.

I could not see anyone but I spoke firmly in Spanish. "I come without arms to speak with Ibran. I am his brother-in-law."

After that I heard a pebble roll—it must have been a sentry going down into the camp to get instructions—and I kept moving toward the crest of the mound, testing each footstep, doing nothing sudden. My body was tensed against an awaited bullet and I was trembling with terror. I had to fight down the impulse to throw myself flat.

I could see piñons to either side of the shale slide. Behind some of them warriors lurked; but I could see no one.

Then I crested the mound and saw the camp fifty feet below me—men coming awake, reaching for their weapons; several Apache with their rifles trained upon me.

I waved the white flag slowly back and forth over my head. I kept walking out of the fear that hesitation might provoke a bullet. Slipping and stumbling on the jagged loose shale I made my slow way into the camp and it took an eternity.

I had to pass a boulder the size of a bull and as I did so I caught a tail-of-the-eye movement imperfectly; I wheeled to find a burly Indian coming at me with a knife.

Someone shouted—Ibran?—but the attacker kept coming and I leaped back, more in desperation than in calculation, with the flag fluttering between us—a shield of sorts: I managed to whip the flag at the knife and snag it against the cloth, deflecting it momentarily.

Voices roared beyond us but my attacker seemed to be charged with madness. We locked together, my grip on his knife wrist, the white cloth crumpling between us. I kicked out desperately and my boot cracked his ankle so that he howled and fell away from me and I tumbled across him still gripping the knife wrist. As I rolled, my shoulder—the bad shoulder—struck rock and pain lanced through me; the shock reduced my grasp and the Apache was very quick, wrenching away, rolling over to get his knees under him, bringing the knife up underhand—I flung myself back away from the blade and in panic lashed the heel of my boot toward his face.

He didn't see it coming in time. It hit him only a glancing blow but that was enough to tumble him over and I scrambled swiftly while he was still dazed—my knee dropped hard across his forearm and I plucked the knife from his hand.

I stood up with a red pulse pounding in my eyes and roared at the men below me: "Is this how you greet your brother?"

Ibran was halfway up the slope by then, slipping and grunting. He stopped and glared up at me. I threw the knife at him in disgust and he caught it effortlessly and almost smiled at me. "That one is always a little wild." It was the closest he would come to an apology.

But I wasn't satisfied; anger and fear lurched inside me. "If you can't control your men any better than that you've got no business leading them."

Ignoring me Ibran climbed past me and kicked the offending Apache savagely on the shin. The man had just got to his feet and the blow knocked him down again. Ibran put his foot on the man's face, turning the head to one side and grinding it against the shale until the man cried out faintly and threw his hands out to the sides in submission. Then Ibran turned to me.

A muscle worked at the back of his jaw; otherwise he was inscrutable. He seemed much bigger than in the old days: it was the air of leadership. With a dry and witty courtesy I didn't expect of him he said, "*Con mucho gusto, hermano.*"

We went down into the camp then and the young men watched me curiously and with baffled suspicion. By a quick eye-count I guessed there to be about fifty warriors in sight, well-scattered along the length of the V parapet; it meant there were twenty others somewhere beyond my view—sentries and the like.

The horse herd was rope-tethered toward the upper end of the parapet to my right in a little pocket of scrub growth. The camp was nothing more than a few open firesites. Apache traveled light

My heart still pounded with exertion and rage. "If he'd killed me you'd have died—a lot of you." I pointed up toward the cliff. It was hard to see against the red sun. "Up there with rifles—and all around you."

Ibran's face drew into a spasm of clenched teeth and drawn lips. "So."

"I haven't betrayed you, Ibran. I'm trying to save your hide."

"Who is it—blacks?"

He meant the Negroes of the Tenth Regiment. I said, "No. Scout company—mostly Indians, like you. You want Indians to kill Indians?"

"Al Sieber?"

"Yes."

He seemed to relax a bit and after a moment I understood why. He couldn't trust soldiers to do the sensible thing but he knew Sieber, at least by reputation, and knew that Sieber was a ruthless killer but would not act capriciously or foolishly.

The trap was working mainly because of the difference in fighting philosophies. The Apache was in the habit of getting in close to spring an ambush. This was the result of his tradition of hand-to-hand fighting. A long-distance ambush was foreign to his thinking and Ibran hadn't been prepared for the idea that we could surround him at considerable distance with long-range rifles.

I said, "They can probably kill half of you before you get out of here."

"How is my sister?"

He had a way of shifting subjects like that. Taken aback I could only meet his eyes and hold my ground. "She's dead, Ibran."

I watched him take it in. His face was not as impassive as he would have preferred.

He said, "Of what did she die?"

"Smallpox. The fever. We had a son, Michael Ibran. The fever took him too."

"They did not die for lack of you treating them good?"

"I wish I could have treated them better but you've seen the smallpox, Ibran. There was nothing I could do."

His face went cold with emptiness; he was withdrawing from me and I couldn't have that. I gripped his arm. "Ibran . . ."

He wrenched himself away. "I've lived this far without any white man's help and I guess I can die the same way."

"And all these others with you?"

"Their choice, *hermano.*"

At least he still called me brother. I said, "Do this in peace. What's the sense getting a lot of men killed?"

"They want to put us on the Camp Verde and make little white men out of us, *hermano* Car-dee. Listen, I don't want to be white. If the spirits wanted me to be a white man they'd have made me one in the first place. I'm poor but I'm free, no white man is going to tell me where to go. If I must die I'll die the same way, free—it's better than being told where to set my feet."

"Ibran, you've got rifles down your throat and impatient men out there with their fingers on those triggers."

He turned and looked at his braves, one to the next. They were watching him, awaiting his signals. They were lean men for the most part, agile and strong—the best hunters of the tribe; unlike Geronimo, Ibran wasn't the sort of man who would attract drunks and wild youths—he was a great hunter and those who chose to follow him knew they would have to be able to keep up with him and that meant only the best men would join him. It also meant if things came to a fight Sieber's scouts would have more than a handful of trouble.

Ibran said, "What do you want of us?"

"I want you to go back home and get back to meat-hunting instead of playing at war."

"The gringos made the war."

"I won't argue right and wrong with you. I won't argue what's fair and what's not fair. You're a practical man—I'll only tell you practicalities. The practicality is you can't win. You've got Sieber against you and he likes nothing better than killing Apache people. And you've got the Yankee army and they've got more soldiers than the Sierra has piñons. Ibran, you just can't win."

"You cannot always go by that."

"What do you want to do, prove a point? You want to prove that you can die bravely? Forty, fifty good men here?"

"Numbers."

"Numbers hell, I'm talking about people. Dead people. One by one, dead." I cast my look over the Indians around us—waiting, angry, ready to explode. I said, "These men are probably the best in the tribe."

"Yes, I believe they are."

"You get them killed, Ibran, who's left to look after the People?"

He reached out and tugged at the lapel of my heavy wolfskin coat. "You, *hermano,* what is it that you want from us here?"

"I want you to ride back to Fort Lowell with Sieber."

"Why?"

"Because I expect it's better than dying."

"There are worse things than dying."

"For you maybe. But for all of them? You're responsible for them, you know. Look—if you stay out, if you keep burning ranches and killing gringos and Mexicans, don't you imagine they will wipe out every Apache they can find?"

He said, "You talk reason to me, *hermano,* but did your people use reason when they massacred my people at Camp Grant? Do they talk reason when they break the treaty promise and remove us to Verde?"

"You are my brother," I replied. It was lame but the only answer I had.

"I will think," he said and walked away from me.

. . .

There was a council among them and it went on for some time, an hour or more; I heard voices lift and drop. I sat on the shale and waited them out and only hoped Sieber's men had sufficient patience.

I spoke negligible Apache and could not understand what was said but I didn't need to. Ibran had spoken first and then had curbed his tongue while the rest of them argued. I thought it probable that he had not made a recommendation; he had simply laid out the situation and the alternatives. Leadership among the Apache was not a fixed matter of hierarchy; the degree of democracy among them was extraordinarily high and a leader remained in his position only as long as he enjoyed the confidence of his followers. It was not up to Ibran to tell his band what to do; they were not people who took orders without question.

The disputations became heated for a time. Angry glances shot toward me frequently. I sat still and tried to maintain an impassive expression, relying for my safety on my tenuous relationship to Ibran. It might not be enough—certainly it hadn't been enough to stop the warrior who'd attacked me with the knife. The only protection I had was each Apache's knowledge that if he attacked me he would have to answer to Ibran in personal combat. And in a group like this there were always those young bucks who might feel ready to challenge the leader, much as stag antelopes or bull buffalo would pick a fight with the herd leader to establish supremacy.

A few wandered near me with cold curious eyes; one man's spittle struck not two inches from me. I only held his eyes until he turned away. But my heart was racing.

As the sun climbed the snipers on the cliff became visible and I saw some of the Apache studying them with speculative hunters' eyes, wondering how effective the fire might be from that far away—the cliff stood perhaps four hundred yards from us. These men were hunters; they had a fair idea of riflery even though most of them were far better trackers than marksmen. Most of them had been raised on bow and arrow.

The arguments climbed in pitch and volume until finally Ibran stood up and injected his strong voice into the proceedings, whereupon the others in the council went silent and listened to his words. I saw dejection on many of their faces and did not envy them their dilemma.

After Ibran finished talking the rest of them muttered briefly among themselves and then the meeting broke up. The members of the council went around and spoke with other Apache and after a while Ibran stood up and walked onto the shale and ceremonially laid his rifle down and backed away from it. Then one by one the others followed suit until there was a pile of rifles and bows on the shale. The Indians stood in a cluster looking up toward the cliff and Ibran sang out, calling the sentries in, and I watched them come in from all directions from their places of concealment. Some of them argued loudly but they were shouted down by the group; in the end the last of them deposited his rifle on the pile and joined the crowd, after which Sieber and Fitz came over the crest of the mound and walked down into the camp to join us.

     · · ·

It was in that manner that Ibran's uprising was quelled in the summer of 1881 and I have recounted it as faithfully as I know how because there have been some wildly absurd tales written about it. Most of them, taking a leaf from Bob Halburton's earlier stage play, have reported great wild battles resulting in the bloody deaths of hundreds of Indians and soldiers.

As one can plainly see by my factual account of the pursuit of Ibran and our encounter in the Sierra, there was neither bloodshed nor battlefield heroics. Those, I am afraid, are the province of fictioneers and entertainers, and I count myself among the latter now, but in those long-ago days I was not a hero but simply a young man doing his best to get along in the world.

BOOK EIGHT

Return from Exile

I STOOD IN THE SHADE of a weatherbeaten cantina keeping watch on the traffic coming through the border gate just as I'd done every day for the past week. Anger stirred in me like a low growl in a wolf's throat. I opened my snap-lid watch and closed it; if anyone had asked me the time I'd have had to look again.

I went back inside. The proprietor gave me a brief look tinged with fear and alarm. Without my asking he poured a drink for me. It was midday; there were no other patrons. I went back to the corner table I had preempted and sat there as I had sat before, neither whittling nor reading but simply waiting.

Finally that afternoon he came. I heard the horse outside and somehow knew it was Sieber. But perversely I sat where I was and did not get up when he limped into the room and sought me out in the dimness.

He stood waiting to be asked to sit down. I did not oblige him. "You took a week," I said. "It's one day's ride."

"You think I have nothing else to do? I had business in the mountains, Colonel. Killing business."

"You ever get tired of murdering Indians?"

He merely stood watching me, volunteering nothing. I said, "Tell me, Sieber. Tell me."

"I talked to Miles. Miles talked to Sheridan. I know this much. Sheridan says he will use his influence with the Secretary of War."

"That all?"

"It may take months to get an answer from the President, Colonel. If we get one at all."

"That all?"

"Yes. That is all."

"Leave a message with the bartender here when you get word for me."

"Yeah." He walked out.

．　．　．

I'd put up my horse in a stable that belonged to two elderly brothers whose time was given mainly to the consumption of mezcal. An Indian boy kept the place swamped out and looked after the stock with indifference. With time on my hands I got into the habit of going there twice a day to see to my horse, as I didn't altogether trust the boy. And I found the stable a convenient place in which to exercise my arm. As its strength had increased I had placed ever heavier tasks upon it until now I was able to lift myself one hundred times so that my chin touched the top of the stable's crossbar beam.

I had arrived in the province a cripple but by the time I made ready to leave it I doubt any man in Sonora had arms stronger than mine.

In the course of the next few days I managed to get thrown out of my boardinghouse and two cantinas. After a few pointless roughhouses I was taken in by the proprietress of a sporting house and employed there to keep unruly clients in line or throw them out, as circumstances might demand, and I remained there a fortnight. (I did not spend two years as a Mexican whorehouse ponce, as one unfriendly journalist has insinuated.) At the end of that time I found a message with the bartender of the cantina where I had met Sieber.

The message stated only that the Secretary of War had prevailed upon the Attorney General to forward my plea to President Arthur. Sieber's letter was cool and brief. I realized I had been too harsh with him for my own good. I did not like the man and had made no bones about it; in terms of the politics of my situation I supposed that had been a mistake. But Sieber was not easy to like. He had a crude personality, an ugly appearance and a cynical single-mindedness that I thought petty. He treated his Indian scouts with contempt and held their allegiance only because they respected his toughness and his man-tracking skills.

Later I came to think more kindly of him; a killer, he was nevertheless a peacemaker and his main sin was that of pride—he was without much morality but his devotion to his job was extraordinary. Probably without him the Indian wars of the Southwest would have been far bloodier. After all, it was Sieber who brought those wars to an end when in 1886 he finally brought Geronimo to bay. But he had killed a great many people to do it and he took too much pleasure in the killings to suit me.

From time to time I have wondered what he had against the Indians. I have heard many wild stories but none of them holds much water; to this day I do not know what his true motives were. Possibly they would have made no sense to anyone but Sieber; he was one of the strangest men I ever met.

After receipt of his message I realized I was not likely to have quick response to my petition. I had a plan in my mind but it required that I be free to move about the United States without being hampered by bounty hunters and hangmen. Were it not for my dedication to this plan I would have found it easy enough to enter the country by stealth; there was an unguarded span of a thousand miles in either direction along the border. But I would not have been able to use my real identity and such a restriction would render my plans unattainable.

For I had plans. I was no longer a youth to be buffeted by circumstance. When I drove my bargain with Al Sieber it was the gambit for an aggressive game which I resolved to play. I'd had my fill of being directed by fate; I intended to make my own fate from then on. The future had taken shape in my imagination. There was lost time to be made up; and a son—my firstborn, who carried another man's name—to be brought to my side. To achieve that I would challenge and conquer the world if need be.

. . .

The border was still closed to me at that time; I could scheme but I had to wait. Knowing it might be months I cast about for employment more suitable than what I had. I found it quickly enough at Candelas—at that time the largest ranch in the world. It sprawled across a good part of the states of Sonora and Chihuahua and its size and power were such that the provincial governments had authorized the management to establish its own law enforcement. My size, strength, marksmanship and reputation enabled me to obtain good employ at Candelas as a private policeman or regulator.

Candelas belonged to the Inca Land and Cattle Company which was a Scottish company in Glasgow with stockholders in many parts of the world. The manager of the ranch was a Scot, Ranald Urquhart, and his fiefdom contained several towns and villages, numerous mines and farms, more than a thousand employees and squatters, and some millions of acres. Ran Urquhart fancied himself a sporting shooter and we had become acquainted in Nogales. We shot a match, I took one hundred of his pesos, and we supped in the Hotel Occidental where he offered me the job.

Contrary to the numerous unfounded yarns that have been spun about my heroic two-gun service as Texas Ranger, Kansas marshal or Arizona sheriff, the truth is I only served as a police officer once in my life and that was during the autumn of 1881 when I enforced the peace of the western sector of the Candelas ranch. During that period I did not hear or fire a single shot in anger. My jurisdiction encompassed some two thousand square miles of mountains and chaparral—four villages, a silver mine and ninety farms. I had to keep alert for cattle thievery but mainly I adjudicated disputes, calmed drunks, prevented fights and pulled steers out of bogs. I ran off two monte sharks and a chicken rustler.

. . .

Ran Urquhart was a square-built man with reddish sandy hair that curled thickly about his head like wire wool. In the service of the queen's regiments he had fought Sherpas, Ethiopes, Russians and Zulus. Then through some family connection he was offered the position of overseer of the Inca Land and Cattle Company's Mexican holdings. He'd had the job four or five years when I first met him; he was good at it. I found him a man of irrepressible enthusiasms—loud, hearty, a figure of great cheerful bravado. If I saw him walking a mile away I could recognize him by his colonial officer's stride—one arm swinging high, the other crooked stiffly to a quirt clamped under the armpit.

He lived with his stout ebullient wife in an ugly house on top of a hill overlooking Pueblo Candelas. I was invited there a few times to dinner and met some of the Sonora gentry.

When Ran Urquhart introduced me to his visitors he did so with an amused twinkle and then guffawed when the visitors, upon hearing my name, gaped at me with sudden fear.

I realized after a while that my years in the Sierra had cloaked me with mystery. Everyone had heard of me—distorted truths and outright lies but they knew my name.

They'd seen some of the dime novels that still, apparently, poured forth from Bob Halburton's pen. They knew I'd been a Hero of the Plains who had turned stage actor, been involved in a "gunfight" in New York, fled for my life, sailed the seas with many a high adventure before the mast, faced Doc Holliday down in Caborca and single-handedly massacred an entire tribe of murderous Apache warriors in the Sierra.

They knew I had killed seventy-nine men, not counting Indians and African headhunters and Malay cannibals. They knew I could converse with pumas and wolves in their own tongues, and could run faster than any horse, and could kill a man five miles away with a rifle. They knew, in short, that I was a raving great wild god of the wilderness—I think some of them honestly expected me to have fangs and claws and the hot snarling breath of a dragon; my legend was the kind with which mothers frighten their disobedient children.

288

I suppose strangers found little in my appearance to belie those myths, for I was very tall and still had my great masses of white hair. I had shaved off the mountaineer's beard but I'd retained the drooping white mustache. I was weatherbeaten beyond my years and had been told many times how particularly bright and penetrating my eyes were. Because of the exercises I'd undertaken to restore my arm I had developed a powerfully muscular physique and of course I was much taller than most men. At that time I still favored my homemade deerskins (last memorabilia of Flower) over store-bought clothes; they were softer yet tougher than cloth. And according to Ran Urquhart I moved in a manner "sinuous, silent and sinister."

All in all I must have presented a startling appearance that did little to discourage the legends.

Actually I encouraged them. I spun many a wild yarn in which I rescued fair maidens from Indian captivity, wiped out entire communities of bandits and generally raised spectacular hell. We were fine liars out West; it is a country that stimulates the imagination. An honest man might come out from the States as truthful as George Washington but the West just naturally stretches facts and pretty soon that honest man will be swapping lies with the best of them.

· · ·

I kept Ran Urquhart's visitors enthralled and often capped our evenings with shooting exhibitions in which I performed some of the tricks I'd learned in my youth from Grandfather Clement Tyree and Fitz Bragg. Mrs. Urquhart had a set of steel-rod chimes which I learned to set up for targets; by lantern light I would play "Old Black Joe" on the chimes from a range of twenty-five feet using Ran Urquhart's .22-caliber revolvers.

Ran's own reputation achieved awesome proportions during this time because he became known as the man who had tamed the wild mountain creature. The two of us enjoyed these leg-pulling evenings immensely but naturally after a while the novelty wore off and people began to realize they'd been hoorawed; soon I was accepted as a man rather than a monster and in truth I found this much easier to get along with.

· · ·

Nate Loving became famous with our show when he toured with us. I first met Nate on Ran Urquhart's Candelas ranch that winter—but our first encounter was hardly propitious.

In my capacity as regulator I was summoned into Pueblo Candelas by the proprietor of the town's tonsorial parlor who had an odd story to tell.

"The Negro comes in, señor, with a little black boy he holds by the hand. The man says to me he wishes the hair cut, the shave, the toilet water, everything. And he says to me give the boy a haircut too.

"And so I cut the man's hair, I shave him, I put on the toilet water, everything. And the man says to me, while I am cutting the boy's hair he will go up the *calle* to buy the cigar.

"The man goes out and I cut the boy's hair. It is ten, fifteen minutes. Then the little boy he says to me, how is it that I am giving him this free haircut?

"And I say to the little boy, the haircut is not free, what makes you think it is free?

"And the little boy says, señor, this man who just left, he stopped me on the *calle* and asked me if I wished a free haircut. I never saw this man before, señor."

. . .

I had to clear out of the tonsorial parlor in order to avoid laughing in the proprietor's face. To him it was a very serious thing. He was owed three pesos.

According to the proprietor's description the "thief" was a big Negro who wore bright-colored range clothes and a Mexican sombrero and spoke good Spanish with a Texas accent. That did not give me a great deal to go on, inasmuch as there were scores of Negro vaqueros on the Candelas payroll. There were more Negroes than white Anglo vaqueros. Most of the vaqueros were Mexican of course; but in those days the border was not a very formal thing and men drifted back and forth across it and hung their hats wherever they found employment. Because of feelings in Texas that were left over from Civil War days and Reconstruction, a large number of Negro vaqueros had sought work in Mexico where there was less likelihood of their being hoorawed or set upon by ex-Confederate whites.

I did not think much of my chances of finding the guilty party; in any case the fellow had given me a good laugh and I felt that was worth at least three pesos, so in the afternoon I returned to the tonsorial parlor and told him I had run into the Negro who had told me of his oversight in neglecting to pay for his haircut and had given me these three pesos with which to pay the barber. I gave the man the money, he accepted my story, and I went on my way. A few more chuckles at odd moments; after that I forgot the incident.

But a few days later a shopkeeper came running up to me on the street and hollered that a wild man was chasing a train. I had better stop the man, the shopkeeper said, before something terrible happened.

I went along to the railroad siding, where the cattle pens were, and sure enough I found a man chasing a train. The train was chuffing along at no great speed, the single wood-burning engine hauling quite a long chain of freight cars, and I saw a horseman riding back and forth curling his lasso into a loop. While I approached on the run, the vaquero began to whirl his loop overhead. He was whooping and laughing like a madman and I immediately discerned that he was drunk.

He was yelling at the train the way a matador would yell at a bull: "Hey—*toro! Toro!*" He rode back and forth across the tracks in front of the advancing locomotive, the spade-cowcatcher missing his horse by no more than a hair.

Then the rider hurled his noose and it settled over the high funnel smokestack of the locomotive. In astonishment I saw the vaquero dally his rope around the horn of his saddle; then he lined out away from the tracks with the obvious intention of dragging the smokestack right off the engine.

But when he reached the end of the rope I saw the line draw taut. I cringed, thinking of the poor horse, but fortunately for the horse the saddle cinch snapped in two and then I saw the vaquero go for a wild ride as the locomotive pulled him through the air—a whooping Negro cowboy waving his hat, riding a soaring airborne saddle without a horse.

It is a sight I shall always cherish in my memory.

But it came to a bone-jarring end soon enough when the rider and saddle struck earth and went dragging along painfully.

All this while I had been running. I was still too far away to reach the vaquero and the train was traveling as fast as I could run. I could not catch him. Evidently the angry engine driver was disinclined to take pity on the vaquero by stopping his train. And in the meantime the vaquero, tangled in stirrup leathers, was being dragged along on what must have been the roughest ride of his life; and the rope was drawing him ever closer to the relentless rolling wheels of the train.

I drew out my revolver, stopped to take aim, and parted the rope with a bullet.

The vaquero rolled over and under his saddle two or three times and then the wild ride ended. He was disentangling himself when I walked up to him.

"Are you all right?"

"Now that's the silliest damn question I ever heard." He got slowly to his feet, testing each joint as he moved. "Amazing. I think everything still works."

I saw the engine driver lean out his cab and look back at us with haughty anger. The Negro vaquero made an obscene gesture in his direction and abruptly whipped out his revolver and began blazing away. The engine driver rapidly withdrew his head from sight.

I batted the revolver out of the vaquero's hand. "All right. Fun's fun."

"Who the hell you think you are?"

"I'm the regulator around here."

"The hell you say."

"I'm also the fellow who just saved your bacon. Calm down. You want a little sobering up."

"You think you're man enough to do that?"

I looked him up and down. "I guess I am, if I have to be."

Then abruptly he smiled, a display of flashing teeth. "In that case to hell with it."

I said, "You've just had a haircut. I think you're the man that owes me three pesos."

. . .

In that manner I first made the acquaintance of Nate Loving. I soon learned that his wild humor was utterly and childishly irrepressible. I remember an occasion when he rushed into a crowded cantina and cried, "Geronimo's busted out!"

There was pandemonium in that cantina until I took him by the arm and inquired, "Where'd he bust out to, Nate?"

"All over his arms and legs!" Nate shouted, and burst into tears of laughter.

On another inebriated occasion he was trying to lasso the cannon on the plaza in Pueblo Candelas and drag it off when I came along.

There just wasn't much you could do by way of civilizing Nate Loving. He had too much fun in him.

Not everyone took it in stride. One of the other regulators caught Nate one time driving a half-dozen steers toward the border. Cattle theft was a serious crime of course. Nate always insisted the cattle were unbranded and he'd claimed them for himself as mavericks but there was some dispute as to the condition of their hides—the regulator who'd arrested Nate said the brands had been scraped off down to the under-skin but Nate claimed he'd had nothing to do with that. In any case the administration of justice on Candelas was rigid and severe, mainly conditioned by the nature of punishments in the colonial regiments that had produced Ran Urquhart, and by the time I heard of the incident Nate's head had been shaved, a two-inch T (for "Thief") had been pricked on his right thigh with India ink, he had taken twenty lashes and then been imprisoned for forty-eight hours. There was no jail on Candelas; like other offenders Nate was imprisoned by being lowered down a dry well on a windlass, ball-and-chain and all.

But when he emerged he wasn't chastened; he didn't slow down a bit.

Nate was employed intermittently. He would get a job for one *segundo* or another—he was a first-rate vaquero and could do things with rope and horse that most men never even dreamed possible—but his prankish wildness soon would emerge and he would outrage the *segundo* with one thing or another and get fired. Then he would go on the drift, wandering from one village to another, gambling and whoring and causing endless ruckus and destruction until he ran out of money and went looking for a job with a *segundo* who hadn't employed him previously.

By the time I met Nate he had just about run out of *segundos* to victimize and was thinking of pushing on to fresher pastures.

He was a self-styled hero and claimed to have been a lawman, Indian fighter, drover, mountain man, six-gun duelist, bank robber, train robber, gold miner, circuit gambler and buffalo hunter. Possibly some, or even all, of it was true. But Nate never told the same yarn twice and I never was able to decide whether there was any truth in anything he said. On separate occasions he told me he'd been born in 1849, 1854 and 1857—in Atlanta, in Philadelphia and in Nagadoches. His father was either a plantation slave or a Baptist preacher (possibly he had been both, I suppose) and Nate was either an only child or the fifteenth of seventeen children.

He was wiry, narrow, not very tall but he had a good strong ebony face. He adorned himself with flamboyant outfits that usually ran to vivid reds and yellows. I always suspected he hadn't been born with the name Nate Loving; there was a famous Texan named Loving who had pioneered one of the cattle trails and I assume Nate took his name from that fellow or perhaps simply adopted it because he felt it suited his personality—Nate was an extraordinary man according to the sporting ladies. On one occasion I am told he went through the entire population of sixteen ladies in one sporting house in a period of less than five hours. When he stumbled downstairs the ladies stood him a five-course dinner and a bottle of whisky on the house, after which Nate returned upstairs and made the rounds again.

So I am told.

. . .

The news and gossip of that time along the border was much to do with the legends of Jesse James and Billy the Kid.

Jesse's myth had achieved a stature comparable to Robin Hood's, partly for the simple reason that he managed to remain at large for such a long period of years—he had invented bank robbery at Liberty, Missouri, in 1866 and was still at it in 1881 when I went to work for Ran Urquhart. Jesse was to be killed the following spring but of course we didn't know that; he was the subject of much speculation and

293

argument—he had many partisans—at that time it seemed as if he might go on forever thumbing his nose at the railroads and bankers and Pinkerton detectives.

Billy the Kid had been killed by Pat Garrett in the summer of 1881 and that too was the subject of much discussion around the cantinas and bunkhouses. Here I was ignorant for I had never heard of Billy the Kid; I suppose most people had not—he only became famous after his death and largely because Garrett made such an issue of having killed him. Garrett's book on the subject—*The Authentic Life of Billy the Kid and How I Shot Him*—had been rushed into print and while it was the next thing to a dime novel we all read it with avid interest.

A few vaqueros on the Candelas claimed to have known Garrett up in Lincoln County where they said he was nothing more than a two-bit saloon drunk, but I never got the straight of it, having a limited interest in the subject. I never met Pat Garrett.

I was most interested in news of Buffalo Bill Cody, who was touring Eastern opera houses with dubious success in a theatrical vehicle written by A. S. Burt and titled *May Cody, or, Lost and Won*. Apparently for sheer falsehoods it put even Bob Halburton's play to shame—it offered up Cody as conqueror of the Sioux, guide for Brigham Young, Civil War hero and so on, ad infinitum. Apparently the show had pretty much worn out its welcome and was not drawing very good crowds, for it ran only limited engagements and these appeared to be few and far between; Cody evidently spent most of his time building up his ranch in Wyoming.

I suspected then—and still do—that audiences were tired of Western stage melodramas because Caleb and Bob and I had skimmed the cream off that particular venture; there wasn't much that Cody could do on a proscenium stage that audiences hadn't seen done before by Cardiff and Rice in *Heroes of the West*.

It was my aim to get back into the show business but I did not see the sense of doing it in theaters and opera houses where the outdoor spectacle of horsemanship and marksmanship was proscribed.

My ideas, at first vague, were crystallized at Pueblo Candelas upon the occasion of the ranch's annual fall roundup celebration. It was there, on Friday, October 14, 1881, that I shall always contend the Wild West Show was born in a hoorawing lark of Nate Loving's. I doubt Nate had any idea he was making history.

.   .   .

The fall roundup occupied a period of some weeks at the end of which all the cattle that were to be shipped to market were driven into the vast holding pens beside the railroad siding at Pueblo Candelas.

The air trembled with the thunder of that multitude. Long trains were drawn up to the chute ramps and the cattle driven into them, seventy-five head crowded into each railroad car. It was a grimy exhausting business and the trains came and went for nearly a week before the last of it was done. By then the vaqueros, like the locomotives, were more than ready to let off steam.

A few bony underweight steers had been culled out, sorry critters destined for the hide factories and boneyards. Two or three boneyard brokers had journeyed to Pueblo Candelas to bid for these castoffs and I heard one of them say in a dry Texas drawl, "Them hat racks is a real buy—all lean meat."

Before being shipped away the hat racks were destined to be employed as running stock for the vaquero competitions of the roundup fete, which took the form of a day-long sequence of events and contests followed by an evening *baile* and an all-night toot.

The fete had evolved from the Mexican tradition of celebrating everything with ritual and drinking and fireworks. In the early days it had been simply a matter of staging a bullfight in which the ranch's boldest vaqueros tried their luck as matadors; the surviving victors were carried off the field in triumph and treated to a wild wingding. By 1881 this celebration had expanded under the influence of the horseback vaqueros; to the *corrida* had been added the numerous steer-roping and bull-riding events that we now know as the rodeo.

In those days nothing was organized with any formality. If a vaquero took it into his head to see if he could ride a wild steer he simply did so, in whatever corral happened to be empty; his friends would sit on the fence and cheer him on until he was pitched off. Sometimes eight or ten such events would transpire simultaneously in various corrals. A vaquero with a saddle blanket in lieu of a cape would be dodging a charging bull to the accompaniment of raucous rowdy *Olés* from boisterous onlookers while in the adjacent corral a horseman with his lariat spinning would be chasing a terrified steer.

I naturally drummed up a shooting event. We fired at tin airtights and sundry other targets for a couple of hours during which large numbers of spectators drifted by to watch me shoot.

There was no real competition from other shooters. Most cowhands are abysmal marksmen, wild romantic tales to the contrary. Often the vaquero uses his revolver as a hammer, pry bar or club; the accuracy of a weapon that has been thus battered and bent is hardly likely to be impressive. And hardworking vaqueros have little time to practice shooting.

Caleb Rice, who in the 1870s enforced the laws of several Kansas cow towns, later told me of a remarkable gun battle that took place in one of his towns—a battle that must prove once and for all the average Westerner's gun-handling skill. Two rival Texas trail crews happened to meet in a small saloon after driving their respective herds to Kansas. Heated words were exchanged, someone drew a gun, a brawl commenced and abruptly all hell broke loose—forty men went to war.

Concussion from the first flurry of gunshots blew out most of the oil lamps but the cowhands kept shooting and Caleb, approaching on the run, had visions of the carnage he would find within.

According to the evidence of lead that was dug out of the woodwork the next day, more than two thousand shots were fired in about two minutes in that confined space.

All the guns were fired empty; then Caleb and his deputies went in to view the massacre.

A horse, tethered fifty yards away up the street, was the only casualty. Not a man in the saloon had been scratched.

So much for the vaunted gun skills of cowhands.

In any case I had no challengers at Pueblo Candelas; I was too well-known. The vaqueros were happy enough to shoot for pesos among themselves but when I stepped forward they stood back respectfully and called boisterously for an exhibition. I obliged them, writing the word "Candelas" in a plank with bullet holes, driving nails into fence-posts and generally showing off. One vaquero threw a handful of six pennies in the air and I punctured them all before any had hit the ground.

I enjoyed putting on such displays but I had no competitors and little chance to earn betting money; after a while I put up my weapons and went along to see what excitements might be taking place elsewhere.

A stagecoach—the regular Friday afternoon coach from Agua Prieta—came up through the pueblo drawn by four teams. As it neared the *portal* of the company sutler's emporium, which was its normal depot, the coach suddenly was attacked by a whirlwind crowd of horsemen who stampeded forward shooting in the air and howling like Indians.

The coach horses bolted and came thundering toward the corrals, escorted by the galloping cowhands who kept whooping and blasting the sky.

They were a colorful gang of ruffians led by Nate Loving in his bright red outfit, all of them laughing fit to split their seams.

The red-faced coachman sawed at his reins and stood up against the brake handle but the teams only stopped when they came up against the fence; they made a bunched squealing tangle and several men rushed forward to sort out the traces while the coachman bellowed oaths at the high-spirited vaqueros.

In the meantime Nate and his henchmen were still riding about, shooting holes in the air and yip-yip-whooping, waving various articles of cloth overhead and all but trampling those unfortunates on foot who happened to be in their midst.

In the confusion a corral gate came open. A steer lunged through the open gateway, hotly pursued by a vaquero, his lariat loop twirling overhead. The vaquero hurled his noose but it fell a fraction short and the steer ran on toward the crowd.

I joined with those who shouted warnings to the crowd—people were about to get impaled on those long horns—but in the general din we were not heard. The steer, with madness in its eyes, thundered toward the crowd. I lifted my gun, ready to shoot it down.

That was when Nate Loving came bursting toward the steer on horseback. At first I thought he intended to head it off. But the steer had too much headway and instead of intercepting it Nate found himself chasing it. The steer was almost onto the crowd then—men reeling back in panic—and none of them had time to get away. I was running full tilt, trying to get a clear shot at the steer through the tumbling crowd.

Then Nate launched himself from his saddle.

He went through the air like a swimming diver; his outstretched hands locked precisely on the handlebar horns; he swung his legs forward and dug his heels in; he twisted the steer's head ferociously.

The steer skidded, slowed, began to tilt over. Nate twisted its head like a corkscrew, horns all the way under. His boot heels dug trenches in the clay.

The momentum came off the charge; the steer fell on its side and slid a few feet farther. Nate disengaged himself and stood up—I saw him haul out his revolver, ready to club the steer but it only reared to its feet and trotted dazedly away. Several vaqueros choused it back into the corral while the crowd yelled happily and men nearly trampled one another to get close to Nate and clap his back and shout in his face.

The little black vaquero came up beaming. He caught my eye and winked.

When the mob began to disperse Nate drawled to me, "Nothin' to it, gringo." He always called me gringo. Mostly the word was a vile insult but Nate's use of it passed for camaraderie. He said, "I seen young Bill Pickett do that lots of times over in Texas. Bulldogging. Puts on a good show, don't it?"

"You do that often?"

"I been practicing it some."

"Would you do it every day if you got paid for it?"

Nate laughed at me. "Now who the hell gonna pay me for that?"

. . .

That afternoon while the raucous celebration went on without relief I saw old Fitz Bragg riding forward through the crowd. Suspecting that he was looking for me, I made myself apparent to him and Fitz gigged the horse, shoving cowhands out of the way. He came along talking a mile a minute but I couldn't make out a word of it; we were surrounded by whoops and yells, the pound of running hooves, the occasional gunshot. I shook my head and cupped my ear. Fitz reined across my bows and pulled back the flap cover of his saddlebag; he, or the horse, threw a powerful stink at me. Fitz pulled an envelope from the pouch and waved it above my head like a peppermint stick held just beyond a child's reach. Then with a beaming grin he rode back toward the railway and I followed along as best I could, prying my way through the crowd in his wake.

He allowed me to take the envelope; then he dismounted arthritically and faced me with an idiot grin. "Go ahead, open the damn thing."

I unfolded the document and glimpsed the printed heading: THE PRESIDENT OF THE UNITED STATES OF AMERICA. My eye whipped down the page—*With regard to the great injustice that has been perpetrated upon you . . . unlawful conviction in absentia without trial or defense . . . And in view of the great and valiant service you have rendered your country in promoting the peace and welfare of White-Indian relations . . . as Commander-in-Chief do hereby confirm your temporary Commission as Lieutenant-Colonel of Scouts in the Army of the United States . . . and do hereby extend, grant and proclaim you absolved, acquitted, and PARDONED IN FULL AND PERPETUITY . . . with my sincere personal apologies in behalf of a sometimes insensitive Government . . . I remain Gratefully and Admiringly Your Ob't S'v't, Chester A. Arthur.*

I did not turn away from Fitz; I didn't mind his seeing my sudden tears.

. . .

I poured the drinks and chalked myself up for the round. The cantina—poor light, splintered furnishings, smells of tobacco and grain whisky and tequila and mezcal and pulque and beer—was crowded to its Plimsoll with a flowing jam of celebrants on their way in from the festivities and out to rejoin them. The gambling tables were packed three deep.

"Thirty-five to one here. *Treinticinco al uno.*"

"Get your money down, amigos."

"Eight to five on the colors. . . ."

"Keno."

"Are you all down, gents?"

We carried the drinks out back into the weeds; a drunk snored under

298

the cantina's back *portal* and a small dog panted in the shade. Fitz said, "What you fixing to do with that shinplaster?"

"Go home and post it in the newspapers. I don't want lunatics chasing me on the belief they'll get bounty reward money for my hair."

"Your hair don't look like it's worth much, you want the truth. All white like that, looks like an old man's scalp lock. You ever think about using some kind of pomade to put color back in it? You can't be, what, a whole lot over thirty years of age, can you? Look like sixty with that white hair and all."

"It's my hair, I don't aim to paint it up fake. People can take it or leave it," I said. "You want a job, Fitz?"

"I got a job."

"How can you stomach working for Sieber?"

"I'll tell you, Albert's the one who'll end this fighting. He's the man to bring peace down here. He'll do it better and faster than any other man alive. But right now we've still got Geronimo and the Apach' Kid out against us. I expect I'll work with Albert until the war stops. And by then reckon I'll be too old for much. What kind of job you had in mind for me? You aim to set up shooting contests again?"

"Not exactly."

"Not exactly how?"

"I'm going to put on an outdoor show. There'll be shooting matches all right but that's just part of it."

"Like a circus you mean."

"No," I said, "not like a circus. I intend to bring the West to people in the East. Not Mr. Barnum's freaks or some kind of Russian acrobats or whatever. I'm going to show them a piece of the true real West—like this roundup that's going on right here today. Catch-roping steers and riding buck-jumpers, all that stuff. People back East, they'll pay money for tickets to see it, I promise you." I grinned at him. "Fitz, you ought to come along. You're a famous man, you're just about the last of the mountain-man pioneers. They'd pay money to see you."

"What, playacting on the stage?"

"No stage. Outdoors."

"Outdoors? I never heard of that kind."

"Nobody has. Yet."

"Well it don't make no never-mind. I guess I'm like Caleb Rice. I don't expect I'd take to playacting much."

"You ever hear from Caleb?"

"No. Hear about him, time and again. I believe he's still punching law up in Kansas there."

I said, "You work out of Fort Lowell. You must know Tucson well enough. I've an old friend named Isaac Singman—a long time ago he said he was thinking he might open a dry-goods there. Do you happen to know if—"

"Sure, sure enough. You can't miss Singman's. Biggest building in Tucson. You mean that rich-son-of-a-bitch Jew is a friend of yours? My, my—I didn't ever know you counted such high-tone friends."

I aimed a mock blow at his face. "All right, Fitz, I just want you to remember one thing. When you and Sieber get done with your war and the army throws you out like an old shoe, you come look me up and we'll get the world by the tail together. Hear?"

·   ·   ·

Fifty miles southeast of Tucson the Bisbee rail spur conjoins the main Southern Pacific line. I had to change trains there and I was pleased to see a poster on the platform wall advertising SINGMAN'S GRAND EMPORIUM—TUCSON'S FINEST.

It was only an hour's journey and it brought me to Tucson on a lovely mild desert afternoon. The town was a great deal expanded since I'd last seen it guiding the wagon train to California a dozen years earlier; it sported high-front buildings and street-corner lamps now, overhead telegraph wires and a large depot of impressive facade. Stretching west along Congress Street were three-story hotels and saloons and shops, even an opera house.

I left my belongings in the left-baggage room and was directed to Singman's Grand Emporium; it was a few minutes' walk. As I passed along the street I drew the curious stares of Tucsonans and one or two scowls; in truth I must have looked a wild creature against those sedate and civilized surroundings.

The emporium's two-story structure spanned an entire block and was rendered loftier by a high false wall bearing ten-foot-high lettering: SINGMAN'S.

Inside the lofty gloom a good many people rattled around—customers and clerks—but the place was so vast it did not seem crowded. There was nothing elegant about it, nothing of the fashionable style of later years; it was a barn of a place and put me in mind of the Sacramento warehouses in which Isaac had done his business a decade earlier. Goods of all conceivable descriptions hung from pillars and rafters; jumbled articles were stacked in haphazard piles; great stacks of crates and kegs made pyramids throughout the cavernous space. There was a rich intermingled aroma of new leather and old sawdust, lamp oil and gunpowder and oily wool and a thousand other things.

I buttonholed a clerk and was directed to the stairs; made my way up into the second story and found myself in a stadium that equaled the lower level; asked directions again and finally found myself at the rear of the place talking to a clerk at an anteroom desk, only to learn that the proprietor was out somewhere in the emporium looking after his customers. I had to prowl the place nearly half an hour before I caught sight of Isaac.

His beard was thick and salted with grey—he was forty or thereabouts but he'd always looked old; to my eye he hadn't changed a bit. He was still slender, a bit stooped, birdlike in his movements. The steel-framed spectacles clung precariously to his nose.

He stared at me in disbelief; came away from his customers lifting his glasses to his eyes to see me more clearly.

"Well," I said softly, "you seem to have prospered."

"My God." He wrung my hands with delight. "I didn't know if you were alive or dead."

"I'll tell you all about it if you'll invite me to supper."

"Done. My God, Hugh, what a marvelous sight you are."

.   .   .

Isaac's coachman collected us in a hansom that had Singman's Grand Emporium advertisements discreetly lettered on the doors. Isaac chattered all the while, a magpie rattle that made me laugh. We rode through tree-lined streets along the Rillito and drew up before a stately Spanish house deep in the shade. "No more sleeping under wagons for you, Isaac?"

He twinkled. "Come and see."

Beside the house in a coach barn stood my old Studebaker wagon—fresh-painted and glistening as if it were brand-new. Its tongues were propped up against the dashboard as if it were ready to be hitched and rolled out.

"You see I haven't forgotten," he said. Then he took my arm and hurried me to the house. "And now you must meet the Singmans."

I drew back, astonished, while he flung the door open and sent his eager call ahead into the house: "Margaret? Margaret—we have a guest!"

Then I heard the piping of children's voices and a woman's quick steps—Isaac urged me inside and in the cool dimness I saw the woman enter wiping her hands on her apron, the dark red hair heavy about her face; then she stopped and the tentative smile fled as her glance fell against me. The apron dropped from her grasp. In an unawares and revealing gesture her hands went to her hair.

Isaac paid no notice. He gabbled on with happy introductions—"my oldest and dearest friend, you've heard so much about . . ."

Maggie. And I remembered a sweltering bedroom in Nogales, the scent of cheap whisky, gold coin on a dressing table.

She said: "What brings you here, Hugh?"

"A good fast train."

Isaac in the end was alerted by our faces. He pushed his glasses up on his nose; then he rocked his hand, fingers splayed. "Hugh, we have no secrets in this house."

"In that case," I said to the woman, "I'm happy to see you. You did me a kindness when I was sore in need of one. Even if you don't remember it—"

"I remember it. I never knew your name but I might have known. So you're the great Hugh Cardiff." She took my hand; Isaac put his arm about her. She stood half a head taller than my friend.

Isaac said, "We take our pleasure in shocking some people but not you, Hugh. I'm pleased you remember each other with fondness."

Margaret said, "Come, Hugh, and meet our children."

. . .

Isaac and I took our whisky and cigars into the parlor. I could hear the rattle of crockery as Margaret and the Indian woman cleared the dining room. He turned up the lamp and sprawled on a settee. "Light and digest," he said. Then we heard something smash in the kitchen—a plate, a bowl, some bit of porcelain—and it only widened Isaac's smile. "She becomes excited when friends come to visit. She's still got a bit of child in her, my Margaret."

"Count yourself lucky."

"I do. I'm sure you've guessed how and where we met."

"Yes."

"Nine years ago. I was only starting my business here then—of course the town was scandalized when we were married. There are still women who cross the street to avoid speaking with Margaret."

"You've got two good boys there."

"I am thankful for that too. The boys have their mother's strength and their father's intellect. I expect great things of them."

"Don't push them, though."

"Only a little nudge now and then. I am sorry about your son, Hugh. I know what a son means. I've no idea what I'd do if I lost one of mine." He blew smoke toward the ceiling. "What star do you follow now?"

"I'm heading East by stages. I've had a pardon from the President. . . ."

"East—and then?"

"I intend to open an outdoor exposition. A show of the West. Isaac, I want to borrow money from you."

"No. I won't lend you a cent." Then he took down the cigar. "I won't have to. You're quite a wealthy man—you can use your own money if you intend to invest in such a foolish venture."

"Come again?"

"You invested in this enterprise of mine, don't you remember? After

302

the fire wiped me out in Sacramento." He jabbed the cigar toward me; his eyes twinkled. "We've been equal partners from the beginning. I was so relieved to see you—there'd been rumors, you know, that you'd been killed by Indians or died of smallpox in Mexico. I don't know what would have become of your wealth if you'd died. I know of no heirs. The thing is, don't you know, half of every penny of profits in my business has gone into your accounts. The firm is registered under both names. Hugh Cardiff and Isaac Singman. We're duly recorded as equal partners in law."

. . .

Clutching me firmly by the arm Isaac marched into the bank. I said, "You've broken your back for a dozen years to build up your business. I didn't lift a finger."

"You made it possible."

"You'd have done it without my money. It might have taken a little longer, that's all. You've got to quit this nonsense, Isaac. Just pay me back the few thousand I lent you and I'll borrow the rest of my needs somewhere else."

"I've never known a man so eager to turn down a fortune. Now stop this childish arrogance and we'll say no more about it."

We stood just inside the door; a woman pushed her way past us and we moved to one side. The woman gave me a peculiar stare and left the bank. Isaac hissed at me, keeping his voice down. "I'm as wealthy as I ever dreamed of being. Do you think I need your money as well? Do you think I could possibly take it? You insult me by refusing it!"

. . .

When I made my way back to the house I found Margaret Singman watching the children play under shade trees. She gave a start at my approach. "My goodness, you don't announce yourself when you move."

"Got a little Apache in me, I guess." I kept my eyes on the two boys.

"You feel awkward with me, don't you? Listen, Hugh, he don't mind about what I used to do for a living. It's not as if I'm the only whore who ever got married, is it. Of course there's a lot of evil talk—I married him for his money, all that nonsense. Well I didn't. He was barely making ends meet when I married him. The store was mortgaged and we lived in a one-room 'dobe for the first two years and I didn't mind a bit of it. I never knew a gentler or more loving man."

Apparently she mistook my silent consideration for suspicion. Her voice lifted defensively. "All right, I was getting long in the tooth, I wanted a ticket out. He asked me and I said yes—I didn't love him, I just wanted a man to support me for a change. But listen, you live with Isaac a little while, you can't help falling in love with the silly sawed-off half-blind leprechaun."

303

I said, "How'd this be, Maggie—I would like to treat you both to the best dinner in town tonight."

She laughed in her throat, a soft and attractive woman full in her skin. "Been a while since I had occasion to put on my glad rags." Then she swayed toward me and kissed my cheek.

. . .

Over the modest shop in Santa Fe hung a huge wooden gun twelve feet long for the edification of those who couldn't read the legend spelled upon it: GUNS—PISTOLS—REVOLVERS—*GUNSMITH*—RIFLES—SHOT-GUNS—AMM'N. *Kevin Tyree, Prop.*

The narrow shop stank of oil and sulfur. A clutter of weapons filled it and the ceiling was pendant with cartridge belts, holsters and scabbards that enriched the aroma with the smell of fresh leather. Beyond the counter was a workbench at which Kevin was bent over a grinding wheel, his feet pumping the pedals; there was the high buzz of the wheel against cold steel. Over his shoulder I saw a place-of-honor rack of hardwood that supported eight or ten gleaming rifles with polished stocks and gleaming blued barrels. Above the rack hung a modest placard: *Rifles Hand-Mfg. by K. Tyree.*

I hadn't seen Kevin for more than fifteen years; he'd been a boy then. But I'd have known him on the street—he hadn't grown old and he bit his lip as he bent his face to the work with the same determined youthful eagerness I remembered from the smithy forge on the Tyree Grant.

When I entered he looked up without recognition. "Be right with you." He hadn't grown very tall and was nearly as frail as Isaac—he was pale and his hair had darkened, very fine and thin on his head—but his voice had gone startlingly deep for a man so small.

He stood up from the bench. The wheel rolled to a stop, pedals flapping.

"Hello, Kevin."

I watched puzzlement creep across his brow; he came forward slowly. "Is it . . . Hugh? Can it be . . . ?"

. . .

"We've spent the past three hours talking about everything under the sun except Libby. Tell me about her."

He bit his lip. Presently he said, "She hasn't changed where you can see it."

"But."

"Well she's still married to Senator Merriam."

"He made that, did he?"

304

"Took him two tries. They're down in Washington—big house, you ought to see the place, quite a palace. Rich. You know, I mean *rich*. Some put the Merriams with the Vanderbilts and them."

"Do you see her?"

"Not much. Letters now and then."

"Well how is she, dammit?"

"All right I guess."

"Kevin . . ."

"Look, Hugh, I know things I shouldn't know. I'm the one she confides in. Guess she doesn't trust anybody else—but it makes things awkward for you and me."

"Why?"

"Why? Because I know Bill's your son, not Merriam's."

"I still don't get your meaning."

"You want him, don't you? The boy. Guess that's inevitable. It's what you came back for, isn't it?"

"What gives you that idea?"

"He's your son."

I said, "Until this minute I didn't even know his name."

"William Phipps Campbell Merriam."

"God."

"Call him Bill. Everybody does except Libby, she calls him William, like the way Mother used to call her Elizabeth."

Kevin went along to the door and hung the *Closed* sign in the window. I said, "What's he like, then?"

"Eleven now. Bright as a whip. Looks a lot like you—tall, got your shoulders and eyes, jawbone, nose. Kind of lazy, guess you could say indifferent. Wouldn't surprise me he grew up arrogant—the way Merriam treats him. Was up to me I'd tell you go get the boy out of there, hell, I'd help you. Bring him out, raise him like a man. But he's my sister's boy. You see why I don't like talking about this, Hugh?"

He'd developed a staccato way of talking as if he didn't have much use for conversation and wanted to get it over with as quickly as possible so as to get back to the dependable precision of his mechanisms. But it couldn't conceal his troubled anguish.

I said, "Your first thought was that I came back to take the boy. What put it into your head? I need to know."

"It's what they all believe."

"Who?"

"Libby, Vern, especially Merriam. Your pardon was in all the newspapers you know. Must have been broadsided by the White House— good publicity for President Arthur, you know. You're still a famous man. All those dime novels. Got a stack of them at home myself. Libby wrote me, said Merriam's afraid you're after the boy."

I said, "Good. It won't hurt him to sweat."

"Look, Hugh, he's one of the richest men in the world. People get in his way he squashes them."

"People try that from time to time. I don't squash too easy."

"You mean to take the boy?"

"In my own time, in my own way." I studied him. "Would she leave him, Kevin?"

It took him a while to examine it. "Can't say for sure. She's made her peace with him. Everybody expects he'll be President before long. She wants that. She's ambitious. Partly for Bill's sake, but I don't know—she's harder inside than she used to be. Colder; you know. Long time since she had anything to warm to except Bill. Hugh, you've been away years. Years and years. She's been living in that house—big chilly palace, rooms so big the light doesn't get up in the corners. She's past thirty. Jesus, she's not the same—nobody is. Ten, twelve years?"

I brooded on that; Kevin went back around the counter to his rack of handmade rifles. He took one down and offered it to me. "Take a look at that."

It was a slide-action repeater, skeletal, very light in weight; a sporting piece with precise caliper screws to set the sights. The walnut stock was hollow-ground to paper-thinness except where it needed bulk for shoulder and hand; the metal fittings were as light as filigree. It was like a feather in my hands.

"Thirty-eight fifty-six one-twenty," he said—caliber 38/100 of an inch diameter; 56 grains of black gunpowder; a bullet weighing 120 grains of lead. He said, "I chambered it for the standard Winchester cartridge case but you load your own powder and bullet—the mold goes with the rifle. Weighs short of five pounds fully loaded. No good for long-range big-game work—too light—but for varmints or targets it's the best rifle I ever made. Shoot your glass balls in the air with that all day long. Slide action, you never have to shift your grip while you shoot."

"How fast is this action when it's loaded?"

"Fast as you can pump it. You know I wouldn't make a slow piece, Hugh. Shoot that rifle so fast you can hardly hear where one shot leaves off and the next starts. Full-length magazine there, spring load—nine in the magazine and one up the spout, ten-shot repeater."

"It ejects out the side," I said. "Up or down?"

"Down and forward. The empties won't get in your eyeline."

A sensible man doesn't choose a rifle without first trying it in the field.

But when I handed the .38-56 back to Kevin I said, "Make me six of them."

His smile went wide. "I designed this for you, Hugh. Twenty years of trial and error in that rifle."

"Not too much error, I hope. A thousand dollars for the six, how's that?"

"No." He turned the rifle over in his hands, snicked it open and looked into the gleaming breech. "A gift, Hugh. And I won't take an argument."

"I'm rich now, I can afford it."

"You can't afford to buy these rifles. You can only accept them."

I had to acquiesce. Then I said, "You mentioned Vern."

"Aeah. Big brother Vern."

"He lives there?"

"In Washington. Not in their house but near enough. Spends time in New York on the high-stakes card tables but I guess he wins some of it back shooting matches. Good marksman, got to give him that. But I won't work on his rifles. He misses a shot, he blames me for it. I don't take that anymore. Not from him or anybody. My rifles hit what they're aimed at."

He smiled in an odd way, crooked; he said, "Vern claims he's the best. Claims he could beat you now."

"He'll get his chance to try."

"You going back on the circuit, then?"

"In a way. I'm going to start an outdoor show. There'll be a lot of guns and I'll need an armorer to keep everything working properly. We'll be using a lot of blank cartridges and you know how they gum up a weapon."

"Any third-rate gunsmith can handle that."

"Well my armorer can hire himself an assistant for that. But I'll stand ready anytime, anyplace to shoot against all comers. That means my rifles need to be in perfect match condition. I'll be shooting exhibitions at every show. I'll be burning a lot of powder and wearing out a lot of steel."

His look was colored by skepticism and I said, "You'll have your own rolling shop. You can carry all the equipment you want. There'll be time to manufacture Tyree rifles and we'll advertise them in the show —we'll advertise the fact that I'm using them. You won't be able to keep up with the demand. You can make yourself a rich man that way if you've a mind to."

His eyes crinkled. "I don't make that many and anyhow I never had much ambition to get rich. But all right, Hugh, I'm your man."

"It'll take time to organize this—I'll send you a wire when we're ready to start. Most likely we won't roll the show until next spring. I can't see opening an outdoor show in the winter."

"Hugh—this scheme got anything to do with Libby and Bill?"

"Maybe."

"Damned if I see any connection."

"Good."

"Good?"

"If you don't see a connection, neither will Phipps Merriam."

"Be obliged if you leave me out of that part of it," he said. "My trouble is I love my sister but I always did love you more than my own real brother. Don't put me in the middle, Hugh."

"I won't. That's a promise."

.   .   .

I changed trains at Raton and changed again at Denver onto the Kansas Pacific line, traveling light.

Part of the journey I was in company with a troupe of nomadic actors who earned their passage around the country by putting on tent-show performances of drama, variety and burlesque. They weren't particularly adept and half of them were drunk all of the time but I enjoyed their company and went along to one of their shows in Colorado; chiefly I remember reading the advertisements on the stage curtain and wincing at the company's wretched rendition of *The Girl in the Gilded Cage*. The encounter gave me a vicarious taste of trouping in the raw, however, and for a while I had misgivings.

The train carried me into Ford County and decanted me at the Dodge City depot. The great cattle pens were nearly empty of stock and the town had a soporific look; the commerce of boom times had passed it by and the paint had begun to chip. Homestead farm settlers had filled up the land and left no graze for the Texas cattle herds; the cattlemen had built their own railroads down into Texas and there were no more drives or drovers. Dodge City had become a farm town.

Faded shinplasters adorned the depot walls. Most of them carried stern warnings about alcohol. Kansas had introduced prohibition and nothing but beer was legal thanks to the Puritan farmers who'd flooded the state since the introduction of the railroad. I saw a lot of boarded-up saloons along the quiet streets.

The yellowest of the shinplasters remained as a wistful souvenir:

Any person who has ever borne arms against the government of the United States of America who shall be found within the limits of the city of Dodge City, County of Ford, State of Kansas, carrying on his person a pistol, Bowie knife or other deadly weapon, shall be subject to arrest.

W. B. Masterson
Sheriff of Ford County

308

Masterson was long since gone by then and so were the post-Civil War feelings that had made a rendition of "Dixie" in Kansas saloons the inevitable overture to a chair-smashing bottle-breaking brawl.

I found Caleb in the barber's tonsorial shop, reading the *Police Gazette* and stinking of bay rum and swigging from a bottle of Dr. Ludlum's Golden Medical Tonic and Blood Purifier.

. . .

We walked the late-afternoon streets, Caleb in a plug hat and sucking on a peppermint Zanzibar. He pointed out the site where Luke Short had killed someone, the window where Dora Hand had been shot to death, the steps where Caleb and Masterson had faced down an angry Texas trail crew. "Bat and me come into this town intending to impress law and order on it if it took a dozen funerals to do it. But I never reckoned on officiating at the funeral of the whole damn town." He looked drawn, older than his years, his hound face wizened.

At the corner opposite the Dodge House he stopped and cocked his head on one side in an old and familiar gesture. "Colonel Dodge used to put up there, and old Dog Kelley the mayor. All dried up now, I expect they're fixing to close the place any day. Don't get nothing but commercial drummers no more. Maybe we got too filled up with self-righteousness behind these badges. Run out the gamblers, run out the drunks, run out the hard cases. Nothing left but dull folks. Upstanding citizens. I'm fixing to move on myself. Soon as my term expires. You know old Bat's back in New York, swears he's never going West again. Hell, Hugh, let's you and me go get ourselves a steak."

He still carried two revolvers in his sash and people still tipped their hats to him; and a few passersby recognized me. My hand was pumped and hearty nervous words stammered about us.

A slender little woman with hard blond hair accosted us outside the Whip-or-Will Café. "Caleb, you look terrible."

"Nobody ever did offer me a beauty prize, that's a fact."

"You look all stove up. You drink too much of that elixir, you'll find an early grave."

"Mary Lee, I don't rightly expect that's much of your—"

"Amelia's been gone almost a year now, isn't it?"

"Ten months, thirteen days."

The woman gave me a helpless look. "You poor bastard." I assumed she was talking to Caleb; she swept past us and away, heels clipping the boards like drumsticks.

In the café we sat on tall rickety stools before the counter. I said, "Those pies look good. God, how many years has it been since I've had a peach pie?"

"You must've been pretty far back in the mountains for a fact."

"Who's Amelia?"

"Used to be my wife, I guess."

"What did she die of?"

"She didn't. She got tired chasing me around from town to town. After a while I guess she forgot who she was chasing."

Knowing what it was like to carry a torch for a woman I nevertheless had the gall to adjure, "You ought to put that out of mind and look ahead now."

"How would you like your steak, Hugh—medium rare or right in the face?"

"There's always been some question in my mind which of us was the bigger fool," I said, "and looking at you right now I still don't know the answer. You're looking like an old man."

"You try getting shot at and stepped on without a thank-you or by-your-leave."

"Then quit."

He said, "I guess not," and turned to talk to the waitress about food.

When those negotiations were concluded I said to him, "In the spring I'll be putting an outdoor show on the road. Come on with me and we'll partner up again. You'll get all the glory you can use."

"Much oblige, I guess, but I've lined up my next job. Going to work for Billy Tilghman down in the Indian Nations. Deputy federal marshal for Judge Parker."

"You just said you'd had enough of that."

"Ever bit of it. But it's what I do. I'm a dandy lawman, you know, I'm about the best next to maybe Tilghman himself. I'll never be hard put to find a job. The pay's all right, you get to keep half the fines, you get bounties now and then. You see these clothes on my back? St. Louis and top price, and I can afford to wear them for working duds. I get respect too."

"That's not what you said a minute ago."

"Old Bob still makes his living writing those fairy tales about me and you. People know me all right. They think twice before they disturb the peace while I'm around. They all scared of Caleb Rice and that's a fact."

"You take much pleasure out of going around scaring people?"

"You know sometimes it's fun. They don't just call me hey-you any-more, I'll tell you that. It's Mr. Rice Sir."

"I can see how much pleasure you take from that. You get a runaway wife and a lot of lonely nights with Dr. Ludlum's elixir."

"You want to go easy now."

"Do I? Is there anybody else around here who'll talk to you that way?"

310

"Mary Lee Plate for one. You just met her outside there? Woman gives me no peace."

"I suspect that's because she cares about you."

"You have any idea how many times I've had to arrest that whore?"

"You'd rather wait for a high-society lady, is that it?"

"Hugh, get off of me now. I'm going to be all right. I'm getting through this bad patch here, I made the mistake of falling in with a pious little preacher's daughter that turned out to be not fit to shine my boots. I guess I can talk about her that way, it must mean I'm getting my self-respect back. Pretty soon I'll start to laugh about what a fool I been. Old Billy Tilghman's picked me to be his right-hand man and that's about the best compliment I ever had. Don't you worry about me."

"This is going to be the biggest fancy show the world ever saw, Caleb. I'd like to recruit you."

"I don't need another dose of your show business. I'm no playactor."

"We used to be a dandy team."

"You want to pin on a badge and we can be one again."

"Not my line of work."

"That's exactly what I just said to you."

"All right, dammit."

"Cheer up, eat your steak. I know where we can get our hands on a jug of Tennessee corn. We'll tie one on good enough to keep you hungover all the way to the St. Louis depot."

. . .

Night came on to hide their dark deeds. Horses were made ready, the dreadful arsenal of weaponry was loaded, and the dark evil leader prepared to give the order to horse. But then from the darkness came the tones of a powerful, yet calm, manly voice that struck terror into the cowards' hearts:

"Hold on, varmints, he's a dead man who moves, for I have got ye all covered!"

For Hugh Cardiff had discovered the trap!

Yet then the dastardly Holliday, filled with treachery and concealing himself behind the mass of a cutthroat henchman, drew his blade and sprang at Hugh Cardiff from behind with a fearful thrust of steel.

But the frontiersman's keen ears forewarned him, and with the speed of a bolt of lightning he spun to parry the deadly blow of the wily villain— thrice Holliday's steel sought to drink his blood, thrice the plainsman's rifle held it at bay while the ring of steel upon steel scraped against the ashen hearts of Holliday's cowardly comrades, not one of whom was man enough, or possessed the presence of mind, to leap into the breach.

Then the plainsman's great fist loomed, and the villain Holliday fell unconscious from the blow, struck straight between the eyes as if he had been poleaxed by a giant!

Quick as a flash Hugh Cardiff's rifle danced toward the others. "Would anyone else care for a fight?"

I had opportunity to do a bit of reading on the train journey East. After two or three examples of Bob Halburton's work I was relieved to open the cover of *The Adventures of Tom Sawyer* by Mr. Mark Twain, which everyone told me I must read. And in truth I found myself much pleased by this nostalgic tale of young adventure; it brought back to mind my own Kentucky youth.

The talk among the traveling strangers was desultory—the weather, the economy. The news at that particular time was unexciting to the extent that the arrest in England of the Irish orator Parnell made headlines. A stirring speech delivered by Senator Merriam was reported in several newspapers; the speech had to do with a dispute that was going on, even then, over proposed treaties with Central American governments and the choice of sites for a ship canal through the isthmus. In a St. Louis newspaper I found an announcement of a forthcoming shooting match in Baltimore—Dr. Bogardus' name was mentioned prominently, as was Vernon Tyree's—and in a dog-eared issue of *Harper's Weekly* I found mention of the closing of Buffalo Bill Cody's stage show, to which the magazine referred as "the end of a short-lived era in theatrical curiosities."

I absorbed everything I could—sucked it in as a desert sucks in rain —for I was a long-time stranger to those all-important rhythms and routines of civilization. As the railway coach carried me into the East I felt more and more self-conscious and ill-prepared.

In Chicago I visited Beadle's—at that time the publisher of Bob Halburton's Ichabod Zachary novels—and, upon identifying myself to the managers, was treated to a glorious evening on the town. Then I was on my way again because they informed me that the always restless Bob had taken up residence for the moment in the plush Astoria Hotel in New York City.

. . .

The woman who answered the bellman's knock was unusually tall— six feet, I estimated. Her outfit was colorful enough, a defiant bold yellow dress, but its severe cut accentuated the length of her bones. Her face was not unattractive, although perhaps longer and narrower than fashion might have preferred, but her expression was weary and harried and suspicious. Masses of fine hair were drawn up in a chignon atop her head; in subsequent times I always had difficulty defining its color— somewhere between red and brown: a kind of rosewood-walnut blend of hues. Her age was difficult to determine on first glance; later I learned she was twenty-nine.

She had in her hand a notepad and pencil and peered with annoyance at the bellman. "Yes? What is it now?"

"I'm sorry, ma'am. This gentleman insisted on coming up."

She transferred her suspicion to me. "May I help you? I'm Mr. Halburton's secretary."

"Would you mind telling him an old friend is here?"

"And what name should I give?"

"Hugh Cardiff."

Her face changed. "My God—you just could be, too."

"My word on it, ma'am," I said dryly.

She glanced over her shoulder. "Well I suppose you'd better come in."

. . .

The front room of the suite was strewn with stacks of foolscap and dime novels: on chairs and sills and floors. The woman said, "Take a seat if you can find one," and went briskly toward the farther door. I watched the sway of her hips.

She closed the door behind her before I had more than a glimpse of the bedroom beyond; I heard the bad-tempered growl of Bob's voice through the partition. I went around looking at the heaps of paperbound novels. *Caleb Rice Takes a Chance. The Guns of Hugh Cardiff. Cardiff's Trek: Being a True and Authentic Account of the Grueling Desert Pursuit of the Notorious Apache Chief Ibran. Adventures on the Candelas. Man of Dodge City: True Exploits Behind the Badge, Featuring the Famous Caleb Rice. The General's Daughter; or, Hugh Cardiff Tames a Savage.*

I was still studying the implications of that latter title with wonder when I heard the latch and turned to hear Bob Halburton's affectionate rumble: "More'n five hundred of them, Hugh, and the public never tires of them. I wrote some of those in less than twenty-four hours each."

"Having read a few of them I wonder why it took you so long."

I said it mostly in jest but then my eye fell upon his face. He looked terrible. He gave me an unblinking bloodshot look, his eyes narrowed painfully. His costume was dismal enough for a preacher's; his hands trembled and when he reached for the cigar in his mouth the back of his hand struck the ash, showering sparks over his suit. When he lurched forward to embrace me the hanging wattle shifted under his round chin. A sickly smell hung about him; I heard him wheeze.

He squinted into my face, grunted and wedged himself into a small armchair. His hips squeezed out under its arms. "My God. You know I never expected to see you again." He prodded the cigar toward the tall woman in yellow. "You've met my secretary, Jeanette Fowler?"

The woman and I inclined our heads toward each other, not without reserve. She moved toward Bob's chair. Possession was evident in the distracted way her hand fell upon his shoulder. She said, "Mr. Halburton has been very ill, Mr. Cardiff."

I could see that for myself. I said, "You look terrible."

"I know I do. It'll pass, they tell me. Influenza, gout, you name it. I'm on the road to recovery, however, mark my words." He gave a reproachful belch, as if his illness had been my fault. "Be that as it may —how the devil are you?"

"Well I reckon I'm better than I've any right to be."

He chuckled at that. "To be sure—considering the vast number of times you've been punctured by knives, arrows and bullets."

"Come on, Bob, I've never been shot but once in my life."

"Ah yes. I sometimes forget the distinction between the reality of Hugh Cardiff and the tales in my books." He cocked a raw eye at Jeanette Fowler. "I'm afraid you'll find him disappointingly tame, my dear."

"That might be a relief." But the smile she gave me had no warmth; it was dictated only by courtesy. She didn't like me, that was plain. Evidently she considered me a threat to Bob; I couldn't fathom why.

He said, "Your shoulder seems to've healed, in any case. Dr. Bogardus was convinced you wouldn't use that arm."

"Dr. Bogardus should have known better. It takes both arms to shoot a rifle."

"Indeed." He grinned maliciously. "Are you out to outshoot the old rapscallion again?"

"Every chance I get. I'm back from a long time's exile, Bob, and it's a long time I aim to make up for."

"That's the spirit. My Lord, what I'd give to be with you—riding the plains once again, fighting off redskins as we used to, hoorawing the frontier with you and Caleb, leaving our mark from Council Bluffs clear to California and back. . . ." He smiled dreamily into the fog of cigar smoke. "Jeanette, those were truly the days."

I let him run down. Then I said, "I want you back with me. It's one reason I'm here."

"No!" It burst from the woman involuntarily; I saw her eyes go wide as if she'd startled herself.

I was baffled. "Ma'am?"

She said, "He's safe here. . . ."

"Safe from what?"

"He's not a well man."

"Nonsense," Bob said. "I'll be back on my feet in no time."

"Yes, you will—but not if you go off like a whirlwind again." She scowled furiously. "Bob's health is fragile. He won't admit it but it's true. I kept trying to persuade him to settle in one place but he'd have none of that. He had to be forever off on a new expedition to find fresh tales of adventure in foreign parts. My God, the horrid journeys we've taken, the bedbug palaces we've seen—it took the influenza to hobble him here, Mr. Cardiff. Otherwise we'd have been off to Arabia a week ago."

Bob said, "How the hell can a writer get inspiration in a hotel room? One must go where the adventure is."

"He's too old for it," she said to me. "He won't admit it but he's fifty-six years old."

"That's not old," Bob said. "I've got another twenty, thirty years in me."

"Not if you keep burning it up at this rate." She went back to me. "Leave him alone, Mr. Cardiff. He needs to rest."

I said to Bob, "How long's the lady been with you now?"

"Couple of years."

She was biting her lip. I said, "I guess I know him as well as anybody. If anything will kill him it's boredom."

"Absolutely dead-on right." Bob smacked his knee with his fist. "If I can't ride into adventure with the wind in my face and a saber gleaming high in my fist, there's no point in living anyway. What's the good of resting? Time enough for that in the grave. There's got to be a difference between a man and a vegetable."

He cocked an eye at me. "I've been trying to get that through her stubborn head but she just won't listen."

"Anybody can get knocked down by a fever," I said, "but you can't make an invalid of him for the rest of his life on that account."

"Hear, hear!"

Her lips were compressed into a thin pale line. "Mr. Cardiff, I've had about enough of this."

"Then go!" Bob shouted. "Get out and take your damned apron strings with you!"

The woman gave me a livid glance. Without a word she strode to the door and went out. The door closed behind her with a slow quiet seething click.

Bob laughed. "She'll be back. At least I hope she will. Been a godsend to me. Don't know how I ever got along without her—you know I never had a head for petty details."

"Geniuses rarely do." I lifted a pile of magazines off a chair, reversed it and sat down vaquero fashion with my legs astraddle the back and my arms folded across the top. "And you've got a genius for promotion and publicity. You're wasting your time pounding out these hack stories, you know."

"I'll tell you something about that. I got ambition once. Saw myself as an impresario of the theatrical world. Why I was going to be the next Phineas Barnum. Perhaps you recall what happened then? I managed ever so cleverly to bankrupt the enterprise. Had it not been for your phenomenal self-sacrifice, a generosity that knew no bounds for it led you to grievous injury and even into lengthy exile, I should still to this day be paying off those debts. And in subsequent years, no matter how much success I may have achieved in publishing, no matter how much money I may have earned, I have systematically and consistently found ways to separate myself from it. This week alone, from my sickbed, I've had to dictate two full-length novels merely to keep sufficient income to pay this hotel's usurious charges, which I had allowed through some oversight to slip into considerable arrears."

"I hope you haven't spent all this time blaming yourself for what happened to me at that shooting match in Brooklyn. That was none of your fault."

"A man can't help but accept responsibility for certain things. If it hadn't been for me you wouldn't have set up that contest."

"You're as foolish as you're fat."

"Sir, I grant you that. A fool and his money . . . I've proved it often enough, haven't I?" He was looking around for a place to deposit the gnawed remains of his cigar. I brought him a glass tray and returned to my chair. He said, "As an impresario I am to be trusted only to the extent that I can be depended on to guarantee ultimate failure of any enterprise to which I set my hand. I may not have learned much over the years, but that much I have come to know."

I said, "Suppose I offered you a position where you didn't have to risk that kind of failure."

"What sort of position?"

"I want you to undertake the publicity and advertising for the greatest show the world has ever seen."

. . .

While he listened to me propose the idea of the show he kept rubbing his thumb across the pads of his fingers.

"Not a play," I said, "not a circus. We'll present our show not on a cramped stage or inside a tent, but outdoors on the wide spaces. Buffalo, horses, vaqueros, soldiers, Indians. We'll show Western life the way it is —roping, riding, stunts, the spectacles of the West. And shooting. Shooting like the world hasn't ever seen before."

The room was thick with his cigar smoke. I went around throwing the windows open; the brisk autumnal air began to push the smoke around. Bob said, "It will take a great deal of money to do the thing properly. A great deal indeed. If you don't have sufficient capital when you take the plunge, you'll never survive. It's what happened to me with the play, you recall. Mainly my own fault, but what matter whose fault it may be? If you run out of money too soon you must either close

316

the enterprise or indebt yourself to vultures. Therefore clearly the first question is, are you wealthy enough to undertake the expense?"

"I think so. What will it take?"

"We must begin by working that out."

"Then you're with me?"

"Did you ever doubt it?"

. . .

Excitement goaded us; we schemed and worked, day and night, hardly noticing the passage of time. Bob would pull the bell rope and presently a bellman would appear; we would summon our meals and drink to the room. I slept in snatches on the front-room divan after clearing it of dime novels. Now and then I went down the hall to my own room for a change of clothing. I hardly visited the luxurious indoor bathroom at the end of the hall, not more than twice in that week, and by the end of it we were both as ripe as buffalo skinners. But enthusiasm for the enterprise made Bob blossom with returning health. Color came into his cheeks; his abundant flab seemed to harden a bit; his eyes grew bright and almost clear, abraded only by the constant sting of tobacco smoke.

We drew charts and tables, worked out figures, proposed and counter-proposed the wildest of ideas; some went by the wayside, others were fitted into the plan. We had to try to anticipate every detail and then estimate its cost.

On the eighth day of our labors we recessed to assuage our exhaustion. In good cheer I soaked in the great marble tub, shouldered into my tailored finery and made my way back to Bob's smoke-encrusted suite. He was fashioning the knot in his maroon cravat. His hair was slicked back, the waistcoat smoothed down over his vast abdomen, his boots polished to a wicked gleam. By the door waited his top hat and elegant ebony walking stick. He looked every bit the man he had been a dozen years earlier, and then some; his stoutness was awesome.

But his face was troubled. "Where is that woman, Hugh?"

"She was in her room a couple of days ago."

"Not anymore. Her luggage is gone."

Our night on the town proved a deflated celebration; Bob's cheer was forced. As he grew drunk he became sullen; his bombast dwindled to grumbles. I helped him back to the hotel and went down to the desk. "Did Miss Fowler check out of the hotel?"

"Yes sir."

"Did she leave word where she could be found?"

"No sir, I don't believe she did."

. . .

Jeanette Fowler had been a clerk in a sundry shop in the village of Brewster about sixty miles north of New York City. Visiting a publisher whose summer home was near the village, Bob Halburton two years ago had chanced to drop in on the shop in order to purchase cigars. A stack of dime novels on a shelf—many of them his own compositions written under a bewildering array of pseudonyms—had drawn his attention.

The tall spinster clerk had inquired if he wished to purchase any of this literary material; Bob had been drawn into a conversation with her. The woman had a jaundiced attitude toward dime stories but she had read a few of Bob's works and pronounced them distinctly superior to the rest in diction and poetic value.

He found Miss Fowler's praise comforting and her attention flattering, for he was not a man to whom attractive women often gave second glance; when he required female companionship it was his habit to pay for it. Miss Fowler appeared happy to dine with him and converse with him and of course he had no defense against that; he was smitten immediately and was overjoyed when she accepted his suggestion that she give up her employment in the drab shop and join him in his travels as his secretary.

She was more than that, of course; companion, factotum, nurse. I did not know to what extent their intimacy might extend; even Bob, who could be rude enough, was not so petty as to boast of his sexual exploits where a good woman's name was concerned, so it was left to me to guess as to their after-dark relations. I made the normal assumptions.

It was clear after that dreary night abroad in New York that Bob missed her much more than he was prepared to admit. The next morning, on some excuse, I left him for the day. As soon as I was out of his sight I made my way directly to the teeming railway station and boarded a northbound local.

. . .

I found her with ridiculous ease; it was a small town, very quiet and lovely under the vivid leaves of autumn. I learned that her parents were farmers nearby. The tram would take me past their gate. I boarded the horse-drawn trolley and had a very pleasant thirty-minute ride, dropped off by the Fowler mailbox and walked across a crackling bed of red and yellow leaves to the porch. There was a stream and an old mill, its wheel no longer functioning; the house was mainly of stone with an upper story of white clapboard.

Jeanette's mother answered my knock and after one look at my unusual height she convinced herself I was a suitable suitor for her daughter. With comical eagerness I was invited inside upon no more introduction than my announcement that I wished to see Miss Fowler if she were at home.

Miss Fowler was not nearly so happy to see me. Her eyes were a bit swollen with the evidence of tears—they were, I noticed, a very dark blue in color—and my arrival did nothing to cheer her up.

Noncommittal monosyllables were exchanged at first until with some reluctance the mother, who was as slender as the daughter but hardly so tall, retired from the room. I had a feeling she probably posted herself just beyond the door with her ear to the wood, so I kept my voice right down. I said, "He misses you terribly."

"Does he? I was under the impression he'd made his choice."

"There's no necessity for him to choose between you and me," I said. "I'm not a threat to you, Miss Fowler. He needs you."

"That's hardly what he said."

"Do we always say what we mean?"

She said, "I came to that room twice. He gave no sign of forgiveness. He didn't retract what he'd said—to get out and go away. The two of you were deep in whatever it is you're doing. It was obvious he had no time for me. I left. I know when I'm not wanted, Mr. Cardiff. I've had many years to get used to it."

"He needs you, he wants you. I don't know what else to tell you— except that I'm fond of him and I'm not going to get between him and his happiness. You're his happiness."

"Am I?"

"Part of it. The other part—Bob's like me, he's got to make his mark on the world. Without a challenge he might as well be dead."

"This challenge you're offering him—I have a feeling it will kill him just as quickly."

"It's his choice, isn't it? Would you deny it to him?"

Her shoulders settled. A bit of a smile illuminated her features for the first time and I was surprised by how it changed her, softened her appearance; I had the sudden impulse to comfort this bony awkward outsized woman. I said, "He'd never allow to it out loud but nothing's going to please him if you don't share it."

"I half believe you, Mr. Cardiff, but I was terribly hurt when he snarled at me so. You only needed to walk in that door and he was willing without hesitation to discard everything we'd built between us. He threw me out. . . ."

"He didn't mean that. You know he didn't."

"I want to believe you."

"He was never a happy man before. He never knew how to be. The best he could do was teach himself how to be indifferent to unhappiness. I think you changed that for him. I know something did."

She said, "He thinks the world of you. To put the shoe on the other foot, I mustn't come between you."

"Come back to him then."

"How can I be sure it will work out?"

"Nothing's ever sure, is it? You can give it a shot, that's all."

We had been speaking in very subdued tones; now and then her eyes would wander toward the door behind which her mother had disappeared. Now Jeanette smiled full in my face and it was as astonishing as sunshine at midnight. As she rose she said, "It will take me a few minutes to pack my things. Will you wait?"

.   .   .

On the train she sat tall and prim beside me. "I suppose part of it was . . . you terrified me."

"I did?"

"I'd read Bob's stories and I heard him talk of you so much. It's always hard to know how much of it is true. I discounted most of it, of course, but you know there's always a kernel of truth in his stories. He extrapolates from reality but he doesn't create things out of whole cloth. Granted he's attributed adventures to you and Caleb Rice that probably occurred in other men's lives—when he's hard-pressed he'll lift the plot of one of his old Wild Bill Hickok stories and simply change the names and the locale and rewrite it with you or Caleb as the hero. But all those stories came from somewhere. That's why he insists on traveling so much. He loves to meet people, get them talking. He gets them drunk. The wilder their lies the better he likes them. He's chronicling the folklore of every campfire drunk in the West, you know. In a way it's a kind of history. No less so than the legends of King Arthur's knights."

I said, "You ever meet Caleb?"

"Yes, last year. He's a sweet little man, isn't he?"

I laughed; she seemed both startled and hurt by my laughter; I said, "I never heard anybody call him that before."

"But it's true, isn't it?"

"Yes, I guess it is."

She said, "Tell me about this scheme of yours that Bob's so smitten with."

I told her my plan for the show. She listened with polite attention but when I was done she obviously didn't think much of it. I said, "What's wrong?"

"It won't do."

"No?"

"How can you control that many wild beasts and wild men on a tour in civilized country? You'll have cowboys and ruffians disturbing the peace everywhere you go. You'll have people hurt in stampedes. Some of those bucking broncos, won't they buck right into the audience? What if people are killed?"

"We'll have to make sure it doesn't happen, won't we?"

She turned her head to give me a sidewise glance. "It seems to me, Mr. Cardiff, that you and Mephistopheles possess a close partnership."

"Well I never looked at it quite like that, ma'am."

Then I was relieved to see her smile. She actually patted the back of my hand.

The rest of that journey, which at the outset I had dreaded, proved to be surprisingly pleasant.

BOOK NINE

The Wild West Show

. . .

I SHOWED the first penciled draft to Bob Halburton in the Astoria Hotel suite. "Maybe you'd like to improve on the wording."

He read it, passed the note to Jeanette and looked at me with one eyebrow raised nearly into his hairline. "Let me see if I have the straight of this. You're claiming you can shoot straighter and faster with a rifle from horseback than any other man can do with a shotgun from a secure stance on the ground?"

"That's the proposition."

Jeanette stared at my scrawled note. "It's foolhardy."

"Foolhardy?" Bob made a face. "It's asinine. At a thousand dollars a head they'll walk away with your fortune in one afternoon."

I said, "You really think so?"

"Isn't it obvious?"

I had to smile; they were so worried.

Jeanette said, "You must be insane, Hugh."

"I should get plenty of takers then, shouldn't I?"

" 'Takers' is the word for it," Bob said. "They'll take you for everything you've got."

He retrieved the notepaper from Jeanette, studied it with gloom and whapped it with the back of his hand. Cigar ashes drifted against it. "I've seen you shoot," he said. "I know how good you are. But this is ridiculous. You've been beaten. You've been beaten on equal terms, let alone against such self-imposed handicaps as these. Why, shooters like Bogardus and Tyree would make mincemeat of you under these terms."

"They would," I agreed, "and perhaps two dozen other shooters I could name offhand."

Jeanette squinted at me, full of accusation. "You've something up your sleeve."

"Sure enough."

Bob was startled. "I don't see it."

I said, "Essence of simplicity, Bob. It only works if I draw plenty of challengers. A broadside like this, posted on quarter-page adverts in all the newspapers, should draw hundreds of amateurs out of the woodwork to try their luck. When will they ever get a better chance?"

"That won't stop you losing to Bogardus and Tyree and the rest."

"Maybe not. Or maybe I'll have some luck that day, who knows? But it doesn't matter, does it?"

"Doesn't it?"

I said, "You don't get this yet, do you? Look, suppose I lose to twenty shooters. And suppose I beat a hundred and fifty amateurs. That's a clear profit of one hundred and thirty thousand dollars."

Jeanette said dryly, "And what happens if your horse stumbles and breaks a leg?"

"I guess we'll just have to allow for a reshoot under those circumstances. In the fine print somewhere."

Bob said, "I still don't see how you can do it faster than they can."

"Shotguns are slower than rifles," I explained. "I'll be using ten-shot Kevin Tyree repeaters. I'll have one in my hand and one scabbarded on each side of the saddle. I'll have my thirty shots ready at hand. Once I start there'll be no interruption, no slowing down. I used to kill buffalo that way—as fast as I could pull the trigger from the back of a running horse."

"Buffalo's a trifle bigger target than a glass ball in the air."

"Not true, Bob. The mortal target area behind a buffalo's shoulder is no bigger than a glass ball—and it moves a lot more erratically." I spread my hands benedictorially. "Faith, my children. With a little luck

I'll beat the best of them. Without it I'll still beat the majority and make a profit. And in any case the publicity will be extraordinary. We need headlines to start the show off."

"I don't believe it," Jeanette said. "You're asking us to help you to financial ruin."

"And the destruction of your reputation," Bob said. "If you make a fool of yourself the ridicule will be deafening."

Jeanette said, "Besides, a running horse has to move—you'll be getting farther from the targets all the time unless you keep riding back and forth. It takes time to turn a horse around."

"I'll have two boys ride in front of me on horseback throwing the balls in the air for me. I should be able to do it in one straight run of a hundred yards."

Bob looked at her. "He's thought of everything, it seems."

"I believe I have," I agreed happily. "Now let's pick a time and place for the match. It should be in the spring, a few weeks before our show opens. We'll have to reserve the shooting grounds."

Bob still clutched my note. He scowled at it. "With ideas like this, what do you need a publicity man for?"

· · ·

On a blustery fall day I waited with my coat collar turned up, watching the train back its linked chain of stock wagons onto the yard siding by the river in Croton-on-Hudson where we had established our winter quarters for the assembly and rehearsal of the show.

Harry Dreier was first off the train. Behind his short red beard the beaming smile illuminated the entire yard. He stumped toward me on his wooden leg and we embraced with a great flood of feeling.

"My God, Harry, let me look at you. You haven't changed a whisker."

"A little gray here and there in the red, maybe. But I'm a healthy bull, Hugh. Lordy if you ain't a strapping heroic figger yourself now."

Wranglers came spilling out of the cattle cars. Harry waved his arm in a circle overhead to draw them to us. "Got a hell of a mob of livestock here."

"Saddle them up," I told him. "We've got a trail drive ahead of us."

"You don't say?"

"All of eight miles to our leasehold."

· · ·

I was at the depot again two weeks later when another friend arrived. Predictably he appeared astraddle the engine's cowcatcher: Nate Loving, spinning his lariat loop overhead and grinning with a thousand teeth.

· · ·

Just before Thanksgiving Kevin Tyree arrived sedately in a passenger coach. We unloaded his trunks of gunsmithing equipment and rifles into the bed of my mud wagon and headed back for the farm.

. . .

It had been a dairy farm and had gone broke from mismanagement. We'd selected it because of the voluminous barns; we needed shelter for our livestock through the Northeastern winter.

On the first of December we gathered in the front room of the house: Bob Halburton, Jeanette Fowler, Harry Dreier, Nate Loving, Kevin Tyree and I.

A map of the United States was open flat on the table. I stabbed it with my finger. "Baltimore. We'll open there in April and move the show north with the spring. Philadelphia, New York, Boston. Then west— Buffalo, Detroit, Chicago, Omaha. South from there while the weather cools—St. Louis, Memphis, New Orleans, Mobile, Atlanta to close out the season. Thirteen cities, two hundred days—that's two weeks' stand in each city, with a few odd days for travel and such. We'll close out the season in November. It's going to be a hard push. Can we do it?"

Harry Dreier said, "What do we use for transportation? We have to drive this mob from town to town on foot?"

"We use our own train," I said.

His lips shaped a whistle. "You're talking about money now."

"I am. Kevin?"

"What makes you think we can sell enough tickets to keep the show open for two full weeks in a town?"

"That's Bob's job."

Bob Halburton said, "Our principal advertising will be poster boards. We'll plaster up thousands of posters within a two-hundred-mile radius of the next-stop city. Every barn, fence, tree and shop window. People may not read newspapers—and if they read them they may not read the adverts in them—but they can't help but see posters if there's a poster everywhere they turn. Now we intend to send out an advance party, occupying three railroad cars, running two cities ahead of us— that's about one month's lead time. Publicity men to whip up attention in the newspapers. Barkers with teaser acts. A sizable crew of bill-posters with brushes, paste barrels, carpenters and lumber to construct temporary billboards. It'll be their job to plaster up thousands of posters —wallpaper the area in the weeks before we arrive. Nobody alive will be unaware of our coming."

Jeanette said, "Millions of people who never see our show are going to see these posters. A hundred years from now those shinplasters will remind people of their heritage. We want to see every aspect of Western

326

life and history represented on them. We're employing the foremost artists and the best lithographers."

"Be that as it may, at the moment I'm less interested in the heritage of posterity than I am in selling this exhibition to the public."

Nate Loving said, "How much all this costing, Hugh? How many of these shinplasters you printing up?"

"They tell me half a million for the season."

Bob Halburton had his notepad out. "Posters run twenty cents apiece in lots of a thousand—that's a hundred thousand dollars for half a million posters. Paper and printing. On top of that we have to pay the paperhangers and in the cities you have to rent billboard space which generally runs about four bits per month per sheet. We'll be spending somewhere up to two hundred thousand dollars to advertise and promote the enterprise—it's the single largest expense on the budget. All told, if you folks are interested, we'll spend the better part of half a million dollars to launch this exhibition and keep it running for one season. At four bits a ticket that means we have got to bring in an audience of one million people in a single season. Big? Yes, we're talking about big. This is no county-fair carnival. We have got to draw six thousand people, minimum, to each and every performance—on the average—before we'll see a penny of profit."

Harry Dreier said, "No wonder you got us carrying two railroad cars full of broke-down arena bleacher seats. Six thousand head of people to each show?" He shook his head violently. "Ain't that many people in the world, Mr. Halburton."

"Oh I think there are. I think our posters will draw them out of farms and caves and holes in the woods to see Colonel Cardiff's Wild West Show."

Harry continued to shake his head in total disbelief. "Remarkable."

.   .   .

The restaurant's tables were crowded and I drew stares as the maître d' threaded a path among them, leading me to the prestigious booth.

Doc Bogardus rose as far as the table's edge would permit and extended his smile and his hand. He had a napkin tucked bib-style into his waistcoat. His hair and spade beard were mostly grey now, just shot with a few streaks of black, but he seemed thinner than formerly and looked in keen-eyed health; I supposed he was near sixty but his vigorous appearance belied it.

When I sat down there was a rush of excited murmurings from the tables nearby; Bogardus and I shared a glance of amusement—we'd both been recognized and, the rivalry between us having been inflated

for so many years in the press, any face-to-face public encounter between us had to be a matter of keen interest to the crowd. I could see
people throughout the room casting surreptitious glances our way. I
said, "If we don't start shooting at each other pretty soon a lot of
people are going to be disappointed."

"I'm afraid we'll just have to disappoint them, then. How are you,
Hugh? You look splendid. White hair becomes you. Does that arm
actually function?"

I lifted it overhead. "Better than ever."

"I'm amazed. What will you drink?"

"Sour mash."

"Of course. I recommend the trout here, by the way."

We spent nearly an hour in casual reminiscence; he was very curious
about my arm, and astonished by my account of the manner in which
I had achieved its recovery. During our colloquy several young sporting
bloods approached timidly and requested our autographs, and we were
happy to oblige them.

Finally Bogardus said, "You've acquired a monopoly on the news
headlines of late, it would appear. First the presidential pardon, then
the announcement of your forthcoming Roman circus, now this utterly
charming shooter's challenge—from the back of a running horse, no less.
I congratulate you on your taste in press agents. Bob Halburton's fine
bibulous hand, I presume."

"Yes indeed."

"Give my love to the reprobate. And Caleb Rice—what of him?"

I told him Caleb was riding for Hanging Judge Parker now as a
deputy marshal under Tilghman and the news seemed to please Bogardus. "It's what he was cut out for, I'm sure. Shooting at inanimate
targets was never his game, although he's got the eye for it—we're
fortunate, you and I. Had Caleb decided to take up the sport seriously
he'd have eclipsed both of us, I'm sure."

"Have you shot much against Vern Tyree?"

"Major Vernon Tyree. Oh yes. Indeed I have." His tone expressed
his feelings toward Vern. "I can't deny he's a superb marksman."

"In your class, Doc?"

"Definitely. We've competed a good many times. I may have the
slightest edge over him in numbers of victories but he's still improving
his skills. At the moment I'd say we were as evenly matched as any two
men can be." He was rolling his wineglass in his fingers by the stem.
"Off the shooting ground, of course, we've no words to exchange with
each other. He knows I detest him."

"I'd hoped he might have grown up by now."

"Perhaps he has. But I've never forgiven him for what he did to you."

"I'm willing to let bygones be bygones," I said. "Doc, I still owe you one."

"One what?"

"One life. Mine. You set my shoulder, you got me out of the country. Without you I'd have hanged. No, let me finish. A long time ago you suggested the two of us ought to appear in a sequence of shooting matches to decide the national championship, inviting all comers to take us on. You remember that?"

"A fond dream. Certainly I remember it. I'd have gone ahead with it even in your absence except for the fact that I couldn't stomach the thought of traveling in company with Vernon Tyree."

"Would you still be interested?"

"With you? Certainly. Say the word. But what of your commitment to the traveling circus?"

"It's not a circus. The shooting competitions will be built right into the program of the Wild West Show. They'll provide the climax to the last day's performance in each city. Thirteen matches during the season. What do you say?"

"I see a risk of corrupting a serious competition with cheap show contrivances."

"It's an honest shooting match. I mean to beat you and everybody else out for the title. I mean to do it straight." I grinned at him. "Now you can't turn down that challenge, can you? The show pays your traveling expenses and a thousand dollars for each match you shoot, plus an additional thousand to the winner of each match, plus another thousand to any shooter in any match where he hits more than ninety-five out of a hundred."

"Can I safely assume you don't intend to put me on a horse to parade up and down shooting from a rocking saddle? I'm a bit old for those shenanigans."

"Doc, I said it was a serious shooting match." I put my hand on the table. "Can I put you on the payroll, then?"

"At a thousand dollars and expenses, am I proscribed from placing side bets?"

"No."

"Any other fine print I should know about?"

"No."

"Then sign me up."

． ． ．

We erected a huge circus tent over the main corral at the dairy farm. Franklin stoves kept the area above freezing while our growing battalion of riders and workers rehearsed their acts.

Harry Dreier was our harried arena master at first. Most of the show's dramatic exhibits were designed by myself and Bob Halburton; the more outrageous stunts were mainly devised by Nate Loving. Kevin Tyree's mechanical inventiveness soon extended far beyond the armory into the creation of special machinery for various attractions, chiefly trick-shooting stunts that I devised by trial and error: for example a maypole attraction that later became one of the crowd-pleasing favorites of the show. Colored glass gewgaws were suspended from long lines attached to a small wheel at the top of a telegraph pole. The entire assembly was set to spinning; then it was my job to ride past the pole and shoot all the gewgaws to pieces while they spun.

We had many a winter conference over annoying details and major difficulties alike. One of the most persistent subjects of dispute and heat was the name of the show. It came up at every meeting. Everyone had suggestions. Jeanette favored a title of her own devising: "Cardiff's Real Wild West Roundup." The others proposed "Cardiff's Pioneer Exposition" and "The Peerless Congress of Horsemen" and "Hugh Cardiff's Combination" and "The Winning of the West" and "Cardiff's Congress of Range Riders" and "Prince of the Prairie: Col. Hugh Cardiff and His Frontier Combination." And for a while Bob Halburton wanted to stay with the original title of our decade-old play, "Heroes of the West."

Finally the day arrived late in January when we had to make the decision because the first posters needed printing. Someone had to break the deadlock. Arbitrarily I chose the title that I felt encapsulated the spirit and intent of our program: COL. HUGH CARDIFF'S WILD WEST SHOW.

And so it remained; and not until many years later after our copyright had expired did any other troupe employ the title "Wild West Show." Cody's show, for those who do not remember, was billed most frequently as "Buffalo Bill's Wild West and Congress of Rough Riders of the World." Our show, being the first, had preemption on the phrase "Wild West Show."

.   .   .

The Grantland Clay Pigeon Company offered Bogardus and me a series of six matches in New York, of one hundred shots each, for which we received quite a sum of money. We shot these competitions at the Brooklyn Driving Park once again, during January and February 1882, twice in snowstorms and once in rain. As I had not shot against serious competitors in a decade I was nervous at the outset but I had been practicing at every opportunity and acquitted myself well enough, taking four of the six from Bogardus and losing the other two only narrowly by one or two clay pigeons.

The matches drew sizable crowds of onlookers and bettors; as they were designed as advertisements for the sponsoring company's clay pigeons, all expenses were paid for us and the newspaper advertising cost us nothing.

The matches whetted the public's appetite for the coming season and particularly for the grandiose horseback challenge I had scheduled for March 25, a Saturday afternoon. Bob Halburton, with misgivings, had begun leaking word of it to the press as early as the previous November; in February our own large advertisements began to appear in the newspapers and on bill posters.

Reservations for competitor positions began to arrive in the post as early as February 8 and it quickly became apparent that there was a surprising number of bloods willing to risk one thousand dollars each on the match. By the closing date for entries—the twenty-third—we had two hundred and sixty-seven competitors signed up for the shoot. The competitions clearly would have to be shot in relays, running over into the Sunday, with shooters' times measured by stopwatch.

The match was something of an anticlimax, for most of the serious shooters regarded it as a grandstand stunt and did not stoop to enter. Through an intermediary I learned that Vern Tyree preferred to bide his time and shoot a fair-and-square match with me rather than take obvious advantage of the handicaps I had proposed for the horseback exhibition. Bogardus came, because I insisted, but his heart was not in it at first; only when I had completed my own run on horseback, splintering twenty-eight of the thirty glass balls in a period of 82 seconds, did Bogardus begin to take the challenge seriously. Then he stepped into the line in his turn, took his stance and shot seriously, smashing all thirty balls without a miss, using relays of pump-action shotguns, finishing his run effortlessly in 67 seconds. I was soundly beaten by him that day and we enjoyed a good laugh Sunday evening after we'd counted out the proceeds: fourteen of the shooters had beaten my score and time, twenty-seven others had beaten my score but not my time (bets were canceled under those circumstances), and after paying out the expenses of organizing the match and cleaning up afterward we banked a profit of nearly two hundred thousand dollars.

It was not a bad weekend's work. It paid virtually half the year's cost of mounting the Wild West Show and it engendered tons of newsprint publicity, most of it of the awed variety punctuated by numerous exclamation points. In a way the nationwide news coverage did us a disservice because it rendered my repeating the success impossible; but I was not inclined to complain about that. People throughout the nation read of my "impossible" marksmanship from the back of a galloping horse; the same people could reasonably be expected to spend half a dollar to see me perform the same feat in person.

. . .

The musicians of our cowboy band on horseback were breathing tentative sounds into their instruments. It was one of our last rehearsals under canvas before setting out for Maryland. Fitz Bragg had arrived only a week earlier after an incessant barrage of daily telegrams from me—I'd taken no mercy upon him for I needed him to shepherd the seventy-five Indians we had employed; they trusted him as they would few other white men. With many a grouse and complaint Fitz had taken charge. Our Indians—we'd had to post bond for every man taken off the reservation to tour with us—were hunters and proud of their skills with lance and bow and arrow. Exhibitions of their marksmanship with these weapons were woven into the scheme of the show.

The band struck up its tune and Fitz rode down the tented corral to where I sat on the fence. We had duded him up in white buckskins not unlike my own and he looked, in his own opinion and mine, right handsome—the very picture of the pioneer frontiersman.

The band's peppy march spread cheer under the canvas. Fitz curled his knee over the saddlehorn and folded his arms to watch Leadville Buck Thompson warm up his explosive whip act. Harry Dreier had found Thompson tooling a team through the farm and had promoted the wagoner on the spot: Buck Thompson did astonishing stunts with the tip of his lashing twenty-four-foot bull whip, which was one article I left to the wagoner after having tried it once myself and nearly slicing off my own throat.

Fitz said, "I never seen such a mixture of colors in one gang of men. You keep all these races thrown together we bound to have trouble, Hugh."

"Most of them were on the Candelas. If they could work together there they can work together here."

"They was fifty miles apart down there, most of them."

In truth we had one of the most richly hued polyglot admixtures I had ever seen or heard of. In addition to our white cowboys and Indians we had a score of Negro vaqueros, of whom Nate Loving was always the most noticeable; we had a score of Mexican hands, notably innocent-faced young Guillermo Rojas who threw knives with more chilling accuracy than any other man I ever saw; we had several Orientals, mostly on the crew and in the mess cook's section but Roku Ohara, our Japanese cowboy, seemed capable of riding any buck-jumper ever born. We even had an "Eskimo" cowboy—actually he was an Aleut Indian from off the coast of Alaska somewhere; he went by the name of Charlie Whalebone and had been a fisherman out of San Francisco before he became enthralled with cowboying. It was Charlie Whalebone who devised the stunt, in our stampede sequence, of pitching off his horse as if thrown, then grabbing a running steer's tail above the tassel and allowing the longhorn to drag him away to safety. It was an exceedingly dangerous trick but Charlie proved he could do it at every rehearsal without being hurt; we left it in the show. Such were the origins of our attractions. They were improvised by real Westerners in the course of devising and rehearsing the show. Our exposition, unlike the circus, was true to Western life and spirit and free from faking, although I admit a bit of dramatic license may have been employed to enhance the excitement. We promised, and gave, a full year's Western adventures in three full-packed hours.

Fitz said, "You know I feel like a kid playing hooky. Albert's still out after old Geronimo down there. That's where I ought to be."

"Sieber enjoys killing Indians. You don't."

"That's just it. He needs somebody keep a rein on him."

"I expect Geronimo and Ibran can do that well enough."

"Ibran for sure. That brother-in-law of yours put a hex sign on old Albert or something. Albert keeps his distance from that old boy."

Ibran was on the Camp Verde Reservation with his band of hunters— for the moment. I was never convinced my little effort at pacification would last. A year later it did not surprise me when we learned Ibran had jumped the reservation again.

I said, "Fitz, I'd appreciate it if you'd quit feeling guilty about running away from the war. You're old enough for a dignified retirement from that nonsense. You know you'll enjoy this if you just let yourself loosen up."

"I'll give it a try anyhow. Here comes your dude friend."

Doc Bogardus came along the rail and joined us to watch Nate Loving practice his bulldogging chase of a longhorn steer full tilt across the corral. When the dust settled and the steer was led back to its pen Nate got to his feet dusting off his flamboyant red outfit and whooped at us out of sheer exuberance.

The cowboy band came marching out on horseback and began its circuit of the corral, tooting up a sprightly "Garry Owen"; Doc Bogardus said, "I'd never have believed what I've seen here the past few days. The equestrian acts alone . . ."

"That's the difference between prettified circus horses and real cow ponies, Doc."

"I've never in my life heard of accomplishments like these, let alone seen them."

I said, "You ought to give a quote to Bob Halburton for the advertising."

"Now what would that do to our presumed rivalry? We're supposed to hate each other." He gave me his conspiratorial smile. "I must return to my sadly neglected surgical practice. I'll see you in Baltimore, then, on the twenty-fourth?"

"Best polish up then, Doc. I beat you four out of six on the clay pigeons."

"A fluke, I assure you."

I laughed as he left the tent; I was in higher spirits than I'd known in years. I felt like an eager boy again.

. . .

In our makeshift office in the farmhouse I pored over the program charts with Harry Dreier and Bob Halburton. Harry said, "You sure you want the stampede there in the middle of the last act? Comes a little close in front of the wagon-train finale, don't it?"

"Where else would you put it, Harry?"

"I honestly don't know. But it's going to put a heavy load on our stock tenders right about then. They'll have to corral them steers and get them calmed down and all at the same time line up the stock for the finale."

I said, "Let the riders pitch in then. They'll be going off the field chasing the stampede. Let them round up the herd themselves—they're in the best position to do it."

"Good idea if the boys don't object."

"Put it to them the right way, that's all. It'll make things easier on everybody if we don't overload people. The work's going to be hard enough as it is."

"That's for certain sure."

Bob Halburton sucked from his flask, sucked from his cigar, coughed, recovered and said, "I had a little talk with Fitz Bragg this afternoon. He's worried about dust-ups between the men. Mexicans against Indians, whites against Negroes, that kind of thing. These men are going to be stuffed together like cattle on that train. They'll be smelling each other's feet all season long. We're going to have fights, Hugh. I see no way around it."

"I doubt they'll have too much steam left after a hard day's work," I said, "but I think the main thing is to give them plenty of team rivalry they can work out on the arena. That's one reason for the races and stock competitions."

"Maybe," Bob said. "But the backstage crew doesn't get a crack at those competitions."

"At least they'll have their own men to root for."

"Just the same it's something we'd better keep an eye on."

Harry said, "I'll tell you one thing might help. If you give me authority to fire any man on the spot if he's caught fighting."

"Done," I said.

Harry nodded. "The pay these boys are getting, they'll think twice before they risk their jobs. It'd take them five years cowboying to earn what they'll get in one season's work with this show."

"If you ask me they're overpaid," Bob said.

"They'll earn every penny of it," I assured him. "What's next on that list, Harry?"

. . .

We had spent six months recruiting, planning, acquiring equipment, designing props. Everything we could think of. But had we thought of everything? Had we mesmerized ourselves into blind ignorance of the faults? We thought we had a grand triumphant exhibition: were we mad, misled, mistaken? Would audiences greet us with hisses, eggs, tomatoes and brickbats?

In the chilly spring evening I stood on the lamplit porch of the farm-house alone with my terror. The plan had seemed foolproof: we'd reviewed it up one side and down the other until we were dizzy. But now at the last moment when it was too late to do anything about it I could see a dozen flaws, a hundred risks, a thousand points where something could go wrong.

Across the farmyard the great tent had been taken down; the corrals stood open, wagon-trucks ready to receive tomorrow's loading. Nearly everybody was off somewhere, away to celebrate the last night's respite before the start of the grueling schedule. We had just short of four hundred employees. I was responsible for them. That night the burden sagged heavy on my shoulders. What if I should fail them?

The money was nothing; I could lose that with equanimity. But I could not so easily lose the respect of four hundred men and women who depended on me, who believed me when I told them they were part of a unique enterprise that would make the world sit back in awe.

I saw Kevin Tyree come softly across the deserted ground. Puffing smoke from his pipe he climbed up onto the porch and favored me with a vague smile. "Got the jitters, then?"

"Guess I have."

The cool stillness seemed ominous, as if a storm were gathering just beyond the horizon. Along the row of tents that the men used for living quarters a few canvas sides were illuminated from within by lamplight; some of the older wiser men would be down there quietly playing cards or reading or writing home to their families and intendeds. But there was no sound; only the occasional thud of a hoof in a stall, the whisper-scrape of wind through the branches.

Kevin said, "You've made no contact with my sister, have you?"

"No."

"Why?"

"I thought you wanted to be left out of it."

"She's still my sister; you're still my friend."

I said quietly, "Make up your mind, Kevin. I'll confide in you if you want it."

"That might force me to choose a side, mightn't it?"

"It's up to you."

He had a shy but engaging smile; it was no surprise he was a favorite of the camp-following girls and it was no secret he made every advantage of it. Thrown into the lusty company of our troupers Kevin had blossomed. I'd watched him grow: he was more secure in himself now, much less afraid of the world.

He said, "I can't hide from it forever. You'd better tell me—then I'll have what I need to make up my mind."

I took my time composing my answer; it wasn't something I'd rehearsed.

I said, "I fell in love with Libby when I was sixteen years old."

"I know."

"Nothing happened between us then, although your father believed otherwise."

"I know that too."

"I carried a picture of Libby in my heart for years."

"She carried yours as well. I suppose you know that."

"Yes. I went down to Virginia that fall we opened the play in New York. She told you about that?"

"She did. She always regretted not going on with you. She's hated herself ever since for turning back. Both your lives might have been so different. . . ."

"Who's to know that? We might have been killed. Vern had that warrant hanging over me. In any case I haven't seen her since then, though sometimes it amazes me to realize it. She wrote to me about the child—it's the last I ever heard from her and that was more than ten years ago. I suppose a true romantic fool could carry a torch that long. Maybe it was my weakness—maybe I'm not strong enough for that. But I met a woman in Mexico and I married her. Then we learned to love each other. And we had a child. And my wife and the child died."

I'd been staring out across the yard; now I turned my gaze on Kevin. "I miss Flower more than I miss Libby. Do you understand my meaning?"

"You can't keep something burning forever if there's no fuel to stoke it with."

336

"That's a mite fanciful, Kevin, but I suppose there's truth in it."

"You're saying you've no burning want for her any longer."

"I don't even know her, do I? I've changed, God knows. I'm sure she's changed as well. She's not the same girl she was then—how could she be?"

"You're right about that, of course."

"I imagine she's suffered a great deal."

He said nothing to that but his silence was a form of assent. I said, "No, I don't intend to pursue her. She's Merriam's wife. She elected to stay with him."

"That was for Bill's sake. The boy."

"It's Bill I'm concerned with," I said. "I don't want him to grow into one of them."

"Well at least he'll grow up rich and privileged."

"That's all right if it's not all that matters to you. But I expect it's pretty dreary if you're not cut out for it. And I can't see a son of mine respecting himself if all he can say for himself is that he inherited money and position."

"So?"

"You are right. I intend to get him out of there."

"How?"

"Well I intend to ask Merriam to turn him over to me."

Kevin watched me bleakly. "Sure."

I poked my jaw out toward the wagons, the stalls, the great camp of tents. "The world's never seen anything to match what we're going to show them. We're going to set this country on its ear, you know. And it's all for one thing, Kevin. It's all to gain a son."

"All right. Tell me how."

"I guess it looks coldhearted. But it's sustained me in dark times— it's given me the will. I lost my son Mike in the Sierra. I've nothing left but my firstborn, the child of my first love. He's *my son*."

"Yes," he murmured.

"I mean to win him—and I mean to do it openly. I won't sneak like a thief in the night to abduct my son by ruse or gunpoint. Listen— questions of parentage and custody are matters for the courts."

"The courts are in Phipps Merriam's pockets."

"I don't expect the issue ever to come into open court."

"No. Phipps couldn't afford the scandal."

"That's the point," I said. "He'll relinquish the boy rather than face that. The strength of my case rests on that."

"So?"

"I need the support of important people in high places to make it work. I need to achieve such a position that my threat of making my claim public will be taken seriously. It would have been useless for a penniless drifter to broadcast claims that a rich senator had stolen his son. I'd have looked like a fool—I'd have been laughed out of the East."

"I see. You aim to make your name bigger than Phipps Merriam's, then."

"Yes. Then he'll have to take me seriously. You can imagine what the publicity would do to his chance at the presidency."

"I don't imagine it would do you much good yourself. It hardly fits the heroic image—a man committing adultery with another man's wife and then leaving the bastard child behind."

"I can live with it. Phipps Merriam can't. That's my edge. When I walk in on him at the end of this season I'll show him that edge and then I'll ask him politely for my son and he'll turn him over to me."

"After which he'll do everything in his power to destroy you."

"Let him try."

"You know there's one thing you're not taking into account. What about Bill? What if he doesn't want to go with you?"

"He probably won't. The way he's been raised it'll take time to straighten him out. I'm prepared for that. He's still my son."

"And what of Libby, then?"

"She'll stay with Merriam or she'll leave him. It's her choice."

"But you don't want her back?"

"Back? I never had her, did I? A few long-ago days in Virginia, a lot of memories, that's all we ever shared, Kevin. It's too late for Libby and me to make any kind of a life together."

"Sort of leaves my sister holding the short end of the stick."

"I'll do whatever I can for her if she wants my help."

"That's a bit cool."

"Is it? I can't help it. She's a full-grown woman, she's got her own mind."

"Down deep you hate her, don't you? You hate her because you loved her for so long and she couldn't be with you."

"No," I said, "God knows I don't hate Libby."

His pipe had gone out. He knocked it against his palm and scattered ashes over the porch rail; then he poked it stem-first into his belt like a pistol. I said, "Does it help you make up your mind, then?"

"I don't know. I'll have to think on it." And he went down off the porch and away toward the bunkhouse that he shared with Fitz Bragg and Harry Dreier.

I watched him until he was out of sight. The conversation had stirred up my old uncertainties and I was in a ragged frame of mind just then, anxious for the show and not sure about the rectitude of my ambitions for young Bill; in an irritable way I swung across the porch and thrust myself inside.

Jeanette sat by the lamp with a book open in her lap. She looked up at me without visible expression; her face was so studied in its guarded composure that I said, "You heard that?"

"I couldn't help it. I didn't mean to eavesdrop—but then I suppose I could have left the room or announced myself. I'm sorry. We all depend on you so much—I worry about you sometimes. Perhaps you'll forgive my listening."

"No harm done."

"Don't be cross with me, Hugh. Please." She set the book aside. "Perhaps I guard Bob's interests too jealously sometimes."

"It's for Bob's sake you're concerned? Don't be. I won't let him down. My private ambitions have nothing to do with the show."

"Don't they? What happens when you've extorted your son away from Senator Merriam? Will you have any reason to keep the show going after that?"

"Expect I will," I said, "assuming it's as successful as we hope it'll be. I'd be a fool to throw it over, wouldn't I?"

"Most men would see it that way. I'm not sure you do."

"No?"

"You're an independent man, Hugh, you don't live by ordinary rules. I can see you happily chucking the whole thing in and taking your son off to the mountains to raise him Indian-style."

"I guess it's possible. But by that time you and Bob may be sick to death of publicizing the show."

"You're probably right. I tend to worry about things too much."

"You're a damn good woman," I said. "I'd be happy to have someone to worry over me the way you worry over Bob." Then I went back through the house to my bedroom.

.   .   .

On a grass sward outskirting Baltimore we opened to a lovely sun-drenched crowd. A few acts missed their cues, there were delays; a steer was loosed into the arena by mistake; there were the hitches that had to be expected in a debut performance. But the company and audience alike took them in stride.

We played to thirty-eight thousand people that day. I am sure every one of them who is still alive remembers it as vividly as I do. We have become an elite and exclusive club, those of us who witnessed the birth of the Wild West Show.

In the grand-opening parade all the riders of the show, one hundred and ninety strong, galloped in concentric circles in opposite directions: great wheels of horsemen lofting flags and banners of all descriptions, led by myself on a palomino stallion with the American flag on my staff.

I remember the noise of it, the smell, the rumble and roar of the audience: we had them with us from the outset.

As our parade filed off the field I passed the flag to Fitz Bragg and turned to gallop along the open end of the horseshoe arena firing from the saddle at a line of bright tinsel-glass balls strung across the opening. As each ball shattered the applause intensified until at the end of the run when I bowed from the saddle, sweeping my hat off, the roar might have been that of a hurricane.

The thrill of that moment beggars description, I was as giddy and enthralled as any child in the audience.

An Indian appeared at the far end of the arena. A mounted vaquero ran at him with brandished knife. The Indian sprinted away and a race ensued, the vaquero on horseback in hot galloping pursuit. The race between the fleet Ute and the well-mounted vaquero ended in a draw; both bowed to the audience—another tidal wave of applause.

A riderless horse was set to galloping; a Pony Express rider on a brisk pinto dashed into the arena, threw his mochila upon the riderless horse, leaped from saddle to saddle and rode on. . . .

Rojas put on a pyrotechnic display of hurtling knives, sinking them precisely into equidistant points along the rim of a revolving wooden wheel. Fitz Bragg and a crowd of buckskinned hunters chased our small herd of buffalo through the arena with an abundance of whooping and shooting of blank cartridges. Nate Loving, whom we billed as "King of the Cowboys," rode comically into this melee, leaped onto the back of a buffalo bull and rode it out of the arena waving his hat to the crowd.

I galloped down the center with revolvers in both hands. A dozen small hot-air balloons lofted swiftly into the air, riotous with colors, and I shot them all when they were high in the air.

Roku Ohara roped and rode a bareback bucking bronco. A vaquero rushed forward asaddle and took him off. Nate Loving dashed around the arena at full gallop, leaned from the saddle and plucked a bandanna from the ground—with his teeth.

Then appeared the artifact that proved, down through the years, the most prominent and best-known prop of the Wild West Show: the Tombstone Mail Coach.

The red-painted stagecoach was an old Concord that had changed hands often enough: the St. Louis Mail Company, Russell Majors & Waddell, Butterfield Overland Mail, Wells Fargo. It had been held up three times and had been attacked by Indians in Apache Pass. It saw service on the Tombstone-to-Tucson run, during which Wyatt Earp briefly rode shotgun for Wells Fargo—one of his few honest law jobs.

We had purchased that particular coach for the show because the fracas at the OK Corral had occurred only a few months prior to our opening and had brought the name of Tombstone to the nation's attention. The old stagecoach would be featured henceforth in all our parades and shows; it was a large coach and could seat eighteen with some crowding, and Doc Bogardus had the idea of inviting local dignitaries to ride as passengers during the holdup skit. Drawn by eight white horses the mail coach was a stirring sight, and except for our regular repaintings it was genuine and authentic down to the last cotter pin and I grew to resent the carping nitpickers who accused us of having built it especially for the show.

When the coach careened into the arena it was, of course, attacked—in what Bob Halburton's programs and fliers described as "a startling and soul-stirring battle for the Tombstone gold coach." The adventure ended in a rescue of the embattled vehicle by scouts led forward at the gallop by Hugh Cardiff and Fitz Bragg, guns blazing. The barrage of deafening gunfire resulted in the visible demise of a score of outlaws, some of whom pitched off their horses with great acrobatic leaps. The coach then shot forward at a gallop, its driver falling over the side, and it was my job to give chase and rescue the runaway. When I drew it to a stop the cowboy band struck up a cheerful march and that signaled the conclusion of the opening act of the show.

Intermission. Our vendors moved through the crowd peddling programs, snacks, magazines and dime novels. Behind the arena the stock crews worked like madmen to ready the next acts.

In our headquarters wagon I did my best to dust off my whites. Harry Dreier and Kevin Tyree were outside when I emerged; both men beamed from ear to ear. No words were needed. I clapped them both upon the shoulders and we walked together toward the arena gate. Up on the arena master's platform Jeanette was sorting notes for Bob Halburton; I saw him suck a surreptitious drink from his flask. Fitz Bragg ambled over to join us at the gate; he couldn't keep the grin off his face. "You was right, Hugh. More fun than a barrel of Denver whores."

The second act of our two-act show began with Bob Halburton at the megaphone introducing my shooting exhibition with a speech about "Guns—The Great Democratizers."

I have always had an extremely modest appetite for orations and had persuaded Bob, by means of dark threats, to keep the speech short. At its conclusion I rode into the arena at full gallop in pursuit of two young boys on horseback who rode ahead of me tossing targets in the air. I swiftly knocked the targets to pieces with rifle and then with revolvers.

341

This was followed without pause by my maypole act in which I broke a dozen glass balls swinging from strings about the high-guyed telegraph pole.

One of the boys hurled a brick into the air—I shot the brick in two on the rise, then shot both halves as they fell.

On that opening day I was charmed by fate: I hardly missed a target all day. The crowd was ecstatic.

Equestrian acts followed: trick riding, roping, wagon races, Nate Loving's comedy ride—under the running horse's belly, out behind dragging from its tail, a vault back into the saddle—and all the time Bob's voice boomed from the megaphone describing the reality of such feats and their place in Western life and recreation.

The stampede followed—virtually all the livestock and most of our horsemen participated; it filled the arena with bawling animals. A few signals were confused and one man was pitched off his horse—a gasp from the crowd—but a vaquero rescued him unhurt and the pageant continued. For a moment there my breath had hung in my throat.

For the protection of the crowd we had erected a fence below the bleacher grandstand; this proved adequate to contain the stampede and there was no real threat to the audience, although I'm sure many in the forward rows had delicious thrills of fear to remember.

While the stampeding cattle were herded out the wide gates four vaqueros drew the crowd's attention with a magnificent display of trick roping and equestrian choreography, weaving among one another as they spun and leaped through their loops.

Then began the lengthy climax of the show, which commenced with the arrival in the deserted arena of a lone scout on horseback who dismounted, scanned the ground for tracks, and began to follow clues toward a copse of artificial brush. Here he was leaped upon by Indians who captured him after a valiant struggle. The scout was then tortured and put to death rather gruesomely by the Indians. All then withdrew from the field and a train of five Conestoga prairie schooners drove into the arena, complete with outriders and livestock as it would have been on the plains. The wagons were drawn into a circle, the teams and cattle corralled within, the saddle horses hobbled without. There was some loud thin dialogue about the mysterious absence of the trail scout, and a warning to all to keep eyes peeled for savages.

Women prepared cookfires while men chopped wood with their rifles ready at hand. A slight youth was featured in this episode, a boy who worked more industriously and eagerly than anyone else.

The audience then began to catch sight of Indians who were creeping up on the wagon camp. Shouts of warning erupted from thousands of throats.

Finally, when all seemed lost, a keen-eyed wagoner at last gave the alarm and fired his rifle.

Instantly the pioneers rushed to their defensive positions. Indians rose up from the grass and attacked; volleys of fire from the defenders drove them back time after time. After a fierce battle the Indians withdrew to regroup and powwow.

In the wagon camp the slight youth set his rifle aside and, armed only with belt revolver and knife, crawled away from the camp into the wilderness. Many in the audience of course took this to be an act of cowardice and there were loud hisses all around.

Now a mounted war party joined the first Indians; there was a quick hubbub among them and then the tribesmen spread out, surrounding the wagon train. The defenders manned their positions bravely, calling encouragement to one another and death to the savages.

Then with a yip and a whoop the Indians attacked.

Shouting, running, shooting—thunder of hooves, crack of rifles, clouds of dust and powder smoke: a melee of action.

In the nick of time, with one wagon's canvas in flames and the field of battle strewn with beleaguered defenders down to their last ammunition, a stalwart band of frontiersmen—led by myself, Fitz Bragg and the slight youth who had earlier made his escape through the Indian lines—came a-gallop to the rescue, blazing away furiously until nearly every Indian was done in. The applause was bombastic.

But then I was leaped upon by half a dozen raging Indians and had to flay about me single-handed until finally I dispatched them all with gun, knife, tomahawk and fist.

The battle was ended. Our heroes remounted their horses and I led them in a triumphant horseback parade across the entire front of the horseshoe grandstand, signaling the end of the day's performance, removing my hat and sweeping it back toward the company lined out behind me.

It did not fail to drive our audience to its feet with wild and thunderous applause that seemed never ready to end.

. . .

That was the sequence of exhibitions in our very first Wild West Show. It set the pattern and remained essentially intact, with inevitable minor additions and revisions, down across a considerable period of years. In size and number of personnel the show grew somewhat from its beginnings but the essential program proved astonishingly durable with audiences throughout the world and we had no reason to effect any large changes in it. Thematically I believe the most important alteration in subsequent years was an increase in the Indian participation in the show and an added emphasis upon the Indian's side of the

343

story; but that came later. At first our show was purely an action entertainment. We made and kept our promise of thrilling diversion.

It was near dark by the time the last visitors departed; nine of us gathered in the headquarters wagon to drink toasts and congratulate one another.

"There is no nectar like applause," Bob Halburton said, "no liquor half so sweet or heady. But I would also point out to you happy children that we took in a shade under twenty-two thousand dollars. If we can keep up even half that pace we'll earn a half million's profit by season's end—and I will drink to that."

I was driven by a wild impulse and lifted Jeanette off her feet to plant a magnificent kiss upon her lips.

Afterward her glance shot toward Bob and a flush suffused her face; I felt a blundering fool; but Jeanette rescued me with a smile that forgave all. She lifted her glass. "Gentlemen"—and she stared up into the champagne—"I give you Colonel Hugh Cardiff."

Most assuredly the day was mine.

.   .   .

Not without hitches and mistakes we settled gradually into the rhythms of performance and popularity. Like Indians picking the bugs off blankets we found and discarded errors and weaknesses. Throughout that first season I doubt we performed three successive shows without making some change in the repertoire or the order of events. But in its essence the show remained the same. We made alterations in costume and hairdo but the lady remained intact. There were no tentative half-steps, no infantile awkwardnesses and few growing pains.

We were vagabonds of course; we lived in tents or sitting up on our private train. Some of my associates suggested that for appearances I should take a suite in the largest hotel but I could not do that; I had to live among the members of the troupe. We quickly developed a camaraderie that never could have occurred if I had behaved like a wealthy mogul who only now and then condescended to visit the children slaving in his sweat shops.

In that respect I should point out that we had numerous children in our employ throughout the years of the show. They were paid a fair wage commensurate with their duties and stations and in defense of our organization I must put on record the fact that we employed only orphans and children whose parents gave written permission for them to travel with us. We had no trouble recruiting young workers; to a boy the Wild West Show was even more glamorous and awesome than a circus.

Among our youths the most coveted job was that of glass-ball thrower, for the throw-boys had to be expert horsemen as well as tire-

344

less hurlers, and they were featured before audiences in flamboyant costumes. Competition for those positions was fierce and I made it a point to hold regular auditions to test boys' horsemanship and the accuracy of their throwing arms. Many a youth who began as one of my many throw-boys grew up to become a regular member of the cowboy troupe. One of them, Mark Hankins, joined us in 1883 at the age of eleven and was still with us, as a trick roper and rider, thirty-five years later. That was a brand of loyalty I shouldn't likely have commanded had I repaired every night to the luxury of a hotel suite.

.   .   .

We soon learned that our visiting audiences were as fascinated by our encampment as by the performances. Almost from the very beginning we opened our camp to the public and allowed visitors to stroll freely about to examine the rope-corral enclosures where our buffalo and elk and longhorns browsed. Citizens poked happily through the tents and tepees of our living quarters. For a while we allowed the children to touch, and even climb upon, the Tombstone mail coach; but then roughnecks began making off with souvenirs from it and we were forced to post a guard on the coach to discourage such road-agentry.

In the tent that was signposted COL. CARDIFF was hung a small museumlike display of Indian and mountain-man artifacts that included duplicate models of the various guns and knives I had carried over the years. For special occasions I carried the originals—those I still possessed—in a locked trunk.

I must admit that the tepees that housed our Indians, while they were of genuine Indian manufacture, were not native to the Ute and Apache who made up most of our portable "tribe." Apache do not live in tepees. When traveling they sleep in the open; when settled they build wickiups, similar to the mound-shaped Navajo hogans; but these structures are not portable, nor would they have suited the rainy climes through which we traveled.

One of Kevin Tyree's most splendid inventions was the audience protector. Our arena was a portable stadium that we carried in sections aboard several railroad cars; when erected it formed a horsehoe-shaped grandstand some 200 yards and by 120 yards in dimension; with practice by the end of the first season our crews were adept at erecting or tearing down the stadium in less than three hours—no mean feat considering its capacity of 36,000 people. (For overflow crowds we added rows of portable bleachers.) After two of our Baltimore performances were postponed because of showers, Kevin proposed that we design a canvas canopy to be erected on a lightweight structure of poles and rods above the audience. Similar designs have been used more recently

345

in horse-racing tracks: the audience is protected from the rain while the show field itself is open to the sky. Unless the rain was terribly heavy it did not affect our performances but even a light rain could discourage thousands of spectators from coming to the show. Once we advertised the fact that the audience would remain dry regardless of inclement skies, our bookings became much more reliable. That single inventive idea of Kevin's probably made the difference between a break-even season and a whopping profit.

We had to make other adaptations as well. Some show grounds did not provide suitable backstops for our shooting exhibitions. Bullets, after all, must have somewhere to go. A bullet does not stop or disintegrate once it shatters a glass ball in the air; its trajectory continues until it falls to earth somewhere. Normally our advance crew was able to hire appropriate farm-field space near the railroad spurs where we might have several acres of plowed fields to use as receptacles for spent ammunition. But this proved impossible in such show grounds as Boston's Beacon Park and Detroit's Princess Rink. Here we were forced to set aside our rifles. In my shooting acts I employed pump-action sixteen- and twelve-gauge shotguns loaded with chilled shot No. 8, and smoothbore revolvers chambered for birdshot. These substitutions were announced to the audience at each performance, and the reasons for them explained. I state this for the record in order to refute certain accusations that have been made against me. It is a fact that some of my competitors used shot shells exclusively but pretended otherwise. On the authority of Cody's own armorers it is known that he shattered glass balls in midair using rifles that had been bored smooth to accept .44-caliber shells loaded with a quarter ounce of No. 7½ chilled shot, while claiming his rifles and cartridges were normal solid-bullet rounds. I never once used shot shells in my exhibitions without announcing the fact. My weapons and ammunition were always subject to examination by the press and public without notice. I have never cheated or defrauded the public.

. . .

As agent-manager and chief publicist of the Wild West Show Bob Halburton had to be priest, bail bondsman, confessor, headmaster, brother, drinking comrade, crying towel, accountant, lawyer, arbitrator, mother, father and God.

The weight upon him was heavy. Bob's health was uncertain; it was not clear to me whether he was indeed ill or whether he merely was susceptible to exhaustion and drink. But it was clear to us all that he was not equal to all the demands made upon him. Quite early I reorganized the distribution of responsibility in order to ease his burden. Harry Dreier, already the backstage crew chief and arena director, as-

346

sumed responsibility for the personal and financial problems of troupers
and crewmen. Jeanette took it upon herself to perform the legwork
of publicity and direction of the advance crew of bill-posters. Dr. Bogardus quickly succumbed to the lure of celebrity and a newfound love
of the show business; he transferred the last of his dwindling surgical
practice to an associate—the same young man who had operated on
my shoulder—and joined us full-time, serving not only as resident
physician and shooting master but also as a sort of official "ruffled-
feather smoother," as he put it—he charmed and placated local politicians and socialites who wanted special treatment or reassurance. It
was Bogardus who first had the idea of inviting prominent local citizens
to ride in the Tombstone coach during the holdup spectacle.

Kevin Tyree looked after the show's endless mechanical needs; something was always breaking down or needing alteration and Kevin's ingenuity never failed to meet the requirements. The work kept him away
from gun designing but he found a satisfactory resolution to the difficulty: during the season he would devote all his attention to the needs
of the Wild West Show, and the money he earned from it would support him through the winter when he could devote full time to his first
interest.

Fitz Bragg had his hands full with our Indians, most of whom had
never seen cities before and were forever in trouble of one kind or
another. It was a high-spirited kind of trouble for the most part and we
rarely had serious clashes; most often if there was a confrontation it
was provoked by ignorant white visitors rather than by our Apache and
Ute, who behaved with far more dignity than did some of the citizens.

One of my own principal jobs turned out to be the task of keeping
Nate Loving out of trouble. Frequently I had to chase him ignomini-
ously down some boulevard where he was attempting to lasso a speeding fire engine or bulldog an unsuspecting ox. When chastised Nate
would always claim he was just trying to stir up a little publicity for
the show.

. . .

I have heard guns praised as grand inventions that extend a man's
reach a thousand times beyond the length of his arm and I've heard
them condemned as vicious brutal implements the very brimstone-sulfur
smell of which attests to their origin in hell.

They are both tools and weapons; being without souls they give
assistance to evil and good alike. I cannot speak for others. In my hands
a gun was never an implement of murder.

In my years of show touring I taught many a youth the rules of
shooting and it was always my first object to teach caution and respect
for the weapon. Mishaps with guns are not accidents; mostly they are

the result of carelessness or ignorance. If any youngster reading this account aspires to equal or exceed the shooting records I have established, let him first acquaint himself with the rules of safety in handling firearms. The experienced shooter who knows and obeys those rules is likely to live to a ripe old age like myself; it is the careless amateur who dies young.

In more than sixty years' shooting I have never had an "accident" unless one counts the explosion of Vern Tyree's rifle against my shoulder. Had he not been careless in refusing to listen to Kevin's warning, that explosion would not have occurred.

I estimate that in my years of shooting I have fired more than ten million rounds. That should make the point clear.

. . .

On the way to Memphis for our September opening the train went off the rails; ties had rotted and sagged, a joint had separated and we were derailed.

Fortunately this inconvenience occurred on an upgrade and we were moving quite slowly; there was no important damage to the train and no one was hurt but we were immobilized twelve miles short of the show grounds and we were scheduled to open the show in eighteen hours' time, the derailment having occurred at nine o'clock in the evening.

There was a misty drizzle and it was altogether a miserable night as we crowded around the listing locomotive to judge the chances of recovering the train.

Our engineer was dour. "We'll have to bring a steam derrick down from Memphis to lift her off. Then they'll have to rebuild the roadbed and lay in fresh ties and rails. It'll be three days before this line's open again. We'll have trains backed up clear from here to St. Louis by then."

"Let's not be concerned about them," Bob Halburton said. "That's the railroad's headache. Our headache, be that as it may, is fourteen thousand dollars' worth of advance sales we'll have to refund if we don't open tomorrow afternoon."

I was looking past him at Kevin Tyree. Faces were ghostly in the lantern light; the engine canted over us like a great dragon in the night, steam still chuffing from her valves as the fire went down.

I said, "Kevin, if you ever had an inspiration this is the time for it."

"Afraid Jock's right, Hugh. There's no clever way to get around it. We've got to get the line rebuilt and winch the locomotive back."

Harry Dreier lurched forward, his peg plunging into the soft muck. "Listen, the train may be stranded—it don't mean we are. I'll set the boys to scouring every farm in the area. Maybe we can borrow enough wagons."

"Harry, I'd take my hat off to you if it weren't raining so hard."

Bob Halburton coughed and wheezed; I saw him slip out his flask. "I doubt we'll make it in this weather even if we find enough wagons."

"We can try," I said. I gave Harry my nod and he set off toward the horse cars to assemble his men and saddle up.

. . .

I remember that night with great clarity. Seldom has a more motley assemblage moved down a turnpike: dogcarts, buckboards, hansoms, mud wagons, dairy vans, traps, Conestogas, buggies, a bright red stagecoach—not to mention herds of buffalo, elk, cattle, horses and the oxen that we used for heavy lifting and dragging.

To conserve weight most of us walked, squishing in the muck, soaked through and miserable, half-blind in the darkness with only a few storm lanterns to guide us.

We loaded our saddle horses as if they were pack mules; we went along with the Wild West Show on our backs. Only the heaviest equipment—the portable arena, the fences, the tons of canvas—rode on wheels. The Tombstone coach was so massively laden that it lurched along almost up to its axles in mud, hauled by long spans of oxen with queues of men on guy ropes keeping it upright and moving.

Daybreak caught us still five miles from our destination. We'd have to go through part of Memphis to get there—either that or detour several miles around, across bridges and back roads. We called a halt while the rain moved away to the east and the sun began to shine weakly through the grey. Cookfires sprang up along the road and the occasional early rider passing us by gave us curious glances and good-natured remarks.

I crouched by a fire beside Jeanette and Bob. His cough sounded serious; I said, "Ride in the buggy the rest of the way, Bob."

"I'm all right."

"Do as he says," Jeanette told him. I saw the concern in her eyes; she was no longer able to hide it.

Bob laced his coffee with sour mash. His hands trembled when he lifted the cup. His eyes had a shine on them.

He said, "Hugh, I've got an idea. Call it a press agent's pipe dream if you like, but hear me out."

"Go ahead."

"We've got to drive this assemblage through a sizable corner of the city. Why not go straight through the center of town?" He gestured with his metal cup toward the endless line of mismatched vehicles and four-legged stock. "Organize this mess into something with a little style and discipline. Put the mail coach up at the head of the line. Put you on your white horse, in costume, carrying a banner—hell, make it the

American flag. Dress it up and make it a parade. Get the cowboy band mounted, break out the instruments, march through Memphis to music. What do you say?"

That is how we began our custom of introducing ourselves to each town by parading our entrance. Bob Halburton's spur-of-the-moment idea, inspired by the dreariest of mishaps, must have given pleasure to millions of people over the years; certainly it increased our attendance considerably, for it was fine advertising. Few people who saw our jaunty parade could resist buying tickets to the Wild West Show.

Unhappily it was the last of Bob's grand publicity notions to aggrandize the show's success. His health declined increasingly and he took to his bed; we summoned physicians to examine him but they came away somewhat baffled and at odds over what was wrong with him. Jeanette shouldered more and more of his duties while Bob issued irascible instructions from his hotel bed.

We played out our Memphis run. The crowds were as thrilled as any but I hardly noticed.

I made time to haunt Bob's room. He sat propped against down pillows, sunk in his flab. I tried to keep up his cheer by regaling him with fanciful versions of my adventures at sea and in Mexico. He exhorted Jeanette to make copious notes of my ramblings for use in dime novels he intended writing.

After our last Memphis performance I set Harry and the crew to packing up the show; then I deserted them to go off to Bob. I found him pale and short of breath, hardly able to lift his head to greet me.

We both knew it was time for a farewell but at first neither of us mentioned it. Bob went on for a bit in short panting bursts reemphasizing his ambition to visit Khartoum and Mecca the following year; no white man had done it. Jeanette sat tall and straight on an uncomfortable wooden chair. Her very presence rebuked me. Bob began to run out of wind and asked me to tell him again about how I'd saved Ibran's life in the desert by carrying him across my back for three days. I began to oblige, coloring the story with outrageous boasts and lies; I was midway through the yarn when he interrupted me, his voice so deep and slow I hardly understood his words:

"Tomorrow you're downriver to New Orleans. I wish I could be with you."

I said, "You'll pick us up in Mobile or Atlanta. I've no fear of that."

"No, Hugh, I believe this is my last roundup. I ought to have my boots on." His grin was wicked but weak.

"Nonsense."

"I'm fifty-seven and I've had a good spin for my money," he said.

Jeanette leaned forward to take his flaccid hand. "I never expected to make old bones anyway. Fat men never do."

Jeanette said, "As soon as the doctors know what's wrong they'll be able—"

"I know what's wrong and so do they. They may not have scientific names for it but they know. I've burned myself out, that's all. I've worked hard, I've rotted my insides with sour-mash whisky and Virginia tobacco, I've seen too many elephants and played too many ninety-hour poker games. Well you can put it on my epitaph that I don't regret it. I damn near invented the dime novel, I sure as hell invented the Western stage show and I was part of the invention of the Wild West. I expect they'll remember Robert Halburton for a while."

The speech exhausted him and he lay with his eyelids fluttering. Jeanette stroked the back of his hand; her tears ran freely and she made no effort to conceal them.

Then his eyes opened and for a moment I saw the old dancing fire in them. "Hugh—there's something you must do. It's just come to me. The Wild West Show must go to Europe. Command performances before the crowned heads of the world. You'll be the greatest entertainment spectacle of the age. Let that be my memorial. . . ."

"I'll do that," I said, "if you'll come along and run our publicity."

"In spirit, my boy. In spirit."

. . .

The show was half through its Mobile booking when Jeanette's wire informed me that he'd died. We cut our run short and the entire company entrained for Memphis. We gave him a funeral that must have delighted his publicist's imagination: three hundred mourners and a dirge played by the cowboy band.

. . .

Our first Atlanta show played to thirty-four thousand people but there was a grey drizzle and a November chill. After dark I repaired in a poor mood to my private tent and broke out a bottle of whisky. I was drinking from a tin cup, not thinking about anything in particular, when I heard a brisk handclap in lieu of a knock. "Who is it?"

It was Jeanette; she stooped to enter the tent. She saw the bottle and cup in my hands and said, "Have you got another cup?"

I found one, poured out a measure and watched her knock it back. She sat down on the edge of my cot. "I've still got Bob's silver flask. I think he'd have liked you to have it. I'll bring it over when I think of it."

"I'd like to have it. As a reminder of him."

"I believe you honestly miss him as much as I do."

"I expect we both loved the bastard, Jeanette."

"Although God knows sometimes he made it hard." A distracted smile fled across her angular face. Then she held out her cup suggestively and I filled it again. She drank half of it down, blinked rapidly against the strength of the whisky, looked uneasily around the tent at everything but me and finally said, "While I was waiting for him to die I spent a lot of time blaming you in my mind. If you'd only left him alone in New York—that kind of thing. Just before he died he talked to me about that. It was as if he'd been reading my thoughts. I suppose I'd let my anger show. He said I should never blame you— he said the only thing he'd have regretted would have been my forcing him to miss this past season. And I realized he meant it, Hugh. He wasn't simply making excuses out of friendship toward you. He thoroughly enjoyed every moment of the birth of this show. It was his greatest adventure and he was right, it would have been unforgivable if I'd prevented him from doing it."

"I'm not sure. To tell you the truth I've been kicking myself around some, on that account."

"I know you have—you've had no bounce in your step since the funeral. That's why I had to tell you this."

"It's not that easy. He might still be alive if it hadn't been for me."

"You mustn't feel that way, Hugh. He wouldn't have wanted it." Then she met my eyes. "I don't want it."

"Thanks for your kindness." I settled back in the camp chair. "We're closing down, end of next week—everything into storage. I'm taking a lease on the Florida line to winter the stock because I don't see any point hauling everything a thousand miles and putting the animals through another northern season."

"Sensible."

"We'll gather back here at the beginning of March to rehearse the new show—we've had invitations from so many cities we can't possibly fit them all in."

"That's good."

She was subdued; I tried to break through. "Jeanette, I'm asking you something now."

"Are you?"

"Asking you to take over Bob's work. You know the job better than anybody else alive."

"I'm flattered. And grateful."

"And?"

"I'm not sure it would be wise. Men aren't in the habit of listening to a woman. I may get laughed out of newspaper offices, which wouldn't help the show. I'm thinking of the show, Hugh."

"Don't you want the job?"

"I'm not sure. Memories of Bob . . ."

"Then what will you do?"

"I don't know. Will you let me think about it before I decide?"

"Of course."

   . . .

I knew that any communication from me probably would be intercepted and therefore I had prevailed upon Kevin to write a letter to his sister requesting that she meet us in Washington on the Saturday after Thanksgiving. It was a blustery afternoon and Kevin and I arrived early and went immediately to the men's bar of the new Hay-Adams Hotel to get warm. We posted ourselves near the door so that we'd be sure not to miss Libby when she arrived in the lobby.

I was unnerved and uneasy. I did not know if she would come; I did not know how we would behave with each other if she did. My feelings toward Libby were ill-defined, impossible to articulate; I had tried to explain them to Kevin the previous spring but my attempt at candor had been lame and inadequate. In short I was afraid: I did not know what feelings her appearance might stir up in me. Love? Anger? Indifference? Would we be strangers or would it be as if no time had passed at all and we were still lovers? Until she stood before me I would have no answer to the question. Intuition and imagination failed me utterly.

"I don't think she'll come," I said crankily.

Kevin spared me a wry glance over the rim of his glass. "She will. I made the letter mysterious—she'll be too curious to stay away. Didn't mention your name, of course. Just said I had to see her on a matter of vital and confidential importance, and I'd be here with a friend."

"She knows you're working with the Wild West Show. She knows who that friend must be. Likely she doesn't want to see me."

"Well it's almost four. Let's just wait and see, shall we? Come on, Hugh, relax, drink your puma sweat, stop fidgeting."

"I'm convinced it's a waste of time. The only way I'll see her is to go to her house."

"Likely get the dogs set on you."

"Your father threatened me with that."

"Old Lobo. Good old dog. No hound, though." Kevin grinned. "Remember when I tripped and fell, almost scared those ducks away? Vern got so mad he almost took a notion to shoot me. Hadn't been for you there, I don't know what might've—"

"Speak of the devil," I muttered; for Vern Tyree had entered the lobby.

   . . .

I made my presence known to him by stepping through the lobby door. When Vern saw me his head rocked back as if from a physical blow. He stood bolt-still.

He wore an expensive topcoat with brown fur lapels and his hands were gloved; his hat was a high flat-brimmed beaver sombrero and his golden hair flowed plainsman-style about his shoulders. He had grown mustaches and beard in an attempt to conceal some of his scars; the facial hair was neatly trimmed and in sum his appearance was dandy and well-to-do. He was thirty-five years old and a handsome man in his prime.

In that moment of silent recognition I looked at once for evidence of the old hungering wildness in his eyes but I did not find it. He looked sure of himself, perhaps even a bit cocky, but the feeling that came off him was one of arrogance rather than hate. I do not know exactly what I had expected but I suppose it had entered my mind that he might care to take up where we had left off at our last encounter a dozen years previously. But he seemed to have outgrown that or at least put a lid on it.

He even came toward me with his hand outstretched and a thin smile on his square bold face.

He did not remove the glove however; and his handshake was brief. "Hello, Vern."

"Well then, Hugh." He looked me up and down. "The Wild West hero in the flesh, at last. You've come a long way. Hello, brother Kevin." He reached past me to clasp Kevin's thin hand. Vern's voice as always was rich and powerful, a great booming organ, and now he carried himself with a composure to match it. He had the look of power.

Kevin said, "Where's Libby?"

"I'm here in her stead." Vern looked at me. "The Senator wants to see you."

"He knows where I am, apparently."

"Not here. It wouldn't do." Vern tipped his head toward the men's bar. "Can I buy you a drink?"

"All right."

We made places at the bar, drawing not a little attention for it was an unusual sight to say the least—two tall long-haired frontiersmen at a genteel saloon bar in the best hotel in Washington. Vern dropped his voice right down. "I can't help but admire your quixotic devotion to my sister even after all these years."

He gave me a dry look followed by a brief smile to suggest it didn't matter—a man-to-man conspiracy of recognition. I saw little point in trying to disabuse him.

Kevin said, "Is she all right?"

354

"She's fine, Kevin, never better."

"How's Bill?"

Vern was looking at me when he answered Kevin's question. "He's a good lad. Doing just fine in school."

"What school's that?"

Vern still didn't take his eyes away from mine. "In whose interest are you asking, Kevin?"

"I'm his uncle. I've got an interest in the boy."

"I see." The bartender set drinks before us and Vern lifted his without looking at it. He tipped it toward me in a careless toast. "Your good health, Colonel." He spoke in a mild pleasant tone but his eyes remained fixed on me and the air around him was charged. When he set the glass down he said, "We've heard about your great successes in the show business."

"We have set the world on its ear," Kevin agreed.

Vern ignored him. "I saw your challenge in the newspapers last spring. I hope you don't think I avoided it out of cowardice."

"No."

"One of these days we'll have a fair square shooting match, Colonel. No horses or gimcracks."

"I'm looking forward to it."

"I expect you are." He smiled. "The Senate's in recess, you know. The holidays and all. Senator Merriam's taking his rest in Virginia. Down at Blaisedell Downs, near Arvonia." He leaned forward a bit; his eyes didn't blink. "I expect you know how to get there, Hugh?"

"I can find it." I gave him a bit of a smile.

"Tomorrow afternoon would be suitable if it fits your schedule. There's a train to Arvonia that leaves Union Station at noon. You can hire mounts at Arvonia depot."

Kevin said, "Is Libby there?"

"Well, it's possible, little brother. The invitation includes you of course. Your brother-in-law's always happy to see you."

"Sure he is." Kevin covered his anger by lifting his drink in front of his face. "You going to be there?"

"No," Vern said. "I've got something to attend to in New York."

"Sportin' lady or sportin' game?"

"Maybe a little of both. Why?"

"You ever think about earning an honest living, Vern?"

Vern made a point of looking around the room as if searching for someone he knew. He had developed a self-control I hadn't seen in him previously. Fitful rages shot through him—they were visible in his facial tics, in the way his knuckles went white upon the glass he clutched, in the quick darting movements of his eyes—but he kept a rein on his voice. "I'll tell you something, Kevin, if a fellow can shoot he doesn't need to work for his keep." His eyes swiveled abruptly toward me. "Isn't that a fact, Colonel?"

Kevin brooded into the amber smear at the bottom of his glass. Vern's gloved finger traced the scar on his face while he stared at me. I could not back away from it; I met his glance until his eyes flicked away. Nothing had been said but I knew his mortal enmity toward me was undimmed. He had tried twice to kill me and it was in his mind to finish the job.

But he only put his empty glass on the bar, tugged his hatbrim down and walked out without a further word.

Kevin said, "What do you make of that? He's up to something—you watch your back, Hugh."

"We'll take things as we find them," I said.

. . .

Riding up along the stretching white paddock fences I felt pangs of memory. Libby and I had begun our brief idyll here.

Negro servants took our hats and coats. We were led from the center-hall foyer into a richly appointed drawing room where a man in livery handed us glasses of dry sherry and told us the Senator would join us shortly.

I stood by the window waiting. Kevin went around the room idly examining the spines of books. There were hunt lithographs on the wall; a trophy head of a grizzly bear hung over the mantel—there was a plaque under it with the engraved information that the 3,400-pound beast had been killed with a .45-90-280 Sharps rifle bullet at a range of 25 yards at Wolf Creek Pass on 12th September 1878 by Major Vernon Tyree.

It took courage to face a grizzly at close range but I gave the bear's head only a cursory glance for I had never been impressed by trophies. I have killed for food; I have killed in self-defense; but I find no pleasures in it that are worth commemorating in taxidermy. Killing is nothing for a man to boast of. There is no sport in necessity, nor necessity in sport.

The majordomo in livery returned to inquire whether we wished our glasses refilled and I took the opportunity to ask the whereabouts of Mrs. Merriam.

"Which Mrs. Merriam, sir?"

"The Senator's wife."

"No sir, I do not believe she is here at present."

We waited a further ten minutes at the end of which a door opened and a Negro manservant bowed Senator Merriam into the room.

356

He was shorter than I'd thought, rather fine-boned; there was a sinuous suavity to his carriage. His face was heart-shaped and the dark hair was combed smoothly back from a widow's peak. He presented himself in jodhpurs and a short black riding jacket— the air of a country gent, his cravat casually undone.

"I'm sorry to keep you waiting. Hello, Kevin, you look well." His voice was strong but surprised me by its high pitch. He sized me up, throwing his head back with an expression of amusement. "Colonel Cardiff—we meet at last." It was purely a politician's smile; nothing behind it.

Neither of us offered to shake hands. Phipps Merriam said to Kevin, "Let us have a few minutes, will you?" and dismissed Kevin by turning his shoulder to him.

Kevin sought my signal; I granted a nod and he withdrew. When the door closed behind him the Senator put his hands in his pockets and stood facing me across the oval rug and I could not interpret the expression on his pale features.

"You wanted a meeting with my wife. For what purpose?"

"That would be between Libby and me."

"No sir. What do you want?"

I took two paces to the right to see his face better. "I want my son, Senator." I felt cool enough; he would acquiesce or he would fight— either way I was prepared.

He was not a man whose face gave anything away. "We're alone here and I shan't argue the point of the boy's parentage. But it means nothing. You forfeited everything when you abandoned him."

"I was forced out of the country. That was Vern Tyree's doing but I'm not sure you didn't have a hand in it. I imagine it would be possible to find out, even now. Do you intend to force me to try, Senator?"

"Go ahead. The warrant against you was valid. We had every right to insist on its enforcement."

"I doubt the public will see it that way, once they find out why you did it. To keep my woman and son from me. It won't look good in the press, Senator—it won't buy you many votes."

"You're a cleverer bastard than I took you to be."

I watched him bite the end off a cheroot. He didn't light it; he kept it between his fingers. "Extortion doesn't quite fit the brute-heroic image I had of you, Colonel."

"How far would brute heroics get me in dealing with a man like you?"

"Not very. But then neither will this tack. You were an outlaw in disgrace, hiding away from justice, and for twelve years you never lifted a finger regarding the boy. That's not a very heroic picture either,

357

Colonel. It would be pitifully easy to puncture those dime-novel legends. The yellow press revels in exposing heroes' feet of clay. A rumor here and there, the suggestion that the President may have been politically motivated in pardoning you as part of his campaign to discredit me— the suggestion that you were indeed guilty of a vile murder in Kentucky. ... It wouldn't take much of a nudge. Your reputation and your Wild West circus would dry up and blow away like an autumn leaf."

None of it surprised me in the least. I let him finish and then I said, "I'm willing to play it that way if you are."

"What?"

"I haven't got a political career to protect. All I want is my son. You can't threaten me with the ruin of my reputation—I don't care that much about my reputation." Then I let him see my cool smile. "It gives me an edge, doesn't it, Senator?"

"My God, but you're a calculating bastard."

Well I'd had a long time to calculate. I didn't reply; I only watched him, conscious in a corner of my mind of the hard cold weight of the Wells Fargo pistol behind my belt; a shabby precaution perhaps but I did not know him and felt I needed to be ready for anything.

I said, "Call it blackmail if you like. I'm sure you're no stranger to it. Either the boy comes to me or I talk to the press. Those are your alternatives—the choice is yours." Then I made my voice hard. "You can have the boy or you can have your try for the presidency. But you can't have both."

"I need to consider this. . . ."

"No. You give me your reply right now. If I leave this room without it I go to the newspapers."

"You pitiless bastard."

"Pitiless? I guess I am, Senator. After you threatened Libby's life and the boy's you gave up all claim on pity."

"She told you that, did she?" He had been looking away; now his eyes darted toward me. "What makes you think it was true?"

"Don't dispute the point. It won't do you any good."

"She's always been flighty. You know that. Sometimes I had to keep her in line. I wouldn't have carried out those threats."

"Then you should have held your tongue." I turned away from him and began to stride toward the door.

"Wait."

I stopped, looked back. He lifted the cheroot and struck a sulfur match; I listened to it hiss. The tobacco ignited and he blew out the match. "Let's talk about the boy's interests. With me he's got the best. With you what would he have? The life of an itinerant circus tramp? No mother? Don't you care at all?"

"I care about getting him away from the influence of you and your kind."

He drew on the cheroot and expelled the smoke to one side. "I'm a politician. I'm always receptive to possibilities of compromise. Perhaps we can find a common interest to pursue. Don't be in such haste to walk out—you'd regret it."

"Then speak your piece."

"Bill believes I'm his father. He's never had any reason to think otherwise. It would come as a terrible shock to him. Imagine what the confusion might do to him—it's a delicate age."

"At his age I was crossing the plains in a wagon, Senator. He comes from tough stock."

"We don't live in pioneer times anymore. He's had the best schools, the finest upbringing."

"All designed to turn him into a worthless rich scoundrel."

"Who's been filling you up with that? Kevin?"

"Senator, I'm about to leave. If you've got anything to say to me get it said."

He rolled the cheroot in his fingers; he was employing it as a prop to occupy his eyes and fill up the time it took him to think things out. I didn't mind. I tasted victory. He concealed his feelings well but I'd seen it shake him when I'd threatened exposure; it was his weakness—he'd do anything to protect his ambitions.

He said, "He's enrolled in the Westlake Academy. He boards there except during the holidays. In the summer he comes home. I don't see why we couldn't arrange for him to visit you during part of each summer. After all, you're an old friend of the family and a celebrated public figure—Uncle Hugh. I'm sure he'd enjoy a few weeks amid the excitement of your circus."

Once again his eyes flicked sharply at me as if to catch me off guard. "You see I'm trying to be reasonable. I'm sure you don't really want to fight this out in the newspapers. I'm sure you didn't come here to use the boy as the instrument of your revenge against Libby and me. You'll avoid a fight if possible, just as I will. We're both grown men."

Then he squinted through the curling smoke. "Of course if I agree to send him to you during the summers you'll have to agree on your part to maintain the fiction of his parentage. He's not to know I'm not his father."

"No good. He's got to know the truth."

"Later on, then, when he's grown up. When he can take it in stride. I'm concerned for his well-being, you see."

"The hell you are," I said. "Senator, I didn't come here to bargain with you."

359

"Then you'd prefer to fight it out in public?"

"I can afford the risk. You can't." I stepped closer to him, forcing him to tilt his head back. "I don't want a compromise. I want my son."

He said, "He's also my wife's son. Don't you think she has something to say about this?"

"Not as long as she's afraid to speak her mind. I don't believe the reasonable mask, Senator—you may as well take it off."

He didn't like looking up at me; it forced him to walk away. "You're probably right. There's no point. We're alone—let me be blunt." He whipped around to face me and it brought him against a cloud of his own smoke; he had to bat it aside. "All right, Cardiff, now you can listen to me. If you ever breathe a word of what you know to Bill or to the press or to anyone else outside this family, I will make things happen to you. An accident perhaps. A gunshot from the darkness. A knife between the ribs. There are a hundred ways. I'm talking about both you and the boy, do you understand? He's not my son, is he? I wouldn't be spilling blood of my own. And I believe the voters would extend their sympathy to a man whose son died in an unfortunate tragic accident, don't you?"

"Do that and I'll kill you, Senator."

"Dead men don't kill."

"This one will. If anything happens to the boy, my friends will do you in. No mistake."

His face for a moment went savage; but then it was gone. Now there was no expression at all.

He said, "We're at an impasse. Very well. Take the boy, you may have him. So long as you keep it from him that I'm not his father." His eyes went wide then. "You don't honestly want to tell him he's a bastard. And it's got to be kept from him. I'm offering to give you what you want—you've got to leave me with the thing I want. No twelve-year-old could keep that secret. It would get out and I'd be ridiculed as a cuckold—I'd be destroyed in Washington. Politics is my life. Take it away from me and I'll have nothing left to lose, I may as well destroy you. You see you've got little choice. But I'm offering you the boy—let that be enough for you. You're a stubborn man, Colonel, but you've met your match. Take what you can get."

He went toward the door, circling past me, trailing smoke. "There's nothing left to say. You may as well get out. When the school term ends in May we'll send Bill to you." He reached for the knob. "Good-bye, Colonel."

Then he regarded me inquisitively; I hadn't moved. He said, "Well?"

"I'll want to talk to his mother."

"Out of the question."

"She's got to hear it from me. I won't trust you to tell her the truth of this thing."

"She's not here."

"I'll be at the Hay-Adams for a week. Send her to me there."

He considered it; he turned the knob and pulled the door open. "If it will keep you out of my sight henceforth," he said, "I'll concede that much."

I wanted nothing further from him. I left without another word.

.   .   .

Kevin and I climbed onto our saddle horses and rode out between the white fences. I felt buoyed—unaccountably thrilled by anticipation. *Libby. . . .*

We had hired our mounts from a livery in Arvonia. It was a good distance to cover and we had not eaten. We went along at a good brisk clip and when Kevin had extracted from me a report on my confrontation with the Senator he made a few cautionary remarks which I found well-intentioned but unnecessary, and after a while fell into a monologue regarding his plans to market his newest ballistic refinement, "the Cardiff Rifle," through one of the mail-order arms catalogs. The Cardiff Rifle was a sporting version of the target rifle he had designed for me. It was a lightweight short-throw weapon with a quick slide action, employing his own design for open sights (a square rear notch, a square front sight with a polished bead) and ideal, Kevin insisted, for small game: anything up to mule deer. The concession he made to mass sale was principally the chambering of this public version of the rifle for standard popular ammunition—he intended to offer the rifle in calibers from .32-20 to .38-40. With considerable excitement he began to explain to me how he was negotiating arrangements with one of the major rifle factories to manufacture the Cardiff Rifle.

"We'll put out a thousand of them over the next year and see how it goes," he said. "The thing is, you see, this slide-pump action's the handiest of all the designs for fast reloading and high-speed shooting but until now nobody's ever licked the problem of looseness in the breech mechanism—"

I *saw* the bullet fired. I cannot explain it any other way. Perhaps it was the puff of muzzle smoke or the shimmer of its heat wave; I only know I saw it, in the corner of my vision, far out across a vast farm field. Kevin later insisted it must have been a wink of sunlight on the gunmetal but I am sure there was no wink; it was the exploding shot itself that I saw. The range was quite long, more than a quarter of a mile, and a bullet takes a certain brief span of time to cross that distance and

361

my plains-trained instincts hurled me to one side, one outflung arm propelling Kevin out of his seat—we were both pitching sideways out of our saddles when I heard the *crack* of the bullet whipping past and felt the burn of it along my sleeve. Had I still been upright in the saddle it would have driven straight through my heart.

· · ·

I fell rolling, breaking the fall with palm and hip, tumbling between the skittering hind legs of the two startled horses—a clod stung my cheek and the horses ran on, Kevin still in the saddle but clinging to one side of the horse, bent low like a Comanche, the horses broke into a gallop and the hidden rifle boomed again and I heard it break a foot above my head as I rolled. Those who have never been shot at may write that bullets scream or whistle or whine; the fact is they *crack* as they pass the ear—like a thunderclap.

I slithered against the base of the white wooden fence and winced from the bruises of the tumble; I fumbled about my clothing for the revolver and pushed it through the fence. I could not see the hedgerow from which the shots had come; I only saw the tops of the trees over there and had to raise my head to bring its base into view.

That time I clearly saw the puff of smoke. He hadn't spotted me; he was shooting blind—or perhaps he'd switched his aim to Kevin, I couldn't tell. I leveled the revolver in both hands; it took but an instant —my instincts were trained to calculate the range, the power of the bullet, the wind—I fired and felt the revolver buck fiercely against my palm; cocked it on the rise and leveled it again, fired again—four shots very fast and then I held fire, knowing better than to empty my weapon. I slid belly-flat along the fence to a point ten feet from where I had done my shooting—and lifted my head for a look.

It later occurred to me that it was the first time in my life I had actually been under fire. At the time, however, the emotion that overwhelmed me was anger. I had been fired upon from ambush by a treacherous coward.

The racket had exploded a flock of birds from the hedgerow; they swooped across the sky. The farm field was calm. Down along the road to my left Kevin, who was not armed, had dismounted and thrown himself flat against the fence—he lay some two hundred feet from me and the two horses were dodging about in the road beyond him.

For a while nothing stirred. I punched the empty cases from the cylinder of my revolver and plugged four cartridges into it, snapped the gate shut and drew back the hammer. Then I poked my head up again, far enough to search the hedgerow. The birds had begun to return but now they wheeled away again—something had spooked them and I lifted the revolver in case a target should present itself: juices pumped through me, I was flushed hot with rage, and in that moment I believe I was more than willing to kill. It is a fury I have experienced very few times in my life and I have always found it terrifying in retrospect.

I heard a muted thrashing from the direction of the hedgerow; the birds circled, the flock corkscrewing above the trees. The racket subsided and after a little while the birds began to settle one by one into the branches.

Then I had just a glimpse of something moving across the ridge-top horizon behind the hedgerow; it was only a furtive sighting—the object appeared briefly between two treetops half a mile away and was gone. A man on horseback, I thought.

He made his try. He missed. Now he's run for it.

I stood up and trotted along the fence, stopping short every few paces, ducking and weaving. But I drew no fire. When I reached Kevin's side he gaped up at me. "Sweet Jesus."

"Let's catch up those horses."

"You mean to go after him?"

"God damn right I do."

. . .

We found the trail in the hedgerow; we followed cautiously, alert for another ambush; but the sniper had made his escape. We lost the tracks in the hard-packed traffic of a main road.

Kevin reined his horse around to follow me back the way we had come. "I wish I had a rifle."

"Well you haven't got anything to shoot it at now."

"It was my bastard brother-in-law. He's set a killer on you, Hugh."

"I'm not sure it was the Senator's doing."

"Come *on,* Hugh!"

I said, "He didn't have time to send a man this far after we left the farm."

"Then he set it up in advance, knowing we'd have to ride this way."

"No. It's not something he'd have set in motion before he found out what I had to say to him."

Kevin's face changed. "It could have been Vern. Couldn't it?"

I said nothing. He gigged his horse forward, alongside me; reached for my sleeve. "Couldn't it?"

I said, "I expect Vern will have six poker cronies to swear he spent this day at a high-stakes game in New York City."

We rode briefly in silence before Kevin said, "I am ashamed to call him my brother."

"You didn't pick him."

"We'll never know for sure, will we?"

"Maybe not." But I intended to keep a sharp eye, a keen ear and my back to the most convenient wall until I found out.

. . .

She came to Washington four days later. We met on neutral ground —the hotel's dining room. She sent a bellman up to my room with word of her presence and she was already in the dining room when I came down. When I entered the room I sought her out and saw her from some distance. The sight of her made my breath catch in my throat— it was as if no years had passed, not even months; we might have parted two weeks ago; she was unchanged, radiant in her beauty.

Then I approached the table and saw the little lines of years and bitterness. By the time I reached her side the illusion was gone. She looked at me as a stranger.

. . .

We were polite to each other in cool voices. We kept it right down almost to a whisper; the room was peppered with late diners.

"Your hair's gone white."

"So they tell me. You haven't changed."

"I did all my changing a long time ago, Hugh."

"Will you have anything?"

"I've had lunch, thank you. A cup of coffee perhaps."

"How's Bill?"

"Well that's what we're here to discuss, isn't it?" She was stripping off her gloves, tugging a finger at a time. Her blond hair was done up under a little hat; she wore a pink dress with stays that accentuated the length of her waist; she was extraordinarily comely as always but I saw no fire in her eyes. She seemed not so much self-assured or mature as simply resigned, as if life had passed her by.

She said, "I've followed your exploits in the press. It all seems terribly exciting. You must be quite a social lion."

"I'm not married if that's what you're asking."

"But you were."

"Yes."

"To an Apache Indian."

"She was a kind and gentle woman."

"I'm glad for you. I'm sorry she died." She smiled, meaninglessly. She laid the gloves neatly alongside her place. "What do you intend to do with my son, Hugh?"

"Give him a chance to grow up to be a man we can respect. That's a chance he hasn't got with Phipps Merriam."

"I've done my best to protect him from that. He sees very little of his fa—of Phipps. I'm sorry."

"It was an honest slip of the tongue. I'm not offended."

She said, "I have devoted my life to William's best interests."

"And naturally it offends you that I want to take him away from you. I'm sorry, Libby. The boy needs a father. He's at that age."

"I shan't quarrel with you."

"Did Phipps warn you not to?"

"Yes. But I wouldn't have quarreled in any case. I've done my very best for William but it hasn't been enough. He needs you."

She stared lifelessly at the table. After a moment I said, "Thank you for that."

"I'd like to come and visit him from time to time."

"Of course."

"Will you put him back in school next year?"

"We'll have to see how things work out."

"He likes the school. It's a second home to him."

I thought: *Maybe if he had something to come home to he wouldn't feel that way.* But there was no point in hurting her by saying it.

I felt a terrible sense of loss: I tried to recall the intensity of my passion toward her but it would not come to the surface.

I said, "Next summer we'll be touring the country with the show until November. Then the next spring we're taking it to Europe. I don't know how long we may be abroad. Maybe one season, maybe five—it depends on the reception."

"Don't make a gypsy of him, Hugh."

"No, I didn't intend to. He'll go to school, whether it's here or in Europe. They've got fine schools over there."

"So I'm told." She picked listlessly at the fringe of the tablecloth. "Is that all you wanted to say to me?"

"I wanted you to know the truth from me. I didn't trust Phipps not to fill you full of malicious lies. I want my son, that's the truth of it, but it's not a selfish thing any longer. I just want him to have the best chance to grow up straight, with some dignity. He'd never have the chance with that pack of varmints and crooks in the Senator's set."

She smiled a bit with one side of her mouth. "You know the strange thing is, Phipps isn't a bad politician. Of course there are all sorts of mutual back-scratchings but that's normal enough. He's not corrupt— how could anyone bribe him? He's already one of the richest men in the country. He's done some good works, did you know that?"

"I'm not surprised. Anything that polishes his reputation."

"If he manages to buy the presidency he won't be the worst president we've had. In fact he'll be quite a good one, you know."

"I don't believe that," I said, "but I don't feel like arguing the point with you. At least you seem content enough with him now."

"I've made my peace," she agreed without luster. She stood up abruptly; her hands moved with vague indecision and then she remembered to pick up her gloves. She said in a whisper so faint I almost missed it, "Oh, Hugh, I've made such a wretched mess of everything," and then she bolted away in tears.

I went after her, threading tables, and only caught up to her in the lobby. "Libby—"

"No, never mind—can't you see it's too late for anything at all?" She kept her face averted. The girl behind the counter handed her cloak over and I draped it across Libby's shoulders; I felt them shake. "I'll be all right," she whispered. "I'm sorry to make such a silly exhibition of myself. Will you get me a hansom?"

We went out into the raw wind; I tipped the doorman and handed Libby up into the hack. She held my hand a moment. "Be a good father to him, Hugh."

Her face turned away. "Union Station, driver." Her hand withdrew.

As I watched the hansom clatter away down the cobblestones I thought of a dozen things I might have said to her.

. . .

I returned to the lobby in a blue funk and was on my way to the stair when a tall figure in yellow barred my way and I looked up in astonishment to see Jeanette Fowler before me.

"I didn't want to intrude," she said. "Who was that, Libby Tyree?"

"Libby Merriam," I replied. "What are you doing in Washington?"

"Looking for you. I've got something important for you. Is there somewhere we can talk?"

I glanced toward the dining room but Jeanette said, "We'll need more privacy than that. I've spent enough time in hotel rooms before—my reputation can stand it if yours can." She gave me a wan little smile that demanded a return in kind; my spirits lifted a bit as we climbed the stair together, Jeanette chattering away about the atrocious weather and the abysmal train ride from New York and the Pendleton civil-service-reform scandal.

As I put the key in the door Jeanette said, "She's a lovely woman."

"What?"

"Your Libby. Strikingly beautiful."

"Well she's not mine," I said, holding the door open for her.

"I saw the way she took your hand, Hugh. You don't need to keep secrets from me."

"There's no secret to keep. You were looking at dead ashes blowing away in the wind."

"My, what a poetic turn you've taken." Her eyes teased me; she eeled

366

past me and dropped her coat across the back of a chair, glanced without interest around the elegant room and plopped herself down on the edge of the bed. "I've been working." She said it with a gleam in her eye that arrested me; she was almost gloating. "And it's a good thing too because otherwise they'd have caught us with our drawers down."

I had to laugh. A year's traveling with the show had made something of a bawd of our Jeanette.

"I'm afraid it's more serious than that, Hugh. We're not going to have the country to ourselves anymore. We have competitors."

"We?" It was the first thing that struck me. "Then you made up your mind."

"Did you think I wouldn't come back? Give a girl a taste of the world and you can't keep her down on the farm."

"Welcome back."

She scrutinized my face belligerently. "Are you honestly glad or would you rather I hadn't come back?"

"I don't know where I'd have found anyone else to do the job as well as you."

She wasn't altogether mollified. "Massa is so kind."

"Jeanette, I'm happy to have you back in the family. What more do you want me to say? If you're asking for a raise you can have one. What competitors?"

"I thought you hadn't heard me. I was doing a bit of advance work in New York and Rochester. I tried to book the New York Hippodrome but it won't be completed in time. But I found out a man named Salsbury had been there inquiring about the same thing—hiring the Hippodrome for a Wild West Show."

"Salsbury?"

"Nate Salsbury. He's working for Buffalo Bill Cody."

"Cody always did know a good idea when he saw one."

"They're advertising several well-known people with their show, Hugh. John Nelson—"

"Old John? I know old John. He used to partner with Fitz."

"And Dr. W. F. Carver—"

"Calls himself the Evil Spirit of the Plains, that one? Well Carver's a first-rate rifle shot you know. Cody'd need someone like that. Drinks too much to keep a steady hand."

"You don't seem to be taking this very seriously, Hugh. They've got Ned Buntline out drumming up advance publicity for them."

"Plenty of room in this country for two shows, I expect."

"Not if Buffalo Bill books into the same cities three weeks ahead of our show."

"Is that what they're doing?"

She nodded. "Apparently Salsbury got his hands on a copy of our itinerary."

"Let him keep it," I said. "We'll change the itinerary." Then I grinned, knowing how Bill Cody hated anyone getting the better of him. "Tell you what, if he's setting his schedule three weeks ahead of ours, what do you say we cut out the first three cities on our itinerary and move the whole thing up six weeks?"

A slow canny smile stretched Jeanette's lips. "You clever dog. You mean put us three weeks ahead of him? My, my, you are a ruthless man."

"I just want to give Bill Cody the message that I was here first. Once he and his advance people know I'm not going to be fooled, they'll change their schedule. There are plenty of towns out there. We don't need to tread one another's heels. He'll see that fast enough."

And he did. Buffalo Bill's Combination opened in Omaha that spring while our show began its season's run in Charleston as originally planned.

I am obliged to digress here to mention the matter of the competition between the Cardiff and the Cody shows. For many years our two shows followed the pattern that we set in 1883—we neither followed nor led one another, but toured widely different areas of the country. Years later, after the turn of the century, when Buffalo Bill was aging, ill, drunk all the time and hard-pressed by both creditors and a wife whose patience had run out, his partisans attempted with considerable success to establish the claim that Cody had been the originator of the Wild West Show and that his Wild West and Congress of Rough Riders was the grandpapa of all the expositions and the most spectacular of them. These claims were made at a time when it would have been churlish of me to contest them—the old man was down—and in some ways they were not unjustified. Buffalo Bill was a public figure before I was; he was older than I, and well-known to magazine readers as a Pony Express rider and Civil War hero before he turned to hunting buffalo and fighting Indians on the plains. By the time I began to make my mark at the Colorado shooting matches, Cody was known to thousands of readers as the hero of dime novels written by Ned Buntline and Colonel Prentiss Ingraham.

When Buffalo Bill began his Wild West and Congress of Rough Riders he did it on a grand scale, benefited from some of our mistakes, and employed the publicity talents of three splendid press agents: Nate Salsbury, Ned Buntline and Major John M. Burke. Buffalo Bill himself was an extraordinarily attractive showman; he had a taste for the sort of bombastic rhetoric with which I had no patience; he wrung every possible tear of sentiment and patriotism from his acts; and over the years

368

his show became more circus than roundup. I saw his show a few times; at its peak it was a glorious medley. It had a twirling merry-go-round, marching cornet bandsmen, organ-grinders, conjurers, gaudy sideshow attractions of all kinds, sword swallowers and flame eaters, freaks, cossacks, dancers, gauchos, Arabian horsemen, aerialists, balloonists, even peep-show machines for the farmboys—*What the Butler Saw.*

He developed the show by instinct—his own and the instincts of his promoters—and his instincts were surer than mine; in many ways Buffalo Bill was wiser than I. (It was his press agent, Major Burke, who prevailed upon Teddy Roosevelt to name his troops "Rough Riders," after the Buffalo Bill show.) Proposals of similarly pyrotechnic grandeur were made to me from time to time by Bob Halburton, Jeanette and the others who directed our publicity, but in many cases I ruled them out. As a youth I had set out to be the world's champion rifle shot. I was determined to prove that claim at every performance of my show, and to the end I remained reluctant to subordinate the honest skills of marksmanship to any tricks of legerdemain or simulation. For many years I resisted the incursion of circus sideshow elements that might dilute the purity of the Western-roundup flavor of our show.

Cody was the consummate showman; I will not gainsay that. The result has been that today Cody's show is remembered more vividly than is my own, and when the public thinks of Wild West Shows it thinks of Buffalo Bill.

Yet his show did no harm to our trade; and since my show continued robustly to tour the nation long after Cody's death, I can hardly seek to blame him for its failures. The competitive rivalry between us was more a matter of press agents' copy than of reality. Buffalo Bill had his partisans, to whom he wasn't far short of God, and his detractors, to whom he was a drunken charlatan; I have never numbered myself among either of them but on balance I did not dislike him and sometimes admired him.

I should like to let the matter rest there.

. . .

We began the 1883 season on April 3 in Charleston and I rediscovered the stirring warmth of the unity between performer and audience.

I was looking forward to being united not only with audiences but also with my son Bill, an event that was scheduled to occur seven weeks hence at the end of his school term. In the meantime, in Charleston and Wilmington and Raleigh and Richmond, I continued to devise new exhibitions to justify the title that the newspapers had conferred upon me, "The King of Crack Shots."

From the outset I had always been willing to oblige spectators who wanted souvenirs of my rifle. I shot coins in midair for them, so long as they provided the coins. My specialty was shooting three-cent pieces, which for those who don't remember them were somewhat smaller than nickels.

During the second season I took to shooting coins out of spectators' fingers. When the possessors of these fingers were children this exploit often alarmed their parents but in many years' shooting I never drew blood.

Doc Bogardus traveled full-time with us during the 1883 season, enjoying it hugely; at heart he was a ham actor. Between us we struck up several profitable competitions, although in order to attract challengers we had to offer to shoot from twice as far away as they did. Once, in Charleston, when a challenger complained about what he thought surely must be the magic powers of my Tyree rifle, I exchanged rifles with him and went on to win the match. With my rifles I regularly outshot challengers armed with shotguns; I always drew applause by shattering glass balls on the rise from full gallop while challengers proved unable to do it from the ground; I set up metal chimes like Mrs. Urquhart's at Candelas and played "Old Black Joe" on the chimes with .22 revolver bullets; and I devised a new trick that enthralled audiences for years: set a glass ball on the ground, shot just under it so that the concussion flipped the ball into the air without breaking it, then shattered it with a second bullet.

Doc Bogardus and I taught ourselves to shoot from both right and left shoulders, to pace ourselves, and during our closing shows in each city we established the pattern of shooting thousand-ball matches *in one hour*. This required relays of numerous rifles on account of the overheating effect; it obliged us to fire a shot every three-and-a-half seconds. We found ourselves quite evenly matched, Doc and I, usually scoring 965 out of a thousand or better; on one occasion in Raleigh Doc shot 983 and at the following match, determined to do him better, I shot 983 as well. I always thought myself Doc's equal but I seldom was able to prove myself his better; I would win a match against him but then he would come back and win the next one.

The real heroes of these matches, in their own eyes, were the throw-boys. My favorite thrower was a youth named Charlie Samuelson who remained with us for four decades in various capacities; in 1883 he was my number-one throw-boy and he always drew laughter from the crowd when at the end of the match he announced in a loud voice, "Heck, Colonel, I'm the one that ought to win all the money—I'm the one that hits the bullets with the glass balls."

It was Doc who came up with one of our more extraordinary public challenges; it proved the downfall of many a local bully. After some weeks this challenge became a regular part of our biweekly matches: we preceded each competition by a warm-up act in which we offered twenty-five dollars to any man who thought he was strong enough to lift one of our rifles to his shoulder one hundred times in fifteen minutes. We pointed out that in our thousand-shot matches we regularly lifted our rifles two hundred and fifty times in fifteen minutes; and we taunted the audience by pointing out that in order to win the twenty-five dollars they didn't need to hit targets or even fire the rifles. All they had to do was lift them.

I kept that challenge in the show for more than twenty years. We had plenty of takers. Over the years I believe we had nine winners, all of them experienced shooters.

During a four-day layover between bookings after our Richmond stand, a financier offered to back Doc and me against all comers in a marathon match—six thousand balls in three days—and to split half the winnings of his $30,000 bet with us. We shot the match, I won it (by only seven balls), Doc came in second with a score of 5,961, and we calculated afterward that the exercise had required that each of us lift ten tons a day.

Most of the spectators who accepted our challenge to lift rifles were local strongmen who were employed in heavy lifting jobs: they were coal sackers or ice haulers with huge chests and brawny biceps. But none of them was accustomed to speed in motion; that was what failed them. They had the strength but not the agility and their muscles would cramp after a while. Only a shooter could win that bet. No circus strongman ever had a chance against us; we proved it time after time. I believe this is all the more remarkable in view of the fact that I had suffered a broken shoulder and the loss of much of my musculature there, and the fact that Doc Bogardus was fifty-eight years old.

. . .

My dear Hugh,

A fortnight ago I was summoned to the Westlake Academy by a telegram from the headmaster. He expressed concern about the state of William's health.

After one glimpse of William I knew the headmaster's concern was not misplaced. He had a pale, thin and listless mien. I immediately bundled him in blankets and carried him away to Philadelphia, where for twelve days we have been consulting physicians and surgeons.

William is under treatment now in the Pitt Hospital. He is resting, complains of no discomfort, but to my eye he is wasting away. The doctors feel there is little hope for his health. The disease has been diagnosed under various names but the Merriam family physician, who is highly reputed here, has broken it to me that William is suffering from leukemic cancer of the

371

blood, that it is incurable, and that the boy has only a short time left to him.

I hope you will forgive the curt formality of this note. As you may imagine I must hold myself in with rigid care. William is all I have lived for.

I could not be so heartless as not to inform you of his condition, nor can I be so cold as to prevent your visiting his bedside. I am at his side at all times and shall expect to see you here at your earliest convenience.

Yours in wretched regret,
Libby

. . .

The doctor was a portly man, gruff and bald and wearing a professionally condoling smile; he intercepted me in the corridor. "Colonel Cardiff? We've been expecting you."

"The boy—"

"I'm sorry, Colonel. Last night he took an abrupt turn for the worse. We had expected him to last out the week, perhaps even the month. It was not to be."

I stared at him, speechless, my mind gone utterly empty.

"I'm afraid he's dead. I'm sorry. Mrs. Merriam has gone to her relations outside the city."

"Dead," I said. *I never saw my son.*

"The funeral arrangements are being made through an undertaker nearby. There will be a viewing Thursday morning. . . ."

I walked away without listening.

. . .

In the afternoon in a fog of unreason I made my way back to that hospital again; I sought out the bald doctor. "I need to know one thing. Is there any chance it could have been poison?"

He was shocked. "Deliberately administered?"

"Could it have been poison?"

He gave me the strangest look; finally he shook his head. "The symptoms . . . No. Not one chance in ten million. I've seen too many cases of blood cancer, Colonel. Far too many to suit me. I know the disease."

"I'm sorry to have troubled you."

He touched my arm. "Sometimes it's hard to accept the fact that Fate deals cruel blows. Perhaps you'd have found it easier to believe in a deliberate malevolence."

He was right of course. I'd been ready to accuse Phipps Merriam of the murder of my son.

"You must have known Senator Merriam's son very well, Colonel."

"I was very fond of the boy," I muttered and left in haste.

. . .

It was not my only suspicion. I went that evening to the undertaker's parlor and insisted on seeing the body. There were objections; the remains had not been made ready for viewing; I pushed it all aside and thrust my way through to the operating cubicle.

I stared without recognition at the wan innocent mask. I had half-expected to see my own face; it confused me that he did not resemble me so far as I could see.

His hands seemed very small. The skin had collapsed across the delicate cheekbones; he looked like an old man dead. The peculiar white color of his flesh repelled me. His hair was dark blond, as mine once had been; he had a straight blade of a nose and a good square jaw and after a moment I began to realize that in those respects he did resemble me after all—it was his deadness that had put me off, the way the cheeks and eyes were sunken, the awful thinness that must have been the result of his illness. Bones jutted starkly through the parchment of his flesh.

The undertaker was a brusque man without the avuncular piety of most. He stood tapping his teeth with a pencil, impatient to have me gone.

I said, "Did you know the boy before he died?"

"Why do you ask?"

"Do you mind answering the question?"

"I knew him. I've had occasion to bury two Merriams in the past couple of years. The Senator's mother and an uncle. The boy came to both funerals. Yes, I knew him."

"Then this is William Merriam. There's no mistake?"

"None. Why?"

"It doesn't matter." I couldn't stand the sight of that room anymore; I had to get out of there.

In my dark suspicions I had believed it possible that Phipps might have rung in a substitute—to fool me into believing my son was dead.

None of these aberrations seemed implausible to me then: I was in a melodramatic fugue.

· · ·

It should have been a gloomy day, sodden with rain, sunless; it would have matched the occasion and my mood. But the sun shone upon a profusion of gay dogwood and cherry blossoms in the cemetery—a day for a birth, a wedding, a festival.

In hired black clothing I stood among the mourners and listened to the intonations and watched the small casket descend into the earth. The ropes were pulled away. Libby knelt to cast earth upon the wood. The Senator stood beside her. He was looking at me across the open grave and I believe it was in deference to my presence that he did not toss earth himself. After a moment his glance softened and I saw that he was trying to extend sympathy toward me, the little of which he was capable. He was not being polite; he was not tolerating my presence; there was more than that in his face. For a moment I saw him put himself in my shoes. I saw him acknowledge his recognition of some part of my feelings. It was a moment after which I always thought more kindly of him and it was a moment that taught me a lesson I have kept to heart ever since: even in the darkest of men there is light somewhere.

I sought some sign from Libby but her face was hidden behind the veil; her hands trembled and she had to be steered away by her husband when the ritual ended.

I did not speak to anyone. I went away alone.

BOOK TEN

Wild Times

I RAN THROUGH the remainder of the season in a bleak fog that infuriated Harry Dreier. Attendance began to drop off; we closed out the season without regrets.

The assassin who had fired upon me in Virginia did not make another attempt. Perhaps he had been restrained. In the belief that the assassin had been Vern Tyree I journeyed to New York after the season closed and made inquiries with the aid of Abner Wingate, the investigator whom I had employed once before. The results proved nothing. Vern Tyree had been in New York at about the time I had been ambushed in Virginia; but he could have gone to Virginia by train and returned the same way.

Nevertheless for a time I went about with my hand close to my revolver and the short hairs aprickle upon the back of my neck.

.   .   .

That was Gotham's Gilded Age. There were all manner of gaudy amusements from Barnum's Greatest Show on Earth to the lively lesser commerce of championship prizefights, dime museums and vaudeville theaters. I explored it all—dutifully and without much interest but in a kind of desperation.

Jim Fisk was long since dead by then, shot in the Grand Central Hotel, and Boss Tweed dead while serving his time. Speculators became millionaire plutocrats overnight and millionaires went broke equally abruptly. I watched Gillette on the boards of the Bowery Theater, went to the Liederkranz masked ball in the guise of Sir Lancelot, lunched with the famous at the Union Club, slept—infrequently and seldom alone—at the Brevoort, and dined in the mansions of old and new rich. In clawhammer suit and silk hat I conquered the city, and didn't care.

. . .

Christmas Eve, a gathering somewhere, I took a woman home—I do not remember her name; she had money and position but at heart she was a lady of Cypriot persuasion. I was indifferent to the festivities and I am sure the woman brought me home only because I was a "catch." We had hardly entered the flat when I began to be troubled by anger and regret because it was only a strange woman in a strange room and as soon as we had mussed the sheets there would be nothing to talk about and I would soon find an excuse to take my leave.

I tasted her breath in my mouth. She sucked my lower lip. A forced urgency to it all; the scent of champagne on her breath. "Say you love me. You don't have to mean it—I'll pretend I believe it." She waited a moment and then turned away beginning to strip things off. Somewhere a clock told two. The woman had a look at me; her fingers stilled. "Now and then can't you give me a smile that doesn't look like the remains of one you've already given to someone else?"

"Sorry."

"God. I wish you'd stop looking like a mountain that's about to erupt." Then she sidled toward me, touched my lips with her fingertip, whispered into my throat: "Even an animal needs a mate, you know."

I pushed her gently away. "I'm sorry, it's no good." I took my hat and turned to the door.

She flounced after me, filled with indignation. "I must be getting old. This is the first time I've ever been thrown out of my own bed by a man. No one would believe it if I told them."

"Tell them anything you like." I pulled the door shut behind me.

Walking back to my hotel through the snow I found myself wondering childishly how I'd have done with her. *Now I'll never know.* Then I smiled to myself. *The hell I won't.* It had been foregone; there'd been no question of doubt; and I lost—instantly and forever—some small but important part of whatever it was that had set me after so many musky women for those past months. I knew there was no longer any anticipation in the chase, no uncertainty; I faced myself with the knowledge that it had only been a dreary game I'd played with myself.

Christmas morning I twisted my head around and learned I'd slept alone and was glad of it.

. . .

January first, 1884, the New Year. Fitz Bragg was in town. I found him drinking corn whisky at eleven in the morning. "God damn you," he welcomed me, "how're you makin' it, boy?"

"All right. Pass me a snort of that tanglefoot."

376

"Happy New Year."

"What brings you to New York?"

Then we both replied in unison, "A good fast train," and had our little old-times chuckle.

He looked incongruous in those civilized surroundings; it was a small staid business traveler's room in the Royale. His saddle-roll warbag was propped on a chair, his Texas boots under it, his big hat on the bedpost. Fitz had gone bald on top but the fringe around the sides fell to his shoulders in a yellowish white cascade. Except among his intimates he never took off his hat anymore.

He made a tent of his fingers and peered through it slyly. "I ain't going to Europe with the show, Hugh. I come here to tell you that."

"Are you all right?"

"Surely am. It ain't for reasons of health."

"Why you'll love it over there, Fitz, they'll lionize you."

"Ain't saying I wouldn't enjoy that, neither."

"What is it, then?"

"Albert."

"Now Fitz—"

"I have made up my mind," he said. "Ain't no use you trying to change it. Ibran's done joined up with Geronimo and they gone out again. Ripe little uprising down there."

"Will it never end, then?"

"I expect this'll be the last time, myself. Most of them Apache getting kind of long in the tooth, like me. The younger ones, any of them any younger than Ibran, they been born and raised on the reservation, they ain't real Indians no more. No—there'll be drunks raisin' ruckuses here and there but I reckon this here's the last Indian war we ever going to see. And I expect that's why I aim to be in it."

"You're too old, Fitz."

"Hell I am."

"You're slow. I saw what happened to Clement Tyree when he got old and slow."

"Well I knowed Clem, he was a good old boy. I would admire to go out with the same dignity myself. A lot better than doing it on a bed in some depot hotel in some junction town in Ohio, I will tell you that."

"Be sensible, Fitz. You've got a lot of years left as long as you don't try to outfight a crowd of Indians one-third your age."

"Never did count on living forever, you know."

"You may not live forever but you'd be a damn fool not to try."

His eyes windowed irony. "I might could say the same thing to you, Hugh. The way I hear you been gallivanting around fixing to kill yourself for whisky and fancy women and no sleep . . ."

377

"A toot now and then cleans out a man's soul," I said. "I'm over that now."

"Well I am happy to know that. Anyway you better find yourself a new old-time mountain man to sit my saddle in that show. Reckon old Colorado Jack Newhall might be willing to replace me."

"Maybe you can be substituted for, Fitz, but you can't be replaced."

"Well I always calculated you sized up pretty good too, Hugh. I have admired to know you."

"I won't change your mind now, will I?"

"No chance of that, son."

"Promise me one thing, at least—don't let Al Sieber run you down any holes like a ferret. Let him do his own dirty work."

"I know Albert better'n you think I do. He won't toll me into no hard places without I want to go into them."

I lifted my drink to him and wished him good luck.

．　．　．

Jeanette's mother, whom I had met only once and briefly, fell ill with a malaise of age that seemed destined to linger. With regret we left Jeanette behind tending her mother when we set sail for Southampton in March 1884.

I was not the first Western shooter to have exhibited his skills in England. Dr. W. F. Carver, the "Evil Spirit of the Plains," before joining forces with Bill Cody had journeyed to England in 1879 and created a small stir with his exhibitions of shooting skill. He had shot for the Prince of Wales at Sandringham and had embarrassed a good many of Britain's top shooters at Bisley and Edinburgh; there is no shooter on earth to match a plains-bred Westerner. But Carver was exclusively a shooter in those days, not a showman, and he had no troupe of Wild Westerners and no show to perform.

As I write these pages Dr. Carver, who is some years older than I, is still trouping with his circus side act, the Carver Horses; he still puts on shooting shows, I am told, although his eye has lost some of its keenness and his hand its steadiness. I should mention that I have had the privilege of shooting against Dr. Carver at four rifle competition meets in America. Dr. Carver won one of those matches and I won three but the scores were separated by very narrow numbers on two of those occasions and I believe him to be every bit Dr. Bogardus' equal with the rifle. At two other meets, however, I licked Carver by substantial scores with revolvers; I therefore put little credence in his claim of being the world's champion marksman. Carver, like the other rifle champions I have met, did not have the advantage of having his shoulder crippled for nearly a decade—a blessing in disguise that forced me to polish my handgun skills to the utmost. I believe the record shows clearly that I am the champion all-around shooter of the world. To this day no one has broken the records I established.

. . .

We journeyed to England with 250 performers, 200 horses, 40 buffalo, 25 mules, 20 Texas longhorns and a grizzly bear that Nate Loving somehow had taught to wrestle harmlessly with him. We had our full 18-piece cowboy band, five Conestogas and of course the Tombstone mail coach. It was an aggregation vastly more splendid than anything that had ever been seen on that sceptered isle.

When Queen Victoria came with her court to a command performance of the Wild West Show it was the first time a British sovereign had ever saluted the American flag, to my knowledge, and it was I who had the privilege of carrying that banner. As I rode forward to the royal box the Queen rose and bowed; the officers and gentry around her doffed their hats and saluted as our cowboy band played first "God Save the Queen" and then "The Star-Spangled Banner." I removed my hat and bowed, the horse dropping obediently to one knee, and as I swept my hat back I heard a ripple of applause. Then I lifted the hat overhead and swung it in a circle and the show began.

. . .

Before we left London the Wild West had become the new English fashion. Young swells and dandies were decked out in cowboy hats and boots with great clinking spurs; riders in Kensington Gardens could not be seen on anything but vaquero and Texas saddles. Medals and jewelry were bestowed upon me by nobles and royalty. I played poker with the Prince of Wales—he won, which was not surprising since I have never played the game well—and during that summer, our first tour of England, we were seen in performance by more than two million people.

In the autumn we started south across the Continent following the climate. We would return in the next summer to Paris; we began the fall tour in Lisbon, then went on to Madrid. In Barcelona, on the spot where Christopher Columbus landed upon his return from the discovery of the New World, press agents posed me with a number of my Indians, one of whom—after having been coached by Harry Dreier and me—announced loudly and in good English, "Some of us wish old Columbus had stayed home." That photograph made its way all the way back to the American newspapers.

Then Tangier, Rome, Cairo, Aden. I had sailed through Suez years ago before the mast; now I made the passage as an honored visitor. Constantinople; Athens; Lyons. It was mid-spring by then, mild and gentle. Our bookings carried us up the Rhine and into the Low Countries; we played command performances before King Leopold II of Belgium and the benevolent William III of the Netherlands.

379

We opened our show in Berlin's Tiergarten in April 1885 before a royal audience that included young Wilhelm who was not yet crown prince but was the grand-nephew of the reigning king and would in due course become the Emperor Wilhelm II, Kaiser Wilhelm; he was accompanied in the royal box by Otto von Bismarck. During my shooting exhibition the young prince seemed intrigued by my clipping the lit tip off a cigar clamped in Harry Dreier's mouth. The future Kaiser came down off the royal box, filled with good humor and—I suspected—abundant schnapps; he insisted I must extinguish his cigar in the same fashion.

The royal request unnerved me but I had little choice. I pulled a bit wide and only managed to nip the ash off the cigar, which seemed to amuse the prince; I was thereafter in his good graces. But years later at the outset of the Great War the newspaper cartoonists and editorialists regretted that I had missed Kaiser Bill's head by so few inches with my bullet. I was obliged to send the Kaiser an open letter in 1917 demanding that he give me another shot at him.

· · ·

Those tumultuous months abroad excited and enthralled all of us, the troupers no less than the audiences; and it was good healing medicine for me, for it kept my mind from personal things; in truth it was to be a long time before my soul recovered from the loss of both my sons.

I felt bedeviled by an inner challenge to continue perfecting my shooting skills and devise ever-more-difficult tricks. I taught myself to shoot six balls in the air at once; taught myself to shoot backward over my shoulder by use of a small mirror; and finally, what I always felt was my supreme accomplishment, trained myself to shoot blindfolded by sound alone. A glass target was suspended from a frame. A boy would toss a pebble at the target, making it ring. I would shoot at the sound—and shatter the target.

Of all the tricks I devised over the years I believe that one is the only one that truly amazed Doc Bogardus.

· · ·

Still, the most difficult challenge I faced in those years was one I accepted before a royal audience in Dresden from the King of Saxony, who offered me a challenge—and a substantial bet—to shoot 250 glass balls on the rise without a single miss.

My previous record theretofore was a string of 153 straight hits during a thousand-ball match with Doc Bogardus. I was not at all confident of my ability to hit 100 in a row, let alone 250, and was exceedingly reluctant to wager my money on it but obviously it was a challenge from which I could not retreat without serious loss of face and revenue to the entire troupe. Kevin and I devoted many painstaking hours to the preparation of cartridges and rifles; finally I stepped forward into the arena on the appointed day before the crusty King and his haughty skeptical court, shot 274 balls without a miss in a period of 37 minutes and stopped shooting when I failed to hit the 275th. When I turned and bowed to the royal box the applause and shouting were deafening even to my gunshot-dulled ears.

That record stood for a number of years and I was the one who broke it.

. . .

We made quite a stir by taking our troupers and Indians on shopping tours and visits through museums and palaces. Doc Bogardus and I chatted with monarchs, played croquet with princes, dined with nobility and shot tourneys against the Continent's finest marksmen. Wherever we traveled I always posted my standard challenge to compete from horseback against gunners on foot. In forty-seven shooting bouts I was beaten twenty-two times but twenty-one of them were engagements in which I took second place to Doc. The sole match that neither of us won was taken by a sergeant from a Scots fusilier regiment whose skill with a Mannlicher rifle had been acquired in battle against sepoys and Sherpas. I never learned what became of him.

We made our last stand of the season in the Bois de Boulogne of Paris. That lovely city lionized us.

We finally embarked from Le Havre on October 19, 1885.

. . .

Our return must have been picturesque for the newspapers next day were filled with descriptions of our arrival in New York harbor. I have a few clippings yet.

Hugh Cardiff stood at the high rail, his extraordinarily tall figure easily recognizable for the long hair waving in the wind, a striking figurehead. Cowboys and roughnecks and Indians crowded colorfully along the rails of the main deck while the masts and rigging were abundant with the fluttering banners of a score of nations, those "conquered" by the Wild West Show along its Alexandrian expedition. Cardiff's famous cowboy band brayed enthusiastic renditions of "Dixie" and "La Cucaracha" and "Yankee Doodle" with vim enough to announce to the entire city how joyful the troupers were to behold the sight of home.

Upon the Customs Dock Colonel Cardiff answered speculations by confirming that he intends to lead his Wild West Show on a grand tour of the United States next year, and averred that he was not disturbed by the recent announcements of similar tours by no fewer than three competing Wild West fairs, to wit those of Col. W. F. ("Buffalo Bill") Cody, Dr. W. F. ("Evil Spirit") Carver, and Major Vernon Tyree.

Col. Cardiff's Wild West will journey west by private train early in November, affording citizens along the route a glimpse of the valiant celebrated troupe. It is Cardiff's intention to treat his men to a winter in the sunshine of his old stamping ground in the Arizona Territory. It was suggested that perhaps with the return of Col. Cardiff to those parts, the current Apache Indian uprising may at last be brought to a close.

.   .   .

I scrubbed off the smell of the sea, wrapped myself in a dressing gown and returned along the corridor to my suite, where I anointed myself with toilet water, combed my hair and began to attire myself. I had that task half-completed when I heard a light knock at the door and went to it clad only in stockings, drawers and trousers; it is my habit to dress from the bottom up, for no reason more compelling than the fact that my father used to dress me in that order when I was small.

I opened the door with my shirt in my hand and discovered Jeanette on the threshold. After but a single glimpse of me she burst into a peal of laughter.

I growled something and stood aside so that she might enter. "I'm sorry," she said as she brushed past me. "You're quite a sight. Do you always greet ladies like this? No wonder you've such a reputation in the boudoirs around here."

I pushed the door shut. Jeanette glowed; she was dazzling; it seemed she owned a beauty I'd never seen before.

Without a word I swept her into my arms and kissed her.

.   .   .

Her sleeping face was composed, gentle, reflecting a quiet content-ment; her hair was spread on the pillow, her hip mounded high under the bedclothes. She opened her eyes drowsily and smiled at me, moving her face toward me. I printed light kisses on her nose, her cheek, her mouth. Sweet and warm, she burrowed against me. "This is so deli-ciously sinful."

"I didn't think you'd come. When you didn't meet us at the boat . . ."

"Oh Hugh, I didn't want to meet you in front of all those people. This is what I wanted, I confess it. The two of us alone." Then she sat up, throwing the bedclothes back, smiling at the way my eyes lingered on her. "Since my mother died I've done a lot of thinking about what's going to become of me. I knew what I wanted but I didn't think I could have it. Then I decided I must try. And here I am." She snuggled down again; my hand traced the long column of her spine. "I'll be a pest, traipsing after you wherever you go. I'll be there when you want me. I'll go when you tell me to go."

"Jeanette, that's ridiculous."

"No. There's a lot of things, little things a woman ought to do for a man. You've got no one to do them for you. I won't be in the way. You

382

see it came to me, while I was missing you so, that loving is more important than being loved."

I was startled to feel the wet of her tears against my brow. I looked up into her eyes. "Stop that now. I can't stand a bawling woman."

"You're so gruff and fierce. You're a giant kitten, Hugh, do you know that?"

"You ever let that news out and I'll shoot you full of holes."

Then we both laughed low and gentle and it was good laughter, cleansing away a great deal.

After a while I said, "It's a wonder to me that this never happened before."

"Did you ever want me before?"

"Expect I did. But you were Bob's woman."

"That was long ago—I wasn't the same woman then. But I'm so ugly, Hugh! Some evil demon got inside my bones when I was twelve years old and I just never stopped growing until—well you see what happened. By the time I was old enough to be sparked by boys I towered over all of them. I am six-foot-one and I've never learned how to stoop, not that it would matter that much. From the time I was fifteen I had a dream I'd fall in love with a great gallant monstrously tall man, as handsome as Apollo and as gentle as a saint, but it was only a dream —the kind a little girl uses to drive away the dark when she's sent to bed. Then I met Bob and he started spinning yarns to me about you. He told me you were six and a half feet tall in your bare feet. At first I thought it was another one of his wild exaggerations—I was sure you were five-foot-seven. I met Caleb Rice once and I was crushed—he was Bob's other hero and he's nearly a dwarf. . . ."

I laughed. "Come on now."

"Well he's very small." She pouted. "But Caleb assured me you were as tall as Bob said you were."

"You pick your men by the yard, do you?"

"I'm too proud not to." She hiked herself up on one elbow and looked earnestly down into my face. "Does my candor shock you?"

"Nope."

"The first time I met Bob I found him a little bit repulsive. He was such a windbag, he smelled of awful cigars and whisky, he had stains on his shirt and his eyes were bloodshot and he looked like an oily pompous fool. You know the only reason I went out with him was I wanted to hear more about you?"

"I didn't get that feeling the first time we met. You chewed my head off."

"By then I was fond of him, worried about him, I wanted to protect

383

him. I mothered Bob—I suppose I needed it then as much as he did. But I've outgrown that. I don't want to be your mother, Hugh. I want to be your woman, for however long you'll have me."

I pulled her down and kissed her roughly and long; she melted against me and the odd thought flashed through my mind that it was the first time I'd ever made love to a woman whose feet touched my own—both hanging over the foot of the bed.

Later I gave an elaborate sigh of mock resignation. "I suppose we're stuck with it, my love. It's obvious what God had in mind when he made us to fit each other." I was flat on my back with my hands laced under my head; Jeanette was at the dressing table pulling a comb through the long fall of her deep red-brown hair. Her quick smile blazed at me in the mirror. It was a smile that did amazing things with her mouth and eyes; I never was able to describe it but it was a smile that once seen could never be forgotten. The sight of it now drew me to my feet and I walked across the room to stand behind her with my hands upon her wide bare shoulders. Jeanette leaned back against me and her eyes went dreamy in the mirror.

I bent forward and kissed her forehead; my hair tickled her and she shivered. I went to my clothes and began to get dressed. "Woman, you've interrupted my night on the town but I expect we can still find someplace open where we can get supper. I'm hungry enough to eat a buffalo."

"Make that two buffaloes. I'm just hungry enough to keep up with you."

We found a herd of New Yorkers still thundering in Delmonico's. A great shout of welcome went up when we entered the restaurant; I smiled and waved my hat to the crowd before I turned it over to the hatcheck girl. I never got that hat back—someone purloined it while we ate—and after that I developed the habit of safeguarding my hat in public places by keeping it on my knee.

The maître d' found us a small table in a corner booth shielded from the crowd. I touched Jeanette's hand under the table and she gripped my fingers, hardly relinquishing them all evening; her eyes shone at me and as for myself I felt a giddy adolescent sort of thrill—I'd long ago had my fill of love-and-forget nights but it was more than that: it was the wonder of discovering what treasure I'd had in my own hip pocket for so long without knowing it. It was like a young boy's first discovery of love all over again.

We mooned at each other and laughed at ourselves; we nuzzled brazenly like children in a hay wagon. "God damn," I kept saying. "God damn."

"Will you quit blaspheming at me?"

384

"Well somebody should have told me about this. I feel like I've a lot of wasted time to make up for."

"Just so long as you let me help you make up for it for a little while." She traced my ear and my lips with her finger. "Oh Hugh, you are such a grand magnificent *man*."

"You ain't half a woman yourself, my love."

. . .

"Now look, I can't spend all week mooing like a moonstruck long-horn bull. I've got to ask you something. It looks like the mice have been playing while we've been away. What's this news about Carver and Vern Tyree running Wild West shows?"

Jeanette's answer was businesslike enough but the glaze didn't go off her adoring eyes and her hand did not leave mine. "Carver had some sort of quarrel with Buffalo Bill Cody. They're suing each other. Carver has started his own show—he ran a small tour for the last third of the season this year and I think he drew fairly good crowds. They say he's a fine marksman but a little careless of where his ammunition ends up—it's only a rumor but I've heard he was shooting nine glass balls on a single rise and by the time he shot the last two or three they were so close to the ground that the bullets ricocheted and wounded two of his throw-boys. But then he apparently doesn't mind the sight of blood—they say he's killed quite a few Indians."

"They say that about me too, you know. I wouldn't believe too much of that."

"Did you ever kill an Indian, Hugh?"

"Neither Indians nor anybody else. But don't ever breathe a word of that." I grinned at her.

"Why ever not? I should think it would be something to take pride in."

"The world would take me for a namby-pamby after all the dime-novel mayhem that's been pinned on me. What's Vern Tyree up to?"

"There are always opportunists ready to follow a trend. I suppose he's one of them. He's had a number of dime novels issued to build up his reputation as a war hero and he's gotten a lot of press by bragging that he's a better shooter than you are. He claims he's challenged you a dozen times and you've never accepted the challenge."

"We'll have to see about that, won't we?"

"He's so brash I doubt too many people pay him much attention. I shouldn't be too concerned."

"Where is he now?"

"Touring South America with a shooting show. He's announced he'll take his Wild West combination on tour here in the spring."

"Find out his schedule," I said. "When I challenge him I want to make sure he's got no excuse not to show up. If he's spreading that kind of rumors they've got to be scotched. I never did understand what drives Vern. He's a fine shooter, one of the best—I know; I'm the one who taught him. Why can't he be proud of it without smearing lies against the rest of us?"

"Some people are born to be destructive, I guess. But he seems to have a particular grudge against you."

"The hell with him. I'll meet him in the spring and settle this." I lifted her hand to my lips. "How would you like to spend the winter out in Arizona with me?"

      • • •

Three of us made the drive out from Tubac in a one-horse runabout: Jeanette and I and the lawyer Martínez. When the sandscraped ranch house came in sight on the hilltop I felt my heart lift. I urged the horse to a canter and then slowed when we approached the yard; I pointed out features to Jeanette—the *portal* where the old clay *olla* had hung, the corral where Kevin and I had fence-walked on teetering boots, the pasture where I'd had my painful steal-the-bacon equestrian education. I was fascinated to see the old rocking horse was there, stripped of paint by twenty years' weather; I could still see little Libby riding it ferociously, blowing soap bubbles from her corncob pipe.

As we rounded the corner of the barn I had an image of John Tyree and Harry Dreier riding out in the rain with vaqueros and Lobo on the trail of Grandfather Clement's murderers. The feel and smell and look of the place flooded me with recollections that poured through my mind too quickly to be grasped and held.

Bits of dry sage rolled in the wind like tumbleweeds. The ranch had the barren sun-dried air of desertion. The adobe needed patching, a windmill—new since my time—stood rusty, the corrals were empty of stock but for a few listless tail-swishing horses. A Mexican hand stood in the doorway of the old sutler's shop watching us drive in; he nodded gravely to the lawyer beside us.

I drew rein and set the brake and gave Jeanette a hand down. The lawyer led us inside.

I did not find it musty, for the air there was too dry, but there was a sad lifelessness in the house. Very little furniture remained—nearly everything had been sold to settle various debts—and the few things there had no value or beauty. In the parlor the old bookcase was dried and splintered, its empty shelves bowed from the onetime weight of heavy volumes: the painted motto across its top was only faintly discernible. GOOD BOOKS ARE OUR BEST FRIENDS.

In the patio there were boards across the top of the well; the crank handle needed oil. Scrubs sprouted among the stone flagging. Most of the windows were boarded over: Libby's room, Kevin's, Vern's, mine, fat María Maldonado's quarters beyond the kitchen. I wondered if she was still alive.

The old master bedroom that John and Marjorie Tyree had shared, and Grandfather Clement's chamber beside it, were not boarded up; apparently the most recent occupants had used those, and inside we found a few beds and rudimentary furnishings, even a Mexican rug. It was the cheapest of homemade hand-hewn furniture.

The lawyer said, "They fought hard to keep it, Colonel. But the drought just went on too long. Four years running."

I was looking at Jeanette. She was going around the place with her lips pursed, touching things here and there—a doorjamb, a wall. I could not fathom her response.

Martínez said, "I must be honest with you. There's no sign the drought will break. It is said the climate here may be changing permanently."

"They could have drilled more wells, couldn't they?"

"To be sure, señor, but more wells would not have provided grass for the cattle to feed upon."

"I heard a naturalist fellow down in Mexico was developing a brand of prickly-pear cactus with no spines that cattle can eat."

"Perhaps. I've heard rumors of it but I've never seen such a thing."

I said, "How much are the Núñez people asking for the place?"

He named a figure. It seemed a bit high but not unreasonable. I could afford it easily enough; I was the next thing to a millionaire after the past four seasons of touring in America and Europe.

Martínez said, "If you'll excuse me for a while—I shall be at the rig when you're ready to go." He withdrew with a certain funereal obsequiousness and when he was gone from the patio Jeanette swayed against me and nuzzled my throat.

She wore a simple homespun dress and a little flat hat, pale blue with paper peonies and the hint of a veil. She had laughed when she put it on but she claimed it was suitable for dusty traveling. I'd allowed as how it was pretty enough to wear on Sundays.

I said, "Dammit, woman. Well?"

"It's so big—such a hard land. So masculine. Why it's as vast as you are, Hugh—it suits you. Such a lovely great manful land."

"But you don't like it."

"I could feel the warmth stirring in you the moment we first set eyes on it. It was your first real home, wasn't it?"

"My home was in Kentucky, you know."

"But you never loved it as you loved this place. I'm getting to know you, Hugh. You've a deep nesting need to settle your roots and you've

387

spent so much of your life moving from place to place—you've only had two homes you ever loved. This one and the cabin where you lived with Flower and Mike. You need this land, I can feel it—it will make you whole, won't it?"

"Then you don't mind if I sink money into all this dust."

She took my arm. "Come on. Let's tell Martínez to get out his bill of sale."

· · ·

When the long parade of our Wild West company rolled into the Tyree Grant just before Christmas one thing struck me with more force than any other incident of that whooping excited day. It was the tears that sprang into Harry Dreier's eyes while he sat his horse in the middle of the roiling confusion in the yard and cast his eyes around from sight to familiar sight.

I reined my horse over beside his and leaned out of the saddle to clap his arm. Startled, he reared around to stare at me.

I said, "You're still the foreman of this outfit, Harry. Get this god-damn mess organized."

His grin fairly split his wide face open. Then he gripped my hand between his callused palms and wept a great flood without shame.

· · ·

Kevin's tool wagon came rutting into the yard and I saw it turn directly toward the old forge shed. I reined the white horse carefully through the milling gang of troupers and caught up with him just as he was dismounting from the wagon. He tipped his hat back and planted his feet, arms akimbo, and took in the scene with a steady deliberate turning of his head. Then he looked up at me. "I know you didn't do this on my account," he said, "but I believe my father and mother would have been proud of this day. Can't explain just exactly what I mean but it's a kind of vindication for the Tyrees. Guess I'll say this just once and then I'll say no more about it. Thank you, Hugh, for letting me come home."

· · ·

We celebrated our housewarming with a bashing great Christmas wingding. Isaac and Maggie Singman came down from Tucson with their children. Ran Urquhart and his wife rode up from the Candelas with a score of old friends from the crews there; they were delighted to see Nate Loving and the other Candelas veterans among our show troupe. Fitz Bragg arrived on muleback from Fort Huachuca near Tombstone, which had become the army's headquarters for the Apache war. We had a wire from Doc Bogardus in New York and a parcel of reward posters—the old murder warrant with my name on it—from Caleb Rice, who was enforcing the law as a United States marshal out of Fort

Smith, Arkansas. Nate Loving and some of the boys immediately ran around posting up the wanted shinplasters all over the ranch, to the delight of all my friends and myself as well. They remained nailed up there until so many years had passed that the weather bleached most of them to pure whiteness; I still keep one of them protected under a smoked-glass frame as a keepsake, not so much of my own checkered past as of Caleb's good-humored thoughtfulness.

As much as possible I was determined to keep the Tyree Grant as it had been in my youth when I had first come upon it in Isaac's peddler wagon. Jeanette had discerned the truth of it: the Grant was my home. I'd done my growing up there.

That thought was strong in my mind when we sat down to eat the greens and beans and the beef that had been roasting on open-fire spits all day long; we had set out the show's long camp tables and the assemblage of hundreds filled the entire open yard. The padre from Tubac offered a prayer of blessing and we all bowed our heads after which Isaac and Harry and Kevin and Ran Urquhart got up and made what appeared to be the first in an endless succession of toasts to Christmas and to me and to absent friends and to the Wild West Show and to God knows what-all. While the cheering ran through the night I sneaked a glance at Jeanette.

She hissed at me, "You absolutely reek."

"Good honest Apache mezcal."

"I thought you'd fallen down in the corral."

She held her nose and made a face. But behind it I saw hesitation and reserve, an uncertainty that had been in her since our departure from the East. I knew the cause of it and felt powerless to change it.

Voices boomed from the assemblage: toasts and speeches to this new winter home of ours, to our grand and glorious future as the greatest show in the world—oratory and rhetoric, bad jokes and hearty cheers. For a while I was swept up in it: and when I looked for Jeanette she was gone.

I spied her then, running with her long ungainly stride, fleeing across the *portal* and into the house. The door slammed behind her and I felt a baffled disorder; I pushed through the crowd, fending off hands and smiles—they were still whooping it up when I plunged through the door and the parlor and the open patio with the thunder of their uproar echoing off the sky.

I half-expected to find the door locked but it gave to my pressure; I thought I might find her facedown sobbing across the bed but she was in the chair facing me, no tears, merely a slight cool frown. She said mildly, "I believe God invented the fist so that we could knock before entering."

"I'm sorry. You looked upset . . ."

"I am. Upset. There are times when one prefers to be alone, Hugh."

"I don't want to leave you alone like *this*."

"Why?" Very aloof.

"We need to talk," I said.

"I suppose we do. I doubt this is the time for it."

"It'll do." I took a seat on the bed, elbows on knees. She met my glance warily.

I said, "You're feeling out of place, aren't you?"

"Like a bull in a china shop."

"It's something you'll get over."

"Will I?"

"In a while it'll become your home as much as theirs."

"As much as *yours,* Hugh?" She shook her head. "It reeks of Libby Tyree. And so do you."

.   .   .

I tried to dissuade her but I suppose I spoke without force; she kept denying my words with her silence. Finally she said, "It's full of ghosts here."

"Maybe that's all they are. Ghosts of dead things. Libby's a long-ago thing in another life I used to have."

"No. You're deceiving yourself. Anyway it hardly matters. You don't need to comfort me, Hugh—I've been happy enough just being with you for a little while. It's all I expected, honestly."

"Will you quit running on like a lunatic?"

"It's not the end of the world, don't you see? I'm a big strong moose."

"You're thinking about leaving, aren't you?"

"Yes."

"Don't."

"Oh, Hugh, don't beg me, it would be a disservice to both of us. If I stayed you'd soon be sick of the sight of me. I'd rather go now and have nothing but sweet memories to keep. I'm a big clever woman and I'll make my way in the world, have no fear. From time to time we'll meet again and we'll have good memories to share—why spoil that?"

"I wish you'd stay." It must have sounded as lame as it felt. For she was right. In every cranny I saw Libby: a girl on a rocking horse, a pubescent prankster, mischievous child-woman, radiant lover. Perhaps my life might have taken a different turn there, had I been practical and strong enough to put senseless dreams behind me. Just then I wanted to sweep Jeanette up in my arms and wring her pledge to marry me. But I did not. It would have been false to her and to myself.

I said, "Give it time—give it a chance."

"No, Hugh. You belong here. I don't. Don't you see—I'd always be an outsider here."

I could have said: Then we'll go somewhere else. We'll buy a place in Colorado or Kansas. But I said nothing at all. Jeanette knew me too well.

In the morning she was gone.

. . .

I had hardly had time to take stock of the sudden loss of Jeanette when another blow fell. Early that spring—it was 1886—a horseman brought a crabbed note which told me virtually nothing but provoked my anger because of its cryptic arrogance: *Come with bearer. Sieber.*

The bearer of the note was a young soldier, a Negro Tennessean, awed by my name and presence; he answered my questions bashfully but with candor—he really had no idea what it was about; the Tenth Cavalry was running Indians across the desert and a lieutenant had pressed the note into the trooper's hand and sent him to fetch me.

"How far from here?"

"They're still on the move, sir. No telling. Several days I guess."

I outfitted a packhorse and, refusing a score of offers of company, set out quickly with the trooper. We rode into the border country, eighteen hours to the point where the trooper had left his unit and then another two days on their track—we were in Mexico by then and the trail of shod hooves grew heavier as scattered groups converged. Reading the sign I could tell easily enough that various scouting detachments had trailed various fragments of an Apache band across these plains, converging as the Apache converged. Pushing hard by the sign of it: the Apache mostly afoot. Here and there we passed the bones of a dead army horse, ridden into the ground.

We found the army's camp by moonlight and announced ourselves to the sentry and passed in through the perimeter. It was short of midnight and the officer of the guard held us by the horse picket line while he went to fetch Sieber. I thanked the young trooper for his guidance and he left me, heading gratefully for his blankets.

Sieber came limping forward half-dressed. He carried a light rifle; in the poor light I couldn't make out what kind. While still ten paces from me he spoke: "It's you, right enough. A man could not that size mistake."

I had known the meaning of the summons, of course; it was only his manner of delivering it that had annoyed me. When he handed the rifle to me I understood well enough. It was the old French needle-gun repeater—the one Fitz Bragg had been shooting at the Denver match the first time we'd met. Nearly twenty years ago.

"He wanted you to have it, Colonel."

Horses whickered along the picket line; sentries walked their posts. There were no fires, nor smell of any. "You've been pushing them to death."

"The Indians? They give us no choice. I know you don't believe this, Colonel, but I am sick to death of hunting them. I am too old for this killing—maybe like Fitz I die soon, eh?"

"Tell me, then."

"They are in the Sierra—just up there. Not far from where you used to live. A *ranchería*. I think they do not have the strength to run more —they will make a stand. Tomorrow, the day after. Either they fight to the death or they give it up. I hope they give it up. There are too few of them, too many of us—Miles has a regiment down here tonight, we have permission from Mexico you see."

"Geronimo?"

"Of course. And your Apache brother-in-law with him. And maybe seventy, maybe eighty men. Not enough, Colonel. Not enough to make a war any longer."

"You haven't told me about Fitz."

"He died. What does it matter how?"

"It matters if you prodded him into it."

"I guess you're never going to like me, Colonel, but maybe you know my word is good? Fitz had two of my Apache scouts, they after four bucks came. Out there on those flats, maybe fifteen mile. Three days ago. Four bucks on foot and Fitz saw his chance to ride them down. With these eyes from that mountain I saw. He was like a crazy man running buffalo—at full gallop, shooting from the saddle. The two scouts went along behind him, I think to protect him maybe. The four bucks just stood their ground. On their bellies, one of them had a good rifle. Fitz killed two of them all the same—a hell of a rifle shot he was —but the one with the good rifle shoot him out of the saddle. Afterward my scouts brought the two bucks in. Their rifles was empty then. They used their last bullets on Fitz Bragg. He prodded himself into it, Colonel. It wasn't me."

Sieber was stiff with me; I suppose he had a right to be.

I said, "He attacked them straight up?"

"He did that."

"Not like Fitz. He knew how to ride low in the saddle."

"He knew this, yes. I think he did not want to."

I nodded slowly, accepting it. "Thanks for the rifle."

"One other thing now. I don't force you this time, I only ask. You talk to Ibran again, like you did before?"

"They've got their backs to the wall this time, Sieber. You've run them down to the bone. They've got nothing left to lose. Will my talking to them change anything?"

"Might bring them home alive, Colonel."

I studied his face. "You know I do believe you mean it, Sieber. You don't want more killing, do you?"

"No sir. It's come to me it's always the best men who get killed. It's only the stove-up bastards like me that living go on."

. . .

As it happened I had my chance to talk to Ibran but not in time to have any effect on events. By the time Sieber and I went into the Sierra at the head of one of Miles's columns of Negro troopers Ibran and his little group had given it up. They had surrendered to an advance party of Apache scouts and we found them sitting around a fire, their arms tied with lariats—they were skin and bone; I could count every one of Ibran's ribs and he greeted me with a wan bleak stare, so dulled I was not sure at first that he recognized me but then he said in a hollow voice, "*Enju,* Car-dee," and I sat down with him and we spoke for some time. Ibran had lost everything by then, everything but his pride. His health was gone—he had a racking cough and I was worried for his life. I prevailed on Sieber to lend me a detail to escort the captured Apache back to Arizona Territory. When Sieber looked upon Ibran I saw, for the first time in my memory, a genuine compassion in Sieber: he smiled very briefly, said, "Sure, Colonel, you take them home," and left us, leading the remainder of the troop on into the Sierra where within a few days they were to corner Geronimo's remnant and force the final Apache surrender of the Indian wars—a muted sorrowful climax to a wild and bloody era.

Sieber did not die in that last campaign. Perhaps he'd have been happier if he had but he lived twenty years, mostly among the Indians whom he had fought so long. He was the supervisor of a gang of Apache who were building a road on the Salt River in 1907 when a rockslide killed him—a curious and somewhat ignoble end for an astonishing man.

At the base camp at the foot of the range I begged the use of a four-horse army ambulance and, together with an escort of Negro troopers, conveyed Ibran and his seven ailing companions back to Arizona. We looked after them in the Tubac hospital for some weeks, much to the displeasure of the local citizenry—I had to post an armed guard on the ward to prevent incidents. I looked in on Ibran several times as we made ready to take the show out for the new season; his health improved slowly and he seemed pleased to see me when I came but the spark had gone out of him and we talked only of neutral things. Neither of us ever mentioned Flower's name.

Against my wishes—I was powerless to intercede—Geronimo's band was placed under military arrest and sent by train to detention camps in Florida where the army felt the Apache would be unable to stir up further risings. Ibran went with them and I did not see him again for some time.

. . .

"Customarily I don't talk business with principals." The dapper man twirled his bowler hat on his finger.

I was cool. "I have no seconds, Mr. Potter. Anyhow it's not a duel, is it? Why don't you state your business? Or if you're afraid I'll out-bargain you then maybe you'd be wise to ask Vern Tyree to send another errand boy."

Potter flushed with embarrassment. He looked around the tent—the desks, the trunks of paper files, the typewriting machine, everything except my eyes. We were playing that week in Portland, Oregon. Heavy rains had canceled the show two days in a row, the downpour was still banging the canvas of my office tent and I was not in the gentlest of moods.

"I'm sorry if I offended you." Potter was a precise little man, nervous and bony. "Now and then I have a weakness for chewing on my own shoe leather. I'm not Major Tyree's errand boy, as it happens. I'm in the employ of the Merriam Industries. We've made a proposal to Major Tyree and he has accepted it, and I've come here to offer the identical proposal to you."

"All right, Mr. Potter. Propose it."

"The newspapers and magazines have given much attention to the pending clash of arms between you and Major Tyree. 'Two Titans of the Plains'—that kind of thing. I'm sure you've seen some of it?"

"Here and there."

"The public's been stirred up over it." Potter twirled his hat and focused his eyes on it. "And they've also followed the preparations of the Bearsted expedition with keen interest in the press. It occurred to my employers that there could be a considerable profit in combining the two attractions. Profit for all concerned—yourself included."

"I don't see what the shooting match has to do with the Bearsted hunt."

"Sir John Bearsted fancies himself a crack sportsman," Potter told me. "He intends to hunt big game on the plains as you know. During the past winter the arrangements for his expedition have been made through the offices of the Merriam Industries. Sir John will be traveling

394

with a large retinue of sporting gents and press correspondents—he intends that his party be not only successful but famous as well. As you know, I'm sure, he has been determined to employ a world-famed frontiersman as his personal guide, and Major Tyree has agreed to lead the hunt in that capacity. The Merriam Industries feel this expedition would provide a splendid setting for the Tyree-Cardiff championship rifle match. We'll profit from it, of course. By sponsoring the match."

When I didn't interrupt with questions or refusals Potter hurried on, his pitch as well-oiled as that of a tripe-and-keister barker. I found his earnestness amusing. "Merriam's intends to provide all facilities and underwrite all costs. And we guarantee a large purse. To be specific, we propose to set up a seating stand to accommodate five thousand spectators. We also propose to guarantee a purse of fifty thousand dollars."

Potter looked up briefly and smiled.

I said, "Where's Merriam's profit in it?"

"In sporting bets, Colonel. Also, the match will be known as the Merriam Rifle Cup, and we expect our industrial sales to be enhanced by the goodwill and by the advertising of our name. We make a great many products besides locomotives, you know. We make gunpowder, for example. We'd expect both shooters to use it in their cartridges, and to allow us to advertise that fact. Would you object to that?"

"I use my own blend. It happens it was formulated by Major Tyree's brother."

"Merriam powders are the equal of any other, you know. We have a contract with the government. Our gunpowder is used in the manufacture of cartridges at federal arsenals."

"I'll use my own powder, Mr. Potter."

"Then simply let us advertise that you used ours."

"I can't do that."

"Well it's a hurdle but we'll see. I'm sure something can be worked out. Now we're proposing to underwrite all costs and to guarantee the purse, which removes all financial risk from your shoulders. You may not feel you need us—I know how accustomed you are to mounting your own public events—but in view of the, uh, strained feelings between the Major and yourself we didn't see much likelihood that either of you would defer to the other in the matter of arranging the facilities, and Major Tyree is anxious that the arrangements don't break down on that account. He feels, and we agree, that both parties might more readily accept a neutral third party's good offices in this respect."

"Vern being the Senator's brother-in-law," I said, "it hardly makes you a neutral third party."

395

"In matters of business I assure you we are."

"I expect the Senator wants the publicity. Warming up for the campaign for the presidency and all that."

"It won't hurt him I suppose. I am being candid with you, you see."

"What date did you have in mind?"

"Fourth of July, naturally."

"What place?"

"The expedition will arrange to be in North Platte at the time. It's suitable, as it has the railroad for public access."

"My show is booked in Denver for the Fourth."

"You've got six weeks to change your bookings, Colonel. It's only a few hours' train journey from Denver to North Platte. You'd miss one day's exhibition, that's all. For that matter the show can go on without you, can't it? What happens when you have a day sick?"

"I don't get sick," I replied. "People buy tickets to see Hugh Cardiff. If I'm not there I refund their money or provide them with rain checks. But the July Fourth shows—there'll be three shows that day."

"I'll tell you what, Colonel, we'll make it July the third if you prefer. That way if you win the match you'll sell out your show on the Fourth. How does that sound?"

Potter was a horse trader and I had the feeling he'd wanted July 3 all along but I only changed subjects on him to see how he'd react. "What are we shooting at?"

He took it in stride and I knew he was cleverer than he appeared. "Glass balls at twenty-five yards' rise. I believe that's customary?"

"How many?"

Potter smiled. The hat stopped twirling. "Best of ten thousand, Colonel."

"In one day?"

"When it was proposed—Sir John Bearsted proposed it, actually—Mrs. Merriam reacted in just that same way, Colonel. She said, 'But their arms will fall off.' Her brother disagreed, however—Major Tyree accepted the challenge. And, I might add, Merriam Industries propose to add a bonus purse of an additional five thousand dollars for each straight run of five hundred or more without a miss."

"Not much chance of that," I told him. "All it takes is a breath of wind or a bullet out of balance."

"Nevertheless."

Sir John Bearsted's idea perhaps—but I had the feeling Vern Tyree had put the bug in his ear. Vern knew about my shoulder; Vern was the cause of it. What Vern was counting on was that my shoulder would weaken in such a marathon endurance match. What he didn't realize was that there wasn't a thing wrong with my shoulder anymore; it was, if anything, stronger than it had ever been. Certainly I could lift as many rifles as Vern could. Let him think he had an advantage—a cocky man was prone to mistakes.

I said, "You're on, Mr. Potter."

.   .   .

During the ensuing weeks of our tour through Oregon I practiced my newest diversion—splitting a bullet on a blade to hit two separate targets—and trained myself with a daily regimen of arm-lifting workouts to prepare for the marathon tournament. I did not lift weights; I lifted rifles. None of the strongman weightlifters who took on our challenge ever won a cent from the Wild West Show; it was frequency of endeavor rather than mass-weight that made for success in a rifle tourney.

By the time we decamped from the fairgrounds in Salt Lake City I felt confident my shoulder would not betray me. Bogardus and Kevin and I spent many hours selecting and adjusting the twenty light rifles I would use in relays during the Merriam Cup Match at North Platte. Kevin developed a flat-nosed 79-grain bullet half the weight of the usual slug—it followed a flatter trajectory than others and pleased me because it takes little metal to shatter a glass target and even the slight reduction meant my day's work would be reduced by a good many pounds of lead.

Still, Bogardus did not conceal his concern. The terms of the challenge match were such that I would be required to lift fifty tons in a single day.

.   .   .

Senator Phipps Merriam was neither large nor athletic. In running two years hence in the 1888 campaign for the presidency he expected to find himself pitted against the incumbent in that office, Mr. Grover Cleveland, who of course was a large bluff hearty fellow known to be partial to a good cigar and the occasional poker game. Senator Merriam was canny enough to know that his own reputation made him appear by comparison somewhat effete and cool. To appeal to the public it is necessary to present the appearance of congeniality and strength—a president must be seen to be a fellow with whom you wouldn't mind chewing the rag in a saloon. During the past year or two the Senator had been attempting to enhance the illusion of his man's-man stature: he'd got out among the public and the wards and rings of local politicians, much as he had distaste for it, and he'd attracted the support of several big-city political machines by slapping the right backs and spreading the money around. According to Kevin there was no question but that the Senator had the political bosses behind him; he would get the Republican nomination; his concern was the winning of popular and electoral votes, and to this end he endeavored to put himself before the public as a man of action.

He had seen an opportunity in Sir John Bearsted's hunting expedition and he seized it by appending himself to the entourage as honored co-host (along with Vern Tyree). Naturally the lavish party was accompanied by a phalanx of correspondents, photographers, sporting gents, politicians, industrialists and trophy hunters. To the Senator it must have seemed a heaven-sent opportunity to be seen performing bold deeds so that his exploits might be flashed across the country into every newspaper and journal. All that remained was to contrive the said bold deeds and exploits, and in this scheme he apparently enlisted the aid of his celebrated brother-in-law; or at least it so appeared in the end. Even today most readers of this account probably remember the astonishing events of that third of July at North Platte—not a newspaper in the hemisphere failed to report them—but, as I was there and in some ways a participant, I feel obliged to report the truth of the incident, shorn of journalistic hyperbole.

At the conclusion of our afternoon show on the second of July I entrained for North Platte together with Kevin, Doc, Harry and indeed most of the members of our troupe, all of them eager to see the match and cheer me on and engage in serious wagering. I cautioned them not to bet too much, as nothing is guaranteed in any contest: I had been known to lose shooting matches and there was also the chance of loss by forfeit, through mishap or misdeed.

We arrived in the evening to find the expedition encamped along a mile or more of the riverbank. Two trains were drawn up on branch sidings at the edge of the village—Merriam trains, private cars richly appointed for the more prominent members of the tour. The rest of the party, along with several thousand newcomers who had arrived to see the match, were housed in a great city of tents.

The Bearsted expedition had hunted the plains for some weeks by then. After the North Platte respite they were to advance ponderously into the Rockies—eighteen wagons to carry forage and luggage; several dogcarts and ambulances for those who disliked the saddle; several score horses and an escort of two hundred cavalry troopers, cowboys and scouts. Apparently the hunt had been a sluggish affair, for each morning the city-on-wheels awakened to the hoot of a bugle but the tourists tended to be slow getting past their hangovers and ablutions, so that the party rarely moved much before noon. Vern Tyree had been playing his frontier-hero role to the hilt, appearing each day in elaborate buckskins and leading Sir John and the Senator and the other sportsmen out on the trail of game—game which Vern invariably produced for the hunters to shoot, for he was wise enough to have sent his scouts out

398

ahead to locate animals and leave hidden messages that only Vern could find. He had made himself popular with the baronet in this fashion. On occasion I heard he had put on fancy displays of long-range shooting that impressed the onlookers. On one occasion apparently Vern had shot an elk at such extreme long range that Sir John had clapped him on the shoulder and cried, "Good heavens, man, I hope your rifle's loaded with rock salt, for otherwise the meat surely will spoil before we get to it."

Senator Merriam had made himself visible at the sides of Major Tyree and Sir John throughout these adventures and the reporter fellows seemed suitably impressed, or so I judged from the newspapers I'd read. They were doing a fine job of making the Senator out to be a bold outdoorsman and brave hunter. He was at particular pains to be seen roving about the campfires of the hired hands, playing poker with the cowboys and otherwise ingratiating himself with Common Men. It was so deliberately contrived that I wondered how the voters could be fooled by it; but he must have slipped handsome sums into the pockets of the accompanying reporters for his coverage was very prominent.

The dudes had just about had their fill of the plains but Sir John had an overwhelming ambition to find and kill a buffalo on his own. He seemed prepared to remain in the West all year to accomplish that goal. Of course the buffalo were all but extinct in 1886—there were fewer of them than there are today; the herds have multiplied since then, largely because a few men like Colonel Cody and myself took it upon ourselves to establish breeding stock on our own ranches.

The nearest buffalo herd that Vern Tyree knew of was my Wild West Show herd in Denver. Near the end of June a group of cowboys had arrived at our encampment determined to buy a bull from us. I was not aware of the transaction until it had been concluded. The cowboys had approached Harry Dreier and offered to pay him ever-more-outrageous sums for a single buffalo bull until, at the figure of one thousand dollars, Harry had acquiesced and sold one of the older bulls to them, putting the cash into the company safe; it was not until three days later, when I asked where the thousand dollars in the envelope had come from, that Harry remembered to tell me about the sale of the bull.

I later learned that Vern's cowboys had loaded the bull onto a train and shipped it to a point near North Platte where they held it in a temporary corral until the morning of July 3. But when I arrived at North Platte I had no knowledge of this; the presence of the buffalo was not explained to me until after the event.

.   .   .

We arrived that evening in force and were greeted by a ceremonious celebration of music and fireworks and shouting. The baronet was there

399

in person, riding in a splendid coach; he stood on the running board to greet us with a sweep of his grey beaver hat—not descending, I think, because he did not wish to get dust on his boots. He looked hardy enough, although a bit florid: a burly fellow in tweeds and jodhpurs, a pinch bottle in one hand and his hat in the other, a broad beaming smile of welcome across his wide muttonchopped face.

I saw a buggy beyond his carriage and recognized the three people in it: the Senator in rough outdoor garb, Colonel Vern Tyree in his fringed buckskins and, seated between them with her hands in her lap, Libby.

A vague smile touched her lips when I caught her eye. She looked wan, I thought, but otherwise unchanged: travail had not diminished her beauty.

I descended from the train at the head of my delegation and removed my hat to shake Sir John's hand. Our eyes were at a level—he on the carriage step, I on the ground. I do not remember what cordialities we exchanged; my mind was on Libby. The crowd swirled about us. I was invited into the baronet's coach and could not refuse him; we drove off from the depot slowly, accompanied by the great shouting pedestrian mob. Sir John offered me a metal cup the size of my thumb and filled it from his pinch bottle and we drank to the morrow's competition. He had a bluff and hearty way of talking—a bit of a simpleton, I thought, but a harmless one except from the point of view of the unfortunate creatures who were forced to indulge Sir John's childish pleasures by providing their heads to adorn the walls of his castle in Sussex. I was surprised to learn he was something of a captain of industry. I was not surprised, afterward, to learn he had inherited it. I suspect his principal ambition was to see if he couldn't spend it faster than the family factories earned it.

I was invited into his railroad car and found it luxurious with splendor. Mr. Potter was there—the emissary from Merriam Industries —and we were joined by Senator Merriam and Vern Tyree. I took note of Libby's absence from the meeting. We discussed the impending shoot in calm voices. "There'll be a ten-minute break in every hour and a one-hour break at midday, if that's agreeable?" And I nodded to Potter.

Vern Tyree held a lucifer to the Senator's cigar and turned a cool eye toward me. "Old Saddlesores," he said, "you're looking fit." A cool smile hovered beneath the scar that I had been told he was passing off as a dueling cicatrix. He wore soft deerskin gloves.

I felt little rancor and no wish to be abrasive. I said pleasantly, "I hear you set South America on its ear, Vern."

"They respect a shooting man down there."

"What iron are you using tomorrow?"

"Winchester carbines, thirty-two-twenties. Shaved down for weight. You're using my brother's lightweights?"

"I am. I'm surprised you don't use them yourself."

"The grips don't fit my hand quite right." The fingers of his gloved hand were curved a bit unnaturally; for a moment I saw a glitter in his eyes.

"He could design them to fit you."

"Kevin seems to have his hands full with other matters nowadays." Vern cut the words off curtly. "Come outside with me, Hugh. I'd like a word with you."

The Senator looked on—I never knew how to read his lizard eyes; he never gave anything away. Sir John ushered us out of the railway carriage with blustery platitudes and abruptly I found myself walking along the cindered roadbed beside the man who, so far as I knew, still regarded me as his mortal enemy.

But he spoke evenly enough. "I want to put something to you." Up ahead of us past the caboose we could see the lights of the tent city. There was a great deal of hooting and laughing; bits of music drifted on the evening air. Vern stopped, twisting one toe back and forth, grinding ashes into the earth. "Last time we shot against each other I said I'd beat you on the shoot and I'd beat you every other way there is. Fifteen, sixteen years ago—Brooklyn—but I remember it still. Well I rode you out of the country on a rail and kept you out for ten years but now you're back in my hair and I intend to ride you again, Saddle-sores, and if you want to know when I mean to stop hounding you I'll tell you—I'll stop when you drop."

There may have been a long-ago time when his ferocious rhetoric might have rattled me but now I took it for a precompetition attempt to shake me up and I let it go by. All I said was, "Keep your powder dry, Vern," and turned away from him.

It was rankling him, I suppose, that I was still alive: he had tried to kill me twice. And he had a frank hunger to be the top shooter in the world. There could be only one champion; no one remembers the second-place contender. Vern wanted to make his mark.

. . .

It was in the back of my mind that Senator Merriam was subtle enough to have brought Libby out here as a way of rattling me. Her presence in the camp put me in mind of a moment many years ago when she'd unnerved me to the extent that I'd batted off a hasty shot toward a sage clump and missed it by half a yard and she'd laughed at me.

I knew she hadn't been traveling with the hunt. She must have come out to North Platte especially for the match. I doubted it was something she would have done voluntarily.

None of that mattered to me. I knew I had to see her.

The Senator was still in Sir John's Pullman car—I could see them through the windows, as they hadn't drawn the shades; they were drinking together, Potter darting about with cigars and drinks. I watched Vern stride away toward the tent camp on whatever errand he had in mind. I went along the train until I found a white-jacketed man carrying a tray of glasses and whisky bottles. I asked the whereabouts of the Senator's lodgings and was directed to a dimly illuminated Pullman car on the adjoining track. My knock there was answered by a plump woman in maid's dress. She left me waiting on the open vestibule while she retired within to consult with her mistress; I waited, somewhat surprised and relieved to find Libby was in. After a moment the door opened and I expected it would be the maid again but it was Libby, drawing a wrap about her shoulders, standing in the doorway with the light behind her so that I couldn't see her face.

"I knew you'd come."

"May I come in?"

"It would be better if you didn't. It might be misinterpreted." She came outside, pulling the door to; she went down the steps and looked up, waiting for me. "Shall we walk?"

    • • •

The river, wide and flat, curled between its low banks and we went at a strolling pace through the trees. Moonlight winked on the water and laced the earth with shadows. The sound of revelries from the encampment reached us faintly.

I had expected anything and expected nothing; she might have shown anger or hate, pleasure or love, anything at all—I had no idea what to anticipate; I knew only that I wanted to be near her, hear her voice and see her face when I spoke to her.

She was subdued. But I could not tell what she was suppressing. Her voice was a murmur without inflection. "Well then, Hugh. Here we are."

She took my hand then, not with urgency but with gentle calm; she explored the backs of my fingers and did not look up at me. "They say you've cut quite a swath with the ladies."

"They say a lot of things." The touch of her hand upon mine sent a thrill through me.

"You haven't married again, though."

"No."

She withdrew her fingers and hugged herself, turning away from me.

We stood amid the trees; her face kept going in and out of the light. Her sadness made me want to engulf her. One step forward; I reached for her arm, a tentative grasp but all the while I ached to hold her—and she pulled away from me, still not turning to face me. "It's no good, Hugh. Too much time—I'm not the same anymore, I'm not the girl you used to know. I'm no good for anyone."

"Come with me, Libby. Stay with me."

She walked away from me into the light and turned to face me squarely. Her chin came up. In the soft moonlight she might have been sixteen again: she was as slender as she had been then. She spoke in the same controlled monotone. "I shouldn't say this to you—I've no cause to break your heart again. But I owe you the truth. And the truth is— I'd marry you in an instant if I could. If I were free to."

"Libby—"

"Don't move. Stand there. I have things to say and I won't possess the presence of mind to say them if you touch me."

I strained, as if at the limit of a chain; but remained where I was.

"I've known for weeks that this would come. I planned it all out, you see. As soon as Phipps asked me to come here. I knew we'd meet—I even knew he'd give us this chance to talk together. He knows there's nothing you or I can win by it. I'm sure he enjoys the idea that he's allowing us to torture ourselves. Because he knows I still love you, Hugh. I've never said a word—but he knows."

She sank down on her ankles, the skirt smoothed over her knees; plucked a long blade of buffalo grass from the earth and began to break it off a piece at a time. "I've tried to keep my sanity since William died. I've done good works—you can't imagine the hours I've worked. Hospitals, missions. I've got the hands of a fisherman's wife. It's not charity, you see—it's to keep me occupied. Without some sort of purpose I'd have been lost. But the irony is, of course, Phipps approves of it—it suits him to have such a dedicated charitable wife, it's good for the presidential illusion he wants to create. I'm the manageress of an empire, did you know that? Not quite the size of Merriam Industries, to be sure, but I'm the chairman of a chain of Christian missions with stations in every part of the world. It's marvelous really—I give and Phipps takes away; the cycle goes on forever."

Then she threw the stalk away and looked up. "I'm sorry. I didn't mean to ramble. I've had time to think it all out, you see, and at first I didn't want to come at all but Phipps insisted—it was a chance to be cruel and he couldn't pass it up. And after a while I decided to play into his hands. If he wants to throw us together then we may as well go along with it. Maybe it's better than nothing."

"Yes."

403

"He won't give me a divorce. How can he? He wants to be president."
She rose to her feet with effortless grace: she was strong, perhaps
stronger than I'd ever credited. Her body was strong because she worked
hard, I suppose, but it was the strength of her spirit I found astonishing.
Phipps Merriam would have broken a lesser woman long ago.

She came into the shadows where I stood; her palms touched my
cheeks and she searched my eyes. "Tell me, Hugh."

"I love you. That's all I can tell you."

"It's all you need to tell me." Her hands went up behind my neck
and drew me down. "Make love to me then. Now—here. It's all we
have."

.   .   .

It had a bittersweet flavor, that night; there was no storm of passion,
only a wistful sadness that infected us both with its gentle warmth. We
drew our clothes on against the chill of the night and lay in each other's
arms in the grass while the moon tipped toward the Rocky Mountains
and the river chuckled past and, out of sight beyond the trees, the great
encampment slept.

For a time we lay undisturbed and I was filled with a contentment
I hadn't known since those stolen nights in Virginia long ago. And I
was even able to think gentle thoughts of Flower without the sting of
regret that so often pricked me and still sometimes overwhelmed me so
that on certain nights alone in the privacy of my tent I had wept. I felt
no sense of betrayal toward her memory; if Flower had been a part of
me then Libby was another part. Jeanette had known I was the kind of
man who is incomplete without his woman; out of love for me Jeanette
had tried to provide that completion but she'd known my love for her
wasn't of that kind—sometimes I felt I'd been wretched to her but it
always came back to the woman who now breathed softly against my
throat: the first love of a faraway childhood, the final love of my searching manhood. I felt giddy with rediscovery: having dreaded the possibilities of this moment I was awash with dizzy relief, so much so that
I thought my heart would burst—and I knew that having found Libby
again I could not let her go.

I was remembering the sweet time when the two of us had gone down
by the Santa Cruz River—wondering how different all this might have
been if Vern had not chanced upon us just then. I hated him for what
he had done to us and I knew nothing on earth could prevent me from
humiliating him in tomorrow's shooting match: it didn't matter how
well he did—I would beat him. . . . The savage resolve swirled through
me and was gone; I printed my kisses on Libby's brow and felt the
tension in her as she crowded against me. Then after a while she went
soft in my arms and I think she may have slept for a bit. I did not sleep.

404

Stunned by the power of this rediscovered passion I knew I must not let Libby away from me again. There had to be a way . . .

Once she stirred and said, "This may be all the time we'll ever have, Hugh." And another time she said, "We can find ways to steal hours together." And then: "But you'd learn to hate me. You're not cut out to be a thief in the night. Accept this, Hugh. It's not a thing you can face standing straight up in the sunlight. There's nothing we can do but choose between dishonor and loneliness."

"I think there's another way."

"No. None."

"I'm going to have it out with the Senator," I said.

Her arms clenched around me. "No. He'll kill us. He'll have you shot."

"We'll see," I said. But the resolve had settled in me. She was right —she knew me, even then, as well as anyone alive did—I had a good many vices but stealthy knavery was not among them. I wasn't cut out for slinking in the night; she was right, I was too stubborn for that, perhaps too arrogant. I would have Libby all to myself—but on my terms, not Phipps Merriam's.

. . .

We parted in a grey predawn chill at the vestibule of Libby's Pullman car. "I'll be all right," she said. "He's a heavy sleeper. And we don't share the same compartment."

"After the match we'll settle this."

"No, my love. You mustn't." We spoke in whispers.

"I want you to trust me in this, Libby."

Briefly and wantonly she pressed her cheek to my chest; her arms behind me clutched my shoulders. "Of course I shall."

Then she was gone inside and I strode away, intending to examine the shooting ground before anyone else might arrive: I knew I must clear my head for the match. I had to put thoughts of confrontation with Merriam away.

I found that after all I was not the first to arrive on the shooting ground. Kevin was there before me, scowling in the dawn. The bleachers were aligned along the south side of the meadow; a judges' platform had been erected and great mounds of glass balls glittered faintly on the earth.

"Are you all right, Hugh?"

"Never better."

"We were worried."

"I'm sorry. Something came up."

He was grave. "My sister?"

I looked back toward the camp. Figures were stirring—fires coming

405

alight. I saw lights in a few train windows. A wrangler was pitching hay into a rope corral. Kevin seemed willing to let my silence close the subject. He said, "I was talking to one of the hands on Vern's crew. He's quitting the job after today. He said they spent a month inching across the prairie on those trains with all these fine upstandin' gentlemen shooting deer and porcupine and even prairie dogs from the windows of the train. They left the injured animals to stumble off and die—the train didn't stop, you see. Harry reckons they left enough corpses along the right-of-way to feed every coyote and buzzard between Calgary and El Paso." He shook his head in wonder. "They surely are fine sportsmen."

I pointed along the throwing ground. "Vern picked this place, I expect."

"The downslope you mean. Yes, I imagine he did. It'll give just an extra fraction of time before the glass ball reaches the ground—it's got that much farther to fall. Give a man an extra tenth of a second or so to make his target."

"Vern always did like to shoot them near the ground if he missed his first try on top of the rise. Never mind," I said, "if it's an advantage for him it's an advantage for both of us."

"Otherwise how does it look to you?"

"I wish there was a little more shade. But it'll do." I put my back to the meadow. "Where's our quarters? I'd best get freshened up."

"Harry'll have the breakfast fires lit by now," Kevin said. "Come on, I'll show you the way."

We went down through the camp—acres upon acres of canvas tenting; along the pathways the heavy grass had been beaten away to raw earth. I took the handshakes of many a well-wisher on my way through the encampment—I am not sure whether it was because of my own popularity or because so many of them resented Vern's high-handed ways and wanted to see him beaten. I felt an indomitable confidence that morning: no man alive could beat me on the firing line that day. I'd found Libby again—I was invincible.

Harry's crew had pitched our Wild West Show sleeping tents on the other side of the railway tracks because there was no space left for us amid the standing camp. We had to go around the cowcatchers of both trains to get there. I found Harry and Doc Bogardus breaking their fast in camp chairs. Nate Loving was twirling a rope for the entertainment of a group of wide-eyed youngsters. Doc and I exchanged some hammer-and-nails conversation about the shooting conditions for the match—the likelihood of wind, the need for deliberate pacing in such a grueling marathon. Kevin came around after breakfast with a buckboard, into which we loaded the cased rifles and ammunition I would use in the shoot. The three of us examined each rifle with care—we used dentists' mirrors in the open breeches to look down the bores.

"Twenty-five yards," Harry Dreier said, "is a long throw for anyone's arm. Have we got enough throw-boys? Likely to wear out a regiment of them."

"Our boys will stand up to it," I said. "They've been training for it."

Kevin said, "They won't let Hugh down, Harry."

Doc Bogardus sat heavy in his camp chair. I suppose he must have been feeling the aches of age in that chilly sunrise—perhaps wishing it was he who would be facing the challenge today; but Doc was too courteous to speak of it. In an attempt to set him easy I began to talk with him about our scheduled meets later in the season—Memphis, Louisville, Cincinnati, Buffalo and the season's closer at Saenger Park in Philadelphia where Doc and I planned a spectacular "grudge match" shooting competition. The press was still maintaining the fiction of a bitter rivalry between us. And it was true on the shooting range that neither Doc nor I gave quarter to each other. To a great extent I attribute my sustained excellence as a shooter to Doc's constant presence in those years: with Doc for an opponent I never could afford to slacken. We kept each other at the peak.

The shoot was scheduled to begin at ten o'clock. At half-past nine Kevin and Harry left us, driving the wagonload of rifles up toward the meadow. I completed my sartorial arrangements: I was still a showman, after all. I'd selected butternut trousers and a grey cotton shirt with stovepipe sleeves that wouldn't restrict my arms—grey so that powder-smoke stains wouldn't ruin its appearance. Knowing I would be on the stand for eight hours or more I chose moccasins in place of boots, to favor my feet. I wore no tunic; I wanted no unnecessary weight on my arms. The hat was my familiar Wild West Show hat, nearly white, high of crown and very wide of beaver brim; I would wear it as far as the shooting ground, doff it to the dignitaries with a gallant sweep, then set it aside during the shoot. I have always preferred to shoot bareheaded. It is best to have the wind about one's face to clear the smoke; and as Caleb had taught me it was useful to keep one's ears moistened and exposed to the breeze.

Doc and Nate Loving and I began the walk to the shoot. We went along past the big Mogul locomotives and were approaching the first row of tents when a commotion drew our attention—shouts of alarm to the right.

Sir John Bearsted was just then emerging from his railway car. I had time, strangely, to notice the leather patches at the elbows of his

407

tweed hunting jacket. Beyond him I saw an astonishing sight: a shaggy bull buffalo thundering down from the trees—straight toward the baronet.

At that moment Senator Phipps Merriam rushed from between two railroad cars to confront the charging bison: the Senator was unarmed and bare-handed.

As was I. I cast about me rapidly: "A rifle, dammit!" But Doc and Nate were as bare of weapons as I was. And then Nate was off on his fleet legs, dashing toward the scene.

I saw a horseman burst from the trees—just where the buffalo had emerged—it was Vern Tyree, his rifle up. Doc and I were running in Nate Loving's wake, Doc falling behind, and a number of things were happening at once: men yelling; Senator Merriam rushing directly into the charging beast's path, waving his arms; Libby coming out onto the platform of her railway car; Nate Loving running past Sir John Bearsted; an armorer pressing a rifle into Sir John's hands; Vern Tyree galloping downhill in pursuit of the buffalo; a great deal of noise—voices, one or two gunshots, the terrible drumming of the bull's hooves. . . .

I heard the shot and saw the puff of smoke from the muzzle of Vern's rifle. He fired from the back of his running horse and the bullet must have severed the buffalo's spine, for the bull's hindquarters went asplay. But it was a long way from death or harmlessness.

Senator Merriam leaped toward the buffalo, crying something in a loud voice—I could not make out the words but afterward someone told me he was shouting that he would save Sir John's life at any cost.

Propped on its front feet the bull flashed back and forth in semi-circles, dashing itself about in throes of pain, whipping itself about too fast for Sir John to get a clear shot past the Senator. Vern seemed to be having some trouble with his rifle—his horse slowed, he wrenched at the weapon.

And Senator Merriam leaped boldly upon the injured animal—seized it by the tail to hold it down.

The buffalo's heaving lunges were huge and violent. The beast was frothing and wild. I ran full-out but Nate was still ahead of me.

The Senator was not a large man; his weight was insufficient to still the beast—he was dragged off his feet.

The rattled baronet fired his rifle. The charge went off when I was rushing past him: flat against my ear it deafened me, rocked me. Sir John had fired point-blank into the buffalo's skull but no buffalo ever died that way—the bullet only bounced off heavy bone, tore up a bit of flesh and further infuriated the bull so that it rolled over, turning upon its back.

Fifty yards beyond, Vern was lifting his rifle again, spurring the horse. At that moment Sir John's armorer was running back toward the train, perhaps in search of ammunition or perhaps in fear—Vern fired the rifle in haste as the horse rushed across the uneven ground; the bullet whined off bone, carving a sudden white streak across the horn of the bull, and I saw the armorer fling his arms up and pitch to the ground in the shadow of the Pullman car.

The Senator, whether heroic or simply insensible with panic, seemed entangled in the lashing tail—unable to loose his hold. He was dashed from side to side while Vern rushed forward on horseback and the baronet fired again, this time into a shoulderblade—I actually heard the whine of the ricocheting bullet. The buffalo made an awful sound in its throat—it heaved itself into the air and fell back upon the Senator and I saw the great head twisting in madness, horns swinging to gore the Senator.

Then Nate Loving fell upon the beast with both hands, a quick sure grasp upon the terrible horns. Sir John fired yet again; I heard the crack of the bullet as it flashed past me. I fell upon the bull, my hands reinforcing Nate's and together we manhandled the dying animal, lifting the great head to keep the horns from the Senator's body. Sir John must have rushed to one side for a clear shot, for a moment later he administered the coup de grace with a clear heart shot behind the shoulder and the enormous hulk shuddered and went still in our grasp.

Doc Bogardus lumbered forward. Vern Tyree leaped from his horse and came running toward us, his rifle still lifted. I waved them forward —the baronet as well: "Lift this thing off him. Help me here . . ." And together we managed to heave the massive twitching carcass off Senator Merriam.

Doc growled, "Give me room here."

The Senator was moaning—barely conscious, I believe; he spoke out in his pain but the words were not distinguishable.

The crowd rushed in to fill the place and I stood up to my full height. Vern stood agape, the rifle forgotten in his fist—I took it away from him and he did not protest; I fired a shot into the air to get attention, and bellowed at the crowd: "Please stand back. A man's injured here— he needs air." Then I turned to some of the onlookers nearby: "Drag that thing away from here."

Then I saw Libby coming through. They were making way for her. I stepped forward in an attempt to hide the sight from her, interposing my body, but she said quietly, "Let me through, Hugh," and I stood aside and watched her stride past Nate Loving and drop to one knee beside Doc Bogardus and her husband.

I saw Doc shake his head and Libby gave him an odd look and Doc, thinking she had misunderstood his gesture, said, "He won't die of it, ma'am, but I believe his spine's been snapped."

. . .

There was a great deal of confusion in the ensuing half hour. A stretcher was brought forth from the nearby town and under Doc's guidance the injured Senator was carried aboard his railway carriage. Libby and Vern went inside with him. I felt it was not my place to join them. With Harry Dreier and Kevin I stood watch at one end of the car while Potter and some others guarded the opposite end—preventing reporters and the curious from access to the Senator's bedside. At first there was a clamor for entry and information. Sir John disappeared within, then reappeared to assure the press with platitudes: the Senator was doing as well as could be expected, so forth. A woman from the encampment was summoned to serve as a nurse in assisting Doc Bogardus. Sir John Bearsted scratched his muttonchops and blustered a bit from the vestibule platform and then turned to me and said in a low voice, "How did that buffalo come to be here?"

I had my suspicions but kept them to myself; I only told him I didn't know where the beast had come from. Sir John said, "I suspect this forces a postponement of the match today."

Kevin said bluntly, "Why should it? Phipps isn't a contestant."

"Out of respect for the honorable Senator. I had thought . . ."

Kevin said, "We're ready to shoot if my brother is."

I had nothing to say to that; Kevin had taken it upon himself to act as my second in the matter and I didn't wish to contradict him but I knew the affair had shaken Vern badly and he might be unable to shoot with his customary deliberation. I told Sir John, "Let's hold off a bit until we've heard from Major Tyree."

A man in jodhpurs came along and from the foot of the car steps addressed the baronet. "I'm afraid we've lost Hoskins, sir."

"Hoskins?"

"Your armorer, sir. He was dead before he fell. A terrible accident, sir."

"Bloody hell." The baronet put his head down, thinking, and then went back inside the carriage.

Shortly thereafter I saw Potter hurrying away afoot toward the town of North Platte, apparently bent on some urgent errand; and Doc Bogardus came out on the platform drying his hands on a cloth. "He'll live, I expect—too mean to die from it."

I said, "This thing happened by design, Doc."

"What do you mean?"

"What happened to Merriam may have been an accident but the buffalo was prearranged. It didn't just happen to wander in, did it?"

"I see what you mean."

Kevin said, "Maybe you don't get it yet, Doc. My brother came out of those trees on horseback behind that bull. What was he doing there on a horse?"

Doc stared at him. "You're suggesting Vern Tyree drove that bull into camp?"

"I don't see any other way to size it up. It was set up as a stunt—the Englishman wanted a shot at a buffalo and the Senator wanted some heroic publicity. And Vern was supposed to cripple the bull with that shot of his from horseback. Then the Senator went into his act—but they didn't count on the size and strength of that buffalo."

I said, "Vern fired too low. A little higher along the withers and he'd have stopped that bull from doing anything but snorting up a fuss."

Doc shifted his glance toward the matted earth where stains of the buffalo's blood had gone dark. "A tragic miscalculation, if that's the case. But how can you be sure of this?"

"No one's sure of anything," I said.

Kevin said, "But the Senator's in a bad way and that armorer's dead from a ricochet."

"I know," Bogardus said. "Sir John told us—the Senator went into a rage."

"He's conscious?"

"Very much so," Bogardus said. "And in a state of wrath—perhaps understandable. He's just learned he's been paralyzed for life. He'll spend the rest of his days in a wheelchair."

. . .

Potter returned in a buckboard in company with several burly citizens in bowler hats. They all carried shotguns and had grim expressions. They entered the carriage by its rear, led by Potter. "Constabulary," Doc Bogardus said.

We soon learned their objective. Within two minutes the policemen reappeared. Two of them had Vern Tyree by the elbows. Vern's hands were manacled behind his back.

At the foot of the steps Vern turned to look over his shoulder. I could not read his glance—but it was aimed directly at me.

Kevin leaped off the platform and ran to the buckboard, intercepting the officers as they helped Vern climb onto the seat. Bogardus spoke softly in my ear: "There goes your shooting match, Hugh. I expect the Senator needed a scapegoat."

I dropped off the train and crossed to the wagon. Vern was talking to Kevin just then; one of the constables was gathering the reins and Kevin stepped back to let them pass. Vern had his eyes steadily on me. He said, "We'll have this cleared up soon, Saddlesores. Then we'll have our shooting match."

"I'm at your disposal, Major."

Vern clapped his mouth shut; his lips went thin and taut. The deputies climbed aboard in the bed of the wagon behind him and I watched it clatter away.

Kevin said, "He's arrested for murder. The armorer."

I scowled at the receding wagon. "That makes no sense. It wasn't deliberate."

Doc Bogardus came up. "It'll get sorted out if it goes to trial. We'll all be there to testify."

And so we were; but the result was not what we had anticipated.

. . .

The trial took place in the Lincoln County courthouse during the week of August 17, 1886. A long procession of witnesses ascended the stand to describe what they had seen on the day when the buffalo had invaded Sir John Bearsted's encampment. The charge against Vern Tyree was murder in the first degree, in the case of the death of Samuel Hoskins by violence.

It was sweltering hot all week and the air was foul in that insanely crowded courtroom.

It was understood by nearly everyone present that the charge against Vern was purely a product of Senator Merriam's enraged vindictiveness. So far as I could see, no false testimony was put forth at the trial. It was established beyond any doubt that the bullet that had killed the armorer had been fired from Vern's rifle. The issue in the trial was not a question of facts. It was the question whether a man should be held maliciously responsible for the death of another man by mishap. No one purported to believe that Vern had intended to kill Hoskins. The tragedy had been an accident; everyone knew that. Vern might be guilty of negligent homicide but none of us could understand the accusation of murder that had been leveled against him.

Kevin's suspicions and my own were confirmed by testimony that came forth at the trial. Vern had indeed purchased the buffalo from my herd, by way of cowboy emissaries, and had driven the beast deliberately into the camp that morning so as to provide Sir John with a target for his rifle and Senator Merriam with a chance to prove his heroism. Miscalculation and misadventure had resulted in the unintended crippling of one man and the death of another. In sum that is what the trial established and I am sure the jury was not misled as to the facts of the case.

On the Saturday morning when the testimony ended, the judge prepared to deliver his charge to the jury. Those of us who had personal interests in the case had inquired into the laws pertaining to it. It seemed evident to all of us that the jury would either acquit Vern or, at worst, convict him of negligent homicide—a crime for which the maximum punishment was a term of three years in prison. With his prominence in the public eye Vern might serve a few months in prison but he would soon be paroled. We all felt confident of that.

Libby was in the courtroom throughout the trial at the side of her husband, who attended the proceedings at the cost of considerable obvious pain: he was cast in plaster from waist to collar, rendering his figure obscenely bulky under the suit of baggy clothes, and he was wheeled in and out of the courthouse each day in a chair to which he was strapped. Except for his testimony—which he delivered in a tight voice pinched with pain—he neither spoke to anyone nor seemed to take much interest in the trial. But he was there every day and Vern hardly ever took his baleful eyes off his crippled brother-in-law. If I had no doubt there had been no murder in Vern's heart on the day of the armorer's death, I had equally little doubt there was murder in his heart now.

Each night Libby came to my chambers; each night we rehearsed our plans. When the trial was over and the Senator sufficiently recovered in strength and wit, I intended to face him. In the meantime we had each other; we needed nothing more.

Then it was the morning of the judge's charge to the jury and we were stunned by it.

. . .

We understood that the basis of the trial was Senator Merriam's vindictive wrath. We understood the power that his money and political position gave him; it had not surprised us when the prosecuting attorney of the county had introduced, as his "assistants," a battery of Pennsylvania and Washington lawyers from some of the most prestigious law firms in the East. There were even suspicions that attempts might be made to bribe the jury—but an unjust verdict in the public eye would surely give grounds for mistrial. We felt, despite Merriam's wild and powerful efforts, that the facts were so clear that justice must be served.

Then the judge spoke his brief charge and we knew that justice had been subverted.

"It is the jury's responsibility to decide the facts in any criminal case," he said, "but it is the court's responsibility to determine the law, as it may apply." The judge was a circuit rider, reputed to be the most learned justice of the Omaha bench. He was a thin man, quite bald,

413

and had maintained order throughout the trial with a stern booming voice.

"The law in this case is quite clear," the judge said, "and is not a matter for dispute amongst the jury. I'm obliged to remind you of the provisions of the criminal code of the state of Nebraska. The law provides that if a death by violence occurs during the commission of, and as a result of, a felonious crime of any sort, then the perpetrator of such felonious crime shall be deemed guilty of murder in the first degree, regardless whether the death may have been inadvertent or premeditated. This statute is popularly known as the felony-murder law Under its provisions a man who robs a bank and then, in fleeing from the robbery, accidentally runs down a child in the street and kills the child, is as guilty of murder as though he had purposefully slit the child's throat."

The judge paused a moment, his eyes moving from face to face along the jury-box rail. "The penalty for the crime of felony murder is the same as the penalty for any crime of murder in the first degree. That is to say, the jury may recommend that the prisoner be executed by hanging or that the prisoner be sentenced to life imprisonment by the state. No lesser penalties are allowed for, in the criminal code."

A murmur of protest began to run through the crowd and the judge banged his gavel. "The testimony in this case may have persuaded you that a prank misfired and that the result was tragic but not criminal in nature. I must point out to the jury that when a man, for whatever reason, endangers life and limb by reckless public behavior, that man is guilty of a felonious offense—the offense of criminal assault. If a cowboy hooraws a town by discharging his weapons with reckless disregard for innocent pedestrians, that cowboy is guilty of felonious assault in the eyes of Nebraska law, and if one of his wild bullets should happen to kill an innocent pedestrian then the cowboy is guilty of felony murder. In the case before us the deadly weapons employed so recklessly by the accused seem to have been two in number—the wild buffalo bull and the defendant's own rifle. It is, of course, up to the jury in its wisdom to decide whether or not the facts presented in this trial have been truly described and faithfully testified to. But if the jury concludes that the defendant did in fact loose this deadly beast of his own volition, and did in fact recklessly endanger the lives of innocent citizens abroad in the encampment, then the jury will have no choice but to find this defendant guilty of murder in the first degree, so long as it is the jury's conclusion that the deceased was killed by a bullet fired as a result of defendant's reckless assault."

The judge went on at some length and then discharged the jury to its deliberations.

414

The verdict was inevitable after that. Vern Tyree was sentenced to life imprisonment.

.   .   .

Patterns of light felt aslant through the bars, crosshatching his haggard face. At first he looked at me without recognition.

Then he came to his feet and stood facing me, a yard of concrete—and a wall of bars—between us.

"I came to offer my help."

A sour laugh. "*You?*"

"You'll be filing appeals. You'll need lawyers—that needs money. You won't be getting money from the Senator anymore."

"I've money of my own. Did you think my show was as bankrupt as yours?"

I saw no point retorting to that; we were far from bankruptcy—we'd been turning them away at the gates.

I do not know if injustice had deranged him but his mind did not seem to be following a straight track. Abruptly and without preamble he said, "Stay away from my sister." He clutched the bars with both fists. "Hear me?"

I knew there was no point reasoning with him. His jealousy where Libby was concerned was obsessive and constant and irrational and perplexing. No words would change his mind.

I watched his knuckles whiten on the bars. He said in a strained whisper, "*Hear me?*"

"You've got nothing to say about that," I told him. "There's one thing I'd like to know from you. A man took three shots at me with a rifle on the paddock road near Arvonia a while back. He was a good marksman—if I hadn't dodged he'd have had me through the heart from a hedgerow five hundred yards away. That was you, wasn't it?"

He went back into the cell and sat down in a corner with his arms wrapped around his upraised knees. His silence in that dim corner told me the answer to my question. He uttered no heated denials—he made no response at all—and I knew that nothing had changed between us. One day he would come to kill me. It had nothing to do with reason; it was a compulsion within him and quite possibly he had as little understanding of it as I had. No matter how long it took, he would come at me again, as he always had.

.   .   .

We played out the season. If my heart wasn't in it completely I tried to make up for it with energy: I gave them what they'd paid to see.

In October we pitched the stadium in Saenger Park and Libby arrived in a dogcart, lovely in her autumn coat. "I've missed you so. . . ."

415

We had been apart for weeks; they seemed months, years. I engulfed her in my arms.

She told me Vern was still in prison; his attorney's efforts thus far had been to no avail—there had been no grounds for mistrial; the judge's conduct of the case had been technically impeccable and they had found no basis for overturning it. They were still trying—ever-new tactics.

"What about the Senator?"

"I haven't seen him. I've kept to myself. He's at the family estate."

"It's just as well. I'm glad you haven't talked to him."

"I think he knows, Hugh. He has spies everywhere."

"It doesn't matter. I'll go up there tomorrow—we'll settle this."

"Not yet. It's not the right time yet."

"We can't keep putting it off, Libby."

"He's not well . . ."

"His mind's well enough."

"I'm frightened. I don't think I can face him."

"I don't want you to," I told her. "You've suffered enough abuse from him. I'll come to you when it's settled."

· · ·

The houseman faced me, stiff in livery. "Senator Merriam is not at home."

"The hell he's not." I stiff-armed the man and strode past him into the enormous foyer. I heard the click behind me and wheeled in time to bat the pocket pistol out of the houseman's hand. I picked it up and put it in my pocket. "Lead the way, that's a good fellow."

"I guess not." He was a big bruiser but not my size. Stubbornness kept him rooted to the spot.

I said reasonably, "Do you prefer I ransack the house?"

A hard glare, then a cooler second thought; he set out up the stairs without another word. I followed warily, leaving distance between us.

I had never been upstairs before in that house. The corridors seemed to run on forever. Here and there in wall niches were exquisite models of Merriam locomotives—I recalled some of those from long ago.

The houseman knocked at a door; a voice rumbled within; he pushed it open and spoke. Then I heard the Senator's voice: "Let him in, then." Petulant, testy.

I waited for the houseman to step aside. Going into the room past him I said, "Don't come up behind me." Then with my elbow I knocked the door shut in his face.

The Senator sat strapped in his wheelchair near a window. There was a book in his lap; he had a robe across him. His face was pale, drawn— an invalid's bloodlessness but the eyes were alive and cruel.

416

"If it's about my wife," he said, "the answer is—"

"The answer is"—I rolled over him pitilessly—"you haven't got much to say about it anymore. I didn't come to ask anything. I came to tell you."

I had the document in my pocket. I unfolded it and dropped it in his lap. He was surprised enough to look at it—I took the pen from the inkwell on the table and pushed it toward his hand. "Sign it."

"I haven't my spectacles," he lied. "I can't read this."

"It's your agreement to grant Libby's petition for a divorce without contesting it. Sign it."

He looked up at me. I planted my feet and contrived a frigid little smile. His eyes went a little wider—I saw fear at their edges; it was what I wanted.

He knew me more by hearsay than by personal appraisal—we'd confronted each other only once before and I had won that confrontation. To him I was an outsized creature of the wilderness, wild and violent, a savage from a lawless frontier who ran with ferocious cronies: I still remembered the glimpse of wonder in his terrified eyes when he'd seen Nate Loving bulldog the buffalo that had him down—Nate's white teeth sinking into the beast's hide. That was a raw direct kind of violence with which the Senator had no experience. He understood wickedness: he understood the manipulations of power, the uses of paper and words, the genteel ways in which destruction and murders could be arranged—but he was not accustomed to dealing face to face with direct physical menace: the threat posed by a man who was willing simply to kill him.

"You've got damn little left, Senator. No legs and no political future."

"Gloat if that's what you came for. I can't stop you."

"A man ought to know his limitations. You forgot yours—wrestling that bull was your mistake, not Vern's. Blame him if you want—you still know you never belonged among men." I spoke with a quiet and brutal contempt. "You're scared of every little thing. It's made you a bully all your life. But now you've got trouble because I'm too big to be bullied."

He said stonily, "It only takes one bullet."

I took the houseman's revolver from my pocket. "That's right," I said, very soft. "That's all it takes." And cocked the weapon.

He regarded it bleakly.

I said, "The divorce won't cost you anything now. You've no need of Libby—and it'll cost you too much to be dog-in-the-manger."

He blinked. Then with a sour malicious grin he drew the legal document across the arm of his chair and poised the pen above it. I watched him, the revolver cold in my fist. He looked up at me in twisted defiance and scrawled a great ragged X at the bottom of the page and tossed it away onto the floor.

"I've called your bluff, Colonel. Now use the gun or get out."

. . .

It would have been too much to expect he would capitulate without resistance; he may have been a coward at bottom but he was a defiant one and was accustomed to dealing with men who would back down in the face of his power.

I wasn't prepared to be thrown by it. I said, "With a little luck you'll live another forty years and mastermind a thousand political maneuvers and industrial victories. You may even enjoy yourself—it's the kind of life that'll suit a devious man. But right now it's the only thing you've got. Your life."

"You already said that."

"Now I know you were listening. If it's the only thing you've got then it's the only thing you've got to lose. So I believe you're the one who's bluffing."

He was looking at the revolver. "Who's to do me in," he said, "if you're lying in your grave?"

"Unlike you, Senator, I have friends."

"I'm tired of your cheap threats, Cardiff."

I started shooting then.

In the closed room the noise was earsplitting. Concussion from the first shot blew out the lamps. I clipped both knobs off the back of his chair—right beside his ears. I put a bullet through the back of the chair, firing through the narrow space between his arm and his ribs—the bullet singed the cloth of his robe. I shot both wheels of the chair, smashing the hubs. With one bullet left in the chamber I ceased firing. Stinging smoke whirled and settled. The Senator sat with his eyes squeezed shut, knuckles white where he gripped the arms of his chair.

I said in a voice without tone, "You'll grant the divorce without contesting it. You'll demand no conditions. You'll never send anyone after us with paper writs or warrants, or loaded guns, or buggy accidents. You'll stay right there helpless in that chair and you'll never lift a finger against us because if you do I'll come for you and I'll shoot you to pieces the way I shot that chair to pieces—a little bit at a time so that it hurts for a long while."

He didn't open his eyes or stir. He was trembling violently—aftershock. I heard footsteps in the corridor and I strode across the room, flung the door open and stalked out with the smoking revolver in my fist. The houseman had a shotgun but mine was cocked and when he didn't fire immediately I knew he wasn't going to: I took the gun from him and let him rush into the Senator's chamber; I went past two gawking maids, straight down the stairs and out. When I climbed into my carriage I threw the houseman's guns into the driveway before I reined away.

. . .

Libby must have heard the wheels of my carriage on the cobblestones. She was on the doorstep when I dismounted. She watched my face anxiously.

I wanted to tell her it was done. But I hadn't really expected it to be that simple. I said, "We'll see. It's up to him now." And she flew into my arms with a great heaving sob.

. . .

Throughout that winter we took precautions against the possibility of the Senator's retaliation; I watched my back a great deal and took care not to expose Libby to danger. We wintered on the Tyree Grant and took our pleasures in exploring old familiar ground: we had both come home.

Our attorneys attempted to serve papers on the Senator. But his door was locked to them; refusing to accept service, he made no communication of any kind. It seemed he had become a recluse. No one was known to have seen him or spoken to him except his own servants and they were a closemouthed lot.

In the spring Libby filed a petition for divorce in the territorial court at Prescott but we were informed she had not resided long enough in the territory and must return again in the autumn of 1888 to fulfill the requirement. A copy of the petition was sent to the Senator but he made no response. Through our agents in the East we attempted to communicate with the Merriam lawyers but they refused to comment.

Phipps Merriam's elected term in the Senate had not yet expired but he stayed away from the Capitol and his seat remained empty. There were rumors that he continued to manage the affairs of the Merriam Industries by correspondence from his locked chambers. He subscribed to every newspaper and journal; he installed his own telegraph line and, not long thereafter, his own telephone exchange. In a way he was fulfilling my predictions—manipulating politics from behind the scenes, helming the Merriam companies with an iron-fisted avarice that astonished even his robber-baron colleagues. But years were to go by before he again showed his face in public.

It would be twenty months or more before Libby could satisfy the residency requirements of the Arizona court. It was not a matter of importance to me; but it loomed in Libby's fears. So long as she remained the Senator's wife she did not feel safe from his reach. More to reassure Libby than to satisfy the law I drove us across the border just after Christmas to the Candelas, where Ran Urquhart was delighted to see us and put on a fandango that ran nearly a week and exhausted half the population of Sonora. At the end of that time, through Ran's influence with the Mexican judiciary, Libby was granted a certificate of divorce. We had no guarantee it would be honored by any United States court but Libby seemed to be calmed by it; at least it gave us a legal position on which to fall back if we had to—if a Merriam warrant sought us out, we could repair to Mexico and be safely beyond its reach. For my own part I had no intention of being forced into exile ever again, but for a long time I did not say as much to Libby.

The Mexican divorce was of uncertain validity and we did not feel it would be proper to marry; and yet as a figure in the public eye I knew our circumstances were precarious. The scandal-mongering yellow press would delight in sinking its sharp teeth into a liaison such as ours; and a showman's popular acceptance is a capricious thing. We knew that from the beginning; I have mentioned it here only to confirm that we did not act out of ignorance of the consequences.

During the next two seasons the Wild West Show suffered a considerable falling-off in receipts. At times we played to nearly empty bleachers. There was nothing to which we could attribute this except the public disfavor that had resulted from the scandal of my living in sin with another man's wife.

To pretend that this state of affairs did not trouble us would be asinine. We were not far into the 1887 season when Libby and I had a bellowing quarrel in our tent that must have awakened half the crew. We were under a terrible strain. I yanked a blanket from the bed and stormed into the night and rolled up under the stars, lying back with blood pumping through my cheeks and misery overwhelming me.

And then Libby came to my side and took my hand. "Oh Hugh. . . . My God, the things we said to each other."

"I love you, Libby, but I don't know how much of this we can take."

"We've got to be kind to each other." She stretched herself beside me: I brought her inside the blanket. "Cuddle me," she said. "I'm so sorry. It's my fault. If it weren't for me—"

"Stop that."

"It's Phipps, isn't it? He's having his revenge by keeping silent. Do you think he knew this would happen? The harm the scandal would do to the show—he couldn't have found a more fiendish way to hurt us both. It's tearing you apart. Your loyalty to the show—to all these good people. They depend on you. If the show collapses you'll have let them down. That's what you can't stand."

"We have each other, Libby. Let's don't let him destroy that too." I sat up. A cloud went across the moon. It was Illinois—we were camped outside Springfield; crickets chirruped in the brush and the grass was damp with dew. We'd played that evening to an audience of 157 people, most of them truant children.

I said, "We're between a rock and a hard place right now. Listen—it's a strain. And everyone quarrels. I'm not giving you up and I'm not giving up on the show. I'm still the best shooter in this world—sooner or later they'll come back for that. This thing can't stay in the newspapers forever. They'll go on to something else. After a while it'll die down, people will forget. The audiences will come back, Libby. We've got to wait it out—ride it out, stay on the bronco until the bell rings. I can do it if you can."

"Do it, Hugh."

"I'll borrow money to keep the show running if I have to."

"Yes."

"I'll pawn everything I own. Except the ranch—we won't give up our home." My brain calculated swiftly. "We've spent a great deal on the ranch and on the show, keeping it running, but there's still some money left from the good seasons. We'll throw in more shooting competitions to raise money—the sporting gents don't care about scandals and piety. There are always shooters who want to beat the champion."

Libby drew me down. "Yes. We'll do it. The strain may not get any easier for a while but we're not going to let Phipps beat us."

I was no longer wrung out; I no longer felt despair. We had decided to brave it out—and it was the decision itself that mattered, whatever the outcome.

In the months that followed we loved and squabbled but it was the squabbling of lovers. The Senator had neither won nor conceded; but we had found our own brand of victory.

We outlasted the public disfavor; soon the Wild West Show triumphed again.

BOOK ELEVEN

Denver
Shooting Match

WHAT REMAINS to be told in this narrative is the true story of my long and sometimes misreported conflict with Senator Merriam and Vern Tyree—a story that ended so strangely that those who only saw it from a distance cannot possibly have understood much of it. It was an acrimonious affair that lasted an unlikely number of years, provided yellow journalists with spice enough for a Roman banquet, and gave rise to a great deal of disputation and error.

By the early 1890s our Wild West Show was at its peak in size and numbers. By outwaiting the Senator and the law, Libby and I won our little triumph: we were married in January 1889. By 1891, as we had hoped, our moral transgressions were forgotten if not forgiven (there was still the occasional hellfire-and-brimstone preacher who fulminated against the Wild West Show) and our audiences had returned. We traveled with 660 troupers, 520 horses; everything on parade. Our private railway train was famous throughout the continent: forty carriages including four water-tank cars, three generator-engines for the electric lighting, miles of wire and rope, nine sleeping coaches, an office car with ticket-office vestibule, and our own 2-6-2 Merriam locomotive.

We were by any measure an immensely successful enterprise. We packed the crowds in, thirty and forty thousand at each performance, sometimes two shows a day after the advent of electric lights. In our best seasons we jammed them in and turned them away and took in nearly two million dollars a season of which half a million were profits, much of which was distributed among the troupers and crewmen.

Our show was described by learned observers as the most thrilling and monumental institution of entertainment the world had seen since the Olympic Games and the Roman Circus.

. . .

It is not my purpose to describe at length things that everybody already knows. The years brought changes. We continued to tour the United States until the 1893 season when once again we took the show abroad and shepherded our wide-eyed Westerners and seasick Indians from Cairo to Ceylon to Melbourne to Hong Kong. We spent 1894–95 in Europe and Russia; we were plagued with ill fortune, suffering blizzards and flooding rains and an epidemic of glanders that forced us to destroy every horse in the company. The bright trappings had to be burned with the carcasses and the stench trailed us for miles between St. Petersburg and Moscow; we replaced the stock with cossack ponies but many of us wept to lose our mustangs. Still, every afternoon we had to swing into the saddle for the show and there had to be horses.

Progress, it is said, must not be impeded. By the time we returned to America to resume our national touring in the 1896 season a change seemed to have swept the nation—I cannot define its nature precisely but it was a kind of growing impatience, an acceleration of the pace of things. We found it no longer possible to settle in for two- and three-week stands, even in the larger cities. The schedule for 1896 contained 146 stands in 187 days, more than we'd ever attempted before; even though we covered a route of ten thousand miles our gate receipts, while respectable, were far below their previous peak.

We were dead-tired; we slept on moving wagons and trains—gave two performances, sometimes three, sometimes only one; then struck the equipment in the dark and rolled out at midnight toward the next day's stand; came creaking into the new town with the grey dawn and paraded through early-morning streets with our animals and wagons and rock-weary troupers to set up once again with that magical hasty contrivance of order out of the jumbled confusion of equipment and canvas and our overstrength battalion of men and women.

Finally the season ended and we returned to our resting grounds in Arizona. We picked up old friends all along the track from Chicago to Tucson and from there it took us three days to drive to our ranch because we had to stop at every ten-cow outfit and hacienda. In Tubac we found every cantina overflowing with old and new friends who had ridden from many miles around to honor us with drinks and tall yarns.

When we finally reached the home ranch and turned the stock out and got ready to put our feet up we found ourselves augmented by a hundred guests; naturally they were free to stay as long as they liked, to drink and hunt with me and swap wistful stories about the old days. It has been said, and truthfully so, that I owned the most overcrewed and unprofitable ranch in the territory; but then we didn't go there to work. It was our place for stretching out. For Libby and me it was home. Back to the east there was nothing anymore but fences and farms and towns where once I'd chased buffalo across empty plains. Down in that forgotten corner of Arizona the world had not yet changed within the boundaries of the old Tyree Grant and I could find grateful peace in the illusion that all was as it had been. Libby and I could pack into the hills and lie in camp and listen to the silence and hear the long-ago voices. . . .

The Gay Nineties. They were that. Mechanical nickelodeon bands; horseless carriages, cigar-store wooden Indians. Flickering five-cent film-strip images. From Tubac you could talk to Tucson on the telephone. I remember velocipede races and dozens of balloonists who came to the Southwest on account of the heated dry buoyant air. The world was becoming modern and the Wild West suddenly became history, a relic and an anachronism like the Confederate veterans and the Grand Army of the Republic marching through town on Decoration Day. As an exhibition we found ourselves in fierce competition with every little town's Saturday-afternoon baseball game. Railing against trusts and crosses of gold William Jennings Bryan focused his acidulous attention momentarily on the Wild West Show and stridently quoted Juvenal: " 'That entertainers have achieved an excess of fame is a symptom of the decay and decadence of Rome.' Let us be pleased with our strength in throwing off such a yoke!" As I have said, I thereupon went out of my way to vote for Roosevelt against him.

. . .

"Remember the Maine" and "Cuba Libre"—the cries of frenzy whipped us toward war in the spring of 1898.

There was amusement in it despite the dire turmoil. Our rival, Buffalo Bill Cody, announced to the world that he intended to rejoin the army and lick the Spaniards with the help of his cowboys and Indian troupers. Cody always claimed to have been an army colonel, although in fact I believe his claim was even more spurious than my own. In any case he blustered his way around the country at the head of his Congress of Rough Riders promising everywhere that he was just about to leave for Cuba and the war. Of course he never went, and was still blustering after the war ended, insisting he was still awaiting his orders from the War Department. I happen to know that General Miles wanted to see if Cody was serious and did in fact issue such orders but Cody, on receipt of them, replied that it would cost him a fortune to close his show and he didn't think it would be proper to put his employees out of work that way. "I would give ten thousand dollars to be with General Miles right now," he told anyone who would listen, but the fact remains he never went. In truth I felt sorry for the old boy then, for I'm sure it was true enough about his concern for his employees and I suspect the bravado about rushing off to war was something his press agents had forced on him. Certainly at his age there wasn't much point in his trotting off to battle. By that time his men had to prop him up on his horse before each show; he was fairly far gone with drink, although hardly as decrepit as some of his detractors made out—after all he did last nearly twenty years more in the saddle and it was grueling trouping. I know; it was an experience I shared.

Nevertheless Cody got a terrible ragging from our people from then on. What had been an amiable rivalry turned sour; there was a great deal of sneering contempt among our riders. "Cody couldn't hit the side of a barn from inside the barn. Couldn't break a glass ball with the buttstock of his rifle. Why doesn't he quit?"

I tried to set them straight. He was a magnificent showman. But my pleadings in his behalf must have been seen by my men as the courtesy of a contemporary; I was within a few years of Cody's age and in fact had been longer than he in the show business. It may well be that age softened my skepticism toward him but I have never believed he was as much of a fraud and charlatan as his enemies made him out to be. When we were all hunting buffalo on the plains no one ever called him a fraud.

When Buffalo Bill's Wild West began to fail in 1900 there was a flurry of conflict between us when his advance crews declared war on us in Milwaukee in a battle for billboard space. For a time there was a melee of skirmishes and action, each group tearing down the other's shinplasters and posting its own bills in their place. Cody's show hired a gang of nearly a hundred hard-fisted roughnecks to defend their paper and after a few serious injuries occurred I decided to leave them to it rather than risk anyone's dying. The word was abroad by then anyhow; our grandstand remained crowded while Cody's weary combination fought for penny droppings.

. . .

Vern Tyree spent those years and more in prison; his every effort to overturn the Nebraska verdict was thwarted by Phipps Merriam's exercise of unseen power. In truth those of us who knew that an injustice had been visited upon Vern were not altogether unhappy with his incarceration. He had twice tried to kill me, I knew that much; and there were other crimes behind him as well. Justice had taken a strange form but in its blindfolded way had prevailed.

426

The Senator remained a prisoner as well, by his own choice never venturing out in public. He no longer held office, of course, but everyone continued to refer to him as the Senator. Never in those years did we have any communication from him, not even the most indirect. Whatever vindictive schemes might have been stirring in his strange obsessive mind were unknown to us then.

The year the century turned was the year of the death of one of my friends: the gallant chief Ibran.

Two years after Ibran's deportation to Florida I had been able to secure his parole on my personal bond. Ibran lived out the rest of his days as chief of the Indian encampment of our Wild West Show, and many hearts I am sure were stirred by his proud rendition of that speech he had first delivered to my ears alone in the Sierra, concerning the honor of the Apache and how we ought to put him on wheels. But Ibran did not thrive on the show business. He felt toward it much as Caleb Rice did. But we made his life as bearable as we could and allowed no one to slight him with indignities. I have never subscribed to the effete notion that all redskins were noble; but Ibran was a true nobleman and was demeaned by circumstances beyond his power to avert. He died without turning to drink (as Geronimo did before his death in 1909) and without giving up hope for a rekindling of pride among his people but nevertheless he died in early middle age and I believe it was because his heart was broken: he simply did not care to go on.

As for the others among my friends of the early days, for the most part they have proved an exceptionally long-lived lot, even as I have. Perhaps it can be attributed to the healthy outdoor lives we all had led. Time, of course, effected changes for some of us. Nate Loving retired from the Wild West in 1899 and astonished us all by promptly taking a job as a conductor on the Santa Fe Railroad. I rode his train occasionally over the ensuing years and learned to my amazement that the great ambition of his youth—provoked the first time he ever saw a train—had been to ride into the twentieth century on a railroad train. Having fulfilled that goal he seemed content for a while; but then a few years later he abruptly quit his railroading job and went out to California with the troupers of the XIT Wild West Combination and joined up with veterans of the 101 Ranch Show in performing for motion-picture cameras in a production called *Ranch Life in the Great West*. Nate's famous bulldogging exploits were recorded on celluloid film and he associated himself thereafter with another performer from that motion picture, the fine showman Tom Mix. Nate is today in his late sixties but still works as a stunt rider in Tom Mix's cowboy movies.

Inevitably some of us parted company in that way or in others. One

427

of the saddest days Libby and Kevin and I had to endure was the day in 1903 when a skittish cow pony threw Harry Dreier into a boulder while he was chousing stray buffalo calves through the badlands of the Tyree Grant. Harry was dead when we found him; he had died without pain, apparently, and still active despite his wooden leg and countless fractured bones he'd endured over the years. He died quickly and with dignity and perhaps he would have wanted it that way, like Fitz Bragg; nevertheless his passing flooded us with sorrow.

. . .

During her years in bondage to Phipps Merriam, Libby had preserved her strength and perhaps her sanity by donating her time and work to charitable causes. Her natural talents for managerial organization had emerged in those years. I have stated earlier in this narrative that my Libby was never the simpering heroine of dime-novel expectations; if she had been of such swooning character I doubt I could have sustained such powerful feelings toward her for the long years of our separations. Beneath her slender appearance of fragile beauty Libby had always possessed keen humor and a will of towering strength. This came to the fore once again as we settled into the annual life of trouping the great show. At first—because of Phipps Merriam's stubborn silent recalcitrance and the journalistic scandal that resulted—I had found myself torn between my dedication to the show and my limitless love for Libby. But after our marriage the dilemma disappeared. Libby did not merely take a hand in running the show; she became its chief executive. We were partners both in marriage and in the show business. It has been a partnership of many years now—and no travails, no matter how awesome, have ever shaken it.

. . .

I trained a fair number of protégés; whenever a young shooter drew my attention with his skill I made the time to coach him. Some of my pupils later took skeet, trap and pistol championships at the leading meets.

By far the finest young shooter who ever came under my wing was Jack Turkin, who must be familiar by now to every reader of this account. Jack first entered my life at the turn of the century when from the ranch-house parlor, where I was reading the latest William Dean Howells, I heard an intense rataplan of rifle fire that drew me outside to find out what was going on.

The racket issued from the hilltop beyond the corrals, the same hill where long ago I had sometimes gone to practice my own shooting. I saw a small figure up there blazing away at targets that lay beyond my view. It was a lovely January day and I gave my legs a stretch, walking up the hill and coming up behind the boy.

He was intent upon what he was doing and remained completely ignorant of my approach; he plugged cartridges into the rifle and shouldered it and flicked his shots off with blinding speed. As I came along the slope I saw that he'd set up a long line of tin airtights and was knocking them down one by one. They were a good three hundred yards from him and he emptied the entire magazine of the Tyree rifle without missing a single one; it was excellent shooting and especially so in view of the fact that he couldn't have been more than twelve years old.

I cleared my throat to announce myself and the boy jumped as if he'd been stabbed. With a sheepish smile he said, "Oh-oh."

"Good shooting," I remarked.

"Yes sir. Thanks, Colonel."

"Mr. Tyree lend you that rifle?"

"Well . . ."

"You just helped yourself, did you?"

"Guess I did, sir. I'm sorry. I'll clean it before I put it back."

"What's your name?"

"Jack. Jack Turkin, sir."

"I haven't seen you before."

"No sir." He didn't meet my eyes.

I sat down cross-legged. "Maybe you ought to tell me about it."

"About what?"

"Your story. Go ahead—I won't bite you. I'd like to know how you come to be here, that's all."

"Well I guess I'm trespassin', Colonel."

"Why?"

"I just wanted to come here, that's all."

"How'd you get here?"

"Hooked rides on some wagons and such. Walked most of the way from Tubac."

"Where'd you come from?"

"Bisbee, sir."

"That's a long way."

"I guess."

"Eaten anything, Jack?"

"Yes sir, they kindly fed me down to the cook shack there."

He was a knobby kid, all elbows and knees and Adam's apple; he had freckles and red hair and a shooter's blue-grey eyes. The Levi's and plaid workshirt were threadbare and the uppers of his boots were coming away from the soles.

"Where'd you get the ammunition?"

"Just picked it up. Cases and cases of it there."

429

"I expect your folks in Bisbee are worrying about you, Jack."

"Ain't got none. See, I was in the county orphanage."

. . .

It was inevitable that we should take him in. There was such devotion in his eyes; he was a splendid rifleman; and he was just five years older than my own son Mike had been when he died. It was like picking up a life over again, twenty years afterward.

Libby took to the lad right away. He had a degree of wildness in him from the beginning but it was easy to attribute that to his upbringing in several orphanages; anyhow it was good to have a spirited boy around—his pranks lifted my spirits. He was a devil for practical jokes, though, and I believe several of the grown-ups on the crew were quite uneasy of him, for you never knew when you might find a horned toad between your bedsheets or a bucket of water balanced atop a door that stood ajar.

Of all the shooters I have come across, Jack was the most naturally talented. He took to it as if he'd been born to it. I found it easier to teach him than it had been to teach Vern Tyree and that is saying a great deal because Vern had been my most successful pupil up to then.

I spoiled the boy terribly. But I felt he deserved it. He hadn't been born to this good life he'd found with us; he had earned it. To be sure, he'd bought his way into our hearts with trespass and brashness, but shyness wins a man very little and in my heart I applauded his bold spirit from the moment of our first encounter.

In the next few years he grew to be a strapping fellow, nearly as tall as I but never as big, for he had a lanky cowboy's frame and the wiry flat-muscled strength that goes with it. He had a natural grace and agility and as he matured he became quite handsome, the freckles receding almost to invisibility and the eyes assuming a permanent outdoor squint that made young women swoon.

Jack first traveled with the Wild West Show in the 1901 season. By July he joined the sharpshooting-team act; by September he had so outskilled the rest that I gave him his own spot in the show. During the next few seasons Jack developed new shooting tricks of his own and by the time he was fifteen he was, next to me, the star shooter of the combination, with high billing on all our posters. The newspapers had dubbed him "Manhood's Answer to Annie Oakley" and Jack more than lived up to it, actually defeating Miss Oakley twice in challenge matches; but in fairness to Cody's favorite lass it must be pointed out that she was past her prime by then. I only shot against Annie once myself; it was in the early 1890s and her marksman-husband Frank Butler was shooting the match as well, along with a score of other shooters. It happened all three of us lost to Doc Bogardus that day.

430

In the winter of 1903–04 Jack begged me to work with him on his revolver training and I obliged happily. Needless to say he found no mystery in it; he learned faster than I could teach.

On his sixteenth birthday, in December 1904, Jack and I shot against one another in a match tournament for the first time. We took first and second place, Jack deferring to me by only seven balls out of five hundred, and afterward when we were scrubbing the powder grit from our faces he looked up at me with a towel in his hands and said, "I believe the day's gonna come when I'm gonna whup you fair and square, Colonel."

"I wouldn't be surprised," I said. "I'm getting old, you know."

. . .

After the turn of the century when our receipts began to dwindle seriously we made a mistake. Or at least it seems to have been one in retrospect. We allowed Jack Turkin and a group of circus-trained promoters to convince us that we had to add sideshow attractions to the combination to boost its popularity. Midgets, freaks, mind readers, jugglers, fire-eaters, snake charmers and magicians came aboard our train to distort the flavor of the Wild West. I never approved of the idea much but I must confess that for a few seasons it did seem to increase attendance considerably.

Then in 1907 we added a motion-picture-show tent with one-reelers, mostly Westerns of course, nearly all of them Bronco Billy films.

Young Jack was quickly enamored of the magic of moving pictures and took to spending more time than he should have around the projectionists and their arc lamps and hand-crank machines and flat square hardboard containers of celluloid.

. . .

It was 1912 and Congress had bestowed statehood on Arizona and the celebrations were wild.

Our troupe headed up the parade through Prescott, the capital, and afterward there were innumerable speeches. I thought my own address to be much the best of them. Here is what I said from the bunting-bedecked platform:

"Ladies and gentlemen, I feel like Cherokee Bill, who stepped up on a platform a little like this one to be executed by the hangman Maledon. When asked for his last words, Cherokee Bill said, 'I came here to git hung, not to make a speech.' That's how I feel, folks. I came here to celebrate, not to make a speech."

And I stepped down. I believe that speech got more applause than any of the others.

Ran Urquhart, who now owned his own ranch over near Willcox, got up to deliver the next remarks and surprised me with them, for I was unaware that any tribute to me had been planned.

"We who have lived the past half century and more," Ran thundered with the remaining hint of a brogue, "we remember that when this great land was a great wilderness with lawlessness rampant and our red brothers fending off the onward tide of progress and civilization—we remember that the pioneer, the settler, the child and the woman knew young Hugh Cardiff as their protector and their defender. Hugh Cardiff was the first man ever to face the war chief Ibran across gunsights—when both men were but children—and Hugh Cardiff won that battle as he did every subsequent one. Settlers felt safe whenever Cardiff rode on the frontier. How little he must have dreamed, in the long ago, that the lonely path of the pioneer scout and great lone hunter would have led him before this great assemblage today and on such an occasion as this. We are proud to stand here reflected in the brilliance of your glory, Colonel, but we old-timers can never forget the tribulations through which you journeyed, ever with head held high, while the path of civilization was still being surveyed, while the howl of the coyote was not yet outshouted by the shriek of the locomotive, nor the free range of the great bison herds narrowed by annihilators and barbed wire, nor the bellicosity of the red Indian drowned by the vast flood of settlers. . . ."

There was more and it rambled everywhere; Ran was drunk. I near fell over containing my laughter but I must admit I took pleasure in the number of times the crowd interrupted Ran's Byzantine tribute with applause. Libby clutched my hand fearfully and it seemed she could not contain her tears, although behind them she bubbled with laughter. With a fond regard that swelled my heart I looked into her shining face and treasured each line that the years had brought, each grey tress of her proud once-blond mane; she was as lovely and magnificent then as she had been in the first bloom of womanhood.

· · ·

The statehood blowout was a high spot in our lives but it did not change the fact that we were engaged in an increasing struggle.

Moving pictures did not kill the Wild West Shows; but they did not help either. By 1913 our one-reel Bronco Billy tent had lost its audience to local town-center bijous to which the five-reel epic productions of William S. Hart were attracting long queues. Jack Turpin kept after me relentlessly: "Hugh, you can't turn your back. We've got to compete. We ought to be making our own moving pictures down here in the off seasons."

It all came together that fall when Caleb Rice paid us a visit at the Tyree Grant. Caleb had retired temporarily from badge-toting and was living on a pension and some savings in Boulder, Colorado; he journeyed to Tubac because he earnestly wanted my advice about a widow woman who had caught his eye. I had no useful counsel to offer, not having met the lady, but it appeared Caleb mainly was gun-shy and wanted time away from the widow to collect his ragged nerves. Under the circumstances I suppose he was more susceptible to Jack's enthusiasms than he might otherwise have been. In any case Jack lost no opportunities to buttonhole Caleb, who of course had lost none of his heroic luster in legend and myth: he was one of the last surviving peace marshals from the frontier. Bending his ear mercilessly, Jack inveigled Caleb into pressing the proposition on me that I had rejected when it had come from young Jack himself.

Jack's ambition had infected Caleb. He pressed me into a corner: "Look, old horse, you may not need money nowadays but I sure do. I'm out to pasture with nothing but a gold watch and a mortgaged two-story in the woods. I don't mind making a passel of money for my sunset days—what have you got to lose?"

Playing on my sympathy with good-humored slyness Caleb thus roped me into the scheme and together the three of us formed the Arizona Mutoscene Company, raising capital from Isaac Singman and other boosterish Arizona businessmen. We set about filming motion pictures in which we attempted to dramatize for posterity the exploits of our youth.

We brought our cameras to the Tyree Grant and employed the cast and crew of the Wild West Show in near-epic attempts to outdo Hart and Mix and the flamboyant silent operettas of Mr. C. B. De Mille.

Having seen the circus-show childishness of Tom Mix's motion pictures and the one-reel idiocies that had been perpetrated by Bronco Billy Anderson on his New Jersey "ranch" we were determined to show the West as it really was.

We proceeded with great gusto, once we had started. Jack Turkin ramrodded the cast and crew, rushed about setting up lights and reflectors, and acted generally as one-man whirlwind and factotum.

Unfortunately however we embarked upon the enterprise with more enthusiasm than ability, more dedication than experience. Much of the time when he was not before the camera Caleb insisted upon wielding it as though it were some marvelous toy version of a Gatling gun. In the parlance of the trade his long shots proved competent enough but his close-ups left something to be desired, inasmuch as he invariably leveled the camera at the height of his own eyes, so that nearly all the other members of the cast—and particularly his co-hero, myself—were cut off at the neck by the top of the screen.

By the time this mistake was realized—after the miles of film had been processed—we had nearly exhausted our capital. We made hasty efforts to photograph the decapitated close-ups over again but then our exposed film was shipped to a primitive laboratory in Phoenix where the lot was consumed in the terrible fire that destroyed the Adams Hotel.

I had to dig deep into my own pocket to satisfy our creditors. Caleb was too dismayed and embarrassed to carry on with the venture. He returned somewhat sheepishly to Colorado; in the end he did not marry the widow lady, but journeyed to Oklahoma to pin his badge on again.

A few months later Jack Turkin came to me hat in hand, embarrassment making him mutter, and with difficulty announced that he wished to leave the show because he had received a handsome offer from a moving-picture company in Chicago to appear as the hero of a series of two-reel horse operas. I hadn't the heart to prevent his going, though I saw little future for him in that undependable fad industry. Libby and I watched him board the Chicago train with considerable lonely sadness in us; he was as near to a son as we had.

. . .

The show no longer made a profit; it ran at a steadily increasing loss, which I made up out of my pocket, but I could not bear to close it down. Too many people depended on it. There were still more than five hundred mouths to feed; we had tried to diminish the payroll by the attrition of retirements and resignations—we were resolved to hire no new personnel—but then we'd learned that 261 of Ibran's Apache were still, incredibly, being held as prisoners of war at Fort Sill, Oklahoma, having been moved there years earlier from Florida; and we took them on with the Wild West Show. One of them, who went by the name of Nino Ibran and claimed to have been Ibran's son, was a high-spirited cheerful rogue who proved as unpredictably raucous as Nate Loving had ever been. On the opening day of his third season with the show, Nino Ibran appeared on the arena in a magnificent regalia including a bonnet made of 250 eagle feathers. It had cost him more than one hundred dollars in a theatrical-costume haberdashery and it was only with the greatest difficulty that I dissuaded him from wearing it during the battle scenes. I relented to the extent of permitting him to wear this proudful possession in the opening parade but I have had some regret about that because I am sure it instilled in a new generation of children the false belief that Apache Indians wore feathered warbonnets.

Nino Ibran put a few light moments into our lives and so did Charlie Samuelson, who had long ago outgrown his job as throw-boy and was now managing our office staff. One time I happened to come by the office in time to hear some of the younger fellows joshing Charlie about some complaints that Charlie's wife had been heard to utter about his potency.

Charlie said, "Hell, I got that all fixed up. I found this apothecary

434

down in Nogales, they fixed me up with these here big iron capsules. I been taking them every night."

"Does that help with your wife?"

"Reckon it surely does," Charlie replied, "long as I keep her headed north."

.   .   .

When the Great War came we contributed our share. Kevin went off to work in a munitions factory in Connecticut. Several of our young men went into the service. Jack Turkin took a leave from Famous Players, where he was a top cowboy moving-picture star by then, and as the world knows Jack achieved a stirring heroic record of bravery on the western front.

The rest of us continued trouping and performed many benefit shows for veterans and the wounded and particularly in the cause of selling bonds for the government.

But we were tired; Libby and I were tired. Every time a man was jailed for exuberance or a horse took sick or an axle broke they came to us about it. I had to wheedle railroad dispatchers to get our shrinking train through in time for the next one-day stand; we lived in those malodorous railway carriages for months on end, jolting on bad track joints, shunting from siding to siding, unloading and performing and loading again, feeding ourselves and feeding the stock, fighting off thieves and charlatans and constables, performing in gales and droughts and rainstorms—snapped by the wind, choked by dust, drowned by downpours—coming into towns that had been stripped of ready coin by a circus four days ahead of us or one of a dozen imitative competitors from Pawnee Bill to the 101 Ranch Show to Doc Carver's Rifle-and-Horse Show. We found the East depressed by crop failures, the Northwest panicked by flood rains, the South deprived by cheap cotton and the prairie states wiped out by dust-drought.

One day outside Mobile I recall our receipts at the matinee were nine dollars and thirty-five cents. It was an empty house; but that dozen visitors had paid for their tickets and we gave them our best show.

For more than a hundred successive stands we lost money. Our notes came overdue time and time again; each time Libby and I reached into our pockets, the profits of years past, and bailed the show out so that it could travel on for one more week or one more day. And all the time we were haunted by the way gallant old Buffalo Bill Cody had died in January 1917, penniless.

.   .   .

Charlie Samuelson—dear loyal devoted Charlie who stayed right with us all the way—became full-fledged business manager of the show in

435

1919 when Libby decided she was old enough to retire from the job with dignity intact. She continued to travel with me, however, claiming she did not trust me out of her sight—I took it as a marvelous compliment, having just passed my seventieth birthday.

Charlie came to me one day with his face as long as a fireman's ladder. "You seen the books, I reckon."

"You don't have to tell me, Charlie."

"It ain't that you're exactly slow in the brain, Colonel, but I hear one time a cannonball hit you in the head and bounced off your head and killed one of the toughest mules in the army."

"I believe that is true, Charlie."

"Colonel, that being the case I have got to recommend that you get yo' dumb ass back home to Arizona and dissolve this goddamn shell of a company while you still got something to dissolve."

I said gently, "All right, Charlie, I will do that just as soon as you show me who's going to feed and clothe and house the five hundred and eighteen people on this train."

"You want to pay them off then pay them off, Colonel. You could give every one of them a year's full salary and still come out ahead of where you're at now."

"It's not just money, Charlie. They need the dignity of having jobs where they can earn their keep."

"Half of them can get jobs any old where. Movies'd be glad to get 'em. The other half, well they too old and broke-down to work anyhow."

"That's exactly what I mean," I said.

"Well if you aim to have it that way you ain't nothing but a stubborn old fool of a man. Now this here jug contains genuine copper-distilled double-rectified sod corn juice and I'd admire to have a share of it with you, Colonel sir."

"All of two weeks old, I bet you."

"Why, Colonel, that's *aged* whisky!"

. . .

Charlie did not know it then but our own pockets had gone empty quite a long time before and I had borrowed substantially from Isaac Singman to keep the show rolling.

The loans were personal but to justify them with his bankers Isaac had been forced to deposit signed notes with them in his accounts so that his books would balance. I had long since sold out my partnership interest to him; these loans were just that and I had every intention of making them good.

Isaac and I naturally had an oral agreement concerning the money I had borrowed from him. It was money lent between friends and there

436

were no interest payments or due dates. But Isaac was infirm; his health failed rapidly and we watched helplessly while he changed, seemingly overnight, into a trembling skeletal apparition. Toward the end it was anguish to be with him but I spent weeks at his bedside while he croaked gentle reminiscences and quoted verses I hadn't heard since my youth. When he died it should have been a relief but I grieved a long while: Isaac had been my oldest friend.

After his death the vultures gathered, for he had left a large estate and his children proved quarrelsome; they were grown to middle age, of course, and Libby and I tried to mediate between them but they were at loggerheads concerning the division of his properties and the management of his long chain of enterprises. We were able to calm them and bring them together but a good part of the estate had been divided among a number of presumably charitable concerns, which in the aggregate proved more greedy and callous than any miser: predatory packs of lawyers fell on the estate. In the name of the estate they sued every creditor. I was not exempted. The suits demanded that I make large interest payments, penalty payments and immediate reimbursement of my loans.

To repay that money to Isaac's estate required sums that I neither possessed nor had any hope of raising. I'd already mortgaged the show itself to a group of Denver bankers, including an old friend named Cletus Hatch, now the president of the Ranchers and Merchants Bank, who in the dim and distant past had been a gambling barker taking bets at my first rifle meet against Doc Bogardus.

The bloodsuckers were draining us and I had nowhere to turn. "You can't get it from a stone," I insisted, but they only replied that in that case I must take advantage of the bankruptcy laws.

Libby said, "That's exactly what we must do, Hugh. Declare bankruptcy and let the bastards go to hell singing for their money."

"But I can't, my love. It goes against the grain. I've got to pay every dollar. But in the meantime we've no choice—we've got to close down and return to Arizona." It was only July.

When I told the troupers they registered their shock not with theatrics or anger or even slow burns but simply by seeming to deflate a little. I suppose they all had known it would come; but I couldn't hold back and I wept before them. I spread my hands helplessly. "Boys, there's nothing for it. We are belly-up."

. . .

It was like a funeral train; the Wild West Show was the corpse. We sold the train itself in Tucson to the Southern Pacific company which broke it up, refitted the sleeping cars and poured it down the line like raindrops into an ocean so that it could never be recognized again.

437

It was in Tucson that I came across a newspaper story—Kevin drew it to my attention; otherwise I'd not have seen it—briefly reporting that at long last Vern Tyree had won his fight for freedom, received a commutation of his sentence from the new governor of Nebraska (a man evidently not in Phipps Merriam's pocket, I thought) and been set free after more than thirty years behind the walls. There was no photograph. I remember mentioning the clipping to Libby, who was as preoccupied as I was; she said that she thought he must be a broken old man by now, but we gave it little further thought. Vern had lost all Libby's affection long ago. I believe Kevin still harbored a muted fondness toward him but he made no effort to communicate with Vern and we heard no more of him for some time.

Phipps Merriam's name had been in the press as well. The Washington investigators into the wartime munitions-cartel scandals had unearthed the Senator's name several times but it seemed he had enough power to prevent being subpoenaed and he never appeared before the committees; his presence lurked in the background of the news stories for some months and then the investigations were quietly quashed and one heard no more about them. Whatever machinations the Senator was manipulating from behind the scenes we had no idea, and little interest in. Our sorrowing attention was focused exclusively on the demise of the Wild West Show—an entertainment, an institution and a home for several hundred men and women that Libby and I had shepherded for more than thirty years.

. . .

I sold the four-cylinder Peerless, which when I'd bought it had represented the apogee of achievement. I wrote to a mail-order house and tried to interest them in selling prints of the famous photograph of me on my horse with my rifle, but we got few takers. The news we were closing the show got out somehow and sped across the country on the wires; several reporters and friends sent money—drafts for fifty dollars, a hundred, one for five hundred; we received about two thousand dollars in such charity and I did not have the heart to rebuff the kind donors by returning it. Libby wrote thank-yous to them all and we gave every penny out, sharing it out among our stranded troupers whom I could not pay myself. Nino Ibran took me aside and with a sly smile slipped into my old hand twenty dollars in crumpled one-dollar bills and made me cry when he whispered, "I wish it could be more, Colonel."

In Tucson on January 16, 1920—the same day Prohibition became law—we went up on the sheriff's auction block: every head of stock, every piece of equipment and memorabilia that belonged to the Wild West Show.

I put my own personal collection of relics and weapons up for auction to raise money for the crew. I saw an old familiar face in the audience and went to sit beside him—it was Cletus Hatch, the banker from Denver; we exchanged small talk, carefully avoiding the realities, and then the auction commenced and when my personal collection went on the block in one solid lot Cletus Hatch began to bid and kept at it until he had outbid everybody else. The collection was knocked down to him for a sum that astonished me—$67,000—and then Cletus leaned over to me and whispered in my ear, "The money goes into the bank to reduce your debt. Makes us just about clear with each other—one less creditor for you to worry about, I reckon. As for that collection, I have got no earthly use for that old junk and I trust Mrs. Cardiff will accept it as a gift from an old friend."

"You can't do that, you damn fool."

"Try and stop me. Look here, do you really want to punish yourself with the rest of this harrowing scavenging or will you come out with me and have a drink? I want to talk to you."

We went east along Congress Street past Singman's to the Santa Rita Bar where I nodded to Burt Mossman and a few other acquaintances; we went back into the cavernous darkness in the most remote corner of the room and Cletus sat me down—I was benumbed and listless then, hardly attending anything. He said, "It may perk you up a mite to know I've got my agents in the crowd there with instructions to outbid any and all contenders for certain items of invaluable property, for example the Tombstone mail coach and that museum-tent full of medals and citations and your presidential pardon. All that will be returned to you and the money from it will go to settle the rest of your debt to my bank, since the money's coming out of my pocket."

"I can't accept such gifts, of course."

"Well I know that, naturally, but I want to give you a chance to earn it back so we can conclude this on a business basis."

"I don't know what you're talking about. I doubt you know either."

"Listen now. I'm a gambling man. Always been a sucker for a high-roller's bet." He grinned without guile.

"What do you want to bet on, Cletus? Which one of these flies will jump off the sugar bowl first?"

"There was a time when I would have—and did. Lost twenty thousand dollars to Haw Tabor once, betting which one of two raindrops would reach the bottom of a Pullman train window first."

"What are you drinking?"

"Coffee, I reckon. That's about all you can buy in here as of today." Cletus sat back and clasped his gnarled hands over the mound of his shriveled stomach. His pants were cinched high like a mail sack; his flesh was alternately pouched and inflated. He said, "I'm the president, manager, majority stockholder and outright owner of the Ranchers and Merchants Bank in Denver."

"I know that."

"I can do anything with that bank I want, consistent with state laws."

"So?"

"Trouble is, you see, I'm eighty-three years old."

"Congratulations, Cletus."

"And one of these days that whippersnapper board of directors of mine is going to up and wheel me away into some courtroom and have me declared incompetent because of senility or some other trumped-up son-of-a-bitching technicality."

"So?"

"Before they gather up enough gumption to do that, I aim to retire."

"Good for you."

"On my terms, not theirs. By God, Colonel, I am fixing to go out in a blaze of glory, I am."

"You asking me to join you in some kind of pyrotechnical suicide pact, Cletus?"

"Well you might put it like that, only I expect we will not only survive it but emerge triumphant."

"I hear you talking. I'm a little deef but not that much so."

"You are still billed as the champion rifle and revolver shot of the world. You are the king of the crack shots, as they say. No one has ever beaten you over the long haul—not even recently, isn't that so?"

"It is. I'm still as good a shooter as I ever was. A little slower but just as straight. Up close I am as blind as a bat but for shooting I have got perfect vision."

Cletus said, "I can't even begin to sum up the amounts of money I have made for myself over the years by betting on you in shooting matches."

"Is that so?"

"At a conservative estimate I would say I've won at least seven hundred thousand dollars betting on you. Possibly as high as one million dollars. And I have never bet against you, sir. Not once in my life since I saw you shoot that time in Denver in the spring of eighteen and sixty-eight."

"That's mighty kind of you to say so, Cletus."

The old man grinned and cackled at me. "Even if it ain't true, hey? But I promise you for a fact it *is* true, Colonel. Of course I lost a few dollars now and then when you got beat by Doc Bogardus or somebody but I knew you had sand, you see, I knew you'd outlast any of them and come up winners in the end, and I just kept putting my money on you and I just kept winning. I will let you in on a little secret here now,

Colonel. You—you personally—have made me a millionaire. Of course my faith in you had something to do with it too, but you were the man on the firing line."

He looked around as if wary of eavesdroppers; I caught a fleck of concern in his eyes as he turned back to face me. "How's your shooting eye holding up, Colonel? The truth now."

"I told you the truth before. There are men who shoot much faster than I do nowadays but there's none who shoots straighter."

"Your word on that, Colonel?"

"Yes sir. My word on it."

"I'm sorry to have pressed the point and I accept your word. You understand why I had to ask. You are what, seventy-one years old?"

"As of next week, yes."

"And you haven't shot a public competition match in a few years now."

"Had my hands full with the Wild West Show, that's all. I'm ready to shoot any man, anyplace, anytime."

"Then I'll tell you what, Colonel. I'll tell you what we're going to do. You and I are going to set up the most grandiose and extravagant and gigantic winner-take-all rifle-shooting contest in the history of the world. We will invite every one of the world's prominent shooters to take part. I personally, and my bank, will guarantee a purse to be funded out of paid admissions and sundry concessions. It shall be a purse big enough to draw big-game hunters from Europe and maharajahs from India and old-time Boer frontiersmen from Africa and the champions from Bisley and Springfield and everywhere. Big enough to draw Jack Turkin and maybe Tom Mix too. And maybe even big enough to tempt Doc Bogardus out of retirement."

Then his voice dropped near to a whisper. "But most of all it'll be big enough to draw the presence and participation of the king of crack shots himself—the only marksman in the world who can still draw crowds. Colonel Hugh Cardiff himself, in person."

I twisted my knuckles; confidence had deserted me somehow. Down the street they were selling off my possessions; I had failed my people; I could hear in my mind the painfully slow scrape-scrape of old Isaac Singman's slippers before he'd died and I wasn't far behind him in age and I'd seen all my friends and contemporaries fade and die and I was reminded how much longer it took me nowadays to climb into a double-rig saddle and I was thinking that the first time I shot a championship match was fifty-two goddamned long years ago and that was an awfully, awfully long time in a man's lifespan. . . .

I pulled my head around reluctantly toward Cletus. "You are talking now about a marathon match, aren't you? Not just one hundred rounds or one thousand rounds. That wouldn't draw any crowds at all anymore."

"No, I reckon it wouldn't. Listen now, I have spent a long time working this out in my head and I believe I know what it will take to do this job and settle for all time the championship of the world."

I said, "One hundred thousand balls, something like that. Is that what you've got in mind?"

"No sir. Hear me out." He was whispering, showing his yellow teeth; a visionary's blinding illumination lit up his eyes and he leaned toward me with ferocious energy:

"Unlimited balls, Colonel, at twenty-five yards' rise. Night and day, day and night, however many days and nights it takes, until there is only one shooter left, until he is the last remaining shooter left in the arena. To stay in the match each man must hit a minimum of ninety out of every one hundred balls thrown. If he hits only eighty-nine he's out, disqualified. If he falls asleep or cannot lift his arms or cannot return to the contest within two hours after his departure he's disqualified. The winner is the shooter who goes on hitting a minimum of ninety out of every hundred balls until he is the last remaining shooter left in the arena."

I only stared at him.

"The ultimate," he breathed, "in marathon endurance tournaments. The most grueling test of marksmanship ever to offer itself for men to measure themselves against. One hundred thousand balls, you say? Who knows? It may be over and finished after five thousand—but it could go on to half a million rounds. Who knows? That's the excitement of it!"

I brooded at him. He licked his cracked lips fretfully. "Well?"

"That's not an old man's game, Cletus."

"You are the greatest endurance shooter ever born, Colonel. You've trained yourself for a lifetime for just this very contest. Can you now turn your back? Can you?"

"God, Cletus, I'm an *old man*. . . ."

"You're the best. The champion of the world. I'm offering you the chance to prove it once and for all."

He looked so youthful then, buoyant with enthusiasm and radiance. "It will draw crowds from all over the globe, Hugh! A once-in-a-lifetime battle, unique in human history, surely never to be repeated! And you're the man who can win it. Can you possibly hesitate?"

"You could do it without me. All the young sharpshooters—Jack Turkin . . ."

"Without you it would be meaningless. Like all the contenders fighting among themselves for Dempsey's spot without any of them ever stepping in the ring with Dempsey. No sir. If you won't compete then

I won't sponsor the match. I will not change my habits this late in my life. You're the only man I can bet on."

His hand, trembling and mottled with cyanotic spots, reached out to cover my own. His glistening old eyes peered into mine. "You can do it. You can. I ought to know—I plan to invest the major part of my fortune in you."

"You're a madman."

Of course he was. I knew it; he knew it; the twinkle in his aged eyes said as much.

He said, "I'm offering no charity. You can bail yourself out—you can win enough to support every one of those precious hangers-on and red-skins and no-goods. Enough to pay off the mortgage on the Tyree ranch and enough for all your needs. Money is freedom, you know that. But you're going to have to earn it, Colonel, and I reckon it'll be the hardest money you've ever earned."

"What if I lose?"

"Then you're no worse off than you are now, are you? If you lose you'll bring me to the brink of bankruptcy but that's my lookout. That's the way I want it, can't you see that? I'm a gambler—what's the point gambling if you're not risking everything?"

"You've got no family to consider?"

"I'm a widower. We never had children. No—there's no one. That's another reason why I want to sponsor this match. It'll be my monu-ment—it'll go down in the history books. The Hatch Tournament. Why, it'll be as famous in history as the Olympic marathon run! Colonel—humor me, but don't patronize me. What is your answer?"

"I must think on it."

I left him sitting there and stepped outside into sunshine so bright it made me wince. I turned and strode up the street, my hands deep in my pockets.

I must make clear that at that time it did not occur to me that Cletus Hatch's motives might be other than he said they were; regardless how implausible the challenge, *he* was plausible. It did not enter my mind that another party might have planted the notion in his mind or encour-aged him to develop it. And to this day I do not believe Cletus had evil intentions. In the end, whether or not the idea of the tournament had originated with him, Cletus dedicated himself to it as if it were entirely his own, and none of what ensued must be blamed upon him.

The challenge had taken me aback; I examined it suspiciously, not because I impugned Cletus' motives but because I doubted my ability to meet it. *I'm a used-up old man,* I thought dismally.

I had not gone far along the street when a tramp staggered near with palm outstretched. I looked into his face—his eyes beseeched me. He was a good deal younger than I; but life had treated him unkindly. I dropped my last four bits in his hand and he scuttled away.

I looked at his bobbing back and told him, "You won't find a drink in there, brother."

But he didn't hear me and went on into the saloon. After a moment the door opened again but it wasn't the tramp—it was Cletus, his face childishly eager as he gaped at me.

I walked back to him. I was thinking of the tramp. I said, "I am not dead yet."

"No sir, you surely ain't."

"Goddammit, I'm a long way from dead. I will shoot for you, Cletus."

. . .

The Cletus Hatch Tournament was scheduled to convene on Saturday, May 15, 1920. Because of a sentimental quirk of Cletus' it was to be held on the premises of what had once been Skinner's farm—the same field where I had shot my very first professional match fifty-two years earlier. There were small farms all about; what had been open country was now paved, built, illuminated and crowded. But the field itself was as it had been; the long ridge behind it was the same backstop against which we had shot before and it was likely there were still lead bullets buried in its loam from the Hawken rifle I had fired in 1868.

Aside from the shooting ground nothing looked at all the same. Where the crowd had once milled behind a primitive corral fence now stood enormous grandstand bleachers constructed at considerable expense by Cletus Hatch's carpenters. Strings of electric arc lamps were mounted in high and low rows to flood the field at night. Dressing-room trailers formed a long row behind the grandstand for the use of the celebrated shooters and those who survived the early weeding-out.

Putt-putting trucks with solid rubber tires and open-keyhole doorways went lurching in and out of the grounds on numerous errands; one of them was a tanker truck that drove back and forth across the shooting field to dampen down the earth and prevent dust from rising. Various outbuildings and sheds had been constructed, virtually obscuring the farm buildings so that an entire town seemed to have sprung up— there were souvenir stands and bookstalls and snack counters and Wild West artifacts, some of them (like the Tombstone mail coach) brought to Denver for the occasion by Cletus Hatch from the Tucson auction. Public chick sales with pull-chain flush toilets had been installed all around the grandstands.

Spread along the full length of the firing line the seats were sufficient to accommodate ninety thousand people.

Every hotel and lodging-house room in Denver was taken; the city swelled to bursting, trains overflowed with arrivals, farmers came lurching into the city in their Fords only to find the traffic jammed from out-skirt to outskirt, tourists doubled up for sleeping space in barn lofts, restaurants ran double shifts and stayed open around the clock to ac-commodate the endless streams of hungry visitors; and Cletus had to hire a platoon of private police to keep early-rising eager beavers from trampling the show grounds to ruin and stealing everything that wasn't nailed down.

There was no question it was a mammoth public event. Cletus had expended fortunes in newspaper advertising from coast to coast and in publications abroad. Applications for places in the shoot had arrived from every corner of the world. A month before the tournament it had become clear that we would be swamped and immobilized by the vast number of entrants if some means of eliminating the unqualified were not devised; Cletus had commandeered baseball stadiums and rodeo corrals for the Thursday and Friday preceding the shoot in order to separate the men from the boys. If a shooter had not proved himself by achieving respectable scores in previous match competitions he was forced to shoot in one of those regional preliminary matches—he had to demonstrate that he could hit at least 85 out of 100 targets thrown in the air. If he failed in it he was refused admission to the main tourney. Only in that manner was it possible to reduce the number of entries to a workable size.

Just the same Cletus informed me early Saturday morning that four hundred and seventeen crack shooters had qualified for the tournament and would be taking their turns in the line.

It wasn't surprising that so many turned up. Even for men who didn't bet on themselves or their favorites there was always the lure of the Cletus Hatch purse—an incredible $250,000 in cash.

Each shooter had to pay a $150 entrance fee in order to compete. Each spectator had to pay one dollar for every day he came to the meet. Concessionaires expected to make goodly sums as well. Cletus' bank, which had financed the meet, would lose no money on the tournament itself; it would break even, purse and all. But that was only a sidelight as far as Cletus was concerned. As he'd said, he was a gambling man; his entire personal fortune was spread out among hundreds—perhaps thousands—of bettors and bookmakers. He informed me he'd bet every dime on me alone.

His crazy faith inspired an equal craziness in me. I knew it was ludi-crous; but I also knew that if I lost the match I was bankrupt anyhow. I shamelessly borrowed every penny I could. I hocked my remaining possessions—all but my weapons and those few items that were precious to Libby—and in all I raised about $12,000, all of which I bet on myself to win. I was able to secure excellent odds on account of my age and

stood to win nearly a quarter of a million dollars if I took the prize—
that on top of the purse, of course; if I won I'd be half-a-millionaire.

I had no physical chance of winning; that goes without saying.

It was the first time since my boyhood that I had risked everything
on a wager. Always before I'd held something back, a rainy-day kitty
in case of loss. But this time it didn't matter. The creditors would get me
anyway. In a strange way it bestowed upon me a great gay freedom; I
went into the tournament light of heart and asparkle with good-humored
cheer.

. . . .

Cletus had offered to put us up in the best suite at the Brown Palace
but we had declined, not wanting to be surrounded by crowds; we'd
rented a little cottage half a mile from Skinner's farm and had informed
no one, not even Cletus, of our whereabouts. But of course the word
got out—perhaps the landlord—and in the end I was forced to beg
Cletus' help in hiring a number of private police to surround the place
and keep curiosity-seekers at bay.

There was considerable concern about the weather in the day or two
preceding the meet. It was extraordinarily chilly for May; it rained off
and on and there was the threat of snow. Cletus was prepared to go
ahead with the tournament in anything short of a full-out blizzard but
there was the possibility that inclement weather would reduce the size
of the paying crowd and—more significant—play such havoc with the
shooters' scores that no real championship could be established.

The evening before the match Libby and I retired early to the cabin
and sat before the hearth's fire. I heard the rain when a gust of wind
blew it against the window. Libby leaned back against my chest until
her white hair tickled my face and I said, "Well, my love, soon it'll all
be over—one way or t'other."

She was reading the *Rocky Mountain News;* she passed it to me—the
paper was full of headlines and sidebar stories about the match. She held
her finger on one of the lead stories and I squinted through my eyeglasses to make it out:

> No publicist or dime novelist has ever contrived a more valiant exploit than
> this, that in his 72nd year the great and legendary Col. Hugh Cardiff should
> take up his rifle again to meet and challenge the world's finest marksmen
> for the title of champion shot of the world. . . .

I set it aside without reading the rest; I stretched my long legs toward
the fire. "They've got to have something to fill the space, I reckon."

"It's true, you know, what that fellow's written there."

"Nonsense. You of all people, my love—you can't sleep with a man and listen to him snore and endure his crotchets and foolishness and still believe any of that hero-legend folderol these hacks crank out. You've counted my warts and memorized my scars and punctured my balloons. You've nagged at me and laughed at me. You chide me all the time for behaving like an irresponsible little boy. You've had to hold my hand and salve my goddamn piles, for Christ's sake. You've got an old beat-up husband living on memories and wishful thinking. Where's the heroics in that?"

She didn't speak for a moment; then she said, "I shouldn't say this because it's unwise to swell a man's head when he already thinks too highly of himself, but I have believed from the moment I fell in love with you—and I have never for one instant stopped believing—that you're a great man, Hugh Cardiff. A very great man. And you know it's one mark of your greatness that you've never once let yourself believe any of the nonsense that's been written about you. But don't you see, that very resistance to falsehood is one measure of your greatness. A smaller man would have succumbed to it long ago. Look at Bill Cody, how after a while he honestly didn't know which were lies and which were truths anymore."

"You just go right ahead and butter the old man up, I don't mind a bit. You want me to roll over so you can butter the other side now?"

"I imagine Daniel Boone probably had piles too, the age he reached. I expect sometimes Mrs. Boone couldn't stand the sight of him. But he was a hero."

"Well, Daniel Boone, sure."

"That's what you are, Hugh. You're the last of the great American heroes, do you know that?"

"I'm always pleased to be a hero in your eyes, ma'am."

She sat up and turned to face me. I saw she was being serious then. She said, "I don't mean Halburton's fictions. I don't even mean the entire generations of children who've been raised on the legend of Hugh Cardiff. That doesn't count, none of it counts—that's only what other people think of you and in the end that doesn't matter. But you are a hero in your own life, Hugh. I don't know many men who can lay claim to that."

I said, "Before you get my head too swelled up to shoot straight suppose you quit talking this nonsense and go poke up the fire there. I'm feeling lazy and I don't rightly want to move just now."

She was moving toward the fire when there was a knock at the door and Libby changed her course to go and answer it. I heard the Pinkerton man say, "Thought we ought to let this gentleman through, Miz Cardiff," and then Libby whooped with joy and I lifted myself off the rug to see past the top of the couch. It was our onetime foster son, the

447

movie star Jack Turkin, and I climbed to my feet delighted to see him.

There was a boisterous round of hugging and kissing and talking. Libby put the coffeepot on the fire and broke out biscuits and jam. Jack, who seemed uneasy, gave us the news of Hollywood and such.

Jack finally said to me, "Can we talk a minute, Colonel?"

"Go ahead."

"Alone."

"Well it's a one-room cabin, Jack. We'll go outside if you want."

"Yes sir."

I shouldered into my coat, got my hat and went out with him; we were followed by Libby's puzzled glance.

The drizzle was batted around by the wind. It stung our faces. The only light came through the windows; it was hard for me to make out Jack's features under the cowboy hat he wore. The cabin had only a tiny lean-to roof over the stoop and it wasn't enough to keep the rain off us.

He said, "It's clearing up over the mountains. Ought to blow off by morning."

"That's good to hear. Cletus Hatch should be pleased."

"It's been a while since we've seen each other, Colonel."

"I've seen all your moving pictures. I keep an eye on you that way. You've done grand for yourself—I'm proud of you, Jack."

He muttered something I didn't catch—it was flicked away by the wind. I leaned toward him and cupped my ear.

"What?"

"I said I don't know if I deserve that. I don't know if you'll still be proud of me after I tell you what I've got to say."

"My ears are still pretty good. You don't have to shout."

He grinned abstractedly at me. I had to respond with a sheepish smile. Too many gunshots had leaded my ears a bit, in truth.

I said, "What's on your mind then?"

"Well I'm afraid I am going to shoot against you tomorrow, Colonel."

"I fully expect you to. What's the matter, son?"

"You see I didn't intend to. I didn't aim to enter."

"Why the hell not?"

"Because I owe you too much. This was obviously your shoot—I know Cletus is your old friend, I figured you two had set this up to be your swan song. Go out in a blaze of glory with that final great victory."

"And?"

"I didn't have any intention of spoiling that for you, Colonel."

"You don't need to worry on that account, Jack. I can still lick you."

It made him smile. "You have got the most indomitable spirit of any man I ever knew, and that's a downright double-distilled fact."

"Then what's all the mysterious bother?"

"This marathon last-man-standing-wins thing, this is a young man's game, Colonel. You're good enough to beat the other old-timers and the young amateurs but you've got no chance to beat me. We both know that."

"You know it. I don't."

"The thing is, Colonel, I don't have a choice now. I have got to shoot against you and I've got to shoot to win."

"I expect nothing less of you. My God, Jack, if I win this shoot and ever find out you held back out of charity to me—"

"You don't understand, Colonel. I've *got* to win."

"Why?"

"Because Vernon Tyree has forced me into it."

. . .

"I didn't want to tell you," he said. "Vern would kill me if he found out I'd spilled the beans to you. I may not be half the man you think I am, Colonel—the truth is I've done some shady things in my time—but I have always been square with you, sir. I know this is the last minute, I should have come to you weeks ago with this but I just didn't have the guts. Now we're right up to the wire and I just couldn't go into that arena with you not knowing."

"Not knowing what? Quit beating about the bush."

"This ain't easy for me to explain, Colonel. You've got to bear with me."

We stood face to face with a yard of rain between us. Somewhere away to the north metal in the rocks brought the lightning down; there was a belated slam of thunder, echoing among the mountains. When Jack met my glance his eyes were stained with the unhappiness of a trapped animal.

"Vern Tyree has never done better than come second to you, Colonel. He wasted his life up until he went to prison trying to best you instead of casting his own shadow. He's had all those years to brood on it and I believe it has burned a hole right through him. He's a warped obsessed man. He's got nothing left except the need to spite you."

"He warped his own life—it wasn't my doing."

"You should have killed him, I think."

"He told you that," I guessed.

"Yes sir. He says it a lot, mainly when he's drunk. One time a few weeks ago he smashed a bottle of whisky and got blood all over his hand, and then he looked at me and yelled at the top of his lungs, 'Why didn't that bastard kill me?' "

"If he ever asks you that question again, tell him it's because I refused to dirty my hands on him. Maybe that'll shut the old fool up."

"No sir, it's too late for that. He doesn't want answers anymore. He just wants revenge. I believe it's the only thing that keeps him alive."

"It'd be a shame if he ever got his revenge. It would only leave a great big hole in him where his hate used to be," I said, "If he's looking for revenge he ought to look to Senator Merriam's door, not mine."

"I guess he does, Colonel, but he can't whip the Senator on a shooting ground, can he? But like I said, he's never understood why you didn't kill him that time his rifle exploded. It's always baffled him—I think it drives him half crazy, wondering. I think he must have gone peculiar back then, when he was growing up."

That was true, I suppose. Even before he'd gone off to war Vern had never been young the way the other kids were young. He'd always had that dark thing in him.

Jack said hesitantly, "And from the way he talks, sir, I'd venture he seems to have an unhealthy and unnatural regard for his own sister, if you'll excuse me putting it like that."

I could think of nothing to say to that. It was a strangeness in her brother that had not gone unnoticed by Libby, particularly in the latter days of her marriage to Phipps Merriam, but if Vern had harbored in-cestuous intentions he had never acted upon them—perhaps out of decorum, perhaps out of a minimal sense of self-preservation. Still, if it was true it could explain the intense hate he'd always borne toward me: jealousy is among the most powerful of the rages.

Still, if he had felt that way toward me then why hadn't he felt that way toward Phipps Merriam?

Perhaps, I thought, it was because the Senator was not man enough to have challenged Vern's sense of his own masculinity.

I said, "Tell me what you mean, now, when you say he's forced you to shoot against me."

"Well you know he's been on the drift ever since he was pardoned. He turned up in Hollywood a little while back and came to see me. I was surprised—surprised by his calling on me and surprised by how he looked. I'd expected to see a stove-up old man."

"And?"

"He's old, I guess, but he sure ain't stove-up. Looks pret' near as good as you do, Colonel. In fact right away he started doing character parts. They got him playing judges and sheriffs mostly—funny when you think about it. I guess partly it's his name, he's still remembered as a sort of famous character from way back when. The Wild West and all that."

"Jack, I'm getting soaked to the skin and I wouldn't mind a bit if we—"

"I'm coming to it, sir. You have to know how it came about. Now when Hatch announced this tournament it appeared right away in the

450

newspapers and of course Vern Tyree took an interest for obvious reasons. I don't know where he got the money, sir, but he's been buying rifles and ammunition and they say he's spent the last I don't know how many months out on the shooting ranges. Practicing."

"Think of that, now."

"He might still be too rusty for competition, of course—"

"Maybe not. I expect Vern Tyree could still be a first-class shooter. He always was."

"Under the circumstances it's mighty generous of you to say so, Colonel."

"Facts are facts. Go on."

"Well he's been coaching a whole crew of young shooters out there." Jack spoke with a bashful averting of his head. "The plain fact is, Colonel, ever since this tournament was announced with your name at the top of the list, Vern Tyree's been bound and determined to see you whupped. He's going to shoot against you here."

"I'm glad of that. Maybe once and for all we'll settle which of us is the champion." I grinned at him to show I was joshing; the truth was, I never expected to come near winning that match—but I expected, by damn, to try.

"He's going to shoot against you," Jack continued in the same dull painful way, "and just to make sure, he's coached himself three, four young shooters too. And plainly it occurred to him I was the one shooter in the world most likely to best you, so he—"

"So he came to you and asked you to—"

"He didn't ask me a damn thing, sir. That's not how he does things. If he'd asked me I'd have said no. He didn't even bother to ask."

Then Jack squared himself up. "Look, Colonel, I've been married three times now and I ain't always done things to be proud of. You hear a lot of crap about Hollywood but some of it's true and I guess I've partaken of a few things I shouldn't have. You see the trouble is I work in a business where the slightest scandal can wreck a man's career overnight. Now Vern Tyree put detectives on me and he confronted me with a few things and said he could bankrupt me if he exposed some of these things in the right places. He said I'd never work in that town again. And I expect he's right. And that's my life, you know. Moving pictures."

"I always believed you had sand, Jack. I can't believe there's any threat he could have made that would force you to do anything you didn't want to do."

"Well he kind of come up on my blind side, Colonel, because this little gal I'm married to now, this is the real thing for me. I love her just a whole lot. And there are things he threatened to tell her—"

"If she loves you she'll live with that, Jack."

"Well I wish I could be sure of that. She's pretty straitlaced and all. Colonel, I can tell you this. I thought about his threats for a while and I thought about going back to him and saying I couldn't do this to you. I thought about telling him to go ahead and ruin me if he thought it would do him any good. I thought about telling him I'd probably kill him if he did, but it would be up to him. I thought about those things but I didn't do any of them. I'll tell you why. In the first place I didn't see why I should let that old man's bitterness ruin the rest of my life. And in the second place he was trying to force me into doing something I might have done on my own if I'd thought clearly about it. I don't mean to take your glory away from you, sir, but this is nineteen and twenty and begging your pardon but your day is past, Colonel, you are an old man now. I love you as if you was my own father sometimes —but when daddy gets old he ought to go and retire and pass the family business on to the next generation. I had intended to stay out of this thing and give you your time in the sunshine here, but Vern Tyree changed my mind about that. I can't honestly say whether he scared me into this or whether he just opened my eyes, through no intention of his own. I will say this, to be honest with you. If I don't beat you on the firing line Vern says he'll expose me to the newspapers and to my wife. I think I'm scared of that, but I don't know if I'd go ahead and do this if that was the only reason. The thing I keep thinking is, it's my turn. You've had your turn, sir. I believe it's mine now."

"Don't count me out just because I'm old, Jack. Old dogs know all the tricks—I still know things you haven't learned yet."

"Point is, Colonel, I intend to beat you. I expect to do it fair and square but I felt I had to tell you the circumstances here."

"Suppose I win. What then?"

"You mean supposing I give it my best show and you still beat me?"

"Don't say that with so much disbelief, Jack."

"Well if that happens, sir, he says he'll ruin me. Of course he may not. Maybe it was an empty threat."

No, I thought. Vern Tyree didn't make empty threats.

Jack said, "I don't suppose it matters much to him whether it's me or somebody else that beats you. Vern wants you beat, that's the main thing. I think he'd like to win this tournament himself but he mainly wants to see you lose. He knows it'll bankrupt you and puncture your pride. And he's made himself all this insurance—training these young shooters and blackmailing me into this."

After a brittle pause he said, "What it comes down to, Colonel, I am not without a choice in this. I could have refused. But I didn't. I aim to shoot against you and I aim to beat you—for my own reasons more than Vern Tyree's, but just the same, I wanted you to know how it was."

"I'm obliged to you for telling me, Jack." I clapped him on the arm. "Now come indoors and get dried off."

. . .

I did not sleep well that night. For all Jack's proud upright candor, the fact remained that Vern Tyree had threatened to destroy his career and his marriage if he didn't whip me on the firing line. If I set out to win the tournament and managed to best Jack Turkin, I had no doubt Vern would carry out his threat. By my own actions I would be destroying the life of someone who was very dear to me.

But the alternative was no happier. I owed it to a great many people to do my best to win. If I failed for lack of stamina or skill it would be an honorable failure; but if I failed for lack of trying it would be a betrayal of those who depended on me and those who supported me with their good wishes or their betting money. I would be letting down Libby and Kevin and Caleb and the grand old man Doc Bogardus who had come out of retirement to enter the Hatch Tournament. And the two hundred men and women who still lived on the Tyree Grant—veteran survivors, with Libby and me, of the Wild West Show.

I saw no way out of the dilemma.

. . .

Caleb and Doc and Kevin arrived at dawn to breakfast with us before we started the journey to the shooting ground. Libby sat down with us and for a while I believe we simply looked around at one another in wonder that we all had survived so long. Doc Bogardus was over ninety years old then—shriveled to half his onetime bulk. But we were all old: Caleb looked about him and made a cheery remark about the waxworks. Kevin, the youngest of us, was sixty-eight.

. . .

Shortly before the nine-o'clock commencement of the tournament I emerged from the dressing-room wagon that Cletus Hatch had kindly provided. Denver constables stood guard outside the door to protect our privacy; I nodded to them and watched Kevin and my team of throw-boys come forward with the heavy boxes containing my rifles. The area was crowded with trucks and wagons and trailers. A considerable traffic of earnest busy people trudged about. I saw a gang of newspaper reporters and photographers beyond the rope fence, restrained there by city marshals. There was a hum of voices that reached us all the way from the stadium.

Libby leaned against my arm. Caleb was helping Doc Bogardus down from the wagon. Doc didn't move too well anymore but he was determined to put in at least a token appearance on the tournament field: he'd be shooting light .22 rifles.

Then I saw Jack Turkin coming toward us from his truck. He looked

453

as if he'd had no better a night than mine. He shook my hand and we both smiled, partly for the benefit of the news people and partly because we both meant it. But in that moment I felt a sour premonition that both Jack and I would be eliminated in the early rounds of the competition, thus solving everyone's difficulties except my own: and in truth I was half-prepared to have it so.

We walked in a tight little knot toward the fenced-in entrance to the tunnel that led under the grandstand into the arena. I felt my heart swell; my shoulders straightened and I flung my arms about Libby and Caleb as we walked forward—Doc Bogardus and Kevin close beside us: the five of us walking in a single rank, shoulder to shoulder—it was a grand heady triumph of its own. We were five who had prevailed. I felt myself fill up with a great warmth.

Then Jack Turkin trotted up alongside and fitted himself in beside Doc Bogardus, lending the old man a hand under his elbow, and the six of us entered the stadium that way and I heard an incredible roar from the audience.

We walked on out into the field and turned to face the grandstands. The applause intensified—I have never heard such tumult. They were on their feet, yelling, throwing things in the air. Jack stepped forward and bowed; Caleb took his bow; there was a renewed round of yelling when Doc Bogardus lifted his old arms to the crowd; and I was heartened enough to sweep off my hat to them as I had done in Wild West Show days—they nearly went berserk then; the applause ran on far longer than courtesy required.

I am sure many of the shooters and serious sporting bettors thought that I was an anachronistic relic and that the serious competition would soon narrow down to younger shooters; but there remained a mass of spectators who had been drawn by the opportunity to see Caleb Rice and Colonel Cardiff shoot— we were relics to be sure, but relics of the heroic age of American legend. We were living reminders of a history that had come and gone before most of the people in that audience had been born. Of course Jack Turkin was better known than either Caleb or I, but I believe most of the spectators did not know him to be an expert shooter; some of them probably thought his presence was a publicity stunt. They were soon to learn better.

I was searching the arena floor for any sign of Vern Tyree but I did not see him. I was sure nothing would keep him away—he meant this match to be my downfall and he meant, if possible, to be the shooter to beat me. After more than fifty years he still wanted to best me.

Jack turned, making as if to examine one of the rifles his seconds were proffering; he said to me, *sotto voce,* "You see that young pair of dudes in the checked shirts over there? Halliwell and Foran. Halliwell's the one with the soft cap on. Those are the shooters Vern Tyree was coaching. They are damn good, Colonel. Halliwell was a sniper in the war—they say he killed more than five hundred Huns."

"Well they're not shooting at spiked helmets today."

"Here's Vern."

I turned and saw him emerging from the tunnel—a smile below the scar, a taut spring in his step: astonishingly he looked half his age—robust, vigorous, a truly handsome man in flamboyant buckskins and white gloves, followed by a retinue of cold-eyed men in business suits. A ripple of tentative applause ran through the crowd; Vern ignored it. He came straight across the grass to me. "Old Saddlesores," he said. There was no quaver in his rich voice. He made no gesture of recognition toward Jack but he did thrust out his hand toward Kevin. Kevin shook his brother's hand without enthusiasm and Vern said, "Doc Bogardus. I thought you'd be dead by now."

"It's the anticipation of outshooting you that keeps me alive, Major." Doc grinned brashly, his false teeth startlingly white.

The crowd was still streaming through the stands, taking their seats and talking with a great hubbub. Officials and seconds were fanning out across the shooting ground. The sky was mainly clear, only a scattering of high cotton-ball clouds, and the morning sun had dried the earth.

Vern said softly, "Look to your laurels, Saddlesores. Today you well and truly retire." And walked away from us, doffing his hat pleasantly to the crowd.

He had not looked at Libby once.

.   .   .

In the Hatch Tournament we used glass balls, although wooden blocks had become favored by most aerial shooting competitors. The use of glass balls was dictated by Cletus Hatch out of deference to me. Wooden targets had come into favor some years earlier because they were cheaper to manufacture, less susceptible to being pushed around by wind, and cheatproof: if a shooter used birdshot rather than solid bullets, the wooden block would give evidence of this. But my preference ran to glass balls, partly because I was used to them and partly because they were more of a crowd-pleaser. I believe one reason why target-shooting exhibitions have waned in favor is that wooden blocks hurled into the air by mechanical traps are rather dull to watch; they neither glitter nor fly apart when hit.

I knew I would be presented with an agonizing dilemma if I stayed long in the race but at the beginning of the tournament I was determined to put on my best show. Regardless of the ultimate outcome I did not mean to forfeit the match too early. Most of the people in the audience had paid to see Colonel Hugh Cardiff shoot. I meant them to have their money's worth.

Beyond that I did not know.

. . .

Cletus Hatch was at the microphone on the central podium, announcing the rules of the shoot to the audience and touting the celebrity of some of the shooters. I shook hands with the line judges and grinned at Doc Bogardus, who was setting up to my left.

During a pause in Cletus' bombast I removed my hat, waved it to the crowd, got a round of applause and spun the hat through the air to my onetime throw-boy, Charlie Samuelson, who caught it deftly and planted it on his own head.

I plugged cotton wads into my ears and selected my first rifle. It felt easy in my hands. I had been in training for several months, had shot every day and felt sure the old man was still capable of surprising a few young upstart shooters.

I saw Vern Tyree move into the line and realized that Cletus must have fiddled with the order of entries; there was no random selection here—he had put his big guns into the line right at the front of the show, no doubt for the benefit of the crowd.

Then Libby came across the field and her face was white. I reached for her arm—"What is it?"

"I won't turn around," she said. "Look past me—beside the tunnel."

I looked and saw. A caved-in figure seated in a wheelchair: an eye shade, a blanket about his shoulders, four hulking men around him. It was too far to make out his features but I didn't need to.

Senator Phipps Merriam.

Kevin made as if to walk past me. I stopped him. "Where are you going?"

"To find out what he wants."

"We know what he wants, Kevin."

Amplified by loudspeakers Cletus Hatch's voice echoed through the arena: *"Let the tournament begin!"*

The bell rang. Boys tossed glass balls aloft and the competitors commenced the shoot.

. . .

I still had the rhythm of the shoot. I suppose it is something you do not lose unless you allow yourself to fall apart, which was a thing I had never done. The balls lofted and arced; they met my aim; I shot them apart—I was like a machine, like Doc Bogardus the first day I'd seen him shoot: I was a veteran, a professional. Steady and nerveless. I set my own pace and kept it, somewhat slower than it might have been at one time but businesslike nonetheless. I paid no attention to the shooters on either side and made my mind blank to Jack Turkin, Vern Tyree, Senator Phipps Merriam: my whole attention went to the mechanics of the job and I did not trouble to keep count as I had full confidence in my seconds and in any case there was no maximum number of balls in this shoot, no fixed deadline.

The rules required that each rifleman had to shoot eight hours out of every twelve—a test of endurance. You could break up your twelve hours any way you wished. I'd decided to start by trying a five-minute break at the end of each hour, then a half hour for lunch, then a two-and-a-half-hour break in the evening for dinner and sleep; and so on.

The only other rule of importance was that you had to shoot ninety out of every one hundred balls thrown in order to remain in the competition. This ruling weeded out all but the most expert shooters in short order. That first morning I had little trouble with that requirement. My first miss took place on the 49th throw, my second on the 128th, and thereafter I had back-to-back straight runs of 105, 211, 79, 140 and 194.

I was not shooting quickly but kept the metronome beat, never missing it even when I changed rifles—the fresh rifle was always at hand, thrust into my hands by Kevin when I was ready for it.

By the time I went off the field to take my lunch—a vast wave of applause carried me off the arena—I'd fired at 3,600 target balls and I'd missed only twenty-nine of them.

I was filled with a savage satisfaction. I still had a thing or two to show the world.

. . .

While I ate my lunch in the dressing-room trailer Libby kneaded my shoulders and Charlie Samuelson sat with his notepad on his knee bringing me up to date on the match that had been taking place around me. He had gleaned some of the information from the judges and the rest from his own observations and those of our happy henchmen, all of them veterans of the Wild West Show.

"A lot of them already been eliminated," Charlie said. "When we come off the field it was down to one hundred and nine shooters left in the match. Timekeepers keeping careful score on some of them because some people shoot a lot slower than others which means you got some shooters ahead on time but behind on targets. This thing ain't too well-organized if you ask me. I was just told that Mr. Hatch will circulate a ruling this afternoon requiring that every shooter must fire at least five thousand rounds in every eight hours to qualify for the next shift. A lot of the boys ain't gonna be happy about that—changin' the rules in midstream—but it can't be helped because otherwise we'd of had some shooters working on their eight thousandth target while some others working on their three thousandth and that would give the big advantage to the slower man. Of course they should've thought of that beforehand but it looks like nobody did."

Certainly it hadn't occurred to me; it should have, considering how I'd slowed the proceedings on this very ground with my single-shot muzzle-load Hawken rifle many years ago.

I gave it a bit of thought and then said after a mouthful of good hot radish, "I don't think that'll matter much after the first day or so. The stayers will be the professionals and the professionals are shooters who don't waste time."

"Yes sir, I expect that's prob'ly right. Now in terms of actual scores, as near as we can calculate them, there is eight leaders running way ahead of the rest of the pack, and you don't need me to tell you that you're at the top of those eight. You're leading the tournament as of now. Jack Turkin's right up with you and Doc Carver's only a few rounds behind. Vern Tyree is tied with him. Foran and Halliwell close by. And Doc Bogardus, believe it or not. And there's also a fellow name of Mackenzie from Scotland someplace, shooting a Lee-Enfield of all goddamn heavy things."

"I always did get stiff competition from Scotsmen," I commented. "There was a Scots fusilier who beat me square in a match overseas once." Libby's hands were soft on my shoulders; I covered one of them with my own. But pain nagged at me inside—I could not help the anguish of the dilemma that lay ahead.

At half-past twelve I went back into the firing line; by then the contest was down to ninety-four shooters and by the end of the afternoon we were down to forty-one and then the lights came on and that weeded out those with weak eyes or poor night vision; when I took a break at eleven o'clock Charlie informed me, not without satisfaction, that Doc Carver had run out of steam and shot a ragged 89 and been retired, and that we were down to thirteen shooters. I was still leading; Vern Tyree and Jack and Halliwell and the Scot Mackenzie were close behind me, and Doc Bogardus—against all credibility—was still in the shoot.

I took a moment to go around to Carver's tent and shake his hand. The old man—he's a few years my senior—was gracious and gallant and wished me luck, and I told him that for my part I admired his pluck and hoped I'd be as spry when I reached his age. Carver laughed at me, a good-spirited old gentleman, Buffalo Bill's first partner and one of the great shooters of all time; he shooed me back to the arena and I resumed shooting into the crisscrossing beams of electric-arc light.

I took my second sleep break in the small hours, as did most of the other shooters; the grandstand was all but empty by then. We most of us expected the shoot to last till the end of the second day or perhaps the early hours of the third—certainly no longer than that. But I began to be concerned that it might end sooner than we'd anticipated, because by dawn on the second day—when we'd been shooting only about nineteen hours—there were only nine of us left in the field: Vern, Jack, Mackenzie, Foran, Halliwell, a Texan named Dan Huston, a circus trick shooter named Billy "the Kid" Dix, Doc Bogardus and myself.

Neither the press nor the public could credit the fact that Doc and Vern and I were still in there fighting, for the crowd began to swell very early that morning and the place became aclutter with journalists and photographers and it was evident they were there to watch Vern and Doc and me. Every time one of us made a long run there was applause; every time we missed there was an audible groan. I could hear individual voices urging us on every few minutes—"Come on Colonel, come on Doc, you can beat these whippersnappers!"

Then in the middle of the morning Doc Bogardus put his rifle down and came across and stood pale and shaking before me. "I have kept up with the lot of you for twenty-four hours, which for a man in his nineties is not too bad. As a medical man I judge myself too near the point of exhaustion to carry on with this. I'm abandoning the field to you young kids." With a grin and a whap of a friendly gnarled fist against my bicep he walked off the field, buoyed off by an ovation of applause which I led. I do not believe Doc's feat of endurance will ever be duplicated by a man that age.

. . .

Caleb Rice, who had not entered in the shoot—it was a rifle shoot only and Caleb had not practiced for years—stood guard at my door while I took my minutes of rest and food and drink. Libby seemed never to sleep—she must have snatched brief naps during my own. Kevin was everywhere at once, inspecting glass balls for flaws, cleaning and supervising the reloading of my rifles, testing the wind and keeping me appraised of its shifts. After a few hours' sleep Doc Bogardus returned to the arena and sat behind me in a camp chair, watching with keen interest. Jack Turkin in his movie costume—stained, like all our clothes, with powder burns and soil—fired away almost casually at a steady fast rate, shattering glass with the regularity of a carpenter driving nails with a hammer. For a while Jack's score drew ahead of my own and he grinned brashly at me; having got the confession off his chest I believe he felt untroubled by conscience and he whole-heartedly intended to win the meet. But during the morning I again pulled even with him and then a bit ahead.

Vern Tyree and his two protégés, Halliwell and Foran, stood on adjacent positions and spoke to no one outside their own coterie. Halliwell's score was, by a small margin, the best of those three—but all three of them maintained scores that hovered near my own and sometimes overlapped it. Several times during my breaks I saw Vern turn and plant his feet and glower mutely at the Senator, whose wheelchair seldom moved from its position at the foot of the grandstand.

Going into the tunnel at ten o'clock I met the Senator's glance. His costume was dismal—a black suit with waistcoat against which his doughy belly strained. His eyes looked filmed; he had the flaccid look of death. He hardly seemed to recognize me.

Cletus Hatch stood beside the wheelchair and when I looked up into his face he flushed deep color and evaded my eyes. I went on into the tunnel, troubled by what I had seen, reeking of gunpowder and trembling a bit with weariness but my mind speeding from one clue to another. I was beginning to see how things fit together. There was more to this tournament than might have been imagined—more, certainly, than I had thought. I knew I had to put my mind to it. The time had come for me to make my decision.

· · ·

The Texan, Dan Huston, shot 87 just before noon and was ruled out by the judges. He retired with flippant cowboy grace—it was an act, I knew; he was disappointed and anyway he wasn't a cowboy at all, he was a test shooter employed by one of the rifle-manufacturing companies. I am sure he must have been worried for his job; I am equally sure his employer was secretly happy that their man, with their rifle, had come so close to winning.

Vern's man Foran also fell by the wayside before lunch, leaving six of us on the line.

I felt pretty good and postponed my lunch break. I went on shooting until two o'clock when I set my rifle aside and took Caleb by the arm and walked him toward the shooters' private gateway that led under the grandstand to the rest area. I said, "I wonder if you'd mind taking Vern Tyree a message from me. Tell him I want to see him in my trailer at half-past four sharp. Tell him to be there or else I'll lasso him out of the line and drag him through this dirt like a pig." I clapped his shoulder and went on, leaving him there with a gaping grin on his wizened face.

I'd decided what I was going to do. With the burden of indecision off my back I slept soundly and only came awake after Libby shook me violently; I realized she'd been talking at me for a while—I'd taken it for a dream. She said, "You've got to get up. Your visitor's due to arrive any moment."

460

"All right. Dammit, woman, you never give a man any peace!" I swung my legs groggily off the specially built cot, sat up and rubbed my face.

"You'd better leave us. I've got things to say to Vern in private."

"Don't trust him—"

"No." I slipped a small revolver behind my belt. "But it's got to be alone."

"I'll stay close by outside if you want me."

"I always want you, my love."

We smiled and embraced and kissed, two silly old people mooning like kids; then she left me.

I latched the door back wide open so that I'd know when he came; I sent Caleb away. Then I lay back and let the muscles go loose. A trick I had learned somewhere along the way was how to let everything go completely loose at every possible opportunity. During a marathon match it prevented cramps and eased fatigue. Over the years I've become a past master at the catnap. I can sleep for three minutes, on my feet if necessary, and come back from it remarkably refreshed.

I heard footsteps at last; and sat up to meet my enemy.

. . .

Charlie Samuelson accompanied him to my trailer. I said, "Take the gentleman's hat, Charlie," and it made Vern flush as I'd known it would. I felt cruel and vindictive just then; I wanted to hurt him any way I could.

Charlie withdrew and left us alone. I didn't offer Vern a seat. He glanced around the trailer, taking in its luxurious appointments—Cletus had spared no effort in attending to my comfort.

Wire-thin veins made circular smudges on his leathery cheeks; his eyes seemed smaller and meaner than they used to be. They beetled at me, little red organs full of the blood of obsessive hate. He was seventy-three years old. I had that thought and then shoved it aside; it was no time to be pitying him.

I said, "Jack told me about your blackmail threat." I studied his face. He was trying to guard it. I said, "That surprises you, doesn't it?"

"Well I don't know what he told you, do I? People tell lies." I was reminded of the feverish gleam his eyes had projected from the dim corner of his prison cell: white-hot, demented.

I said, "I will tell you something about myself—I have never taken a human life—"

"I always did take you for a yellow coward."

"—but I tried once. When you fired on me from ambush in Virginia. If I could have I'd have killed you then."

461

"You'd have been better off if you had," he said. There was something odd about the tone of his voice just then: perhaps he was thinking, *And I'd have been better off too.*

He pulled out a pocket watch and looked down at it. "We'd better get back in the line."

"There's time."

"Too much time, Saddlesores."

I said, "If I lose the match you'll have your satisfaction but that's not my concern just now. If I win after all—"

"You'll never win," he breathed. "Not this time." I saw fifty years' pent-up rage in his snarl.

"Vern, listen to me now. You've paid more than thirty years of your life for your crimes. I'm not your enemy—I never was. No—hear me out, let me finish. I'll shoot against you out there and I'll take my chances and so will you, but I am not your enemy. If you've got an enemy left in this world it's that old man in the wheelchair."

"His turn's coming, Saddlesores. But yours is now."

"He set this match up, you know."

"Aagh," he said in disbelief.

"You took his legs, Vern. I took his wife. That's how he sees it. He's got a soft core—I faced him down once and he's never had the courage to come after us head-on because he knows he'd die if he did. But now he thinks he's found a way to get vengeance against all of us, you and Libby and me. His devious style's written all over this tournament."

"You're senile."

"I believe he put the idea for this match in Cletus Hatch's head. I believe he's counting on your stubborn pride and mine. He knows the rivalry between you and me is too strong to let either one of us quit. He means to watch us break—he means to watch us go on until we drop. We're lifting fifty, sixty tons a day with these old muscles, Vern. He expects we'll cripple ourselves, maybe kill ourselves. He could be right. You and I, we're too damned old for this."

Vern watched me unblinkingly: years of pent-up hate. "You've tried every way you could to break me, Saddlesores, but I am still here and I am fixing to leave a record behind me on this shoot that'll stand and be remembered long after you've turned to forgotten dust. You're the man I was put on this earth to beat. It was all written down in the book before you or I was born—you think you can turn my head aside with shrewd talk about Phipps? Don't you worry your head none about old Phipps. I have got things in mind for him. But you come first. You always come first, Saddlesores."

He stood under the low ceiling with his head bowed as if in prayer; he was not looking at me; he spoke again, briefly, as if to himself. "You

462

don't know how a man keeps himself alive inside for thirty years. You don't know what goes through a man's head all those years with walls around him and animals for company. You don't know how many men I had to kill in that place to keep myself pure. They never proved it on me but they knew." He was scowling, as if momentarily baffled, having lost the track of his thinking. Then he looked up, savage again: "We saw the newspapers. I saw it when you took my sister away and besoiled her. But I stood up to that test, just like all the others. I wasn't put on this earth to be broken. But by God *you* were!"

It exploded inside him: he lunged at me in fury. We grappled, tumbling about the wagon—I hit my head a painful crack as we tumbled across the bunk and I groped for his wrist and we struggled in ferocious silence—I heard the raging whistle of his heavy breathing; he had the furious strength of all that wrath he'd kept bottled under incredible pressure and he must have learned everything there was to know about fighting and I believe the only thing that kept him from my throat was the massive corded rifle-lifting strength of my own arms but I could feel the brittle strain in these old bones and while we heaved and grunted and strained at each other I knew I could not prevent him from overcoming me.

I heard him catch his breath in his mouth; I felt his grip shift—then with amazing force he flung me over onto my face before I could brace against it: and he had my left forearm in a beartrap grip, twisting up along my spine until agony shot through my shoulder—an agony I hadn't felt in forty years.

His final thrust against my wrist, twisting the arm that last notch, made me cry out. Then he had the revolver from my own belt: I felt it when he pulled it free, heard him get to his feet and step back.

I sat up, clutching the burning shoulder in my right hand. Vern faced me with the gun in his fist. Breath sizzled in and out of him. "No," he said. "No, I don't kill you now. First I have to beat you out there on the shooting ground." Then his lips peeled back, exposing gaps in his teeth. "Saddlesores—hear me. You fouled my sister. You didn't leave her fit to live. I'll make you a sporting proposition then, one champion to another—you win this match I'll go away and take care of my business with old Phipps. But you lose it to me and so help me God I'll kill Libby and you both."

The revolver clattered to the floor; he was gone.

I sat up and lifted my arm. The pain receded. He had pushed it far enough up my back to have dislocated a normal shoulder from its socket —but mine was not a normal shoulder. I swung the arm back and forth: a twinge, a final dim stab where he'd bruised the flesh, then no pain at all.

I thought dismally, *I shall be forced to kill him.* And knew I couldn't do it. Not in cold blood.

. . .

I left the trailer swinging the arm. When I arrived on the line Vern was stunned to see me lift my first rifle effortlessly. I held it in a loose grip, not quite pointed at him but not quite pointed away from him. He stood fifty feet away and there were men between us and I did not speak but I was sure he understood me. We would continue the shooting match as if nothing had taken place between us. After the match we would settle up. Not for a moment did I believe his promise to let it drop if I won; Vern was not a man of honor.

I did not see how I could prevail in the end. If he came at me straight up I would defend myself; but that wasn't his way—he could come at me through Libby and probably from the darkness. . . .

. . .

We shot through the afternoon and into the evening. Young Billy Dix was cocky: it was his downfall and he dropped out after seven o'clock and an hour later the Scot Mackenzie began to shoot erratically, which was not surprising inasmuch as we all had been shooting steadily twenty-six hours out of the last thirty-five.

Halliwell, the young sharpshooter from California trained by Vern, kept his scores up with those of Jack and Vern and myself. He was a heavy bull of a young man with a thin vicious mouth; I did not like his look.

My eyes were raw and I was deaf from the pounding. In the breaks Libby brought me cups of warm beef broth and they helped revive me. I answered her questions about my confrontation with Vern, but said nothing to her of his intentions.

Senator Merriam sat day and night with his arms folded across his chest and no visible expression on his pasty cheeks.

Halliwell was talking in fast low tones with his armorer, a sharp-faced man who according to Kevin was a talented but somewhat shady gunsmith from San Francisco. I was much too far away to hear any of their low-voiced talk, even had my ears been young, but it was clear they were arguing. Halliwell was exhorting the armorer to do something and after a while the armorer nodded and went back to the rank of waiting rifles and selected one and carried it back to Halliwell, who jacked the lever half open to glance at the cartridge within. Halliwell's cruel mouth was pinched into a thin line. He flicked a sidewise look at Vern Tyree, who did not notice it, and then moved back into his position in the line.

I had no idea of the meaning of what I'd seen. Determined not to let

464

it distract me, I lifted my rifle and called for the throw and resumed the steady dreamlike beat of the shoot.

. . .

The rifles sprang to life in my hands under the lights that evening. Libby stood not far behind me, not so much patient as avid: she never tired of watching me shoot. Her eyes sparkled and danced. I forgot everything—even Vern—as the song and beat of the shoot carried me high. I might have been a youth that evening. In the first forty-two minutes that followed the supper break I had one incredible straight run of 776 balls—breaking and nearly doubling the record I had myself set many years earlier.

It was mitigated by the fact that the miss that ended the run threw me off-stride and for a while I couldn't seem to hit more than twelve or fifteen in a row without missing one; I shot 91 out of 100, then 93, then 91 again.

At eleven I paused for a few minutes' rest and while I swabbed my eyes and limbered my arms and legs Kevin walked around with me talking in a rapid worried low voice.

"Can't figure it out. Maybe my tally's not the same as the judges' but I compute in the past two hours this Halliwell kid has pulled forty balls ahead of everybody else." Then he turned away from me. "I intend to look into this," and he was gone.

I went back into the line; Charlie Samuelson tipped my hat to me and said, "My boys hitting a whole lot of your bullets tonight, Colonel. Reckon they'll use up a bucket of liniment on their arms."

I resumed shooting under the lights. The arc lamps were carefully placed behind the line so as not to be in our eyes but they made for strange shadows in the air through which the rising balls went rippling; one's eye had to be especially keen not to be fooled. But the difficulty was the same for all of us.

At the midnight break I saw Kevin marching forward with several men in tow. One of them was Cletus Hatch. Kevin presented himself before me and opened his hand. In his palm I saw a .32 cartridge. Kevin worked the slug out of it with pliers and upended the case into his hand. A little heap of gunpowder appeared. He spread it across his palm with a finger and I saw tiny pellets amid the powder.

"Look how the butt-end of the slug's been hollowed out," Kevin said. "I stole this when they weren't looking. He's using fine shot in his cartridges—*behind* the bullet. No wonder his score's perked up."

I plucked the hollowed bullet from his hand and turned it over in my fingers. "Clever piece of work," I remarked.

"Christ—that all you've got to say?"

465

Cletus Hatch said, "We're on our way to throw him out of the match, Hugh. These marshals are with me to make sure he doesn't stir up a ruction."

Kevin hissed, "My black-hearted bastard of a brother—"

I said, "Vern didn't put Halliwell up to this, Kevin. The most important thing in the world to him right now is to beat me on the square."

I was watching Cletus Hatch's face. To either side of us the rifles cracked on—Vern, Jack Turkin, Halliwell.

Kevin and the marshals were turning toward Halliwell's line position. I stayed Cletus Hatch with my hand. "Tell me one thing." I sent my glance across the ground toward the man who sat shadowed in the wheelchair. "Whose idea was this match, Cletus?"

He made no audible answer but his eyes turned to follow the track of mine and it was all the reply I needed.

I said, "He must have sworn you to secrecy. It's all right, Cletus, I've no quarrel with you."

"He had notes against my bank stock—"

"Never mind." I extended my hand.

He looked at it and hesitated. "Hugh—I lied about those bets. I didn't bet it all on you. I spread it around."

"Any sensible betting man would."

"No," he said, "I won't shake your hand. I wouldn't foul your hand that way." And walked away from me with his shoulders bowed. I believe, however, that after a while he was relieved to know it was out in the open. I bore him no grudge. But at least my suspicion had been confirmed.

The marshals escorted Halliwell out of the stadium; Cletus returned to the microphone, called for a moment's halt in the shooting and informed the crowd that Mr. Halliwell was withdrawing from the tournament because of irregularities that had been discovered in the ammunition he was using. This caused a rush of reporters, two gangs of them—one group converged on Cletus and the others chased Halliwell and the marshals through the tunnel. I put my back to all of it and called for the throw; Vern and Jack and I resumed the shoot.

• • •

It came to be about three o'clock on the morning of Monday the seventeenth of May and we had been nearly two full days in the line and there were just three of us left; more than half the crowd was still there, expecting it to be decided soon. We all took a break and I saw Vern's head jerk back when he looked at me—I stepped across to Charlie and murmured, "Let me borrow this awhile," and took Charlie's revolver and slipped it into my belt, for I did not wish to have Vern at my back in his present frame of mind when I had an empty rifle in my hands. I suppose I could have asked for his arrest but I'd have had slim grounds for it and it would have appeared I was trying to win the match by underhanded means. There was nothing to do but wait out the finish.

In the break Jack approached me and said with infinite sadness, "I'm sorry, Colonel. You deserve to win this for sheer courage alone. But I intend to take the victory, sir."

"Do your damnedest then, Jack."

I went across the arena. Libby waited by the shooters' gate at the mouth of the tunnel. I went toward her but then averted my steps and the four big men around the wheelchair stiffened; one of them looked pointedly at the revolver in my belt. I lifted my hands slowly and folded my arms across my chest as I approached. One of the bodyguards showed me a bulldog pistol and kept it in his hand, hidden from the crowd by the fall of his coat. I stopped beside him and looked down at the Senator.

The old man wore smoked glasses, perhaps to protect his weak eyes from the smoke of the shooting field. He removed them slowly—all his movements were painfully slow and his hands shook with a palsy. His eyes had a glaze on them but his mouth was grim.

I said, "Enjoying the show, Senator?"

He said nothing.

I glanced at the bodyguards, who had shifted positions: two of them stood behind me. "You needn't fear me," I told him. "You don't look well, old man." I said it very gently. "You ought to be on a soft mattress between satin sheets."

"Thank you for the advice." His voice was icy.

I said, "This may go on awhile. You can't be very comfortable here. Go to bed, Senator—I'm sure you'll be one of the first to hear the results, no matter where you are."

"Your concern for my comfort is most touching, Colonel."

I said, "I'm trying to tell you, Senator, you're exposing yourself in easy range to a man who's had thirty years' good reason to hate you— a man with a loaded rifle in his hands."

"I'm aware of that."

"You think these thugs can protect you from that?"

The Senator's hands scrabbled at the robe across his lap—knotted old fingers picking as if at fluff. He did not reply to my question and I understood with sudden clarity what he had in mind. He *wanted* Vern to shoot him—I believed that: he wanted Vern to hang for murdering him. He knew he was dying and he did not wish to die alone.

He was looking past me. I did not need to turn my head to know he was looking at Libby. I said, "She bears you no malice."

"That's good of her." He bit the words off. "She always did have a childish charitability to her. Well she needn't fear me much longer, Colonel."

It confirmed my previous thought but I did not speak of that. I said, "I'm sorry for you, Senator," and immediately felt a touch of shame: by pitying him I had achieved a sort of revenge, I suppose, but it had a shabby feeling.

He leaned forward in the chair with great effort. His voice quivered with intensity. "You'll win this match, won't you?"

"If I do it'll be for my reasons, not yours."

"Win it, Cardiff. Win it." Then he sagged back in the chair and tremulously lifted the glasses to conceal his eyes.

.   .   .

The light of dusk and the light of dawn are the worst for shooting and we avoided them, using those hours for rest and meals. The three of us went back into the line about half-past eight Monday morning. I felt somewhat refreshed but the weariness was beginning to infect me and I suppose it slowed my step a fraction because Jack intercepted me. "It's enough, Colonel. They've had their show. Look—most of them have gone home."

"Well I still feel all right. These folks paid their money too. Let's show them a little fancy shooting, all right? No point ending this thing too early in the day." I winked at him and went on—reached for my first rifle and let my call sing out so everybody in the stands could hear:
"Throw!"

.   .   .

She swabbed my eyes with a solution of borax and camphor. I lay back and was instantly asleep.

Charlie shook me awake. "Time, Colonel."

"Where's Mrs. Cardiff?"

"I reckon she couldn't bring herself to wake you up again, sir. You're really pretty damn played out you know."

"What time is it?"

"Two in the afternoon."

"What day?"

"Tuesday, sir. Ain't hardly nobody left in the grandstand."

"Are Major Tyree and Mr. Turkin ready to shoot?"

"Yes sir."

"Then let's get out and join them, what do you say?"

.   .   .

"Darling . . ."

"Yes my love."

"Are you listening to me?"

"Mmmm."

"I know this prize would be worth a lot of money to us, Hugh, but you can't be a mogul in the cemetery. Your shoulder is really bothering you now, isn't it?"

"A little. Not too bad. Where's my clean shirt?"

"Doc Bogardus thinks you should quit now, darling."

"Uh-huh. Where's that other shirt, dammit?"

"You're not listening to me, are you?"

"Of course I am. Here it is. I knew I had another one."

"No. You hear me talking but you're not really listening. Doc insists—"

"Doctors always want you to quit. Doctors told me I'd never use this arm again. That was damn near fifty years ago, my love. Never listen to a doctor. What time is it? How much time before I go back in the line?"

. . .

I awoke with chilled feet and had to struggle to sit up. The pasty unfamiliar face hovered in the lamplight. I said, "Doc?"

"I've given you another injection of morphine to calm the pain in that arm. I have to tell you this again—are you awake and comprehending me?—if you continue this punishment much longer you'll surely lose the arm. It will have to be amputated. In the past five days' shooting you have lost thirty-five pounds in weight and I doubt your system will be able to withstand the shock of amputation at your age and under your current overstrained condition. You're an old man, Hugh. You have got to give this up now."

"Well pretty soon anyway, Doc. Thank you for your ministrations. What time is it, anyhow?"

"Just after midnight."

"Well I'm a bit overdue in the line then, aren't I? So if you'll excuse me I'd better get my boots on here. Mind stepping aside just a little there? Thank you."

. . .

When I went to leave the trailer Charlie barred the door. "Get back there now and lay still, Colonel. You're finished." There were tears in his eyes.

I pushed him gently aside. "Not finished just yet, Charlie." I stepped down to the ground. Spasms ran uncontrollably along my punished legs; I had to square myself up with an effort of will in order to take the first step. The wind drove right through me and I tucked my face toward my shoulder against it while I made my way toward the white arc lights of the arena. Specks of dust, or perhaps it was snow, twirled against the arcs; twice, behind me, Charlie spoke but went almost unheard—I

469

hadn't the strength to answer him. I plodded on into the tunnel and on through to the shooting ground.

Libby came from the shadows.

"You look heartbreakingly beautiful, my love."

"Oh, Hugh—don't you understand? Too much courage can be as fatal as too little. . . ." She saw I was not going to give in. Her eyes slowly filled with tears. She pressed her hand to her temples and for a moment she turned away from me but then she ran against me, clasping me tight in her arms, shuddering.

I stank of liniment and poultices and the sweat of heat treatments. I stepped away from her and began to turn toward the line. Libby threw her head back and smiled—she managed somehow to smile for me and I shall never forget that moment. She whispered: "God bless you then, my darling."

. . .

I was a bit lightheaded from the morphine. I attributed my stumbling to that. I found a little knot of men standing around the shooting line— Vern and Jack of course, and Doc and Caleb and Cletus Hatch and a couple of judges. I glanced at the stands—not a soul except one man with a notepad open on his knee; a reporter, I was certain—someone had to report the outcome of this match, even though it was anticlimax, and I guessed that the pool of reporters probably had drawn straws to see which one of them had to stay behind and cover the rest of it; that poor soul had lost. He was hunched back on his elbows, snoring mouth pointed at the sky, and I knew when he awoke he'd have a blinding headache.

And there at the foot of the stands I saw the man in the wheelchair and his four hard men.

. . .

In the cold wind Cletus Hatch's voice was almost whipped away; he sounded as fatigued as I was. "Gentlemen, I personally would be willing to call it a three-way draw at this point—God knows you've proved yourselves equals and the betters of any other shooters alive. But there are some millions of dollars in wagers resting on the outcome of this tournament and it must be decided. A winner must be declared and it must be seen to have been a fair decision. Still, it's time we wrapped this up. It has gone on far longer than anyone dreamed it would. I'd like to ask you three if we may agree to a change in the rules so as to conclude this matter before it kills anyone."

Cletus was watching me; then his grave glance switched to Vern Tyree, whose drawn face was so grey with smoke that his eyes seemed illuminated from within it.

470

Cletus said, "If we can agree, then we can safely conclude the tournament today. I propose a simple rules change. Whichever shooters first miss one ball are the losers. The winner is the man who hits more consecutive targets than his two opponents. Straightforward and I believe decisive, don't you agree?"

I said, "That suits me if Jack and the Major agree to it."

I saw the smile of relief cross Jack's face. He was drained, I could see; his eyes took longer to blink as he watched me.

"It's agreeable," Jack said.

It seemed to me that Vern Tyree had to wait to get his breath before he spoke; but oddly of the three of us I am sure he looked the freshest. When he did speak it was in an obstinately discordant voice: "Strangers' bet money isn't the only thing riding on this. I expect we're all eager to have it finished—but I won't have it said that the rules were changed out of deference to old men. We're deciding the rifle championship of the world here. Are we children, to change the rules when the going gets rough?"

I said to him, "You're playing into the Senator's hands, Vern."

He wheeled toward me. His mouth quivered. "I won't lose it this time to any tricks of fate. I'm not willing to gamble the championship on a misfiring cartridge or one glass ball that's out of round. You won't cheat me of it again."

Cletus said dismally, "If you all can't agree then we've no choice but to go on under the existing rules. At your convenience, gentlemen, be so kind as to resume your places in the line."

I swiveled slowly on my heels, surveying the empty grandstand. I heard Doc Bogardus say, "It's insane."

Caleb took my sleeve—lightly for he did not wish to hurt my arm; he knew the pain I was enduring. "Goddammit, old horse, quit it now. You've got nothin' left to prove here."

Libby, behind him, spoke in an oddly warm voice. "He won't listen, Caleb. He's stopped listening to anyone."

Then she came forward. "You're destroying yourself. You're doing what *he* wants you to do." She tossed her head toward the distant malevolent figure in the wheelchair.

I said, "Let's get this done," and turned to go into the line. As I came past Charlie Samuelson I said, "Just for the sake of interest, Charlie, how many balls have I shot so far?"

"One hundred and forty-two thousand, sir. Give or take a few hundred."

"Well that's pretty good, I expect. How many have I missed?"

"A little over two thousand."

"That's a shame. Shouldn't have missed that many."

"It's an average of one miss out of seventy, Colonel. Ain't but two other men alive can match it. You don't need fret none."

· · ·

My eyes felt sticky and the arm honestly was giving me quite a lot of trouble, the muscles all swollen up and inflamed and whatnot. I didn't dare switch to left-handed shooting again because it would throw my rhythm off and I couldn't afford that.

We'd been shooting for a while, I don't know quite how long. I knew I'd shot one good string by then, something over a hundred straight. I was taking my time though. Then I turned to hand my empty rifle to the boy and accept the fresh one but a fist gripped my sleeve and I turned to see Jack there glaring at me.

"Goddammit," he hissed. "You got to quit this now, Colonel."

"No sir, I guess not. I haven't quite played out my string yet."

"Don't you remember anything I told you, sir?"

"You mean what Vern said he'd do to you if I didn't lose. Now you've interrupted my rhythm here and I don't take kindly to that. Why don't you go on back over there and pick up your rifle and we'll finish this thing."

He was in tears. "I just don't understand you at all."

"You can win this shoot," I said, "but you've got to beat me fair to do it. I'm not going to hand it to you, Jack. If you're man enough to beat two frontier-bred men then I guess Vern and I are man enough to accept losing it—at least I am—but I will not default it. I won't cheat. Now come on, Jack, I'm too tired and too old to stand here arguing with you. Let's finish this thing." I reached out—a twinge in my shoulder —and gripped his forearm. "You can beat us if you're good enough. That's all you have to keep in mind right now."

"That's just it, Colonel. I'm not sure I'm good enough any longer."

I knew I had him then.

And I did.

Jack missed eleven out of his next hundred.

· · ·

Vern and I had practiced and exercised and trained with grueling dedication for the tournament but I suppose other men had as well. We knew what we were about, he and I; that was what it came down to at the end when we were the only contestants left on that empty smoke-stinking field. What we lacked in youth we made up for in the canny ability to conserve ourselves. Doc Bogardus had taught me every economy of effort. All I had to do was hold the rifle up throughout the fifteen-shot magazine run.

But dear sweet Jesus it was getting hard to hold it up.

I forced my mind to think of nothing at all except the targets. I had long since stopped calling for throws; Charlie made the calls for me. When a rifle went empty Kevin would lift it from my grasp and fit the next one snugly into my hands so that I did not need to lower my arms. I saw the tears in his eyes but I ignored that too.

Once I thought I heard Libby weeping. I did not look.

The man in the wheelchair was still there—an apparitional lump, guarded by his four silent men beneath the empty stadium.

Kevin said, "Time to break, Hugh. Two o'clock." He took the rifle from me.

I lowered my arms slowly, afraid they might snap.

Charlie spoke. He had to say it twice before I heard him. "He's going slower than you, Colonel. He's got another two hundred balls to catch up."

"How am I doing, Charlie?"

"You hit ninety out of a hundred that time."

"Not so good."

"Jesus God, Colonel . . ."

Then I heard a thump. It was not a very loud sound and my ears were done for but perhaps I felt it in my soles, for the sound drew me around and I almost lost my balance because my feet weren't working very well but when I looked toward Vern he was standing with his arms half-raised and a bewildered slack face and his rifle lay on the ground at his feet: he must have dropped it and I saw him bend down to reach for it before his seconds could get to him. He lost his equilibrium and pitched forward, tipping over on a shoulder and falling on his side.

Two men bent over him and Doc Bogardus hobbled toward him but Vern began to bellow, his voice hoarse but amazingly loud, vile epithets that drove the two armorers back while Vern groped for and reached the fallen rifle. But it seemed he could not close his left hand upon the forestock and the rifle drooped—held only by his right hand around the pistol grip—and a roar of agony and outrage burst from Vern's lips as he struggled to his knees, weaving there like a drunk with the rifle dangling from one hand. Doc Bogardus stood a few paces from him but Vern yelled at him to keep away.

Vern's terrible raw eyes swept across me; an expression of bewildered disbelief settled upon his face. He was trying to get to his feet but only fell over on his back. Then I saw him slither around on his side, kicking at the earth with his heels to propel the spin. Mad fires raged in his eyes. With a mammoth bellowing effort he lifted the rifle in one hand—

I saw the muzzle waver past me and suddenly I knew what he intended and I shouted and took a step forward but it was too late because the rifle cracked.

It had been aimed straight at Senator Phipps Merriam.

. . .

The four bodyguards clustered about the wheelchair and I glimpsed the glint of their guns with one quick glance but I spared no further attention to them; Cletus and several armorers were crossing the arena, giving the bodyguards no clear shot. I rushed stumbling toward Vern —he had jammed the buttstock into the earth and was jacking a new cartridge into the breech, his eyes fixed upon my face while the rifle swung toward me—I recognized the cruel hunger in those eyes for I had seen it before.

Tripping, stumbling, I drew my revolver.

But the rifle dipped toward the earth before it had traversed onto line with me. I saw the struggle with which Vern attempted to lift it. His jaw worked with childlike concentration. His hand clutched at the grips. His left arm flailed about him as if he had lost all control over it; his right fumbled with the weapon but only managed to discharge it into the earth and the recoil kicked the rifle out of his grasp.

I bent down on one knee and pushed the rifle out of his reach. "It's done, Vern. It's finished."

He began to weep then.

. . .

My head swam. Caleb and Libby lifted me to my feet. Kevin stood with a rifle, aiming it at his brother who lay curled up twitching, trying to hide his tears.

Doc Bogardus limped toward us from the wheelchair. "The bullet caused no bleeding. That means there was no blood pressure. The Senator was dead before Vern shot him. He died sitting there in the chair watching this. No telling how long ago."

They carried me out of the arena.

Libby's tears washed over me. "You silly stubborn magnificent fool —do you really think you've proved something by this?"

"Why yes, my love, I think I did, I think I proved something."

Jack Turkin was there. I swam in and out of awareness; I recognized their faces—Doc Bogardus scowling over me, Libby hovering protectively near, Caleb, Charlie, Cletus Hatch chewing his lip, Kevin with deep sorrow in the lines of his face.

I saw Jack's fists clench and open, clench and open; I summoned him with a toss of my head. "Vern won't carry out the threat."

"When did you know? That time he came here to the trailer? Days ago?"

474

"Yes."

"And you didn't tell me then? My God, Colonel, you should have told me. You know I might have backed off. I might have given it to you without you having to go through this—"

"I had to win it fair and square, didn't I? I expect Vern did me a favor hanging that threat over you. It meant you would do your best."

"You proud beautiful old man. I never knew such damn-fool stupidity in my life."

"I never claimed I was very bright," I said.

. . .

I fooled Doc Bogardus. My arms are nearly as good as new. I don't shoot competitions anymore—I don't need to—but I still shoot for pleasure. Now and then folks come to visit the ranch and I oblige them with a few rifle tricks. We have quite a successful outfit here on the Tyree Grant—Libby and Kevin and I, and Doc who always sits in old Grandfather Clement Tyree's place at the table. We provide longhorns and buffalo and horse stock for rodeos and moving-picture companies and we sell some of the best beef cattle in the West from our range here.

Like a scorpion maddened by the heat Vern Tyree tried to sting himself to death at the end of the Hatch Tournament. He is still alive but I understand he will never be fit enough to leave the hospital. There is a strange justice in how it all ended: Vern and the Senator each achieved their revenge upon the other.

Charlie Samuelson is foreman of the Tyree Grant now. Cletus Hatch retired from banking but I hear he is still a tough man to beat at a poker table. Jack Turkin comes down once in a while to visit. Sometimes he brings along a Hollywood crew and shoots one of his movies on the ranch.

Jeanette Fowler passed away in her sleep a year ago after a long happy marriage to a lumberman in Saskatchewan.

Caleb Rice is still in harness in the new boom town of Odessa, Texas, where he is chief of police—a more or less honorary title, although I hear he still arrests the occasional bootlegger. Caleb is the last of the great peace marshals. I do not count Wyatt Earp, who is very much alive over in California somewhere; as I said before, Wyatt Earp was never the marshal of anyplace.

I will be around for a while yet. My health is excellent and I aim to hang around to see if anybody beats my record and lays claim to the title of champion rifle shot of the world. I do not believe anyone will ever do it but I mean to stick around to make sure. I might be coaxed out of retirement to prove it, or at least that is the threat I make to Libby when she gets on at me.

It was Libby who convinced me that the truth needed to be told about the old days and those not so old. At first the publishers of this narrative wanted to send a professional writer out here to "collaborate" with me on this memoir but I refused to have any of that. I am a literate man, having grown up on the great books under the tutelage of Isaac Singman who was one of the finest teachers ever born, and I felt that this account had to be written in my own poor words because the truth is not simply a matter of facts or allegations. No professional writer has shared my life's experiences or learned how to sort out wishful memories from true ones.

In conclusion, may I say that I hope to see you all in the year 1949 when you are invited to my 100th birthday celebration. And in the meantime I am confident this account will in some way assist the generations that come after me to understand some things about truth and legend and myth and the way one leads to another.

When he read the manuscript of this book Jack Turkin said to me, "Dear Lord, Colonel, you have had your share of travail and tribulation." Well, that may be. But I do not know of any man alive or dead who has ever been so fortunate as I in his gathering of friends, or in his wife.

AFTERWORD

Author's Note

THE FOREGOING WORK is a novel and is not intended as a *roman à clef*. The major characters are creatures of the author's imagination and the novel should not be regarded as a basis for historical guessing games. A few of the minor and peripheral characters did exist—Buffalo Bill, Wild Bill Hickok, Wyatt Earp, Al Sieber, Doc Carver, Doc Holliday, some others—and some of the incidents in the lives of the characters of the novel are drawn from events in the actual lives of scores of nineteenth-century Americans; but the novel often attributes events taken from the lives of several historical persons to a single character in the novel. The characters themselves are not intended to represent or replicate the personalities of specific historical figures.

Still, the astute reader who is versed in the history of the American West may recognize an astonishing number of incidents in this novel. Nearly all the incidents (apart from those concerning the fictitious personal lives and conflicts of the protagonists) are based upon, or at least suggested by, facts.

The history of the West was recorded by observers who sometimes were unreliable: debunkers, partisans, purveyors of hyperbole. This novel is not intended as a history. But Cardiff's point about fact, legend and the relationship between them is valid. The American West was the birthplace of the American Myth.

477